Charles S. Gleed

The Kansas Nemorial

a report of the Old Settlers' meeting held at Bismarck grove, Kansas, Sept. 15th and

16th, 1879

Charles S. Gleed

The Kansas Nemorial
a report of the Old Settlers' meeting held at Bismarck grove, Kansas, Sept. 15th and 16th, 1879

ISBN/EAN: 9783337378837

Printed in Europe, USA, Canada, Australia, Japan

Cover: Foto ©Andreas Hilbeck / pixelio.de

More available books at **www.hansebooks.com**

THE

Kansas Memorial,

A REPORT OF THE

Old Settlers' Meeting

HELD AT

BISMARCK GROVE, KANSAS,

September 15th and 16th, 1879.

CHARLES S. GLEED, EDITOR.

ILLUSTRATED.

KANSAS CITY, MO.:
PRESS OF RAMSEY, MILLETT & HUDSON.
1880.

TO THOSE

WHO RESCUED KANSAS FROM THE PERILS OF SLAVERY, AND WERE
FIRST IN HELPING HER TO WAYS OF PLEASANTNESS
AND THE PATHS OF PEACE, THIS BOOK
IS INSCRIBED.

NOT a grave of the murdered for Freedom
But grows seeds of a wider Freedom,
Which the winds carry afar and sow,
And the snows and the rains nourish.

WALT WHITMAN.

Wallace, Kansas,
Sept. 19th, 1879.

NOT a grave of the murdered for Freedom
But grows seeds of a wider Freedom,
Which the winds carry afar and sow,
And the snows and the rains nourish.

WALT WHITMAN.

Wallace, Kansas,
Sept. 19th, 1879.

THE KANSAS MEMORIAL.

PRELIMINARY.

THIS book is a report of the meeting of the Old Settlers of Kansas, held at Bismarck Grove, on the line of the Kansas Pacific Railway, near Lawrence, September 15th and 16th, 1879. The meeting was held as a celebration of the twenty-fifth anniversary of the settlement of the State, and as such was of extraordinary interest.

The first Old Settlers' celebration at Lawrence was held September 15th, 1870. A celebration was held annually thereafter until 1877. Up to this time these gatherings had been of a local character. At the meeting in 1877, it was determined to have no celebration in 1878, but to make that for 1879, a more general one for the whole State of Kansas, and to make preparations for it on a scale commensurate with the importance of a gathering intended to commemorate the lapse of a quarter century since the settlement of Kansas was begun. To take charge of such preparations, the following committee was appointed:

James Blood, Robert Morrow, E. A. Coleman, Joseph Savage, C. L. Edwards, Joseph P. Root, Cyrus K. Halliday, Charles B. Lines, Joel Grover, Ferdinand Fuller and Charles W. Smith, the last named gentlemen being chosen secretary of the committee. At a meeting of this committee held April 10th, 1879, a committee on invitations was appointed, as follows:

James S. Emery, Robert Morrow, and Charles W. Smith. Charles Robinson was also appointed a committee to confer with railroads in relation to transportation. At a meeting held August 6th, the State Historical Society was requested to coöperate with the committee in making arrangements for and conducting the

proceedings of the celebration.   J. S. Emery, Sidney Clarke, and
O. E. Leonard were added to the committee on transportion at
this meeting, and it was determined that the Celebration should
continue through two days, Monday and Tuesday, September 15th
and 16th, 1879.   On the 20th of August the following officers and
committees were designated:

President — Charles Robinson.   Marshal — Samuel Walker.
Assistant Marshals—H. B. Asher, and John P. Ross.   Committee
on Barbacue—E. O. Coleman, C. L. Edwards and T. H. Kennedy.

There are reasons why a brief history of Kansas would be appropriate in connection with this report.   There are reasons to the
contrary.   In the opinion of the editor the time has not yet
arrived when a full and impartial history of the stirring events which
transpired during the territorial government of Kansas, culminating in the admission of the State to the Union as a free State, can
be written.   For, while the line of demarcation between the pro-
slavery and free state parties was strongly defined, and the issue
clearly made up, yet neither side brought to the contest a solid
organization.   Each party was composed of factions, agreeing
probably upon the main issue involved, but differing, often widely,
upon minor points.   There were free state men who demanded
total abolition; others who were content to save Kansas alone;
and still others who cared little for the slavery question, one way
or another, but much for the preservation of the Union, whose
danger they wisely comprehended.   On the other hand there were
pro-slavery men who believed in the institution of slavery on general principles; others who maintained, with Douglas, that the doctrine of State's rights was paramount to that of universal human
liberty; and yet others who lost sight of the slavery question in
their anxiety to dismember the Union.   On both sides, also, there
were adventurous men without convictions of any sort, and selfish
men who sought only their own supereminence, being regardless
alike of private and public welfare.   Of the chief actors in the
early troubles, many are now alive, and, as participants in the
exercises at Bismarck Grove, gave in their own words, as recorded
here, their version of the story of Kansas.   But the testimony is
by no means all in, and for the editor now to say which of the
many conflicting statements and opinions is best substantiated by
the weight of evidence, would be a premature and, under the circumstances, an ungracious task.   It must be many years, there-

fore, before this snarl can all be disentangled and the mysteries of it made plain.

Certain facts, however, in regard to the general outline of Kansas history should be borne in mind; and first, there are in Kansas history the four following well-defined divisions :

I.   The period prior to January 1st, 1857;

II. The period subsequent to January 1st, 1857, and prior to January 1st, 1861—practically to the commencement of the rebellion; '

III. The period subsequent to January 1st, 1861, and prior to January 1st, 1865; and

IV. The post-bellum period, from 1865 to the present time.

Within the first period are included the pioneer days proper, and the struggle for free soil. This struggle was squarely ended by the date above given. The second period may be characterized as the period of political organization, during which occurred the bitter struggle for leadership among the old free state leaders. This culminated in the election of Lane to the Senate, April 4th, 1861. The third period was the war period, during which the people of the State were in an uncertain, turbulent condition, isolated from other parts of the country, unsettled in their purposes, and apprehensive of calamity of every sort. The fourth and last period covers the years since the war, during which the immediate effects of the war have been almost wholly obliterated by the wonder-working hand of progress. These years, though not without their times of trouble and discouragement, have been years of peace and prosperity, witnessing an era of material advancement the like of which has rarely been recorded on the pages of history.

Kansas in 1854: What was it? Only a vast unexplored territory stretching from the Missouri river westward to the Rocky Mountains. A few settlements clung to the eastern border; agriculture had scarcely pushed a rifle's shot into this wild domain; Indians roamed at will over the great plains, swooping down now and then upon the scattered settlements with murderous intent; buffalo in countless herds tramped the boundless prairie to the hardness of pavement; a few faithful missionaries established schools among the tribes; the people were heterogeneous, poor and almost purposeless. Politics stepped into the arena, and the air was filled with strife. The territorial government was formed, and armed conflicts took place; fire, rapine, pillage, bloodshed, robbery and a general chaos enveloped Kansas. Bleeding Kansas they called it then. After awhile, Kansas was erected into a State. People flocked into the new Commonwealth and a new era was inaugurated.

Out of the smoke and clouds of the earlier conflict has arisen a Commonwealth greater in its present achievements and far greater in its inevitable future than the most sanguine pioneer could have prophesied. A quarter of a century denotes but a small part of the world's duration. Locate it back beyond the days of our grandfathers, and it would, perhaps, cover but few important events; but that quarter of a century which marks the early days of Kansas, is an era of moral and material progress unexampled in the history of nations. Whatever of strife the exigencies of politics may have engendered in the past; whatever differences of opinion may have been entertained; whatever of local disturbances may have occurred in the earlier days of Kansas, happily for her and happily for all the people, the acerbity of those days belongs to the past alone and serves only as a milestone in the history of the State. There were times of strife, now the hour is one of peace.

Something should be said here in regard to the place where the old settlers assembled—Bismarck Grove. One of the best brief descriptions of it was by Noble L. Prentis, author of "A Kansan Abroad," who wrote: " One of the things which may be considered worthy of a little Kansas self-gratulation at this quarter-century celebration is the creation of such a place as Bismarck Grove. Originally, we believe, a beer garden and dedicated to Gambrinus, it has been transformed into a beautiful place, one of the finest for out door gatherings in the West. It has afforded an opportunity to gratify a Kansas passion—that for advertising. The glaring poster and the modest but insinuating ' dodger ' have made Bismarck Grove much better known in Kansas than the names of the four Evangelists. The Kansas Pacific has become, in a business way, a promoter of free speech, and every variety of it. Here in Bismarck Grove, in the course of a few weeks, the friends of temperance have held the greatest meetings in the interests of that reform. Here clergymen and laymen have labored on the bulwarks of Zion, and, following them, came the Liberal convention, where the opponents of orthodoxy marshaled their forces, all classes of dissent being represented, from the mildest protestant against eternal punishment, to those so bitter that they recalled a criticism on Lord Amberly's infidel book, 'What can Jesus Christ have done to Lord Amberly, that he assails him with such violence?' Speaking of Bismarck materially instead of spiritually, the trees are broad in their shade, the grass is green, the tents, the cottages and the tabernacle afford ample shelter, while the lakes, wells and fountains furnish an abundance of water for all purposes. Bismarck is a good place, and a credit to Kansas."

In conclusion, those who may chance to be interested in this book should write with the editor in thanking Hon. F. G. Adams, Secretary of the Kansas State Historical Society, for having performed the most important part of the work of preparation. To him and the Society, which he so ably represents, the people of Kansas are indebted for that which none but future generations will know fully how to appreciate.

ORGANIZATION OF THE MEETING.

ENERAL JAMES BLOOD, of Lawrence, Chairman of the Old Settlers' Committee of Arrangements, called the meeting to order. Prayer was offered by Rev. Richard Cordley, D.D. Dr. Cordley made a simple yet comprehensive and powerful prayer. He alluded to the guiding and protecting power of God in the past, and especially during the dark and bloody period of early days; to what the State had become, and what yet might be before it. He prayed that Kansas might always be true to the principles for which its early settlers had made so many sacrifices.

At the conclusion of Dr. Cordley's prayer, Gen. Blood announced the officers of the meeting as follows :

President—Hon. Charles Robinson, first Governor of Kansas.

Vice-Presidents—Ex-Gov. Thos. Carney, Ex-Gov. J. M. Harvey, Ex-Gov. S. J. Crawford, Ex-Gov. Geo. T. Anthony, Gov. J. P. St. John, Hon. S C. Pomeroy, Ex-Lieut. Gov. Green, Hon. Geo. A. Crawford, Hon. E. G. Ross, Hon. D. W. Wilder, Col. Wm. A. Phillips, Col. D. R. Anthony, Col. John A. Martin, Col. Samuel Walker, Hon. Robert Morrow, Hon. Sidney Clarke, Hon. John Martin, Gen. Chas. W. Blair, Hon. S. N. Wood, Hon. F. P. Baker, Judge S. D. Lecompte, Hon. T. S. Huffaker, Hon. Sol. Miller, Wm. Hutchinson, Esq., G. W. Hutchinson, Hon. E. N. Morrill, Hon. B. F. Simpson, Hon. James Hanway, Col. Kersey Coates, Hon. Geo. Graham, F. Fuller, J. G. Sands, Hon. C. V. Eskridge, Hon. Jacob Stotler, Hon. M. M. Murdock, Hon. W. R. Wagstaff, Capt. E. A. Coleman, Hon. James S. Emery, Hon. Len. T. Smith, Gen. C. W. Babcock, Hon. Chester Thomas, Hon. P. P. Elder, Hon. D. C. Haskell, Hon. Thos. Ryan, Hon. John A. Anderson, Gen. Charles Leonhardt, Hon. C. B. Lines, Judge John T. Burriss, Capt. Oliver Barber, Hon. James F. Legate, Hon. H.

Miles Moore, Dr. E. G. Macey, Wm. Yates, Esq., John H. Shimmons, Col. John Ritchie, Judge L. D. Bailey, Col. S. S. Prouty, Hon John Speer, Col. N. S. Goss, Col. D. W. Houston, Hon. John T. Lanter, Hon. John W. Scott, Hon. John R. Goodin, Capt. James Christian, Hon. Orlin Thurston, Hon. Geo. A. Reynolds, Hon D. P. Lowe, Col. H. S. Wilson, Hon. Ed. R. Smith, Col. James D. Snoddy, Capt. A. J. Shannon, Col. Josiah E. Hayes, Hon. A. D. Downs, Judge S. N. Latta, Hon. Josiah Kellog, Capt. W. I. R. Blackman, Col. J. R. McClure, Henry Hyatt, Capt. N. Cradit, Hugh Cameron, Rev. C. H. Lovejoy, Rev. J.W. Clock, Dr. W. L. Challis, Hon. George W. Glick, Rev. Pardee Butler, Hon. S. D. Macdonald, Maj. H. H. Williams, Joseph Bliss, Rev. S. L. Adair, Hon. Cyrus Leland, Maj. A. S. Johnson, Sam. Kimball, Hon. S. O. Thacher, Hon. Ira J. Lacock, James S. Huggins, Maj. Martin Anderson, Col. D. H. Horne, Hon. F. W. Giles, Hon. J. W. Farnsworth, J. S. Gordon, Esq., Col. H. D. McMeekin, Dr. F. L. Crane, Hon. James Rodgers, C. S. Colman, Ed. Smith, Rev. J. W. Fox, Hon. Henry Fox, Capt. G. W. Umbarger, Elder B. R. Reed, John Hammond, Rev. Richard Cordley, Ed. Barton, Maj. T. H. Kennedy, Mrs. Samuel Walker, Mrs. E. A. Coleman, Mrs. S. N. Wood, Mrs. S. J. Willis, Mrs. J. Savage, Mrs. O. A. Hanscom, Mrs. M. E. Lane, G. M. Simcock, Hon. R. G. Elliott, Hon. Isaac Sharpe, Capt. John Armstrong, Hon. J. C. Burnett, Hon. P. B. Maxon, Hon. Wm. Martindale, N. B. Blanton, Hon. Henry Bronson, Capt. S. Kauffman, Hon. W. A. Johnson, Capt. Charles F. Garrett, Capt. F. B. Swift, Hon. O. A. Bassett, B. W. Woodward, F. A. Bailey, Hon. R. W. Luddington.

Secretary—Hon. F. G. Adams, Secretary State Historical Society.

Assistant Secretaries—Hon. J. K. Goodin, Hon. D. B. Emmert, Hon. J. C. Hebbard, Hon. T. D. Thacher, Capt. A. R. Banks, W. H. T. Wakefield.

ADDRESS BY CHARLES ROBINSON.

The opening address was delivered by Ex-Governor Charles Robinson, and was as follows:

Friends and Fellow Citizens:

Before proceeding with the order of exercises as prescribed by the Committee of Arrangements, I must be permitted to thank the committee for their partiality in asking me to preside on this occasion.   To be selected for such a position at the celebration of the twenty-fifth anniversary of the settlement of Kansas, I regard as the crowning honor of my life.

During the quarter of a century closing with this year, many events have transpired of vast import to our State and nation. While twenty-five years from May last not a legal settler could be found on Kansas soil, nor a dollar of taxable property, nor a mile of railroad or telegraph line, the census of 1880 will probably show one million of inhabitants, two hundred millions of dollars of taxable property, and three thousand miles of railroad and telegraph lines in our State.

While twenty-five years ago the States of our Union were part free and part slave, and four millions of people were held in bondage, neither slave States nor slave men can be found throughout our land.

Before the opening of Kansas to settlement, two methods were advocated to dispose of the "irrepressible conflict" between freedom and slavery—one was a dissolution of the Union; the other, paper provisos by Congress against the further extension of slavery. But the passage of the Kansas-Nebraska bill changed the conflict from the forum and halls of Congress to the plains of Kansas. Foreseeing this result, while this bill was pending in Congress, a member of the Massachusetts Legislature gave the alarm, and called upon the anti-slavery forces to change front, and prepare to meet the enemy on his chosen battle-field.   He immediately set about procuring two charters for emigration societies, one from Connecticut and one from his own State.   No sooner was Kansas open to settlement than the contest opened between freedom and slavery; and opened not for Kansas alone, but for the entire country.

Warren D. Wilkes, in the Charleston *Mercury*, thus states the issue :

The importance of securing Kansas for the South may be briefly set forth in a positive and negative form. By consent of parties, the present contest in Kansas is made the turning point in the destinies of slavery and abolitionism. If the South triumphs, abolitionism will be defeated and shorn of its power for all time. If she is defeated, abolitionism will grow more insolent and aggressive, until the utter ruin of the South is consummated. * *
* All depends upon the action of the present moment.

Charles Sumner, on the night of the passage of the Kansas-Nebraska bill, said :

Sir, the bill which you are about to pass is at once the worst and the best bill on which Congress ever acted. * * * It is the worst bill, inasmuch as it is a present victory of slavery. * * * Sir, it is best bill on which Congress ever acted, for it annuls all past compromises with slavery, and makes all future compromises impossible. Thus it puts freedom and slavery face to face, and bids them grapple. Who can doubt the result ? * *
* Thus, sir, now standing at the very grave of freedom in Nebraska and Kansas, I lift myself to the vision of that happy resurrection, by which freedom will be secured, not only in these Territories, but everywhere under the national government. * * * Sorrowfully I bend before the wrong you are about to commit; joyfully I welcome all the promises of the future.

Was this issue actually joined? In the spring of 1855, at a meeting of proslavery men at Leavenworth, among others the following resolutions were adopted :

Resolved, That the institution of slavery is known and recognized in this Territory ; that we repeal the doctrine that it is a moral or political evil, and we hurl back with scorn upon its slanderous authors the charge of inhumanity ; and we warn all persons not to come to our peaceful firesides to slander us and sow seeds of discord between the master and the servant, for much as we may be driven, we cannot be responsible for the consequences.

Resolved, That a vigilance committee, consisting of thirty members, shall now be appointed, who shall observe and report all such persons as shall openly act in violation of law and order, and by the expression of abolition sentiments produce disturbance to the quiet of the citizens, or danger to their domestic relations ; and all such persons so offending shall be notified and made to leave the Territory.

The usurpation called the Territorial Legislature, sitting near the Missouri border, enacted the following :

SECTION 12.   If any free person, by speaking or writing, assert or maintain that persons have not the right to hold slaves in this Territory, or shall introduce into this Territory, print, publish, write, circulate or cause to be introduced into the Territory, any book, paper, magazine, pamphlet or circular, containing any denial of the right of persons to hold slaves in this Territory, such person shall be deemed guilty of a felony, and punished by imprisonment or hard labor for a term of not less than two years.

Here is the challenge.   How was it accepted?   At the first opportunity that offered, at the Celebration of the Fourth of July, 1855, the issue was publicly joined, not only for Kansas, but for the country.   The speaker on that occasion, on behalf of the free state men took up the glove as follows:

"These," gentlemen and Christians, "repel the doctrine that slavery is a moral or political evil," and "hurl back with scorn the charge of inhumanity," and warn all persons of different views from their own not to come to Kansas, for they shall be "made to leave the Territory!" if they do. "Made to leave the country!" indeed.   Well, a "right smart" good time of it may our neighbors have in making all leave Kansas, who will not bow down and worship the calves they set up. "Made to leave!" Gentlemen, look at that beautiful banner (presented by the ladies to the "Stubbs"). Think from whence it came, and of the motives which prompted its presentation, and then think about being *made to leave* your country for no crime. One thing appears evident if *we* are made to leave, the ladies will be ashamed to follow, and will let us go alone.   *   *   *   *   *   Again, "If the people of Missouri make it necessary, by their unlawful course, for us to establish freedom in that State, in order to enjoy the liberty of governing ourselves in Kansas, then let that be the issue.   If Kansas and the whole North must be enslaved, or Missouri become free, then let her be made free. Aye, and if to be free ourselves, slavery must be abolished in the whole country, then let us accept that issue.   If black slavery in a part of the States is incompatible with white freedom in any State, then let black slavery be banished from all.   As men espousing the principles of the Declaration of Independence, we can do no less than accept these issues."

At the first general Territorial Convention of the free state men, after the passage of the Leavenworth resolutions, and the enactment of the slave code by usurpation, the following resolution, drafted by Ex-Gov. Reeder, was adopted :

"*Resolved*, That we will endure and submit to these laws no longer than the best interests of the Territory require, as the least of two evils, and will resist them to a bloody issue as soon as we ascertain that peaceable remedies shall fail, and forcible resistance shall furnish any reasonable prospect of success."

These brief extracts from the public utterances of the time are sufficient to show that the charge was made and accepted in terrible earnestness. On the one side was the slave power of the country with all the machinery of the Federal Government at command; while on the other was a handful of earnest men and women, inspired with the spirit of liberty, and with such moral and material support as was afforded by the Emigrant Aid Associations and freedom loving men of the country.

How this contest was waged; how this small number, with three hundred miles of hostile territory between themselves and their sympathizers, managed to defy and resist the usurpation and usurpers and baffle the Federal officials, history must record. It is sufficient for this occasion to know that Freedom to-day is triumphant throughout the land.

Kansas can perhaps be pardoned for not only claiming the credit of the first local victory, but was the first State to accept the challenge of the Slave Power when it laid violent hands upon the government. When Kansas went into the Union, seven slave States stepped out, and eight others were on the point of going. Under these circumstances, when the destinies of the nation trembled in the balance, and the bravest seemed to hesitate as to the course to be taken, Kansas gave no uncertain sound. In her first official paper, she advised that the nation should do as she had done, accept at once and forever the issue tendered. In her first message she said:

A demand is made by certain States that new consessions and guarantees be given to slavery, or the Union must be destroyed. The present constitution, however faithfully adhered to, is declared to be incompatible with the existence of slavery; its change is demanded, or the government under it must be overthrown. If it is true that the continued existence of slavery requires the destruction of the Union, it is time to ask if the existence of the Union does not require the destruction of slavery. If such an issue be forced upon the nation, it must be met, and met promptly. The people of Kansas, while they are willing to fulfill their constitutional obligations toward their brethren in the sister States to the letter, cannot look upon the destruction of the fairest and most prosperous government on earth, with indifference. If the issue is presented to them—the overthrow of the Union or the destruction of slavery—they will not long hesitate as to their choice. * * * * * While it is the duty of each loyal State to see that equal and exact justice is done to the citizens of every other State, it is equally its duty to sustain the Chief Executive of the nation in defending the government from foes, whether from within or without, and Kansas, though last and least of the States in the Union, will ever be ready to answer the call of her country.

How well she kept her pledge to the President, let the muster rolls answer. If I mistake not she furnished a larger percentage of her population for the war, and lost a larger percentage in battle than any other State.

So much for Kansas and Kansas citizens; but great injustice would be done non-residents did we attempt to claim all the credit for the grand results of the last quarter of a century. At the opening of Kansas, slavery seized upon every town and district except such towns and districts as were settled by the agency of the Emigrant Aid Society. Without those settlements, it is safe to say, Kansas would have been a slave State, with not even an attempt at resistance. Without the Emigrant Aid Society these towns would not have been, and without Eli Thayer, Amos A. Lawrence, Edward Everett Hale, Wm. M. Evarts and their co-laborers, that society would have had no existence. And these men would have been powerless with all their machinery had not the Liberty party and free soil campaigns, under the lead of the Birneys, Hales, Julians and others been fought; and these campaigns would have been still-born had there been no Garrisons, Parker Pillsburys, Theodore Parkers and Wendell Phillipses to cry in the wilderness and prepare the way for the agencies that followed.

Another class of actors rendered invaluable service near the close of our struggle and must not be forgotten on this gala day. The Walkers, Stantons, Denvers, Forneys and other conservative Democrats, by their impartial and honorable course prevented much bloodshed and cut short the struggle, perhaps years, by crushing out fraud and giving the government to the legal majority as demanded by the Organic Act.

Also to our former pro-slavery antagonists who have so honorably acquiesced in the result, we most cordially extend the right hand of fellowship We have reason to believe that many are well pleased with the institutions of the State, and all are willing to forever close the "bloody chasm" that once divided us.

In conclusion, let me congratulate Kansas and our guests and all friends of Kansas, that the close of the first quarter of a century from its settlement finds peace and good will among all its inhabitants, and unprecedented prosperity throughout its borders.

SONG OF A THOUSAND YEARS.

At the conclusion of Governor Robinson's address, Messrs. Thomas H. Edwards, Wm. C. Edwards and Captain Henry Booth, of Larned, sang the following appropriate song, written by Walt. Whitman, the venerable poet, who had accompanied Col. Forney to Kansas and was present at the celebration:

> Lift up your eyes, desponding freemen;
> Fling to the winds your needless fears;
> He who unfurled your beauteous banner,
> Says it shall wave a thousand years.

CHORUS—A thousand years, my own Columbia!
   ' Tis the glad day so long foretold!
   ' Tis the glad morn whose early twilight
   Washington saw in times of old.

What if the clouds, one little moment,
   Hide the blue sky where morn appears—
When the bright sun, that tints them crimson,
   Rises to shine a thousand years.

                 CHORUS—

Tell the great world these blessed tidings!
   Yes, and be sure thy bondman hears;
Tell the oppress'd of every nation,
   Jubilee lasts a thousand years.

                 CHORUS—

Envious foes beyond the ocean!
   Little we heed your threat'ning sneers;
Little will they—our children's children—
   When you are gone a thousand years.

                 CHORUS—

Rebels at home! go hide your faces—
   Weep for your crimes with bitter tears;
You could not bind the blessed daylight,
   Though you should strive a thousand years.

                 CHORUS—

Back to your dens, ye secret traitors!
   Down to your own degraded spheres!
Ere the first blaze of dazzling sunshine
   Shortens your lives a thousand years.

                 CHORUS—

Haste thee along, thou glorious Noonday!
   Oh, for the eyes of ancient seers!
Oh, for the faith of him who reckons
   Each of his days a thousand years!

                 CHORUS—

Governor Robinson, as President of the Old Settlers' Meeting in introducing Judge Usher, and referring to the arrival of delegations from different parts of the State, said he well remembered arrivals from the same localities in former times for the defense of Lawrence, when our neighbors from across our eastern border made hostile incursions. Once a multitude of them were camped in the Wakarusa bottom. When we saw the Topeka and Leavenworth boys coming, we were glad and welcomed them to our assistance in saving our homes. So we now welcome them on this day to our hearts and homes. He then introduced Hon. J. P. Usher, formerly Mr. Lincoln's Secretary of the Interior, now representing the city of Lawrence as its honored Mayor.

Judge Usher spoke as follows :

Since the organization of society, men have been accustomed by appropriate methods to commemorate great events in their career, as well as the acts and deeds of their benefactors, their heroes and their statesmen. Especially are they prone to do this if the benefaction, the event, act, or deed has resulted in eradicating an insufferable evil, or in the establishment of a great and lasting good. It is in commemoration of such acts and deeds that we have assembled to-day.

The especial significance attached, is not that we are to commemorate the first settlement of a new and wilderness country, accompanied by hardships and sufferings such as were encountered by the Pilgrims of Plymouth Rock, or in the settlement of the Northwestern Territory ; yet it is called the Old Settlers' Meeting, and we have met here to commemorate the settlement of Kansas, a settlement which, for causes which I will briefly explain, inaugurated a fearful and bloody struggle, to be determined only by a constitution afterward to be adopted, declaring whether Kansas should be inhabited by freemen only, or by freemen and slaves.

At the request of the citizens of Lawrence, I have been deputed on this occasion to extend to the citizens of the State and from abroad their cordial greeting and welcome. Our citizens are here in large numbers, and, as there are many among them now fathers and mothers who were unborn when that fearful struggle raged, I may be pardoned in wasting a few words in explanation of the great significance of this meeting, by giving a brief narrative of the causes which led to that contest.

Kansas, though of immense proportions, is but a part of that vast domain which was ceded to the United States through the instrumentality of Mr. Jefferson, seventy-six years ago. Missouri is a part of that domain. When that State was admitted into the Union, March 6, 1820, after a long and fierce debate, it was by

2

Congress enacted that slavery and involuntary servitude, otherwise than in punishment for crime, should be forever prohibited in all the Louisiana Purchase north of latitude 36° 30'. This law was called the Missouri Compromise, and, unrepealed, protected the territory in which Kansas now is from the curse of slavery.

But, by many acts of Congress, Kansas was not subject to settlement, until May 30, 1854, when what is known as the Kansas-Nebraska Act was passed. Many Indian tribes had by treaty been allotted large tracts of land now within the State of Kansas, and, by force of these treaties and acts of Congress, all citizens were prevented from intruding into the Territory, and the army of the United States was employed to defend the same against all who might come.

By this act of Congress of May 30, 1854, the barriers so long existing against the settlement of Kansas were removed; but in the removal of the same, through the omnipotence of the slave power in Congress, the Missouri Compromise was by the act repealed. Mr. Clay acquired great and lasting renown for the part he took in securing the Missouri Compromise act; but having died in 1852, after having successfully carried through the compromise measures of 1850, Congress had the temerity to declare in the Kansas-Nebraska Act that these compromise acts were inconsistent with the Missouri Compromise act, wherefore that act was repealed; and, further, that in and by said Kansas-Nebraska Act it was not the intention of Congress to legislate slavery into any State or Territory, nor to exclude it therefrom, but to leave the people thereof perfectly free to form and regulate their domestic institutions in their own way. The act further provided "that in all cases involving titles to slaves, writs of error or appeals should be allowed and decided by the Supreme Court without regard to the value of the matter, property or title in controversy."

Men, philanthropists, and statesmen who had long struggled and indulged the pleasing hope that there was a growing sense of the inhumanity and wrong of slavery, were shocked and horrified at this law. They plainly saw that, instead of the realization of their hope that the shackle was about to fall from the slave, new shackles were forged; and, while yet in dismay, the decision of the Supreme Court in the Dred Scott case was announced, deciding, as it was said at the time, "that a black man had no rights which a white man was bound to respect." The claim was that slavery was protected by the Constitution of the United States, and this because slaves were property, and that for Kansas or any other Territory or State it only required appropriate laws securing to the holders of slaves adequate means for protecting them in the right to slaves to enable them to exercise the right of enslaving men and women everywhere.

From this brief statement of the condition of affairs at that day you will observe how important it was to the slave holding interest to secure a legislature which should pass laws adequate to enable them to maintain their right to hold slaves in Kansas. They reasoned well that an executive who would sign and approve the Kansas-Nebraska act, would appoint a governor who would approve an act establishing slavery. Accordingly, to make sure of the accomplishment of their purpose, Missouri, then dominated by slavery and devoted to its behests, sent into Kansas bodies of armed men who appeared in numbers at nearly all the voting precincts and by menace and brute force took possession of the polls, drove the free state men away, voted and caused to be returned as elected, and their names to be returned to the governor as elected, an out and out pro-slavery legislature. It was in vain that Governor Andrew H. Reeder, of Pennsylvania, sought to overhaul and purge the polls and correct the returns. The legislature met and made haste to pass an act which became a law, as the legislature pretended, though never approved by the governor, whereby it was enacted, that whoever should entice a slave to escape from his master, should, upon conviction, suffer death; whoever should deny the right to hold slaves in the Territory of Kansas, should be imprisoned not less than two years and suffer other penalties. The blind and unreasoning zeal of that legislature is well displayed in the report of the judiciary committee of the legislative council, the higher branch of the Territorial legislature—a copy of which report I have procured, and which is as follows :

The Committee on Judiciary, to whom was referred a bill entitled an "Act to punish decoying slaves from their masters," respectfully report that they have had the same, for some time, under advisement, and recognizing the correctness of the provisions of the act, but one question has occupied the attention of the Committee, and that is the character of the punishment prescribed in the bill. At first presentation of the subject, there was an apparent severity which seemed not to be in consonance with the crime, and, viewing the offense in the light of grand larceny alone, the genius of our institution and the prejudices of the day in which we live, at once discard so extreme a punishment. But when we view the offense in its peculiar bearing upon our institution at this particular time, it assumes more the character of treason against the laws than an ordinary crime, which but affects the parties immediately interested, or the immediate community in which the offense may have been committed once, may, in its incendiary tendency, lead to consequences of the most fearful character, as well upon our political as social institutions; it is an offense, the frequent occurrence of which, we may well imagine, might light the bonfires of civil war and result in bloodshed more fearful than a thousand murders. We are, therefore, in view of this, prepared to sanction the penalty of death, and respectfully recommend the passage of the act.   R. R. REES, Chairman.

When I say that the member of the legislative council whose name is attached to that report as chairman of the judiciary committee, was, in his nature, one of the kindest men in the world, for it was my privilege to know him for many years as such, it only shows how imperious and exacting were the demands of the slave power upon the men deputed to do the work of fastening slavery upon Kansas, and of persecuting and driving out those who sought to make this the dwelling-place of freedom.

In addition to the passage of this most atrocious law, the legislature adopted, in mass, the statutes of the slave State of Missouri, with its slave code, and after passing some other special acts, adjourned. Governor Reeder was removed by the President, Mr. Pierce, and he left the Territory in disgust, and I believe to avoid insult and personal injury, in disguise.

Then it was that the anti-slavery sentiment all over the land was aroused, and with firm resolve determined to defy this pretended law. John Speer, here, publisher of the "Kansas Tribune," denounced and defied them. He published in large and glaring letters, "I deny the right of any person to hold slaves in the Territory of Kansas."

Material aid was contributed, without stint, by the adversaries of slavery, throughout the free States, and in addition to those who intended to make their permanent homes in Kansas, there came many others with no other intent than that of joining in the fray in behalf of freedom. In the meantime the pro-slavery party was not idle; they were vigilant; in Kansas they were vigilant, and all along the carrying places where they had dominion and sway. They controlled the transportation upon the Missouri river, and established a rigid surveillance upon all boats ascending the river. Emigrants with or without arms were treated alike; they were stripped of all they had and required to return from whence they came. Such, in brief, were the obstructions which the emigrants encountered, that they were compelled to abandon the more easy way by the river and resort to the tedious and more expensive way through Iowa; and so by that way they came in wagons and on foot. The first advantage was altogether in favor of the pro-slavery party. They, as it were, had choice of grounds, and struck the first staggering blow; but the advantage thus secured, was not to last. The struggle fiercely raged, and after a few months it became apparent to the careful observer, that the cause of freedom was steadily being advanced. The issue remained on trial until 1861, when by the adoption of the Wyandotte Constitution the advocates of freedom secured a complete and lasting triumph. By that Constitution there has been secured to the people of Kansas, all the great and valuable rights ever contended for by philosophers and statesmen, among which, and they are fundamental, it is ordained that there shall be freedom of speech, freedom of the press, the inviolability of the person from enforced servitude except for crime, and all monopolies are prohibited. Free colleges and free schools are established, and the system has been organized upon such basis as to secure their endurance forever. Without attempting to pass into detail, of all the valuable provisions of our Constitution, it is enough to say, that although the government of the United States did not leave the people free to determine, by their Constitution, what their domestic institutions should be, the people did, against all governmental influence, against the tyrannical use of the army, against the profligate use of the public money and abuse of the appointing power, make Kansas free. And after more that twenty years of established freedom there has been paid to the institutions of Kansas and to the work of the old settlers, the highest compliment that has ever been paid, in my judgment, to the political work of men.

A people, after having borne the lash for 200 years, toiling unrequited under the stings and pains of the lash, near two thousand miles away, having turned the yoke of their oppression, cast about to find some land where they could enjoy equal rights with their fellow men, and of all places on the face of the green earth, Kansas was found to be the haven of refuge.

Who that stands in the way and receives in his sheltering arms the hare by hound pursued, does not instinctively resolve to save the life of the timid creature from its relentless pursuer? The emotion that prompts this is not altogether human, as it seems to me, but an emotion which proceeds directly from the power and influence of the omnipresent and merciful Deity.

Neither they of the exodus, nor those who flee from oppressive laws in other lands, need to have the principles upon which our government is founded asserted in their behalf.

My friends, I now want to explain to you in brief the reason why we are here at this celebration. It is to commemorate the inauguration of a State possessing institutions which should remain forever of the best and most exalted character possible for humanity to invent. I have shown to you and you know that the effort to establish such institutions has been crowned with wonderful success. It now but remains for me to say why in my opinion Lawrence should welcome you in this glad gathering.

In the midst of all the turmoil and suffering of the pioneers of free Kansas, Lawrence was the head. Hanging well on the borders of the Indian reservation, it was the first practicable and proper place for the location of a town beyond the Missouri border upon the Kansas river not reserved for Indian occupany. Twenty-five years ago they came, the pioneers of freedom, and located in Lawrence. One of our most estimable citizens, one whose place can never be supplied, I fear, Secretary of the State Board of Agriculture, says in his report that Lawrence was then called the city of freedom. That in Lawrence, and only in Lawrence could a man at all times say that he was opposed to slavery without being in danger of losing his life. It was in Lawrence that the weary persecuted ones in other parts of the Territory found repose; with John Brown among the number. (Applause.) John Brown, who, when he struck that final blow at the slave power, that blow which caused that haughty power to tremble throughout its entire domain, and, in its frenzy, to rush to those measures which caused its destruction—John Brown the hero who, in that fatal hour at Harper's Ferry, standing with one son dead at his feet, with one hand feeling the pulse of another son whose life blood was oozing, and with the other hand holding his rifle, commanded his men with the utmost composure, encouraging them to sell their lives as dearly as possible—this old hero whenever in his Kansas sojourn, he would seek repose in safety, where none but friends dwelt, would repair to Lawrence. (Applause.)

The fact, my friends, is well known that Lawrence was the only place in the entire Territory where free state men could utter their sentiments. For this thing, Lawrence suffered. In one day nearly two hundred of her citizens, before the sun had gone down, lay cold in death. There are few, if any, among the survivors of twenty-five years ago who were here in Lawrence to witness the horrid scenes, which at different times transpired in the devoted city. But there are many who have come since. The pioneers have children and those who have come to settle since have children. It is well that they know these things, and I have tried in a brief way to-day to speak somewhat of them. I wish them to be kept memorable. I wish the great truths which these people came here to establish and did establish, to be forever kept bright and clear in the minds of the growing and rising generation. I wish them to know why they are here in Kansas. I wish them to know the advantages of being here, and why they enjoy these advantages. We have cause to rejoice for many things. We have cause to rejoice that those among us who were of the opposing forces during this terrible struggle have cause for joy twice to our once. (Applause.) They rejoice because they were defeated; we rejoice because of our success. They see the mistake and error and now wonder why they were led to do these things. We all rejoice that they do think so. We rejoice altogether that we are of one common mind, that upon this great subject in which the welfare of mankind was buried up, that it has been terminated for the right; and we all believe that it is right. Men of all parties exchange congratulations that the difficulties have gone by and that all are now ready to join hands and go on in building up our glorious State, and in sharing the blessings of its institutions. It is the aim of all that our school system shall be brought to a better condition than that of any other State in the world. That these accumulated funds, now amounting to hundreds of thousands of dollars, shall be cared for and preserved until every child living among us, of whatever race or nationality shall have the benefit of it; and that the school fund shall be so devoted as to promote virtue and right. We rejoice that we have the best State in the whole Union, possessing such a mild equable and salubrious temperature. Kansas is in the very geographical center of the United States, and our population has now grown to a million. It has only been within a few years that we have been able to increase our numbers and our possessions; for until after Appomattox there was no time when men could peaceably follow their avocations in the State. All this great advance has been made in a few years. Then my friends let us rejoice, but don't let us go crazy. Don't let our friends from abroad think that we are standing on our heads, that we are disposed to forget who made us. We simply claim to be free men, made so through noble sacrifice of these pioneers gathered here to-day; and you see in us what free men, such free men, are. No man is taken to account for any opinion he has or may utter; whether it be political or whether it be religious, or of whatever nature. All say and do as they please, and say and do it in peace and without injuring anybody. That is the condition which we have reached under the Kansas-Nebraska act. (Applause.)

But I am taking up too much time. I know well enough there are many here who were present in those trying times, and I know they have come here as gladly as I have, and as you have. We hope to hear many of their voices to-day in re-counting the scenes of the early times, and I will not detain you. Providence is smiling upon us to-day in giving us this beautiful sky and this lovely air. We of Lawrence rejoice that you from all over Kansas have come to celebrate with us to day. All the old people, all the young people, of Lawrence, bid you welcome. In their behalf I bid you welcome. Let us go on in our work and after the two days shall have gone by, may it be a scene long to be remembered. May it be a scene which our children here to-day shall remember until their hairs are gray and their heads bowed down by age; remembering the difficulties these old settlers passed through in order that liberty might be preserved, and peace and prosperity reign among us in all this rich and prosperous state of Kansas.

THE CANNON "EIGHTEEN-FIFTY-SIX."

The cannon which was brought out from Milwaukee, Wisconsin, in 1856, for the defense of the free state men, and which is now kept at the state capital, had been brought from Topeka for use on this occasion. At the close of Judge Usher's speech, and at intervals between speeches, it was made to talk with its old-time energy.

TELEGRAM FROM GENERAL POPE.

The following telegram was received from General John Pope, of Ft. Leavenworth, and read to the meeting:

FORT LEAVENWORTH, Sept. 15, 1879.

Hon. John Speer, Bismarck Grove:

I will be with you on Tuesday, but cannot make an address; so I wish my name withdrawn from the programme.

JOHN POPE.

Whereupon Mr. Speer offered the following resolution, which was passed with immense cheering:

Resolved, That the old settlers always recognized the patriotic army of the Union, and that we surrender to General Pope, and invite him to visit us upon his own terms.

The hour of noon having arrived, the President announced an adjournment to 2 P. M.

AFTERNOON SESSION.

Gov. Robinson, in calling the meeting to order, said: As an evidence that universal harmony has taken the place of the strife of twenty-five years ago, I wish to announce that Thos. E. Irvine, who has charge of our salutes and is superintending the firing of that cannon, the "old 1856," was brought up a strong pro-slavery man, and was in the rebel army. And yet I do not know a man on the ground that is more jubilant than that same gentleman.

ADDRESS OF WELCOME BY COL. C. K. HOLLIDAY.

Introducing Col. Holliday, Gov. Robinson said: We all take a great pride in the capital of our State. It is one of the most beautiful towns in this country, to say nothing of Kansas. It has a brilliant future before it, and those who are here twenty-five years from to-day will see it a city of not less than fifty thousand inhabitants. I want to introduce to you a certain gentleman, but before doing so, I want to tell a little anecdote.

In 1854, after we had started Lawence, a party came here to Lawrence from the east under the auspices of the Emigrant Aid Company, and reported to its agent at this place. A committee was accordingly appointed to look at the country and find a location for this new company, and they went up as far as Topeka and Fort Riley, and then south and back to Lawrence. The committee saw three places where the country had so many advantages that they failed to make a selection, and they could not make a report in favor of any particular place. Well, the party said, "what shall we do?" I suggested to them, "the little place up here at Topeka," but said I, "if you say anything about it here in Lawrence, the chances are that some Yankees will go up there and jump the site. You had better go or send some four or five trusty men up there to squat upon it at once." Before the company arrived on the ground, a young man of fine address, good clothes, good looking, came to our settlement at Lawrence, from Pennsylvania. He introduced himself to the agent of the Emigrant Aid Company. The agent looked him over from head to foot, took several days to make his acquaintance, and finally concluded that he was just the man to superintend the erection of the capital of the State of Kansas, and so he sent him up there to represent the Emigrant Aid Company in the town of Topeka. He is now here to make an address of welcome in behalf of the old settlers of Kansas. I introduce to you, Col. C. K. Holliday.

Col. Holliday spoke as follows:

Mr. President, Fellow Old Settlers and Fellow Citizens:

This is no ordinary assemblage. This is no ordinary occasion. The assemblage is composed of the founders or early settlers of a great State. The occasion is to commemorate the early settlement of the State; and, looking back from the standpoint of a quarter of a century to measure the success of this great undertaking, and to contemplate, perhaps, from the success of the past —possibly, with a little vanity withal—the still greater success in store for them in the quarter century to come.

It is an impulse of the human heart to pay homage to the originator of any great movement having for its object the welfare of mankind; the discoverer of any great invention which contributes to the good of our fellow men; the promulgator of any great truth which is calculated to make men better, wiser, or more prosperous. To the founders or settlers of a great city, or great State, the highest meed of honor is due.

Surely, then, the meed of "well done" must be accorded to those who, a quarter of a century ago, bidding "good by" to their homes and friends and all the world held dear, turned their backs upon the lands of their births and their faces toward the setting sun. They came to subdue the desert; for did not all our geographies teach us that that vast and almost unknown plain between the Missouri river and the Rocky Mountains was the "Great American Desert?" They came to subdue the desert, and out of the desert to make a State; and in so doing to suffer all the dangers, toils and privations incident to the herculean task; to endure hunger; to suffer cold; to encounter fevers; to run the risk of border strife; to guard against savages; to contend with death. And now, at the expiration of a quarter of a century, it is well that those of the old settlers who still survive, with the kindly sym pathizing thousands of later settlers, should assemble together in re-union, as we are doing here to-day, rest a moment, review the great work accomplished, and take heart for the accomplishment of still greater achievements in the future.

They came—a quarter of a century ago—to subdue the desert and erect thereon a State. To-day the State is erected in all its magnificent proportions; to-day the "Desert blossoms as the rose."

"What hath God wrought" was the divine recognition in the first message ever transmitted by the electric telegraph. May we not with equal fervor and with equal faith, ask "What hath God wrought?" when we behold the wonderful transformation that has taken place upon the plains of Kansas in the quarter of a century just closing.

No such transformation—no such change—has ever been made, in the same length of time, heretofore, anywhere upon the broad surface of the globe. Then, a quarter of a century ago, an absolute void, and absolute waste, a—nothing; nothing at least but the earth, the air and sky. Now a State with nearly a million souls, ranking with the great States in population and wealth among all the States in the Union, and leading all the great States in some of the staple productions of the soil, and leading most of them in the other staple productions of the soil.

But I am reminded that it is not the productions of the soil, but—

"Men, high minded men,
Who know their rights, and knowing, dare maintain,
These constitute a State."

Then, I ask, where are the laws more liberal, or more just, or more conscientiously administered? Where do temperance, virtue, morality and religion find more cherished homes? Where does education shower her blessings more kindly, or more profusely upon rich and poor alike, and upon the children of all nations, races, colors, creeds and sects? The archives of our governments, both state and federal, exhibit the astounding fact that Kansas furnished more of those brave and heroic soldiers who, in in the great rebellion, upheld the banner of the republic high above the blazing clouds of battle, than she had citizens eligible to vote.

This, then, is the State we exhibit to-day, and these the men who compose it.

"Men, high minded men, who *knew* their rights, and knowing *dared* maintain." Men with the stern convictions and high moral courage of the descendants of Plymoth Rock, and the chivalrous dash and daring of the descendants of Jamestown combined; men, "who in peace prove their faith by the sweat of their brows, and in war by the blood of their hearts."

If so much has been accomplished in the twenty-five years gone by, amid the hardships of frontier life, the terrors and dangers of border strife, and the devastation of a great internecine war, with all the hindrances incident to the settlement of a new and remote country, what may not be accomplished in the twenty-five years to come? That distinguished gentleman and earnest friend of Kansas in her early history, and of freedom everywhere. Hon. Eli Thayer, predicted a year ago while riding with some friends through the State, that at the termination of the next twenty-five years Kansas would rank in population and wealth as the second State in the Union. I put the prediction on record to-day, not so much that it flatters our pride to be told that we shall soon be next to the first in the grade of States; but that when our children assemble again in Bismarck Grove—then a park in the city of Lawrence—at the half centennial celebration, they may pronounce a proper eulogium upon him who has been our unswerving friend in our darkest hours, and now lights up our pathway of State by this brilliant prediction of our future.

While I may not have pinions to follow my friend as far as he has gone, yet *I* may say, and I say it reverently, employing the language of the apostle, that "eye hath not seen, neither hath ear heard, nor yet hath it entered into the heart of man to conceive, the glories which shall be revealed" in our great and prosperous State; in the near future, as occupying the grand central position in the Union, in the language of Pierre Soule, "a hundred States shall revolve around her and strive for the honor of saluting her Queen."

On a day, and on an occasion, like this, all reference to political topics should be sacredly avoided. All are invited to participate in this great ovation to the successful founding and the successful building of a State; and no utterance must fall from my lips that could wound the most sensitive heart. But that which was politics a quarter of a century ago, has become history to-day; and brief as my remarks should be, they would be incomplete if I did not advert to the position Kansas was forced to assume in the determination of the greatest governmental problem of the century, and the greatest question of human rights and human freedom determined in any age.

"Come on, then, gentlemen of the slave States," said Mr. Seward, when all further effort to resist the passage of the Kansas-Nebraska bill, and with it the repeal of the Missouri Compromise became useless, "since there is no escaping your challenge, I accept it on behalf of freedom. We will engage in competition for the virgin soil of Kansas, and God give the victory to the side that is stronger in numbers, as it is in the right." By the passage of that act the wall which had excluded slavery from the free Territories beyond the Missouri was broken down. Under the doctrine of "popular sovereignty," the controversy was transferred from Washington to Kansas, from Congress to the people. And what Congress had not the manliness nor the courage to do, the people of Kansas—the old settlers—had both the manliness and courage to accomplish. Congress broke down the wall, and said to slavery, "go!" The old settlers, God bless them, a remnant only of whom I see around me here to-day, said: "Thus far shalt thou come; no farther; here let thy proud waves be stayed."

Mr. President, I want to be prudent; I want to be conservative; I don't want to be inconsiderate; but it does seem to me that no sterner devotion to principle, no more heroic action, has ever been exhibited in the whole world's history than that exhibited by the early settlers of Kansas in their successful resistance to the spread of human slavery over the virgin prairies of their State.

How our blood tingles! How our hearts beat! How our admi-

ration leaps from our excited brains, as we read of the three hundred Spartans who stayed, at the Pass of Thermopylæ, the mighty
army of Xerxes in its impetuous march. But how vastly greater
was the endurance, the courage, the heroism of the men and
women—of the early settlers—of Kansas, as they successfully
resisted and beat back this more than Xerxes pro-slavery host from
the limits of their Territory.

In the logic of events, this preliminary skirmish and repulse
had almost necessarily to be followed by a grander movement
along the whole line, and the great four years' conflict which
ensued between the national government and the seceding States—
or, more properly speaking, between freedom and slavery—was
but the continuation of the struggle begun in Kansas in her early
territorial days. As years go by, the importance of that great
event will become more and more conspicuous! And the historian
will assign to Kansas, and to the brave sons and daughters of her early
territorial days, the honor of having turned the current of human
affairs and human government into the channel of universal liberty; that the defeat of slavery—the slave power—of the slave
spirit—upon the plains of Kansas was the defeat of the same power
and the same spirit in our own and all other nations; and that the
triumph of freedom upon the plains of Kansas was the triumph
of freedom throughout the circuit of the globe.

In the attainment of this grand result, the distresses inflicted
upon the early settlers will never be recorded by human hands!
the poverty entailed! the sufferings borne! the privations endured!
the lives sacrificed! Yet, in view of the great good to mankind,
of the universal emancipation of the human race, as the glorious
compensation for the poverty, sufferings and privations endured,
and lives sacrified, I even bless the troubles in which our Territory
had its origin, and almost envy those whose lives were offered up
in a cause so just. Their distresses may never be recorded by
human hands; but are they not all recorded, for future good, by
Him who numbers the very hairs of our heads, and who suffers
not a sparrow to fall to the ground without his notice?

Our good friends here at Lawrence inaugurated this quarter
centennial gathering two years ago. They then said when we get
to be twenty-five years old we will have a big meeting, and it shall
be local. But other good friends at Leavenworth, Topeka, Atchison and all over the State, said: "Here, we are twenty-five
years old, also, and you must make your meeting general. And
they said: "Yes, we will make it general." And then it was all
at once remembered that Kansas in her early struggles, and, in
fact, ever since, had some very warm and earnest and distinguished
friends in the older States, and we said, "maybe these good friends
would like to come out to Kansas and see what 'manner of men'
they had been befriending for 'lo, these many years.'" So they
were invited, and they said they would come. And then Judge
Adams, with the Historical Society at his back, said this is getting

interesting, I guess I had better look into this thing. So Judge Adams and his Society were invited. And then the new settlers, who are beginning to outnumber the old settlers by a million or two, and who, I am afraid, are not quite as modest as the old settlers, said, "Oh, we are going to that 'Old Settlers' meeting' at Lawrence, whether we are invited or not." You see they are not very modest. So we came to the conclusion to invite the new settlers, also, as we knew they would come whether invited or not.

. But we said we will steal a march on the new settlers in this; we will hold it as an old settlers' organization. That an old settler shall preside, and another old settler shall be secretary, and another old settler shall do the first talking, and the distinguished friends of the old settlers from abroad shall make the big speeches; and thus we will mortify the new settlers. For, I think I had better tell it out, if there's any one thing under heaven that a Kansas man, be he old or new settler, would rather do than any other thing it is to hold an office or make a speech.

But we think, Mr. President, we may heal the wound we have thus inflicted in the breasts of the new settlers by promising that at the next quarter centennial they may "run the machine." God help us all.

Some one—now a new settler, then an old settler—I hope as worthy a man, will occupy your seat. Some other than the present speaker will be delivering the opening address; and most of us shall have joined that other and larger gathering of "old settlers," on the other side of the river, among whom is he whose "soul goes marching on."

That the strong friendships forme l amid the dark and troublesome times of our early history may be quickened; that old acquaintances may be revived; that new friendships and acquaintances may be formed; that the old stories may be told again, and the old songs sung; that pleasant remembrances of those who shall be with us again here no more forever, shall be revived; and that after a delightful two days' gathering for all, we return to our homes inspired with higher hopes, animated with a loftier appreciation of each other; with enlarged views for the prosperity of our State; with a profound regard for our whole country, and an acknowledgment of that divine goodness which sustains us all, in behalf of the old settlers, I bid you each and all a cordial welcome and kindly greeting to the quarter centennial reunion and celebration of the old settlers of Kansas.

TELEGRAM FROM MR. P. B. GROAT.

Gov. Robinson read the following dispatch from Peter B. Groat, General Passenger and Ticket Agent of the Kansas Pacific Railway, a gentleman to whose enterprise and liberality, the Governor said, was largely due the gathering of the multitude who had come to this celebration. The telegram was as follows:

INDIANAPOLIS, Sept. 15, 1879.

Governor Robinson :

I regret my inability to be present with you all, to-day, at Bismarck Grove. Please present my best respects to the old settlers of Kansas, with my best wishes for the future exalted prosperity of our glorious State. May all persons with you to-day live to reassemble on many joyous occasions; and may peace, good will, joy and plenty crown all with supreme happiness.

P. B. GROAT. ·

ADDRESS BY GOV. JOHN P. ST. JOHN.

GOV. ROBINSON: It has been suggested by our friend who has spoken in behalf of the old settlers that this celebration has grown upon us. It started somewhat as a local affair. It has been extended from one class of citizens to another, and finally to the whole State, and we could not do less than to ask the representative of the State to be present and speak for the State, extending, as I know he will do, words of welcome to all. I take pleasure in introducing to you Gov. John P. St. John.

The Governor spoke as follows :

Mr. President and Fellow Citizens :

I learned that I was expected to participate in the exercises of this day only last Saturday. I look upon this as one of the great occasions in the history of Kansas, and every one who talks to you ought to have an opportunity to prepare what he says.

My friend Col. Holliday has said that this is peculiarly an old settlers' meeting. I do not know whether I am included in the list or not. I believe, however, that I was here before my distinguished friend. I was in Kansas *twenty-seven* years ago. The only difference between my friend and myself is that he staid and I did not.

I have watched, however, with great interest the history of the State, and when we call to mind the fact that but a little over a quarter of a century ago, the Territory which now constitutes the State of Kansas was laid down upon the map of that day as a part of the "Great American Desert," and then witness here to-day 20,000 citizens, representing almost every portion of our State, that upon that same desert has sprung up, as if by some magic power, with its population of a million people, we are impressed with the fact that truly the progress of civilization of the day and age in which we live is wonderful.

I shall not talk to you old Kansans who were here in the beginning about the history of our territorial days. You know it. Your lives constitute a part, or rather the brightest pages of that history, and I leave you to tell the people about it. You are familiar with it. You lived in the midst of the events as they transpired, and none can tell it so well as you whose lives have made it. Many States have been admitted into the Union without any apparent struggle or commotion, but not so with Kansas. There was an irrepressible conflict between slavery and freedom being waged in this country, and it seems that God, in his wisdom, had willed that here in these broad prairies, in the geographical center of the Union, on Kansas soil, the liberty-loving freemen of this land should settle that conflict, and none know better than you old settlers how well the task was done, and how thorough was the consecration of this soil to the cause of human liberty.

It was not, Mr. President, in my opinion, the beauty of these broad prairies or the richness of their soil, that induced you to come to Kansas Territory. I believe, sir, that yourself and those who came with you were actuated by a higher and nobler motive. You came to battle for a principle, and to make the Territory of Kansas *forever* free, and the result of that battle was the entering wedge that opened the way to the total destruction of the accursed institution of human slavery, and makes Kansas to-day the pride and admiration of the civilized world. We are told that in the olden time, at the building of a great temple, a peculiar stone was found, that was neither oblong nor square, and it was cast into the rubbish. After a while it was found that the structure could not be completed without this particular stone, and then it was that the workmen went to the rubbish and took from it this stone, and with it made the building complete. So, as the workman took from the rubbish the stone so necessary to make the building complete, you old settlers took Kansas, as it were, from the rubbish of the land and made it the grand keystone in the mighty arch that cements and holds together the union of the States that constitute this great nation.

What is the harvest that we are reaping to-day from the seed sown by you twenty-odd years ago? Let us see: A free State and a free nation; a free ballot and free schools, with five thousand free school houses; freedom of speech and freedom of the press, with full protection to the life and property of every law-abiding human being; a permanent school fund of nearly $1,700,-000, with sufficient school lands when sold to swell the amount to $13,000,000; our state institutions in successful operation and paid for; nearly three thousand miles of railway; a state debt of only about $1,000,000, two-thirds of which is owned and controlled by the State; our obligations met promptly with the cash as they mature, commanding a premium everywhere; contracting no new debts, but paying our way as we go, while having nearly one-half million dollars in the treasury of our State with which to do it; and a population of nearly one million people—as law-abiding, temperate, moral and loyal as are found anywhere. Here, to-day, where 20,000 people are congregated in this beautiful grove, not a drunken man is to be seen—not a profane or unpleasant word heard, no revolvers, no policeman, and no necessity for any. This is the harvest of a State planted in freedom.

Many of the slaves made free sixteen years ago by the proclamation of good Abraham Lincoln (God bless his sacred name) are
now ragged, breadless and penniless, fleeing from the tyranny and
oppression of their late masters, asking for shelter and a chance to
earn their living in this, to them, the "promised land." Let us
Kansans in our treatment of these unfortunate people, not blot out
or mar a single page or line of the grand history of Kansas, in behalf of freedom, but rather let us, remembering the sacrifices of
her early martyrs to human liberty, keep our doors in the future as
they have ever been in the past, without regard to politics, religion, race, condition or color, open to every human being, willing
to obey our laws, and put forth an earnest effort to better his condition and make for himself an honest living. Let us do our whole
duty, and God will take care of the results.

And now, Mr. President, in conclusion, it is my pleasant
duty, in the name of all the good citizens of Kansas, to extend to
each and every man, woman and child here to-day a cordial welcome, and to our friends from abroad I desire to say (turning
toward Hon. J. W. Forney and Walt Whitman), though it has
been many years since the early struggles in Kansas, we have not
forgotten that you were our friends, and that with the pen (which
is mightier than the sword), as well as your money, you extended
to us all the aid in your power, and for the true friendship that you
have ever shown us, and for your presence here to-day, I know I
but express the sentiment of every citizen of our State in extending
to you our heartfelt thanks, and a cordial welcome, trusting that
God may ever guide and protect you, as well also our State and its
people.

THE OLD BAND.

In making the announcement of music by the "old band"
Governor Robinson said: In 1855 you remember we had the
Wakarusa war. When we were preparing for the defense of Lawrence against the twelve hundred men who came from Missouri
and had their camp near Franklin—a town below, on the Wakarusa—people came here from all parts of the Territory to aid in our
defense—from Topeka, from Leavenworth and all around. Those
were serious times. News came in one day that George W. Clark,
a pro-slavery man, living between Lawrence and Lecompton, had
shot and killed Thomas W. Barber. I will not attempt to depict
the consternation (perhaps that is not the word) but the stupefac-
tion that came over our little band as we were gathered on that
occasion. The funeral proper of Thomas Barber was held the
next spring. His remains were removed from their temporary resting place to a permanent one. At least one of the members of
the band that played on that occasion (the first settler's band I

believe that ever played in Kansas) is with us as a musician to-day and will remain during the meeting. The old band will now entertain you before the next address." [See chapter on Old Band by Joseph Savage.—ED.]

ADDRESS BY HON. GEO. A. CRAWFORD.

Introducing Ex-Gov. Geo. A. Crawford, Gov. Robinson said: You all remember Gov. Walker, Gov. Stanton and others of their class who came among us. You all remember that when we concluded to vote for members of the Territorial Legislature in 1857, that although we knew well enough the free state men had a majority over the pro-slavery party, we were all very much afraid we should be swindled out of the election. We would not consent to vote until Gov. Walker had given the most solemn pledges that we should have a fair election. The election was held. The voice of the people would have been beaten had it not been for the manly action of Gov. Walker in throwing out the bogus votes. You remember how many instrumentalities were employed about that time to defeat us, and you know the true friendship manifested by Hon. Geo. A. Crawford and Govs. Walker and Stanton. Several of the friends who stood by us in those days are here and will address you. Hon. Geo. A. Crawford will now introduce to you one of those noble men.

Mr. Crawford came forward and spoke as follows:

FELLOW KANSANS—Your Committee honor me with this moment of your time to present your distinguished guest because he is my friend. To me it is an inestimable pleasure that he has been yours also. Long years—long years ago—he was presented by the only one capable, himself. Then, though distant, he found Kansas an altar of sacrifice, and grandly he made the immolation of himself in your cause.

Let me introduce him as a Pennsylvanian, that, in honoring him we may honor the State that bore him. Disparaging nothing of the efforts of others, and leaving to others to present different claims from different standpoints, I may say of Pennsylvania that in our crisis when the then slave Territory was being bound in the prison house of a slave constitution, she took that sober second thought of hers, reconstructed her forces, and came with her army of rescue, her Democratic Governor, Wm. F. Packer, at the head—antidote to Buchanan. In Congress her Democratic Congressmen, Hickman and Montgomery led the fray, and in his Democratic press Forney thundered.

Let us never forget, whilst gratitude is "the memory of the heart" that Pennsylvania gave us those Democratic Territorial

3

Governors—Reeder, Geary, Walker—the first driven out in disguise, the second spat up, and the third permitted to resign, but each true to freedom and to Kansas as once the panting heart of the slave to the north star. Among these honored names let me not forget that old Pennsylvania Whig and Republican, late citizen of Lawrence, Judge George W. Smith, free state Governor elect under the Lecompton Constitution. In the "white winter of his age" he made it summer where he went, warming and being warmed by the hearts that love him, and the sunset of his life was a full orbed splendor, cloudless as his character and resplendent as his services.

In this galaxy of Pennsylvania names let me mention that one of "fortune's dimmer stars"—poor old Dutch Charley Torrey of "Alt Berks," only factotum in the office of Surveyor General Calhoun, who muttered doubtful English, smoked his old pipe and was nobody, yet he was spy for freedom. When Maclean had sworn that the fraudulent returns of the election were in Missouri with Calhoun and then returned to hide them under the wood pile at midnight, the old factotum was watching from the window. He reported to another Pennsylvanian—Gen. Brindle—who reported to yet another—Col. Sam. Walker—and by morning Sheriff Walker and his Lawrence boys were digging in that wood pile and found the famous candle-box and the bogus returns, by which the free state men were to have been cheated of the election. [Here the candle-box, now in custody of the Historical Society, was handed the speaker who said, "yes, I recognize it as an old acquaintance."—ED.]

So the Lecompton pro-slavery constitution thus exposed, would have had the Pennsylvanian—the free state Judge Smith at its head if it had been adopted by Congress.

Col. Forney and you his friends with him, say to old Pennsylvania, mother of so many of us, home of my kindred, grave of my ancestors, that she need not blush for her record in Kansas.

We recognize in one guest a representative of that great city of the Declaration of Independence whose chart of freedom has been re-written with larger meaning in the blood of Kansas, a city endeared to us as the battlefield of our Centennial triumph. We may feebly repay in the person of her veteran editor some of that hospitality which in 1876 embraced the whole world and yet had ample room for the representatives of Kansas.

But not so much to the Pennsylvanian or the Philadelphian as to the man himself do we extend this grand ovation. It would be difficult to measure his services and sacrifices for Kansas.

Editor of the great daily of Philadelphia, *The Pennsylvanian*, his fame touched the bounds of the republic and he was elected Chief clerk of the House of Congress, and became editor of the *Washington Union*, organ of the then dominant National Democracy. Seeing what a fire-brand the slavery question had become, and how it endangered the Union, he sought and achieved that absorbing ambition of his life, the election of Mr. Buchanan, in the interests of pacification and on the basis of fair play to the " squatters." It was a memorable struggle, " Kansas and the Union " the watchword, and Pennsylvania the battle-ground. Col. Forney was chairman of the Democratic State Central Committee, and managed the campaign, and to him Mr. Buchanan owed his election.

Then, when Pennsylvania's president refused to sustain Gov. Walker in his efforts for fair elections in Kansas, and in his opposition to the Lecompton Constitution because of its non-submission to a vote of the people, Col. Forney opened up the batteries of his great newspapers against Buchanan and against the Lecompton Constitution. He sacrificed his leadership in a triumphant party to help the weak and to defend the right.

It was a grand fight against an almost solid south and a solid administration. Douglas, in whose honor your county, here, is named—born leader—led the battle in the Senate against Buchanan and the Lecompton Constitution, whilst Seward, Sumner, Chase and other great Republican leaders dealt heavy blows. The great guns of Forney chimed in chorus. Yon sun never rose nor set on a grander victory for God and humanity.

Prior to his departure for Washington, I had visited Judge Douglas in Chicago to assure myself of his opposition to the Lecompton Constitution. The other day—Sabbath day—standing by his Chicago monument, there came the memory of a ride from Washington to Philadelphia. He was fresh from his victory—still red-hot with the rage and rapture of the fight. He kept me on the platform of the cars all the way, whilst he smoked and *cooled off.* Arrived in Philadelphia, his first exclamation was, " Let us go and see Forney."

That sentiment is your own and has largely brought you here. You, too, are impatient to " see Forney," and I am proud to present him.

ADDRESS OF COL. JOHN W. FORNEY.

Col. John W. Forney, of Philadelphia, then spoke as follows : *Ladies and Gentlemen, Gov. Robinson, Gov. St. John, and my Friends :*

Although I have printed what I intended to say, I am tempted, before I read the cold pages that will to morrow be read by perhaps a million people, to say something else. I am recalled by this extraordinary reception, and by this flattering introduction, to remember what Queen Catherine said when the news came to her of the death of Cardinal Woolsey. There sat by her side one of her servants, who, appalled by the bitterness of her invections against the wily churchman, said to her, " My good lady, now let me speak the better part of Woolsey," and so when she said of the great man that he had some good qualities, the servant captured her mistress so that when she finished she said, "Dear, honest Libby, when I die let me have no better chronicler than you." And so I say to you of our friend Crawford. I want no better chronicler of fame than what he says for Pennsylvania, for me and of our native Commonwealth Here we meet in a common congress, and here all the States meet around a common fireside of peace and freedom and fraternity. We have met here to talk over the scenes of twenty-five years ago, the mere mention of which always fills my heart with pride, and I am right glad that dear old Pennsylvania found such an orator in Gov. Crawford.

And now, ladies and gentlemen, while I read to you what I have printed, I will try to articulate it so as to be heard by all the persons comprising this vast assembly. I have entitled my paper the

LESSON OF KANSAS.

If I had been commanded to choose one spot on the globe upon which to illustrate human development under the influence of absolute liberty, I could have chosen no part of God's footstool so interesting as Kansas; and if I had also been ordered to fix the time for the experiment, I would have found no period like the present. And what is best of all, you yourselves have fixed both the place and the time. I come by your invitation. I feel I am welcome, not only because it is pleasant to myself, but chiefly because it is agreeable to you. We wanted to see each other, and I know how I have longed to look into your eyes, and to take you all by the hand. It is twenty-five years since we began to be familiar with our names; twenty-five years since many now present first saw the light; twenty-five years during which we have seen thousands laid away in the silent chambers of the dead. This is not a long time, friends; not much longer since that graceful tree began to grow; not much longer since that lovely woman began to be called mother; not much longer since that handsome man began to feel himself a part of this magical Commonwealth. But what a cycle of war and wonder has it been! How much has been crowded into a little! You remember the Arabian legend where the fisherman drew to the shore in his net a small vessel, which, when opened spread into a massive figure of light and glory that covered all the land. That was like Kansas. And Kansas was only yesterday. Yesterday an infant, to-day a giant, to-morrow who can tell? Who could have foreshadowed this colossus twenty-five years ago, in 1854, when Lawrence was a city of tents, and kind Dr. Robinson gave shelter to the wandering stranger?

And now as distant commonwealths and empires are reading the marvelous answer to this question, you would hardly tolerate me if I attempted to repeat the story you have written yourselves, or to take or carry you through a world of your own creation. You do not visit St. Peter's to tell the Romans of its centuried glories; nor Westminster Abbey to preach to the English of that ancient cathedral; nor Shakespeare's home to recite on the spot the wondrous romance of an inspired life. You go there as I come here, my friends, that you may draw from the text of a great fact some thoughtful and resounding lessons for others.

In 1854 the Whig party was dead, killed by the Know-Nothings as the Anti-Masons had suicided the Anti-Jackson party in 1833–35 In 1854 there was no Republican party. In 1852, two years before, the Democrats had carried the whole country, and as a presage to the dissolution of all antagonism to that great organization, its giant foes, Henry Clay, died in Washington, June 29th, and Daniel Webster, at Marshfield, Massachusetts, October 23d, in the same year. In November following, the most illustrious soldier of the republic, Winfield Scott, running as the Whig candidate for the presidency, received but 42 electoral votes out of a college of 296, and was defeated by one of his bravest subordinate generals, my own personal friend, Frank Pierce, who got 254 electors. All the West was Democratic; all New England but Massachusetts and Vermont; all the Middle States, including Ohio and New York; and every southern State but Kentucky and Tennessee. Both houses of Congress, the Supreme Court of the United States, the army and the navy, the press, the social aristocracy, and, in a large degree, the church, were dependants, tributaries, echoes, and defenders of slavery and the Democratic party.

In two years from that time the Kansas-Nebraska bill became the law. From that hour the fate of slavery was sealed. A party of that revolution, and a friend of the much derided popular sovereignty doctrine, I claim to speak for those who resolved at all hazards that there should be a true, and not a false sovereignty. They were not holiday soldiers. They voted for the Kansas and Nebraska bill, meaning no pledge to a glittering generality, but to a sound religion. Others understood it differently; the ultra slave holders, as a snare and a delusion, believing all Democrats would finally come to the heresy that slavery could be carried anywhere under the Constitution, and the ultra abolitionists that it was Congress, and not the people, that had the ultimate decision of the greatest question nearest the people.

I am not here to-day to revive old issues, but I claim that it was the doctrine of a righteous popular sovereignty that gave liberty to Kansas and Nebraska; and that the Democrats who followed Douglas, and fought Buchanan, who gave up office, party, social position, and even life itself, rather than yield their faith, deserve to be remembered with special honor on this silver wedding of the Republic of Kansas.

We must not forget that the Northwest was ripe for revolt against slavery long before the repeal of the Missouri Compromise. There was hardly a Democrat in the organized States of the great empire between the Ohio and the Lakes, and from the Upper Mississippi to St. Louis, that had not been shaken by the conflicts over the Wilmot Proviso and the admission of California. Great thoughts had been planted in the minds of your earlier statesmen by two great hands over three-quarters of a century before; and they grew and brightened in your Bentons, your Casses, your Dodges, your Douglases, your Wentworths, your Trumbulls, and other Democrats of the generation that began with the administration of John Quincy Adams.

And when the presidential election of 1856 came to be decided, the cause of freedom in the Northwest had got too strong for falsehood. Already the Northwest, the bulwark of the Democracy for many years, was getting weaker and weaker in its allegiance to slavery; and nothing saved a part of it to the Democratic candidate for president that year but a voluntary and efficient pledge to the Douglas doctrine in the Kansas and Nebraska bill. An old statesman had been nominated for that high office by the Democracy, and a very young man by the just organized Republicans against him; and nothing prevented the success of the latter but the broadest assertion of the right of the people of these twin Territories to decide the question of slavery for themselves   In my relations to that event I can only say what I have said a thousand times before, that I had been so solemnly impressed by events under the administration of Franklin Pierce, and by my long experience in Washington, and a full knowledge of the deep conspiracy of the slavery chiefs to force their peculiar institution upon our public domain, that if James Buchanan had not convinced me of his sincerity on this great issue, I should have cordially supported General Fremont for the presidency.   No man knew this so well as Mr. Buchanan himself, and if he had not authorized me to pledge him to you—if I had not daily, hourly, by word and deed, declared that his administration would not obstruct the course of a free ballot in this Territory, we could no more have carried Pennsylvania for him, to use an old simile, than I could storm Gibraltar with a pocket pistol, or sail through the air in a gossamer balloon!   And when in the year following I found that he was preparing to break this pledge, I boldly denounced that betrayal, and together with thousands of other Democrats, took the case before the people, and in 1858 saw a verdict in favor of Kansas so overwhelming, that, from that day, with two immaterial exceptions, Pennsylvania has never voted the Democratic ticket. A single fact will show how, in that glorious era, an unbought people turned upon public servants who had violated written and public faith.   In 1856 Buchanan's majority in Pennsylvania was 607; in 1858 the Democrats were beaten by 26,987; and the delegation in Congress was changed from twelve Democratic and thirteen opposition in 1857, to three Democratic and twenty-two Republican and anti-Lecompton.

But I dare not open the volume to which this tempting chapter invites me; and yet here I stand in Lawrence, Kansas, named after a distinguished citizen of Massachusetts, with my old friends,

Eli Thayer and George W. Julian, who began the great work of organization and victory twenty-five years ago, and not only in Lawrence, but in Douglas county, which brings back the name to which I have just directed your attention. And I find it impossible to restrain the other thoughts that come rushing to my lips in such a presence; backed by such a past, and beckoned by such a future. Indeed, I seem to stand among many eloquent recollections and examples. The figures of the heroic dead; the faces of the heroic living, the moral heroism and physical courage of that tremendous personality, John Brown, and his compatriots; the earlier martyrdom of Elijah P. Lovejoy, whose great brother I knew so well, and whose fearless arraignment of the South for the murder of Elijah I heard on the floor of Congress; the souvenirs of James H. Lane, Samuel C. Pomeroy, Richard Realf, Amos A. Lawrence, Joshua R. Giddings, Charles Sumner, Henry Wilson, David C. Broderick, John Hickman, Anson Burlingàme, and last, not least, Abraham Lincoln, Edwin M. Stanton, Salmon P. Chase, William H. Seward; these reappear to me to-day, not only because I knew them all, some of them most closely, but because they were your champions, and some of them died in fighting for your cause. The tragedy of August, 1863, the Quantrill Massacre, was a new consecration of liberty, another trial in the great crucible of destiny.

But Lawrence has other memories. To me as a Pennsylvanian it is singularly and sadly interesting. Indeed the history of this region, Territorial and State, is redolent of my native Commonwealth.

Pennsylvania not only sent you the Delaware Indians, but three early territorial governors, Reeder, Geary, and Walker. They were all Democrats, high in the councils of their party, identified with the pro-slavery influence. Reeder at the head of the bar in his own district, Geary a gallant soldier in the Mexican war, and afterward first mayor of the city of San Francisco, and Walker, who removed to Mississippi in his youth, which he afterward represented in the Senate of the United States and in the Cabinet of President Polk, and always as the mouthpiece and apostle of extreme southern ideas. A native of the same State, I shared their confidence during many years. The Kansas-Nebraska bill became a law May 30th, 1854, and a few days after, the late Asa Packer, also of Pennsylvania, and myself, called on President Pierce, and recommended Andrew H. Reeder for the appointment of Governor of Kansas, not believing at the time that he would accept. His character was so high, and his ability so distinguished, and his integrity so marked, that we felt, if he would accept, this promising Territory would secure a superb executive, and the true principle of the organic law a congenial interpreter and advocate. To our surprise and delight the President responded to our appeal, and Reeder, to our equal surprise, accepted the place. He was a lawyer of large means and great practice; and he left a home of elegance and refinement to come out to this then distant domain; and when he reached here he was accompanied and followed by a large constituency. My own heart went with my devoted friend. I knew his courage and his honesty; I placed high hopes upon his rare administrative and executive powers; and I waited for his report as I watched his career in the still unorganized Territory of which he was the first executive.

This is what he said to the people at his home in Easton, Pennsylvania, in 1854, when he received his appointment. It shows his devotion to the great Democratic party, and his broad and far-seeing nationality:

The event which has brought you here, my friends, is well calculated to suggest most interesting reflections upon the wonderful progress of our country; and you will excuse me for relating an appropriate incident that occurs to my memory. In 1848, when California was almost an unknown region, and without even a territorial government, I was a delegate in the National Convention of the political party to which I belong, and I recollect that a member in the course of his remarks intimated that when that body should assemble again, a delegate would claim his seat there from the State of California. It seemed a wild and extravagant prediction, entirely out of the bounds of probability, and yet it touched a responsive chord in the sense of manifest destiny and pride of country that dwells in the bosom of every American; and the building shook from the floor to the roof with the shout that hailed it. In 1852 I was again a member of the Convention, and the wild prediction was realized. I found delegates from the State of California, who had come from the very shores of the Pacific Ocean, casting their votes like old denizens of the place.

Now we find that two embryo States are about to be organized beyond the Missouri, although within six days' travel of our Atlantic coast. We pass to them over 1,500 miles of a country teeming with wealth, and commerce, and business, and swarming with population whilst the very starting point of the journey was, but a century ago, itself a frontier, protected by the bullet and the rifle from the savages who prowled around it. Some idea may be formed, too, of the resistless force of the populous wave which has spread like an inundation over this vast continent, from the interesting fact that in this very Territory of Kansas to which my friend has alluded, we find like an uprooted tree carried by the flood, the fragment of the tribe of the Delawares, on whose proper native soil we now stand, and whose fathers waged deadly war upon ours; here in our valleys, where the scream of the locomotive seems to chase the very echoes of the Indian's yell.

But this is not a theme to be discussed in these desultory remarks. It is a subject for thoughts to fill a world, to amaze future generations, and to convert history into romance. We can not discuss it now, and I will close by thanking you once more for this congratulatory call, and by the earnest assurance that whatever may be the result of senatorial action, or of my own action upon the honor which the President has conferred up me, these expressions of confidence and approbation, which it has evoked from my fellow-citizens and friends, will ever be cherished in my memory, are giving to the appointment its greatest value; and whether now or hereafter, in whatever circumstances I may be placed, present or absent, on the banks of the Delaware or at the base of the Rocky Mountains, my heart will always kindle with affection and regard for the kind and faithful friends who have cheered my path by their confidence and devotion. I give you as a sentiment—

"MINNESOTA, KANSAS and NEBRASKA, destined soon to add the 32d, 33d, and 34th stars to our national ensign, and to prove the pathway of empire to the Pacific."

Observe, my friends, there is no declaration here of party or personal opinion. His mind was as clear of prejudice as the youngest child in this vast crowd; if there was any bias it was certainly not against slavery. No missionary ever went forth with a purer purpose, or covered with more fervent popular blessings. I had not long to wait before he wrote to me of his reception in Kansas. He found law defied, life and property unsafe, freedom of speech and the press punished by a pro-slavery mob, his own person in constant peril, and daily demands made upon him to oppose all men and measures but those in the interest of slavery. The effect upon my mind was instant and conclusive. I had had previous occasion to notice the intolerance, and to resist the insolence of extreme southern men in Washington. No one had gone farther than myself to extenuate their conduct to northern men; few had done more by printed and spoken word to find excuses for some of their leaders. But these revelations of Governor Reeder were·too much for me. They aroused my solicitude for my distant friend, and my deep detestation of the means resorted to for his destruction. I took his letter to President Pierce, and I must do him the justice to say that at first he recoiled with manly indignation from the shameless spectacle, and joined me in denouncing the persecution of my friend; but the power that subsequently bullied and finally broke down James Buchanan when he attempted to keep faith to his solemn pledge, was too much for President Pierce. On the 31st of July, 1855, my friend was removed from his post, and on the evening of that day the President's private secretary came to inform me of the fact. My own position was delicate and responsible. I was the editor of the National Democratic organ, the *Union*, and in those days that personage was always designated by the President, or appointed after consultation with him. I resolved to resign my post if I was called upon to approve the proscription of my friend Governor Reeder; and I mention the fact, also to the credit of President Pierce, that I held my place till the December following without a word in support of the policy that lost Kansas the first brave governor, in the columns of that paper while it was under my control.

Three other governors followed him—Wilson Shannon, of Ohio, J. W. Geary, of Pennsylvania, and Robert J. Walker, born in the same State. Shannon was removed because of his inability to aid the elements arrayed against the people of Kansas. Geary followed Shannon, and resigned at the end of six months, and Walker followed Geary, and resigned at the end of seven months.

The injustice and cruelty to Reeder were surpassed by the treatment of Geary and Walker. There was no mercy for either. They all came here Democrats, but they could not close their eyes to wrong so palpable as to excite horror and amazement everywhere else but among those who had resolved to force slavery upon this virgin soil. Reeder was born in the old Tenth Legion, where to be a Democrat was to be with a successful party, and for gifted men like himself to rule and lead. Geary was born in Democratic Westmoreland, which still votes against the Republicans by a large majority, and Robert J. Walker, born in Northumberland, for many years one of the strongholds of the same party. These three historical men have all been called home, but before they died they became terrible witnesses against the Democratic party, and their eloquent testimony of the dreadful persecutions, frauds, and murders to force slavery upon Kansas, constitutes a volume of proof which has gone to thousands of hearthstones; converting almost millions to the great principles of Thomas Jefferson and Abraham Lincoln. All the former Democratic fortresses in the North have crumbled to the dust. The West, that once voted unanimously on the Democratic side, is now almost unanimously Republican; so of New England, and so of the Middle States. On the Pacific coast the same republican rule prevails; and I predict that when the eight Territories of Arizona, Dakota, Montana, Utah, Wyoming, Idaho, New Mexico, and Washington, ripen into States, each will be controlled by the same inspiration, and gravitate. into the same supreme sisterhood. In this grand consummation the chief contributor was Kansas. Her martyrs are the marshals of this transcendent destiny. On her map she marks every school house with a star, and she will soon be girdled by new constellations. Her newspapers have become the messengers of new evangelism. Her railroads have opened her fruitful solitudes to a grateful and continuous exodus, and have welded her into an indestructible unit. At the genesis of her great work, the incomparable Sumner spoke as follows in 1856:

A few short months only have passed since this spacious mediterranean country was open only to the savage who ran wild in its woods and prairies; and now it has already drawn to its bosom a population of freemen larger than Athens crowded within her historic gates, when her sons, under Miltiades, won liberty for mankind on the field of Marathron; more than Sparta contained when she ruled Greece, and sent forth her devoted children, quickened with a mother's benediction, to return with their shields or on them; more than Rome gathered on her seven hills, when, under her kings, she commenced that sovereign sway which afterward embraced the whole earth; more than London held, when, on the fields of Crecy and Agincourt, the English banner was carried victoriously over the chivalrous hosts of France.

And now, twenty-four years later, when fruition has baffled prophecy, and the young republic has broadened into an empire, and these shining savannas are opened to all the races of man, alike those who fly from the wars of the Old World, and from the double pestilence of the old South, we can only accept the lesson of Kansas, and wait for the still greater world's quickening in her womb!

I said, a few moments ago, that the seeds of this tremendous transformation were scattered by two great minds more than three-quarters of a century before Kansas was settled and organized— George Washington and Thomas Jefferson, of Virginia, the first

American abolitionists. The Declaration of Independence, written by Thomas Jefferson, and his public record, prove his inherent hostility to human slavery, and his devotion to absolute human equality, and the last will and testament of George Washington establish his own deep-rooted hatred of the whole idea of property in man. The ordinance making all the Northwest Territory free was Jefferson's conception, and to the last his best thoughts were given to the education of the people and to religious liberty. But there is one measure which is so rarely referred to, and which has borne such magnificent results, that I feel justified by all the exigencies of the hour, and the memories of this anniversary, in recalling it to your mind. I mean the purchase of Louisiana in 1803. How few Americans out of Kansas ever think that Kansas was a part of this grand acquisition, and how few that this same Virginia slave-holder was not only the real author of the great ordinance that made the whole of the Northwest free, but that he organized the expeditions of Lewis and Clarke, the discoverers of the Rocky Mountains and the road to the Pacific; that Zebulon Pike, who penetrated to the sources of the Upper Mississippi, and gave his name to Pike's Peak, in the Rocky Mountains, was appointed and sent forth by the Virginia author of the Declaration of Independence!

But it is of the Louisiana purchase that I desire to speak to-day, and of the part played by the South, led by Virginia, in subsequent additions to the public domain. It is a fact that nine-tenths of the territory acquired since the organization of the Government has been mainly acquired under southern administrations, and every foot has been cleansed of slavery by the doctrines planted in our system by Thomas Jefferson, a Virginia statesman! It was a Southern President that gave us Louisiana. It was a Southern President, James K. Polk, that gave us California. Two Virginia Generals, Zachary Taylor and Winfield Scott, defeated the Mexicans, and gave us California and New Mexico, and the latter made the treaty, aided by Nicholas P. Trist, son-in-law and executor of Thomas Jefferson, which secured this vast empire. It was another Virginian, Sam Houston, that secured the independence of Texas and added it to our Union; and it was a North Carolinian, Andrew Jackson, that aided another Virginian, President Monroe, to secure Florida in 1821, as in 1815 Jackson had aided President James Madison, also of Virginia, to drive back the British when they attempted to capture New Orleans, the capital of Thomas Jefferson's Territory of Louisiana.

Observe how logically these magnificent acquisitions followed the great first example of Thomas Jefferson; and how irresistibly his original declaration in favor of human liberty finally controlled all government action.

Add the acquisition of Florida in 1821; the annexation of Texas in 1846; the acquisition of California and New Mexico in 1848; and at a glance you see what southern statesmen and sol-

diers have secured to our national domain. I am not here to-day
to speak of northern sagacity, courage, or patriotism. As Daniel
Webster said in his reply to Hayne, of South Carolina, in 1830:

I shall enter no encomium upon Massachusetts; she needs none. There
she is. Behold her and judge for yourselves. There is her history; the
world knows it by heart. The past, at least, is secure. There is Boston,
and Concord, and Lexington, and Bunker Hill; and there they will remain
forever. The bones of her sons, falling in the great struggle for Independence, now lie mingled with the soil of every State from New England to
Georgia; and there they will lie forever.

I address another audience to-day.

It is to the South that I would read this lesson of Kansas. It
is to leaders like Jefferson Davis, of Mississippi; R. M. T. Hunter,
of Virginia; Alexander H. Stephens, of Georgia; George S. Houston, of Alabama; George W. Jones, of Tennessee; and J. W.
Throckmorton, of Texas, that I would affectionately recommend
this interesting study.

Thomas Jefferson was the real leader of the movement that
made the abolition of slavery necessary for the preservation of the
Union; the author of the policy which added to the old thirteen
States a domain larger than the area they first occupied; and all
those who succeeded him were in sympathy with his known anti-
slavery convictions, excepting only James K. Polk. Let us repeat
for a moment the significant truth—that Monroe, who made the
treaty with Spain that gave us Florida; and Jackson, who fought
the battle of New Orleans in 1815, and commanded the army in
Florida in 1821; and Houston, who secured the annexation of
Texas; and Scott and Taylor, who defeated the Mexicans and
made the acquisition of California inevitable, were all in sympathy
with the anti-slavery sentiments of Thomas Jefferson, and primarily
devoted to the preservation of the Union at all hazards. And as I
recur to Jefferson's passionate and persevering efforts to secure Louisiana at the time the great Napoleon was preparing for his gigantic struggle with the European monarchs, seventy-six years ago,
I often wonder whether he saw through the clouds of the future his
mighty mission. He seems certainly to have been gifted with a
strange and overmastering inspiration. Having resided for years
at the French capital, he acquired a new love for his own great
ideal of human freedom, among that impulsive and agreeable people. He had seen king-craft face to face only to despise it, and he
prefigured a universal republic before the blood and flame of the
first French Revolution. His pictures of the reigning sovereigns
of Europe, seven years before the Revolution, makes Louis XVI
a fool; also the kings of Spain, Naples and Sardinia; the queen
of Portugal an idiot; and so the king of Denmark; the king of
Prussia a hog in body and mind; Gustavus of Sweden, and Joseph
of Austria, both crazy; and George of England in a straight-
jacket. Such was continental Europe when it became the easy
prey of the great Napoleon, who held Louisiana in his clutch, and

to get it from whom was Jefferson's eager desire. Benjamin Franklin, before his death, had proclaimed in 1787, in the same spirit of prescience : "I would rather agree with the Spaniards to buy at a great price the whole of their right on the Mississippi, than sell a drop of its waters. *A neighbor might as well ask me to sell my street door.*" What a romance the struggle of his ministers, Livingston and Monroe, to induce Napoleon to sell Louisiana. The wild excitement along the great rivers at that early day, while this negotiation was pending, is still remembered; the strange uncertainty of Napoleon ; the intrigues of his ministers ; the sleepless nights of President Jefferson; and his abounding joy and gratitude, when at last the ambitious First Consul consented to sell that priceless territory to raise money for his projected invasion of England. We were a poor people seventy-six years ago, and the millions asked for Louisiana was more than we could afford. Besides, to make such a contract was a distinct violation of the National Constitution, which made no provision for our holding foreign territory, or incorporating foreign territories with our Union. But Jefferson did not stop. He did what Jackson did at New Orleans in 1815, when to save the city he defied the judicial opinion of Judge Hall, and what Abraham Lincoln did between 1861 and 1865, in the great crisis of the rebellion. Now let the tranquil historian speak of that transcendent act of the great Republican President, Thomas Jefferson, and I read it here on a part of the magnificent empire he secured to human liberty. I quote from Henry S. Randall's great book :

No conqueror who has ever trod the earth to fill it with desolation and mourning, ever conquered and permanently amalgamated with his native kingdom a remote approach to the same extent of territory. But one kingdom in Europe equals the extent of one of its present States (The State of Nebraska contains 335,882 square miles.) Germany supports a population of thirty-seven millions of people. All Germany has a little more than the area of two-thirds of Nebraska, and, acre for acre, less tillable land. Louisiana, as densely populated in proportion to its natural materials of sustentation as parts of Europe, would be capable of supporting somewhere from four to five hundred millions of people. (Its area, not including Texas—afterward improperly surrendered from the purchase—and the region west of the Rocky Mountains, is not far probably from a million square miles. But for all practical purposes and results, the purchase extended beyond the mountains to the Pacific; and Texas should have been ours without a remuneration.) The whole United States became capable, by this acquisition, of sustaining a larger population than ever occupied Europe. The purchase secured, independently of territory, several prime national objects. It gave us that homogeneousness, unity, and independence which is derived from the absolute control and disposition of our commerce, trade, and industry in every department, without the hindrance or meddling of any intervening nation between us and any natural element of industry, between us and the sea, or between us and the open market of the world.

It gave us ocean boundaries on all exposed sides, for it left Canada exposed to us and not us to Canada. It made us indisputably and forever (if our Union is preserved) the controllers of the Western Hemisphere. It placed our national course, character, civilization and destiny solely in our

own hands. It gave us the certain sources of a not distant numerical
strength to which that of the mightiest empires of the past or present is insignificant.

A Gallic Cæsar was leading his armies over shattered kingdoms. His
armed foot shook the world. He decimated Europe. Millions on millions
of mankind perished, and there was scarcely a human habitation from the
Polar Seas to the Mediterranean, where the voice of lamentation was not
heard over slaughtered kindred, to swell the conqueror's strength and
"glory!" And the carnage and rapine of war are trifling evils compared
with its demoralizations. The rolling tide of conquest subsided. France
shrunk back to her ancient limits. Napoleon died a repining captive on a
rock of the ocean. The stupendous tragedy was played out; and no physical results were left behind but decrease, depopulation and universal loss.
A republican President, on a distant continent, was also seeking to aggran-
dize his country. He led no armies. He shed not a solitary drop of human
blood. He caused not a tear of human woe. He bent not one toiling back
lower by governmental burdens. Strangest of political anomalies (and
ludicrous as strange to the representatives of the ideas of the tyrannical and
bloody past), he lightened the taxes while he was lightening the debts of
a nation. And without interrupting either of these meliorations for an instant—without imposing a single new exaction on his people—he acquired,
peaceably and permanently for his country, more extensive and fertile do-
mains than ever for a moment owned the sway of Napoleon—more extensive ones than his gory plume ever floated over.

Which of these victors deserves to be termed "glorious?"

Yet with what serene and unselfish equanimity, which ever preferred
his cause to his vanity, this more than conqueror allowed his real agency in
this great achievement to go unexplained to the day of his death, and to be
in a good measure attributed to mere accident, taken advantage of quite as
much by others as by himself. He wrote no laureled letter. He asked no
triumph.

And now, in the presence of the almost incredible fruits of the
providential work of the third President of the United States,
Thomas Jefferson, I may again ask : Does it not seem as if he saw
what was to come ? And if in the unknown and inscrutable system of nature, his great spirit looks down upon this scene to-day,
he may enjoy a rapture greater than the angels, who never knew
mortality, and cannot define the unspeakable bliss of a glorious
work done on earth to be rewarded in heaven. And if he could
speak to-day, if he could arise from the dead, whose silent company he joined with John Adams, of Massachusetts, on the 4th of
July, 1826, he would turn from this dazzling harvest of his own
sowing, to those of his own section who still refuse to follow the
doctrines of the fathers of the old Democracy, and to gather the
fruits of the early Jeffersonian policy. Had these doctrines been
followed these fruits would now be shared by the South equally
with the North and West. Every step since the Southern departure
from the Jefferson standard has been followed by mischief to the
South. Every step that the North and West have taken toward
the Jeffersonian standard has been followed by prosperity to those
sections. The territorial system, by which millions of acres of
square miles have been added to the 850,000 square miles of the
original thirteen colonies, was a southern, or rather a Jeffersonian system, begun by the author of the Declaration of Independ-

ence, and carried forth by the disciples I have named in marvelous chronological succession. And its results would have been shared in providential profusion by the South, *had the Southern statesmen been inspired by the great ideas that have made Kansas the increasing wonder of the world.* "Thomas Jefferson," says a recent critical writer, "was the model American citizen, whose writings contain more to instruct and guide his countrymen in the duties of citizenship than those of any other man. His very faults had more of virtue in them than the good deeds of other men. He was a Democrat by nature. He was a Democrat because he was truly an intelligent man; because he saw things as they are, not as they seem. His heart would have told him that all men are brothers and equals, if his great mind had not discovered it." He was always a Republican, and to the last wrote himself down as a Republican.

Democrats of the South, your real leader has won the great fight. Strange that he should have conquered the Federalists of the North who voted against the purchase of Louisiana, and that his ideas should have conquered the Whigs of the North who opposed the annexation of Texas and the acquisition of California. And yet it is not strange, because they finally saw that all these acquisitions were not to extend but to stop the advancing tide of human slavery. But it is doubly strange that the South, that helped to press these great acquisitions, refuses at the eleventh hour to seize the advantages they have now the right to share. Can they not see that they are losing under a leadership that is fatal now, and must be more and more fatal every hour? Robert J. Walker, fifteen years ago, when sent forth by Mr. Lincoln to Great Britain to assist the Union cause during the Rebellion, wrote a series of letters for English circulation, comparing the old Slave and Free States in population, industry, commerce, and intelligence. His book electrified all Europe. But had he lived to make a contrast between Kansas and Kentucky, or between Kansas and Louisiana, what a picture he would have drawn! His living contemporaries in the South still refuse to study the great lesson. They are like blind men in a land of light; deaf men in a land of song; they can neither see nor hear. The world is changing around them, and they live in it unchanged. They hug their delusions to their withered breasts, and dance their weird dances in their skeleton carnivals, listening only to the dreary strains of their ghastly theories, without dreaming that the Vesuvius of the Census is coming on to exhaust them!

Ah, gentlemen of the South, the great Virginian would have builded better. Had he been here, he would never have allowed John C. Calhoun's ideas to indoctrinate the South; and if he had failed to stop the poison, he would have demanded, at the close of the civil war, and in the face of the generosity proffered to the South by the North, "both hands full," that his people should not be held back in the new race for empire. He would point them to the gigantic growth of the North under free institutions and the abolition of human slavery, and he would have proclaimed from this part of his Louisiana purchase, that Kansas was the last and most prodigious product and proof of the justice and beneficence of his prophetic labors. He would say, in words of solemn warning, that whether the southern Democratic leaders desired it or not, the fiat had gone forth, and they could no more resist the current than Canute could arrest the sea; and then he would talk to the long-deluded masses of the South, and implore them to seize the golden opportunities all around them, and to act for themselves and by themselves, without the reckless pilots that had led them into the storm, and had neither purpose nor capacity to lead them out.

Such would be the master's voice were he alive to speak out. Let me, his humble follower and interpreter, add that there is still time "to recover arms." The South is full of wealth, genius, eloquence, and invention. The mighty elements that helped to make and fire the Revolution are not dead. Harness these elements to progress; inspire them with Jeffersonian liberty; and before the nineteenth century closes its doors, the old Southern States will be abreast of the new Western Republics, and the next silver wedding of Kansas will find Texas divided into four empires, each as grand and potential as Kansas is at present, and from the Potomac to the Rio Grande, an athletic liberty as strong as that of Massachusetts and Pennsylvania to-day.

And now, ladies and gentlemen, I beg to return to you my heartfelt thanks for your kind reception; and I assure you that my visit to Kansas has been full of inspiration and satisfaction; and I return to my labor at home with the hope that I may visit you again in the future. But whether I do or not, I beg to assure you that I shall always have the kindest feeling for this grand republic.

MUSIC.

At the conclusion of Col. Forney's address, the orchestra and chorus, under direction of Dr. J. D. Patterson's skillful baton, gave one of their wonderful renditions of "O Hail Us, Ye Free," from Ernani. After this, the meeting adjourned to meet at 7 o'clock, p. m.

EVENING SESSION.—The Old Settlers' Love Feast.

A larger assembly than that of the afternoon filled the Tabernacle by 7 o'clock to hear the old settlers talk over the scenes and incidents of the early days. Hon. John Speer, one of the Vice Presidents of the meeting, presided.

ADDRESS BY L. F. GREENE.

Mr. Speer introduced Capt. L. F. Greene, who spoke as ollows:

Mr. Chairman, Ladies and Gentlemen:

So many memories come thronging to my mind at this moment that I scarcely know where to begin. This is an hour of triumph —a call for gratitude and renewed consecration to the principles of liberty. Sixteen years ago, Gov. Willliam H. Seward said in a speech made in Massachusetts street, Lawrence: "If I should ever grow lukewarm and cold in the great struggle now going on in this new world, I will come back here to Kansas, and, in the presence of a great State saved to freedom, at her shrine renew my devotion." In that spirit, we gather this day to celebrate this, our twenty-fifth year; and, in looking back through the past eventful years, on and up to this good hour so full of hope and promise, may we not without presumption, without fanaticism, trace a power above man's power, a wisdom above man's wisdom, in the fortunes and destiny of Kansas?

A nameless sorrow fills our hearts when we miss so many dear, familiar faces of the early pioneers who have gone from us. Their bodies are joining the silent dust in that narrow temple of rest and reconciliation in the mysterious fellowship of death. Their spirits are in the presence of Him whose service is perfect freedom. I see behind me (pointing to a portrait of Gen. Lane) a trace of the existence of one whose name will be forever linked with our early history—one whose best years were given to the struggle for free Kansas; whose rough, sad face is yet so well remembered; who sank down under life's heavy load just as we were entering the shining land of peace; and let me in passing, in the moving lines of the great Quaker poet, pay tribute to his memory:

> " O, Mother Earth, upon thy lap
> Thy weary ones receiving,
> And o'er them, silent as a dream,
> Thy grassy mantle weaving,
> Fold softly, in thy cold embrace,
> That heart so worn and broken,
> And cool that pulse of fire
> Beneath thy shadows old and oaken.

> "Shut out from him the bitter word
> Of hissing and of scorning,
> Nor let the storms of yesterday
> Disturb his quiet morning;
> Breathe over him forgetfulness
> Of all save deeds of kindness,
> And save to smiles from grateful eyes,
> Press down his lids in blindness."

In our history we may now witness, with becoming pride, the moral of that beautiful Persian fable of the fairy doomed at times to wear a humiliating disguise, and to those who received and treated her kindly, she came afterward, in her celestial form, to crown them happy in love and triumphant in war. So, in Kansas in the early days, the genius of liberty, disguised, often came to

4

our cabin doors in the form of a poor fugitive slave on his glad
way to freedom.　But she now comes in her divine form to crown
us with her grateful benediction in the presence of these glad thousands.　And here and now, in this grand presence, with the mighty
engines of our ripe civilization sending the pulsations of our life-
tide from ocean to ocean, thundering along the base of the mountains at the frontier of Aztec civilization, may we not say, reverently, gratefully, as did the great Judge of Israel when he looked
back upon Israel's pilgrimage and deliverance, "'Thus far the
Lord hath brought us.''

AN OLD DOCUMENT.

Mr. C. H. Crane, of Osawatomie gave some interesting facts
in regard to the historic town with which the name of John Brown
has been so much associated, and then read a copy of the original
indictment found by the territorial court of Lykins county in 1856,
against John Brown and his companions for conspiracy to resist
the bogus laws.　The following is the document:

United States of America,
TERRITORY OF KANSAS, ⎱ ss.　　　•
County of Lykins.　　 ⎰

　　In the United States Court of the 2d judicial district, sitting
in and for the County of Lykins, and Territory of Kansas, May
term A. D. 1856.
　　The grand jurors summoned, empaneled, and sworn to inquire
in and for the body of Lykins county, in the Territory of Kansas,
on their oaths present, that O. C. Brown, John Brown, Sr., John
Brown, Jr., O. V. Dayton, Alexander Gardner, Richard Mendenhall, Charles A. Foster, Charles H. Crane, William Partridge, and
William Chestnut, late of said county, being persons of evil minds
and dispositions, on the 16th day of April, 1856, and on divers
other days and times, both before and after that day, in the County
of Lykins, and Territory aforesaid, did unlawfully and wickedly
conspire, combine, confederate and agree together mutually to aid
and support one another in a forcible resistance to the enactments
of the laws passed by the Legislature of said Territory of Kansas,
let the attempt to inforce such enactments come from whatever
source it may.
　　And the grand jurors aforesaid do further present on their
oaths aforesaid that the said O. C. Brown, John Brown, Sr., John
Brown, Jr., O. V. Dayton, Alexander Gardner, Richard Mendenhall, Charles A. Foster, William Partridge and William Chestnut,
of said county on said 16th day of April, 1856, and on divers other
days and times, both before and after that day, in the county aforesaid, unlawfully and wickedly did conspire, combine, confederate
and agree together forcibly to resist and oppose the collector of

taxes in and for the county and Territory afor. said, and to use all the means and force necessary to prevent the execution of the laws of said Territory authorizing the assessment and collection of taxes to the evil example of all others and against the peace and dignity of the Territory of Kansas. WILLIAM BARBEE,

Attorney *pro tem.*

Indorsed as follows:

May Term, 1856, No. 4 Court, Criminal Conspiracy.

Kansas Territory vs. O. C. Brown, John Brown, Sr., John Brown, Jr., O V. Dayton, Alexander Gardner, Richard Mendenhall, Charles A. Foster, Charles H. Crane, William Partridge, William Chestnut. A true bill.

J. T. BRADFORD, Foreman.

Filed May 30, 1856.

CHAS. P. BULLOCK, Clerk.

(A true copy.)

I, L. McArthur, Clerk of the District Court of the U. S. and Territory of Kansas, in 2d judicial district of said Territory, certify that I have compared the above with the original and certify the same to be a true copy thereof.

In testimony whereof I have set my hand and affixed the seal of said Court at office in Lecompton this 7th day of August, A. D. 1857. L. McARTHUR, Clerk.

ADDRESS BY GEO. W. BROWN.

MR. SPEER:—I want to introduce to you one of the earliest of Kansas pioneers, a man who occupied a prominent part in the history of Kansas in the early period as an editor. Although in those days there were differences of opinion and some disputes among the free state men, we may now consider them to have been mere love spats to be soon forgotten. I take pleasure in introducing to you Dr. Geo. W. Brown, formerly editor of the *Herald of Freedom*, now of Rockford, Illinois. Dr. Brown began by giving a vision of what our State would be in 1900, which he first published nearly twenty-five years ago, and which now seems to have been almost prophetic, so accurately are events justifying the predictions then made. The speaker then said:

Mr. President, Early Settlers and Citizens of Kansas:

Plutarch informs us that Solon made a law prohibiting persons from attending entertainments too often, as it encouraged effeminacy and indolence, while he required persons to attend when invited, otherwise it would be discourteous to those hospitably disposed. Fourteen years absence from your State has saved me from censure under the first of these provisions, while my presence on this occasion, in obedience to the request of your committee of invitation, exonorates me under the latter requirement.

It gives me pleasure to join you on this occasion, to commemorate the 25th anniversary of the first settlement of this great and prosperous State. Few of us who looked out upon these broad prairies twenty-five years ago, had any just conception of the mighty changes that awaited our action. As we looked abroad over the extended landscape all was—

> " Vast as the sky against whose sunset shores
> Wave after wave the billowed greenness pours."

We inhaled the health-laden atmosphere as it came sweeping down from the north and felt that each particle of it was fragrant with freedom. We looked upon its soil and saw there the elements of perfected physical manhood. The rains descended in grateful profusion; and a cloudless sun vitalized the whole, and assured us of a glorious fruition. Turning our eyes eastward and southward a dark and threatening cloud was visible. It was portentous and impenetrable to human vision; and yet we trusted time would sweep it away, and light up the horizon beyond with brilliancy and beauty, and make all a scene of perpetual joy.

Many a day of gloom was ushered in, but with earnest faith and resolute endeavor, we pressed forward, conscious that we were sustained by the true and good everywhere. Finally, our desires were more than realized. A free Commonwealth, giving protection and security to every citizen was fully established, under whose ægis your population has swollen in a quarter of a century to numbers closely approximating a million.

Flowing directly from this as a natural result, all the wide national domain north, west and south of us was converted into free States and free Territories. Incidentally to this, as day follows dawn, the entire American Republic became a nation of free men, realizing the prophecy of Whittier in 1856, whose letter of regret because of his inability to be with us will probably be read in our hearing, filling us all with sorrow :

> " Whereso'er our destiny sends forth
> Its widening circles to the South or North,
> Where'er our banner flaunts beneath the stars
> Its mimic splendors, and its cloud like bars,
> There shall free labor's hardy children stand
> The equal sovereigns of a slaveless land."

No one then living, even in his wildest dream, dared anticipate what we to-day witness. Amid discouragements, such as no people ever had to contend with before—cruel poverty, protracted drouths, destroying pestilence, wasting famine, desolating war, and the stealthy hand of the incendiary and assassin,

YOU HAVE TRIUMPHED !

Shelley, seventy years ago, with poetical vision saw, and in glowing beauty described the glorious transformation. Before reading let me revive your recollection by stating that in all our maps printed prior to 1854, all that vast region lying west of the Missouri, extending thence to the Rocky Mountains, now embraced in the limits of Kansas, was marked as "The Great American Desert, inhabited by buffaloes and roving tribes of wild Indians." I read from Shelley's Queen Mab:

> "These deserts of immeasurable sand,
> Whose age-collected fervors scarce allowed
> A bird to live, a blade of grass to spring,
> Where the shrill chirp of the green lizard's love
> Broke on the sultry silentness alone,
> Now teem with countless rills and shady woods,
> Cornfields and pastures, and white cottages;
> And where the startled wilderness beheld
> A savage conqueror stained in kindred blood,
> A panther sating with the flesh of lambs,
> The unnatural famine of her toothless cubs,
> Whilst shouts and howlings through the desert rang;
> Sloping and smooth the daisy-spangled lawn,
> Offering sweet incense to the sunrise, smiles
>   To see a babe before his mother's door,
>   Sharing his morning's meal
>   With the tame and stately buffalo
>   That lies down at his feet."

Whilst I am fully conscious that you wait with impatience the better things in store for you from the eloquent gentlemen from abroad, and the champions of free institutions at home, I know you will excuse me a few minutes longer while I read the closing paragraph of a leading editorial, published in the *Herald of Freedom*, an old-time paper which all the old settlers of Kansas, I trust, will remember with some satisfaction. I read from a copy which my good wife found, with twenty-three additional numbers, under a carpet, in house-cleaning time, where they had been placed by a former owner of the property, being all that now remains to me of the fruitage of fourteen years of continuous journalism, six of which were in Lawrence. The complete and bound files of all my papers, with twenty-five sets of the *Herald of Freedom*, which I had preserved with great care to present to the historical and literary societies of Kansas, when properly organized, were burned at that terrible Quantrill Raid, on the 21st of August, 1863, when near two hundred of your best citizens were ruthlessly slain, and your homes were destroyed by fire.

You will please remember while I read that I left Kansas on the morning after President Lincoln's assassination, the 14th of April, 1865, at the close of the rebellion, while yet the blackened ruins of your crumbling walls remained, though here and there new structures were rapidly rising, among which was the Eldridge House, now the Ludington, the successor of the Free State Hotel. The north side of the river was yet covered with the primeval forest, and the Delaware Indians with their tribal relations, were in full possession of their reservation. I returned again but a few days ago, my first visit since leaving, not delaying till the year 1900, as suggested in the editorial I shall read you.

In this connection allow me in few words to state a fact which should pass into history, that the first number of the *Herald of Freedom*, consisting of 21,000 copies, at a cash cost to me of $600, was printed on my power press at Conneautville, Pa., and completed on the 21st of September, 1854, though bearing date a month later. The press was immediately taken down, boxed and shipped to Lawrence. The cylinder and much of the working part was broken at the destruction of the office, May 21, 1856, and though originally costing, without addition of freight, $2,250, I sold the old iron to Kimball Brothers for $40 to be recast and appear in other forms. Of the first number of the paper the entire edition was distributed at my expense, not to the press for complimentary notices, but to passengers on every western bound railroad train from Buffalo, Albany and Boston, to encourage emigration to this country, to which I was about going, I bringing with me a party of nearly three hundred, all raised by my own individual efforts, mostly in western Pennsylvania, some of whom have come several hundred miles from the interior to cheer us with their presence to-day.

For fear you will think I have but recently written and printed the papers from which I shall read, it gives me pleasure to learn that your State Historical Society has gathered with much care, has bound, and will carefully preserve such portion of my labors in Kansas as they could get possession of, comprising nearly all the numbers issued, and that you can verify my reading by consulting No. 44, Vol. 2, of date June 27, 1857, some twenty-two years ago.

I repeat, please remember that this description is an imaginative one only, written in 1857, with no prospects of a civil war, a Quantrill raid, of blackened ruins, with no intention of ever leaving Kansas, and of course, with no idea of returning to it in fact twenty two years after. In the light of what is realized to-day, and the nearness of the year 1900, who will suggest that nearly the only prophecy remained to be fulfilled, the trip from New York to San Francisco at an average rate of sixty miles an hour, will not be fully accomplished? I am only saddened with the reflection that if permitted in reality to meet with you on that day so few of my worthy co-laborers will remain to give me a cordial, fraternal greeting with which they have all welcomed me at this, the almost exact half-way station.

Let us visit Lawrence in 1900, and see what is passing there and then. We left it in its youth, just at the close of the civil strife, and hardly recovered from the discord and confusion produced by vandal hordes from beyond the rolling Missouri. Then it was a little hamlet upon the prairie, though giving promise of an energetic, thriving city, rising from the far-stretching plain beside the winding Kaw, where the wigwam of the savage and the forest stood in unison.

Before we came, huge posters stared us in the face, headed, "New

York and San Francisco—through in three days!" and leaving the splendid depot at Duane street, we are buzzing away toward the West, at an average rate of sixty miles an hour, taking breakfast at St. Louis and supper perhaps in Lawrence, where we leave the train, which stops but a moment and then speeds on its way, with a precious freight of lives to where the Sierra arises in majesty above the rolling waves of the Pacific. Crossing the splendid bridge, a single span over the river, we take the Massachusetts street cars for the Oread House, a mile or two from the depot, where we sit down to a magnificent collation served up by the good-humored host; and while engaged thus, revert to the trying old days of the "St. Nicholas" and "Metropolitan," when bacon reigned supreme, and hominy held the important part of aid-de-camp. Later came the more modern and comfortable hotels of 1857, among which we recollect the Morrow and Central Houses and commodious Whitney, close to the antique ferry.

After supper we regale ourselves by a stroll through the city, visiting places which were of interest in times agone. Passing down the street, we come to the Free State Hotel, diminutive in comparison with the more splendid structures on either hand, though standing as a memorial of other days. When last we looked upon the spot, it was rising Phœnix-like from the ashes, while around were strewed the ruins caused by vandal hands. Far to the south stand, on both sides of the broad thoroughfare, beautiful and substantial edifices, which, fifty years ago, would have been a pride to eastern cities. A Babel-like sound comes from the busy denizens of the street, and the bang of closing shutters mingles with a strain of music from the balcony of Metropolitan Hall. In what was once a handsome glen just beyond the ravine stands the church of our recollection like the old Dutch edifice of Sleepy Hollow, serving to call to the memory of age a passing thought of early days on the Kansas border, when the gruff challenge of "Free State or Pro-Slavery?" rang out upon the air, and *Lane's ragamuffins!*—in Border Ruffian parlance—were encamped upon the prairie sward. Other streets of equal beauty traverse the city. New Hampshire, Winthrop and Vermont streets are models in their way, and many a gem of architectural beauty pleases the vision as we pass along. We left them with an existence hardly more than a name; we return to old familiar spots as having no superiors in the State. All, all is changed! On either hand we read the evidence of progress, architectural, agricultural, mechanical and scientific. The old woods of the Delaware reserve are standing no longer. In their stead are the superb residences of our citizens, and thither now they have mostly retired. The sonorous peal from yon towering spire strikes the hour of ten; the gas lights burn brightly far adown the street, like an extensive torch light procession. Here and there we see crowds trooping home from the various places of amusement, some toward the Oread, and thither we wend our way.

We have visited a portion of Lawrence in 1900—when shall we visit it again?

Gladly I witnessed the almost complete realization of this ancient dream; and in many respects more than fulfilled. Joyfully I greet my old-time fellow-laborers for the freedom of Kansas, each one of whom did the best he knew to accomplish the desired result; sorrowfully I drop a tear with you as I recall the immortal dead who fell to secure the great boon of freedom to this fair land; trustfully I look forward to the year 1900, when, in my eightieth year, if living, if health and pecuniary circumstances will admit, I shall hope again to greet some of you; again grasp your warm hands, while we, with tender memories, will recount the glowing virtues of those gone before, as we now do those who have preceded us, before taking my own final departure for the land of the unknowable and unknown.

A KANSAS SONGSTRESS.

Noble Prentis in *Atchison Champion :* "After Mr. Brown's reading was concluded, Miss Zella Neill, of Lawrence, with orches-tral accompaniment, sang, 'With Verdure Clad.' The sight of this modest, sweet-faced, plainly clad young Kansas girl, singing, seemed to this, possibly, sentimental writer, a more attractive vision than all the aged politicians he remembers to have met in Kansas. She sang like a bird, without self-consciousness or any of the vanities technically known as ' frills.' That the State has produced such a singer in twenty-five years ' from the sod,' is glory enough for one day. The young singer was applauded, not with 'faint praise,' but with a tumult of joyful hands. The applause rose and rang again and again, until Miss Neill came forward and repeated the selection. At its close some fellow in the crowd sang out, ' Good for a new settler,' whereat there was a great laugh and cheer. Gov. Robinson remarked that in this case the honors were divided between the singer, who was a new settler, and the orches-tra, who were partly new and partly old settlers." The words of Miss Neill's song were as follows :

> " With verdure clad the fields appear,
> Delightful to the ravished sense ;
> By flowers sweet and gay
> Enhanced is the charming sight.
> Here fragrant herbs their odors shed ;
> Here shoots the healing plant ;
> With copious fruit the expanded boughs are hung ;
> In leafy arches twine the shady groves ;
> O'er lofty hills majestic forests wave."

ADDRESS BY HON. JAS. F. LEGATE.

GOVERNOR ROBINSON: In early times, when it was a little dangerous to live here, one did not know what was going to hap-pen from one day to another. I remember when the Congressional Committee was here taking testimony ; they had started for Topeka and had stopped at Tecumseh to take some testimony ; I remem-ber that that committee was composed of John Sherman, now Secretary of the Treasury, and several others. Mrs. Robinson and myself went up one day and met them at Topeka. I think it was at Tecumseh we met one of the grand jurors, and he informed us that the free state government was to be broken up ; that the governor of that institution was to be indicted ; and, when it sat

in Shawnee county, the Topeka Legislature was to be indicted—
and we found that what he there said was carried out. One of
that grand jury was James F. Legate. We had a duel in our first
constitutional convention, but it was bloodless. I was going to
say that I was acting as second for one of the parties. They
passed a resolution in the convention that anybody that took part
in a duel should be expelled, so I turned my case over to James
F. Legate, who will now address you.

Mr. Legate spoke as follows:

Mr. Chairman, Ladies and Gentlemen:

I came here to-day hardly expecting to speak, or expecting, if
called on, to draw largely upon the only speech I ever made in my
life, which was to an agricultural society up in Doniphan, and I
confess to you that I am not only grieved, but chagrined, to find
that the first speech that was made by Governor Robinson was
composed of about one-half of that speech of mine Governor
Robinson should have done better and should not have remembered so well what Sol. Miller printed. The other half of his
speech was made up out of his message to the first Legislature,
and what Charles Sumner had said. There is one thing that I can
say and that is, that that portion of his speech which was a copy
of mine was a most elegant address. I did not think that any one
else would draw upon that speech, but it seems that my friend
Holliday also reads Sol. Miller's paper, and he, likewise, appropri-
ated a portion of it, which I don't think was exactly fair, so I am
a little vexed at him. He went back to the days of Lycurgus,
and brought him back here and made him one of the old settlers.
Well, I was tolerably satisfied when *he* got through, but up comes
Governor St. John, who pulled out his old geography and went
over the Great American Desert, almost word for word, as I did up
in Doniphan. I don't think it exactly fair of these gentlemen to
thus rob me of the chance of making a speech. I then began to
think of Geary and Brindle and old Judge Smith, and had woven
in my brain the material for a pretty good speech—but, my God!
George Crawford went over the same ground, and the Lord only
knows what he would not have covered up if he had not stopped.
My Doniphan county speech is therefore exhausted. What, then,
is there left for me to talk about? We are here to-day to review
the events of the past; and there are many things in the past that
we have seen and realized, that taught many a lesson for the present and future. We have heard a great deal to-day about the
early settlers of Kansas and the early settlement of Lawrence.
Sometimes I laugh to myself about those early settlers. There
was not one of them—no, not one—who realized the work he was
doing. Why, I remember, twenty-five years ago, when the free
state men of Kansas (and that meant Lawrence, Topeka and a few
fellows over in Leavenworth) would hold a convention as often as

the Yankees eat in hay-time, and that is three regular meals a day and a luncheon between. And a solemn convention it would be, too, with Dr. Chas. Robinson, President; Geo. W. Brown, Secretary (with now and then Joel K. Goodin or John Speer for Secretary); and about a dozen awfully ragged, deplorably forlorn looking cusses (who wanted to get back east again, and hadn't the money to take them there,) to make up the audience. And that convention would solemnly resolve, like the three tailors of London, that *we*, the people of Kansas Territory, resolve that *we* will make this a free State. And Wm. A. Phillips, Jim. Redpath and Hinton would report it, and it would make two and a half and sometimes three columns in the New York *Tribune*.

I remember, among the early conventions, the celebrated Sand-bank Convention. Gen. James H. Lane came to the Territory and stopped at Lawrence to get a jug of—water. He did not want to get contaminated by abolition principles, but when he came to get the jug of—water he was pleased with the Yankee settlement and concluded to stop. Then followed a series of caucuses, as we would call them—"private seances" such as no one ever saw outside of Indiana. Then began the trouble of making him a good settler; he did not become a convert just then, but he did afterward. Well, they had the famous Sand-bank Convention —a Democratic affair. I was a little tinctured in those days with the same peculiar disease, but somehow I did not take kindly to that sand-bank conclave. It was composed of Dr. Wood, James Christian, Joel K. Goodin, (he doesn't answer?), Joe Speer and old Judge Curtis, a handsome gentleman who looked like President Lincoln. There was also a young fellow named Jas. S. Emery, whom they used to call "the young man eloquent from Maine," who addressed the Sand-bank Convention on the question of the dissolution of the Union, saying, in substance, that if South Carolina or Louisiana should take umbrage at the action of the Abolitionists in Kansas, and should go out of the Union, there would be a conflict of arms and a fratricidal war such as no history had ever recorded; and denouncing in strong terms the action of the Abolitionists. Old Judge Curtis (who had one tooth protruding three or four inches and tobacco juice running down each side of his mouth) sat in solemn dignity during that speech, gave an occasional twist to the little wampum that he had about his neck and saying, "Well, I think you are about right, but I don't care a d—n what you do." Joe Speer made a speech, but Joe Speer was not as conservative as Lane. My friend Emery was not very conservative; he was a staunch Douglas man, and expected to get Kansas into the Union as a Douglas Democratic State. But, when he had finished his speech and the others were talking, he amused himself by picking up pebbles and skipping them on the river. A young man, who was lying on the bank above the convention, at this point shouted, "Y-y-u b-bet-better q-qui-quit this thing," and the convention adjourned. That was the only attempt to make a Democratic organization until after Kansas had become a free State. Then there were not offices enough for all the aspirants in the Republican party. That young man, by the way, is worthy of more notice. He came to this State with one who has since become distinguished as a newspaper man. He says that when they reached Chicago the gentleman had $700—more money than *he* ever dreamed of having. (The young man had "nary a red.") They stayed in an hotel, and, before retiring, piled up all the furniture in the room against the door, and says the anxious possessor of the $700: "Charlie, what shall I do with this money? If I should lose this $700, I never could start a printing office in Lawrence!" The young man replied: "John, I'll t-tell y-you w-what; you g-go to bed and s-sl-sleep on the ba-back side, a-an-and if any-b-body c-co-comes in to rob us th-they w-will try me f-first and ge-get dis-discouraged and g-go away." This sagacious young man was afterward employed in a printing office in Topeka, during the Topeka constitutional convention. A man by the name of Dickey died and a eulogy had been pronounced upon him, which, among other expressions, contained something like the following: "Let us gather around the grave of our departed friend and shed a tear to his memory." In "setting up" the article, the meter of that sentence did not suit the ideas of the young printer, so he changed it and read the proof himself; and in the morning, when the paper came out, the solemn sentence read: "Let us gather around the grave of our departed friend, Dickey, and shed a tear or two, or, perhaps three, to his memory."

I came here to-day expecting to hear impromptu speeches, but those devilish reporters have compelled the fellows to write out their speeches, and, at the suggestion of those reporters, they have written ones that would take me at least a month or six weeks to get up. So what I have to say will simply consist of reminiscences of the past.

As I said in the beginning, there were but few who realized the work they were doing. There were but few who realized that they were active participants in a conflict which was to settle the momentous question of freedom or slavery. Men seldom know the ultimate purpose for which they are moved to act. So the men in those early days scarcely dreamed of the ultimate result of their actions. Governor Robinson will pardon me for telling something which was private once, but is public now. The Governor is and always has been a cold-water man. Well, I remember that at an entertainment given in honor of Fred Stanton, the Governor gave the following toast which he drank in cold water, but which I want you to understand some of us drank in whisky: "Here is —— in for making the tin!" And there was as much truth as poetry in that, for ten to one—yes, a hundred to one—came to this Territory to better their conditions, financially, rather than from any motive of philanthropy or abolition principles. Men came here as Democrats—men came here as pro-slavery men—who

have performed work and accomplished deeds in the cause of freedom that entitle them to be perpetuated in history as much as those
who came here imbued with no other sentiment than that of antagonism to slavery.   There was Gen. James H. Lane, for instance,
(and I was never counted among his friends, politically,) who
came here as near a pro-slavery man as a man could come and
come from a northern State.   He came here with the conviction
that all that portion of the country in which rice, cotton, tobacco
and hemp could be raised, and which he regarded as only products of slave labor—putting in the word hemp—rightfully belonged
to slavery, and it was only when he became convinced that the
first three products could not be raised successfully here that he
dreamed of espousing the free state cause.   Still, no man ever
lived in Kansas who left behind him a more glorious history, even
with all his errors and shortcomings.   No man ever left behind
him a history of which his widow, his children and his grandchil-
dren could be more proud than that of Gen. James H. Lane.   I
say this, detracting nothing from my friend, Governor Robinson,
who came here imbued with the New England sentiment that slavery was wrong under all circumstances and all pretensions, in all
climes and in all times.   I take nothing from his history of which
he has reason to be proud and of which future generations will ever
feel proud.   As I said on another occasion, (and not at Doniphan,
either, for I am going to quit on that speech,) there are three men
in Kansas whose history never can be forgotten.   Their names
are Governor Chas. Robinson, Gen. James H. Lane and old Osawatomie Brown.   The balance of us in those days were privates
and will sink into oblivion; they alone form specks on the great
ball of revolving time.

Nevertheless I am glad to be here to-day.   I am happy to
have the opportunity of talking to you, for I can only talk.   I
can't make a set speech.   I have not the power in my weak, diminutive frame to send the ponderous words rolling forth as did
my friend, the stalwart Crawford, this afternoon.   Nor was I suf-
ficiently a mechanic to adjust that arch stone of which the Governor spoke, or even view the performance "with a critic's eye."
But I came here to have a good time, to be free and easy, and
not to be "gawked at" and scared to death.   But I would not
hold a manuscript up before you, as some of my illustrious prede-
cessors have done, for all the world.   The only time in my whole
life that I ever saw Governor Robinson scared, was to-day.   When
he pulled out that manuscript his knees actually knocked together.
My friend Holliday did better, but that was owing to the fact that
in his youth he wore good clothes.   Good clothes give a young
man an *entre* to good society, and in good society one gets used to
being stared at.   So he passed through the trying ordeal without
shaking much.   But Crawford quivered—and I don't know which
made him quiver the most—the sight of all of you folks looking
at him or the thunder of his own big words.   Well, taking up the

broken thread of my reminiscences of early times: Long years ago I came to this Territory, like a great many others responsive to the sentiment of Governor Robinson's toast. I came here with a few dollars and I have a few left to night, but not quite enough to pay that fellow for bringing us over. I got trusted for that. I have seen a great many things. I remember the Wakarusa war and a great many of its incidents. I remember that it was a scientific affair. You see I am a scientific fellow. I happened to be running a township line, of the public survey, and I ran it right through that celebrated camp of Sheriff Jones' Missouri militia. I knew Sheriff Jones and wanted to know what he was doing up here. He said : "I have come up to find those G——d d——d Yankees. I came up here as sheriff of Douglas county and arrested an old man by the name of Jacob Branson, and they rescued him from me." I left my outfit in the Wakarusa bottom and came up to Lawrence where I found the people in council. I talked with Governor Robinson and found out that they were getting ready to fight, and I thought I would turn in and help them. The Wakarusa war was fought, and I am sorry that as a matter of history, my friend Governor Robinson said to-day that Major Clark shot this young man Barber, just outside of Lawrence. He never shot him at all. Jim Burns was a young man full of blood and hell, and retains all the hell yet, and was over here with Sheriff Jones' militia, and Major Clark was not the man who shot Barber, but Jim Burns was, and was indicted by a pro-slavery grand jury for shooting him. Right is right. I was here to take Major Clark's place, and had it not been for you Abolitionists, I should have had it. You decoyed me into one of your abolition meetings and I was like all the other fellows, ass enough to go to making speeches. I told them I wanted this a free State, but I wanted it a Democratic State. George W. Brown was then publishing a paper here. He was a fellow with a good deal of distinction. He called me "Gen. Legate, of Mississippi." He induced me to deliver a speech, which he afterward published in his paper, in which I said that I was a free state Democrat, (which was true,) but that when the time came, that by voting I could make Kansas a free State, I was ready to perform my part of the task. There was a fellow in Washington, who went from Mississippi, by the name of Ed. Wright, who was taking Geo. Brown's paper, and after seeing that speech of mine in it, he wrote to me that my cake was all dough. Had it not been for that speech, I might have been the same Indian agent that Major Clark was. I immediately went up to see Calhoun and got a job surveying.

The Wakarusa war taught the Missourians that they were meeting a force in this Territory with as great determination, and as daring a spirit as their own, which they must overthrow before they could take slaves to the Territory of Kansas. It disheartened them. Governor Shannon—the newly made Governor—had just come fresh from Ohio, imbued with all the sentiments of proslaveryism, and they expected that he would use not only the power of the Territory, but also that of the general government, to crush out the spirit of liberty and put, in its place, the institution of slavery. Near the conclusion of that bloodless war, (with the exception of the death of young Barber,) he came to Lawrence, filled to the brim with the spirit of which you may guess. However, Governor Robinson and Lane were more sagacious than either Shannon or his advisors, so they made a treaty. The army was disbanded, and the Missourians went home disgusted alike with Governor Shannon and the prospects of making Kansas a slave State. There was also a convention up here at Big Springs, and another set of resolutions and another report to the eastern press. This convention was the basis of the Topeka constitutional convention which framed the first constitution for free Kansas. Reeder contested the seat of J. W. Whitfield, the proslavery delegate elected October 1, 1855. I rode over the Territory with G. P. Lowrey, taking testimony. Sometimes I was Justice of the Peace, and sometimes he was Notary Public, without any seal, but the testimony was good all the same. Out of that contest came the investigation by Congress. The Topeka constitution had been submitted to the people and adopted. A list of officers had also been elected under that constitution. It was about time for the assembling of the Legislature. I was honored, as I have been oftentimes, by holding distinguished positions in the State of Kansas, by being a member of a grand jury, and what a sweet-scented(?) jury it was! Uncle Jimmie McGee and myself were members from Lawrence. We had a caucus semi-occasionally. There were seventeen members all told. Uncle Jimmie and I were temperate, but there were at least fifteen bottles of whisky in the room all the time. The first and most important case to be decided by that grand jury was the indictment of Sam Wood and John Speer. I have forgotten whether it was John Speer for assuming to hold an office that he was not legally elected to, and Sam Wood for resisting an officer, or *vice versa*. Attorney General Isaacs was sent for. Like a great many Yankees, I was inquisitive, and it was a very important question to be decided, in my mind. So I said to him: "You have John Speer charged with treason. Under what law or circumstances do you make his offense treason?" "Well, sir," said he, taking hold of the flask of whisky, "the facts are these : A man who pretends to hold an office, having once held that office, and is defunct, and assumes to still hold it against the constituted authorities, commits treason." Said I, "What about Sam Wood?" He replied: "If a man undertakes to carry out the decrees of such an officer, he commits treason also." I thought that was good enough. There were thirteen votes—Stewart not voting. Uncle Jimmie McGee and I voted no. It came up again, when Robinson, George W. Smith, George W. Deitzler, Gaius Jenkins, George W. Brown and Governor Reeder were indicted. We discussed it in all its forms, but we indicted them. The next thing was this "cussed" Emigrant Aid Society. They had built a hotel here in Lawrence with about a foot and half of wall above the roof, and fitted it up with port holes, and they called that the Fort. It was designed to protect the town against the officers of the law from executing the decrees of court, they said. About that time I remembered that I had a pressing engagement out at old Judge Wakefields. So I went out a-foot, (that is the way we used to ride a good deal in those days,) and got a pony and saddle there, rode up to Tecumseh, where I had a talk with John Sherman, Gov. Robinson and Mr. Howard, and I gave them a pretty clear idea of what was going on—that is, I intimated it to them. I then went back to Judge Wakefield's, slept about an hour, walked over to Lecompton, and was arrested for contempt of court. I went into the court room and the court wanted to know what excuse I had. I gave a truthful answer, as I always do. I said I went over to Judge Wakefield's, went to sleep and had overslept myself. I was excused and I went back to Judge Wakefield's, got the pony and came over to Lawrence. I do not think Governor Robinson was there at the time. I believe he had pressing duties which called him east, and he went as far as Lexington, where he found a stopping place. He came back by way of Leavenworth to Lecompton. They made some arrests in Lawrence, and then they went about abating the nuisance of the Fort Hotel. They had a cannon on the opposite side of the street, and old Atchison got down on his knees, took deliberate aim at the hotel, but shot clear over it and struck the hill near where a crowd of women were who had left the town for safety. Their gunners were so good(?) that they could not hit the whole side of a hotel across the street. However, they finally demolished it.

I give another incident coming under my observation illustrative of those time.

Governor John W. Geary had a little fellow by the name of Jones for one of his secretaries. I happened to be in Lecompton on a certain day after the Governor had had a little difficulty with a fellow by the name of Sherrard. He had spit upon the Governor—a little matter of indignity. They were having a little indignation meeting there, and I happened to be on the list of the men to whom the subject of resolutions was referred. I believe it was myself, Dr. Wood, a man by the name of Stewart, and some others, I cannot think now who they were. I got up some resolutions expressive of my sentiments. Stewart reported them to Sherrard, who sent word back that he would kill any man who would read those resolutions. I was not on the die worth a cent, so I went up there and read the resolutions, holding them in one hand and a revolver in the other. I was not as large as I am now, but I stood still. I have seen some ludicrous things. I remember one young fellow who thought there was more safety in flight than standing and looking on, so he ran and hid behind one of those machines that were designed for use in constructing the capital building. He had got right under it when whack! whack! came a couple of bullets against it, and he rolled out crying, "Oh! oh! don't! don't!" I was here when Quantrill came. I got out. I was the best pleased man in the State when I got on this side of the Kaw. The last time I ever saw Charlie Hart, *alias* Quantrill, was in the hotel, and I gave him ten dollars to get medicine. I believed him to be honest, and I believed him to be a second John Brown. But I was mistaken. Well, as I said before, I was here when he came to Lawrence. I had a little colored boy who came into the room where myself, wife and children were, saying that "the bushwhackers are in town." I got up in less than a minute. My wife said: "Now don't be scared." I was not scared, but I could not find the button holes in my clothes. I did not like the looks of things. I got on my clothes, went out into the street and saw them butcher three men, firing shot after shot into them. I heard these men plead for their lives in tones that would penetrate hearts of steel, and yet I felt so paralyzed that no emotion of pity, sympathy, or anything akin to it, sprang from my heart, notwithstanding the piteous pleadings of these poor victims for even one moment more of life. I walked around until I got a good opportunity to get into a house and then walked into it in a hurry. It was full of women—Swedes, Germans and Americans. One would say something in one language and another would make a reply in some other language. I went through that house as if there was something in the back yard that I wanted. There were four rows of corn in that yard and I took the middle row. I did not take the outside row. I kept right on, and if there is any race horse that can make better time than I made, I would like to see him. I went down through the tall hemp and corn, and then through some tall grass and bushes and all at once I came upon a man lying on his back, who threw up his hands and feet and cried out, "Oh! don't! oh! don't!" and I was more scared than he was, but I said: "Who are you before you die?" And he said: "Why, Legate, it's Solon! Don't you know Solon?" We made friends in a moment, for it was a time when we had to make friends quickly. I continued my race and he followed. When we got to the river we were in a terrible stew about getting across, the only way being to swim. He turned and went back and I jumped into the river, but I notice I backed up under the bank so closely that even a mosquito could not find me. Several of the bushwhackers came along and I heard them talking, oh, so sweetly(?) They saw the tracks leading back into the bushes, so they turned back and I struck out. I made the best time possible, and I am certain that no Missouri river boat ever ploughed the water quicker than I did. They came back after awhile and amused themselves by shooting at me. They leveled a very large gun at me, resting it against a tree, and took deliberate aim. I could see clear to the bottom of the barrel, and could see the ball shining down there, but strange as it may appear, I was just as certain that it was not going to hit me as I ever was of anything in this world. I got out all right and started for Leavenworth at once, where I had some pressing business. I went to an old Indian woman and asked for a horse, and she replied in a lot of Indian gibberish, and that was all I could get out of her. So I went out and gobbled a horse and started for Leavenworth. I do not want to stop to criticise the actions of Tom Ewing, but I believe to-day as I believed then, that if Tom Ewing, now of Ohio, but then a general in the army, had taken my advice he would have captured Quantrill. There were seven steamboats at Leavenworth which he could press into service to transport his eleven hundred men to Kansas City, where he could head Quantrill off, but he went to De Soto instead, and got there just in time to see that noted bushwhacker and his men go out of the State.

I have detained you longer than I intended. I am like Geo. Crawford, when I get to talking I do not know when to stop. I expect to be here at another twenty-five year celebration. I expect Gov. Robinson to be here also. And I know Geo. Crawford and Emery will be. And John Speer will be here for seventy-five years; twenty-five years after I am dead. I hope that this meeting will serve to refresh the memory of the old settlers and impress on the minds of the new, the trials through which the early settlers passed to make Kansas a free State. The making of Kansas a free State made the nation a free nation. I hope it will serve to give every man a generous reward for his deeds in those days; believing, as I do, that there is a Power above and beyond men that guides, directs and controls; believing that neither the Emigrant Aid Society, Governor Robinson, Gen. Lane, John Brown, or anybody else is entitled to that enormous credit that some men seem ready to accord, but thinking that each and all were but instruments in the hands of a Power Unseen, whose purpose was to take from this country that relic of barbarism, the curse of slavery. That is all there is in it. I thank you all, ladies and gentlemen, for your kind indulgence and flattering attention.

ADDRESS BY COL. S. N. WOOD.

Mr. SPEER: We have an old resident among us this evening who is well known to all of you. He came to this State during its darkest hours and has passed through some very narrow places since that time. I mean Col. S. N. Wood, and I have the pleasure of introducing him to you now.

Mr. Wood spoke as follows:

Mr. Chairman and Ladies and Gentlemen:

I do not know why I am called upon to make a speech. I came here by accident. I had no intimation until yesterday morn-

5

ing that I was expected to say anything on this occasion, or I would have done like my friend, Legate, and prepared a speech two hours long and committed it to memory. And then, after the whole history of Kansas has been mapped into one speech, if I had undertaken to say anything, Legate would get up here and say I was copying some of his speeches; so that it places me in a very embarrassing position. There is another reason why I should not talk here—I was not sent to Kansas by the Emigrant Aid Company; I did not come from Boston, and I never was a Pennsylvania Democrat. And these are at least two good reasons why I should not say anything. I don't expect there ever was as big a coward in Kansas as I was in its early settlement, because I never got into a fight—if I did, I never got killed. I want to say right here that I expect to attend the next Quarter Centennial, and I expect to listen to my friend Legate giving the history of the next twenty-five years at the Centennial.

I really do not know what to talk about here to-night. We have heard a great deal about Pennsylvania, Thomas Jefferson and George Washington—and I want to say a word here for Thomas Jefferson. I recollect, in the early history of Virginia, that he said, "Indeed, I tremble for my country when I reflect that God is just and that his justice cannot sleep forever." Yet I do not think that Virginia is entitled to any credit for making Kansas a free State; neither do I think that the Pennsylvania Democrats are entitled to any credit for making Kansas free, for I want to say right here that what we used to call "The Stubbs" did more to make Kansas free than all the governors that ever came here from Pennsylvania. Why, all that can be s id of those old governors is that they were not as bad as we expected, and as they were understood to be; and after they got here and became acquainted with us, they found we were not near as bad as they had expected. I recollect when the word came from Shawnee Mission, in 1855, that Governor Reeder wanted to see some of his friends at Shawnee Mission, two wagon loads of us went down. We understood they were going to force him to issue certificates of election to men elected by force and fraud. We were ready to meet them, force with force. But the certificates were issued all the same, with two or three exceptions; and they might just as well have been. Reeder lacked moral courage; but he got right, finally, and so did Geary and the rest. They came here all wrong, and we had to convert every one of them. They did not come here with very much that was good about them, as I recollect them.

I was going to say that during our Wakarusa war, there were two ladies here who went where men dare not go—through the border-ruffian lines, across the Wakarusa, and procured information and returned to Lawrence. They did more to make Kansas free than all the Democratic governors that ever came here from Pennsylvania. I recollect the ladies of Lawrence who used to meet at my house, day after day, and make cartridges; and these ladies, and the men who fought, are the ones who converted the Democratic governors of Pennsylvania and made Kansas free. Now I never was a Democrat—I never expect to be.

I came here from Ohio. I have not heard Ohio mentioned, I believe, in this celebration; and it always did occur to me that there was her Chase, who helped to make Kansas free, and her Giddings and Wade—God bless them! We had about as many Ohioans in Kansas as people from any other State. I think, in 1860, when the census was taken, that we had more Ohio people here than all New England had. I recollect very distinctly that in the first free state Legislature we ever had, there were more Ohioans in the Legislature than there were members from any other State—and Ohioans never want office, either. I can prove that by President Hayes, at any time.

If you will allow one word of egotism here, I want to mention a circumstance—so Legate can put it in his next speech. When the Kansas–Nebraska Bill was pending before Congress, we had an indignation meeting in the town where I lived, in Ohio. I was studying law, at the time, with a firm, both of whom were Democrats. I took an active part in that meeting. I denounced the Kansas–Nebraska Bill and squatter sovereignty.

Mr. Brumback said: "The bill will pass, and then what will you do about it?"

I said: "If that bill passes, I, for one, will go to Kansas and help fight the fight over again!" [Applause.]

I recollect I was cheered, but I did not think what I was saying at the time. I had no idea, then, of going to Kansas, but in the course of the next thirty days the question was asked me frequently when I was going to start. It became evident to me, as to everybody else, that the bill was going to pass. One night I went home and told my wife, as quick as the bill passed, I was going to Kansas, and asked her what she would do. She said if I went she was going also. The bill passed on the 30th of May, and, on the 6th of June, we—that is, myself, wife and two children—were on the road to Kansas. And we had never heard of the "Emigrant Aid Company," either.

When we came up into Kansas, Mrs. Wood and myself and the children, (we came in a wagon which we had brought with us from Ohio, by Cincinnati and up the river—we drove up on the old California road,) I remember we met two good free state men, Mr. White and Mr. Yates. We camped with them; the next morning they showed us their claims, which now take in all the country where the towns of Bloomington and Clinton are built. We thought there was considerable land to the acre. We went back to Independence, Missouri, by the Santa Fé road. I was raised a Quaker and opposed to fighting—on principle. We camped one night on Bull creek, and it rained very hard; in the morning, all around was cold and wet. McCamish, who kept a trading house, came down to see if we wanted breakfast, and invited us to his house to dry and warm. We met a stranger, I afterward learned, Mr. Brady, of Missouri. He evidently took us to be Missourians. I let him do all the talking, answering with monosyllables. Just as I was getting up from the table he said:

"There are some men who say we have no right to bring our slaves here, and hold them as property."

I said: "That is my position exactly."

He says: "Explain."

I said: "You bring your slaves into Kansas. I swear out a writ of *habeas corpus* requiring you to bring your slaves before some court, to show by what authority you hold them. You can't plead the constitution of the United States, for that don't say anything on the subject. You can't plead the laws of Missouri, for they have no jurisdiction in Kansas. You can't plead the laws of Kansas, for we have passed none, and your slaves would go free."

He replied that he had but one reply to make to such argument, and that was with his revolver and a rifle.

Before he had the words hardly out of his mouth I had my revolver out, and at his breast and said:

"God damn you, I would just as soon argue in that way as any other."

He then politely informed me that he did not intend anything personal.

We used to have a good deal of fun in those old times. I do not think that we realized what we were doing, half of the time. I recollect when I first came to Kansas, I had been to Westport. They had held a meeting there and resolved to hang every white-livered abolitionist that dared set foot in Kansas, and every man north of Mason's and Dixon's line is an abolitionist. I wrote it up. It was the first letter that was ever written from a free state standpoint, from Kansas. It was published in the *National Era*, Washington, in June or July, 1854 It was copied into the Missouri *Republican*. I was in Westport when the *Republican* came with it in, and heard the letter denounced on all sides, and threats to kill the author. It was copied extensively throughout the States. That night I staid with an old man between Westport and Independence, and he spent the whole evening almost in reading that letter to me. He said to me: "If I ever set eyes on that man I will shoot him at sight." I came very near telling him that he was lying about it, but I did not, fearing it might prove true, and let him go.

I think the first emigrants sent out by the Emigrant Aid Society came here in August, 1854. We were living about two and a half miles west of where Lawrence is now located. We had but few squatters before that time. We had already, however, organized a squatters' association. At the first meeting we had fifteen squatters present. We came near having some trouble in it. Just about the time we had met, and were getting ready to commence business, up came about thirty armed men from Missouri, who wanted to know where the meeting was to be held. We were attending a house-raising and busy at work at the time. There was not a man at that house that knew anything about the meeting. But after they had got tired of waiting, and we had asked them to help us, they finally left. After they had gone, and we had got through raising the house, we had the meeting and appointed our officers. Before our next meeting the first New England emigrants came, and we re-organized.

I have ridden through Westport time and time again, when I was pointed at, and heard the remark, "There goes that abolitionist." One time I had been to Kansas City with Judge Wakefield. On our return we stopped at the post-office for mail. The Judge staid in the buggy. I went into the post-office. Dr. Earl was post-master. The office was in the back end of a drug store. Whilst getting the mail, for the settlement, the drug store filled up, and the talk was about me. I knew I' must face it, and finally, adjusting my revolver, stepped into the drug store, with my arms full of mail matter. A large, tall man said, "here comes this damned stinking abolitionist."

"Now," I said, "if you were not a damned stinking puppy, I would notice you."

He made a lunge for me. I stepped aside and he passed me before he could gather himself up. I laid my mail down, clinched, and raised him from the floor, and threw him backward. He grabbed for my hair, and scratched my face a little. I grabbed his hair with my left hand, and struck him in the face with my right fist. He bled furiously, and cried "Take him off," And I was raised from him. Judge Wakefield came in puffing, and said:

"Mr. Wood has been in bed sick a week."

I laughed at the idea, took up my mail, and asked the Judge if he was ready to go. He said, "Yes."

I bowed and said: "Good-night, gentlemen," and we were soon at the Quaker Mission. I was never insulted in Westport afterward. This was the first time in my life that I ever hurt a man for telling the truth, but I went on the idea that the truth would not do to tell on all occasions.

After the first New England Emigrants came to Mt. Oread, the Border Ruffians undertook to scare them badly. I remember word was sent to my house (the same word was sent to the party on the hill), that unless we left before a certain night, that we would all be tarred and feathered. But we did not go. And when I met one of the men the next day, who had made the threat, I asked him why they had not done what they said they were going to do. He said the reason was that they could not find the feathers.

I said: "We have got two feather-beds. If you will furnish the tar, we will furnish the feathers and see who will get the most of it." (Laughter.)

I had loaned all my arms to the Yankees on the hill, and, on the second night, I told my wife I would go down and camp with

the Yankees, thinking if they were frightened, or driven off, we
should all have to go, but the first attempt would be made on the
Yankees, if made at all.   I got down there about dusk, and we
put matters at the tents in order.   Sam F. Tappan and myself went
on picket duty.   It was very dark.   We were in a ditch at the road-
side.   A small body of horsemen passed us.   We knew from their
conversation that an attempt would be made to frighten the Yankees.   They were joined by two others at the next house, when
they returned.   We remained until they were opposite us, and
within twenty feet, when both of us sprung up, and I ordered :
"Make ready!   Take aim!   Fire!"

Bang, bang, went our pistols in the air, and the whole party
left on a gallop.   I do not know but they are running yet.

There is one other incident that I must relate in our early
history.   It was the attempt to cut down Governor Robinson's
house.   Robinson was building a house on Mount Oread, near
where the old University stands.   Colonel Deitzler (it was the first
time I had met the Colonel—as true a man as ever lived) came to
me, and said, "Dr. Wood, Babcock and Co. have gone up to cut
Dr. Robinson's house down."

I asked :   "Where is the doctor?"

He said :   "He is away from home."

I said :   "They ought not to cut the house down in Robinson's
absence."

He said :   "Well, what shall be done?"

I said :   "If you will stand by me it shall not be done."

He said :   "I am with you."

I said :   "Say nothing, but get your arms and meet me at my
house in five minutes."   I went at once to my house, put on my
hat and two navy revolvers.   By that time Colonel Deitzler was at
my house, and we started for Mount Oread.   As we ascended the
hill I looked back, and the whole city seemed to be following.
Babcock was chopping on the southeast corner-post—Dr. Wood
the south center.   There were some fifteen of them.   The carpen-
ters had quit work.   I left Col. Deitzler at the corner, with Babcock, and stepped to the center-post, where Dr. Wood was chopping.   I stepped between him and the post, and facing him, looked
him square in the face, with his axe raised as if to strike again,
which he could not do without hitting me.   He asked: "What
does this mean?"

I replied :   "It means that not another blow can be struck on
the building.   You were too cowardly to make the attempt when
Robinson was here, and you shan't cut his building down in his
absence."   "Not another blow, gentlemen," said I.   There was
much swearing and threats.   We said :   "We know nothing about
the merits of the case.   Won't argue it, but you shan't cut down
this house."   Dr. Wood swore he would fight a duel with Dr.
Robinson.   I said :   "I am Dr. Robinson's friend.   I will accept
the challenge now and name the weapons.   You shall take a box

of pills of your own make, Dr. Robinson the same, and sit straddle of a log, and see who can eat the most of his own pills and live." It turned the storm into a laugh, on all sides, and the fight was over, and the house saved, until afterward burned by Jones' posse, when the Free State Hotel was burned.

Ladies and gentlemen, my five minutes are up! I don't want to occupy your time any longer to-night. [Cries of "Go on, go on!"]

When we old Kansas men get to talking about Kansas times, it is hard to stop. And it is almost impossible to give the history of those old times without giving our own personal history, to some extent. We have saved Kansas to freedom. Slavery has been wiped out in this whole country, and I am satisfied with the work that I have done toward it.

I believe that I built the first frame house, built in Lawrence. My Yankee friends were camping about in tents and log sheds, and I went to work and built a frame house. I built that house 14 by 16, with two rooms in it, one down stairs and one up stairs. But it was never full. We lodged in that house as high as twenty-five in one night. It was all of split timber and split boards.

A great many hardships were endured in those times, and the reason that we succeeded was because all that we had was dedicated to the cause of freedom in Kansas.

Eli Thayer, and the "Emigrant Aid Society," made a great excitement in Missouri, and especially about Westport. I represented that 40,000 New Englanders were coming out, and excitement ran high. At one time I had been to Kansas City, and on my return to the settlement I stopped at the noon station, on a stream between Westport and the Wakarusa, and while my horses were eating I went out to the road, and took my axe and peeled off an elm tree and wrote on it that,

"Eli Thayer claims forty miles square for the New England Emigrant Aid Society, of which this is the center."

The Missourians soon got the idea that Thayer was in the State, and $1,000 reward was offered for him dead or alive. I went to Westport with D. R. Anthony, and when a Missourian wanted to see Thayer, I said:

"I am Eli Thayer, what do you want?"

He wanted nothing.

One of the first suits that I had in the Territory was when a man named Adams had claimed a piece of land that Dr. Harrington had settled on. The Governor recollects it well. Almost everybody turned out to the trial. I reasoned this way: Adams was a Missourian, and if he can get Harrington's claim, some other Missourian will come and claim any piece of land that any of the Yankees here settled on. And we have got to beat Adams at all hazards.

Only two of the six jurymen drawn were present. We agreed to try with three men. Of the others, one was a free state man and one a pro-slavery. The great point to be gained was the other juryman. Every lawyer knows how important it is to get a jury that you can rely on in the trial of any cause. And this was no exception to the rule, I assure you. We both tried every way that we could think of, to get the other juryman to suit ourselves, but could not make it.

Finally, Adams said: "Make us a fair proposition."

I suggested to him that we would name all the men we wanted as witnesses, he do the same, and then the Judge should name three men from the bystanders that were left, and not witnesses. This seemed to please him, and he assented. I asked them to name their witnesses. They did so. I spent a few minutes marking down the names of our witnesses, and when I was done I had got every man down as a witness that I did not want on the jury. From the bystanders Judge Wakefield named three. They marked off one and we one. And in this way I succeeded in getting the jury I wanted, and gained the case. It would have gained almost any case.

Now, it has been said that we are going to have another Quarter Centennial, twenty-five years from now. I expect to be at it. And I think we have got about as much work to do in the next twenty-five years as we have done in the last twenty-five years. I do not think that labor is more than about half free now. We have got to go to work to save the country from the money power, as we did from the slave power.

Thanking you all for your kind attention, I bid you good-night. (Great applause.)

ADDRESS BY H. MILES MOORE.

MR. SPEER:—I want to introduce to you now a man whose service to the free state cause was valuable beyond all estimation; because, coming from Missouri where he was prominent for his ability and public spirit, he took up his residence at Leavenworth among the first settlers of the place, and there boldly avowed himself a free state man; and there maintained his opinions against the fury and hate of a pro-slavery population, three to one against the free state men. That man is H. Miles Moore, and I now ask him to come forward and speak to you.

Mr. Moore made the following remarks:

Mr. President, Ladies and Gentlemen, and I may be pardoned if I add, Old Friends:

I see before me many old and familiar faces, whom I have known here in Kansas for the past quarter of a century, during all those days that "tried men's souls." To many of us, then young, the silver threads of age are mingling among the gold. The lateness of the hour will not justify me in making any extended remarks, as I might have done, had the time or occasion permitted. I have listened during the day and evening with no little interest to the labored and in some instances tiresome speeches of some of those who were apparently forgetful of the true objects which have brought this people together on this memorable occas on—this family reunion of the "Old Settlers" of Kansas and their friends—this "love feast" as the good old Methodist would call it. The sweet refrain of most of those who have already sung their song, has been to glorify the great and good Governor Reeder and other Democrats of Eastern Pennsylvania, also the "Emigrant Aid Society," of Massachusetts. A stranger unacquainted with the facts and listening to these speeches and addresses, could not avoid coming to the conclusion that to Gov. Reeder and the "Emigrant Aid Society," all the credit was due and all the glory was won, which saved Kansas to freedom and the right, and cast a halo of light along the pathway of her brave sons and daughters, many of whom suffered untold pe ils, and some even death that we might be free. I would be untrue to history, untrue to humanity, untrue to freedom and the memory of her slaughtered sons, untrue to myself and my God, were I to allow this occasion (though brief it may be) to pass without opening my mouth in defense of the memory of those brave men whose bodies lie mouldering on the bleak hill-side of "Pilot Knob," near Leavenworth, or like the lonely grave of poor Roberts, by the road-side, unmarked even by a single stake, which the good old Indian Tonganoxie covered with stones, that the coyotes might not rob it of its treasure. These, and a hundred other brave men laid down their lives that we of Kansas might enjoy the blessings of this day ; not one of them came to Kansas under the auspices of, or received one dollar of assistance from the "Emigrant Aid Society," in any manner or form whatever. No doubt that association did a vast amount of good in its way. It assisted many to come to Kansas who would never have been able to reach here with their own unaided resources. It erected mills and machinery, and furnished settlers with implements of trade and husbandry ; it cultivated, to a certain extent the arts of war and peace. True, many who came out from New England under its guidance, made but a temporary stay in the Territory. They knew nothing of the trials which beset the pathway on every hand of settlers in a new land, and especially in "Early Kansas," they were not prepared to wrestle with the stern realities of a border life. Soon disgusted with its iron rigor, with desperation they seized their gripsacks, and the same Missouri River steamboat that brought them to our shores, on its return from up the river, sped them on their homeward way. The vessel that bore Cæsar and his fortunes carried but an ignoble load compared with those *brave heroes* and their *luggage*. True, some of these noble souls returned many long years after to greet us, and even now, and here, perchance, are boasting of their *early* settlement in Kansas, and of their valiant deeds for her welfare, most of which, however, were done at a re-

spectful and safe distance from danger, among the rugged hills of
their beloved New England.   Let not any one on this occasion seek,
even by comparison, to rob the brave sons of Ohio, Illinois, Indiana,
Iowa, and last but not least of our sister State Missouri, of their proper share of the glory of redeeming Kansas from the thralldom of
slavery.   Many from the latter State settled in the border counties,
some with their slaves, and at least if not prejudiced in favor of
the "peculiar institution," were willing and anxious that the vexed
question should be settled under the provisions of the Kansas-Nebraska bill, by the *bona fide* settlers in the Territory, and not by
armed hordes from Missouri or elsewhere.   The outrages perpetrated upon their political rights by these invaders at the first and second elections in the Territory, and the threats then made by those
ruffians, advertised them of what they might reasonably expect at
future elections, and they were not disappointed.   A hundred
brave men at least, in Leavenworth city and county alone, mostly
from Missouri, banded themselves together and resolved that they
would not longer lend their aid or even countenance such outrages
upon the freedom of the ballot box.   For an honest expression
of their opinions in this behalf, they were persecuted by day and
by night, and finally driven from their homes, hunted like wild
beasts; others were murdered in cold blood, like Brown and
Bimmerlee, Phillips and the lion hearted Shoemaker, and a score
of other brave and gallant spirits, who gave up their lives at Leavenworth alone, for opinions' sake.   It was an easy matter in those
sad days of 1855 and '56 to be a free state man or even an
abolitionist at Lawrence, where all were of one mind and thought,
but a very different question to entertain, much more to express
free state opinions at Leavenworth, where four-fifths of the people
were most violent pro-slavery zealots, and he who dared to assert
his manhood boldly and bravely, carried his life in his hands, at
the muzzle of his trusty revolver, each hour of his life, by day and
by night.   This is no fancy sketch of a vivid imagination, but stern
realities of every-day life.   The most sacred ties of friendship and
of blood were basely disregarded.   The sacred obligations taken
at the fraternal altar were ruthlessly trampled under foot, and those
who dared but allude by word or sign to those sacred obligations,
were denounced as traitors, spurned with contempt, and driven
like dogs out of the town to Fort Leavenworth, or aboard steamboats at the levee.

Those who came from Missouri had no place of refuge or
safety to flee to but to Lawrence, and there they aided those people
in their troubles, with their strong arms and willing hands.   And
right here may I not add (by way of parenthesis) that never on a
single occasion did Lawrence send out her Macedonian cry to
Leavenworth for aid to assist her to beat back the hordes of fiends
incarnate that threatened her with destruction, that the true men of
Leavenworth did not right heartily, and with alacrity, respond to
that cry.   From the day of the "Wakarusa War," in December,

1855, to that memorable day and night of September 15th, A. D. 1856, which closed the war, when the gathering hosts of slavery, led on by Atchison, Stringfellow, Reed and a score of lesser captains, swarmed with their legions around the little village of Franklin, lowering like the pall of Egyptian midnight over that devoted city of the plain, vowing death and destruction to that Spartan band, who had gathered within its sacred and hallowed precincts, resolved to save the last altar of freedom and their household *penates*, or perish in their defense. All our would-be leaders (save Gen. Lane, who was at Hickory Point with the Topeka boys), had long ere this, fled to places of safety in the far east. Of the less than three hundred brave men and devoted women who stood in that breach, to guard the portals of our temple of liberty, over fifty true and tried men were from Leavenworth city and county, ready to do and die, if need be. But the great and good God who watches over the destinies of nations and protects His people, sent His guardian angels in the persons of Col. Philip St. George Cook and the U. S. troops under his command, to save us in the hour of our great peril. When the morning sun arose over the eastern hills a wall of mailed warriors stood between the doomed city and the hosts of Sennacharib, and at his word of command they melted away like the dew upon the mountain-top before the golden orb of day.

MR. PRESIDENT, my heart grew weary and my soul was sick within me, as I listened with close attention to all of the speeches delivered from this platform to-day and this evening. With scarcely a single exception each speaker seemed to vie with the other in lauding to the skies the memory and acts of our first Governor, Andrew H. Reeder, and apparently with marked and studious effort ignored the memory and mighty deeds of that grand old hero, the ''Grim Chieftain,'' as we delighted to call him. The sound of his clarion voice alone was worth a hundred Reeders. He did more to make Kansas a free State, than all the pigmies who have lived and died in her borders, and who have sought to blacken and sully his good name. Though dead, his memory still lives and will continue to burn with perennial brightness in the hearts of the friends of freedom everywhere; his deeds will be emblazoned on the scrolls of fame in characters of living light, among the names that were not born to die. The history of those days, when written, will award him merited justice, and Kansas, his first love, the idol of his heart, will ere long honor herself, by erecting a shaft of Parian marble to his memory, upon which shall be engraved in letters of purest gold, with a pen of iron and a point of a diamond, his many gallant and noble deeds of patriotic devotion to that fair land which to-day holds his sacred ashes.

I come not here to-night to pronounce a eulogy upon General Lane; he needs none at my hands, were I equal to the task. Although not here in person, I feel that his pure and angelic spirit is hovering over us, at this very hour, and bidding us God-speed in this good work of celebrating our natal day of freedom. He

might ask, as I now inquire, why have those who have already
spoken, neglected, forgotten, or ignored those noble and gallant
soldiers, Abbott, Shore, McWhinney, Cutler, Cracklin, Blanton,
Mitchell, Bickerton, Ritchie, Whipple, Brigden, Harvey, Williams,
Walker, Leonhart, and a host of others, good and tried men, whose
names should be cherished by a brave people.   These heroes, ever
true to freedom, drew their trusty blades, and, rallying their faithful clans, led them on to victory or death.   These were the *true
men* of Kansas, who deserted not their posts in the hour of danger,
or turned their backs to the storm of iron rain and leaden hail, but
faced it, daring to brave the dangers of death, if need be, that we
might live and be free.   Heroes who scorned the thought to fight
and run away, that perchance they might live, to boast hereafter
of their brave deeds done in former days, when poor Kansas, like
her great Grecian prototype, bled at every pore.

MR. PRESIDENT, I have no disposition to speak a harsh word
of any of the old settlers of Kansas, much less of those who bore
an honorable part with us in its early struggles.   But why, may I
ask, is the necessity for all this glorification over Governor Reeder?
He may have been, and doubtless was, a most excellent and worthy gentleman, a sound Democrat and a friend of President Buchanan.   I must confess I never had a very exalted opinion of him,
or his career as Governor of Kansas Territory.   He landed at Fort
Leavenworth the 7th day of October, 1854, and was met with great
cordiality and kindness by the people of that vicinity.   By the terms
of the " Kansas–Nebraska Act," the Governor had the sole power
to locate the temporary seat of government of the Territory.   He
had not been here a week before he commenced negotiations with
the Town Company of Leavenworth, to secure shares in that town,
upon the express condition that he would locate the Temporary
Capital at that place.   Your humble speaker was the Secretary of
that Town Company and knows whereof he speaks.   We gave him
five shares (sixty lots) in the original town of three hundred and
twenty acres for a mere nominal price, and he gave us his word of
honor that he would place the Temporary Seat of Government of
the Territory there.   How well he kept his word let the history of
the town of Pawnee show, located a few months after, on the military
reservation of Fort Riley, by himself and his friends, one hundred
and fifty miles west of civilization.   So unblushing a fraud was this
act that even the " Bogus Legislature" of 1855 could not endorse
it, and what they could not sanction would make an honest man
leave his country.   This model Governor shortly after left his own
loved Kansas on a flat-boat, and came back no more to let the light
of his benign countenance shine upon us, till he made a sickly
effort to be elected to Congress, but ignominiously failed, more on
account of his own cowardice than from the want of friends.   The
free state men of Kansas were made of sterner stuff than to tolerate
effeminacy in their would-be leader.   He afterward sought to contest the election through the agency of the " Investigating Commit-

tee of Congress," who came here to take testimony in the summer of 1856. He employed attorneys to manage his case before the committee, who traveled all over the Territory to see the witnesses and prepare his case. One of those attorneys was arrested at Leavenworth by a mob, in the presence of one of the members of the commission, and thrown into prison to prevent his further examination of the witnesses. Reeder failing to secure his seat in Congress, declined and refused to pay those attorneys a single cent for their services, although in some instances they had spent hundreds of dollars and weeks of time, and suffered ignominy almost beyond endurance to aid him. Such was the experience of some of us with the first Governor of Kansas.

Mr. President and Friends, allow me one word further, and I will not weary your patience longer. If I have said aught to wound the feelings of any one, in my desultory remarks, let the mantle of charity be thrown over them. I feel that it is good for us to be here to-night. It is well that we should meet together and renew our vows of fealty to our common country, re-kindle with a burning coal, snatched from the altar before the throne of God, the slumbering fires of liberty in our breasts, talk over with one another those old scenes and trials of other days, and baptize anew our hearts with the love of liberty. What spot in all this broad land is more sacred to freedom than this? Around the name of Lawrence cluster a thousand illustrious memories of the past. Was it not the Mecca of our salvation in the days that tried men's souls? Let us ever respect and revere its almost holy name. 'Ere the cycle of time shall have revolved another quarter of a century, how few of us, of the "Old Guard" of 1854, 1855 and 1856, will meet on this sacred spot to celebrate those eventful days! The places that now know us shall then know us no more forever. May we so live that our memory shall be kept green in the hearts of those who shall come after us. May our children's children rise up and call us blessed. May Kansas be better for our having lived in it and performed our duty well as became good and true citizens of this great Commonwealth.

ADDRESS BY WILLIAM HUTCHINSON.

MR. SPEER:—We have one of our oldest settlers here this evening, one who has passed through many a thrilling scene in the State. Many of you remember Wm. Hutchinson when he was an active worker for the cause of freedom, and you will now have the pleasure of listening to him.

Mr. Hutchinson's remarks were as follows:

Pioneers of Kansas:

The early settlement, organization and growth of a State, like the establishing of a national government, is an event that will be ever the most dear to those who shared in its hardships and endured its sacrifices. To the actors upon such a stage, the impressions are life-long. They know the best of all, the cost of its struggles and personal sacrifices, and the value of final triumph. Already, a generation has passed, since the conflict of moral forces, that fired the hearts of so many brave men and women to settle in the Territory of Kansas, became a thrilling chapter in our country's history. The deeds and achievements of the Kansas pioneer will soon pass from personal recollections, and day by day the imprint of those stern experiences will grow more dim, as the natural vision fades, as the actors are rapidly passing off the stage, until those who remain of you, to commemorate your own deeds of faith and devotion, must, however unwillingly, bear the title of "venerable men."

Humanity itself is not older than the sentiment that became the inspiration of the Kansas emigrant, as he bore the torch of liberty in one hand, and a Sharpe's rifle in the other. There was then a midnight summons to awake. There was then humanity's roll-call for volunteers to strike a blow for a great moral, as well as political victory. It was not from the administration then in power, nor was it distinctively from the pulpit or the press. It was a spontaneous impulse in behalf of a portion of crushed humanity, and like the sullen murmur of the winds, it foretold the coming storm. There were no dazzling illuminations. It was more like the pensive twilight, or a sort of unheralded dawn, but it glimmered from the prophetic West. There were songs and peans, written and sung, and our sweetest poets were invoked, to hasten forward the Kansas tide. One of the earliest responses was from the gifted New England poetess, Lucy Larcom. Like campaign songs in a political crisis, I well remember how her well known "Kansas prize song" thrilled the millions I have not yet quite forgotten all its prophetic lines. I was so anxious to refer to it here that I wrote to the authoress a few days ago for a copy as I could not find it in any of her published works. She answered that she too, had unfortunately forgotten the most of it, and had kept no copy. She could only give the first stanza from memory, as follows.

> "Yeomen strong, hither throng,
>   Nature's honest men!
> We will make the wilderness
>   Bud and bloom again.
> Bring the sickle, speed the plow,
>   Turn the ready soil;
> Freedom is the noblest pay,
>   For the true man's toil.
> Ho, brothers! come brothers,
>   Hasten all with me!
> We'll sing upon the Kansas plains,
>   The song of Liberty."

Those of us who rallied under the inspirations of such songs, have now after the span of one generation met to mingle congratulations, and to thank the dispensation that has brought them together under the blue canopy of a Kansas autumnal sky, illumed by the luminary that will shine evermore for all, with no more darkening clouds to hide it from the face of a brother man ; but, first and brightest, will it shine on for the millions then in bondage. The picture needs no retouch by the pencil or tongue of rhetoric, to portray the relationship between the courageous devotion to principle which upheld and led forward the little band of Kansas crusaders, with more than the zeal of the ten righteous men who saved their city, and the fruitions of this harvest hour, in which after a quarter of a century, not this State merely, but the whole nation is reaping of the seeds here sown, and rejoices in the name of a free and prosperous people. Manifest destiny will never permit the hands to be turned backward upon the dial of our national career. Our century clock has struck one, and its echoes have hardly ceased, when the quarter signal sounds for our adopted Commonwealth.

There has been no period since our government was founded when a celebration of this character would have been more fitting, because the struggle between despotism and freedom is not ended, either among the citizens of our own country, or among the great family of nations. There is something in our political structure, that is yet inharmonious. The call of Abraham to a new land ; the leading of Israel through the Red Sea ; the adventure of Columbus for a new world ; the migration of the Pilgrims in the little May Flower, through the perils of winter storm, were no more pointed by the finger of fate ; were no more a revelation of the Omnipotent Wisdom that tempers the dispensation of men and nations, than is the present exodus from the Southern States to these borders, of thousands of the colored race, in search of the promised land. It is doubly significant, therefore, that the State of Kansas should become the modern Palestine for the colored people, as they flee from the valley of the American Nile, because of the oppression of the modern Egyptians.

Having said this much publicly, I have by way of parenthesis my private opinion on this subject of colored emigration, wholly averse to their wholesale settlement in Kansas. I have not been able to see how either the South—the colored people—or Kansas are made better thereby. I hope they are not severally made worse, but it is safe to predict, that long before they have wandered forty years in the wilderness, their problem will be solved, in accordance with the appeals of our truest humanity, and the light of our highest civilization.

This is no occasion for recounting the multitude of important events that fill the everchanging panorama of the twenty-five years since the first emigrant party, numbering twenty-five, camped on Mount Oread, Aug. 1, 1854. Few indeed of that noble band are now living, and fewer still are now present to celebrate the event. Volumes might be written in adulation of the living, and in eulogy of the dead, who once formed that Spartan band; but a word only must suffice. I will not even repeat the names of all who are already engraved upon the scroll of the honored Kansas dead.

The stream of the Kansas pioneers has been thickly studded with notable events that deserve a mere mention. Let us for a moment throw upon the canvas in panoramic order these floating islands: The long white-tented trains of thousands hurrying west-ward to Kansas; the Whitfield election; the bogus Legislature mostly from Missouri and its bogus laws; Sheriff *alias* Marshal Jones, and his reign of injustice; Cols. Buford and Titus and their desperadoes; Marshals Donalson and Fain, who vie in their zeal to serve their slave masters; the murder of Barber and Phillips; the Big Spring Convention; the Topeka Constitution; the disper-sion of the Topeka Legislature by the regular army under Col. Sumner; the imprisonment of Robinson, Deitzler, Jenkins and Brown; the arrival of John Brown and his four sons at Lawrence; the battles of Hickory Point, Black Jack and Osawatomie; the two battles of Franklin, and of Bull Creek under Gen. Lane; the Shannon or Wakarusa war; the march on Lecompton; the indict-ment of the Free State Hotel and two newspapers at Lawrence by Judge Lecompte; their destruction by a posse of twelve hun-dred Missourians led by Marshal Jones, in pursuance of an order for abatement as a nuisance, from said U. S. Judge; the killing of Doyles, Wilkinson and Sherman; old John Brown and Henry Clay Pate; old preacher White and the fighting preacher Stuart; the Stubbs of Lawrence, the hardest worked and poorest paid soldiers in Kansas; the ladies who made the cartridges and bandages, ob-tained the ammunition, and bore important dispatches through the border ruffian lines; the outrages in Leavenworth; the de-fense of southern Kansas, in 1857-8, by John Brown, Captains Montgomery and Jennison; the Topeka boys as conductors on the underground railroad, and last but not least, the ladies of Law-rence one hundred strong, armed with axes and hatchets, march-ing to the doors of every rumseller in Lawrence, demanding an unconditional surrender, and spilling in the gutters every drop of liquor in the town. These, Mr. President, are a few of the inci-dents that distinguished early Kansas, from other States, and made strong the faith of her people

The first colonists, like all who came after them, took their lives in their hands and hazarded all. Some for freedom's cause, others for fame, others for fortune. Whatever their motives, they soon found themselves closely identified and knit into a sort of *commune* that is known in no other relation. Disaster, or struggles for existence, make near and lasting friendships. Who will ever forget their near neighbors in Kansas, in 1854-5 and '6? their companions in camp and garrison, or their allies when fugitives, during the reign of border ruffian terror? I well remember the appropriate phrase Gov. Reeder used when addressing the people of Lawrence in 1855, relative to his feelings toward them, when he said " he felt in his heart as if bound to them with hooks of steel." It is somewhat in acknowledgment of that sentiment, that I have traveled some 1,500 miles to share with you the pleasures, and to mingle in the anniversary exercises of this hour. Although I have recently traveled but a few days in Kansas, I am more than gratified with what my eyes have beheld, and emotions are evoked in revisiting these once familiar scenes, that can find no expression in words. The reality has outrun the wildest fancy. Could you have looked out from Mt Oread twenty-five years ago through the glass of the future, and had your vision swept across all the broad plains and valleys of the State; could you have painted all the thriving towns, the myriad of improvements that pertain to all the varied industries of city and country life, with all the rose hues that the veriest enthusiast can boast, you would have been happy indeed, to have equaled in your prospective, the reality that Kansas presents to-day in the number and enterprise of her population, the vastness of her agricultural resourses, the extent of her internal improvements, the high standard of her literary institutions, and in all the material and social elements of a rich and sovereign State composed of nearly or quite 1,000,000 people. I apply the term sovereign to all that relates to the material greatness of the State. While in supreme devotion to the very elements of constitutional government, Kansas is the most loyal of the loyal.

All paintings excel in value as they approach the reality in life. So will the events in our lives be classified as they severally impress upon our memories their foot-prints, so that when we behold them in reminiscence, they will vividly recall the light and shade of a past life. This 15th day of September, 1879 is a pinnacle of grandeur, is therefore like the highest mountain peaks the view from which may well be compared to Tupper's proverbial description of—

> " A volume in a word, an ocean in a tear,
> A seventh heaven in a glance, a whirlwind in a sigh,
> The lightning in a touch, a millennium in a moment."

But the imagery or conception of no poet is needed to fill all our hearts with pleasant memories, and to lead all to exclaim as we behold this marvel of a career in the history of a State—"it is well." The outstretching past is a mosaic of life's pleasure and gloom, and with a pioneer, the colors are well set The stream of time will never be without its floating islands. A few clouds in the heavens, rather adorn than mar the landscape picture. Kansas has been no elysian field. Its birth was during a storm at sea, when the ship of State was in imminent peril, and no daughter of Neptune ever had a severer struggle for existence or a more squally time in infancy. Refractory children often turn out to be the smartest in the end. This Kansas child was the first, I believe, in the national family, that has ever ventured to strike its foster parent during its minority. Insubordination is not to be drawn from the fifth commandment, but it is now the verdict of history,

6

that in our Kansas conflict, the voice of the people was the voice
of God, and the "wayward sister" is bidden "go in peace." No,
the experience of our State will never be lost in either a national
or an individual sense. The government has learned that an "irrepressible conflict" is not easily repressed. The men and women
of early Kansas have learned, that in laboring to lay deeper and
broader the foundations of our free government, there is a reward
more enduring than gold or silver.

To look back to those days of the log cabin, the turf house,
and the thatched roof, it seems that the intervening events far more
than fill the measure of an ordinary life-time. It is a long way
from the Wakarusa camp-fires, to the Bismarck Tabernacle. I
well remember a scene that bore some resemblance to this, many
years ago in Washington, when Frederick Douglass, before an
audience of a thousand people both black and white, well mixed,
in one of the largest churches in the city began his two hours lec-
ture by saying—"It is a long way from my master's corn-field to
Dr. Sunderland's pulpit."

That, too, was a span of some twenty-five years. He then,
as we now, could repeat—

> "Oh! fields still green and fresh in story,
> Old days of pride, old names of glory,
> Old marvels of the tongue and pen,
> Old thoughts which stirred the hearts of men,"
> Will o'er us still their visions cast,
> Though one score years and five have passed.

May we all profit by these sweet memories that glide so un-
bidden o'er the scenes that will in the near future abide only in
the archives of our country's history. Then will follow upon the
stage of this westward bound empire the teeming millions of coming generations, after our sands are run. *They*, too, will act their
part, for a brief space, and then,—

> "Darkly, as in a glass,
> Like a vain shadow they pass,
> Their ways they wind,
> And tend to an end,
> The goal of life, alas!"

ADDRESS BY JUDGE BORTON.

Hon. L. W. Borton being introduced, spoke as follows :
Ladies and Gentlemen:

I am not, in all respects, an old settler. But I came in Governor Medary's time, and was appointed a notary public for Arapahoe county, Kansas. That was at the time when the Kansas
country extended to an indefinite distance to the westward, and
all the Rocky Mountain country was included in Arapahoe county;
I went out to the mountains and my services were called into
requisition as a notary public. I had to get up a seal and there
were no seal engravers in the mountains; but there was a printer's

office out there, and the printers helped me to bend some type metal around, and we stuck in some type, and I had a seal. That seal went with me wherever I went and sanctified deeds for mining property throughout Montana, Idaho, Utah and all the mountain region. Everybody, everywhere, in those days respected a seal under the authority of Kansas. I hail from away out on the frontier, in Cloud county, now. I have been living among the gopher hills and caves and dug-outs of the West for lo! these many years, killing rattlesnakes and lapping sorghum. But I thought I should have a finger in the Kansas *salvation* pie, and so I am here. And I rejoice from the bottom of my heart. With me it is not so much a question of how we used to feel, as of how we do feel now—and I feel good.

ADDRESS BY GEORGE W. HUTCHINSON.

Mr. G. W. Hutchinson, of Kansas City, was introduced. He said:

Mr. President, Ladies and Gentlemen:

I shall not detain you more than five minutes. I came here this evening to a love feast. I feel now something as the boy felt when he expressed himself at a camp-meeting. One little fellow had become converted and he gets up and says: "I feel good!" Another fellow, thinking he would not be outdone, said: "I feel bully!" And still another one, more enthusiastic than either, said: "I feel better than these fellows, I feel more than bully—d—n bully!" It is unnecessary for me to give anything in eulogy on the free state men of Kansas in its early days. I don't care anything about Pennsylvania—I am one of those fellows who came from Vermont; there are but very few here to-day. Mr. William Hutchinson used to be my partner in business with John H. Wilder. I remember well how I felt on a certain occasion when Jim Lane, as we used to call him, called the boys to him in front of my store —that Quantrill did not think was good enough to burn down; he got upon a box and said: "Boys, we are going out to fight these infernal scoundrels, and some of you may fall; if you do, you will fall in a righteous cause, and you will be carried by angels to Abraham's bosom. Boys, you are going to meet the enemy out there toward Bull creek, and I know you have to go and make this fight on green corn, for that is all you have to eat. The infernal Missourians have cut off our supplies, and it is they who have reduced you to this extremity; and, boys, you will make some of them bite the dust—and how different will be their portion! In hell they will lift up their eyes and call for you boys of the free state party of Kansas to bring them a drink of cold water. But you know your duty. Be good to Kansas, to your wives and to your sweethearts—and don't you bring the scoundrels nary a drop."

ADDRESS BY REV. C. H. LOVEJOY.

Mr. Speer: There are very few old citizens who do not know the speaker whom I am about to introduce. He was the chaplain of the first free state territorial Legislature, and gave the Lord the first official notice that the Legislature was legally elected—I mean Rev. C. H. Lovejoy.

Mr. Lovejoy said:

I do not rise, Mr. President, to make a speech. As has been said by friend Speer, I had the honor of being elected three times to the Legislature of Kansas. Two of these Legislatures were declared illegal; one was the first free state territorial Legislature. Of this Legislature, our friend, H. Miles Moore, was one of the members of the House of Representatives, and I was employed to pray for that body of men, and I tried to do the best I could. Sometimes I felt as though it was rather up-hill business, and at other times I succeeded tolerably well. I took my place, usually, at the right hand of the speaker of that body, Col. Geo. W. Deitzler. Miles Moore sat near by, at my left. They all sat, usually, when I prayed, but I stood; it was customary for Methodist ministers to kneel. I did as well as I knew how in presenting the case of that body of men to the throne of grace. I took occasion to refer to the difficulties that we had been passing through; and, as has been already remarked by friend Speer, in my prayer I said that the Lord well knew the difficulties we had to contend with in this country in establishing a free government, and took occasion to be thankful, as I was, that we had been successful thus far. When I got through with my prayer, Miles Moore whispered in my ear that that was the first time the Almighty had been notified, officially, of our difficulties in Kansas. That is all I want to say at this time.

ADDRESS BY R. A. VAN WINKLE.

Mr. Speer: We have not the original *Rip* Van Winkle with us to-night, but we have here one of his descendants, an old resident of Atchison county, and he will address you now.

Mr. Van Winkle said:

Mr. President, Ladies and Gentlemen:

I am not in a very good condition to make a speech—I am not in very good health, rather feeble and hoarse—but I will say a few words. I should think, from my experience and observation, that the free state men of Kansas have done a work for America and the world that we ought to be proud of. I have had the honor of acting with them since 1855. I found them an honorable, upright and straight forward people; I found them energetic; I have found them always right and defending the right. They have never failed to honor a call in behalf of right and justice.

True, I never had any occasion to be in any of these fights. I lived in a portion of Kansas which escaped the troubles, and I am entitled to no honor for saving Kansas to freedom. I am a Kentuckian, and Kentucky was between the two fires during the war and achieved no honor in the war. I do not speak of Kentucky to humiliate her and place her beneath her sister States. She once had an honorable record. No State has so good a record as Kansas in the great struggle. I see those present from many other States—from all parts of this country—from Massachusetts, from Vermont, from everywhere. But the contest against slavery commenced here, and through the courage and sacrifices of the people of Kansas, the contest culminated in the destruction of slavery. I must differ from my friend Legate. He says that he believes in an over-ruling power; I say this is the progress of humanity. It is the natural progress of humanity to fight these fights, right or wrong, and right will in the end prevail. I thank you, ladies and gentlemen, for your attention.

ADDRESS BY GEN. JOHN RITCHIE.

MR. SPEER: Our next speaker will be Gen. John Ritchie, and I know you want to hear from him before we close this meeting.

Mr. Ritchie's remarks were as follows:

Mr. Chairman, Ladies and Gentlemen:

As I am called upon to say something in this "Old Settlers' Meeting," I will say a word about what has been claimed as having saved Kansas. It was neither the Emigrant Aid Society, nor the Pennsylvanians, nor any other class or organization that made Kansas a free State. I say it took us all—backwoodsmen from Indiana, Ohio and all the Western States, as well as the men of principle sent out by the Aid Society of New England, and the politicians from Pennsylvania. There was need for all classes; and every Kansas man knows, or ought to know, that the rough hewn western men and boys, who went in on their instincts as to what was right and wrong, as to what was square and fair in squatter's rights, took a full hand in all that was done in beating down the pro-slavery power on the soil of Kansas. I don't want to take any just credit from any society, nor from any State, in this thing; but I remember once, in the spring of 1855, on one occasion, about forty high-toned men, who came out to Topeka from the far East to fight against slavery on principle, when they heard of the approach of a force of border-ruffians to "sack" the town of Topeka, those forty men of principle took to their heels and left the Territory, running through grass as high as their heads and declaring, as they went, that Kansas was a barren country that wouldn't produce anything. An education of mere principle didn't give men backbone; but I don't mean to say it weakened anybody. Some of us came out to make our homes here, if we liked the country, and to fight slavery out if it undert ok to crowd in here. Others came simply to make their homes, without any thought of a fight of any kind; but, when the fight came on, there were as many of these as of any kind, who just went in and stood up to the rack and did a full share of the work till Kansas was made a free State. These classes of the "saviors of Kansas" have not quite a fair share of silver tongued orators to speak for them here to-day, so I thought I would put in my little say-so in their behalf.

ADDRESS BY E. A. COLEMAN.

MR. SPEER:—It is getting late but before we close I want you to listen to a few words from another old settler, and then we will adjourn for the night. I have the pleasure of introducing Captain E. A. Coleman, of Douglas County.

Mr. Coleman spoke as follows:

Mr. Chairman and Fellow Citizens:

I do not know that I have got anything to say, but if I had it seems to me that at this late hour it would be better not to say it. I would like to talk to you five or ten minutes though. As this is a sort of a love feast, we talk about what we know. There are a thousand and one things that tend to make up the history of the State during the last twenty-five years, that never will be known unless they be thrown out on some occasion like this. There are quite a number of things that I would like to tell many of the new-comers, and many of the old, things they do not know. In some things I disagree with my friend Legate and others. I want to say to my friend Legate and others that nineteen-twentieths of all the people who came here to settle in Kansas in 1854, did not come here to make "tin," as has been insinuated here to-night. There was a great principle that underlay it all. The day the news was received in Boston that the Kansas-Nebraska bill had been put before Congress, I went to call on an old gentleman in Boston and he asked me what I thought of Kansas. I replied that if that bill passes, I will be one of the first men to go to fight for Kansas. You know that bill did pass. I fitted up and started as quick as I could. I came here not to better my condition. I had a good business and was making money. I brought my little all and I spent it you know how. I said that slavery was local and not national, that it ought to be shut in and it would die out where it was of its own disease. That is why I came to Kansas; to check the spread of slavery. I always did everything that I could to make Kansas a free State. My house was always open. I have met lots of men here to-day who have slept in my house in con-cealment, up stairs night after night.

I was one of the first settlers in Kansas, coming here in October, 1854. I want to say to you that on the 10th of April, 1855, (mark the time,) I was in Missouri stopping over night with a

Baptist minister, not a Methodist, but a Baptist minister. On Sunday morning, he says that he could not be with me over Sunday. He showed me his library, and said he had to preach that day. He says, "You can amuse yourself as best you can and I will get through as quick as I can and return, as I want to talk with you." When he came back supper was all ready; I sat down to the table on his right. He said, "Mr. Coleman, I was up at Brother So-and-So's to-day, at Independence, and what do you think he said after I told him I had a couple of Yankees stopping with me?" I said that I guessed he said we would steal all your negroes before you got back. "That is exactly what he did say," replied my host; "he said that we must raise a committee of 200 men and go up to Kansas and drive you fellows out." I barely remarked, you can tell him the next time you see him that he can send up all the committee that he wants to—that there is one man who will not leave under any circumstances—but, before he comes, he had better read Yankee history well.

Adjourned.

FORENOON SESSION.

The meeting, Tuesday morning, Sept. 16th, was called to order by Vice-President John Ritchie, and was opened with prayer by Rev. C. H. Lovejoy. Mr. Joshua Davis was introduced and said that in coming from Leavenworth to Lawrence in 1856, he was met by three gangs of border ruffians. He was tied to a wagon by one of them, but on giving the Masonic sign he was liberated. They returned to him his Sharpe's rifle, but the next gang took it away from him, swearing he was an Abolitionist. He escaped, got to Lawrence, obtained some of the scattered type from the Abolition press, melted them into bullets, and shot them afterward into the ranks of the enemy.

Rev. J. W. Clock was called out, and referred humorously to his ten years experience in Kansas. Could not quite say, as one did yesterday, that he would not give one square inch of Kansas for the whole of the particular State (Pennsylvania) glorified by G. A. Crawford, but he liked Kansas and was here to stay.

ADDRESS BY MRS. LUCY B. ARMSTRONG.

COL. RITCHIE:—It is a good time now for some of the ladies to speak in this meeting, and I take pleasure in presenting to you one of the very oldest settlers and one of the best of the pioneer women of Kansas, Mrs. Lucy B. Armstrong of Wyandotte.

Mrs. Armstrong said:

I think that I, of all who are assembled here this morning, have the most reason to be proud. When a discussion was held among the people of the Wyandotte nation, during all of one night in 1848, in reference to the stand they should make on the slavery question, George I. Clark said, "Let us hold on in our opposition to the slave power; and in fifty years we will be proud of it." They did hold on and this morning I *am* proud of it.

The Wyandottes brought *themselves* to the Territory; and as the United States Government failed to furnish them lands they bought land and provisions for themselves; Silas Armstrong being their contractor. There were among them two hundred church members, in a population of seven hundred. Where else has been the colony, in which there was so large a proportion of church members? They bought the land for their new home in October, 1843, and in April, 1844, they had built and occupied their first church—the first church built by the *people* in the Territory. Brother Speer in the Kansas City *Times* of Sept. 7th, says that the first free state school ever established in the Territory was established at Lawrence in January, 1855. The first school established in the Territory was at Wyandotte, and my husband, J. M. Armstrong, was contractor for the school house, and taught the first school in it; commencing July 1st, 1844. He was a lawyer, but could not practice law then, the Territory not being organized. The school was free—*white* children in the neighborhood were permitted to attend. The Wyandottes were the first in the Territory, except a few of our Baptist brethren to oppose slavery. In the winter of 1843 and 1844, the Wyandotte council enacted a law forbidding the introduction of slaves into their nation. We had our border ruffian war before you had yours. We were mobbed; and after my husband's death, the ruffians would sometimes shoot into my yard and call us abolitionists. More than three-fourths of the Wyandottes were anti-slavery. Those who were pro-slavery were descendants of Virginians who had been taken prisoners.

The Wyandottes sympathized with you in your struggle and a Wyandotte was the messenger that warned Lawrence of the invaders in December, 1855.

In May, 1856, when Lawrence was besieged, the border ruffians in our neighborhood were elated and encouraged in their persecution of free state people. That day I started to Ohio and the next day one of them came to my house and asked for that —— abolitionist. He was answered that I had started to Ohio. Doubting it, he searched the premises, but not finding me returned to the house, and as he passed out of the door through which he had first entered, he stabbed the wall next the door three times, saying with an oath, that if that abolitionist were there he "would run her through that way." God preserved my life by leading me to start to Ohio the day before.

The Wyandottes were always true to the Government of the United States. They were efficient soldiers and scouts in the war of 1812. Some were in the Mexican war, and almost all their young men were in the war for the preservation of the Union. I taught a Wyandotte school for four years after my husband's death, and almost all the boys that were my pupils enlisted in the United States service for that war. One dear, good boy was killed in the battle of Wilson's creek, another was afterward wounded and taken prisoner by the rebels and died, it is supposed, and a number contracted consumption by exposure in the army and died. I am not in the habit of making speeches, but I do sometimes speak in love-feast, and wanted to speak in this one. Indeed, I felt last night like doing it voluntarily as we do in our church, for I wanted to say that the Wyandottes were among the first settlers of Kansas, and that they were first in opposing slavery.

ADDRESS BY MRS. LOVEJOY.

Col. Ritchie:—I have another lady, one of the earliest of the pioneers, whom I will now introduce, Mrs. Lovejoy.

Mrs. Lovejoy said :

I am not accustomed to speaking in camp-meetings, but I have a good Methodistical voice and strong lungs, and I believe I can make these ladies and gentlemen hear me to the farthest portions of the building. God bless these old settlers, these old Kansans, these old pioneer wives. We women really thought you were not going to give us a chance for our lives. We have gone through just as much as any of you. As the alpine traveler, when he gets down to the foot, can stop and look back and glance over the path and see the perilous places he has passed through, and the deep dangers he has escaped in more than one instance in safety, so we can look back now and see what great difficulties we have passed through in our early days. My mind goes back with lightning rapidity through twenty-five years past, and takes in what has been wrought here. In 1854 we christened Kansas, and oh! I remember it well. Everybody seemed to be enthused with the spirit of freedom's crusade. I remember the great political camp-meeting in 1854, down in New Hampshire, where the men of the entire country were assembled, and the question was : "Who will go to Kansas; who will volunteer to rescue that Territory from the clutches of the slave power; who will turn back slavery and save the country from its blighting influences for all time?" We finally reached Kansas among the crusaders, and oh, I am so glad I am here to-day. We mothers have passed through a trying ordeal, but we can look back over the ground with a swell of pride in our hearts when we think of the glorious results as we have them before us now. I hope I may be able to live long enough to attend another of these meetings, and to meet my friends as I have done since I have been here.

ADDRESS BY CAPTAIN THOMAS BICKERTON.

It was announced that the Captain of the old free state artillery was present, and in response to the announcement he was loudly called for, and in his address he said:

Ladies and Gentlemen :

I am glad to be here and to meet my old comrades on this occasion. It is my opinion that the first settlers of Kansas with the education they had had, and the instincts for freedom and justice they possessed, could not help doing just what they did do. The same number of men and women from any other part of the world, with the same ideas of right and wrong, would have done precisely what we did, and the results would have been the same. In my opinion we, as a nation, have little to be proud of when we come to consider that we had to resort to the wholesale murder of each other to right such awful wrongs and abuses as were being perpetrated upon that portion of the human race we had so long held in slavery. I believe that the time will come when the future generations will look back upon the present as among the barbarous ages; I mean the age in which we live now, for there is not a civilized nation yet on the whole earth. Nations who settle their disputes by killing men have no claim to civilization.

Mr. President, I cannot make a speech to-day. I believe in works more than words. I would like to make a remark or two by way of advice, and as I am very radical, you will be left to do as you choose with regard to the advice. First with regard to temperance. Let me assure you that the shortest road to that end is to allow the women to vote. Vote for female suffrage. Mix up a few women with the men that you send to Washington, and the thing is done. Study God more, and money making less, in order that the coming generations may be born with strong healthy bodies and sound minds, and with high moral instincts. Let me assure you that it is better to give your children the teachings of God and nature, than all the artificial stuff that you could give them from now on to the end of the world. Now that we have done a good thing here in Kansas, about which we rejoice, let us go on, and endeavor so to live and act as to become loyal to ourselves, and hasten on the good time when all the present evils of the human race shall be known no more in the land.

DISPATCH FROM JAY GOULD.

Gov. ROBINSON:—*Ladies and Gentlemen :* I would like to read a dispatch just received from S. T. Smith, General Superintendent of the Kansas Pacific Road, in answer to a dispatch forwarded from this place to Jay Gould, asking his presence here to represent one of the material interests of our State. The dispatch is as follows :

KANSAS CITY, Sept. 15, 1879.

Hon. Charles Robinson :

Mr. Gould is in Chicago, and requests me to convey his thanks for your kind invitation to attend the re-union of the old settlers of Kansas, now in progress at Bismarck Grove, but his arrangements are all made to go west via Omaha, and he will be unable to accept.

S. T. SMITH.

LETTERS FROM ABSENT FRIENDS.

GOV. ROBINSON: — We have a programme that has been printed. I am sorry to interrupt this love-feast. We hope that every man who has a word to say will have an opportunity to say it before we get through. For myself, I like the love-feast better than anything else. But we have some public men from abroad who have been a part of our history, and I think we ought to give them an opportunity to say something, and I think we will all have an opportunity to hear them. In the course of the arrangements for this celebration, the committee of invitation received letters from a number of distinguished friends of Kansas in the early times, who were invited to be with us, and who could not come. Hon. James S. Emery, Chairman of the Committee, will read some of these letters.

Judge Emery then read the following letters :

LETTER FROM COL. H. T. WILSON.

Hon. Charles Robinson : I am pleased to address you as an old settler of Kansas. I am a Kentuckian by birth. I joined my brother Thomas at Ft. Gibson. He was sutler at that post in 1834. Ft. Gibson is located on the east bank of the Grande River, one mile from its mouth, where it enters into the Arkansas River, in the Cherokee Nation, 50 miles west of the Arkansas state line. Fort Gibson was occupied by twelve companies of the 7th Infantry, commanded by General Arbuckle. Whilst at Fort Gibson I had to do a great deal of riding through the Cherokee and Creek nations; also the Chickasaw and Choctaw nations. The two first-named nations lay on each side of the Arkansas River. The two last-named nations border on the Red River, which is the line of the State of Texas. This is a fine farming country, as also a fine stock country. Some of the Chickasaws and Choctaws, when slavery existed, raised and shipped 150 bales of cotton per year, down Red River, to market. While at Fort Gibson, I learned to talk the Cherokee and Creek languages. I remained with my brother Thomas nine years at Fort Gibson. Fort Scott was located in 1842 as a military post. The officers then here knew me, and invited me here to be sutler at Fort Scott. I came to Fort Scott in 1843, and was appointed sutler. I found the post in command of Major Graham. Ft. Scott was occupied by three companies— one of dragoons and two of infantry. Very soon fine frame quarters were built for the officers and men. Ft. Scott was pleasantly located, five miles west of the Missouri state line, and was designed as a check on the Osage tribe of Indians, who were then located on the Neosho River, forty miles west of Fort Scott. Here I learned to talk the Osage language, in selling them goods and purchasing their buffalo robes and buffalo tallow. Some of this tribe were pretty hard customers. After occupying Ft. Scott a few years the Government, through its officers of the army, found there was no great necessity to occupy it, and it was abandoned as a military post. The Government had expended upward of $200,000 here in improvements, and neglected to take a military reserve, which is equal to a deed or patent. Ft. Gibson and Ft. Leavenworth have military reserves. The buildings at Ft. Scott, a few months after the troops left, were advertised for sale through the newspapers: "The houses without lands." At this sale there were but few persons, because of the wording of the notice of the sale—"the houses without land." But few persons wanted to purchase a house without land.

A military post is a pleasant place to live; the officers of the army are pleasant gentlemen to be with, and do business with. In advance of the day of sale I prepared a protest—protesting against the sale of the houses—claiming the land where the building stood, under the pre-emption law of 1842. Major Howe, of the army, came with his auctioneer from Ft. Leavenworth to make the sale. The Major called to see me, and stopped with me and my family. I found the Major a gentleman. He allowed my protest to be read before the sale of the buildings commenced. The sale was completed and title given to the purchaser. The sale of all the Government buildings was less than $5,000. This ended the military claim to Ft. Scott.

The West is a large country and filling up fast by emigration from the older States, and the day is not far distant when the Cherokee, Creek, Choctaw, and Chickasaw Nations of lands will become a new Territory, giving to all heads of families in the four named nations a quarter section of land, including his or her improvements, without charge for the land, the government ceasing to pay them annuities. This, in my judgment, will soon take place. This is a fine country of lands and climate, and will some day be a fine State. There is more intelligence in these four named nations of Indians than many persons would suppose. The whites are not allowed to settle in these four nations, except by marriage or as laborers.

Kansas is a good State of lands and climate. Emigration to Kansas will soon make it a densely populated State.

While a Kentuckian I lived under the senatorship of the Hon.

Henry Clay, one of the most able men of his day in Congress. The day has come when we had better lay politics aside, and select able men to represent us regardless of party. Life is a lottery.

With great respect,

H. T. WILSON.

AN INDIAN VOCABULARY.

Mr. Wilson appended the following list of Indian words and phrases and their translation :

Cowah . . . . Horse.
Muccasupa . . . . Coffee.
Shawnee . . . . Sugar.
Stilabaca . . . . Shoes or boots.
Hoscaw . . . . Calico or domestic.
Nannahue . . . . Tobacco.
Peciea . . . . No good.
Largana . . . . Good.
Warnumbarue . . . . Something to eat.
Paup-Pusa . . . . A baby.
Ninka . . . . He is gone ; it is gone.
Wabuska . . . . Flower.
Howa . . . . How do you do.

LETTER FROM HON. J. M. S. WILLIAMS.

BOSTON, September 3d, 1879.

Gentlemen : I have delayed answering your invitation to attend the re-union at Lawrence, on the 15th instant, on account of the hope that I might be able to accept it. But I am not to have the pleasure. I would like very much to be with you and witness, in part, your present prosperity; and contrast it with what Lawrence was, when I first visited it, about twenty-five years ago. The saving of Kansas from slave power was a severe but successful struggle, and our success was owing mainly to the fact that the free state men of that early day were men of ideas, and were therefore fully capable of using Sharpe's rifles to advantage in the acquiring and retaining their right to vote, which right was so persistently attempted to be withheld from them by the same tyrannical power which now overrides the personal liberty of our colored brethren in a large part of the former slave district. The negroes not having, as our settlers did, the education to enable them to stand for their rights, with Sharpe's rifles, are now forced to flee to obtain the privileges which your State so opportunely affords. But the time will surely come when, all over our vast country, the rights of all will be respected; when the negro and the Indian will have equal rights at the polls with all other American citizens, and all who assisted in the founding of Kansas as a free State, have the satisfaction of knowing that your success is contributing largely to such a glorious result. Yours very respectfully,

JOHN M. S. WILLIAMS.

LETTER FROM MAJ. EDWARD DANIELS.

ST. PAUL, MINNESOTA, Sept. 12, 1879.

Hon. Sidney Clarke: I am greatly disappointed that I cannot
be at the re-union of the early settlers of Kansas. Will you bear
my greeting to the survivors of that Spartan band who held at
fearful cost and risk the Thermopylæ of freedom for a continent
on the plains of Kansas. Few know, personally, better than I do
upon how slender a thread hung the momentus issue of slavery or
freedom during those "dark and bloody days." The world's history has no brighter page than that which records the intrepid
deeds, the sublime courage, the unfaltering faith in a great cause,
and the heroic endurance of the free state men in Kansas.
Reduced in numbers by the sternest tests of manhood till they
scarcely exceeded Gideon's band, they were made invincible by
the strength of truth. They held in their keeping the ark of the
covenant, and the destiny of the uncounted millions who were
destined to people the mighty West. They were worthy of the
sacred trust, and while freemen tread the soil which they guarded
from the invasion of slavery, their brave deeds will be told with
pride and their memory will grow brighter with the passing years.

I recall the names of three men, not residents of Kansas, who
should be honorably remembered at your meeting: 1. Hon. Timothy
O. Howe, of Wisconsin, late U. S. Senator from that State, who,
earliest among the prominent public men of Wisconsin, gave his
time, money and personal influence to the cause; 2. Edward D.
Holton, a distinguished citizen of Milwaukee, who also came forward in the earliest days of the struggle, and presided over the first
Kansas Aid Society of Wisconsin, giving generously himself and
using a commanding social influence for Kansas; 3. Gen. J. D.
Webster, late chief of General Sherman's staff, and in 1855 city
engineer of Chicago. A soldier by education, he early saw that the
battle was to be won by putting the means of defending the right
vote in the hands of the free state men. For two years as
President of the executive committee of the National Kansas Committee, located at Chicago, he gave his time, energy and money
freely to the work. His social influence was thrown into the scale
and did as much as that of any man in the nation to vindicate
Kansas from the aspersions of her enemies, and to bring about the
vast inflow of aid which she at last received from the lovers of
liberty in the North. Among newspapers, the *Tribune* was chief
for free Kansas, and Joseph Medill and Horace White deserve
lasting honor in Kansas for their persistent and able advocacy.

With fraternal good will,

EDWARD DANIELS,

Formerly Agt. of Emigration for Kansas Nat. Com.

LETTER FROM GEN. B. F. STRINGFELLOW.

ATCHISON, KANSAS, Sept. 14, 1879.

Dear Sir: I had hopes until last evening that I would be able to be present on the anniversary of Lawrence, but have now to regret that I am not a *freeman* but under *obligations* which will compel me to be absent.

Freedom is not yet absolute, and this is one of the many occasions where I am forced to admit myself a *slave*, and would be glad were there any "underground railroad" by which I might flee from my bondage and be with you.

It would be a special pleasure to present myself as one of the witnesses that, widely as we may have differed in other days, we are all now heartily united in efforts to promote the prosperity and happiness of our common country.

Hoping that the meeting may be most pleasant, I am your obedient servant,

B. F. STRINGFELLOW.

LETTER FROM GOV. SAMUEL J. CRAWFORD.

WASHINGTON, D. C., Sept. 7, 1879.

MY DEAR SIR:—I regret very much my inability to attend the Old Settlers' Meeting, in Lawrence, on the 15th and 16th insts. Nothing would afford me greater pleasure than to be present on that occasion, and nothing would prevent my going except imperative duties requiring my presence here.

The meeting cannot be otherwise than of the greatest interest to all in attendance, and especially to the pioneer veterans who stood side by side in the long continued "irrepressible conflict," which began in earnest with the settlement of Kansas, and ended in triumph with the abolition of slavery. From 1854 to 1865, Kansas was nothing less than a military camp. Two determined armies confronted each other in the open field. Many battles were fought. Many lives were sacrificed. But now the conflict is over; slavery is dead; Oxford and Kickapoo forgotten, and peace restored.

You, and others who stood at the helm throughout the storm, and in the end witnessed the crowning of your efforts with such complete success, ought to meet, celebrate and receive congratulations. All Kansans should be there and participate in the festivities of the occasion, because all now are equally interested in the history of our glorious young State, and in the achievements of those who made it what it is.

The Spartans, at Thermopylæ, stood firm; the Trojans, at Troy, were slow to yield; the Romans, under Cæsar, were invincible; and Napoleon's great army, at Waterloo, melted away; but none, even in the trying scenes of those days, displayed more devotion to principle, and more genuine courage and heroism, than did the pioneer settlers of Kansas, in the struggle through which they passed.

I, therefore, trust that the Old Settlers' Meeting may be a complete success, and that the fondest hopes of its projectors may be realized to the fullest extent.

I am, very respectfully, your obedient servant,

S. J. CRAWFORD.

LETTER FROM JOHN G. WHITTIER.

BEAR CAMP HOUSE, W. OSSIPEE, N. H., }
Eighth Month, 29, 1879.   }

Gentlemen:

I have received your invitation to the 25th anniversary celebration of the first settlement of Kansas. It would give me great pleasure to visit your State on an occasion of such peculiar interest, and to make the acquaintance of its brave and self-denying pioneers, but I have not health and strength for the journey.

It is very fitting that this anniversary should be duly recognized. No one of your sister States has such a record as yours—so full of peril and adventure, fortitude, self-sacrifice, and heroic devotion to freedom. Its baptism of martyr blood not only saved the State to liberty, but made the abolition of slavery everywhere possible. Barber and Stillwell, and Colpetzer and their associates did not die in vain.

All through your long, hard struggle I watched the course of events in Kansas with absorbing interest. I rejoiced, while I marveled at the steady courage which no danger could shake, at the firm endurance which outwearied the brutalities of your slaveholding invaders, at that fidelity to right and duty which the seduction of immediate self-interest could not swerve, nor the military force of a pro-slavery government overawe. All my sympathies were with you in that stern trial of your loyalty to God and humanity. And when, in the end, you had conquered peace, and the last of the baffled border ruffians had left your Territory, I felt that the doom of the accursed institution was sealed, and that its· abolition was but a question of time. A State with such a record will, I am sure, be true to its noble traditions, and will do all in its power to aid the victims of prejudice and oppression who may be compelled to seek shelter within its borders. I will not for a moment distrust the fidelity of Kansas to her foundation principle. God bless and prosper her!

Thanking you for the kind terms of your invitation, I am, gentlemen, very truly your friend,

JOHN G. WHITTIER.

LETTER FROM HON. I. S. KALLOCH.

SAN FRANCISCO, July 10, 1879.

GENTLEMEN:—I acknowledge with pleasure your invitation to be present with you on the 15th of September, to participate in a "general reunion of the men and women who took part in settling Kansas." Nothing would afford me greater satisfaction than to be with you, and nothing but distance and pressing cares at home could prevent me.

In the light of history, few men and women will occupy a more illustrious place than the brave pioneers who settled Kansas and preserved and consecrated its sacred soil to freedom and the rights of man. While it was not my pleasure to be with them in person, I was with them in spirit and contributed whatever influence I had to the holy enterprise in which they were engaged. And it is a pleasant memory to me that I afterward knew them personally and co-operated with them in my humble way, to lend efficiency, enlargement and energy to the noble young Commonwealth which they so gloriously founded. From across the Sierras I stretch the hand of cordial friendship and fellowship, and wish you a fitting and happy festival on the "day you celebrate."

Very respectfully,   I. S. KALLOCH.

LETTER FROM JAMES FREEMAN CLARKE.

JAMAICA PLAIN, Mass., July 25, 1879.

Gentlemen of the Committee : I received your previous letter of invitation to the "Kansas Old Settlers' Celebration" and immediately answered it, but I infer that my letter to you miscarried. In that I expressed my regret that I should probably be unable to attend the celebration. I well remember those times which tried men's souls, and I highly value a certificate of stock in the Free State Kansas Association which was given me at that time. Just at the time that I received your first letter I lost a dear friend, a member of my church, Mrs. Samuel Cabot. She did as much as any one in New England to help the free settlers of Kansas during those terrible times when the slaveholders of Missouri overran your Territory. She organized and carried on the Society, which had its branches all over New England. which sent food, clothing and money to Kansas. She was a modest and retiring lady, but when this appeal came she stepped forward to the front, and did the work of many common men. Let us not forget the women, who, with the men, helped to leave Kansas to freedom. Hoping you will have a happy celebration,   I am yours,

JAMES FREEMAN CLARKE.

LETTER FROM HON. WM. M. EVARTS.

DEPARTMENT OF STATE, WASHINGTON, Aug. 8, 1879.

Gentlemen : I have to acknowledge the receipt of your kind letter of the 24th of June, inviting me to be present at the celebration of the twenty-fifth anniversary of the settlement of Kansas, on the 15th of September next. It would certainly give me very great pleasure to meet the "old settlers of Kansas" upon so interesting an occasion, and while I regret that I cannot positively foresee that

7

it will be in my power to do so, I shall cherish the hope that I may be able to visit Kansas at the time appointed for the celebration. I am, gentlemen, very truly yours,

WM. M. EVARTS.

LETTER FROM HON. JOHN SHERMAN.

TREASURY DEPARTMENT, WASHINGTON, July 7, 1879.

Gentlemen: I have to acknowledge the receipt of your kind invitation to attend and speak at the gathering to be held on September 15th, at Lawrence, to celebrate the twenty-fifth anniversary of the settlement of Kansas.

I regret that, by reason of official duties, I will not be able to participate in the celebration and contribute my recollections of my first visit to Lawrence in the spring of 1856, when it was truly in its infancy. The house in which we slept was not plastered, and unfinished in many respects, and I was glad to take shelter under the hospitable roof of Gov. Robinson. We held the official meeting of the committee of investigation in the tavern of Miss Hall, if I remember the name correctly.

The wonderful growth of Kansas since that time is probably as great as that presented by any of your western States, marvelous in their development.

With an abiding faith that your progress will be as rapid and remarkable and honorable in the future, I remain

Very truly yours,   JOHN SHERMAN.

LETTER FROM HON. E. B. WASHBURN.

SHELDON, VT., July 16, 1879.

Dear Mr. Crawford: I have duly received the invitation to be present at the Old Settlers' meeting at Lawrence, on the 15th of September next. I am spending the summer East with my family, and will not venture home until after the time designated for the meeting. I regret, therefore, that I will not be able to be present on that interesting occasion.

I knew much of the early settlers of Kansas, and no braver or truer men ever upheld the banner of human liberty. I participated in all the action of Congress which attended their early struggles, and according to the measure of my ability, did all in my power to strengthen their arms in their hand-to-hand fight with the slave power. And how gloriously they won! Through fire and blood they planted free institutions on your virgin soil, and in a quarter of a century was seen to grow up a great, prosperous and patriotic State, which has excited the wonder and challenged the admiration of mankind.

Trusting that you may have a very happy and successful reunion, believe me,   Very truly yours, etc.,

E. B. WASHBURN.

LETTER FROM SENATOR JOHN J. INGALLS.

UNITED STATES SENATE CHAMBER, ⎫
WASHINGTON, June 28, 1879. ⎭

Gentlemen: I shall have much pleasure in being present at the reunion in Lawrence, September 15th, unless unavoidably detained elsewhere. The occasion will be historic, and the retrospect cannot fail to be instructive to mankind.

Though not one of the earliest settlers of Kansas, my citizenship only dating from 1858, I was a "friend of freedom" from the beginning, and came as soon as I could.

I shall be glad to do anything in my power to contribute to the interest of the anniversary.   Yours,

J. J. INGALLS.

Mr. Ingalls was unavoidably absent, and the letter was read to show that he wanted to be present.

LETTER FROM HON. LYMAN TRUMBULL.

CHICAGO, ILL., July 7, 1879.

Gentlemen : It would afford me real pleasure, if circumstances permitted, to join the "Old Settlers" in the celebration at Lawrence, on the 15th of September, of the twenty-fifth anniversary of the settlement of Kansas, an event that marks an epoch in our country's history, as the beginning of that struggle which culminated in the nation's redemption from the curse of human slavery.

Few now on the stage of action appreciate the hardships endured and the hazards encountered by the brave men and women who made Kansas a free State. The recalling of those events, after a lapse of a quarter of a century, will nerve the arm and cheer the heart of every friend of freedom who hears the story. I have to regret that I cannot be with you to participate in the celebration.   Very respectfully,

LYMAN TRUMBULL.

LETTER FROM AMOS A. LAWRENCE.

NEAR BOSTON, July 22, 1879.

Gentlemen : Please to remember me affectionately to the old settlers. I thank you for remembering me in sending out your invitations for the 15th of September, and if I were to make a journey anywhere, that would be preferred. But my occupations, or else the habit of staying at home, makes journeying unpleasant, and, besides that, I am forced to adhere to certain habits, in order to keep tolerably well. If you will be good enough to send me the printed account of the proceedings, you will be doing another favor to   Your friend,

AMOS A. LAWRENCE.

LETTER FROM N. S. STORRS.

Medicine Lodge, Barbour Co., Kan., Sept. 12, 1879.

Hon. Charles Robinson, Lawrence, Kansas: Circumstances prevent me from being at the Old Settlers' Celebration, on the 15th and 16th inst., and as I was a resident of Lawrence in 1855, '56, and a part of '57, and took part in the war of those days, I would like to be at said celebration. I forward you the names of Derrick Updegraff and Mr. Blanton, who are living here. Mr. Updegraff went to Tecumseh in 1854, from Iowa. Mr. Blanton owned Blanton's bridge, south of Lawrence, in those days. We are all well, and would like to see the old grounds we ranged in defense of freedom in Kansas. Wishing you a happy time, we are,   Respectfully yours, etc.,

N. S. Storrs.

LETTER FROM D. F. PARK.

Pleasanton, Kan., Sept. 15, 1879.

Gentlemen of the "Old Settlers'" Meeting, Bismarck Grove, Kansas: Dear Sirs: I came to Kansas in August, 1854; have lived near here ever since, and would like to be with you to-day. Allow me, as an "Old Settler," to suggest that a register of name and post-office address of all persons now in Kansas, who have lived here continuously for twenty-five years, be now made and kept for future use. To assist you in carrying out the above suggestion, I send you names, with post-office, of all men now in Linn county, who have lived here full twenty-five years.

Came in spring and summer of 1854: D. W. Cannon, Mound City, Kan.; William Park, Mound City; James Osborne, Mound City; Ben Bunch, Mound City; James Barrick, Pleasanton; D. F. Park, Pleasanton; W. H. Murray, Pleasanton; Jo. Conley, Barnard; Ingram Lusk, Centerville.

Came in the fall of 1854: J. D. Hobson, Pleasanton; Enoch Estep, Pleasanton; W. B. Perry, Pleasanton; H. J. Dingus, Mound City; A. R. Wayne, Mound City.

Yours very respectfully,   D. F. Park.

LETTER FROM MARY L. REYNOLDS.

Kanwaka, Kan., Sept. 15, 1879.

To the Old Settlers' Reunion: My father, James Fuller, and mother, Eliza Fuller, three brothers and myself, moved to Kansas in November, 1855, from Wisconsin. We settled two miles west of Osawatomie. I was only twelve years of age, but I remember the day that Reid brought in his band of four hundred drunken men to murder, destroy and plunder. It was August 30, 1856. We were all sick with the chills, but my oldest brother, William, who belonged to Capt. John Brown's company. He had come home on furlough the previous evening. They took him prisoner at our house, and no doubt, if they had known who he was, they would have shot him on the spot. They went but a few rods from the house, where, to my brother's astonishment, there lay, in the middle of the road, lying on his face at full length, cold in death, the Captain's son, Frederick Brown— shot by the advance guards. You can imagine his feelings, prisoner to such a band of outlaws. But he had to pass on, and not show the slightest sign of acquaintance. They took him to the front ranks during the fight, and he stood the fire from both sides. After the fight they tied his hands behind him and tied him to the hitching post, in front of Mr. Sharkey's store, and set the store on fire, and went off and left him until the town was burned. After that they returned, and the four hundred stopped at our house. They took my father out of bed and made him walk, to see if he was able to be taken prisoner; but they concluded he was too sick to bother with him, so finally they let him alone. Nearly every time the mail came in, there was a posse from Missouri ready to ransack the letters. For over six months we never got a letter out of the office; we would find them opened and thrown away by those outlaws. We never heard from my brother for two weeks. You can have but a faint idea what our feelings were, or our anxiety was, unless in like circumstances. He was one of the nine prisoners sent to St. Louis. From there he went to Wisconsin, where our sister resided. The following winter he returned home. It was one grand rejoicing. I think we suffered more during the early times than we did during the civil war, although one brother died in the army.

I could write more, but perhaps this is sufficient. I always attend the Old Settlers' meetings when I can. I wanted to do so this year, but as I could not, I send these facts.

Most respectfully,   MRS. MARY L. REYNOLDS.

POEM BY MRS. KATE R. HILL.

Mrs. Kate R. Hill, of Manhattan, read the following poem, entitled "The Old Folks."

Oh, blessings on the Old Folks,
  As once again they meet
In the sunset's glow, rich-hued, we know—
  With memories grand and sweet.

Oh, blessings on the Old Folks
  As they retrace, in thought,
Thro' life's young day the darkened way
  With care and danger fraught.

From Fatherland and kindred torn,
  In those stern days they came
And found a cross that must be borne
  In Freedom's holy name.

The red man on his hunted path
  With threatening eye looked back,
And Liberty's foul foe, with wrath
  And murder in his track,

Came sweeping o'er the prairies vast,
   Unheeding Nature's charms,
And woke the answering cry, at last,
   " Rise, Freedom's sons, to arms."

Long waged the fierce, the cruel fight,
   Till the watchmen, from the towers,
Cried " Ring the bells for God and Right!
   The victory is ours."

But ah! on Nature's emerald breast
   Was left a crimson stain ;
And ever, where the heroes rest,
   Must fall the tears of pain.

Oh, blessings on the Old Folks
   Who, 'mid their cares and woes,
With toil could cause the wilderness
   To "blossom as the rose."

God's blessings on the Old Folks,
   Who, from life's garnered stores,
With furrowed brow in the gloaming now
   But wait for the golden oars.

They are pressing close to the river's brink,
   And we know, by their trustful eyes,
From the Unknown Land they will not shrink,
   They are going home to the skies.

ADDRESS BY COL. D. R. ANTHONY.

Gov. Robinson : — I shall have to call upon one of the vice-presidents to preside during the morning.   Col. D. R. Anthony, one of the original pioneers of Kansas, will now take the stand and preside.

Before taking the chair Col. Anthony said :

Old Settlers, New Settlers and Young Settlers :

I feel that it is unfair to call me out at this time, after listening to the grand, noble and matured speeches of yesterday and this morning from the lips of such men and veterans as Robinson, Holliday, Usher, St. John, Crawford and Forney ; men who spoke the burning words of freedom and truth which will pass into and make an important part of the history of our glorious young Commonwealth.   I feel almost incapable of adding one word to that which has been said, but I also feel a great interest in this immense and wonderful gathering of the early pioneers of our State, and the importance of the occasion tempts me to say a word upon the sentiment that has brought us together.

I well recollect the time, twenty-five years ago last month, when the then almost unknown, but now known and honored by

all freedom loving men, Eli Thayer, of Massachusetts, wrote to me
at Rochester, N. Y., requesting me to join the emigrant aid party
then about starting from the East to settle in the then Territory of
Kansas.   I promptly accepted the invitation and joined the party
at Rochester on its way to the land of border ruffians.   At St. Louis
we met the agent of the New England Emigrant Aid Company,
Doctor Charles Robinson, one of the shrewdest, ablest, truest and
most devoted advocates of humanity in the West.   By his direction
our party proceeded by steamer "Polar Star" to Kansas City, Mo.,
where we were met by Col. Blood and Chas. H. Branscomb,
agents of the company, who guided us to the spot wheie Lawrence
now stands, the place mentioned by Charles Robinson as the natural location for a town as far back as 1848.   In this way the town
site of Lawrence was located.

When I returned to New York the following month the people
of that great State, composing what was known as the old Whig
party, and the Kansas and Nebraska party met in mass convention
at Saratoga Springs for the purpose of organizing the Republican
party, that grand old party which has, since its creation, transformed four millions of slaves into freemen, saved this Union from
destruction at the hands of the slave power, and made this country
forever the home of the free.   I was at that convention when the
Republican party was formed.   Horace Greeley, Henry J. Ray-
mond, Thurlow Weed, Eli Thayer and hosts of other veterans in the
cause of human freedom were there.   Eli Thayer introduced your
humble servant to that vast throng as one who had seen the wonders
and the glories of the promised land, and one who had just returned
to tell the story to the thousands who were anxious to go West and
help make Kansas free.   I well recollect with what trepidation I
spoke for the first time in my life to the tens of thousands of people
gathered there, and that the uppermost thing in my mind then was
the magnificent agricultural view which I had witnessed from Mt.
Oread, the place where your University now stands.   I spoke to
them of the richness and productiveness of Kansas soil, of what a
magnificent country it was, of its capabilities, and what the future
had in store for those who had the courage to go there and help
build up and develop the natural resources of the country, and
above all, save it from the curse of slavery.   From that time to this
there has been a greater growth in population, and grander material
improvements in this State than were ever made in any other State
of this Union in the same period, of twenty-five years.   Then we
had nothing but the brave hearts and hardy hands of a few hundred
almost penniless men and women, who came here for the highest
and holiest purposes that ever actuated the human heart.   What is
our condition to-day?   We have a country as fine as any in the
world.   We have a State four hundred miles long and two hundred
miles wide; situated right here in the very center of the United
States of America.   A country where all the fruits and vegetables,
and grains and minerals are produced with greater ease and in

more liberal quantity than anywhere else in the world. The exc‑ dus from the South may send a few thousand colored men into our State, or for that matter the whole negro population of the South, but our State is so large that if they were well scattered you would hardly be able to find one of them.

You might bring all the men, women and children in the United States, including all the multitudes of all crowded cities of the East, into this State, and place them equi-distant from one another, and no two of them would be within speaking distance. Bring them all here, and you will find the soil of Kansas will sustain them all.

The fact is, there is not a man present here to-day, or for that matter anywhere else, who does, or can, comprehend the extent, the magnitude and the capabilities of our State. Indeed the human mind cannot comprehend the extent of 52,000,000 acres of land. They know that we raise annually 30,000,000 bushels of wheat, and 130,000,000 bushels of corn; but they don't know how much land it takes to make fifty-two millions of acres, nor how big a pile it takes to make thirty million and one hundred and thirty million bushels of wheat and corn. Therefore I say, that while people talk over these big figures, they yet really have no idea of the extent of our country, nor of the magnitude of the crops we are raising annually. None of us comprehend the future, none of us know what the future has in store for us.

I have just returned from a trip through the East. I have talked with business men, the merchants, the bankers, the farmers and the laboring men, and I find that there is a better and more hopeful feeling existing among them than there has been for the last ten years. They all feel confident not only that values have got to the bottom, but are absolutely looking up. Confidence is restored, values are settled, the prices of industries are advancing, and the people of Kansas may confidently look for an era of prosperity and happiness during the coming ten years unprecedented in the history of any country in the world. Under these circumstances we may well be proud of Kansas.

Twenty-five years ago there was one sentiment in the North in favor of consecrating the great northwest territories to freedom. Eli Thayer organized that sentiment and made practical use of it in settling Kansas with men of one idea, devoted to making it free. He was confessedly the utilizer, the practical man of the period, one who had the courage, the ability and the singleness of purpose needed to do the work then in hand. Kansas owes him a debt, equal to that of any of her early friends, and I am glad to announce, that a bust of Eli Thayer will soon honor a place in the halls of our State Historical Society. In common with you all, I am sorry he cannot be with us to-day, that he might see the wonders, which he helped to create.

A patriotic letter from our dear friend will be read by the Secretary, and Kansas will record her gratitude to one of her truest and best friends.

I do not stand here to give all the credit to Eli Thayer for making Kansas free. I would give credit to all the grand old heroes, Horace Greeley, Thurlow Weed, Charles Sumner, Henry Wilson, U. S. Grant, and the thousands of more practical men, who emigrated here and personally did the work. Nor would I forget the old Pennsylvania Democracy and other Democrats, who, while in our early days, were opposed to freedom, yet in the latter days, when the final struggle came, refused to be dragooned longer in the interests of slavery, but manfully stood up and extended to us a helping hand.

I would give credit to all. I would not deprive anyone of that which is due him or her for the part taken in making Kansas what she is to-day, free, and the most prosperous State in the Union.

I hope we will remember the "lesson" that was read to us yesterday, the "LESSON OF KANSAS." Let us not forget it. Let us see to it that history records the truth. Do not allow history to record a lie. Let it not be forgotten, that twenty-five years ago the army, the navy, the courts, and the whole power of the national government and its appointees were invoked to make Kansas a slave State. No Federal judge or other official dared disobey the commands of the slave power. When the Hon. Samuel D. LeCompte, Judge of the United States District Court at Lecompton, delivered his famous charge, defining "constructive treason" to the United States grand jury then in session, and when that grand jury indicted the Free State Hotel at Lawrence as a nuisance, and then under command of a United States marshal proceeded with a posse comitatus to batter down that hotel with cannon, sacking and then firing it, the court remained silent as the grave while this outrage was perpetrated, and not till long years afterward did he even attempt to explain his then apparent silent approval of the vandalism of his marshal, grand jury and court officials. President, Congress, Territorial Governor, Judges, Courts and Federal officials dared not to lift a hand to prevent the destruction of that Free State Hotel. Let these facts go down into history, and don't let us attempt to wipe them out. We could not if we would ; we ought not if we could.

Let us not forget what Judge Usher said to us yesterday. That R. R. Rees, the chairman of the committee on judiciary in the legislature of 1855 made a report over his own signature in which he recommended the passage of a law, that the talking, writing or publishing of anything in favor of making Kansas a free State, was a felony, and should be punished with death.

During the border ruffian war this man was appealed to by Nelson McCracken, a brother Mason, for help, to prevent his being driven out of town by the Blue Lodge. His appeal was unheeded. A brother whose wife lay at the point of death, appealed to Mr. Rees, the master of his lodge, for the privilege of remaining a few days with his sick wife. His appeal was to a deaf ear. At the time Haller shot Lyle, Capt. I. G. Losee appealed to the master of his lodge for aid. The reply was : "to h ll with Masonry in these times." At a later day Edward's book defending the Quantrill massacre at Lawrence found a refuge in his home. To the day of his death no word of regret for the course he had pursued in the dark days of old border ruffian rule ever escaped the lips of this man. Can we, ought we to forget these things? Ought not history to record the truth? This man was as kind and gentle as a lamb in his personal relations with his fellow men. You could not meet a better man face to face than he was. He was in later years my friend. I have voted for him for office, but I frankly admit I had to choose between him and an old border ruffian judge. This man never performed any great patriotic or philanthropic work in his whole life, which would cause him to be remembered and honored by posterity. He could only, parrot like, repeat the ritual of Masonry. To-day the Masonic order is erecting to the memory of the man who dictated that infamous law of death, a monument more magnificent and costly than was ever erected to any of the grand old heroes of Kansas.

Again I say let us not forget the "Lesson of Kansas." The meetings of yesterday and to-day have a significance and importance which we at this time can hardly comprehend. Let us say and do only that which we will be proud to see chronicled in press and pamphlet. The eyes of the people of these United States are upon us. Let the coming time find us all better and purer, determined in the future as in the past, to stand by the right.

And now I will close by reading the letter of Mr. Thayer, in reply to the invitation to be present at this celebration.

LETTER FROM ELI THAYER.

Col. Anthony read as follows:

WORCESTER, MASS., Sept. 6th, 1879.

My Dear Friends: I do not see any chance of my being able to attend the meeting of the Old Settlers on the 15th inst. This is the greatest disappointment of my life; for the Old Settlers of Kansas are nearer and dearer to me than any other mortals upon the earth.

The ties of blood and the bonds of kinship can never rival the attachment which binds me to the men and women whose devotion to freedom secured its decisive victory and permanent triumph. This country and the world owes more to them than to all other living men, and the day is not distant when history will acknowledge their transcendent worth and work. They were triumphant in the great battle against slavery in which our northern politicians had been invariably defeated.

Zealous to maintain and perpetuate the union of the States, ever acting in accordance with law and the constitution, they gave to freedom works instead of words, and an army of settlers instead of an array of sentiment.

May God bless the Old Settlers of Kansas.

ELI THAYER.

COL. ANTHONY :—As your acting chairman for the time be-
ng, it devolves upon me now to introduce to you one of the most
distinguished of the citizens of Kansas, one who by vote of the
above State was called on three times to represent the State in the
lower House of Congress, and who filled the responsible post with
great ability and satisfaction to the people. I introduce to you
Hon. Sidney Clarke, who will, in turn, introduce to you a co-
laborer of his in Congress who was a most useful friend of Kansas
in the early days.

Mr. Clarke spoke as follows:

Ladies and Gentlemen:

In presenting to you the distinguished gentleman who is next
to occupy your attention, I should not be justified in detaining you
with any extended remarks. The great conflict which resulted in
the freedom of Kansas was a fierce antagonism between two distinct
and dissimilar civilizations. It was a mighty conflict between the
wickedness and brutality of the slave power on the one hand, and
the sublime and beneficent influences of freedom on the other. On
the one side were displayed the worst passions of mankind, insti-
gated by the craft, the ambition and the avarice of a brutal and
barbarous system, while on the other was the grand phalanx of
freedmen, the free instincts of a free people, the marshaled hosts
of a triumphant civilization based upon the highest exemplification
of justice and equal rights. As the men of Missouri, of Georgia,
and of Alabama were mostly the pioneers of slavery upon this soil,
so the Free State settlers were the crusaders of freedom, whose
noble purposes were fired by the matchless inspiration of a great
and sacred cause. And here let me say that to the men of no State,
and of no particular section of the North, belongs the special hon-
or of making Kansas free. Indeed, sir, so great was the strength
of the slave power, and so vast its interests, and so persistent its
purposes, that it took all the forces of freedom, all the combined
work of the friends of liberty in the Eastern, and Middle, and
Western States, to make the victory complete. New England did
nobly and well. At this Quarter-Centennial celebration of the
founding of this Commonwealth of freedom, let us do high honor
to the men whose activity, and eloquence, and ability in our behalf, made it possible for us to commemorate this day. The names
of William Lloyd Garrison, Charles Sumner, Wendell Phillips,
Theodore Parker, Eli Thayer, John G. Whittier, Amos A. Lawrence, John P. Hale, Henry Wilson, Edward Everett. Hale, as
well as many others of the statesmen, the orators and poets of New
England, will be gratefully remembered in the final history of the
Free State struggle. But not less conspicuous were the noble men
of the Empire State, William H. Seward, the philosophical states-

man of his time; Henry Ward Beecher, always eloquent and true; Horace Greeley, the constant friend of humanity and freedom everywhere—always condemning the wrong and battling for the right, and Gerrit Smith, the large hearted, courageous and munificent friend of humanity. All fought the battle of free Kansas with commanding ability.

So also with the men of Pennsylvania: from the standpoint of the Douglas Democracy, sincere and able John W. Forney did noble and effective work with his ready pen and eloquent voice, and he is with us here to-day, our honored guest, a living witness to the marvelous achievements of the triumph of freedom here. And there was another man in Pennsylvania whose memory will live in the history of our conflict to the end of time. I refer to that grand old man, the great commoner, the unflinching advocate of free Kansas—Thaddeus Stevens. Ohio was not less alive to the exigencies of our critical situation, and her public men and her press and people spoke out for freedom in thunder tones. Salmon P. Chase crowned his great reputation with immortal fame by the fight he made in Congress and elsewhere for the pioneers of liberty; while Benjamin F. Wade, stalwart, valiant and true, and with more than iron will, upheld the standard of our cause, and brave old Joshua Giddings scarcely ranked below any in the glorious contest. Owen Lovejoy spoke the sentiments of the friends of freedom in Illinois with words of burning indignation; and the cause of freedom in Kansas had such noble men as Timothy O. Howe, B. Gratz Brown, Frank P. Blair, Jr., and Joseph Medill, in all the Western States, to arouse the people to the impending danger. To all of these—some now dead, and some yet living— and to thousands more, we now render the highest honor for their unselfish devotion to our cause.

But the brave, determined and faithful men who upheld on the soil of Kansas the Free State banner, true in purpose, unselfish in action, loving liberty and hating slavery, and caring little for fame or fortune, were not wanting in faithful and eloquent champions. Martin F. Conway and Marcus J. Parrott should be remembered to-day for their great work for freedom. Both have been overtaken by misfortunes which merit our deepest sympathy, while the efforts they made for our deliverance from slavery command our lasting gratitude. And what shall I say of our greatest leader—the life and soul of our conflict, the Napoleon of the Free State struggle—Gen. James H. Lane. To him more than to any other eminent citizen of Kansas are we indebted for our final victory. With surpassing ability, with restless activity, with diversified civil and military qualifications, and with an enthusiastic purpose and unflinching patriotism, James H. Lane was the one great leader whose life and action was a constant inspiration to all who struggled and suffered for the establishment of a Free State.

But I must not detain you longer. It has been made my pleasant duty to present to you as the next speaker a statesman eminent in the history of the nation, and one of the earliest and ablest friends of free Kansas. In 1856 his eloquent voice was heard in Indiana and throughout the North in our behalf, as it was heard in Congress years before in behalf of the universal freedom of mankind. I present to you not only one of the most devoted and eminent of the friends of freedom in Kansas, but a man whose whole life has been a continued protest against injustice and wrong in all their forms. As the friend of Kansas in her hour of need, as the most conspicuous advocate of the Homestead Bill, as the defender of universal liberty in its highest and best sense, the Hon. George W. Julian, of Indiana, will live in the minds and hearts of his countrymen as long as history endures. I now have the honor and the pleasure of presenting him to you.

ADDRESS OF GEORGE W. JULIAN.

The chairman introduced Hon. George W. Julian, of Indiana, who spoke as follows:

Mr. Chairman and Fellow Citizens:

Before proceeding to read from the paper which I have prepared for this occasion, allow me to express my sincere regret that I lack the health and voice to address this magnificent assemblage in an old-fashioned off-hand speech. I am perfectly aware that standing behind a written manuscript to read what one has to say, seems to you Western people an awkward and embarrassing performance. You have a right to a better entertainment; and I must hope that the speakers who are to follow me will not disappoint your wishes in this respect. Let me say, however, a word further. I am exceedingly glad and gratified to be with you here to-day. I am glad of the honor of being here by your invitation and wish. I am glad of the privilege of having lived in this wonderful dispensation of Providence. The fact is, whole years are now crowded into days; whole generations are crowded into a few years. The history of our people to-day is freighted with great problems of humanity and progress that, a little while ago, nobody attempted to grapple with but a select few. Now our little boys and girls are in a fair way to outstrip their fathers and mothers in a fundamental knowledge of free government, and of the rights and advantages of citizenship in this free Republic.

And ladies and gentlemen, there is another side to this subject which strongly impresses me now. Nearly a third of a century ago, when I entered upon political life, I was thrown among the leading men of the North. And now I am reminded that I am standing almost alone to-day, of those who were privileged to work in the cause of human rights in those days. Charles Sumner, Horace Greeley, Joshua R. Giddings, Salmon P. Chase, John P. Hale, Henry Wilson, all of those men with whom we started in the vigor of manhood, have gone down to their graves and crossed over the river of death. I am getting more and more alone. I have something of a feeling of loneliness as year by year goes on. It is therefore exceedingly gratifying to me, indeed, to be here, for I have seen so many of the survivors of the old time and had the pleasure of shaking them by the hand. I have here greeted some score of friends who have told me they voted for Hale and Julian in 1852. I am glad to see so many of the old men still alive and among us; it reminds one of the times when it tried a man's nerve to take sides on the great questions that were agitating the people; it displayed more than ordinary patriotism in all those who took such a stand, and I have always felt proud of them. But, my friends, to avoid being tempted into making a speech, and to avoid talking about the past in which my heart would get the better of my head, allow me to proceed to the little task that is before me.

The anniversary which we have met to commemorate to-day revives many fading and mingled memories. It touches our gratitude and pride by reminding us of the signal victory of civilization over barbarism, while it saddens all hearts by recalling the precious sacrifices which that victory involved. It takes hold on the grandest epoch of our national history, and links itself to the heroic struggle of the Republic for its life. A generation has passed away since the pioneers of Kansas entered upon their rugged and perilous work, and in facing the new generation which has come to the front, it cannot be out of place to refer to some of the great historic facts which explain the origin of their struggle, and give it its due rank in the march of American progress.

The slaveholders' raid into Kansas in 1854 had its genesis in the victory of the South in 1820. That was the entering wedge to all the terrible results which have followed in its train. The well understood policy of our fathers was the territorial restriction of slavery, and in their vocabulary restriction meant destruction. Slavery had reached the condition of inevitable decay even in the States which had taken no measures for its abolition, and could only hope to preserve its life by diffusing itself over fresh lands. To forbid such diffusion was to doom it to suffocation and death. In a very comprehensive and practical sense, therefore, the founders of the government were abolitionists, although they did not unfurl the banner of immediate emancipation; and when their policy of restriction was essentially modified, and to that extent abandoned, it was morally as well as logically certain to whet the appetite of the slave power for new demands. This was practically illustrated more than a quarter of a century afterward, in our war with Mexico, and the attempt to spread slavery over the Territories acquired by conquest. Another sectional conflict was the natural result, in which the ancient policy of restriction was vigorously reasserted under the name of the Wilmot Proviso; but the South finally achieved another signal triumph, in the memorable compromise measures of 1850. By these measures some seventy thousand square miles of free soil were surrendered to Texas and to slavery, with ten millions of money as good measure. A new fugitive slave law was enacted, which armed the slave hunter with the power to swear away the liberty of any man, woman or child in the free States; for his ex parte, interested affidavit was made conclusive evidence of the fact of escape and of the identity of the fugitive, while the certificate of the commissioner for his removal was made final and conclusive upon all courts. The rights of the non-slaveholding States were thus completely trampled down by this monstrous stretch of centralized power, while it was further provided that their people should become the constables and slave-hounds of their Southern brethren. The army and navy were also placed at the service of the claimant, and the harboring of a fugitive was not only made a felony, but magnified by judicial interpretation into constructive treason. These compromise measures further provided that the Territories of New Mexico and Utah might be admitted into the Union with or without slavery, according to the wish of their people, thus dealing with slavery and freedom as matters of total national indifference, and authoritatively accepting "the gospel of devil take the hindmost." This was the beginning of the baleful dogma of "squatter sovereignty" in the Territories, and the subsequent conspiracy to plant slavery in Kansas was simply an ugly sprout from the grave of the Wilmot Proviso.

In the year 1852 these compromise measures were incorporated into the platforms of the Whig and Democratic parties by their respective national conventions. The Democrats pledged themselves thereafter to "resist" the discussion of the slavery question in Congress and out of Congress, under whatever shape or color it might be attempted; and the Whigs solemnly resolved that they would " discountenance " such discussion—make mouths at it everywhere —world without end. The questions which formerly divided these parties had ceased to be the basis of their strife, and each was crawling in the mud at the feet of its Southern master. That this state of our politics would pave the way for further and more intolerable aggressions was perfectly inevitable. In an atmosphere so thoroughly impregnated with sulphur, border ruffianism in Kansas could not fail to be spawned upon its virgin soil by spontaneous generation. If the principle of "popular sovereignty" was right in New Mexico and Utah, it was right in Kansas and Nebraska. The slaveholders simply followed up the logic of their work, and their unchecked power over Northern politicians very naturally emboldened them in their new schemes of lawlessness. The repeal of the Missouri Compromise was thus resolved upon as the next thing in order, and it was finally accomplished by an act of Congress, approved on the 30th of May, 1854. It could not be considered at all surprising, in view of the complete debauchment which the slave power had wrought in our politics. Was any remedy possible? Could the latent conscience of the Northern States be roused and organized for resistance? The prospect was not flattering. The sufferings and sorrow of your people kindled a pretty widespread and intense indignation; but the evil momentum of the old parties seemed irresistible.

The moral ravages and political whoredom of slavery were everywhere painfully visible. The difficulty was further aggrivated by the Know-Nothing movement which then made its apparition in our politics, and threatened to balk the anti-slavery feeling produced by the Kansas excitement, through its mischievous and indecent crusade against the foreigner and the Pope. The great body of the old Whigs, and a large division of the Democrats entered the lodges of this secret order. In fact, the people of the Northern States, as a general rule, hated the negro far more than they hated slavery. Their hostility to the institution was a sickly and evanescent sentiment rather than a robust conviction. The popular watch-word and rallying-cry was "the restoration of the Missouri Compromise;" but every intelligent and sincere anti-slavery man saw that this was a deceptive, and therefore a false issue. To restore this compromise would be to propitiate the spirit of compromise, which had been the great curse of our country. It would be to re-affirm the binding obligation of a compact which ought never to have been made, and from which we should seek the first practicable opportunity to escape. It would be to go back, by the shortest route, to the compromise measures of 1850, and the Whig and Democratic platforms of 1852, instead of forward to the complete separation of the National Government from slavery by making the breach of this time-honored compact, our exodus from the bondage of all compromises. The repeal of the Missouri restriction was only a single link in a great chain of measures aiming at the complete supremacy of slavery in the government, and thus inviting a resistance commensurate •with that purpose. It was not the wickedness of violating an ancient bargain between the North and South, but the cold blooded conspiracy to blast an empire with slavery, which appealed to the popular conscience; but the popular conscience was slow in responding. Hating slavery geographically was the order of the day. Men who could talk very eloquently about border ruffian outrages were often as careful to disavow "abolitionism" as if slavery had the stamp of divinity upon it. When moralizing about the duty of keeping covenants, and deploring the reopening of an agitation which had been happily settled by Congress in 1850, they protested with uplifted hands, against the policy of marrying the negroes or setting them free among us. Even many of our old free-soil friends, and some of the anti-slavery men of a still earlier day, seemed in danger of losing their way in the muddled and nebulous condition of our politics which then prevailed; for they crept into the invisible conclaves of the new secret order and seemed to follow it as their new Messiah, while mustering under some very strange captains. I am sorry to say that this was especially true in Indiana, as my old Hoosier friends will bear witness, whose welcome faces I recognize to-day.

But the signs of progress were, nevertheless, quite discernible. The seeds of liberty were germinating in the propitious soil of current events. The purposes of desperate men are often providentially overruled. The hierarchy of scoundrels that resolved to blacken your soil with slavery by organized robbery and rapine unwittingly served the very cause they sought to crush. Atchison and Stringfellow were useful northern schoolmasters. The enlightening influence and saving grace of the Black Code of 1855 should be duly acknowledged. The outrages of 1856, and the dispersion of your Free State Legislature, were undoubtedly powerful make-weights in the march of freedom. The picturesque popular triumph of border ruffianism in 1857, by the help of voters whose names were carefully copied from the Cincinnati directory, and the arrest of leading members of the Free State party as traitors, did a grand work in the spread of anti-slavery principles.

The adoption of the Lecompton constitution could not fail to serve the same ends. The terrible trials through which you were called to pass were probably necessary to save the Republic from stagnation and death. The hideousness of slavery had to grow to its full stature, and display all its devilish enormity, before the American people would engage earnestly in its overthrow; and the fires of freedom were now finally lighted, which could never be quenched till liberty should be proclaimed throughout all the land. The old Whig party mercifully disappeared in 1854, availing itself of the Know-Nothing movement as a sort of underground railroad on which its members could securely escape from their old masters, while another great mercy was vouchsafed to the country in a formidable disruption of the Democratic party. The defeat of the homestead act at the bidding of slavery, the Dred Scott decision, and the merciless enforcement of the fugitive slave law, did their part in strengthening the anti-slavery sentiment of the free States. On the 24th of February, 1856, after an exasperating and protracted struggle, freedom achieved its first decisive national victory in the election of Banks as speaker of the House of Representatives. As early as 1854 Republican parties, on a broad anti-slavery basis, had been organized in Michigan, Massachusetts, and many other States, and the leaven of freedom was evidently spreading. Know-Nothingism gradually retired from our politics, while trimmers and conservatives began to accept a position of subordination under the comprehensive and positive anti-slavery policy which claimed the leadership of the new movement. On the 22d of February, 1856, the first National Republican convention was held at Pittsburg and the party formally organized. On the 17th of June following it nominated Fremont for the Presidency, on a very radical and ringing anti-slavery platform, and there was a romance about his life and name which seemed to make him prëeminently the man for the hour. The honor of first naming him for the Presidency, and of starting the popular tide in his favor, belongs to the honored president of this

8

convention. In unbounded and jubilant enthusiasm the Fremont campaign has had no parallel in our national politics, and it was borrowed chiefly from the great tragedy then in progress in Kansas. Such masses of earnest, orderly and intelligent men and women I have never seen assembled, and the whole land was made vocal with spontaneous eloquence and music. It was a mighty educator of the people, and to this extent a real national triumph. Anti-slavery principles were thoroughly discussed, and took root in thousands of hearts that had never before been touched. Old party lines were consumed in the fervent heat of the new move-ment, while political cowards and dough-faces where made to tremble in anticipation of the reckoning which they saw pre-figured in the general commotion. Fremont was defeated; but the moral power of the large vote he received was felt throughout the nation, · and saved Kansas from the clutches of slavery, as the Free Soil movement of 1848 had saved California. In fact, the defeat of 1856 may have been fortunate. As a statesman Fremont was nearly unknown to the people. Congress would have been against him, and only a partially developed anti-slavery sentiment could have given him its support. It was a formative period, rather than a time for courageous and energetic action. The revolution so hope-fully begun might have been arrested by half-way measures, pro-moting the slumber, rather than the agitation, of anti-slavery truth; while the irritating but helpful nostrums of Buchanan's adminis-tration, which afterward filled up and rounded out the horrors of slave-breeding desperation, might have been lost to the country.

Indeed, with all the aid which freedom could extract from the madness of slavery, the admission of Kansas as a free State was accomplished by a prolonged and most distressing trouble. The triumph of freedom in 1860 was only secured by a division in the Democratic party, caused by the stupid and shameless surrender of the body and soul of James Buchanan to the slave power. Mr. Lincoln was a minority President, and the country, even then, had no adequate moral preparation for the crisis which confronted it. We were saved by the perfectly splendid madness of the enemy. The slave-holders occupied a fortified position, and could certainly plead no desperate necessity for their infernal leap at the nation's throat. They had the Supreme Court on their side. They had both houses of Congress; and as a peace-offering we proposed to surrender our national Territories to the ravages of slavery. We were willing to abide by the Dred Scott decision and the fugitive slave law.

So feeble was the grasp of the conscience of the people of the free States upon the nature of their quarrel, and so long had slavery fed upon the manhood of the country, that they even proposed the incorporation of the Lecompton constitution into the constitution of the United States, by an amendment, making slavery perpetual. But the same providential madness of our foe followed us as our ally throughout the struggle. You know how reluctant we were to strike at slavery as the cause of the war and the obstacle to peace, and how anxiously we sought to save the Union and save slavery with it. We were equally unwilling to arm the negroes as soldiers, and afterwards to arm them with the ballot. After the close of the war, and these people had furnished nearly two hundred thousand soldiers to aid us in preserving the national unity, we deliberately proposed to hand them over to the mercy of their old masters, on the single condition that they should not be counted in the basis of representation. It was not the ready and spontaneous humanity and sense of justice of our people, but the iron hand of necessity, invoked by the sublime folly of the enemy, which signally marked our pathway through the fearful conflict, and at last made certain the great and enduring fruits of our victory. Let us frankly tender our acknowledgments to the respectable and popular personage who is understood to appear only in black costume, and whose name is not fit to be mentioned in polite society.

The lesson embodied in the facts to which I have thus hastily referred is two-fold. In the first place, they teach that the work of reform has certain normal limits, which cannot be overpassed by human effort. It must obey the inevitable conditions of progress. It is with communities as with individuals. Every man is the product of his antecedents. His character has been stamped upon him by his ancestry, and by external influences, as to which he had little choice. In the sun and air of favoring conditions, and through the exercise of his will, a good deal may be done in modifying native tendencies, but it is as impossible wholly to escape the logic of his personality, as it would be to run away from his own shadow. It is equally impossible for society to cut the thread of history from behind it, and bound to some ideal height of perfection and blessedness by a single leap. Reform mistakes its mission when it attempts any such folly. Not absolutely, but in a very large sense, progress must be a growth. It demands time, patience, and the helping hand of friendly circumstances. The temperance movement involves the general uplifting of society itself, and there is no short cut or royal road to its accomplishment. Reforms would be unnecessary if humanity had reached its possible maximum of enlightenment; but that millennial day is rather too far off to concern the present generation. We must deal with humanity as we find it, ready made to our hands. Reformers themselves are not angels, or even perfect men, and the raw material with which they are obliged to deal makes their work exceedingly difficult.

The truth of this was painfully realized by the pioneers of your State, and by the leaders of the anti-slavery cause everywhere. Their enterprise appealed to all that is best and noblest in enlightened humanity, and arrayed against them all the forces of incorrigible ignorance and barbarism. While they were compelled to make themselves of no reputation, they were cheered by no hope of reward, or of immediate success. Forsaking all the prizes of life which worldly prudence or ambition could covet, they took up the heaviest cross yet fashioned by this century as the test of real character and heroism. They never under-estimated the difficulties of their task. They were no fanatics, or dreamers, respecting the future. They did not suppose that the new heavens and the new earth for which they toiled, would ever salute their vision. They saw the world about them lying in darkness, which antecedent causes had produced, and without foolishly quarreling with unmanageable facts, they soberly and resolutely dedicated themselves to the work of doing *their* part in righting the wrongs of society. They could at least oil the machinery of progress, and smooth its pathway, instead of handing it over to the unpitying logic of events, and the ugly friction which is always threatened by a cowardly and stupid conservatism.

In the second place, while the progress of reform has its essential limitations, we are taught the supreme value of individual effort Society is not a growth, in the sense in which we speak of the growth of a plant, or an animal, which proceeds in a certain predetermined order. It is largely molded by efforts voluntarily put forth for the purpose, and so far it is a manufacture, as well as a growth. The notion that progress is to be wrought out by gradual development, and that all forms are to be superseded by social evolution, is as indefensible as it is demoralizing. This theory takes the poetry out of life, and reduces humanity itself to a machine. It strikes a deadly blow at personal responsibility, and belittles human character, which is above all price. It practically confounds the distinction between right and wrong. It threatens to dethrone conscience, and substitute development for duty. By committing all social questions to the working of inevitable laws, it dishonors the heroes and prophets of every age, through whose labors and sacrifices our present civilization has been made possible. If social progress has been evolved, it has also quite as certainly been propagated. It is not simply the product of law, but the fruit of human toil and sacrifice, purposely embraced for the improvement and regeneration of the race. We have already seen how the wrath of man has been made to serve the truth, and how beautifully the sincere strivings of faithful souls are supplemented by the blindness of their foes. The history of the anti-Slavery movement is the history of great moral leaders, without whose unquenchable zeal and perfect self-renunciation, the Republic would have drifted to destruction. Their devotion to a great and holy cause was a fascination, and has called forth the enduring admiration and perfect love of mankind. When the church and the State joined hands with slavery as the new trinity of the nation's faith, they believed in God, in justice, and in the resistless might of the truth. They broke in pieces the great political and ecclesiastical organization of the land, and their moral appeals and persistent labors were the rills that finally blended in the grand river which swept slavery from our soil. Who would discrown these martyrs to liberty and high priests of reform? Who now doubts their power as grand factors in the emancipation of a race? Who questions the great lesson of history, that "all mankind at last inherit what is sown in the blood and tears of the few?" For myself, I am sure that God does not mock His faithful children, or suffer their labors to come to naught. Justice is certain. The souls of your hallowed dead are still "marching on," while history will weave into the brightest pages of her story the memory of the men whose toils and struggles for the freedom of your great Commonwealth became the introduction and prelude to the freedom of the nation.

HALE AND JULIAN.

At the conclusion of Mr. Julian's address, Col. Anthony said: "I am requested to ask every man in this audience, who voted for Hale and Julian, to stand up and raise his right hand and stand until counted. I count 55. Now, all those who voted for Julian for Congress in 1852, will please do the same. I count 10."

ADDRESS BY MAJ. GEN. JOHN POPE.

In the midst of Mr. Julian's address the train bringing Gen. Pope arrived, and the battery fired a salute in his honor, during which the speech was suspended. When Gen. Pope entered the tabernacle three rousing cheers were given in his honor, and the audience were almost determined that he should address them then, so at the end of Mr. Julian's address Col. Anthony said: "While I was in the army in Mississippi, General Sheridan once placed a guard of eight men over a peach orchard, in order to keep the boys from stealing the peaches. The boys in my old regiment went down there and captured the guard, stole all the peaches, then released the guard and put them in possession of the peach orchard. General Sheridan sent for me and reprimanded me; and that was the end of it. Yesterday General Pope was over at Leavenworth, and he could command; but to-day, the soldier, and man who has a heart full of sympathy for progress and every thing good, is here. We old settlers have got the power. Let us take the General prisoner, and let him feel how it is to have some one over him. Let us force him to come forward and acknowledge us, and thank us for thus honoring him. He is compelled to come."

General Pope said:

Ladies and Gentlemen:

I assure you I esteem it a great honor to have been invited to participate with this goodly company in the celebration of an occasion so full of interest. There are few if any present to-day, who came to Kansas at an earlier day than I did.   I came as a soldier, pure and simple.   I tramped on foot and on horse back over the greater portion of Kansas in those early days.   It was my misfortune to be absent from this State during the most eventful and interesting period of its history; from 1854 to 1865.   It is scarcely to be expected therefore that I have anything to tell you of the early struggle and of the final triumph; a history to which we have been listening and which I hope to continue to listen to during the day from the lips of the eloquent orators whom you have summoned here for this purpose.   It was neither my wish nor my expectation to be called upon to deliver an address upon a subject with which you are much more familiar than I am.   I shall rely upon the considerate kindness that prompted you to invite me here to allow me to sit by and look on.   There is no man who has a warmer feeling for the welfare of this State than I have.   The time is not far distant, when Kansas will have a place in the first rank among this great sisterhood of States.   Even now you all have a right to feel proud of the trials you suffered in the early days, to establish free institutions in this new State.   I trust you will receive my excuse, and allow me to be like yourselves, a silent listener to the good speeches to be made here to-day.   [Applause.]

THE BARBACUE.

Gov. Robinson announced that the heads of the table at the grand barbacue would be occupied by Mr. Hale, Gen. Pope and Mr. Forney.

ADDRESS BY ROBERT MORROW.

Col. Anthony: It becomes my duty to introduce to you one who is an honest man, one who is governed by principle.   It has been said that but few men in Kansas are actuated from that motive.   I believe that the majority act from principle.   I believe that Governor Robinson could no more be untrue to human liberty than he could be false to himself, or his own country, and I believe that the gentleman that I now introduce to you is equally true to principle.   It is only those men who have hearts and who are true to us, that we should really love to honor.   It gives me great pride and pleasure to introduce to you the honorable Robert Morrow.

Mr. Morrow said:

Mr. Chairman and Fellow Citizens:

I was put on the programme not for the purpose of making a speech, but only to introduce an old friend and acquaintance, Ex-Senator Howe of Wisconsin.

Some thirty odd years ago, we were pioneers together in the then Territory of Wisconsin.   I aided by my vote and in my humble way to place this gentleman on the bench of that State.   He was afterward chosen to represent that State in the Senate of the United States three consecutive terms. Commencing his term of service as senator, with that of the administration of Abraham Lincoln. It was at that critical period in the history of our country, that he was called to the councils of the Nation, when the fate of this great Republic was so uncertain. He aided in molding much of the legislation during the war, as well as that of reconstruction after the close. No taint of corruption, or breath of slander attached to his name.

While serving as a senator on a salary of five or six thousand dollars a year, he did not become a millionaire; while serving as a senator he did not become the silent partner of jobbers of bank syndicates, or credit mobilier. When Oliver Ames pulled out his old memorandum book, that destroyed the reputation of so many public men, he did not fear the same. He served his State and his country faithfully and honestly. I need not tell you what pleasure it would have given me to introduce so distinguished a man as Ex-Senator Howe of Wisconsin, but I most sincerely regret that he has been unable to attend. I have a letter from him which I will read, in which he sends his regrets and his good wishes to the old settlers of Kansas. Senator Howe was an anti-slavery man and always a warm friend of Kansas. We heard yesterday what the Pennsylvania Democracy had done toward making Kansas a free State, as well as what Massachusetts and the Emigrants' Aid Society had done. Last night Sam Wood claimed that the honor of making Kansas free belonged to Ohio. Well, Ohio is a modest State and her citizens do not like to hold office. I only wish we might have heard from one of the great north-western States in the person of Senator Howe. I will now read Senator Howe's letter:

LETTER FROM HON. TIMOTHY O. HOWE.

MR. MORROW read as follows:

GREEN BAY, Sept. 9, 1879.

My Dear Sir: After diligent search I can find no practical way by which I can join the Old Settlers of Kansas on the 15th inst., consistently with the duties devolved upon me here.

I regret this. It would give me great pleasure to aid in celebrating the 25th anniversary of the founding of your State. The occasion will be replete with interest and I hope will not be without instruction.

It is somewhat startling to reflect that only twenty-five years ago, the fair domain of Kansas was flung down as the wager for which Freedom and Slavery were to do battle. Then Slavery had her principal magazine in Missouri, while Freedom had hers, in Massachusetts, and so the conditions of the conflict did not seem quite fair.

Perhaps the framers of your organic act spoke with literal truth when they declared in the 14th section, that it was the true intent of the act ''not to legislate Slavery into any Territory or State, nor to exclude it therefrom.''

But whatever may have been the real intent of the act, there were few there who did not believe its actual effect would be to fasten Slavery upon Kansas. In this respect we have been happily disappointed.

I hope those who next week may be privileged to see, what free labor has done for Kansas in twenty-five years, will candidly admit that the architects who laid the foundations of your State builded better than they knew.

And when they reflect that the election of President Lincoln was mainly a popular protest against the organic act of Kansas, and that four years of bloody civil war was in turn only a sectional protest against the election of President Lincoln, I hope it will be conceded, that truly wise and prudent architects would have built quite as well, more intelligently and more cheaply.

Wishing for the future of your State all that prosperity which her brilliant past predicts, I am very truly, your ob't Servant.

T. O. HOWE.

TEN TIMES ONE ARE TEN.

Gov. Robinson :—Many of you have seen the little book called "Ten Times One Are Ten." I believe the Congregational Church over here has a club of young people named after this little book, "Ten Times One Are Ten." I suppose that one of those belonging, perhaps, to that club has sent up this little basket of flowers for the author of "Ten Times One Are Ten." Perhaps she will excuse me if I say her name is Katie L. Ridenour. The author will be here this afternoon, when this little basket will be presented to him.

ADDRESS BY HON. C. B. LINES.

Gov. Robinson :—You have all heard about the Beecher Rifles, and the Beecher Bibles. I have now the pleasure of introducing to you one of the old settlers of Kansas, who will tell you all about the rifles and the Bibles, Hon. Charles B. Lines, of Wabaunsee.

Mr. Lines said :

Mr. President:

We certainly ought to congratulate each other that we are here to-day, under such auspicious circumstances, to celebrate the 25th anniversary of the founding of what has already become the great State of Kansas—great in its area—in its vast resources, agricultural, horticultural, mineral, pomological, climatical, etc. In the constantly and rapidly increasing multitudes of its people, from every clime and country of the earth, intelligent, progressive, moving on with apparently a common purpose to develop our vast possibilities into the great central State of the greatest nation on earth. In addition to the material resources of our State above referred to, it is pertinent also to refer to its educational and religious progress and advantages, its schools and colleges which so vastly exceed and excel any and all other States when at twice the age of our own, and its churches and Sabbath schools, which are sufficient for all our own necessities in the older settlements, and go with the tide of emigration over the prairies and toward the frontier, till from nearly every section over the entire country, where human habitations exist, the voice of the living preacher and the songs of salvation are heard, but leaving to the future historian the task of describing the capability and growth of Kansas, its resources, etc., in detail, our duty for the day will have been performed, if, in connection with the rejoicing, we note down for the benefit of our children and children's children, such facts and reminiscences as our experience may furnish, of the early settlement, trials and triumphs of our people. Although in conflict with good taste it is nevertheless a necessity in detailing facts, to refer often to the participation of the narrator in the scenes described. In the present case it will be obvious to all that such a necessity exists. My own home for 49 years was in New Haven, Conn. Of course there was born in me a hatred of despotism, and my first inspiration was from the atmosphere of freedom. To digress a moment, an old friend from one of the great and noble States of the West, who addressed you this morning, having in mind only the numerical force of his State, gave utterance to the belief that she contributed more toward saving Kansas to freedom than all New England, whereas the history of the past 250 years has demonstrated that the world is more indebted to New England for its intellectual and moral power, its inventive genius, its philanthropic and Christian activities, its self-sacrificing devotion to universal liberty, than to all America besides. So obvious is it that most of the streams of intellectual, inventive and moral progress that are fertilizing the world take their rise largely in New England, that to leave her out or attempt to belittle her agency in the great work of saving Kansas to freedom, would be as absurd as to omit the sun in a treatise on the origin and power of light. But to return, it will be my purpose to give you a very brief sketch of the origin and work of the "Connecticut Kansas Colony." Prior and immediately subsequent to the passage of the "Nebraska Bill," so called, an intensely quickened interest was awakened among the liberty-loving people of New England, and at New Haven, in the autumn of 1855 a series of public "Anti-Nebraska" meetings were held, and crowded with our most intelligent and influential citizens. Addresses were made by a large number of our clergymen, lawyers and business men. The question in all these meetings was, what can we do to save Kansas to freedom? During the winter Eli Thayer, the great organizer of emigration in Massachusetts, visited New Haven and attended several of our meetings for consultation. He was then especially laboring to raise money in aid of the "Emigrant Aid Society," of Massachusetts, but also to promote the cause in other ways, and did much to increase the interest already awakened in our community. During these discussions my own mind became more and more impressed with the fact that if Kansas was saved, it must be by friends of freedom moving there to live in sufficient numbers to outvote the slavery propagandists; and with this view at a public meeting on the evening of February 17, 1856, my intention was announced to organize a colony and at an early day emigrate to Kansas 'to help plant the institutions of freedom and Christianity upon her virgin soil. The next day notice was published in the city papers, and after visiting Hartford, Middletown, Winstead, Meriden and several other localities and addressing the people, the books were opened and in a few days about eighty-five names were subscribed, several of whom, however, for various reasons, did not become permanent members of our organization. Our first meeting was held on the 7th of March, 1856, at which time there were ninety names on the roll, fifty-nine of whom signed the articles of agreement and constituted our company; leaving New Haven on the last day of March and reaching our destination at Wabaunsee on the 28th of April, 1856. A few days previous to our embarking, a public meeting of the members of the colony and other citizens was held in the North Church to hear an address from Rev. H. W. Beecher. After the address a statement was made by the president setting forth the origin and aims of the company, in which it appeared that no provision had been made for weapons of defense, whereupon the venerable Prof. Benjamin Silliman requested the audience to linger a few moments, when he appealed to them asking that then and there this deficiency be supplied. His address was promptly responded to, Mr. Beecher pledging $625 for one half the number required, provided the other half was subscribed by the audience, which was soon accomplished. This action, engineered as it was by Mr. Beecher, gave our company the soubriquet of the "Beecher Rifle Company." This being conspicuously published in the New York *Times*, with the account of the meeting and republished in St. Louis, came near causing us trouble from the "border ruffians," on the Missouri river; but by a cool and determined purpose to maintain our right, though threatened, we were "severely let alone." The colony was fully organized at New Haven with all its plans, including that of securing "every man a farm," and the colony a "town site." Thus our company originated; and on the eve of March 31 held a farewell meeting at Brewster's Hall presided over by Prof. Silliman, from which we were escorted by a military and fire company to the steamboat, and were soon on our way to take part in the struggle that culminated in making Kansas free, and eventually in securing liberty to our whole country, and giving the cause of universal freedom a powerful impulse throughout the world. Had we and others with whom we co-operated cowed before the threats of the propagandists, human liberty would have been set back indefinitely, and if freedom shrieked when Kosciusko fell, what would have been its pang had Kansas yielded to the power of slavery, but it was otherwise ordered. Let us then be grateful to God that we were permitted to participate in the conflict and rejoice in the victory.

For one, standing as I now do on the confines of life and death, with all the plans, the successes and the failures of my life in deeply interested review, excepting only when at the age of 17 I consecrated my life to the service of God, and the important event a few years later which made me a husband, I remember no act with more satisfaction than the resolve to leave the home of my children and of my ancestors, reaching back more than 200 years. The graves of my children, the church and its members with whom for over thirty-five years I had taken sweet counsel, my pleasant dwelling and its surroundings, its fruits and flowers, with neighbors and friends not a few to make a new home in the "Great American Desert," to interlock my destiny with strangers in what seemed an uncertain conflict to save this fair land to freedom and Christian civilization. Yes, I am glad and grateful that my steps were guided thither, and am confident that by far the larger number of our colony were also animated by a similar feeling, and could their history be written, this statement would be fully vindicated here. We reached St. Louis without encountering any special incident, and on Friday, April 4th, embarked on the steamer Clara for Kansas City. The boat was overcrowded so that many of us could not find room to lie down, even on the floor, and in many other respects we were rendered quite uncomfortable. To all of us the life was new and strange, but our purpose was fixed and we moved on. We were provided with Bibles, hymn books and a minister, and when the Lord's Day dawned upon us we asked permission of the captain of the boat to engage in divine worship to which he readily assented, remarking that it would be a novelty and probably the first Christian worship ever held on the Missouri river west of St. Louis. We had, of course, a mixed but attentive audience. Before reaching Lexington information reached us that we should not be permitted to pass that point. We took occasion to make the acquaintance of some very decent "border ruffians" on board and told them we should not be hindered from traveling on the "King's highway" without a vigorous resistance. The president therefore, upon the request of the board of directors designated ten of our stalwart men to stand by our luggage and defend it at all hazards. On arriving a large number of armed ruffians came on board and uttered sundry denunciations of the Yankee abolitionists, but as they looked into the faces of courageous men, well armed they exhausted their zeal in vile language, while we moved on our way rejoicing. Arriving at

Kansas City we met all sorts of demonstrations from the " ruffian" camp. The city was full of excitement, our arrival was being looked for and many threats were made, to the effect that we should not enter the Territory, on the borders of which the city was located; but as we left the boat we gave the captain and crew each three cheers, to which they heartily responded. We then went to the principal hotel and called the company to order in the sitting room and proceeded to appoint committees, one to go into the country to buy cattle and another to procure wagons and other necessary articles, and the next day with thirty yoke of oxen and a suitable number of wagons, we crossed over into Kansas, and everything was beautiful. The very air seemed unlike any ever inhaled before as we

> " Crossed the prairies as of old our fathers crossed the sea,
> To make the West as they the East, the homestead of the free."

The next day we reached the young city of Lawrence, the Mecca to which every Free State pilgrim sooner or later turned his weary feet. We were cordially welcomed, and in the evening were formally received in the upper room of a "shake" building, the best and only hall in the city, not more than 16x24 feet, and rather risky for so large a gathering. We spent the Lord's Day here and walking out in the morning with a late deacon of our old North Church at New Haven, we were so electrified with the pure and balmy atmosphere that we instinctively remarked, "What a splendid place to make love." We lingered about Lawrence several days while different committees were reconnoitering the country in quest of a location. In the meantime our pioneer committee were heard from, who had been at Wabaunsee, and were greatly pleased with that section of country, but the company moved on to Mission creek where, after a few days, our original committee met us and the president with two others returned from a visit to Wabaunsee, and the reports being unanimously in favor of that locality, except one who had been personally smitten with Topeka. We broke camp and with three hearty cheers for Wabaunsee (the name meaning dawn of day), our new home, we turned our faces toward the setting sun, singing as we traveled,

> "As when a weary traveler gains
>   The height of some o'erlooking hill,
> His heart revives if o'er the plains,
>   He sees his home though distant still."

We reached our destination April 28, 1856, and all seemed satisfied and happy. We found some half dozen settlers located about upon the creeks, only two of whom were able to shelter any of our company. We, however, utilized the few tents we had, hunted up a deserted cabin in the woods, and all by some means if not "on board broken pieces of the ship," found shelter and a resting place.

The deserted cabin was about twelve feet square situated on

the bank of a creek in the woods—put there no doubt to hold the timber, as the land was not yet surveyed. It was the "claim" of a former State Superintendent of Public Instruction in Maine, a gentleman in bad health who died a few months after our arrival. Six of us in the midst of a heavy Kansas shower, broke into this cabin the rain drizzling through the roof and beating in between the logs. Spiders and other vermin common to deserted buildings were abundant here. Our company consisted of the doctor, deacon, president, a young man who came out for his health, and two other young men. We found a primitive bedstead, round poles running lengthwise with legs driven into them and sticks tied crosswise about eight inches apart, on which was an old mattress filled with hay. The bedstead was six feet long by three feet wide. We found also a frame of a table made in the same way, about three feet square, with three long oak shingles or "shakes" laid loosely across for a top. The table was about four inches higher than the bedstead. We placed it against one end of the bedstead at right angles and four of us packed ourselves upon it to sleep, after having made our supper upon "mush and molasses," that being the best our market afforded. The doctor, an extra large man, placed himself upon the outer side one way, the president at right angles the other way, the others packing themselves in the remaining space the best way they could, the entire space affording to each person an average of four feet six inches in length and eighteen inches in width. One of the others had with him a hammock in which he found comfortable lodgings. The other, as he said, found two split oak shingles, six inches wide and three feet long, on which he placed a few straws, and lay down among the spiders, and thus we dreamed of the loved ones left behind. Of these six persons two were afterward members of our Territorial Legislature, both of whom had recently been representatives in the Legislature of Connecticut, and one of them was the first Lieutenant-Governor of Kansas, and afterward minister to Chili, another was deacon and Sunday-school superintendent of the North Church in New Haven; two of the young men died in Wabaunsee; the other who slept on the two shingles, among the spiders, is now a very successful wholesale manufacturer of beef in New Haven, and is arranging to raise and fatten a portion of his stock in Wabaunsee; the deacon returned to Connecticut, and the president alone remains on the ground. We immediately set about making provision for our necessities by constructing a company tent about sixteen to twenty feet long and perhaps twelve feet wide, with berths arranged much as they are in steamboats. Our store was kept in the tent, our company meetings were also held there, and at least a dozen of the members made their home under its shelter. Others boarded in the families or lived in their own tents, and very soon several log cabins were put up, some of which remain to this day. About this time five wagons left for Kansas City to bring up a saw mill belonging to two of our members. We

learned that the road below Lawrence was so infested with ruffians
that it was deemed unsafe to proceed until we met Col. Sumner between Lawrence and Leavenworth in charge of a company of U.
S. Cavalry, and were then satisfied that we should be protected.
Returning from Kansas City we passed near the camp of "Buford's
men," the South Carolina invaders, but as the U. S. troops were
camped near by we were not molested, and stopped for the night
in the same vicinity near a well where some settler had been driven
off.   One of the troops informed us that after arriving on the spot,
they found the body of a free state man, recently hung, in the
well, and pointed to the grave where they buried him and to his
clothing scattered on the ground.   A little further on the next
morning we met some honest settlers from Missouri, who informed
us that a boy had that day been shot down from his horse while on
an errand for his widowed mother, because in reply to a question
he said he was in favor of free State.   About the same time Mr.
Luther H. Root, a member of our camp, was coming out of Kansas City with a load of household goods and was stopped by a company of ruffians and taken into the woods to be hung.   The tree
was selected and the rope adjusted when Mr. Root asked a few moments respite to pray for his family "up in the Territory," which
was denied by the leaders, when one of their number interfered
and said, "I have a family also," and protested against proceeding any further and asked Mr. Root if he would promise not to
harm them if they would let him go.   He replied in the simplicity
of his Christian heart, "I never injured anybody," and after rum-
aging his wife's bureau and the other baggage they left him.   But
these details must not be protracted.   We proceeded on our journey and reached Wabaunsee without molestation and amid many
difficulties, started our mill and found full demand for all the lum-
ber it could make, but the resources of the people were soon exhausted, and as we could make no crop except here and there a
little "sod corn," many of our young men left, and those who remained were poorly provided for; much suffering was endured during the fall and winter.   In August we were called upon to aid in
defending Lawrence.   We sent down two of our number to learn
the condition of things.   They were taken prisoners by the border
ruffians near Lawrence and threatened with hanging, but were finally released.   Soon after our "Prairie Guards," a company of
about thirty men armed with Sharp's Rifles, in response to a call
from the "Committee of Safety," proceeded to Lawrence to aid in
defending that city.   There was great scarcity of food, and the region around about the "Historic City" was swarming with enemies.
When all danger was over the company returned, worn down with
fatigue, and physically deranged, for want of proper suste-
nance and protection from the weather.   They had a hard time of it
through that first winter, which was an uncommonly severe one.
In the month of August of the same summer, the president, according to his original plan, returned East for his family, but as

the Presidential election was pending, and the cause was largely if not exclusively being based upon the conflict for the freedom of Kansas, he was pressed into the service without time being given for a much needed rest and physical recuperation. Consequently he was after a few weeks' labor, the campaign being exceedingly exciting, laid aside with complete nervous prostration and unable to return, and had but little hope for a time of ever breathing the air of Kansas again, but rest brought such a degree of restoration that during the winter about $4,000 was secured to aid in building a church and school house in Wabaunsee both which were built and the meeting house when completed was among the best in the Territory. In the following spring a church was organized and a temporary meeting house erected. In the winter of this year, 1857, two very exciting free state conventions were held at Lawrence, Gov. Robinson presiding, the object being to determine whether, in the event of Congress admitting Kansas into the Union as a State under the Lecompton Bogus Border Ruffian Constitution, we would recognize the act. At the first meeting we decided unanimously that we would *not*— under the influence of a patriotic determination, kindred to that manifested by our fathers at Philadelphia in '76, who resisted tyranny at all hazards. To me it seemed that life itself must not be preferred to the liberty we demanded, and such was obviously the prevailing feeling when the convention adjourned. We were called together again on the 23d of December and for two days debated the same question, some of our leading men having changed their attitude. During these two days not less than ten able and eloquent speeches were made on each side of the question, when it was decided by a vote of 75 to 64 that we would not recognize the act should Congress admit us under that infamous instrument, brought forth at Lecompton by John Calhoun and the Missouri ruffians associated with him. Notwithstanding this vote, however, a few of our excellent free state men led by Geo. W. Brown into the basement of his office, deemed it best to get up a ticket and elect it if possible and they did so, but the vote was by no means a general one. Not a ballot box was opened in Wabaunsee county and the same was true of many others. But the ticket was elected and no harm grew out of it, as the State was not admitted. This same subject was brought up in the Territorial Legislature in the early part of February following. The message of President Buchanan had just been received, submitting the Lecompton constitution and recommending our admission under it. A bill was promptly introduced providing for the punishment of treason, providing in direct terms that any person who should attempt to run a government in Kansas under the Lecompton constitution shall be deemed guilty of treason and upon conviction thereof shall suffer death. The hall was made to ring with the most eloquent speeches, similar in character to those that echoed from old Independence Hall and rocked the cradle of liberty in Boston in 1776. Had Buchanan been there to listen to his ideas in regard to the insignificance of the people of Kansas might have been somewhat modified, and had he heard the defiant declaration by all the speakers in which they hurled back the contemptible falsehood contained in his message and indicated their firm resolve that civil liberty shall not find a grave upon the plains of Kansas until her soil is moistened by the blood of her sons, and that they would resist the despotic effort of the administration to crush out our liberties with the same spirit and for the same purpose that animated our fathers in 1776, he would at least have been interested. The several speakers planted themselves upon true ground. They handled the President very much as John Adams did George the III, in the convention that enacted our Declaration of Independence. Subsequent to this as the freedom of Kansas was substantially assured, the development of the country was rapid and her history is now before the world. Our participation in the war is a matter of record. Our contribution of men was greater in proportion to our numbers than that of any other State, and Wabaunsee furnished her full quota, from the families connected with our original colony who remained in Kansas. There were ten who went to the war, of whom one became a captain, one a surgeon and three lieutenants. One, Capt. E. C. D. Lines, at the head of his company and in the advance while in pursuit of the enemy, was killed. From our community there were not less than twenty not connected with our colony who were in the army, one of whom, a son of Clark Lapham, was killed.

In the civil service there has been, from the members of the colony, one Foreign Minister and Lieutenant Governor, one Senator, four members of the House of Representatives, one chairman County Board for ten years, one Pension Agent and Land Office Receiver, etc., etc., besides sundry minor positions. It is supposed, also, that for general intelligence, moral and religious standing, the community occupies a very respectable position. One fact more indicative of the substantial character of the Connecticut Kansas colony. It was fully organized with all its plans matured before leaving New Haven and faithfully adhered to them until, by the organization of local governments under territorial and state authority, our original compact was no longer needed, and we believe this was the only colony that preserved its organization after reaching the Territory, during the first eight years of our history. Of the original members of our colony eight only are living in Wabaunsee, one in Wyandotte, one in Manhattan, one in Topeka and one in the country near Topeka, but of those who have descended from original members of the colony, or became connected with them by marriage, including all who have settled here because the colony was here or because of their connection or acquaintance with some of its members, the number would embrace fully three-fourths of our entire community.

In reference to the material prosperity of the settlement, it may be truly said that while none have become wealthy we have no paupers, but all are comfortably situated—have good farms with fine orchards, excellent religious advantages, the entire settlement uniting in the same house of worship with no sectarian antagonism. Our schools are of a high order and a condition of things generally exists that leads our people when assembled in any considerable number, to unite at the beginning or at the close in singing:

"Praise God from whom all blessings flow,
Praise Him all creatures here below,
Praise Him above, ye heavenly host,
Praise Father, Son and Holy Ghost."

ADDRESS BY THOS. W. CONWAY.

Gov. Robinson: — We have still another gentleman to speak before dinner. He has a letter to read, from one of Kansas' old friends and a most useful citizen in the early times, a man who is well known to you all. Before reading the letter, the gentleman will make a few remarks about your old friend. I introduce to you Gen. Thomas W. Conway. General Conway said:

Much has been said in eulogy of the various States that contributed so much talent and money and sinew of war to the great State of Kansas. I think I can mention a Southern State, to be added to the catalogue of States contributing to your liberation and freedom, in mentioning the State of Maryland, the State that gave you Martin F. Conway. [Applause.] It is a melancholy task assigned to me to-day to providentially have his letter, written from his room in an insane asylum, placed in my hands to read to his old pioneer friends of Kansas. It is a peculiar coincidence, one that melts my heart. I came from New York, at the earnest solicitation of Mr. Pomeroy, to speak for the negro of the South, whose friend Kansas is, to-day, in his emergency. But the first duty that Providence seems to have assigned me here, is to read this long and touching epistle which I hold in my hand. I saw an eminent physician in Washington, the other day, and he told me that, whatever Martin F. Conway's mental condition may have been before, he regarded him now as perfectly sane, and this letter gives evidence that this physician's opinion was correct. The letter is as follows:

LETTER FROM MARTIN F. CONWAY.

St. Elizabeth, D. C., Sept. 3, 1879,

Hon. John P. St. John, Governor of Kansas: Sir:—I see by the newspapers that the original settlers of Kansas, commonly called "The Old Guard," are to have a reunion at Lawrence, on the 15th of September, to celebrate the anniversary of the triumph of the free state cause. I am one of the Old Guard who cannot be with them on that occasion. I, therefore, write. I arrived in Kansas, from Maryland, on the 16th of October, 1854, a little over three months after the passage of the Kansas-Nebraska bill. I was the only free state man elected to the Council of the Territorial Legisla-
9

ture. I was a member of the first popular convention held in the Territory ; also, of the convention which framed the first Free State Constitution. I was the first Chief Justice of the State elected by the people. I was the president of the Leavenworth Constitutional Convention. I was the first representative of the State admitted to a seat in the Federal Congress. I was the first member from Kansas of the National Executive Committee of the Republican party. At this time I was only thirty-two years of age— A. D. 1860 — and no man stood higher in the popular estimation throughout the country. I have now been two years and ten months confined in the Government Institution for the Insane at this place, that is to say, St. Eliza-beth, near Washington, D. C., within full view of the Capitol — A. D. 1879 — aged 50 years.

I am a citizen of Kansas. I have never voted in any other State, except the first vote of my life, in my native State. For ten years past I have been detained in this district. I address myself to you as the chief officer of the State of my adoption, and ask you to represent my case to the people there-of, especially to the Old Guard, if not to the Legislature itself. I am not insane ; no symptoms of insanity have ever been truthfully ascribed to me. I am held simply on pretense of insanity.

Very truly your obedient servant,
M. F. CONWAY.

General Conway concluded his remarks by saying :

Those who believe in God and who believe that God hears prayers, who love Kansas and who love the memory of Martin F. Conway, should take that poor man, to-day, in their prayers to God, that if there be any derangement in his mind yet, God, in his mercy, may remove it.

Adjourned to 2 p. m.

THE GRAND DINNER.

The dinner, one of the great features of the day, which thousands had come to partake of, was indeed a grand affair. The barbecue proper took place just south of the tabernacle. The roasted ox was there, as were also hogs, sheep, and other good things, and thousands ate and enjoyed it. But to have gathered the whole vast throng about the tables would have been an impos-sibility, and to have even filed them past would have occupied a much longer time than the managers had set down for the dinner hour. So here and there, under every tree that offered shade, were gathered groups of people, who spread their repasts upon the green grass. To a looker on the scene was one of the most pleasing that could be imagined. Those who had, gave to those who had not, and all ate and were filled.

AFTERNOON SESSION.

POEM BY GEO. W. BROWN.

After the opening of the afternoon session, Tuesday, Sept. 16th, some brief proceedings were had before entering upon the formal speeches. First came a poem by Dr. Geo. W. Brown, which is here reproduced, in connection with a letter which Dr. Brown subsequently wrote, as follows:

ROCKFORD, ILL., Sept. 30, 1879

Gov. C. Robinson: — When I asked you, on the 16th inst., at Bismarck Grove, the privilege of reading the poem "Swear Ye Now, O My Brothers," which the immense audience listened to with rapt attention, neither of us were fully conscious how well we were building. Let me state the facts:

I met J. G. Haskell, Esq., of Lawrence, on the car, as I came down from Topeka, on Saturday afternoon, before the Old Settlers' Convention. He stated that he had a partial file of Vol. 1, of the *Herald of Freedom*, left him by his deceased father. On the 16th, just as I was about to partake of a camp dinner with my brother-in-law, A. R. Leonard, Esq., Mr. Haskell handed me No. 1, Vol. 1 of the *Herald of Freedom* to look at, exacting a pledge to return it to him in one hour. I had not examined that number before for more than twenty years. Stepping into the canvas tent with paper in hand, turning to the fourth page my eye instantly fell upon the poem under consideration. Remembering that I had parodied it, in 1854, from one written by Wm. Oland Bourne, and adapted it to Kansas, I read it aloud. My friends were so delighted they insisted it ought to be read to the Old Settlers, as a specimen of the inspiration of the early pioneers; and in the language of another, "I thought so too." Hence the reason of my request, which you, as chairman of the convention, so cheerfully granted.

Though anxious to hear Mr. Hale's address, which immediately followed, my obligation to return the paper pressed me, and I left the rostrum to comply with my promise. On reaching Mr. L.'s tent I opened the paper, and on the third page, second column, under the title " Pennsylvania is Coming," read an account of the organization, on the 16th of September, 1854, of the party which I took out with me to Kansas, from Pennsylvania. As I read, the incidents connected with that organization burst upon me with great force. I had called the meeting at Boynton's Hall, Conneautville, to assemble on the 16th of September, 1854, as will be seen by reference to the paper. The heads of families and such persons as had previously promised to accompany me to Kansas, responded to the invitation. We formally organized with a Constitution and By-Laws, and I was made President, and *ex-officio*, Master of Emigration. The outside forms of the *Herald of Freedom*

with an edition of 21,000 copies had already been worked off, and
I was about to commence press-work on the inside, delaying only
to give the proceedings of the organization of our own party. Con-
cluding our labors, and wishing to inspire my associates with the
anti-slavery character of the enterprise, we had so solemnly undertaken, before adjourning, I asked them to rise while I should read,
asking them to lift their hands to heaven at the place of the oath,
which all did with alacrity.   How well that oath was kept, history
and the present prosperity of Kansas abundantly testify.

*Twenty-five years from the day and hour from the time of reading
that parodied poem to my Pennsylvania Company, I read it again to the
assembled thousands at Bismarck Grove,* forgetful in the excitement of
its second reading, the important part it had already performed.
Are not these facts worth a place in Kansas history?   Please find
a copy of the adapted poem below.

Very truly yours,   G. W. BROWN.

SWEAR YE NOW, OH, MY BROTHERS!

Lo! the Land of the West! where the Freeman shall rise,
   In the pride of his birth, with his standard on high,
And shall point to the East, where the flush of the skies
   Gives the promise of Freedom that never shall die!
And the sun as he wheels in his chariot of day,
   Shall convey from the East, and the lakes of the North,
In the flash of his beam, and the light of his way,
   Holy vows of the Freemen that utter them forth.

Shall these plains ever sound with the cry of the slave?
   Shall these vales ever moan o'er the shackle and chain?
Shall the Kansas bear down with its wealth to the grave,
   Reddened drops of the blood wrung in anguish and pain?
Say, oh, Freeman! canst thou in these valleys foredoom
To the bond, and the lash, and the night of despair,
To the grave of the soul, and the heart's rayless tomb,
   Countless throngs that shall toil in their misery there?

Let the Southron go back with his chivalric claim!
   Shall the Freeman yield up when his life is at stake?
Let the Everglades welcome the depth of the shame,
   While Freedom the bonds of the victim shall break.
There is land enough now with the curse of the slave,
   And the day shall arrive when that, too, shall be free;
Stand ye firm, Freemen all! ye shall now dig the grave
   Where the shackle, and chain, and the fetter shall be.

By the vow that was sworn on the altars of old,
   Where our fathers stood up and appealed to their God;
By the blood that was shed, richer far than the gold
   That allures to the land where the Indian has trod;

By the free air we breathe, and the soil that we love,
And the hopes springing forth of the depths of the soul;
By the RIGHTS OF ALL MEN—by the Ruler above,
Not a slave shall be found where the Kansas does roll!

Swear ye now, oh, my brothers! the vow liveth long!
It is freedom that calls you from sleeping to-day!
If ye quit you like men, ye shall echo the song,
O'er the hills and the vales, in your glorious array!
And the age shall give birth to an empire of hope;
And the land shall bring forth of her treasures of peace,
While the rivers and streams, leaping down from the slope
Of the mountains of gold, shall the riches increase.

ADDRESS BY JOHN P. JOHNSON.

Hon. John P. Johnson of Doniphan County was called upon and came forward and spoke briefly. He said:

I came to Kansas early. The Kansas-Nebraska bill established two Territories, and made the dividing line the fortieth parallel of latitude. The pro-slavery people said, it was the understanding, though not expressed in the bill, that north of the line was to be made a free State and south of the line a slave State. Whether there was any such understanding or not, I was assigned the duty by Mr. Pierce's administration of running the line: of marking the boundary line between Kansas and Nebraska. I came out in the fall of 1854 and ran the line, and I became a permanent resident of Kansas. However much I may have been a Pierce Democrat to begin with, I was always a free state man, and put in my vote with those who helped to keep slavery from Kansas.

ADDRESS BY JAMES HANWAY.

Gov. ROBINSON: I will introduce to you an Old Settler who has not only helped to make some of the history of Kansas, but has contributed not a little to its written records: Hon. James Hanway of Lane.

Judge Hanway said:

Mr. President, Ladies and Gentlemen:

I was not here when the vote was taken, as to those present who cast their ballots for Hale and Julian in 1852, of which I am told there were fifty-six in number. I wish to add one more to the number and to say, that I not only voted that ticket but I was also a delegate to the convention at Pittsburg, which nominated the candidates.

I will add a remark concerning the picture which is known as "John Brown's Cabin," taken in the year 1871, by Barker, photographic artist of Ottawa, Kansas.

As every little incident connected with the history of John

Brown, the hero of Harper's Ferry, when on his mission work in Kansas, during the troubles which took place during the early settlement of the Territory, is regarded with especial interest, I will extend my remarks and relate how the picture came into existence, and to correct a slight error which has by some means been transmitted with the circulation of the picture. I have been informed that one thousand of these photographs were sent to the Centennial for sale or distribution; it is therefore proper that the public should know the exact facts concerning the accuracy of the remarks printed on the back of the photograph.

When the Hon. C. C. Hutchinson was writing his book entitled "Resources of Kansas," he wrote a letter to me making certain inquiries concerning John Brown's visit to my residence, and to relate other personal recollections of the old hero. In the meantime he engaged Mr. Barker, of Ottawa, to take the picture of the old log cabin. On a very windy day Mr. Barker made his appearance and I rendered to him what little assistance I was able. The "Resources of Kansas" was published, and a picture named "John Brown's Cabin" appeared on page twenty of the book. Then followed the comments:

"The above cut is from a photograph taken for this book by Barker, photographic artist of Ottawa, Kansas, who has copies for sale. It is a view of the only building now standing in which John Brown, the abolitionist, ever lived in Kansas. No less than six of those who fell at Harper's Ferry upon the occasion of Brown's raid into Virginia, had eaten and slept in this cabin. The figure with the uncovered head is the venerable James Hanway, and the other Mr. Wasson, who were neighbors, companions and friends of Capt. Brown. The former at one time lived in the cabin, when it was that old Mr. Brown wrote his famous parallels under the roof. (See Redpath's Life of Brown, page 218.) Through the doorway and against the open space made by the fall of the huge old-fashioned chimney, may be seen the ends of ox-bows suspended to-day.

"These tell the story of the 'piping times of peace' which have come since the day that John Brown threw himself into the jaws of death to rescue an oppressed people. The cabin, now rapidly falling into decay, stands in Franklin county, about one mile from Lane post-office."

The paragraph which I take exception to is the one which says: "It is a view of the only building now standing in which John Brown ever lived in Kansas."

This conveys the impression that Brown made this cabin his residence when in Kansas. This is incorrect, for there were other cabins in which the old gentleman tarried when on trips from place to place. On North Middle Creek, on the farm of Mr. Day—eight miles southeast of Ottawa—John Brown caused to be erected a cabin for the purpose of pre-empting the claim for his brother-in-law, Mr. Day, the father of the present occupant of the farm, but I never learned that he ever lived on it; for after the month of May, 1856, he was never stationary, but all the time on the war-path, until he left Kansas for a season.

After the Pottawatomie tragedy occurred, the John Brown Jr. cabin, with a valuable library, were burned down by the ruffians. This cabin was located a short distance south of the Day cabin.

The other sons of John Brown had claims about one-and-a-half miles south—now known as Brown's Run.

As soon as the negative was obtained, Mr. Barker struck off a large number of pictures—"John Brown's Cabin." I wrote a note to him to inquire why he had the words "John Brown's Cabin" printed on the picture, thinking it might mislead those not acquainted with the facts of the case.

He said it occurred thus: When the printer undertook the job to print what is now found on the back of the picture, he asked Mr. Barker, the artist, what name it should be known by. Mr. B. had not thought about this part of the subject. The printer, therefore, suggested the name of "John Brown's Cabin," and Barker consented. So much for the name.

The cabin, the picture of which has been so extensively circulated in all parts of the country, has, however, many interesting reminiscences connected with its history which may be referred to in a very few words:

In the Spring of 1856, I secured a young man to hold the quarter section for my son—John S. H., till my family moved to Kansas, the following Spring—in 1857. He took possession of it and pre-empted it, the same year, my family living in the cabin till the year 1859, then removed to my present residence on the high prairie.

The cabin was what was termed a pre-emption cabin, and John Brown had nothing to do with the building of it, or made it his special home. He was always a welcome visitor.

There are other reminiscences connected with the old cabin, which may be of some interest to the general reader.

Colonel James Montgomery, when pressed by the pro slavery officials of Linn county, always found a safe retreat from his border-ruffian enemies. Others of the jayhawkers, as they were called, frequently found an asylum here during the border troubles. Kagi, Jerry Anderson and others, who cast their lots with the old hero, and who fell at the Harper's Ferry raid were frequent visitors. Other Kansas heroes have entered its portals, such men as Stewart, the fighting preacher; Maj. J. B. Abbott, who afterward became better known as one of the rescuers of Dr. Doy from a Missouri prison, confined on a charge of running off fugitive slaves. Dr. J. H. Gillpatrick, and the self-constituted court to arbitrate the conflicting pre-emption claims of Linn county started from this cabin to organize themselves into "Squatters' Court of Claims" which resulted in producing a beneficial effect in harmonizing the conflicting parties, free-State and pro-slavery.

An incident illustrative of life in Kansas in those troubled days, may properly be introduced while we are speaking of the old Log Cabin:

One morning about nine o'clock, ten or a dozen persons were seen making their way at a lively gait in the direction of the old cabin. Every man was ornamented with a couple of navy revolvers, and in addition a Sharp's rifle was hanging from his side. Occasionally might be seen a large bowie knife or an "Arkansas toothpick," as they were sometimes called; the boots forming the scabbard, the handle of the frightful weapon stuck out a few inches above the tops which were generally of red leather. Their long shaggy beards, their long military buckskin gloves and their general appearance produced a momentay feeling of surprise. They rode up before the cabin door and halted, one of the party, the late Dr. Gillpatrick inquired if breakfast could be obtained for ten, they were in a hurry, and had many miles to travel before sun-down. When an affirmative answer was given, they dismounted, each man leading his horse to the shed to be fed.

My wife (which by the bye was very natural) began to ask some leading questions. Dr. Gillpatrick who had been intimately acquainted with the family for many years replied, "No questions must be asked," the request was obeyed, but every member of the family wondered the more "what does all this mean." A hasty breakfast was prepared and the party sat down to the table. From the back of each chair the navy revolvers were suspended by a belt. My wife laying her hand on the revolvers on the chair occupied by the "fighting preacher," Stewart remarked :

"We are told in Scripture to entertain strangers, for thereby we may entertain angels unawares, but I would not suppose angels would carry with them such instruments of destruction as these." The "fighting preacher" dropped his knife and fork, and turning half round in his chair, remarked : "Madam, if they traveled in Kansas, they would soon find it was necessary."

This breakfast party was the "squatters' court," organized to arbitrate the contested claims of Linn and Bourbon counties. One word concerning the "famous parallels," written by old John Brown, after he had rescued eleven slaves and brought them to Kansas. Mr. Hutchinson, in his "Resources of Kansas," says, these "Parallels" were written in this famed old cabin. I expect I am responsible for this remark, for I so reported to Mr. H. at the time he was collecting materials for his book. The "Parallels" were dated from the Trading Post; this was very proper that they should be. A few days after, John Brown, Kagi, and Jerry Anderson spent several days with us, prior to the removal of the eleven rescued slaves—the latter had been kept within a few miles of the cabin for nearly a month, and cared for by a few friends of the slaves. One morning the old captain read over the "Parallels," and asked my opinion respecting the publication of the paper, etc. He said he was going to send a copy to the New York *Tribune* and another copy to the Lawrence *Republican*. Kagi that morning started for Osawatomie, and it was my impression that he took with him the two articles and placed them in the post-office.

Soon after Mr. Hutchinson's book was published, I was informed that this fact was called in question, stating that they were written at the Trading Post. The article referred to I never read; of course I know not what were the points in question. The circumstance is not very important, whether they were written at the Trading Post, or "under the roof of the old cabin." One fact I can speak with confidence, that John Brown read the "Parallels" to me before they appeared in print.

Another incident I have forgotten to relate in the proper place: It was in this cabin that the Pottawatomie rifle company under Capt. John Brown Jr., stacked their arms when they paid a friendly visit to Judge Cato's court, in April, 1856. The free state settlers were anxious to learn what position Judge Cato would take in his charge to the grand jury, concerning the celebrated "Bogus-laws" of the Shawnee Mission. This visit of our citizens was construed by the court as a demonstration unfavorable to the execution of the Bogus laws. Before daylight the next morning, Cato and his pro-slavery officials had left—they were on their way to Lecompton, and the grand jury was dismissed from further labor. This was the first and the last time that this section of the country was visited by pro-slavery officials.

A few years after the photograph was taken, the logs of the old log cabin became rotten and unsafe for even stock to shelter under. It was pulled down and cut up for fire-wood. A few stones of the chimney remain scattered on the ground; and this is all that remains of the memorable old cabin. The spring still flows as in former days. Most all of the old residents have died or moved away. In a few years more the reminiscences connected with the cabin and the old military parade-ground will have passed away, and no one will remain to tell of the early scenes of pioneer life on the banks of the Pottawatomie.

The wife of old John Brown was never in Kansas to my knowledge. He had a daughter married to Thompson, and one or more of his sons had brought their wives with them. They left soon after the Pottawatomie tragedy took place.

ADDRESS BY JAMES S. EMERY.

Gov. ROBINSON:—I take pleasure in introducing to you one of the earliest and most faithful of the pioneers of Kansas—one who has taken a lively interest in getting up this celebration, and to whom the success of the gathering is largely due, Hon. James S. Emery, of Lawrence.

Judge Emery said:

Fellow-Citizens:

We look backward to-day. We looked forward twenty-five years ago. When we began the work of founding a State in the new Territory of Kansas we had high hopes and large expectations. In the entire realization of all these hopes and in the complete fulfillment of these expectations, we come up from all parts of our young Commonwealth to celebrate, with fitting ceremonies, what the orator of yesterday so happily termed "the silver wedding of the Republic of Kansas." It will be for others—our children—when many of us now here shall have found out the great secret of this life, to celebrate the golden wedding of what shall then be an empire of human souls. We are deeply interested in the impartial verdict, which history shall put upon record. We have lived largely in the public eye whilst that record has been making. Our privileges have been great, our opportunities have been vast, our post, these past years, though one at times of danger has been high and honorable. The world has expected much of us. How much we have achieved for the good of mankind the muse of history, years hence, alone shall say. But let us not glorify ourselves to-day. If we have wrought well, it has been because our times happen to have fallen upon a period of grand opportunity—of storm, of unrest, of change, of a revolution in the two kinds of civilization that once took root upon the Western Continent—the one at Jamestown, the other at Plymouth Rock. But standing here beneath a September sun, at the closing up of almost a generation of human life led upon these prairies, with plenty on the earth and splendor in the heavens, in the presence of this vast assemblage, I think I may affirm of Kansas' history what Mr. Webster, in high debate, once affirmed of Massachusetts' history. He said, "The world knows it by heart; there let it stand." He further said, "The bones of her sons fallen in the Revolution lie mingled with the soil of every State from Maine to Georgia." So I say of Kansas' history. The world knows it by heart; there let it stand—the bones of her sons fallen in the Rebellion, beginning at Wilson's Creek, lie mingled with the soil of every Confederate State. Hence I come to offer no apology for that history—it needs none. It began to be made when slavery dominated in every department of the government—it ended when freedom was firmly intrenched in the free soul of a strong young State.

I have said our times fell in a period of storms, and I think I may say that from the hour the first settlers crossed the Missouri State line in 1854, up to the climax in this war of civilizations, eleven years later, at Appomattox, Kansas was but one vast military camp. We began here at the time when Mr. Greeley wrote these ominous words: "It is all blackness, without a single gleam of light, a desert without a single spot of verdure; a crime that can show no redeeming spot." We began here at the time of the real opening of the Rebellion. As the eloquent orator so well said two years ago, in your hearing, on the very spot where we now stand: "While others go to Charleston to see where the first gun of the Rebellion was fired against Sumter, I come to Kansas to see where the first gun of the Rebellion was fired, on the 30th of March, 1855, against the ballot box."

Upon our record, begun under such untoward circumstances and ending in the full tide of prosperity and glorious promise, the contemporaneous judgment of our country has been most lenient and most flattering. Mr. Seward, the foremost statesman in the anti-slavery conflict, said of us on our streets in 1860: "Henceforth if my confidence in the stability of the American Union wavers, I shall come up here to learn that the Union is stronger than human ambition, because it is founded in the affections of the American people. If ever I shall waver in my affection for freedom, I shall come up here and renew it; here, under the inspiration of one hundred thousand free men saved from slavery. Henceforth these shall not be my sentiments alone, but the sentiments of all. Men will come up to Kansas as they go up to Jerusalem." And now the Quaker poet of America, in the fullness of his years, and whose failing health and strength only have prevented his presence here to day, sends greeting these golden words: "No one of all your sister States has such a record as yours—so full of pride and adventure, fortitude, self sacrifice. Its baptism of martyrs' blood not only saved the State to liberty, but made the abolition of slavery everywhere possible." That opinion alone, connected with the immortality of Whittier's genius, settles forever the question which lifted itself directly in the path of every free state settler, a quarter of a century ago, as he first stepped upon the virgin soil of this infant Territory, what shall the verdict be? Fifty years hence, in the clearer sunlight of the coming age, the historian will search out such opinions as these—these of the statesman and poet—as his supreme authority, in indicting the world's judgment upon our acts, and here, I ask, may we not rest our case?

At this glad yet solemn hour we have with us distinguished friends who have journeyed half-way across the continent to enter into our rejoicings. You come strangers to our section, but your names are household words around every hearthstone in every Old Settler's cabin in Kansas. We have made the record to which I alluded because you and others like you have stood by us and fought our battles with us before the American people. All along the weary and dusty way, the Old Settlers have turned their eyes backward toward the older States for hope and encouragement. The two Hales, the Sumners, the Thayers and the poets of New England, Seward and Greeley, of the Empire State, Forney of the Keystone, Chase and Giddings, of Ohio, and Julian, of Indiana—these men and others have been our pillar of fire by night and our cloud by day. Kansas never could have emerged from the wilderness with songs of deliverance upon our lips, but for their leadings.

This fact alone, it seems to me, constitutes your glory and our own exceeding great reward.

Before presenting the distinguished orator of to-day, allow me to call for the Marseillaise hymn of America, "Old John Brown."

ADDRESS DR REV. EDWARD EVERETT HALE.

After the hymn, Mr. Emery, taking Rev. E. E. Hale by the
hand, said : It is a great joy, Mr. Hale, now for me, to present
you to the largest assembly that ever convened within the limits of
our young State.

New England sends her greeting to Kansas to-day. You are
proud of your own State. New England is as proud of you as you
are of yourselves. You rejoice in your matchless prosperity. New
England rejoices with you. You try hard, but you cannot try hard
enough, to forecast the future which is before you. There are
those in New England who paint as brilliant pictures as the boldest
of you can do of your achievements that are to be. As the news
of your congratulations of yesterday flashes up the Connecticut
valley, and across the Merrimac, and down to the farthest township on the Aroostook, there are thousands of fathers, and mothers,
and brothers, and sisters, who read, even as I am speaking, the
words of your pride and enthusiasm. They rejoice with your joy.
They recall your memories of blood and of sorrow. They pray
with your prayers, and they hope with your hopes.

New England has been indebted to Kansas for one great deliverance, and that, I may say, came before Kansas herself was
born. The Kansas-Nebraska bill, and the men who made it—and
I was glad to hear yesterday that among the bad men who made it
there were some very good men—the Kansas-Nebraska bill cut for
the men of conscience in New England the cruelest bonds that ever
tied their hands. It was somewhat as my friend Mr. Forney found
himself—free to do what he chose, and to lead Pennsylvania at
his will, after James Buchanan had gone back on him ! It has
been the distinction of New England from the beginning—from the
time of Pym. and Eliot, and Hampden, and Cromwell and Winthrop—that she has always mixed up in her politics a great deal of
conscience. People who do not understand her are apt to ridicule
her new parties as "conscience parties," as they ridiculed them
once as "Puritan parties." All the same, that is her way. In such
a community, men of conscience, which is to say men of honor,
felt terribly the entanglements which, in the process of time and
the developments of this nation, were woven about them by the
compromises of the Constitution, and of 1820. But with the courage of conscience, a very large majority of the best men of New
England held their allegiance to the unpopular and even cruel legislation which had followed on those compromises, because they
or their fathers had given a pledge and that pledge had not been
withdrawn. The South held them to the compact; it held them
to it with a cruel hand and insulting tyranny. The Abolitionist
party winced under this insult, so as to accept the alternative which
the Calhouns and Jefferson Davises wished for. The Abolitionist party was willing to condemn the Union as heartily as even Calhoun, or

Davis or the Kentucky resolutions of old times condemned it. It was willing at any moment to cut the tie, and let the slave States go with their horrid odium; let them sink to the deepest bottom where God might choose in the ocean of disunion. But, to the great body of New Englanders of either political party, this seemed as unmanly as it seemed unwise. They did not think they escaped the responsibility of this leprosy by sending the leper into the des· ert shrieking, "Unclean, unclean." They had taken the benefit of the union and of the compromises. They did not see that they had a right, when the other side was presented, to repudiate the contract because it came hardly. "Repudiate" was no word of their invention nor of their politics. It belonged to another state and another social order.

LAW AND LIBERTY.—Those are the mottoes of New England.

"O Law! fair form of Liberty! God's light is on thy brow;
O Liberty! thou soul of Law, God's very self art thou.
One the clear river's sparkling flood that clothes the bank with green,
And one the line of stubborn rock that holds the waters in;
Friends whom we cannot think apart seeming each other's foe;
Twin flowers upon a single stalk with equal grace that grow.
O fair ideas! we write your names across our banner's fold;
For you the sluggard's brain is fire; for you the coward bold.
O daughter of the bleeding past; O hope the Prophets saw;
God give us law in liberty, and liberty in law!"

The New Englander does not know and cannot tell to which of the two his fanatic allegiance is more close. And when the two seem to be parted, when he must choose between one and the other, then comes the tragedy of his history.

Such a crisis had come in 1854 and in 1855.

The old Whigs of New England and the old Democrats of New England hated slavery as thoroughly as you do; but their hands had been tied, till on one blessed morning of emancipation, the passage of the Kansas Nebraska bill set them free. That reason have they and their sons for being grateful to Kansas, even before she was born!

In fact, the announcement that a cool proposal was made to open Kansas to slavery waked the whole conservative North to union. Men had had a theory, till then, that the Southern statesmen were men of honor. They supposed that at least they would hold to their word. And now and here was the announcement, that the promise of thirty-three years, confirmed by "no end" of enactments, was to be falsified. Men who had fought against the Missouri compromise to the last, had all the same assented to it after it had passed. Missouri had been admitted under it, and Arkansas and Florida; and now they were told that, because the time had come when the other side of the bargain was to be enforced, now it was torn to tatters. The honor of the South, so blurted on every breeze. proved to be a mere name. The solid South had no hesitation in saying that, in holding the nation to the

compromise, it had meant nothing.   It had driven a harder bargain
than ever a Connecticut peddler made ; but the moment it had its
pay it meant to break the bargain without even giving one nutmeg.
In that proclamation of her shame, the South released all her
Northern allies, in all parties.   As Mr Forney has told you, even
when the Southern congressmen voted for "Squatter Sovereignty,"
they voted merely in a fashion of speech for a gilded generality.
In such double-tongued breach of faith, the solid North was set
free.   Who can keep faith with liars ?

The announcement released for action on the side of freedom
two sets of men, who had till now been held back, enraged at their
own inaction.   There were the older men of both political parties
—silver-gray men—who had held themselves bound in honor to
maintain the compromises.   There was the young generation
which had never voted for the Missouri compromise nor in any way
assented to it, which, all the same, had been chafing under the lash
both of anti-slavery orators and of Southern slave-masters, as they
ridiculed the Northern dough-faces.   Such young men had seen no
field for action.   The abolitionists simply proposed a dissolution of
the Union.   This was, at bottom, but a confession of defeat.   Of
what use to the slave to take a desperate measure like that in the
hope of avoiding responsibility ?   They thought that this was but
a very unsatisfactory proposal.   And to go to anti-slavery fairs, to
sustain anti-slavery journals, to sign anti-slavery petitions, to work
the under-ground railroad, seemed to young America but a very
milk-and-water business, even though the orators proclaimed dissolution, and begged men to avoid complicity with slavery.   Hundreds of thousands of such young men were chafing with indignation ; not suppressed, because there was no field for the issue.

At last the bell struck for both these sets of handcuffed men.
The South, by a mysterious madness, repudiated the Missouri
compromise.   A fair field was given young America for the battle,
and on the instant young America picked up the glove.

Whoever thought that those fatal provisions were "glittering
generalities," which gave to the first settlers here the right to establish forever your fundamental institutions, soon woke to a sense of
his folly.   Indeed, any man who, in his study of history or in his
forecast of history, keeps out of sight the processes of emigration,
shows that he knows very little of the philosophy of history.
Why, there have been men, and wise men, who have thought and
argued that no tribe or nation ever made any substantial advance
without this divine help of the advent of a superior race !   So the
Peruvians were uplifted by the Incas; so the Gauls were civilized
by the conquering Romans.   And, though one may not make that
extreme statement, it is safe to say that the very courage, patience,
endurance, enterprise and restlessness which go to the make-up of
an emigrant, are qualities which, of themselves, by a law of
natural selection,   "winnow out the best wheat" from the harvest
of old lands for the planting of new.   If any man doubt this, let

him study the blessing which Hengist and Horsa brought to England in that Anglo-Saxon emigration of tribes whose names we retain so proudly to this day Let him study the awakening by which Anglo-Saxon England in its turn was blessed by the invasion of the Normans. Let him study the new life which Italy received in the emigration of the Lombards. Nay, let him study the results which came to Spain in the invasion even of conquering Visigoths. And with us this Genius of Emigration, who had been chafing in the prison whose door the Solomons of another generation had sealed, who was now set free by the fated folly of Jefferson Davis and those other fishermen of the South who were throwing their nets and dragging here and there—he was no bottle-imp to be fooled with by a conjuror—he was, he is and he will be, one of the great elemental powers which move forward the civilization of the world.

The "glittering generalities" of the Kansas-Nebraska bill said: "The first settlers shall settle its institutions forever." What more could our neighbors here in Missouri ask? Jefferson Davis supposed, and Mr. Atchison supposed, that our friends here in Independence, Platte City and Westport would step over the boundary between night and morning, and in an hour stamp slavery on your soil forever. When that was once done, they knew that no freeman would ever come upon land thus cursed. Witness South Carolina, witness Arkansas, witness Mr. Davis' own Mississippi. What freeman had ever migrated to such "sacred soil?" Such was the hope and plan of squatter sovereignty.

But alas for the plan! The free North took up the words, and made of them no "glittering generality," but a terrible reality.

"The first settlers shall decide this question? Very well, we will be of the first settlers."

It is in such words that young America answered the great challenge—when, as I said, young America picked up the glove.

All that was needed was some form of organization, enough to show all adventurers that they were not alone. Here was the great Northwest, full of young men and women who had drunk in freedom with their first breath. They had grown up under the ægis of Nathan Dane's ordinance, the freedom ordinance of 1787, whose language has been copied in every free-ordinance from that day to this day. They were used to the prairie, used to the open air, used to campaigning, used to be free. They had been held in the leash by their allegiance to law. The ordinance of squatter sovereignty was no gilded generality to them. It released them, and they sprang into the field at the call of Liberty. Thousands upon thousands of such men were ready to go down the Mississippi, to go up the Missouri, to make their homes here—our friend Sam Wood has told you how—the moment the prairie was open to them.

And for what did they come? For liberty of religion? They had that at home. For bright jewels of the mines? Thank God,

they have never found them in Kansas.   For virgin soil or homestead farms?   They could have those in Iowa, in Minnesota, or in
Nebraska; and that without a struggle.   If all they wanted was
freedom, freedom for themselves and freedom for their children,
those were to be had for asking, without the flash of one shot-gun,
without the crack of one rifle.   But these men wanted more.
They wanted more and they won more.   It was for other men's
children that they looked forward.   It was for the future of the
whole country that they looked forward.   That the advance of
slavery should at last be arrested, which had been as steady as it
had been stealthy since Eli Whitney invented the cotton-gin.
These settlers from the Northwest meant to establish that barrier,
and to establish it forever—a barrier against which the surf tide of
slavery should break, and dissolve like the invisible spray which
plays over the porphyry headlands of New England.   " Thus far
shalt thou come and no farther, and here shalt thy proud waves
be stayed."

It is this utter unselfishness, this fanaticism, if you please—I
like the word—of the Northern movements, when the Northern
mind is possessed with an idea, that the Southern leaders never
could comprehend and for which they never provided.   They do
not comprehend it to-day, and that is the reason why they do not
provide for it to-day.   Mr. Jefferson never comprehended its
grandeur nor its terror.   In the only conversation I ever had with
Mr. Calhoun, he occupied the whole time in describing this divine
frenzy for an idea, as it existed in Cromwell's Puritans.   But it
was clear to me, even then, that he had no conception of its
pent-up wrath, all ready to burst upon him and his, when the rolling wheel should strike the stroke, and the descendants of the
Puritans, in the grand fanaticism of the nineteenth century, should
be set free.   Jefferson Davis and his crew did not suspect it, when
in the glee of triumph they gave a joyful assent, as Mr. Forney
told you, to what they thought these glittering generalities of
squatter sovereignty in the Nebraska Act.   No more did General
Beauregard suspect it when he fired the fatal shot against Sumter.
With that shot began the ceaseless march of hordes upon hordes of
Northern freemen, the descendants of Cromwell and Hampden,
and the men who charged at Naseby and Marston Moor, who
would march and bleed and die and conquer, till · the meanest
slave in the whole land was free.   And no statesman, Northern or
Southern, will ever rightly lead this country, or rightly apprehend
its forces, who does not understand the devotion of the North,
when it is roused in one of its divine frenzies to an idea.

Now I am proud of my own Puritan blood.   I am glad that I
descend from a regicide.   I am glad that my children descend from
the pilgrims of Plymouth Rock.   I am glad that my ancestors came
over to the bay with Winthrop and with Dudley.   That Puritan
emigration was a noble emigration for conscience' sake.   But, all
the same, let me say, and that not for the first time, that the next

great emigration for conscience' sake contained one additional element of moral grandeur. In 1620, those Englishmen from whom you are born left their homes in England to make other homes in New England according to the divine pattern, as they thought God had given it to men. A noble desire indeed, and kindly has God answered it. But in the next emigration for conscience' sake, which came after two hundred and twenty-five years, came when the freemen of Ohio and Indiana, Illinois and Iowa, and Michigan, the freemen of the great Middle States, and the freemen of poor, cold, storm-beat New England, marched and rode, and sailed, and fought, up rivers, over prairies, through friend or through foe, that they might plant Kansas, there was one other element of nobility which that first emigration did not know. The Puritans sought to make a State for themselves and their children. You sought to save a State which you saw endangered, to save it forever for God and for mankind.

In this movement there was only one point of weakness. It is to this hour the weakness of all emigration. It is the danger that comes to the lonely emigrant. "It is not good for man to be alone." It would certainly happen that the Atchison people would put our friend Mr. Butler into the river. It would certainly happen that Barber would be murdered in the wilderness. It would be easy to pick off one here and one there. The great Northern movement must have the strength and magic of the great Christian word "together." There must be some organization, though it were the simplest, to give unity to the Northern movement. The lack of such unity would be certain failure, and here it was that the boding prophets prophesied failure. For the slave-holding interest was a unit, from the nature of the case, and acted as a unit without even meaning it or intending it. It was organized already. The institution it was pledged to, compelled its unity of action.

It was at this point that Eli Thayer's work, in organizing the simple, abused, misunderstood Emigrant Aid Company, has an exquisite interest, as it proved it had an infinite value. As Gov. Robinson told you, before the fatal bill passed Congress, Eli Thayer had his charters from Massachusetts and Connecticut. Before the bill passed Congress, Gov. Robinson and Mr. Branscomb were here, in the work of the Company, looking up sites for settlements. Before the year was ended, nearly five hundred emigrants from New England sent forward by this Company were here. They were not one-tenth of the emigration of that year. But what was important was that they were in compact settlement. They were in towns.

Now towns, gentlemen and ladies, towns and cities have always been the fortresses of freedom. It was so in the crisis of Kansas.

I need not remind you of what Mr. Wood said so well yesterday. Why did not the ruffians wipe out his little cottage, and leave him and his dead in the doorway? Because they must first handle Lawrence. What struck the real terror into marauding companies, till they found marauding a bad business? It is, as he told you, "the Stubbs" that are worth more than twenty "resolutions," and the "Stubbs" always form themselves in the intimacies · and confidences of men together. Man is a gregarious animal. We separate, and we are broken, as Æsop said, like the stalk of a dead sun flower. They tie us in faggots, and there is no heat so hot as the blaze of the burning!

Let me, then, in a few words describe the methods of the work of the Emigrant Aid Company. I have often heard it described, but almost always it was misrepresented.

In the first place, it never hired a man to go to Kansas, or offered any inducement under heaven to tempt him to go, if he did not mean to. All that stuff of the time about shipping paupers to Kansas was so much clear falsehood. Good heavens, we had no need! The whole of the East and North and Northwest was on the alert. Men and women were wild to go. We never paid any man's passage. We never gave a cent toward any man's passage; not so much as a paper of popped corn to feed him on the way. If he went, he bought his own ticket; and when he came, he selected his own home. Only we kept our traveling agents coming and going; we sent one of them with every party of settlers. These parties were apt to hold together, and from such parties grew such towns as Lawrence, Topeka, Manhattan, Osawatomie and more. All we had to do with the settlers was to induce them to keep together. *Together* ought to be the motto of Kansas.

But the Company had other business as pressing. Mr. Mill or Mr. Spencer would tell you that these new communities must go forward only with such assistance as only the instincts of capital will supply. But I can tell you, my friends, that capital is very shy about sending steam engines and saw-mills and grist-mills and printing presses into regions which are the scenes of warfare, and where people who carry them are unpopular. It was the business of our Company to step in and do what timid capital was afraid to do. So soon as a settlement was made in Lawrence, it was our business to put a saw-mill here, and I dare say many a man who had never heard of the Emigrant Aid Company when he left Ohio was glad to have his logs sawed by the Emigrant Aid Company's saws. We used to head our appeals for money in New England with the words, "Saw-mills and Liberty." Where there was a saw-mill, there would be a town, we said. Where there was a town there would be a company of "Stubbs," and, when you had companies enough, you were sure of liberty.

So when our friend Mr. George Brown came to us, and told us of his grand enterprise of the *Herald of Freedom*, we were glad to risk $2,000 with him in that operation. And when his type was thrown into the Kansas river here, we were not sorry to hear that it had been fished out to be cast into cannon balls to fit the old Sacramento twelve-pounder.

But perhaps the machinery that will interest this audience now was more portable machinery.

In the spring of 1855, my friend Mr. Deitzler came on in haste to New England, to say that fighting was certain, and that you must have more weapons. The breech-loading rifle was then a new and costly arm. It was then that we gave to Sharpe's Rifle Company, of Hartford, the first of a series of orders which became historical. In the next year, Henry Ward Beecher won the nickname which he has never lost, "Sharpe's Rifle Beecher;" and I fancy there is no nickname of which he is more proud. With your permission, I will read the answer of the company to that order, and then I will ask our friend Mr. Adams to accept that letter as an historical document for his society:

Sharpe's Rifle Manufacturing Co., }
Hartford, May 7, 1855. }

Thos. H. Webb, Esq.:

Dear Sir: Annexed, find invoice of one hundred carbines, ammunition, etc., delivered Mr. Deitzler this morning. For balance of account, I have ordered on Messrs. Lee, Higginson & Co., at thirty days from this date for $2,155.65, as directed by you.

We shall be pleased to receive further orders from you, and will put up arms at our lowest cash prices to the trade, with interest added for time. The sample carbine for your use shall go forward immediately.

Our negotiations with you, I trust will be entirely confidential, as the trade in Boston and elsewhere might take offense if they understood we had made you better terms than we grant to others.

Your obedient servant, J. C. Palmer, Pres.

You know the history of that invoice, and of the invoices which followed. You can tell where our mountain howitzer is to-day, and I can tell you where it came from. But I must not dwell on such memories. It was our happy fortune to send to Kansas, in her infancy, the bells which should proclaim liberty to the land, the clocks which should tell the time from the towers of her churches, the books which children should study in her schools, the Bibles which men should read from her pulpits, and the precious chalice with which, at the Lord's table, men and women should unite in the cup of fellowship and communion. Selfish capital, eager for a reward, ought to have supplied these things, according to the theorists. But selfish capital did not do any such thing. These necessities of life were sent to Kansas, not by the meanness of greed, but by the voluntary contributions of men and women who were willing to sacrifice everything for an idea. These belong to the sleepless "fanaticism" of New England.

I am bound in mere gratitude to Dr. Stringfellow and Mr. Atchison, and our friends at Westport and Independence, and in all the border counties of Missouri, to say that they did everything they could to help us in our work in New England. My part of that work was lecturing up and down the country, and feeding the

New England press with its Kansas news.   And never had a public speaker better backers than I had, in your well-meaning friends,
the border ruffians.   In my first year, 1854, we collected and expended in Kansas about thirteen thousand dollars.   Our friends in
Missouri were kind enough to multiply this little sum by four or
five hundred, and they proclaimed to the world that we were
spending five million dollars in the Territory.   If, in any part of
America, there were of those people whom Col. Legate described
with so much humor last night, who wanted to "better their condition," they were attracted by this announcement.   It is possible that even now, in this moral and high-toned community, you
have heard of men who, if they knew that five million dollars were
to be spent at Topeka, would like to be present at the spending.
I am speaking, I dare say, to those who wept for Barber's death,
and R. P. Brown's and Dow's.   But for every drop of those men's
blood, some brave man left the North, determined to avenge him.
It is by one of these dramatic coincidences which make men think
that the eternal Nemesis acts with human fashions and with
the laws of time, that it happened that while the embers of
the Free State Hotel were yet smoking, on that sad day when
Senator Atchison was riding with his company, pensive or triumphant, through Massachusetts street, here—Preston Brooks
struck Charles Sumner from behind in his seat in the Senate.   Before New England heard of your insult here, she knew that her
own son had been wounded nigh to death by a man with the spirit
of a murderer.   The two typical blows were struck which are
needed to awaken and confirm indignation.   The two deeds were
in fact the same.   They sprang from one spirit.   They aroused
one wave of indignation.   They appealed to the same rule of righteousness, the "power which works for good" and sways the destiny of nations, and they brought with them the same vengeance.
     But I speak too long.   New England has long since rejoiced
in the flow of the great Northwestern wave over these beautiful
prairies.   To that wave she contributed four or five thousand of
her sons and daughters in the very years of battle.   She never has
been ashamed of them or their record.   The Emigrant Aid Company, which I represent here, placed $125,000 in this Territory.
No subscriber to that fund ever received back one cent from the
investment.   But all the same we had our dividends long ago.
They came in Kansas free, a nation free, in the emancipation of
four millions of black men, and in the virtual abolition of slavery
over the world.
     The Company's operations afterward need not be described.
In Western Texas, we did what we could.   When the time came,
we directed a few thousand free men into Florida ; and when Florida
gave her righteous vote for a Republican President, that vote was
due to no vulgar fraud, but to the organized emigration into Florida
of Northern freemen ten years before.
     The past is secure, gentlemen and ladies; the future is in your
hands.   See that it be not unworthy of your history.

Gov. Robinson : — Ladies and gentlemen, I am glad to be able to announce to you that Mr. Forney will address the meeting a few moments.

Col. Forney said:

Ladies and Gentlemen :

I really feel as if I were an intruder to-day. My part of the drama was played yesterday, and yet I cannot refrain from expressing my satisfaction and wonder at the scene which I have witnessed to-day. A year ago, just a year ago, I saw what is regarded in France as the most interesting and original and instructive of all their religious festivals. The great *fete* of the St. Cloud or of the sun which lasted for seven days, and I was there every day. And I confess as I passed through this marvelous crowd this afternoon and witnessed the strange changes that have taken place here within the last twenty-five years, and saw the courteous manners, the happy faces, a singularly athletic population, marvelous display of horses and wagons, and all the evidences of honest industry ; and still more than all, the sobriety so marked, so decorous, so exemplary—I was filled with pride. It cast in the shade the habitual temperance of the French themselves. I am impelled to say, and I do say, that we have before us here, perhaps, the noblest offspring, and the noblest results of the great liberties which have been secured by the Pilgrim Fathers, whose distinguished representative you have just heard now. The results that have been achieved in these twenty-five years have been achieved by a sound sentiment promulgated by the original Abolitionists — the great primitive leaders of thought. These victorious and determined and daring men of whom you have heard so much just praise, were impelled to action as the result of that thought. Those of the class of which I claim to be a representative, came after the white slaves of the North were liberated by a movement which began with the Abolitionists of New England, a movement which culminated when the Kansas-Nebraska act was passed on the 30th of May, 1854. Those of us who came in afterward at the eleventh hour, were laggards, brought along by the sentiment due to others. But in the end we did something—contributing, sincerely contributing, to the great results you are celebrating to day. I thank you again and again, ladies and gentlemen, for the permission given me to speak here.

Gov. Robinson : — As our state has grown to such immense proportions, we have some here to-day that were not here yesterday, and some who have never seen our Chief Magistrate, and I therefore, take pleasure in introducing Gov. John P. St. John, who will speak to you a few moments.

Gov. St. John said:

Mr. President and Fellow Citizens :

This is certainly one of the pleasantest hours of my life. It is pleasant because I see so many bright and happy faces here. I am not here to say an unkind word of any one. In fact, I think that any man who would say anything to mar the pleasure that all seem to enjoy in being here, ought to seek a more congenial clime for grumblers than is found here in Kansas.

With no unkind feeling toward our neighboring State of Missouri or her citizens, whom we gladly welcome here to-day, but simply for the purpose of showing the difference between the growth of the government planted by you Old Settlers, here in Kansas, and the one planted by the old settlers of Missouri nearly sixty years ago, I call your attention to the fact that Missouri is three times as old as Kansas. No one will deny that Missouri's natural resources are equal to those of any State in the Union. She has splendid soil, just as good as is to be found anywhere, excepting, perhaps, in Kansas. But take out Kansas City, (which is supported and fed by Kansas), St. Louis, St. Joseph and Sedalia, and there is scarcely sufficient real, wide-awake, live, energetic spirit left in the remainder of the State to organize a town meeting. Missouri, financially, is depressed. Kansas is strong and prosperous. Missouri, socially, is *sour*, and looks with distrust and suspicion upon the immigrant seeking a home within her borders, while Kansas gladly welcomes every body willing to obey our laws and join us in building up our State and making it prosperous and great. In population Missouri is barely holding her own, while young Kansas increases at the rate of 150,000 a year. Of this number at least 100,000 cross Missouri to get here—hence cannot be ignorant of the fact that there really *is* such a State. The reason for all this is plain—Missouri was born of *slavery*—Kansas, of freedom. [Applause.]

In all this vast assemblage of at least 25,000 people you will not find a single specimen of the long-haired, broad-brim, big-spurred gentry of the brush, carrying a brace or more of revolvers; in fact, you will not see a revolver on the ground. Not a drunken man is to be found; there are no intoxicating liquors, no policemen or necessity for any here. Everybody is in a·good humor, ready to shake hands with his neighbor, without caring whether he is native or foreign born, Democrat or Republican, or whether, when admitted into the church, he was sprinkled or "plunged." He only recognizes the fact that he is one of God's creatures, and that it is true merit after all that makes the man.

When talking of Kansas, we cannot help but feel a little like a young American who was traveling in Europe. He was one of those fellows who think that no place on earth is equal to America. When he was shown the capitol of a foreign land he would say, "That is very nice, really magnificent, but you ought to see *our* capitol at Washington, if you would see something worthy of your highest admiration." When shown one of their largest rivers he would first compliment it, but close with the declaration that it was a mere spring branch when compared with the mighty Mississippi, the Father of Waters. So he continued until it became monotonous, and the boys concluded that they would see if they could not place him in some position where he would acknowledge his country beaten. With this end in view, they got him drunk, and laid him out in a coffin and placed him in the catacombs. Then they hid themselves away to await results. He seemed to sleep soundly through the night, but just after daylight he awoke, finding himself in a coffin. He did not know what it meant. He was bewildered and said, "Am I crazy, sick or drunk? Where am I, what am I and who am I?" At last, looking upward and seeing the many thousand human skulls peering down upon him from every direction, he exclaimed, "Ah, I understand it now. It is as clear to me as the noonday sun. This is the grand morning of the resurrection of the dead, and I, an American, am its first fruits. Hurrah for America." [Applause.] So, when this State, springing from a Territory organized by you nearly a quarter of a century ago, is compared with other States of the Union, the result is such as to make us feel like exclaiming, "Hurrah for Kansas." You Old Settlers laid the foundation Those who came after you have nobly helped to build upon it. May we all, remembering our duty to God and humanity, unite our efforts in making Kansas, in her moral and material resources, the pride and admiration of the civilized world. [Applause.]

LETTER FROM ELI THAYER.

Gov. Robinson: I have been spoken to two or three times for the letter of Eli Thayer that I supposed had been read this morning. It is very short. Now all I have to say at this moment about him is, that there never was a man found in the United States who would have done what he did, and if there had not been an Eli Thayer, or some such man, I believe to-day that Kansas and the country would have been filled with slaves. [The letter follows the speech of Col. Anthony elsewhere given.]

ADDRESS BY REV. DR. CORDLEY.

Gov. Robinson: We have with us this afternoon one who has been here so long that memory scarcely goes to the contrary, our old Congregational minister, Dr. Richard Cordley.

Dr. Cordley said:

Ladies and Gentlemen:

I have no speech to make, but the Governor insists on my saying a few words; and in that olden time of which we are speaking, we all obeyed the word of Governor Robinson as the law of the land. I thought it needless that I should speak, for I made my speech here in Lawrence years ago. My speech was eighteen years long, and was delivered from the pulpit of the Plymouth Church across the river, the pulpit which was graced and honored last Sabbath by the presence of our distinguished visitor, New England's honored son, the author of "'Ten Times One Is Ten," a sentiment fitly illustrated in the twenty-five years' history we commemorate to-day.

Then I hardly feel like intruding among the scarred heroes who have appeared on this platform.   I have no special tales to tell or special claim to make.   I am not from Pennsylvania, like so many who have spoken, and I never marched with the Douglas Democrats when they saved Kansas and the Union.   I am not from Ohio, like so many others, and so I never can have an office. I am simply from Michigan, a State which lays claim to no special service, and yet a State which never asked a favor and never shirked a duty.

I am not disposed, however, to concede these special claims, of localities, or classes, or persons.   It was not Pennsylvania, or Ohio, or New England that saved Kansas; it was not Douglas Democrats, or Radical Abolitionists, or black law recruits; it was the rising sentiment of freedom in the land, which saved Kansas. The whole grand army of freemen can claim a part in that conflict, and in that victory.

I can see unity, too, in another matter where others have expressed diversity.   The sentiment has been expressed here very often and very devoutly, that the deliverance of Kansas was not due to any human wisdom, but to the wise guidance of a good Providence.   But one friend from Atchison county, last night, insisted that there was no Providence in it, and that God had nothing to do with it, but it was all a part of that "progress of humanity" which is ever making toward better things.   Now I believe in the "progress of humanity" as heartily as any one.   But to me this progress is not a blind drift which comes, no one knows whence, and goes, no one knows where, and results in, no one knows what; but to me the "progress of humanity" is an intelligent thing, guided by divine wisdom and sustained by divine power.   Therefore, I believe this progress will be continuous, lifting mankind higher and higher, and that by and by the "Kingdom will come," when freedom shall be universal, and truth and righteousness shall reign among all men; when the dream of the poet shall be fulfilled when he sings: "Ever the right comes uppermost and ever is justice done."

ANNOUNCEMENT BY MR. P. B. GROAT.

Gov. Robinson :   I have got the chap here that I read you a dispatch from yesterday.   A man who has done more than any other man to make this gathering a success. He has just arrived from Indianapolis. I have got him by the hand and his name is Groat.

Mr. Groat said:

Ladies and Gentlemen:

I do not deserve these complimentary remarks. I simply came up here to make the announcement that special trains will leave here for Topeka, Leavenworth and Kansas City to-night, after the evening meeting, in addition to the regular trains this afternoon. That is all.

ADDRESS BY T. D. THACHER.

The Chairman next introduced Hon. T. D. Thacher, who said:

Mr. President:

It is a matter of regret that the state of Mr. Whitman's health precludes the possibility of his presence here to-day, and deprives us of the privilege of listening to the poem which we had hoped to hear from his own lips. He was present yesterday, but the fatigues of travel and the excitement of the occasion have precluded his presence to-day. Had he been here, I should perhaps have said in introducing him that I first met him in New York many years ago, when the Kansas struggle for liberty was still being waged, and his sympathies were all on our side. How could they have been otherwise? Despotism does not produce poets. It takes the love of liberty to produce either poems or poets. The whole history of Kansas has been one of the grandest and most magnificent of poems. I know of no incident in the life of John Brown so worthy of the genius of a painter or a poet as when he was being led to the scaffold he stooped down and kissed a little black child, and went on his way to death.

Much has been said here about who saved Kansas to freedom. In my judgment it was the work of no one man, but that of the masses of her people who loved liberty and hated slavery. It was their toils, their struggles, their sufferings, their unquenchable and unconquerable love of freedom which won for us and our children the fair heritage which we to-day enjoy.

ADDRESS BY DANIEL W. WILDER.

GOV. ROBINSON: There is one gentleman on the stand that I know you all want to hear. I want to introduce to you one of the most efficient workers, although not one of the earliest, we ever had in Kansas, the Hon. D. W. Wilder, of the St. Joseph *Herald.*

Mr. Wilder said:

Ladies and Gentlemen :

The State of Missouri seems to be fair game with you all here to-day. Your Governor has alluded to it in unpleasant terms, and nobody has a good word for the State of Tom Benton, Frank Blair, Gratz Brown, Franz Sigel and Carl Schurz. The border ruffians, in their own "devilish" way, precipitated the conflict, but the men I have named and thousands like them were the friends of free Kansas, although living in slave States. That was especially true of the German element in Missouri and all through the South.

When the national conflict followed the Kansas rebellion, Blair, and Brown, and Sigel led regiments to fight your battles as well as their own. Frank Blair's name goes into history with Nathaniel Lyon's, as the hero statesmen of 1861—the two men above all others who saved Missouri and Kansas to the Union. When history is written, the wretched ruffians who came here to bully, to steal and to kill, will cut no more figure than so many horse thieves and assassins, while the men of ideas, John Brown, Charles Robinson, Gen. Lyon and Frank Blair, will be found on one monument, built upon the solid earth of two States and uniting them in a perpetual Union of freedom, civilization and the arts of peace. You cannot leave the good Missourians out of a history in which their bad brothers were such noisy brawlers.

And when States, and men, and political parties, are claiming so much credit, for freeing Kansas and freeing America, I hear very little said here to-day of our old-fashioned Abolitionists, William Lloyd Garrison and Wendell Phillips. I tell you, gentlemen, that they were the fathers of us all. [Applause.] I thank Mr. Hale from the bottom of my heart, not only for the noble speech made here to-day but for the glorious life he has lived, but I cannot forget that Garrison, Phillips, Sumner and their reviled fellow-workers created the public sentiment that made free Kansas possible. They made Kansas, and no celebration of Kansas can be complete that does not have the name of Wm. Lloyd Garrison, inscribed all over it in letters of living light. [Applause.]

ADDRESS BY MRS. S. N. WOOD.

Gov. Robinson: Some of you no doubt remember the valuable services rendered by two ladies on a certain occasion in our early troubles. One of those ladies is present now, and I know you want to hear her. Her name is Mrs. S. N Wood.

Mrs. Wood said ·

It seems to me but a very short time and yet it is a good while. There has been a great deal done in the last twenty-five years since my husband came home and told me he was going to Kansas, and asked me if I wanted to go. I told him that if he went, that I wanted to go too. We took our wagon and started to Cincinnati. We had two little children, one a little baby and the other a couple of years old. We came from Cincinnati to St. Louis on an old steamer of some kind, and from there up the Missouri, and landed at Independence. We stayed there a little while and then came out into the Territory and made our home here. While we were at Independence a meeting was held at Westport, at which a resolution was passed declaring that they would hang, kill or drive out all Northern men who came to Kansas. We were very quietly warned of this just as we left Independence. Well, we came on, and met no great difficulty, and came to Kansas. But you have the history of all our troubles here, from the speakers who have preceded me. The times looked very dark sometimes. I think if I could have looked forward and have seen what was in the future for us, I should have shrunk from it, but we were enabled to meet the difficulties as they came along. We never lost our faith in the triumph of freedom, in the ultimate triumph of right. We have never become alienated from our home. Here we have lived and here we expect to stay. Kansas is dearer to us to-day than ever. Here we expect to remain and be buried.

ADDRESS BY JOEL K. GOODIN.

Gov. Robinson: I wish now to introduce to you a man who in our early days had a great deal to do with the running of the territorial government in one position or another. He will not take but a moment to show himself. I mean Hon. J. K. Goodin.

Mr. Goodin said:

Mr. President, Ladies and Gentlemen:

I am very glad to meet you. You remember last night when Jim Legate made his speech some one in the crowd called out "louder" and he told them to come a little nearer. I will speak as loud as I can and try to make you all hear me.

About four years ago I went back to Ohio where my father lived (and there's where my friend Wood came from), and I attended an Old Settlers' meeting, and they called upon me to make some remarks being an old settler through my father. I told them that I thought it enlarged a man to come west, that I thought I had grown a little taller—a little wider—a little brainier—had more knowledge—better ideas—better perceptive faculties—better and greater conceptions of what constitutes man, humanity in general by going out west and settling in a new State like Kansas. That is the way I talked then. But I had no idea that I had become a great man by having come to Kansas; that I had really grown to be a hero among heroes. (Laughter.) That I was such a brave soldier as all the Kansas boys have been shown to have been in all these speeches yesterday and to-day. (Renewed laughter.)

I came to Kansas early with my family—during the pendency of the Kansas-Nebraska bill and before its passage. I settled here about the 27th of May, 1854. At that time I certainly had no de-

finite idea that I was destined to become one of a race of heroes
on Kansas soil. Beyond a doubt we have done as well as the settlers in any new State. The common necessities which attend life
on the frontier attached to all of us. Settling in a new country involves trouble, privation, deprivation—everything indeed that is
different from what we left in our homes in the Eastern States.

I came here not knowing what I would have to endure ; but I
simply came knowing nothing about the country, where I was going
to settle, or anything connected with it. I squatted down yonder
on the Wakarusa—before a single Yankee settled on Mt. Oread. I
bought a farm of one of the Curlews ; gave him fifteen dollars and
a shot-gun.

I remained there one day after another, one week after another,
finally put up a cabin—my wife and myself— and we lived there.

Then there was a convention called at Lawrence and I was
nominated for clerk and secretary, then the same thing occurred at
the conventions held at Big Springs, then at the Topeka constitutional convention. I made a record of what the boys did, of their
big resolutions and everything. But all these things were thrust
upon me without my really knowing what I was doing, without
really knowing what they were doing either. (Laughter.) I took
it for granted. (More laughter.)

Then came the election for the Legislature under the constitution and somehow or other I got a position in that Legislature. I
don't know how. I think Jim Lane, and Governor Robinson and
John Speer had something to do with it. I don't know but that
they all helped. It was a very important position for me to hold,
but I never got any money out of it. (Laughter.)

I lived four miles from town. I walked from my cabin to
town time and time again ; in the severest weather of winter to attend those free state meetings ; sometimes writing day and night.
In the course of time came on the vote under the Lecompton constitution ; then we split. Some determined that they would not vote
at all ; others determined that they would. Then came the struggle,
and after the struggle then came the power into the hands of the
free state party and Kansas was saved. Now I don't believe that
Governor Robinson—I don't believe that Jim Lane—I don't believe
Jim Legate or anybody else, not even myself saved Kansas (Laughter.) But I do believe this, that every single effort that was made
here in Kansas, coupled as it was with the efforts that were made
in the East, through all parts thereof, and in every direction, all
contributed to the salvation of Kansas. And I think that the man
who will assume that *he* saved Kansas, or that any particular *thing*
saved Kansas, is assuming that which he cannot maintain. It took
all, it took everything that we could do.

We had many antagonistic elements to deal with. The elements were largely Democratic. Early in the day it was not a political contest in the strict sense of the term ; we were driven just where
we were driven. I came here a Democrat ; was asked " Are you

a free state man?" "Yes!" "Well, then you are a damned Abolitionist." So then I concluded if I had to be classed with Abolitionists, then I had to vote with the "damned Abolitionists." And
there's where I have been voting for the past fifteen, twenty or
twenty-five years (except when I "selected" my man you know)
because the necessities of the case drove me there. There's an
idea! I don't believe the Republican *party* is entitled to one particle of credit for making Kansas a free State. But I do believe
that the *people* of Kansas are entitled to the credit in addition to the
assistance they received from the East, and that we made Kansas a
free state *not* by force of arms, but that it was because of our having
more votes than the pro-slavery party. This is true in every respect.

If we had not had more votes at the time of the rejection of
the Lecompton constitution, the pro slavery party would have
beaten us. I want to say this—I am glad that I am not to listen to
these laudatory speeches more than once in twenty-five years, because all these honors piled upon me year after year would finally
make me stoop-shouldered, and begin to look old. Still it may be
of some service for my children and children's children to know
what a great *hero* I have been, in order to communicate it to the
generations far beyond.

ADDRESS BY HON. JAMES ROGERS.

Gov. Robinson :—I see an old free state man here, who has
done great service in his own county—Osage—and I will ask him
to say a few words to you.

Mr. Rogers said:

Mr. President:

I have been called out to speak a few words only in commemoration of the services of those of whom I have spoken, and here
I suppose I ought to stop; but a voice from somebody in the audience, inquiring "if their were no women in Kansas during the
early struggles?" has emboldened me to take the liberty to make
a brief reply.

Let me say that there were not only women here during all
that fearful ordeal, but ladies were here also—and ladies of the
highest type of womanhood; ladies in virtue, refinement and cul-
ture; ladies who had not only enjoyed all the comforts of happy
and beautiful homes, but many who had been nursed in the lap of
luxury and ease. I am more than surprised that amidst all the
splendid eulogiums that have been poured out here to-day upon
the men who took part in the great strife for freedom, I have not
heard one word uttered in behalf of the early women of Kansas.
This, Mr. President, is not as it should be, for they are equally
entitled to praise with "the lords of creation" for the successes of
those early times.

I know well what the early women of Kansas endured. I
know their privations, their hardships and their dangers, and I

know how uncomplainingly they bore up against them.   To those
of you who were not here let me say that you have no conception
of their difficulties, trials and dangers, nor the courage—high
moral courage—with which they met them.   Living as they did in
little, rude, unsheltered cabins, scattered over the bleak prairies,
often miles apart; the husband called out to defend the border, or
to go to the Missouri river for provisions, the woman for days was
left either alone or with her little children, in a country infested
with malicious and vindictive men of the border, or with the lurk-
ing semi-savage Indian whose tribes were scattered all over the
Territory, with no one, save perchance a faithful dog, to guard her
against the surprise and attack of those revengeful barbarians.   It
has ever been a matter of profound astonishment how she arose to
that sublime courage that mocks at fear and makes manhood feel
ashamed.   It seems to me that she must have been inspired of
heaven during all those dark hours of our distress, for when the
man grew weak, the woman grew strong.   When the men became
timid, the women became the more brave.   When the men despaired,
the women inspired them with hope.   When the man cursed and
gave way to his evil nature, the woman prayed and was calm, and
relied on the justice of God with unfaltering faith to lead us through
that sea of troubles.

Those of us in the remote West were often cut off from the
great rivers, our only source of supplies.   We generously divided
until the last morsel was gone, and then for days had nothing to
eat.   Sometimes our women grated green corn on the bottom of a
tin pan with holes punched outward, the result of which she baked
into cakes, which, with baked green squash was our only means of
support.   While the men were engaged in building, breaking the
soil and fencing, the women, with instinctive ingenuity, were
gathering from the forest and field something to assist to make
our corn meal and "hog meat" palatable.   And then came sickness upon us, with not half enough of the well to take care of the
sick; but amid all these afflictions woman never faltered.   She
never once said "turn back."   She was as true to the voice of
liberty, justice and humanity as the needle to the pole.   Her better nature had prompted her to solicit her husband, father or
brother to come to Kansas, and to follow him hither as well; and
when the storm and darkness settled thick around us, she was our
guiding star, our pillar and cloud to lead us to the promised land.
I remember well hearing good Judge Schuyler relate how his feeble
and failing wife urged him to leave his happy home in the State of
New York and come to Kansas and battle for freedom.   I know,
if he were here to-day, the women would not need a friend to
champion their cause.

Mr. Schuyler said: "My wife said, 'go, Phillip.   Buckle on
your armour, and go out and fight for the cause of freedom in Kansas.   I cannot go with you, but I will remain behind and take care
of the little ones and use my influence to urge others to go.'   And

every week came letters from her urging me to stay and cheering me on, but for which I should have turned back in despair ; and when her tongue had ceased to speak and her pen to encourage me, which was in the midst of our troubles, it henceforth seemed that she ever stood by me, and that I could hear her whispering in my ear words of hope and cheer until the day of our triumph."

Such was the character of all the free state women of Kansas. It would be invidious to mention names, as it is impossible in a few brief moments to do them justice. But when the true history of Kansas shall be written—as it surely will be—there will be heroines as well as heroes, and her part in the great struggle for liberty, justice and right, will form the brightest in it. All honor to the early free state women of Kansas; all honor to her devotion to liberty and the cause of God; all honor to her moral courage, which rose superior to all danger and restrained the passions of the stronger sex, and inspired them with courage and hope. I tell you but for the women of Kansas it would have been abandoned in one week, and instead of these free institutions which are the pride and the boast of to-day, Kansas would have been surrendered by those who have been here so highly eulogized, and this goodly land, with its fair fields, its fruits and flowers, would have been the heritage of the oppressor and the oppressed—and that too, perhaps, forever.

ADDRESS BY LEONARD WORCESTER.

Gov. ROBINSON :—The Old Settlers' band has given us music more than once during this celebration. We all remember how much they cheered us, all through the early days—and how too, they mingled their notes with our sorrows in times of trouble. I will call upon one of their number to say a few words to you.

Mr. Worcester said :

Mr. Chairman, Ladies and Gentlemen:

If I had been asked what was the one thing farthest from my expectation to-day, I would have, perhaps, said it was I should have been asked to stand before you here and say anything to you. I have no great record to show. I have done no great thing. In my small way with my friends here, with the old Lawrence band, we tried to infuse enthusiasm into the hearts of the sons of Kansas whenever they were going out to their work, or whenever they came home. But I, by myself, could have done nothing, would have done nothing and was nothing. But my friends here have helped me and the friends were kind enough to say that we did cheer them a good deal, and helped them. Our first work that I remember of, was done at the funeral of Barber who had been buried in the town, was taken up and removed to the cemetery on the hill. That was the first work in which I took a part in Kansas,— in company with four or five others; from that the old Lawrence Cornet Band grew, and lasted after I left the Territory. I left in

1859. But I am glad to hear that my going away did not do away
with the music of the old band by any means, and I was more glad
to be here and see you all together—see all the faces that I used
to know in the troublesome days.   I thank you.

THE OLD LAWRENCE BAND.

The Old Lawrence Band which added so much to the pleasure of the meeting is thus written of by Mr. Joseph Savage, of
Lawrence:

The appearance of the Old Lawrence Band at the quarter centennial celebration of the settlement of Kansas, suggests that its
history be written.

In 1854, Aug. 26th, the writer had made up his mind to go
to Kansas with the second party which started out from Boston,
August 29th, or the Wednesday following.   At church, August
26th, James Sawyer concluded to follow me to Boston on Tuesday,
while I was to go down from Hartford, Vermont, on Monday.
Upon going to the depot at Boston on Tuesday to meet Mr. Sawyer, I was surprised to find three others with him, my brother, F.
Savage, Mr. N. Hazen and Mr. A. Hazen, all members of our
Hartford band, with myself, except Mr. Sawyer.   They had our
four horns along, i. e., one e flat copper key bugle, one brass post
horn in b flat, one b flat cornet, and one b flat baritone.

On Wednesday at the Boston depot a large crowd gathered to
see us off, for the excitement of going to Kansas had already set
in pretty strong, and the papers chronicled all little events connected with our exodus with faithful minuteness; so they said that the
Kansas emigration took along a band of music with them, and
another new-wedded pair went out to spend their honey-moon.

At the depot the large audience sang auld lang syne, to the
words of our poet Whittier:

" We cross the prairies as of old,
    Our fathers crossed the sea," &c.

Dr. Webb was particularly enthusiastic over this song   Our
band (of four) played the tune through before singing, and an in-
terlude of the last strain between each verse, and also as the cars
rolled out of the depot and the crowd hurrahed to us, we in return
gave the usual military cheers.   A little more playing was done on
the cars as we passed along the New England villages, and a little
more on the lake boat from Buffalo to Detroit, Mich., and I think
a trifle more while going up the Missouri river.   The copper bugle,
played by A. Hazen, and the b flat baritone only remained in
Lawrence that fall.   We often, on still moonlight evenings, played
national airs and songs, much to the delight of the settlers gathered
around to listen and applaud.   We also sang often and much with
S. N. Simpson and others, A. Hazen accompanying on the violin,
and myself the horn.   This was the last of our music till the Fourth
of July, 1855, when we had a big celebration in the grove north

and west of the town near the river. A. Hazen never came back
after 1854, but O. Wilmarth came with a c clarionet and a Mr.
Harlow, from Randolph, Vt., came with a melodeon, or reed
organ—with these we accompanied a very good choir of singers,
and besides gave some instrumental pieces upon the platform
erected for the occasion. One of the latter pieces was " Home,
Sweet Home," and it was listened to with evident interest. " Yankee Doodle" and " Hail Columbia " were also rendered with good
effect, for the time, place, and occasion all combined to make it
memorable. Many Indians were present, and some made addresses, one (Pechowkee) said: " Many a red man has watered the
tree of your liberty with his blood." Harlow died that season; and
O. Wilmarth, from R. I., and myself used to play the Portuguese
hymn or " Dead March " up the hill to the cemetery at funerals.
How many times we two played alone I do not now remember,
but it must have been several times. In the fall of 1855 my brother, F. Savage, came out again and settled here, he being one of
the original four made an addition of one. Some time the next
spring, I think in May or June, 1856, Mr. Leonard Worcester
came here and lived at Mr. John Hawse's, midway between my
brother and me. He had a half crescent shaped cornet, and used,
for diversion, to play out of doors in the evening. We heard him,
and after several days we invited him to play with us. He readily did so, and then we had three horns. With these we sere-
naded the new town or city and also the steamboat which had made
a trip up from Kansas City and was lying at our wharf.

Our town grew during the summer and we began to talk up a
bigger band. It was one Sabbath afternoon after church that
Worcester and I went to the residence of Mr. Samuel Kimball to
induce him to join the band. He had two brothers, Edward and
Fred Kimball. All sang well and they had a violin and bass viol.
The Kimballs consented to join us if we could raise the necessary
horns. After some consultation it was decided to borrow one
hundred dollars and send Mr. Worcester to St. Louis for them.
We all gave our joint note, and my brother, F. Savage, furnished
the money. The horns were bought, and the band began in earnest. The Kimballs proved to be workers in music, and Ed. and
Fred soon became good performers.

During the troubles of 1856 we often went into the city, at
the invitation of Gen. Lane, to play national airs in order to drive
away homesickness, and I think it did, for the boys would brighten
up and appear highly pleased. The soldiers were all volunteers and
it took all these combined efforts to hold them together. We also
played at a good many funerals of free state men and others: Barber, Shombre, and one after another as they fell. Thus we pros-
pered until the fall of 1863—in the interim John Ross beat the
bass drum, Abram Wilder the tenor drum, and E. P. Fitch fixed
the lanterns and worked the cymbals.

Also, during this time—I think in 1856 or 1857, Mr. Samuel

11

Newhall joined us from Boston, and Worcester left for the Indian Territory, and Mr. McCoy, from Ohio, led us, and George Banks beat the bass drum in J. Ross's place. Our best days were 1863 when we bought a new set of silver horns all around, of Hall, of Boston. Gov. Robinson erected a stand at the head of Massachusetts street, and we were giving open air concerts weekly in order to pay for our new horns and other equipments. Ours was then a fine band, the music harmonious and all well rendered. But the Quantrill raid on the 2d day of August, broke us up, Fred Kimball, E. P. Fitch, and another member, I do not recall his name, were killed outright. Mr. McCoy, our leader, was so shocked that his health, already delicate, gave out and he died not long after with consumption. Our band had seen its best days and gradually dwindled away as an organization. But we went into the service as a band in the Price raid in 1864, and were gone two weeks on the border. In 1870 or 1871, we had a reunion at our Old Settlers' Meeting on Sept. 15th. At our Quarter Centennial Mr. Worcester comes to us from Greensburg, Indiana, where he is settled as a music teacher and leader of a band and a dealer in musical instruments. He left us as a single man and now he comes back with a son seventeen years of age, and a good musician also.

Mr. Samuel Newhall comes from Ouray, Colorado, where he has located some mines. Mr. Samuel Kimball still lives here and runs the iron foundry as he did in 1856. Mr. Ed. Kimball died several years ago; he was a fine musician. The Savage brothers are both living near Lawrence on farms of their own.

This comprises the old band, viz: the two Worcesters, two Savages, Newhall and Kimball—all that are at the quarter-century celebration.   ·

ADDRESS BY GOV. SHARPE.

The Chairman introduced Gov. Sharpe, of Morris county, who said :

Mr. President, Ladies and Gentlemen :

I most certainly would be ungrateful were I not, under these circumstances, to return to the honorable president of this assemblage my most sincere thanks for the flattering manner in which he has called me to your attention.

But I will tell you the first thing that I told him to tell you : it was why I was not elected Governor of Kansas. I know that I ought to have been, but I did not get votes enough. I believe that I have got just as good grip as any of these more distinguished individuals who have preceded me. I have just as much to the square inch and as many square inches as any of them that have ever lived in Kansas. When I made the effort in 1870, I ran 3,000 or 4,000 ahead of my ticket, and had I had 30,000 or 40,000 more votes I would have occupied the gubernatorial chair. I believe that should I ever run again that I can increase that majority. I never fought, bled or died for Kansas, but I have been here a little over twenty-three years. I am proud to say that I came from Pennsylvania—and if Kansas did not gain by my exit from Pennsylvania, I have no doubt but that Pennsylvania did. As there has not been a speaker who has preceded me, except one or two of our invited guests, but that have told you and entertained you by the hour of what great things they did for Kansas, you will certainly pardon me if I mention what great sacrifices I made for Kansas. This may be very good to you folks who hear it and it may not; but I will give it to you for what it is worth, and if it is not worth anything it will be worth as much as a great deal of the clap-trap that has been given to you yesterday and to-day. I was a Democrat before I came to Kansas. I lived in Lancaster county, Pennsylvania, where I was born, reared and educated. I was a young lawyer and had just been admitted to the bar in the spring of 1856. My father was a warm friend of James Buchanan, who was then running for President. I was very enthusiastic in the election of Buchanan. I made speeches around in the country school-houses, and did everything I could—and I thought I helped to elect Buchanan. I believe I did. It was my first vote. In the fall of 1857 he issued his first message to Congress, in which he urged the admission of the State of Kansas into the Union under the Lecompton constitution. You will all recollect that Stephen A. Douglas, then in the Senate of the United States, took issue with him. Mr. Buchanan telegraphed to Lancaster to the chairman of the Democratic executive committee, and he immediately called that committee together, and they passed unanimous resolutions endorsing his Kansas policy. That committee was called together by its chairman. The resolution was made, perhaps, in Washington—I do not know where—but it went through endorsing the policy of the administration on the admission of Kansas. I denounced the resolution, taking sides with Douglas. My friends said if I was such a Kansas man I had better come to Kansas. In less than three weeks I was on Kansas soil, and I have been here ever since. I am proud, as I know you are proud, that you are here celebrating this event—the twenty-fifth anniversary of this State. In doing that we are proud because we have laid in twenty-five years a great and glorious Commonwealth. We have made a State, a great and glorious Commonwealth, containing to-day, perhaps, nearly a million of human souls. We have, in addition to that, brought into existence one of the grandest systems of education any State in the Union has ever conceived. Let me just say one word here about our education. Our worthy Governor said one word about agriculture in the last two years. I wish to call your attention to one other fact equally as important. When Kansas was admitted into the Union as a State of 1861, you will find that there were a little over 4.000 children between the ages of 5 and 21 years in the State. That number has grown from 4,000 to 266,000 pupils in our schools, and from 110 school-houses in 1861, to nearly 6,000 in 1878. And all this, in conclusion I must say, was brought about by, and we are entitled to give the credit at least to one of our great Governors, Harvey, the distinguished gentleman who scooped me for Governor. We are not only building up a great State, but we are going to be the central State of this Government. I thank you, ladies and gentlemen, for your attention.

[The multitude in attendance was so great, on the afternoon of the second day of the meeting, that all could not be heard in the tabernacle; and a division was made, a portion of the crowd gathering in the grove at a distance, where several of the speeches which follow were made.]

POEM BY DR. F. L. CRANE.

THE CHAIRMAN: We have here one of the oldest citizens of Topeka—one who was always associated with us in every effort for the good of Kansas. He has composed a poem which, with a few words of preface, will now be read. Dr. Crane read as follows:

It is a matter of familiar knowledge that Missouri could not have been admitted into the Union as a slave State in 1821, without an agreement on the part of the slave oligarchy in Congress that their "peculiar institution" should thereafter be limited to the line of 36 deg. 30 min., north latitude, in any Territory belonging to the United States. It is also well known that the repealing of the eighth section of the Compromise Act by the Kansas–Nebraska bill in May, 1854, was a violation of that agreement.

In order by legitimate means to secure the country to freedom, thousands left their comfortable, and sometimes elegant homes in the East, and made homes in Kansas, that they might outvote the slavery extensionists.

These latter came, also, in great numbers, many of whom brought their slaves with them, and it is a matter of history that warfare was the result, and that, when fully tested, the right prevailed.

The government, in the meantime favored the slavery extensionists, and for freedom it sometimes looked very dark. For us there was danger of appearing to be in opposition to the government, to the extent of being nominal traitors.

This, the free state men determined to avoid, and the writer of this, in company with Colonel Cyrus K. Holliday, the president of the Topeka Association, called upon Colonel Sumner at his tent on the morning of the fourth of July, 1856, the day on which the free state Legislature was dispersed by United States troops, assisted by pro slavery men; and we assured him that there would be no resistance to his authority by free state men in Topeka that day.

Seven weeks previous to this dispersion of the Legislature, elected under the Topeka Constitution, and five days before the sacking of Lawrence, viz : On the 16th day of May, 1856, there occurred at Topeka an extraordinary rain storm, in which hailstones fell as large as pullet's eggs. The copious rain caused a stream of water between Jackson and Van Buren streets, and west of my house, at No. 114 Kansas avenue, say one hundred feet in width. After the storm, I saw in the West, from my second story window, an emblematic picture, made up of clouds, in the otherwise clear sky, which was clearly defined, perfect, and is accurately described as follows : A female figure was on her knees, with face veiled and head bowed down, with the resemblance of a liberty cap at her feet. Before her were represented three men, decreasing in size as if in perspective, armed and dressed alike; the tallest and central figure in the picture was armed with a dagger in his right hand, the sharp point of which was over the neck of the humbled female, with his arm in position and apparently nerved to strike ; the left hand clenched and held a little back, and the right foot forward as if marching.

The second masculine figure was smaller than the first, and the third smaller than the second, making an artistic pyramidal picture which remained intact, no part of it being wafted away by atmospheric motion, no brim of a hat, no arm, limb, point of a dagger, or tassel of the liberty cap at the feet of the Goddess; but after about seven minutes of close observation, I discovered that the whole picture was becoming thinner and less distinct and soon vanished, leaving the western sky cloudless.

On the black nimbus cloud which covered the eastern hemisphere there soon appeared two perfect bows with a bright mock sun on the horizon in the center and rays extending from the mock sun to the zenith, to the north and to the south. Very beautiful.

I have endeavored to put a few pages of words together in a form that may assist to preserve a few contained facts in the archives of the Historical Society of the State of Kansas; the gist of the repeal of the eighth section of the Compromise Act; our early struggles for liberty, and the picture emblematic of its distressed condition, and the bright phenomenon in the East emblematic of the condition of humanity when daggers, etc., shall be made into pruning hooks and other useful implements and peace shall reign.

PROLOGUE.

I.

'Tis not intended by this to enact,
That slavery shall, or shall not be a fact
In this virgin land. Let settlers agree
By voting ; thus make it slave soil or free.

II.

Thus Congress, this question opened anew;
As a consequence this together drew
Contending legions who burst the bubble,
While Lincoln settled this brainy men's trouble.

III.

Men from the States; men with pro-slavery aims,
And some from the border, for sham, took claims,
But they did not wait for the people to vote
Ere they brought slaves with each up-river boat.

IV.

The thirtieth of March was a day of some note;
We went to Tecumseh intending to vote;
But we—the crowd of armed ruffians noting—
Declined to collide; none of us voting.

V.

One stranger showed the election a sham,
In Stinson's door with a hand on each jamb;
Armed with revolvers, a dagger in each
Bootleg, and shot-gun in easy reach.

VI.

Many were like him armed in a ravine,
Around and in the house; and there was seen
Old man Gilpatrick, kicked and driven away,
He would not "vote right on the goose" that day.

VII.

At all the polls 'twas known this hellish game
Was played with open and unblushing shame;
And it has since been played with increased rigors,
By vicious Southern whites to bulldose niggers.

VIII.

Unused were free state men to such turmoil,
As new to them as the unbroken soil;
Which seemed as new as if untouched by man,
Since it was formed by the Almighty's plan.

MEETING OF THE PIONEERS FOR CONSULTATION—THEIR DELIBER-
ATIONS AND PROTEST.

IX.

'Tis meet that we do now consult,
　Regarding those armed wights,
Who for kind words give us insult,
　Pretend we have no rights,
Prowl 'round in squads and frighten wives,
　Have banners, ('bate your breath,
For there we see for threatened lives
　Displayed,) *"Slavery or Death."*

X.

We treat all comers brotherly,
　And give to all good cheer,
But those armed villains swear the free
　Yanks shall not settle here.
They have their secret words and signs,
　Are organized they say,
Sworn to enforce their base designs,
　To kill or drive away.

XI.

We had our homes ere we came here,
　Could there have lived in peace,
But distant murmurs filled the ear,
　Nor would forebodings cease.
A holy cause called loud and well,
　Here we were by it led,
In order slavery to repel,
　Nor let it further spread.

XII.

We have a mission to perform,
　We Kansas pioneers,
A conflict irrepressible
　Excites the nation's fears.
Where is our boasted freedom now?
　Her Goddess cannot stand　・
When might makes right that makes her bow
　To powers that rule the land.

XIII.

Might ruling right hath now its hour,
　And strong and proudly stands,

High and imperious with all power
　That patronage commands.
Might hath repealed a compromise,
　Made by the Southern will,
And threatens now to call her roll
　Of slaves at Bunker Hill.

XIV.

Might forces freemen to catch slaves,
　Who flee toward the north star,
If so-called law can make them knaves.
　And do what they abhor;
But time shall put in power the right,
　The slave shall yet be free,
And with his master legislate
　In Congress equally.

XV.

We write to friends, they scarce believe
　The statements written there,
Of pro-slave treatment we receive,
　Of insults we must bear;
Of 'lection frauds in which we're wronged,
　And legislators made,
At polls by border ruffians thronged
　With arms and foreign aid.

XVI.

Shall we with no official power,
　With those who have, contend ?
And shall we like the menials cower,
　And with officials blend?
They say that we should own our kind,
　Domestic "helps" should own,
That lords and ladies then would find
　All their worst troubles flown.

XVII.

Thus might persuades us, but we scorn
　The bribe.　Shall Freedom's Knights
Forget that they are freemen born
　T' establish human rights ?
We have sped here from every State,
　Few coming from the South,
We mean by very numbers' weight
　To close the tyrant's mouth,

XVIII.

And sheathe the dagger in his hand;
  The Goddess shall arise,
Progress in time will then be grand,
  Behold the brilliant skies !
Abundant from the central source,
  The rays of light extend
With bows, a token that the course
  Of progress shall not end.

XIX.

Our government in any view,
  We will forever prize;
But laws made by the ruffian crew,
  We will not recognize.
We see a contest here begun
  By men who freedom hate,
A "wave "* must take to Washington,
  The saviors of the State.

RESTORATION OF THE GODDESS OF LIBERTY.

XX.

Now we congratulate our friends
  On this benign occasion,
When peaceful years have made amends
  For the late war's abrasion ;
On being e'er victorious,
  In what we tried to do,
From making Kansas glorious,
  To helping freedom through.

XXI.

But few who came here free state men,
  E'er thought of interfering,
With slavery in the States where then
  It had a firm appearing.
By gross injustice on the part
  Of the administration,
Radical thoughts were given such start
  As ere long ruled the nation.

---

*" Ride into power on the wave of prosperity."—SAM'L J. TILDEN.
As reported in the Chicago *Times*, of August 14, 1879.

XXII.

Let us believe that higher powers,
    Than those of earth control,
This beautiful, bad world of ours,
    With each immortal soul ;
And yet each is accountable
    For all his earthly acts,
That "Great Book" memory will tell,
    In time all weighty facts.

XXIII.

Dear pioneers, or saint, or sage,
    Honor to you is due,
Of history, the brightest page
    Was written here by you ;
For here you won 'gainst patronage,
    A victory sublime,
An era in Columbia's age,
    To be revered through time.

XXIV.

Proclaim it ! The great civil fight
    Was erst with us rehearsed,
Kansas succeeded for the right,
    Else all had been reversed;
Delayed the time when wars shall cease,
    By universal act
Of world's commissioners, and peace
    A bright millennial fact.

ADDRESS OF THE GODDESS OF LIBERTY TO HER WHILOM ENEMIES.

XXV.

Soon as the Goddess took her place,
    She mercifully said,
"Go now misguided men who this
    ' Unpleasantness ' have led
And till your devastated soil,
    Your bondmen I make free ;
'Tis meet that you now learn to toil,
    Enjoy sweet liberty.

XXVI.

"Never forget that you had long
  Been challenging a fight;
You passed pretended laws, the wrong
  To nullify the right.
You fostered feelings sectional,
  By men in Congress led,
And answered Sumner's telling speech
  By stealthy blows on head.

XXVII.

"You're freed I now may to you state
  From many things you feared,
You now may Christians tolerate
  Whose conscience is not seared ;
You now the young may educate
  En masse in common schools,
For ignorance is not a great
  Need there where freedom rules.

XXVIII.

"Books for your Sunday-schools ; to mend,
  Need not be *visaed ;* pruned
Of every word that might offend
  Ears sensitively turned ;
Incendiary papers may
  Be mailed in the P. O.,
An Abolitionist his way
  Sans peur of hemp may go.

XXIX.

"Now you may all in peace rejoice,
  And be good friends again,
But say no more one of your boys
  Equals three northern men.
No doubt the past has been quite hard,
  The moral is—do right,
Like chicken cocks in same yard,
  The whipped will no more fight.

XXX.

"Ask not again for compromise,
  The time for that has passed,

Each for himself must realize
  A play for him is cast,
In which he acts for others' good
  As well as for his own,
Let—and I trust I'm understood—
  No selfishness be shown.

XXXI.

" When 'tis habitual to act
  For all, and none afraid
Of any who may virtue lack,
  But proffer them their aid
To mount progression's ladder, see,
  How beautiful the sight—
Communities in harmony
  Have duties ever light.

XXXII.

"Whether in this millennium
  Treasure for all appears,
In common as has been foretold
  By those who are called seers,
Is not now plainly evident
  To unassisted sight,
But honest men who legislate
  For all will do it right."

THE GODDESS OF LIBERTY TO THE KANSAS PIONEERS.

XXXIII.

My friends your mission does not end
  With these few years of care—
A life eternal you shall spend,
  With good or bad somewhere;
And idle you'd not wish to be,
  Nor would you sing for aye,
But still assist and teachers be
  To darklings who do pray
To be assisted to ascend
  To higher spheres of light,
Where roses bloom and flowers lend
  Their charms to please the sight;
Where many mansions are prepared,
  By the Great Father given,
Where those who lived and loved on earth
  May love and live in Heaven.

The Chairman introduced Maj. J. B. Abbott, who spoke as follows:

Friends and Comrades:

This is indeed a glorious occasion, a happy gathering of old, true and tried friends. Such a meeting as we have witnessed to-day, occurs only in the life-time of the few. Such friendships as we witness here, are only generated among true men and women, and under severe trials and dangers. And such friendship is more than full remuneration for all the suffering that produced it.

The most of the early settlers came here to better their condition, make homes for themselves and educate their children in the art of agriculture; but the defenders of the "peculiar institution" had decided that Kansas must, at all hazard and at whatever cost, become a slave State, and their first plan was to drive out of the Territory every shade of anti-slavery men, from the Garrisonian Abolitionist to the most doubtful free state Democrat, and thus the principle of self or home defense produced an alliance that was not weakened during the struggle that followed. If the left wing of this alliance could not always endorse the universal equality sentiments of the right, yet they hated the slavery propagandist far more intensely, which answered all purposes for the work that had to be done. We were not driven out, and at last Kansas was admitted into the Union a free State.

How proud were its citizens of the new Commonwealth, and well were they satisfied with the results of their labor and hardships, and thus had they been doubly paid. But the demon of slavery had been sowing broader than he had dreamed, in his endeavor to subjugate and drive out the people of Kansas. For the wind he had scattered over the then small settlements of the Territory, he was soon compelled to reap a full-grown whirlwind in nearly half of the States of the Union, and now, thank God, and all the lovers of justice and equal rights, who have helped in its cause, we are living, not only in a free State, but in a constellation of free States, the wonder and hope of the world.

Kansas, although in her 'teens, has her school-houses and schools, which rank with any State; railroad facilities unequaled by States twice its age, a proud reputation for her agricultural products, is almost free from debt, with a million of inhabitants with broad and liberal views, full of honest enterprise, and watchful to secure every possible good to the State of their adoption and creation. In view of all these results, how insignificant appear the "troubles of Kansas." We have been paid an hundred fold for all we have been called on to endure, and millions are on the road to the enjoyment of that freedom, which they might have never known, had even the few scattered settlements of Kansas been less true to the principles of human rights.

I am reminded, almost daily, and especially as I converse

with the friends here, that our numbers are thinning out, and it is not unlikely, if the facts were known, we should find that the majority of our old comrades have passed over to the spirit-world beyond, and to me it is a pleasing thought, that while they are invisible to us, yet they may be gathered here, mingling with their friends, and enjoying with us this reunion and festal scene, rejoicing over the victories of right and justice and a world's progress. And now in closing, let me say, that e'er another decade shall have rolled around, we will have passed on to the glorious meeting and and joyous greetings of our old comrades, and entered upon the results of our labors. This let us believe, and in this let us be satisfied.

ADDRESS BY COL. DANIEL H. HORNE.

THE CHAIRMAN: — In the darkest hour of our trouble, Kansas had no truer and braver friends than were found in Topeka. I take pleasure now, in calling upon one of the truest and bravest to say a few words to you.

Col. Horne said:

Ladies and Gentlemen:

This occasion reminds me of a trip I made to Lawrence in 1855, when the people here were glad to see me; in the time of the Wakarusa war. I marched from Topeka with a hundred men. We came with music—fife and drum—and, with some drilling on the way down, we were enabled to present quite a soldierly appearance. The Lawrence people at first took us for border ruffians, and they began to get out of our way; but when we marched in front of the Eldridge House, which was Robinson's headquarters, and I halted the men and presented arms, they soon saw who we were, and were very glad to see us, and gave us three cheers.

Allusion has been made to the services of different men in the early Kansas times. I regard Gen. James H. Lane as one of the men who did most for Kansas. No one did more than he to inspire the men and get them into action when any emergency arose. He had a wonderful power over men; and that power was exerted for the good of Kansas and of the country in a great many instances. His style of speech in haranguing the people was very peculiar and very effective. I have now in mind an instance which occurred during the war: Lane had three regiments of infantry to form. A recruiting meeting was held at Topeka, at the Congregational church, and it was packed full to hear Lane. Many persons were present who had traveled with Lane all over the Territory during the troubles. He told them it was their duty to enlist; that they would be ashamed of the name they bore if they allowed this war to pass over without their having a hand in it. They did not start enlisting as quickly and as briskly as Lane thought they ought to, and he began to feel disappointed. But Charley Lenhart, who was present, spoke out, and made a remark which explained the difficulty. Says he: "Lane, we don't want to have anything to do with infantry. We have always been in the saddle." Lane drew himself up and pointing his fore-finger in his peculiar manner, he exclaimed: "I was just coming to that point. I was just going to say, that the Government will furnish saddles, and the Government will furnish bridles, and Missouri, she has plenty of horses, and we can all ride." That removed the difficulty. The boys began to put down their names, and recruiting went on fast enough.

Now, as one who went through all the Kansas troubles, I want to say, and I want to give it in as my testimony, that I consider there were two men to whom Kansas owes more, and to whom is due more credit than to any two others: These were Charles Robinson and James H. Lane. And I do not want them separated. Their names should both go down together as the two men whom the people should most honor for services done for Kansas in the early times.

Some claim that Lane was opposed to Government troops, at the time the pro-slavery government employed them against Kansas; that he was disposed to have the boys fight the Government troops. That is not true. Lane always respected the Government troops. Whenever we came in sight of the troops he always had us present arms; and the next thing, you would see him begging tobacco all along the line for our boys. I know there was not a disloyal hair in Lane's head, even when loyalty to the Government was almost a crime against Kansas.

I want to speak a word about the old gun whose voice we have been hearing on this occasion. I know there are a good many bigger guns than that, now-a-days. But in 1856 it was a very big gun. It was a very big gun when we drove the Missourians out of Atchison with it. It was a big gun when it went, under Captain Bickerton, down on the border, early in the war. We tried to burst this gun when Robinson was elected Governor. We tried to burst it when Lane was elected to the Senate, and when Kansas was admitted into the Union. We have been trying to burst it ever since, on all occasions in which the interests or glory of Kansas have been involved. And here the gun is, to-day, to speak its loudest tones in this great celebration.

Adjourned to 7 p. m.

TUESDAY EVENING.

Governor Robinson being absent, Col. S. N. Wood, one of the Vice-Presidents, presided.

ADDRESS BY HON. JOHN SPEER.

The chairman introduced Hon. John Speer, who spoke as follows:

Mr. President, Ladies and Gentlemen :

Unlike several of those who have preceded me I do not appear reluctantly before you, but I may say that I am gratified at an opportunity to address this vast audience, embracing the gallant pioneers of Kansas—the men and women who gave freedom to this grand Commonwealth.   Aside from the gratification of looking into your faces, and the pride of being thought worthy to address you, there have been many things said from this stand which make me anxious, for the truth of history and justice to the brave pioneers, to be able to reply and to give my views on a struggle in which I trust I may say, without egotism, I was more than a mere spectator, and frequently an active participator.

I desire to refer especially to the attempt to give credit to the early official authorities of Kansas for saving the Territory and the State to freedom.   I would not detract one iota from the credit due them for the discharge of their duties ; but had their policy been pursued, not only would Kansas been given to slavery, but the institution would have been extended westward into New Mexico, Arizona, and even southward into provinces which the slavery propaganda contemplated acquiring from Mexico.

As Col. Forney has told you, he and others secured the appointment of Gov. Reeder as the first Executive of Kansas ; but this was long years before he and his compeers threw their weight in behalf of the cause of free Kansas, and Gov. Reeder, although a good *man*, an able lawyer and a statesman, was a Democrat, in unison with the Administration of Franklin Pierce, by whom he was appointed.   He believed in what the slavery propaganda called the guaranties of the constitution.   He believed that the slaveholder had a right to bring his " property " to Kansas, while the decided " Abolitionist "—a term applied to all men who did not believe that slavery was the "corner stone of the confederation "—held that freedom was national and slavery limited to territory in which it was specially established by local statutory land. A few of the John Brown stamp of men believed that slavery was such a violation of the laws of God that it ought to be resisted by every conceivable means, without regard to human enactments ; but the large portion of the original free state men were opposed to slavery as a matter of political policy.   I would not say that Gov. Reeder was not, in his private opinions, of this class.   But he came here to carry out the policy of the organic act, as his oath required him to do.   I do not know that even his official associates knew his private views upon slavery.   Surely he never expressed enmity to the institution until after the school of severe experience taught him that there was no middle ground for him on that question--· that he must either justify the invasion of the country and fraudulent voting and fraudulent returns, and every possible outrage, even to the murder and expulsion from the Territory of every free state man, or take refuge among the free state men for protection, in asserting the commonest rights of humanity.   The turning point came in the returns of the election of the 30th of March, 1855—the first election of members of the Legislature. At least 1,000 men came to Lawrence from Missouri to vote, but not requiring all of them, about 300 were detailed to go to Clinton, and the elections in both places were controlled by Missouri mobs. At other places elections were carried by smaller numbers in the same way. It seems incredible in this age that men should have come from other States armed with revolvers, knives, shot guns, rifles and artillery, with tents and camp equipage, encamping the night before and striking their tents the morning after election, carrying the returns of their own fraudulent election with them. But such is the fact. They surrounded the ballot box, drove the judges appointed by the Governor from the polls, and declared their own judges elected. This was followed by affidavits of the facts sent to the Governor, and on the day appointed for canvassing the returns, a body of armed free state men surrounded the Governor, and a heavy saber lay concealed under the damask cloth on the Governor's table, for his protection in the decision of the result. The annunciation had boldly been made that the setting aside of these returns would cost him his life, and nothing but the knowledge of intended resistance saved him. From that day onward his official life was one of insult and abuse. Thus l e was almost literally driven into the free state ranks. His official head was cut off soon after by the Administration, for the simple discharge of a sworn duty. He soon became a trusted and honored leader of the free state party; but for this alleged betrayal of the South, his life was sought, he was hunted "from pillar to post," and finally compelled to escape from the Territory in disguise as a deck hand on a steamboat. It was in this school of the persecuted free state men that he learned new lessons on freedom never taught by Democrats since the days of Jefferson.

Gov. Shannon followed Reeder, and his history is known, but even his head went to the block, because he was unable to inflict slavery upon Kansas. Personally there were few better men, but he was in no sense a promoter of freedom in Kansas.

Gov. Geary was a "National Democrat," and was selected by President Pierce, not to promote freedom in Kansas, but because he had been an officer in the Mexican war, and was a man of great executive ability, who was believed to be capable of putting down the "rebellion in Kansas," as the free state organization against slavery and usurpation was called by the pro-slavery invaders and the Democratic leaders. He secured control of United States troops, issued a proclamation disarming all organized bands, and by the government troops arrested and placed in the Lecompton prison, 101 free state men who had just captured a pro-slavery fortification at Hickory Point. With all this effort at putting down the free state men, who were protecting their homes, he was insulted and spit upon—I do not mean figuratively spit upon, but his face absolutely spitten in—because he would not commission a drunken pro-slavery murderer to the office of sheriff; and when a large body of armed free state citizens assembled at Lecompton to denounce this outrage upon a Governor who differed from them, the meeting was assailed, shot into, and the assailant who had spitten upon the Governor shot down in his tracks. On this, pro-slavery assassins stalked abroad in the land. The life of the Governor was in constant jeopardy. And here arose the anomaly —unparalleled in the history of the world—of a ruler compelled to arm his prisoners, but recently captured, for his personal protection against the partisans whom he had been sent to sustain! He was compelled to flee the country, and soon after resigned or was removed.

Then Robert J. Walker, of Mississippi, a life-long supporter of slavery—the former senator of Mississippi—was appointed, with Secretary Frederick P. Stanton, of Tennessee, for Secretary of the Territory. If Reeder and Shannon and Geary and their associates had been failures in the pro-slavery mission-field in the attempts of the Administration to establish slavery in Kansas, it was expected that two such missionaries of slavery as Walker and Stanton would cover themselves with glory in the solution of the imbroglio of Kansas. Stanton came first, and he "bearded the lion in his den," by making his maiden demonstration in Lawrence, where, in a public speech, he told the people he had come to "enforce the laws, and that they must obey." This declaration met a universal response. "Never." "Then," said he, "it is war to the knife, and the knife to the hilt." Speakers arose who boldly defied him to enforce the "bogus laws," and if I recollect right, Gov. Robinson made a very firm speech in defense of the rights of the people and in defiance of the laws. And Stanton, the pro-slavery apostle from Tennessee, took his first lesson from the men who defied "the laws." Recollect, these laws made it a penitentiary offense for any man to deny that slavery legally existed in Kansas, and death to feed a runaway slave. On the day that that law took effect, as editor of the Kansas *Tribune*, I published a bold, defiant article against the legal existence of slavery. No man could vote without swearing to support these iniquitous laws.

Thus every free state man was practically disfranchised. Gov. Walker was a statesman of ability, and he saw no way out of the imbroglio except by protection to all voters alike; and he traversed the Territory delivering speeches, promising the people protection against their invaders and a fair election. Under these promises, for the first time since the election of March 30, 1855, the free state men entered into an election on the day fixed by the "bogus-laws." This gubernatorial action was not in the interest of freedom, but in the desire to do justice to all—or rather to preserve peace as the best mode to sustain slavery parties. These men were both on the side of slavery. The election was held, and nearly every district in the State carried by free state men. A few days after rumors were afloat that fraudulent poll-lists had been made up at Oxford, in Johnson county, Kickapoo, in Leavenworth county, Lightning Creek, in McGee county and at other points, sufficient to give the pro-slavery men a majority. These reports, which were soon verified, aroused the utmost excitement among the free state men. I was a candidate for the Legislature in the district of which Lawrence was a part, and in which the Oxford fraud was perpetrated. If successful, it would have secured certificates to eight representatives in the Lawrence district, eight in the Leavenworth district, two in the Linn district and three in what was called "the nineteen disfranchised counties," and some others—enough to make a clear pro-slavery majority of the thirty-nine members of the House, and a similar majority in the Senate—or Council, as it was called. The perpetrators of this fraud expected that Gov. Walker and Secretary Stanton, as the board of canvassers, would take the position that they could not go behind the returns; and the free state people then had so little confidence in them as to believe that their partizans had not "reckoned without their host." I will not assert that they were ready to perpetrate such an outrage, but I do unhesitatingly express the belief that there were good grounds for the fears of the people. In this state of excitement Gen. G. W. Deitzler and I—both free state candidates for the House—visited Oxford on a tour of inspection, but could ascertain nothing of the facts in regard to the vote. Although we went incognito, we were only able to ascertain from the pro-slavery men who constituted the population of Oxford, that "they voted a heap," and there was a "a powerful sight of people out." We did ascertain, however, that in all the cabins of the district there were not over sixty adult male inhabitants, and that it was doubtful whether a single man there had a right to vote, as the territory was on an Indian reserve, which, by the organic act, was "excepted out of the boundaries and constituted no part of the Territory of Kansas." At Olathe we found the returns in the hands of the pro-slavery probate judge, showing that Oxford had cast 1,628 votes. It was afterward ascertained by the accidental discovery of the name of a distinguished anti-slavery statesman upon the poll-list, that the judges of election had used an old Cincinnati directory to aid their fertile minds in the discovery of enough of names to fill that long list intended to defraud the people and continue slavery in Kansas. It was written in a clear, clerical hand, a beautiful manuscript, regularly sworn to, with all the essential "red tape"— the very counterpart of a poll-book where 1,628 Missouri tobacco-spitting, whiskey-drinking "sqatter sovereigns" had enjoyed the elective franchise.

As Gen. Deitzler and I returned from Oxford, we met, near Blue Jacket's ford, six miles east of Lawrence, a body of 16 men— armed to the teeth—in a hack and on horseback, who openly avowed that they were going to Oxford to hang Batt. Jones, Ganatt and the other man—I forget his name—who, as judges of that elec-

tion, had attemp.ed the outrage.   They were no braggadocios.
They had "blood in their eyes," and "meant business." The
judges heard of them, believed they were in earnest and fled to
the Snibar hills, afterward the resort of Quantrill.   These men on
their mission met Walker and Stanto.1, and boldly avowed that
they would hang the judges or any man who should sustain the
outrage.   I will not be so uncharitable as to say that those threats
were the controlling power which induced them to throw out the
Oxford returns as "evidently similated and fictitious."   That
would be only a matter of opinion.   What I state is history, and
reasonable men can draw their own conclusions.   Even after they
had thrown out these returns, Judge Cato, the special judicial instrument of slavery, the appointee of the Administration, issued a
peremptory mandamus to compel them to issue certificates to the
pro-slavery candidates by virtue of the Oxford vote, which, to their
honor be it spoken, they disregarded.

This gave the free state men legislative control; but, in the
meantime, the Lecompton constitution had been formed, and by a
one-sided vote, largely augmented by fraud, was declared adopted,
and was ready for congressional action on the opening o' Congress
on the first Monday in December.   By the law, the legislature did
not meet until January, 1858.   In this state of things, Gen. James
H. Lane commenced a canvass of the Territory, holding meetings
to urge the Governor to call the Legislature in extra session, to provide for a fair vote on the Lecompton constitution.   He traversed
the Territory, sometimes on horseback sometimes on foot, addressing assemblies in villages, in school-houses and under the trees.
While he was thus agitating, forming and arousing public sentiment,
the free state members of the Legislature assembled at Lawrence,
and petitioned the Governor to call the Legislature in extra session.
Before this petition could reach Gov. Walker, he had left Kansas,
never to return—disgusted if not affrighted at the state of things.
Instead of being the "noble Pennsylvania Democrat who saved the
Territory to freedom," he was a most intensely disgusted propagandist of slavery who failed to plant the institution, had "saved his
bacon," and transplanted himself to a more congenial political
climate, under the protecting ægis of James Buchanan.   In this
dilemma the legislators elect deputed Shaler W. Eldridge to carry
their petition to Frederick P. Stanton, who, by the absence of
Walker, became ex-officio Governor.   He represented himself to
Stanton as a business man and not a politician, who saw the signs
of the times.   He told Stanton that, in view of the Oxford outrage
and the Delaware crossing fraud—one of them to get power in the
Legislature and the other to secure slavery by the Lecompton constitution—and in view of the fact that the free state men had abandoned their old position of non-action under the "bogus-laws"—
under the solemn promises of the Governor and Secretary—that
unless relief was vouchsafed at once by calling the free state Legislature, such scenes would be enacted in Kansas as had never been

witnessed in the worst days of the California vigilance committees, and that men would be found hanging on trees with their crimes printed on their backs and across their hearts. He was successful, and returned with the promise that, if a majority of the Legislature would pledge themselves to go into no other legislation than that necessary to secure a fair, just vote on the Lecompton constitution, the Legislature should be called immediately. The pledge was given and the proclamation issued.

Your speaker was appointed to carry the news to Lane, at Leavenworth, and found him addressing a large audience in Stocktons Hall. As we entered, a tender-footed, pseudo free state man was speaking in denunciation of Lane, as an agitator whose "imprudent" measures were calculated to produce public disorder and bloodshed, and asserting that it was ridiculous to expect that the Governor would call that Legislature together to work mischief. I waited near the door and allowed Lane to proceed a few minutes in reply, when I pushed my way through the crowd, pulled Lane by the elbow, and said: "General Stanton *has* called the Legislature." No man can describe nor imitate the tragic, magic manner of the "grim chieftain's" announcement: "I have the honor to announce to the trembling, cowardly conservatives and the fiendish, devilish, pro-slavery villains, that Stanton has called the Legislature, and that slavery and its minions in Kansas are consigned to a political hell!"

And yet we have heard at this meeting, in beautifully rounded sentences, that to the instrumentality of Pierce and Buchanan we were indebted for the salvation of Kansas. The oratory sounded well; but, alas! that it was so far from true. That I speak the truth of history, I appeal to the noble band of pioneers left to bear me witness. The worth of Lane in the field and on the forum; of the Legislature in council; of Eldridge as the representative; the enactments of the Legislature, and the triumphant vote against that infamous slave constitution, constituted the culminating point in the redemption of Kansas from the thralldom of slavery. And then we heard that Brindle, Pierce's receiver of public moneys, was an instrumentality in "saving the country." It seems to me that at the mention of his name, every intelligent free state man must have had instantly photographed upon his brain the picture of the old *Lecompton Union*, the organ of slavery, with its glaring head-lines, "cursed be Canaan;" with his Scriptural quotations to show that the patriarchs of Israel were slaveholders—the original Calhouns, Wade Hamptons, Haynes and Breckenridges; with his citation of St. Paul when he sent Onesimus back to his master; the curse upon Ham as a "hewer of wood and a drawer of water!" his vivid descriptions of the "little water drops" which the good Lord, in his careful providence, had put under the cuticle of the African as coloring matter to keep the pot-black from showing, and the kinks which He put in his hair to save the necessity of combing; and all the long list of quotations,

which John Brown—the fanatic on the other side, if you please—
called blasphemy against the Almighty.   His better nature may
have warned some easy-going Democrat that his life was in danger,
or he may have told something which exposed murderers—but as
an instrumentality in making Kansas free, he was an utter failure.
    There were men, Democrats—Pennsylvania Democrats—who
did giants' work in the cause of freedom, but they were the humble
in the walks of life, and not the statesmen of the Administration.
It is in justice to them that I was impelled to say that I wanted to
speak.   If this were an ordinary town meeting, errors might go
for what they are worth, and utterances die with the breath that
uttered them; but—

> " A chiel's among ye takin' notes,
> And faith he'll prent 'em,"

the enterprising secretary of State Historical Society, having secured a short hand reporter to preserve the speeches as history.
    The Emigrant Aid Society has had its advocates, the Governors
and lofty officials have had theirs; but the poor, the honest, the
self-sacrificing rank and file have had but meager justice done
them.
    There were Democrats, Pennsylvania Democrats—Democrats
from all parts of the Union—men from the South as well as from
the North, who did great work in the cause of free Kansas, asking
only the reward of a clear conscience.   It is in their behalf that I
speak—would to God that I was capable of doing them justice.   I
think of such Democrats as William Y. Roberts, of Pennsylvania,
since renowned in the history of the State; of Robert Klotz, who
was disinherited because he turned traitor to Buchanan Democracy;
of G. W. Deitzler, who brought the first Sharp's rifles to Kansas to
defend our homes.   Injustice has been done to such men—unwittingly, I have no doubt.   Kansas was the grave of Governors and
the reform-school of Pierce and Buchanan Democrats.   The liberal,
freedom-loving spirit of the world was represented in the Kansas
struggle.   I think of the brave old George Keller, who was driven
from his home; of R. P. Brown, ruthlessly murdered at Easton;
of —— Mitchell, who was thrown into the Tecumseh prison and
bucked and gagged; of Wm. Phillips, carried from Leavenworth
to Weston, Mo., tarred and feathered, sold at auction to a negro
for 6¼ cents, and afterward murdered at Leavenworth, all Ken-
tuckians; of Josiah Miller, a South Carolinian, who shook the
Carolina dust from his feet and allied himself with the free state
men, his life put in jeopardy and tried by Buford for treason to
South Carolina; of Frank Swift, a brave boy then in his minority,
who came from Maine, was wounded at Wilson's Creek and did
more for freedom than all the Governors sent to Kansas; of Wm.
A. Phillips, representing the Highlands of Scotland, with his
trenchant pen as well as his sword; of Pomeroy and Robinson,
the acknowledged leaders; of G. W. Brown, with his able paper;
and his aged father, drilling troops under the lessons he had learned

at Plattsburg, in 1812; of the good Presbyterian elder, Capt. Lyon, the father of Mrs. S. N. Wood, who had learned to drill men in the war for "free trade and sailors' rights;" of Philip Schuyler, Cyrus K. Holliday, John Ritchie, Dan. Horne, Charles F. Garrett, A. D. Searl, George Earl, Charles Stearns, S. J. Willis. Oh, I wish I could think of them all, and that their names could be enrolled on the tablets of fame!—that year by year the children of Kansas, who enjoy the freedom they won, might come up to this grove and look upon them as the Romans were wont to gaze upon the images of the Gracchi! The men who made Kansas free belonged to no State, to no class, to no nation; but were a combination of freedom-loving spirits of all nationalities. When the good Jimmy McGee said to the men throwing up the rifleworks at Lawrence, "Work away, boys—there's 2,000 bushels of corn in Jimmy McGee's crib, and while it lasts ye shan't starve!" it was the liberty-loving spirit of the Methodist Irishman that spoke for freedom; and when the cuticle on the forehead of the brave Tom McIlheney was cut at Hickory Point, it was the blood of a Catholic Irishman, who inherited the spirit of O'Connell and Emmett, that trickled over his forehead; and when Breyman lay suffering in a Lecompton prison, it was the liberty-loving Teuton that was persecuted. When the free state man's friend, the educated Indian, replied to the inquiry as to his views on slavery, "God made white man—God made red man—God made black man—but God never made slave," he was a missionary in the anti-slavery cause without knowing it. When the poor old colored man, called by the boys "the jack of spades," insisted that God sent Lane to bring him out of slavery, he "didn't care what kind of man he was, he knowed God sent him jis' as soon as he come," he but rudely uttered the sentiment so beautifully expressed by the eloquent divine, Rev. Dr. Cordley, when he attributed the great work in free Kansas to a Higher Power than any earthly instrumentality. Most emphatically did He use the humble free state men "His wonders to perform" in the salvation of Kansas from an oligarchy which had ruled the nation since its foundation. They stood in the Thermopylæ of freedom, and not only drove back the tide of slavery from Kansas, and stopped it on its onward strides to the new Territories beyond and to proposed acquisitions from Mexico, but they inaugurated a manful resistance, which culminated in breaking the shackles of 4,000,000 slaves, and establishing universal freedom throughout the nation.

LETTER FROM GEORGE W. DEITZLER.

Col. Wood: You will now listen to a very interesting letter, to be read by Judge Emery, from a very useful and an honored citizen of Kansas in early times.

Judge Emery said:

I hold in my hand a letter which I desire to read, I found the letter at the post office when I went there this evening; and I am glad there are so many to listen. I hardly expected to find so many here to listen to it. I did not think you had got so fired up with this Old Settler sentiment as to lead you to come here the second night in such numbers. This leads me to say that we began this celebration thinking that we could hold it one day. It widened on our hands and we thought we would hold it until the next day about noon when the trains would leave. On the second day it got still bigger, and we thought we would hold it throughout the day, and now it has got into the night. This letter I will now read. It is from General George W. Deitzler. I take it that many of you do not know Mr. Deitzler. I can say that he was a true man and came to Kansas at an early day and lived here many years and then went to reside on the Pacific coast. He was Speaker of the first free state House of Representatives, in 1858, and Colonel of the first Kansas regiment during the war. I will read:

SAN FRANCISCO, Sept. 8th, 1879.

JUDGE J. S. EMERY AND OTHERS, COMMITTEE OF OLD SETTLERS, LAWRENCE, KANSAS.

Gentlemen :—I regret exceedingly that it will be impossible for me to accept your kind invitation to attend the meeting of Old Settlers of Kansas, at Lawrence, on the 15th inst.

Time is making sad inroads upon our ranks. We are passing rapidly away, soon the "Old Guard" will have none of their number left to call the roll. It is gratifying to observe that your State Historical Society is collecting the materials for a full and correct history of the stirring events of 1855 and 1856, and no doubt justice will be done to the people who periled their all in securing freedom to Kansas as well as thos: generous and patriotic men and women who inaugurated and sustained the aid Societies which proved such valuable instrumentalities in the furtherance of the cause. Among the latter stands the able and truly good man, Hon. Eli Thayer, whose letter of acceptance of your invitation published in the Lawrence *Journal* recalls an incident of 1855, to which I beg to refer briefly. Some six weeks after my arrival in the Territory and only a few days after the Territorial election of March 30th, at which time Kansas was invaded by an armed force from the Southern States and the actual free state settlers were driven from the polls, Gov Charles Robinson, than whom no truer or braver man ever espoused the cause of free Kansas, requested me to visit Boston with a view of securing arms for our people, to which I assented. Preparations were quickly and quietly made and no one knew of the object of my mission except Gov. Robinson and Hon. Joel Grover. At Worcester I presented my letter from Gov. Robinson to Mr. Thayer, just as he was leaving Oread Home for the morning Boston train. Within an hour after our arrival in Boston, the executive committee of the Emigrant Aid Society held a meeting and delivered to me an order for one hundred Sharps' rifles and I started at once for Hartford, arriving there on Saturday evening.[*] The guns were packed on the following Sunday and I started for home on Monday morning. The boxes were marked "Books." I took the precaution to have the (cap) cones removed from the guns and carried them in my carpet sack, which sack would have been missing in the event of the capture of the guns by the enemy. On the Missouri river I met Hon. John and Joseph L. Speer, for the first time. They did not know me, but may remember the exciting incidents at Boonville and other points along the river. I arrived at Lawrence with the

[*] See order in address of Mr. Hale, page 147.

" Beecher Bibles," several days before the special election, in April, called by Gov. Reeder. But no guns were needed upon that occasion, as the ruffians ignored said election, and when the persons elected upon that day presented their credentials to the Legislature at Pawnee, they were kicked out without ceremony.

I have not referred to this transaction from any motives of personal vanity, but simply to revive a feeling of gratitude toward Mr. Thayer and his associates for the kind and patriotic assistance rendered by them to the free state people from the beginning to the end of the great struggle which terminated, happily, in the overthrow of American Slavery, and to show how promptly they gave attention to the business which took me to Boston. Those rifles did good service in the "border war" and their movements in the hands of the brave and fearless Stubbs would furnish incidents for a very interesting chapter in the history of the Old Settlers. It was perhaps the first shipment of arms for our side and it incited a healthy feeling among the unarmed free state settlers, which permeated and energized them until even the Quakers were ready to fight. The temptation exists to say more while I am up, but I must forbear. I beg to be remembered by all and trust the Old Settlers will have a jolly good time at this and at all future meetings.

Very Respectfully,   Geo. W. Deitzler.

THE OLD SETTLERS' STANDING COMMITTEE.

Judge Emery: I have another matter that I wish to present you. We wish to perpetuate these gatherings. Of course we do not expect such gatherings as this every year; but I move that the chair name a committee of five whose business it shall be to have charge of and get up the annual Settlers' Celebration that we have been holding some ten years here at Lawrence, in Douglas county, and name the secretary. That is all the organization we ever had; and we must have it kept up. I move the chair appoint a committee of five (and I do not want to be one of them) whose duty it shall be to manage this matter.

John Speer: I second the motion.

The motion was then put and carried.

The following were appointed the committee: E. A. Coleman, Samuel Walker, Samuel Kimball, Joseph Savage, William Yates, and C. L. Edwards, secretary.

ADDRESS BY MRS. SARAH PINKSTON.

Col. Wood: I rise for the purpose of introducing Mrs. Pinkston. Some of you knew her in our early days as Miss Sarah Lyon, afterward as Mrs. Mack. I knew her as a mere girl in Ohio, before Kansas was open to settlement. Her father was a deacon in the Presbyterian church, and was of such stuff as they used to make martyrs of. I recollect he was once indicted under the Fugitive Slave Law for riding along the road with a colored man.

It was thirty years ago that a cousin of mine came to our house near Mt. Gilead, Ohio, and says, " Can I have your team to-night?"

I answered, "How many this time?" He said "Ten." I bantered him to go in the day time. He said, "I will, if you go along with me." I accepted, and at nine o'clock three young men with a four-horse team and ten fugitives in an open wagon, were on the road. We went twenty-two miles, to old Benjamin Gass' in Richland county where we left the fugitives, and went to William Lyon's and stayed all night. It was the first time I saw the young ladies, one of whom not this one, I afterward married. Sarah Lyon came here with her parents in July, 1854, and settled on the California road above Lawrence. The first death was at my house; a young man by the name of Pomeroy. Sarah Lyon helped to nurse him, rode in the wagon with, and steadied the coffin as it ascended Mt. Oread. She was the first young lady in Lawrence. She afterward married John Mack and lived here in Lawrence until two years ago, when she was married to E. W. Pinkston of Chase county, where she now lives. Ladies and Gentlemen, I now introduce Mrs. Pinkston.

Mrs. Pinkston said:

The inspiration of this hour, of this day, of these two days, should bring forth such eloquence in prose and poetry as to immortalize the writer, but we leave such eloquence to abler ones, to Edward Everett Hale, John P. St. John and others, whose whole lives are a continuous poem, and I will tell the simple story of pioneer life.

One bright May morning in 1854 the family of William Lyon left the dear old home in Ohio to make a new home in California. "Man proposes but God disposes." Sickness in the family prevented further arrangements for the California trip, and after a few weeks' sojourn in Independence, Mo., the third week in July, 1854, the family consisting of the father, mother, Mrs. Adams the eldest married daughter, Sarah, youngest daughter, aged 17 years, William Lee, youngest son, aged 15 years and S. N. Wood, and wife (daughter of Mrs. L's), and two little children named David and Wm. Lyon, took up their line of march for Kansas and liberty, for they had learned to their consternation and surprise that there was no liberty even of speech in Missouri.

Wm. Lyon was an old pioneer of the Wm. Lloyd Garrison stamp in the anti-slavery cause. He had stood up in the face of the mob years before and spoken words (now appearing prophetic), that made the friends of slavery tremble with apprehension. He could not submit to live long in a place where the freedom of speech was not allowed, and where the institutions he had fought for twenty years flourished with all its attendant evils. They soon learned that a liberty-loving and slavery-hating Ohio family could not live in safety where the monster had eyes on all sides watching them.

Kansas with Indians, wolves, camp fires, houseless on the prairie, was preferable; anything to get away from where "The trail of the serpent was ever over them all."

Two weeks before the first party of the New England Emigrant Aid Company arrived in Kansas, that little band of emigrants toiled up the hill and rested on the very spot where now stands that noble building, the Kansas State University. The two hours' rest on that hill will never be forgotten. How vast the country seemed to that lonely little party. For miles around the scene was unbroken by the work of human hands. The quiet, good-natured oxen standing patiently in the shadow of the high covered wagon, seemed like part of the family. No wonder. Not a sign of human habitation or of animate nature in all that vast expanse of country, only the few gathered around the wagon resting and enjoying that glorious view, calling the attention of each other to different points of beauty. The mother called the attention of the party to some object just visible above the tall prairie grass. She said it looked like a small pen of some kind. The natural conclusion was that it was an Indian hut. In that same "little pen" Mr. Paul Brooks kept the first dry goods store in the city of Lawrence. The party passed on and pitched their tents four miles farther west on the old California road.

Thus commenced that new, queer, half-Christian way of living, a home without a house. I remember what an effort mother made to keep in sight the old landmarks and dear old home ways. The family altar was established, the blessing asked at table, an extra plate laid for the stranger. Often was our camp-fire a beacon light to the benighted traveler and seeker after a claim. Our tent was pitched a half-mile north of the California road near a spring. That was a temporary arrangement, however, for father's claim was south and near the California road. Just north of the road where we lived three months in the tent, G. C. Brackett now has his fruit and nursery farm. Good water was not plenty those days and the spring was a treasure, but the spring began to fail and it was suggested to dig it deeper. S. N. Wood took that for his job, while father hauled green boughs from the woods two miles north of us, with which he made a welcome shade over the door of the tent, extending out about ten feet; also one for Mrs. Wood's tent. We were more comfortable after that. The hot August sun had been almost unbearable in the tent. Other tents were soon pitched near us, until we had quite a cheery little settlement.

Mr. J. C. Archibald, J. D. Stevens, Mr. John Maley and others, all members of the first New England party, were our neighbors.

The weather was hot and dry, the spring failed again, and we suffered for good water. Father hauled water in barrels from the creek two miles north of us. Everyone was ready to take a drink when he drove up with a fresh supply. One Saturday noon a violent thunder storm came up. Fortunately for us father was at home.   The other men were all away looking for claims or hunting.

The storm came on in such awful grandeur, such magnificent fury as we had never witnessed before.   The thunder rolled and crashed over us.   The rain poured down in torrents.   The wind blew as if it would sweep the prairie clean.   It required the united efforts of the family to hold the tent in place.   Mrs. Wood was alone in her tent a few rods from ours.   Her two little boys came to grandma's tent but a little while before the storm came on.   Mrs. Wood's habitation was soon in ruins, and she ran through the pouring rain to us.

The tents belonging to the gentlemen were all down and blown about.   After the violence of the storm had passed it remained cloudy and threatening and turned cold.   Our neighbors returned to their fallen homes.   The night came on early and dark.   Everything was soaking wet and cold—no fire; no supper, and not even a place to sit down.

Father was equal to the emergency, how he did it I never knew, but he soon had a blazing fire under the cover of green boughs that had nobly withstood the storm.   As the bright cheerful fire lighted up the prairie, father called out to our neighbors to come. They waited for no second invitation for they were wet, hungry and cold.   Some of them had walked miles that day and were glad to get even a wooden stool to sit on near the glowing fire.

Now was mother's opportunity to show that she was, too, equal to the emergency.   She always baked on Saturday.   That day she had her bread ready to bake when the storm came on.   With true housewife care she managed to protect her bread, and when supper time came she had a panful of very light sour dough but no bread.   By the use of a little soda she soon had good light biscuit, and while Mrs. Wood baked them in a Dutch oven mother made a boiler full of coffee, and every one was served with hot coffee and bread and nothing else, but it was a feast.   These new-comers cannot realize the situation, but we old settlers can understand it perfectly.   The dark night; the threatening clouds overhead; the blazing wood-fire casting a weird light far out over the tall prairie grass still dripping with rain; around and near the fire, seated on wooden benches, a little company of men fresh from comfortable New England homes, unused to anything like "roughing it," mother, the tall dignified lady, with the assistance of her daughters, serving refreshments that were as thankfully received as more delicate viands would have been under more favorable circumstances. Father, the returned Californian, was in his element.   He was always "given to hospitality," and it was a real pleasure to him to entertain those houseless strangers.   It was a picture worthy an artist's best efforts.

All were cheerful and talked of far-away homes and hopeful of future homes in Kansas.   One wondered what the effect would be if the group and surroundings could be set down in Boston Com-

mon. Another remarked, "Wouldn't it make the natives stare?"
Mr. Archibald, in that characteristic way of his that we all so
well remember, said as he passed his tin cup for more coffee,
"Well, it is a good thing to have women-folks around." The sentiment was echoed by the others. Mother appreciated the compliment.

The next morning the sun rose in all his regal splendor, as if
to repair the damage done by the storm. Tents were set up, beds,
blankets and clothing were spread out to dry. Soon all things were
in comfortable order again.

When the cabin was built we moved into it and lived all winter without floors, doors or windows. As it was called the best
house on the road we could not complain.

By this time a flourishing city of tents had sprung up as if by
magic, and was called New Boston, Yankee Town and Thayer. It
was finally named Lawrence, in honor of Amos Lawrence, of
Boston. About this time an adventurous Missourian brought a
barrel of whisky in town to start a saloon with. It was left un-
guarded during the night. In the morning when the would-be
whiskey seller returned to his "foundation of a fortune," he found
that some anti-whisky men had been there before him and his hopes
of future wealth had all run with his whisky into the ground
through a half-inch auger hole, bored through the bottom of the
wagon box into the barrel. Every one in the little city looked so
perfectly innocent and sober in the morning that he could accuse
no one of the deed. He retraced his steps with a lighter wagon to
a more congenial clime, a wiser if not a richer man.

On the memorable 30th of March, 1855, when Kansas was
first invaded by Missourians who came in by hundreds to vote for
members of the Legislature and other territorial officials, they
would ride up to the house and ask the way to Douglas, one place
of voting. One rode up to the door and asked if he could get
"something to drink." Mrs. Adams answered. "Yes, sir," and
when she in that quiet lady-like way that was characteristic of her,
handed him a glass of cold water, his look of blank astonishment
was perfectly ludicrous, and he said, "Oh, I want something stronger
than that." She replied, "This is what we drink." He, no doubt,
was thinking of the inevitable whiskey barrel found in the cabins
of his own class of people. During the day many others called for
something to drink and turned away disappointed.

Volumes could be filled with the varied experiences of the first
settlers of Kansas, but the half will never be told.

Our pioneering was not all ills and darkness. We could make
merry over many things that in Ohio would have annoyed us. Perhaps it was the increasing health and physical strength of each one
that caused the happy change. Then we had the lovely prairie
flowers that were a continual source of wonder and delight, and
then a never-ending panorama of beauty, of hills and valleys,
lights and shadows ever before us. Kansas was then in her christ-

ening robes, young, fair and beautiful. Her sponsors were the
brave, self-reliant sons and daughters of freedom, who promised to
protect and educate her in the ways of liberty, justice and equal
rights. She was baptized with the most precious blood of the land,
that of husbands, sons and brothers. Her sponsors have been true
to their trust. Through trials and darkness she has come up to
that high standard of perfection that their most ambitious hopes
could desire. To look back over the long reach of twenty-five
years it seems almost incredible that we have survived it all. Could
the Old Settlers have foreseen the storm of terror that was to sweep
over Kansas and last so many years, surely our hearts would have
failed us. But when the storm broke in all its fury upon us, and
our only hope was for all hands to " hold on to the tent," everyone
was ready, and when the clouds were the darkest, and the lightning of burning homes, and the thunder of death shots, it made
the stoutest hearts quail. Then it was the Old Settlers who stood
firmly at their posts and outlooks until the storm had passed and
the glorious sun of freedom shone out upon them.

The night has passed away and we enjoy this bright, this glorious noontime.

One by one we are passing away, emigrating alone to the new
untried country. Our number is being reduced. While we remain
here let us remember each other, and as we meet year after year
at our reunions, while there is one of us left, let us give the nation to know and understand that we belong to the F. F. Ks.

ADDRESS BY THOS. W. CONWAY.

Col. Wood :—I will now introduce to you a gentleman who
will talk to you about a class of people that the struggle in Kansas
emancipated from slavery.

Gen. Conway said :

Mr. President, Ladies and Gentlemen :

I am surely a newcomer, though my namesake and relative
is one of your old comers, and I noticed to-day when his name
was mentioned that he has a very warm place in all your hearts.
I have not been indifferent to the great and wonderful history
of Kansas. I was reminded to-day when I heard the mention
of Sharp's rifles of what I had to do with Kansas in the early
times, when I was a college boy in a university in the State of
New York. On one vacation day when I was down in New York
City, I thought to myself I would go over to Brooklyn and hear
Mr. Beecher. Just a little while before a kind friend had sent me
a New Year's present of a hundred dollars. I thought myself
very rich with the hundred dollars, and I had most of it in my
pocket when I went over to the Plymouth church, in Brooklyn, to
hear the great minister. The topic that he preached about was
KANSAS ; and the subject I thought was chiefly rifles. An appeal

was made for money, to help you people who were the Free State Pioneers of Kansas; and I thought to myself as God had been so good to me as to put it into some kind friend's heart to send me a present of a hundred dollars, that I would be ungrateful if I did not in turn try to do good to somebody else and give part of that hundred dollars. So I put my hand into my pocket and took out money enough to pay for a rifle to send out here where my relative was struggling with the rest of you in behalf of liberty in Kansas. So, then I am an old citizen to the extent of a rifle. If I had been a little older then, as old as I am now, I have no doubt but that I should have brought the rifle and come to Kansas myself. Now, I have enjoyed this meeting immensely to-day. If I had time I would like to tell you what a Jerseyman thinks of you, but I have not time. I have seen more of Kansas than I ever did before. I am reminded of the time I went to a Chinese theater in San Francisco. I went there with an English speaking Chinaman. I asked him what the actors were talking about. He says, "Chinese." Pretty soon the thing changed and another actor came on and says I, "what are they talking about"? He says, "Chinese," Another curtain ran up and I asked the same question and he says, "Chinese," and so it went throughout the evening's entertainment. Well, now, it is so here. If some one were to ask me what you were talking about I should say "Kansas." If somebody else were to ask what you are talking about I should say "Kansas." I am glad to hear you men and women talking so much about Kansas. Kansas in your heads and Kansas in your hearts. You have got a grand record and a grand history, and I am proud of it. My friend said that I was interested in the exodus. Well, I suppose you all know that. I lived in New Orleans for about eleven years, from 1863 to 1874. I was six years the Superintendent of Public Education in the State of Louisiana after the war. I was connected with the army in various important positions. I am conversant with the condition of the people of the South, and if I were not in favor of the exodus I should be untrue to my manhood. I should be untrue to my knowledge of the Bible. I should be untrue to its principles of grand civilization. I am in favor of the exodus, and I am doing all in my power to enlarge it and give it power, dignity and importance. I am in favor when a building is on fire of rescuing the men and women and children in that building. The South is on fire; the fire of hell reigns in the South. The fire of persecution, the fire of outrage, the fire of denial of rights, the fire of poverty and oppression, the fire of trampling on liberty, and where that kind of fire burns I am for rescuing the people. I met a distinguished citizen of Kansas in New York the other day and he said to me, "General, I want you to go out to the pioneers' meeting, they will be glad to see you." "Well," I said, "it is 1,500 miles away, and it is a long way, but I have long wanted to go to Kansas any how," and so I came. I think I have grown about five feet since I came here. I like you. I like you men and women and children. I like your spirit and your love of Kansas. Speaking of the exodus in Kansas reminds me of what some committees with which I am connected in Washington told me to say. They told me to "tell the people of Kansas for us, God bless them for their kindness to the poor negro." Well, now, I think I have been honored with an important message—a very honorable message—"God bless them for their kindness to the negro." The poorest and meanest and most despised of our people; kind and forgiving and patriotic. Nineteen-twentieths of them Christians belonging to some church, trusting in the same God with the white man that oppresses him, having but very few friends in the South and not a great many more in the North. I meet them on the Mississippi river and I ask them, why are you going to Kansas? They said because Kansas people are humane and kind. Their heads are level in regard to Kansas. If a negro in Kansas has occasion to bring a suit before one of your justices, he will get justice in the court. That is one reason why the negro comes to Kansas. If he works for a man and that man agrees to pay him the wages and then violates his contract, that negro knows that in nine hundred and ninety-nine cases out of a thousand the public sentiment of Kansas will demand justice for him. Don't be alarmed about too many negroes coming to Kansas. You are not going to be troubled with them in that great proportion. I am authorized while I am in the West by negroes themselve who have money and who are organizing into colonies of 2,000 to 3,000, more than a dozen of them have written to me, while I am in the West, to go down into New Mexico, Arizona and Colorado, and see if they cannot get a body of land ranging from a million to two million acres. And I find people in the North ready to furnish the negroes the money to buy this land and make them independent land-owners, and by working upon it as the farmer upon his land, earn their own living. The negroes that are coming up this fall and winter from the South are not coming up as paupers, but or-ganized into colonies. Their plan is not to a llow anybody to join these colonies who has not got money enough to pay their way and buy land when they get up here. We have more than 13,000 applications from Illinois for work for them. You are not going to be troubled. I have 4,000 from Ohio. I have some from west-ern Pennsylvania and western New York. I had a gentleman write me the other day from Minnesota, saying that 500 or 600 could get employment away up there. My own judgment is that they better not go as far north as that.

But I must close. This grand occasion must be of great in-terest to you. Your talks to-night ought to be short. I was afraid I had come 1,500 miles and was not going to get a chance to talk. I never heard no many orators in one place as I have heard here these two days. You are all members of Congress or fit to be, or going to be. You are in favor of woman's rights; and so is my wife and she manages to have them. You are liberal; you are up, on all things, and up so high that a short man like me cannot reach them at all. I leave you to-morrow, and I leave you with very pleasant recollections. I am delighted with my visit among you, and if I live twenty-five years from now, I hope to come over and join in your next quarter-centennial celebration. I am going to write to Martin F. Conway in his unfortunate condition in that asylum down in Washington, and I am going to tell him how you received his letter to-day and how his name was received. I think it will do his soul good. I think when I get back to Washington, on my way to New York, I will stop and see him. I know what it is to be confined in-doors rendered utterly physically helpless. I know what it is to have some cheering voice come from abroad and from some friendly heart. I know how invigorating it is, and I know that Martin F. Conway will be very glad when he learns how kindly his letter was received. We ought to take the case of Martin to God and ask Him that he may be relieved from any trouble of the mind and that he may be restored to health again.

ADDRESS BY HON. JOSHUA WHEELER.

The chairman introduced Hon. Joshua Wheeler who said :

Mr. Chairman:

For the information of my friends I will state that I never was a Democrat. I do not know that I can claim to be an Old Settler. It has been twenty-two years since the 1st day of October with my family—a wife and two children—crossed over the Missouri line into Kansas. A company of neighbors left the State of Illinois during the present month and started for the territory of Kansas. We came overland bringing our wives, our children, our cows, our horses, our oxen and our implements to farm with. We were nearly four weeks making the trip. We came through the State of Missouri and crossed the Missouri river at St. Joseph, remaining there a short time in the town of Elwood which I think has since been washed away by the Missouri river. I settled in Atchison county and many of you Old Settlers know the reputation of Atchison county at that time. It had been but a short time before that General Lane had visited the city of Atchison and a mob prevented his speaking and the secretary of this meeting, the secretary of the Kansas State Historical Society came within a very little of losing his life on that occasion. We had conventions then nearly every day in the week and we had some brave free state men in the county of Atchison. Some of them did everything in their power for the country and one of those men was Hon. S. C. Pomeroy. I took a deep interest in the Kansas-Nebraska Bill when it was pending in Congress. I have not forgotten the last speech made on the passage of that bill by William H. Seward in the Senate when he challenged the men of the South to meet the North and make the struggle here in Kansas. Well, they did meet it. I do not regret it. We have seen troublesome times. Our wives and our families

13

have gone through many hardships of pioneer life for at the time we settled in the State you will recollect that it was just at the money crisis of 1857. Part of the time we had to pay four per cent. per month for money. We had to live very sparing, but we have stuck to it, and I like to look back and think of what we have gone through since that time.

Thank God that the State of Kansas has taken such an active part in this great struggle which this nation has gone through. I rejoice that the people of this State have been true to the great interests of human freedom.

ADDRESS BY REV. WILLIAM BISHOP.

Col. Wood: I will now introduce to you a gentleman from what used to be the western frontier of Kansas, Rev. William Bishop.

Mr. Bishop said:

Mr. President, Ladies and Gentlemen :

I cannot claim that I am really an Old Settler, and therefore I cannot tell what a great many others have told here in their speeches, the important part they took in the great struggle. But I have been here about twenty-one years, and therefore I am of age. I am happy to be allowed to speak at this great love-feast. I claim that I did not come from Massachusetts, nor Ohio, nor Illinois nor in fact from anywhere in the United States. I came from another State beyond the ocean. I have been very much amused, that, with all the speeches I have heard, only one fact has been established, and that is that Kansas has been saved. The question as to who saved Kansas reminds me of the conundrum, "Who struck Billy Patterson?" A great many claim that they have saved Kansas. Now the fact is that what they have said is true in no little degree, I have no doubt. They all did their part, and had their agency in accomplishing this result. But after hearing Col. Wood and Hon. Mr. Legate and all these men I was reminded very much of the old preacher when he was preaching to the Jews. His text was "He goeth about as a roaring lion seeking whom he may devour." And says he, we will inquire first, who the devil he is ; and second, what the devil he is seeking; and third, what the devil he is roaring about. (Applause.) Now when I heard these men roaring I asked what were they roaring about. (Applause.) They were going about like roaring lions who have devoured a great many good men in Kansas. Now the fact is that Kansas was saved by the proper agencies of Pennsylvania, Massachusetts, Illinois and of many other States, and of some not from any of the States. It was saved by the Yankees, Pennsylvania Germans, Irish, Scotch ;—all the nationalities in the world were engaged in saving Kansas. But pardon me if I mention one or two names that have been ignored apparently in this great work of saving Kansas. I say that no man in his proper sphere in the early history of Kansas did more to bring the right kind of an element into Kansas, and use it after it got here, than Col. William A. Phillips. And you will pardon me if I mention another man that now lies asleep in this cemetery over here. His name has never been mentioned; and yet I believe he established the first free state paper in Kansas. I refer to Josiah Miller. And now let me mention still another man who has been under a cloud for some years past; but we should not forget his services to Kansas. He also has been virtually ignored; yet no man did more to promote the interests of the State and the people than he did during his career. I mean Samuel C. Pomeroy. But Kansas has been saved; and well saved, too; although to do this, it was necessary to pass through the border ruffian war of the Rebellion. If Kansas has grown to its present status on the western prairies through all these trials what will it be in the next twenty-five years to come? Let us prepare for this battle and inscribe upon our banners the glorious victories we achieved in the past, and go forward doing our whole duty and trust to God for the result.

ADDRESS BY E. A. COLEMAN.

Col. Wood :— I will now call on one of the old guard, one whom you all know to have been always reliable when duty called; he will tell you some things he knew about.

Mr. Coleman said :

Ladies and Gentlemen :

It has been said, sir, that we were writing history on this occasion to' go on record. Such being the fact, it is absolutely necessary that that history should be correct. In regard to one fact, I want to say one word to corroborate what my friend here says; in regard to the position that Gov. Stanton took at that time he referred to: There are people here who recollect the circumstance to which I am about to refer. It is a stray leaf. It will be recollected by the people of Lawrence and vicinity that before Gov. Walker got here Gov. Stanton came down to Lawrence to make a speech. He got up on the rostrum or platform of the old Cincinnati Hotel and went on with his speech, and said that he, as Governor of Kansas Territory, was bound to see that the laws were carried out to the letter. Robert Morrow, standing by my side, said: "Governor, what laws do you refer to, the territorial laws or the laws of the United States?" He said, "Both." Standing by him I spoke out and said: "We will obey the laws of the United States, but the laws of the Territory, never!" and in this many others joined with me, crying out, "never! never!" "Then," said Gov. Stanton, rising up on his very tip-toes and throwing his arms high in the air, "then, gentlemen of Lawrence, it is war to the knife and the knife to the hilt." But after that assertion he soon crawled down and slipped out of the back door. That is what I call a' stray leaf.

One thing I want to say about "Osawatomie Brown." His name has hardly been brought before the Old Settlers. Osawatomie Brown, it is well known, came, as the rest of the settlers in 1855 did, and brought his family and household goods. But before taking a claim, as the balance of us did, he settled down near the border—near the Missouri line. The border ruffian war commenced in 1855, and John Brown and his sons came here to Lawrence and with us, insisted on fighting them, and fighting them to the death! It is well known that Gov. Robinson, through his intrigue with other men, tried to get old Gov. Shannon drunk and then make a compromise with him and get him to send the Missourians back.

I want to tell you of another fact that I call a stray leaf. John Brown frequently visited me at my house and stayed with me. In fact, my "latch-string was always out" for all such men. John Brown knew where his friends lived, and could go to them night or day. That evening we ate supper out-of-doors in the shade of my cabin, at five o'clock. As soon as supper was over Captain Brown commenced pacing back and forth in the shade of the house with his hands behind him. The conversation was pretty general. My wife stood by the dishes and I sat in my chair with my heels upon the table. I finally said: "Capt. Brown, I want to ask you one question, and you can answer it or not as you please, and I shall not be offended." He stopped his pacing, looked me square in the face, and said: "What is it?" Said I, "Capt. Brown, did you kill those five men, or did you not?" He replied: "I did not; but I do not pretend to say they were not killed by my order, and in doing so I believe I was doing God's service." My wife spoke and said: "Then, Captain, you think that God uses you as an instrument in His hands to kill men?" Brown replied: "I think he has used me as an instrument to kill men, and if I live I think He will use me as an instrument to kill a good many more." He went on and said: "Mr. Coleman, I will tell you all about it, and you can judge whether I did wrong or not. I had heard that these men were coming to the cabin that my son and I were staying in" (I think he said the next Wednesday night) "to set fire to it and shoot us as we ran out. Now, that was not proof enough for me; but I thought I would satisfy myself, and if they had committed murder in their hearts I would be justified in killing them. I was an old surveyor, so I disguised myself, took two men to carry the chain, and a flagman. The lines not being run, I knew that as soon as they saw me they would come out to find out where their lines would come." And taking a book from his pocket he said: "Here is what every man said that was killed. I ran my lines close to each man's house. The first man that came out said: 'Is that my line, sir?' I replied: 'I cannot tell; I am running test lines.' I then said to him: 'You have a fine country here; great pity there are so many Abolitionists in it.' 'Yes, but by

God we will soon clean them all out,' he said. I kept looking through my instrument, making motions to the flagman to move either way, and at the same time I wrote every word they said; then I said: 'I hear that there are some bad men about here by the name of Brown.' 'Yes, there are, but next Wednesday night we will kill them.' So I ran the lines by each one of their houses, and I took down every word, and here it is, word for word, by each one. [Shows wife and me the book.] I was satisfied that each one of them had committed murder in his heart, and according to the Scriptures they were guilty of murder, and I felt justified in having them killed; but, as I told you, I did not do it myself."

He said: "Now, Mr. Coleman, what do you think?" I told him I thought he did right; so did my wife. This statement we are both willing to be sworn to as the truth of it if it would do any good, but it would not, as we are known, and have been for twenty-five years in Kansas.

I thank you; and I will leave the platform to some one else.

ADDRESS BY WILLIAM HUGHES.

COL. WOOD: I want to introduce to you one who is now one of the most prosperous farmers in Douglas county, but who, when a mere boy as it were, as a member of Captain Bickerton's artillery company had nothing to fight for but his rights and the Kansas home he had in prospect. I refer to Mr. William Hughes, and I hope he will come forward.

Mr. Hughes said:

I am one of the boys from Pennsylvania, born again into the anti-slavery fold by my Kansas experiences. It is true I came as a mere boy. I came simply to make a home and an honest living. But the outrages against the free state men brought me into the field, and I did my best for the cause of freedom. I know a good many Democrats—such as the McGee boys, for instance—who did valiant service. There was no neutral ground then. I remember seeing Mr. Wood, the Chairman, disarm Sheriff Jones. I was in the fights at Franklin, Fort Saunders, Fort Titus, Lecompton and Hickory Point. I escaped arrest with the one-hundred Hickory Point prisoners by being detailed to bring Frank Baldwin home wounded. I saw the free state prisoners brought in from Fort Scott with shackles on, and was one of the free state men who disarmed their captors and took the boys to a blacksmith shop and cut off their shackles.

I make no pretensions as a speaker, but the Lord has preserved me, and I now feel independent, and thankful for the part which I was permitted to take in the great struggle for human freedom.

The following was offered by Hon. Sidney Clarke, and adopted by unanimous vote :

Resolved : That we cannot adjourn this meeting without expressing our profound sorrow for the loss of the Old Settlers of Kansas who, since our last reunion have passed over the river to the other side. For each and all we shed the tears of regret, and say, farewell.

ADDRESS BY MR. WAKEFIELD.

The Chairman introduced Mr. Wakefield, who said :

Ladies and Gentlemen :

It is late, but as others have spoken so fully of the leaders among the free state men, and have given the leaders so much credit for what they did in the early troubles in Kansas I will speak a word for the boys, one of which I was at the time. It was the young men and the boys that did most of the fighting and scouting and endured most of the hardship of the border wars. Most of these young men were in the war of the Rebellion and made honor-able records as soldiers, no less than nineteen of the company known as the Bloomington Rangers in 1855 and 1856 having held commissions during the war. This company was the first one organized in the Territory, it having elected officers and commenced drilling in June, 1855. Our company was formed into a secret organization; every man was sworn by a terrific, double-geared, iron-clad oath to be true to the cause, under penalty of death; was sworn to kill any one who betrayed us, and to always rally to the company rendezvous when notified; or to the assistance of his neighbors; and to obey without hesitation the orders of the company-officers, or a vote of the company.

Our place of meeting was in a dense piece of timber, in a lonely and unfrequented place, the regular hour being nine o'clock P. M., where we compared notes of the enemy's movements and laid plans for future operations.

Members of the company were notified of a meeting at nine o'clock P. M. by leaving a piece of blank paper two inches square at their residence, or pinning it to their door if not at home—as a good many were keeping "bach" and liable to be absent from their cabins in the day-time. If the piece of blank paper was cut three-cornered, it meant business at once, and for the one receiving it to rally at rendezvous immediately, armed and ready for action.

It was generally conceded in those days that no other company did more or better service than the Bloomington Rangers, Capt. Sam. Walker commanding. But credit is due to a great many companies, and to a great many individuals who were not leaders. It is the duty of all to collect up the history of all such organizations, and of the worthy acts of all individuals who made sacrifices for the good of Kansas, and in that way alone can the true history of Kansas be recorded and preserved. The State Historical Society is doing a good work in drawing out reminiscenses from the Old Settlers and gathering them into its collections of the materials of Kansas History.

ADDRESS BY W. C. GIBBONS.

COL. WOOD: I will now introduce to you an old settler who has on other occasions talked temperance to you, in this grove and elsewhere, Dr. W. C. Gibbons.

Dr. Gibbons said:

Mr. President, Ladies and Gentlemen:

I was born an Abolitionist and came to Kansas an Abolitionist. On the 18th day of October, 1854, I left my home in the East and started for Kansas. I came up the Missouri river and landed in Kansas City. Then I didn't know how to get up here as I didn't have a dollar. I borrowed a dollar from a man there and started up on foot to what was said to be Lawrence with my pack on my back. On my way up, a few miles this side of Kansas City, when I didn't know where I was going or where I should get anything to eat, or how I would get along, I met a man with his wife and children and a span of horses, and he says, "Throw your pack in the wagon." That man was my dear good old friend Mr. Coleman. On November 3d, 1854, I landed here, so I have a little claim to old settlership. What I have done for Kansas I did as many another man did. We arranged for the work and we went into it not knowing what the results would be, and I am very proud to stand here to-night with these men and women at the twenty-fifth anniversary of the settlement of Kansas. One by one we will pass away, and perhaps very few of us will be here on the fiftieth anniversary. I hope to be here then. I will then be 69 years of age. Well, I can live that long, I see no good reason why I should not. [Laughter.]

Now we must attend to work. One good man here said, "Let's get ready for the battle for the next twenty-five years." Kansas is free, America is free, and we glory in the fact that we live in Kansas. Now let us go on in our manhood, and show that we are worthy of the name that these reporters are wafting over the civilized world. The very fact of this large gathering here at Bismarck we should be proud of. Let us continue, let us love it better, bear it in our hearts and souls, the standard of Kansas. Never let it drop. Let us go on cheerily, grandly, nobly working out the problem of our lives, and the problem of the life of Kansas.

The chairman introduced Mr. Armstrong, who said :

Ladies and Gentlemen :

I was an original Garrisonian Abolitionist, and always acted with the Abolition party before I came to Kansas. I voted for Martin Van Buren when he was the anti-slavery candidate for President. I well remember the excitement in the State of New York and in New England when the Kansas-Nebraska bill passed. I took that occasion to make a move. I had been wanting to go farther south, and I then resolved I would come to Kansas and help to make it a free State. So I shaped things as fast as I could, and on the 1st of November, 1854, I left western New York for Kansas. I arrived at Kansas City, I think, on the 17th of November, or on the morning of the 18th. I went out to the livery stables to see if I could find some one going to Lawrence.

The first man I met was the notorious Sam Wood. There he is, president of this meeting (pointing to Mr. Wood). I looked at him, and he said he was running an express up to Lawrence. I looked at him some more and found he was scarred up a little ; he looked a little rough, and after a little while I found that he had had a little battle over the slavery question at Westport, and had got his nose a little skinned. But I made arrangements with him to carry our baggage, our trunks. There were five of us in the party. I arrived in Lawrence on the night of the 20th of November. I could tell many things but I've not time. There's any amount of the history of Kansas that is yet unwritten. I am not accustomed to speak in public. I wish to say, however, that wherever there was work to do, in 1855 and 1856 and afterward, I was always on hand and ready to answer to the calls of my comrades and my country. In 1855 I think, I was, in the hands of Providence, instrumental in bringing James H. Lane to Lawrence. That spring I met James H. Lane on a boat on the Missouri river the morning after leaving St. Louis. I had been in Kansas in 1854, and with Gov. Robinson up as far as the Blue. He took a crowd of us up there. Lane was on his way to Kansas, and when he found out that I had been in the Territory, he wanted to learn all about the country. Thomas C. Shoemaker, Land Receiver at Kickapoo, was with him, a pro-slavery man as well as Lane, and Lane expected to locate at Kickapoo or Leavenworth. I gave them a general description of the country from the mouth of the Kaw river up to where Manhattan now stands, and of all the country. The location of Lawrence and the Kansas bottom pleased my eyes better than any where else, and I gave them a glowing description of it, and told them that I believed that Lawrence was the place where we should eventually build up a great city. I know I did prevail upon Lane to come to Lawrence, for three days after I got here he came up here with his family.

Lane soon began to come over to the free state side. He came over gradually, and finally got to be one of our main leaders. And we could not have done without James H. Lane; nor without Dr. Robinson, and I hope they will always live in the memory of every Kansan.

I am the first person, I believe, that had the colored children taught to read and write in Kansas, eight of them, in my house or cabin, on Washington creek, in Douglas county, in 1856. I also started an underground railroad in 1857 from Topeka to Civil Bend, in Iowa. I hired a closed carriage and span of mules. I lived at Topeka then. I took up a subscription to start the thing, and amongst the number that gave me money was Dr. Charles Robinson, who was at Topeka at the time. He gave me ten dollars. I think Sam Wood gave five dollars and Maj. J. B. Abbott five. They were attending the Legislature. I don't remember all who helped start the first train on the underground railroad, and I helped establish the depots from Topeka to Civil Bend, Iowa.

Our friend there, Dr. Patee, was talking a while ago about Bull creek. Some said there was no shooting done there. I was an advance guard, going to Bull creek with Lane and five men. I did a little shooting down there. One of them was that noble man who was shot down on the streets of Lawrence in the Quantrill raid, Capt. Bell. He was one of the best friends that Kansas ever had. At Bull creek Bell, Keller, Mitchell and a young man from Boston and myself made up the advance guard. This Mitchell was formerly from Kentucky. When we came to Bull creek the pro-slavery men had thrown out their pickets on each side of the road, and they ordered us to halt. They wanted to know who we were. We had Capt. Mitchell for spokesman to talk to them and we calculated to drive them, but after considerable talk and a little swearing they were a little fooled as they could not make out who we were. After a while Capt. Mitchell ordered me to give them a shot. Well, of course, I was willing to give them a shot, and I think I got my man. I know I got his hat and coat anyhow. Gen. Lane formed upon a ridge about half a mile west of Bull creek. There was a ravine intervening between where the two parties were formed. The pro-slavery men formed on a ridge just east of the creek, Lane to the west of them nearly a half a mile. They began forming in line on both sides of the road. After we got the cavalry in position they sent down three men toward our lines. As they came riding down the hill Lane says: "Armstrong go down and drive them men back." So I went down with my Sharpe's rifle and fired away at the three advancing men at long range. I fired a good many times as fast as I could. It had the desired effect to cause them to turn and get out of the way as fast as their horses could carry them, our boys shouting and cheering as the frightened men ran. So there was shooting done at the battle of Bull creek at two different times to my certain knowledge.

The Chairman introduced Mr. A. R. Green of Lecompton, who said he must be excused from making a speech; but he desired to make a motion as an act of justice to a worthy early settler who seemed to have been forgotten by the committee on officers. A quarter of a century ago George W. Zinn, then an old man, settled at Lecompton and made him a home; and through all the stormy period of 1855–7 that convulsed the Territory upon the slavery question, he was an active, efficient and faithful free state man; never wavering in his devotion to freedom or yielding an inch of ground to the slave-power. His cabin was often a beleaguered fortress, but it stands to-day one of the monuments to free speech. I move that the name of George W. Zinn be added to the list of vice-presidents of this meeting and I am sure that the adoption of this motion will give the old man more pleasure than the many flattering indorsements he has received from the people of his township, his county and his representative district.

The motion was then enthusiastically adopted.

COL. WOOD: I now want to present to you Dr. E. L. Patee of Manhattan, who was a very early settler and a very useful free state man in the most trying times.

Mr. Patee said:

I am happy to meet so many Old Settlers on this occasion; so many of my old and time-honored friends whom I scarcely ever expected to see again. Times have so changed, thousands have settled among us giving us a nearer neighborship; circumstances have forced new acquaintances, and new friends, making Old Settlers' reunions a matter of necessity in order to perpetuate old acquaintance, and the memories of those who, though not forgotten are too far from us in this fast age of our young State, to call upon, to visit, as we once did, to ask the time of day, hear the news, borrow or lend, or warm our feet. We congratulate every man, woman, child, and ourselves on the glorious strides we have made in this, our first quarter-century. Yet in our happiness we are sorry that some who once met with us are not here. I can notice nevertheless the sorrow is lessened in the joy I feel in beholding their portraits in conspicuous places. By these we know they are not forgotten, and in my imagination I feel their influence as I did feel in their presence in days gone by. Among others I notice the likeness of one whose shadow I think was a little longer in the world than any other one in our State; and as ever, I now like to honor him even in death. I think he was a great man. Some see fit to throw dust at his greatness, still I know, as they must, that they can do him no harm. That man was *James H. Lane.* May God rest his ashes; and may his soul rest as peaceful as his life was useful. May the generations of history be as true to him as he was true to liberty. I shall never forget my first acquaintance with him. It was in the fall of '56, when Buford and his Border Ruffian Gang marched into our Territory from Westport, Missouri, intending to make a war of extermination on all free state men in Kansas.

Lane was then in Topeka, had a few men without ammunition. Runners came to Manhattan for help. Powder and lead was needed. Among us we arranged to obtain it of Robert Wilson, then the sutler at Fort Riley, who was a warm pro-slavery man, by causing him to believe it was to go to Buford. The plan worked well although we were forced to "take water" and float down in a skiff on the Kansas river, while soldiers were scouring the woods and prairies after us; we landed about three o'clock in the morning at Topeka all safe. At once all of us but one, who stood with the skiff reported to Lane's head-quarters who received us with caution keeping us there until he sent others to find out the truth of our report; in a short time all were satisfied, and by sun-rise that morning we were marching to meet the "foe," who were reported to be fifteen-hundred strong. By the light of the next morning we were drawn up on the hills overlooking the enemy, who were camped in the valley of Bull creek. A few of us were placed in different places to make us look as big as possible while horsemen rode from one place to another to lend as bold an outlook as we could to the array. Thus we were presented to the enemy's sentinels, who gave the alarm to their camp; and such a skedaddling, I never saw before, some mounted two on one mule, some ran off on foot, while more cut the lariat and rode off single, all disappearing; to leave the camp, tents, and equipments an easy conquest to our little army.

The first of the enemy that reached Westport reported all dead but them, and the next the same and so on until all were home safe, while we held the field with a bloodless victory for we did not fire a gun. Under the circumstances I think this was much the best tactics, and good evidence of a soldier and great man to which he gave additional proofs. And I am very sorry to see the *small point* against him, that a few *poor sheets* have seen fit to spread before the world. I am glad to be able to stand here to-night as I do to offer thanks to the Hon. Sidney Clarke for his noble article in defense of this hero of Kansas, whose very name did much good work to secure law and order in the darker days of our State and during the days of our great national peril that followed.

COL. WOOD: I see the Hon. James Rogers, of Burlingame, here and I am sure you would all like to hear a few words from him.

Mr. Rogers said:

Mr. President and Fellow Citizens :

This call upon me to address this meeting at this time is entirely unexpected, and but from the fact that up to this time no mention has been made of several of the most prominent men of my part of the State and men the peers of any of her earliest settlers, I could not have been induced to give utterance to a single word. Not that I would pluck a single laurel from the brow of any one whose name has been mentioned, but simply that I would have justice done to all. I glory in the names of the leading pioneers of Kansas, and the least of them are entitled to all the encomiums that have been bestowed upon them to-day, but I came here for another purpose than to make speeches. I came here to meet old familiar faces, to greet old friends and to grasp honest and earnest hands. But as I look over this vast assembly of intelligent faces and reflect upon what changes have taken place in this Territory within the last five and twenty years, what "thronging memories" rise up before me. My tongue is unable to give utterance to my thoughts, and language is inadequate to express them.

Everywhere we see change, change, change! Since I first put foot on the soil of Kansas political convulsions have taken place not only in Kansas and throughout the United States, but all over the civilized world.

I remember well when I first placed foot upon Kansas soil. It was the very spot where Fremont camped in his overland tour to the Pacific. It then seemed to me to be hallowed ground. I remember well how my young wife and I trudged along, hand in hand, over the old Santa Fe road toward our new and unseen home in Central Kansas. What a great, broad and beautiful thoroughfare it was, broad, smooth and hard as Massachusetts street in Lawrence to-day. It was early spring and the trains of canvas-covered wagons that later whitened the great natural thoroughfare for hundreds of miles, had not yet commenced to move. All was one vast open prairie. From Westport to Council City (now Burlingame), there was not more than half a dozen dwellings, and these were cabins or shanties. Now a forbidding looking coyote starts up and slinks away in the tall grass, casting a leering look at us as much as to say, "what business have you here?" Now a crow calls out "kaw, kaw, kaw," at us, meaning by tone and gesture that we were on forbidden ground. Now a prairie hawk flies near and cuts a few circles over our heads and flies away as if to tell his more familiar neighbors, the Indians, that we were invading a place sacred to solitude and savage life. Now we meet with a more fiendish and forbidding looking class of animal, the border ruffian, who mutters out to us the interrogative, "Why don't you uns stay in your own country and not come out here to steal our land and run off our niggers" And following this by an imprecation that, "You will soon be trotting out of Kansas faster than you came in."

Those great commercial thoroughfares that then extended across the Territory from the Missouri to the Rockies and into New Mexico, where are they now? They have been plowed up and fenced up until scarce a trace of them can be found. They have been converted with the rest of the country into fertile fields of waving wheat and luxuriant maize. In lieu of these great arteries of trade and traffic we have great lines of railroad stretching out their Briarean arms over the whole State, and across the plains and mountains into Colorado and New Mexico. From 8,000 people when I came here, we have grown to more than 800,000. The whole country has been converted into fruitful farms and covered over with dwellings and school houses, and along these great iron ways have sprung up a hundred villages, towns and cities. The border man, with his unholy institution, like the rest of the wild beasts, has disappeared before the advancing contagion, and those institutions which were the boast and pride of the slave power are to day held in scorn and contempt by the liberty-loving people of Kansas. But, Mr. President, I forget myself. I rose to attempt to do honor to the illustrious dead and among those whose names figure in the early settlement of this Territory none was more worthy of a grateful remembrance than that of Hon. Philip C. Schuyler, commonly called "Judge Schuyler." He was the peer of any of the early pioneers and I had almost said he was "the noblest Kansan of them all." He had all of the virtue and but few of the vices of the men of those days. He was a fine dignified gentleman of the old Dutch Aristocracy of New York. He had the blood of the Schuylers, the Ten Broecks and the Van Rennsselaers of Revolutionary memory in his veins.

He once told me he ran for the office of "judge" on the ticket of Birney, and thereafter ever acquired that soubriquet. I well remember the first time I met him. It was in the office of the elder Bennett, of the New York *Herald*. He excoriated him most genteelly for the course of the *Herald* toward the free state party of Kansas.

I believe that lesson had its effect, for from that time the tone of that gazette was very much modified toward our party here. Nor shall I ever forget what scorn and contempt came over his usually placid face as Col. Sumner marched into the old State House at Topeka, sword in hand, and disbanded the convention there assembled July 4th, 1856.

Judge Schuyler was elected Secretary of State under the first free state constitution, and also to the same office under the Lecompton constitution.

The free state convention which assembled at Lawrence to

nominate candidates for state officers under the constitution voted to put no ticket in the field. Judge Schuyler, G. W. Brown and some others bolted the convention and having met in the basement of Brown's office put a full ticket in the field. For this conduct they were dubbed by the Radicals as "Brown's Cellar Kitchen Cabinet." The election of this ticket and the subsequent defeat of the constitution of the slave party vindicated the wisdom of their course.

It was not all peace as you may suppose among the free state leaders in those days. Those old liberty-loving gladiators hacked away terribly at one another sometimes, but when the clarion of war sounded its free state notes, they came together as one man. All domestic discord ceased and the cry of "Down with slavery and up with liberty," echoed along the line. The name of another, no less conspicuous, who figured in those early troubles, and who had left the classic halls of learning to come to Kansas, was that of James M. Winchell. He probably possessed finer literary taste and acquirements than any of those men of his time. Like Schuyler he first settled at Council City, was its first Postmaster and afterward laid out the city of Superior; was frequently elected to the Legislature; was chosen president of the convention that framed our present constitution; was the war-correspondent of the New York *Times* at Washington, and recently died near New York, having just written a finished and popular poem for the Atlantic Monthly, to which he was a regular contributor. It can be truthfully said that no man had an equal influence with him in our first legislative bodies. At one time he stood high for Senatorial honors. A more ardent, energetic and devoted champion the free state cause never had.

Another name not unworthy of notice is that of Hon. Samuel R. Canniff. He had office thrust upon him. He was not a talker, but following the advice of Greeley, who said, "The workers will beat the talkers every time." He worked faithfully and fervently.

Among the young men in our part of the State who figured on the side of freedom was one whose name I cannot pass by in silence. It is that of Hon. O. H. Sheldon. How enthusiastic I had almost said, how wild he was. He figured largely in our first Legislature. He was a delegate to the convention that nominated President Hayes, and died about a year ago a member of the State Senate.

Last, but not least, is the name of Henry Harvey. He was in religion of the sect of Quakers. He did most effectual work in bringing in supplies and goods contraband of war for the fighting boys. He had once been the U. S. Agent for the Shawnees, and had written and published their history. He had resided in the Territory some twenty years before its admission by Congress. He spoke the Indian dialect and visited all the different tribes and did most effectual service in keeping them on good terms with our party. He settled near Burlingame in what is now known as Harveyville, in Wabaunsee county.

And now, as I have said, Mr. President, I rose merely to say a word in memory of some individuals who had not been mentioned here, and thanking you all for your attention, I will close.

THE BRANSON RESCUE.

The following was written for the Old Settlers' meeting by Maj. J. R. Kennedy, now of Colorado. It gives an account of an event which occurred on the night of November 26, 1855, near the Wakarusa, a few miles southeast of Lawrence, and which was the origin of the "Wakarusa War."

COLORADO SPRINGS, 1879.

My Dear Friends:— It was, I think, in November, 1855, about ten o'clock one night that Miner B. Hupp came to my house in Free State Valley, and called to me to come out. In those days a call to "come out" was not always to be obeyed, but I knew his voice, so I went to the door, telling him to come in. He answered that he could not do so as he was in a hurry, that he wanted me to go with him; for a party of pro-slavery men had gone to Hickory Point to arrest Jacob Branson, who was the principal witness against Coleman for the murder of Dow, and it was the general impression that they would hang him or make way with him in some manner, so it was the intention to make an attempt to rescue him, let the consequences be what they might. Telling him to wait until I got my coat and gun — a Sharp's rifle — I went into the house, getting them in a hurry, while my wife got the children out of bed, wrapping them up the best she could. I took two of them and started for the house of our nearest neighbor, C. Holloway. Miner having gone on, had Holloway out and ready. They called to me to hurry, which I did, placing the babies about fifty yards from the house and running until I caught up with the men. They were on the double-quick, for Miner said he wanted to square accounts with two of them who had threatened and abused him a day or two before, and that he was afraid "the ball would be over before we got there."

The place of meeting was at Maj. Abbott's house, and when we reached there we found quite a body of men. Maj. Abbott was absent, but his wife was present — cool and cheerful — helping the boys fix up their guns. Abbott had gone over to Esterbrook's to see if he could hear or see anything of the parties who had gone to arrest Branson, as it was about time for them to be coming back, it being nearly 11 p. m. Two men had been sent out to watch the pro-slavery crowd, and it was thought the matter would be well attended to, as Berkaw was one of the men — but nothing had yet been heard from them.

We had been together about half an hour, talking and expressing opinions as to what would be done if the party would come, and as to whether they had gone another road and eluded us, or had taken Branson to the nearest woods and hanged him. I was too much excited to be still, so kept going out and in and reporting. Presently Maj. Abbott returned from Esterbrook's without any news. Then there was another interchange of opinions and guesses as to what had been or would be done. While I was standing by the door, still on the watch, I heard Philip Hupp — and no braver man ever lived — say, "Well, boys, I tell you what's the matter; they have taken Branson and crossed the Wakarusa at Cornelius' Crossing, and have him at old Crane's hotel. All we have to do, and what we ought to do, is to march right down there, and if Branson is in the house, tell him to come out; that he is a free man and will be protected." Just at this time I walked out a little from the door, and looking south saw fifteen or twenty mounted men riding slowly along the road toward the house. Stepping quickly back to the door, I caught Maj. Abbott's eye and beckoned him to come out, which he did. I showed him the men, and exclaiming "that's the party," he rushed into the house, telling the boys they were coming, and to go out quick. Mrs. Abbott handed the boys their guns and they did go out with a rush; Abbott going first followed by Philip Hupp; then came Capt. Hutchinson, Paul Jones and others. We turned to the left around the corner of the house into the road a few rods in front of the horsemen. Phil. Hupp was the first man who crossed the road. He said afterward he was watching the man on the gray horse, Sheriff Jones, and he did watch him sure enough. Next to Hupp was Paul Jones, and both were armed with squirrel rifles. Next came Capt. Hutchinson, armed with two large stones; next were Holloway and myself, I thinking Capt. H. was a good man to stay with, as he had been three years in the Mexican war. The rest of the boys ranged along the side of the road near the house. This was about the order we occupied when the party approached close to those in the road and very close to those by the side of the road. Mr. Hupp being in front and seeing the boys scattered along from where he was to the house, called out, "Boys, what the h—ll are you doing there? Here is the place for you." They then all crowded rapidly up in front of the other party, when one of them said, "What's up?" Maj. Abbott replied, "That is what we want to know," which remark was followed by a shot on our side. The Major had a self-cocking revolver, and he had, in the excitement, pulled it a little too hard causing it to go off. Then the question was asked him again by the other side, "What's up?" Thinking of what Mr. Hupp had said in the house, I remarked to Maj. Abbott "Ask them if Branson is there." He did so, and the answer was, "Yes, I am here, and a prisoner." Three or four of our men spoke at once — Major Abbott, Col. Wood, and others whom I do not remember — saying, "Come out of that," or "Come over to your friends," or perhaps both were said. Branson replied, "They say they will shoot me if I do." Col. Sam Wood answered quickly, "Let them shoot, and be d—d; we can shoot to." Branson then said, "I will come if they do shoot," starting his mule. The man who was leading it let the halter strap slip though his hands very quietly. The rest of the pro-slavery party raised their shot-guns and cocked them. Our little crowd raised their guns and were ready in as good time as the others. Sam Wood and two or three of our men helped Branson. Wood asked Branson, "Is this your mule?" "No," was the reply, whereupon Wood kicked the mule and said, "Go back to your masters, d—n you." In the mean-time Branson had disappeared and was seen no more by these brave "shot-gun" men.

About this time some one of them said, "Why, Sam. Wood, you are very brave to-night; you must want to fight." Col. W. replied that he "was always ready for a fight." Just at this mo-ment Sheriff Jones interposed, saying, "There is no use to shed blood in this affair, but it will be settled soon in a way that will not be very pleasant to Abolitionists," and started to ride through those standing in the road. He did not then know old Philip Hupp, but soon made his acquaintance, and I do not think he will be stopped by death any quicker than Phil. Hupp stopped him that night. Just as soon as he started old Philip set the trigger and cocked his old squirrel rifle quicker than he or any other man ever did it before, and said to Sheriff Jones, "Halt, or I will blow your d—d brains out in a moment." He stopped and stayed right there, saying gently to Mr. Hupp, "Don't shoot." There was then a general talk among all hands, and we were told about the "Kansas militia, 3,000 strong, that in three days' time would wipe that d—d Abolition town Lawrence out and corral all the Aboli-tionists and make pets of them." However, Col. Sam. Wood and others out-talked them so bad that they were glad to get away on any terms.

Miner Hupp, who wanted to square accounts with his two men, was prevented by his father from doing so. It was not his fault, for he had a "bead" on them several times, but his father was watching him all the time after he got Sheriff Jones in shape.

This is about my recollection of it, at least as well as I can write it. I could tell it all if I were there with you, and could sit down and have a square talk with you face to face. I regret very much that I cannot be there. According to my recollection, the names of the men who took part in the rescue were: Maj. J. B. Abbott, Capt. Philip Hutchinson, Paul Jones, Philip Hupp, Miner B. Hupp, Collins Holloway, Edmond Curless, Lafayette Curless, Isaac Shappet, John Smith, William Hughes, Elmore Allen, Col. S. N. Wood, —— Smith, and your old friend and comrade,

J. R. KENNEDY.

CLOSING ADDRESS BY S. N. WOOD.

The last address of the meeting was made by Col. S. N. Wood who spoke as follows :

Ladies and Gentlemen :

The time is drawing nigh when this meeting must close. I had intended to talk a little myself in closing, but we are all getting too tired. A mighty revolution has taken place in the past twenty-five years. We have met here from every State in the Union. What once seemed a crime has proved often to be only a prejudice. Our prejudices have worn off and we feel better towards each other. Mrs. Wood chided me for using profane language last night when speaking of the Bull creek affair, but I was reciting history and included it in quotation marks. It was my first oath and seemed to come as if from inspiration. No other language could have been understood. We have had a glorious reunion. Let us aim to take a step higher, and in advance. It should be the determination of every man and woman to make the world a little better for having lived in it, and we ought to be a little better for having lived in this world, and we should try to place our children on a higher moral plane than we occupy. The next twenty-five years, in my judgment, will witness mightier revolutions than the past. Ladies and gentlemen, we must close. Please sing that beautiful song beginning, "My country 'tis of thee, sweet land of liberty."

The whole audience responded to the invitation, and that old song, breathing the spirit of liberty, was rendered with unusual power.

Register of the Old Settlers' Meeting.

In order to give persons an opportunity to make a record of their presence at the Old Settlers' meeting, the Secretary of the Historical Society prepared a register with headings embracing the following items: "Name; date of birth; place of birth; date of settlement; place of settlement; where resided since; present residence; occupation; politics; remarks." The register is preserved by the Historical Society. In it upwards of 3,000 names were entered. They are here given, with the principal items as written opposite the names in the register.

Name, Place and Date of Birth.	Place and Date of Settlement.	Present Residence
Anderson, James S., Va., 1827.	Topeka, 1860.	Topeka.
Anderson, Emma, Va., 1834.	Topeka, 1860.	Topeka.
Adams, J. W, Vermont, 1839.	Grant, 1872. [March, 1855.	Lawrence
Ainsworth, R. M., Dayton, O., 1829.	Leav. county, Wyandotte Res ,	Kansas City, Mo
Ashbaugh, L. S., O., November 21, 1821.	Lawrence, April 1, 1870.	Newton.
Anderson, Mary E., Va., January 6, 1846.	Lawrence, April 1, 1865.	Douglas County.
Anderson, Mrs. Janie, N. Y., March 1, 1864	Atchison county.	Atchison.
Anderson, Geo. S. W., Ripley, O., Sept 4, 1850.	Topeka, May 12, 1873.	Douglas County.
Allison, P. H., Concord, N. H , November 23, 1846.	Lawrence, May 29, 1876.	Salina.
Armstrong, R. B., Westport, Mo., October 20, 1843.	Wyandotte, December 10, 1843.	Wyandotte.
Armstrong, Mrs. R. B., Bronnhelm, O., Nov. 21, 1843.	Wyandotte, May 20, 1868.	Wyandotte.
Allison, Mrs. L., Battle Creek, Me., April 13, 1844.	Eudora, April 1, 1859	Norwood.
Apitz, C E., Canton, Ill., February 5, 1859.	Lawrence, June 4, 1859.	Lyndon.
Allen, Thomas, Park county, Ind . Sept. 18, 1837.	Leavenworth Co , Nov. 1, 1854	Jefferson Coun .
Allen, Charles, Park county, Ind., February 11, 1841.	Leavenworth Co., Nov. 1, 1854.	Leavenworth Co.
Anderson, John, Sweden, June 16, 1835.	Lawrence, December 16, 1865.	Lawrence.
Andrews, Stillman, Sutton, N. H., February 22, 1821.	Lawrence, October 8, 1854.	Lawrence.
Asher Mrs. M. B., New Castle Co., N. Y., Oct. 31, 1810.	Lawrence, December 16, 1878.	Lawr'ce. (Mother of six boys, all Rep'ns.
Abbott, James B., Hampton, Conn , December 3, 1818.	Lawrence, October 10, 1854.	De Soto.
Abbott, Mrs. E. A., Hartford, Conn., Sept. 25, 1831.	Lawrence, October 10, 1854	De Soto.
Atkins, Thomas S., Coles county, Ill., Dec. 2, 1854.	Pawnee county, May 10, 1876.	Pleasant Valley.
Adams, Calvin, N C., September 18, 1818.	Near Lawrence, June 10, 1854.	
Atherton, Annie M., Plymouth, N. H., Oct 23, 1843	Sumner, October 14, 1855	Lawrence.
Atherton, E. P., Bolton, Mass., 1829	Sumner, October 14, 1855.	Lawrence.
Albach, Henry, Big Stranger Creek, Sept. 8, 1863.		Lawrence.
Adams, James N., Montgomery Co., Iowa Sept. 4, 1847.	Lawrence, November 10, 1858.	Leavenworth Co
Adams, Chas. N., Montgomery Co., Iowa, Sept. 27, 1855.	Lawrence, November 10, 1858.	Leavenworth Co.
Armstrong, Wm. H., Madison Co., O., Jan. 28, 1842.	Osage County, March 1, 1875.	Douglas County.
Adams, J. W., Mo., November 26, 1819.	Lawrence, Nov. 16, 1854.	Perry.
Ashbaugh, Mrs. S G., Providence, R. I., Jan. 25, 1816.	Topeka, August 15, 1859.	Topeka
Ashbaugh, Osco, Topeka, August 18, 1867.	Topeka, August 18, 1867.	Topeka.
Allen, A. W., Gloucester Co., N. J , February 4, 1839.		Lexington, Mo.
Allen, E. C., Gloucester Co., N J. June 2, 1810.	Lexington, Mo.	Lafayette Co., Mo.
Adams, Martin, N. C., March 18, 1820.	Near Lawrence, June 12, 1854	Jefferson County.
Abbott, V. J., June 20, 1841.	Paola, September, 1859.	Lawrence.
Abbott, Mollie, December 24, 1859.	Paola, December 24, 1859	Wakarusa.
Anderson, Welhelmina, Sweden, February 9, 1839.	————, August 26, 1860.	Lawrence.
Anderson, Laura G., Ft. Smith, April 1, 1861.	Lawrence, February 14, 1865.	
Asher, W W., Kirksville, Mo , June 17, 1842.	Lawrence, March 22, 1866.	Lawrence.
Ayer, Omar H., Plattsburg, N. Y., Dec. 25, 1825.	Wakarusa, Douglas Co., Dec. 1863	Wakarusa.
Anderson, Charlie, Boone county, Mo., May 16, 1832.	Lawrence, October 20, 1861.	Lawrence.
Adams, M K , Bellefont, Pa., May 20, 1829.	Lawrence, May 29, 1879.	Lawrence.
Andrews, S H., Scituate, Mass., November 16, 1835.	Kansas Falls, April 4, 1857.	Lawrence.
Andrews, Hattie A., Lynn, Mass , September 5, 1845.	Lawrence, March 21, 1866.	Lawrence.
Andrews, Mollie A., Lynn, Mass., December 6, 1860.	Lawrence, March 19, 1866.	Lawrence.
Andrews, Allison, Ind , January 13, 1856.	Vinland, March 19, 1869.	Coal Creek.
Anderson, Lewis G., Ill., August 25, 1833.	Lawrence, April 22, 1855.	Linwood.
Anderson, Mrs. John, Orabro, Sweden, May 13, 1832.	Douglas County, May, 1860.	Lawrence.
Anderson, Miss John, Iowa, March 11, 1859.	Douglas County, May, 1860	Lawrence.
Anderson, Mr. John.		Lawrence.
Aller, H. M., New York, July 5, 1824.	Leavenworth, August, 1860.	Leavenworth.

Name, Place and Date of Birth.	Place and Date of Settlement.	Present Residence
Armstrong, N. H., Berkley county, Va.	Leavenworth, September 1, 1857.	Tiblow, Wyandotte County.
Armstrong, May, Geneva., Ill., February 24, 1863.	Mound City, 1862.	Lawrence.
Adams, Franklin G., Rodman, Jefferson county, N. Y., May 13, 1824.	Ashland, Riley Co., Mch. 27, '55	Topeka.
Adams, Harriet E., Cincinnati, O., May 18, 1837.	Leavenworth, April 19, 1856.	Topeka.
Adams, Jessie, Leavenworth, Kan., July 26, 1856.	Leavenworth, July 26, 1856.	Topeka.
Adams, Azubah, Atchison, Kan., January 13, 1859.	Atchison, January 13, 1859.	Topeka.
Adams, Henry J., Lecompton, Kan., August 21, 1861.	Lecompton, August 21, 1861.	Topeka.
Adams, Harriet, Kickapoo Agency, Kennekuk, Kan., February 20, 1867.	Kickapoo Ind. Ag'cy, Feb., 1867.	Topeka.
Adams, George, near Atchinson, Kan., Oct. 10, 1869.	Near Atchison, Oct. 10, 1869	Topeka.
Adams, Margaret Louisa, near Waterville, Kan., April 13, 1873.	Near Waterville, April 13, 1873.	Topeka.
Adams, Samuel, Topeka, Kan., December 3, 1877.	Topeka, December 3. 1877.	Topeka.
Allen, Jennie, Iowa, July 22, 1858.	Lawrence, March, 20, 1860.	Eudora.
Adams, G. L., Mo., August 31, 1852.	Lawrence, October 1, 1851.	
Adams, Mrs. Eliza R., Washington county, East Tenn., January 10, 1808.	Lawrence, September, 1805.	Lawrence.
Adams, Mary D., Topsham, Me., January 1, 1862.	Douglas County, Nov., 25, 1865.	
Anderson, Thomas, Hanover Co., Va., June 10. 1784.	Lawrence, October, 1868	Lawrence.
Abbott, Allen H., Rockport, Ind., Feb. 14, 1841.	Pottawatomie County, 1856.	Shawnee County.
Ashbaugh, A., Columbus, O., April 19, 1809.	Topeka, August 3, 1859.	Topeka.
Allen, Martin, Monroe county, O., June 29, 1829.	Hays City, Ellis Co., Sept, 1872.	Hays City.
Andrews, Mrs. M H., Scotland, May 7, 1828.	Prairie City, December 7, 1858	
Ashby, George W., Christiansburg, Ky., May 29, 1829.	Prairie City October 16, 1857.	Chanute, Neo Co
Allingham, J. J., Co. Kent., August 2, 1821.	Leavenworth Co., October, 1800.	Reno, Leavwth Co.
Anderson, Sarah B., New York, February 17, 1817.	Clinton, May 12, 1855.	Clinton.
Allan, Hannah Jessie, Ill., July 19, 1850.	Douglas Co., February, 1855.	Reno.
Allen, A. F., Sharon, Washtenaw county, Mich., Dec. 27, 1836.	Girard, Crawford Co., Apr. 27, '74.	Vinland, Doug Co.
Atkinson, Wm., England, March 5, 1825.	Leavenworth City, Nov. 5, 1854	Olathe, Johnson Co.
Ashby, Jennie, Baldwin City, February 14, 1861.	Baldwin City, February 14, 1861.	Baldwin City.
Ashton, John Q., Mercer county, Pa., Sept. 22, 1830.	Osawatomie, September 29, 1859	Lawrence.
Ashton, Priscilla D., Westmoreland county, Pa., Jan. 13, 1830.	Osawatomie, August 5, 1859.	
Andrews, W. W., London, Eng., April 27, 1844.	Lawrence, February, 1865.	Lawrence.
Armstrong, John, Oxford, Canada, June 8, 1826.	Douglas Co., November 20, 1854.	Topeka.
Andrews, E B, Wells River, Vt., June 25, 1837.	Clinton, March 1, 1864.	Topeka.
Adams, James A., Ky., December 22, 1821.	Lawrence, April 8, 1857.	Lawrence.
Asher, Charles F., Iowa, July 21, 1850.	Lawrence, 1868.	Lawrence.
Adamy, U. B., Chemung Co., N. Y., Nov. 13, 1831.	Linn Co., May 25, 1861.	Lawrence.
Abbott. Mrs. L. A., Havershill, O., Sept. 18, 1848.	Atchison County, 1855.	Shawnee County.
Allen, Ellen H., Lawrence, September 18, 1860.	Lawrence, September 18, 1860.	Douglas County.
Adair, S. L., Paint Valley, O., April 22, 1811.	Osawatomie, Miami Co., Mch., '55.	Osawatomie, Miami County.
Anthony, D. R., Adams, Mass., August 22, 1824.	Lawrence, August 1, 1854.	Leavenworth.
Armstrong, R. B., Westport, Mo., October 20, 1843.	Wyandotte, December 10, 1843	Wyandotte
Armstrong, Lucy B, Oxford, Montgomery county, O., July, 31, 1818.	Wyandotte, December 10, 1843.	Wyandotte.
Akers, Moses, Floyd county, Ky., January 28, 1812.	Leavenworth, May 8, 1856.	North Lawrence.
Atwood, S. P., Chittenden, Vt., January 18, 1842.	Lawrence, March. 1879.	Lawrence.
Adams, Sidney, Ill., Aug. 25, 1852.	Lawrence, September, 1857.	Lawrence.
Acher, D. J., Waterford, Con., March 24, 1834.	Lawrence, March 27, 1857.	
Andrews, Mattie A., Lynn, Mass., Dec. 5, 1845.	Lyon, March 19, 1866.	Lawrence.
Anderson, Eliza A., Pittsburg, Pa., Dec. 29, 1818.	Lawrence, May 16, 1855.	Lawrence.
Andrews, Orrin D., N. H.	Lawrence.	Lawrence.
Apitz, E. F., Lanton, Ill., December 27, 1859.	Lawrence, June 10, 1865.	
Atwell, R. H., Johnson, Vt., March 7, 1840.	Topeka, February 2, 1857.	Kansas City, Mo.
Ackerman, Theodore, Fond du Lac county, Wis., Aug. 22, 1848.	Russell, April 21, 1871.	Russell.
Atchison, J. R., June 14, 1844.	Lawrence, August 21, 1857.	Lawrence.
Adams, John Quincy, Va., July 28, 1841.	Black Jack, April 10, 1858.	
Adams, Mrs. Anna M., Chester Co., S. C., January 20, 1844.	Lawrence, April 20.	
Adams, Robert J., Leavenworth Co., May 24, 1871.	Lawrence, May 24, 1871.	
Adams, Mark Orliff, Douglas Co., October 29, 1872	Lawrence, October 29, 1872.	
Adwer, George M., N. H., June 12, 1635.	Lawrence, December, 1865.	
Anderson, O., Iowa, August 27, 1859.	Lawrence, July 15, 1860.	Lawrence Coal Creek.
Andrews, Elizabeth, Ind., November 26, 1826.	Vinland, March 19, 1869.	
Adams, Eleanor, Lawrence, December 8, 1862.	Reno, December 8, 1862.	Reno.
Adams, Annie, Lawrence, January 21, 1864.	Reno.	
Altenburg, Marie, Wis, April 22, 1846.	Lawrence, June 7, 1871.	Lawrence
Atwood, Sam. F., Boston, Mass., March 21, 1828.	L'vnw'th & La'ence, July 10, '56.	Leavenworth.
Allen, Walter N, N. C, March 29, 1834.	Leavenworth, March 10, 1857.	Meriden, Jeffsn Co.
Alder, E M, Hanover, N. H., July 17, 1833.	Lawrence, Kan., Spring of 1855	Lawrence.
Alder, Engene, Lawrence, June 21, 1876.		Lawrence.
Abbott, Mrs. A, Norwalk, O.	North Lawrence, Oct. 11, 1865.	Lawrence.
Archer, Mrs. D. L., Ill., June 16, 1845.	Leavenworth, 1858.	Lawrence.
Allen, Jennie E., Vt., May 15, 1839.		Meriden.

Name, Place and Date of Birth.	Place and Date of Settlement.	Present Residence
Breymann, William, Hanover, Germany, June 30, 1817.	Little Wakarusa, Douglas county, July 18, 1854.	Clay Center.
Breymann, Ferelda J., Madison Co., Ky., Feb 12, 1820.	Little Wakarusa, Douglas county, July 18, 1854.	Clay Center.
Breymann George G., Boon Co., Mo., Dec. 13, 1842.	Little Wakarusa, Douglas county, July 18, 1854.	Clay Center.
Booth, Henry, Yorkshire, England, May 11, 1838.	Manhattan, September, 1856.	Larned, Pawnee Co.
Booth, Freddie, Manhattan, January 4, 1868.	Manhattan, January 4, 1868.	Larned, Pawnee Co.
Bailey, L. D., Sutton, N. H., August 26, 1819.	Belvoir, April 2, 1857.	Lawrence.
Bristol, Mattie J., Edinburgh, O., Nov. 9, 1861	Lawrence, 1870.	
Bell, Dr S. B., N. J., 1821.	Johnson county, 1857.	Rosedale, Kan.
Baldwin, J. C., Chenango Co., N. Y., Feb 6, 1806.	Douglas county, October, 1859.	Douglas Co.
Brown, J. C., Harden Co., Ky., June 29 1812.	Douglas county.	
Bodwell, H. E., Huron Co., O., July 12, 1831.	Palmyra, Doug. Co., Apr. 6, 1856.	
Bonebrake, P. I., Eaton, O., September 25, 1836.	Topeka, June 8, 1859.	Topeka.
Bonebrake, M. L., Ind., October 12, 1830.	Topeka, June 8, 1859.	Topeka.
Blood, Eliza J., Vt., May 26, 1838.	Lawrence, September, 1855.	Lawrence.
Brass, Sarah A., Columbia Co., Pa., July 23, 1824.	Douglas county, September, 1857.	Douglas Co.
Bangs, W H., Stonebridge, Canada, April 19, 1840.	Lawrence, 1868.	Lawrence.
Barlow, John H., Mass.	———, May, 1879.	Lawrence.
Burdick, F. D., M. D., Ill., September 16, 1852.	Atchison county, May 5, 1866.	Lawrence.
Bracht, Henry, Lancaster, Pa., August 12, 1852.	Topeka, January 6, 1870.	
Baldwin, A. S., Harwington, Conn., June 23, 1829.	Clinton, Doug. Co., May 2, 1855.	Clinton, Kan. [Co.
Brown, L. J., Putnam Co., O., March 8, 1830	Clinton, Doug Co., May 9, 1856.	Richland, Shawnee
Beckwith, E. B., Smithport, Pa	Lawrence, January 15, 1879.	Lawrence.
Bastian, H., Lehigh Co., Pa., February 2, 1844	Big Stranger, Sept. 4, 1868.	Lawrence.
Bradford, J. H., Oxford, O., 1817	Manhattan, July 20, 1878.	Manhattan.
Bean, C W., Corydon, Ind., October 20, 1854.	Stranger Valley, April 1, 1855.	Springdale, Kan.
Ballard, D. E., Franklin, Vt., March 20, 1837.	Washington Co., April, 1857.	Ballard's Falls, Washington Co.
Bridges, James, Ill., April 9, 1845.	Franklin, September, 1854.	Leavenworth Co.
Brass, William, Columbia, Pa., July 27, 1816.	Kanwaka, September 10, 1857.	Kanwaka.
Brooks, Albert G., York York Co., Me., Nov. 18, 1838.	Lawrence, January 15, 1860.	Lawrence.
Butler, Oliver, Ind., December 2, 1835.	Miami County, April 4, 1864.	Douglas Co.
Butler, R. E., Ind., Dec 14, 1835.	Miami County April 4, 1864.	Douglas Co
Babcock, Mrs. C. W., Ohio.	Lawrence, 1867.	Lawrence.
Barnes, S. O., Va., June 30, 1853.	Spring Hill, March 27, 1879.	Lawrence.
Boles, C. W., Winona, Minn., December 8, 1860.	Lawrence, August 31, 1877.	Lawrence.
Burnett, J. C., Morrisville, Vt., March 19 1825.	Mapleton, April, 1857.	Russell.
Bechtel, N W, Cincinnati, O., August 17, 1854.	Leavenworth. April 1, 1860.	Valley Falls.
Brownlee, James, Downey Co., Ireland, March, 1842.	Shawnee County, October, 1857.	Fulton Co., Ill.
Burnett, H. C., Morri ville, Vt., October 4 1869.	Mapleton, April, 1857.	Lawrence
Betner, James, Green Co., Ind., July 22, 1817.	Marion, May 14, 1858.	Kanwaka.
Ballard, Jos., Ind. December 22, 1838.	Lawrence, December 2, 1866.	
Brown, Wm., Caven Co., Ireland, November 15, 1837.	Wakarusa, Doug. County, March 4, 1859.	Wakarusa.
Byerly, Maria, Westmoreland Co., Pa., Oct. 25, 1822.	Willow Springs, July 4, 1854.	Douglas Co.
Bodwell, L. M., Danbury. Ct., September 11, 1843.	Baldwin City.	Baldwin City.
Bichet, Francis, France, March 11, 1812	Cedar Point, July 4, 1858.	Florence.
Bayless, W. H., Broome Co., N. Y., March 13, 1839.	Highland, May 29, 1855.	Highland
Briggs, C F., O., April 12, 1833.	Manhattan, January 4, 1856.	Manhattan.
Brass, Cloyd, Kansas, October 9, 1863.	Lawrence, 1860.	Lawrence.
Bothel, James, Indiana Co., Pa., July 31, 1828.	Burlingame, November 4, 1854.	Burlingame.
Burlingame, S. W., Caldwell, O., June 1, 1816.	Lawrence, October 25, 1873.	Douglas Co.
Borton, Lewis W., Cambridge, O., September 1, 1831	Lecompton, February 20, 1859	Clyde.
Buckingham, Henry, Norwalk, O., May 28, 1830.	Leavenworth, November 20, 1850.	Concordia.
Bradbury, Leonard, Summerset Co., Me., Feb. 20, 1813.	Gardner, January 22, 1857	Paola.
Bangs, Mrs. C. W., Boston Mass., April 24, 1840.	Lawrence, September 10, 1868.	Kansas City, Mo.
Barteaux, A. B., St. John, N B., July 18, 1859.	Lawrence, May 12, 1865	Lawrence.
Bodwell, Anson G., Simsburg, Con., June 3, 1801.	Topeka, December 5, 1857.	Topeka
Bristol Frank, New York City, February 11, 1859	Lawrence, July 25, 1879.	Lawrence.
Bowles, James T., Hinsdale, Mass., November 16, 1842	Lawrence, April 6, 1870	Lawrence.
Beek, C. B., Brook Co., Vt., March 29, 1830.	Douglas County, April 6, 1850.	Baldwin City
Brown, G. W., Essex Co., N. Y., October 29, 1820.	Lawrence, October, 1854.	Rockford, Ill
Brown, Mary A., Mandell, Essex Co., N. Y., Sep, 10, '25.	Lawrence, October, 1854.	Lawrence.
Baker, Mrs. J A., Vt., May 19, 1829.	Douglas County, May 25, 1860.	
Boles, J. Lewton, Louisville, Ky., July 24, 1860.		Lawrence.
Booth, Isaac, Cadiz, O., August 27, 1838.	Larned, March 10, 1877.	Larned.
Bell, Lola, Walworth, Wis., March 23, 1854.	Lawrence, November 17, 1870.	Lawrence.
Bell, Mrs. Sarah, Quimans, N. Y., Dec. 11, 1808	Lawrence, January 25, 1871.	Lawrence.
Bell, Manley, Walworth, Wis., September 2, 1847.	Lawrence, April 30, 1869.	Lawrence.
Bell, Nellie, Monroe Co., N. Y., Feb. 15, 1854.	Lawrence, April 10, 1871.	Lawrence.
Boyd, Wright, Mo., Sept. 15, 1861.	Nemaha County.	Nemaha Co.
Bond, S. W., Hamilton, Ind., April 20 1853	Douglas County, May 13, 1865.	Marion Tp.
Brooks, W. W., Clay Co., Mo., December 25, 1855.	Lawrence, October 1, 1860.	Lawrence.
Bunker, Mrs. H. A., Lincoln, Mass., December 8, 1826.	Topeka, Kansas, January 14, 1856.	Topeka.
Boles, C. W., Winona, Minn., December 8, 1860.	Lawrence, August 31, 1877.	Lawrence.
Brillin, W. F., Ill., June 22, 1856		
Blake, William G., Iowa, October 11, 1855	Leavenworth, February 20, 1883.	Leavenworth Co.
Baker, C. M., Rochester, Vt., July 20, 1817.	Topeka, February 29, 1865.	Topeka.
Brannor, W. R., Ind., 1852.		Silver Lake.

Name, Place and Date of Birth.	Place and Date of Settlement.	Present Residence
Boyd, Wm. A., Philadelphia, February 3. 1859.	Lawrence, July 9, 1869	Lawrence.
Byram, F. W., Knox Co., Ill., December 9, 1860.	Jefferson County, 1864.	Chase Co.
Bowen, D. E., Peru, Mass., May 31, 1817.	Douglas County, March 15, 1857.	Douglas Co.
Bodle, C. E., South Eaton, Pa., June 6, 1851.		Lawrence.
Bonebrake, J. H., O., June 26, 1830.	Big Springs, June 2, 1860.	Lecompton.
Borebrake, S. W., Ind., July 1, 1838.	Big Springs, June 2, 1860.	Lecompton.
Bennett, Rev. Geo R., Albion, N Y., June 22, 1841.	——, June 22, 1879.	Lawrence.
Benedict, S. S., Bennington Co., Vt. Nov. 9, 1844.	Wilson County. June 25, 1868.	Guilford.
Barricklow, H. V. D., Indiana August 7, 1849.	Baldwin City, 1855	Baldwin City.
Blood, Kate, Lawrence, January 30, 1862.	Lawrence, January 30, 1862.	Lawrence.
Burkhart, John M., Smithville, Ind., July 29, 1854.	Newton, March 17, 1879.	Newton
Brown, Clara. Mercer County, Pa., April 20, 1840.	Osage County, February 22, 1858.	Carbondale.
Brockelsby, William, Marion, O., April 29, 1832.	Lawrence, May 10, 1859.	Lawrence.
Brockelsby, Mrs. W , Marion, O., April 2, 1834.	Lawrence, May 10, 1859.	Lawrence.
Bangs, C. W., Campton. L. C., December 19, 1834.	Lawrence, March 1, 1868	Kansas City.
Bangs, Albert. Stanbridge, C. E.	Lawrence, March 20, 1857.	Lawrence.
Blackman, W. I. R., Troy, O., December 12. 1824.	Lawrence. April, 1855.	Lawrence.
Barber, W. I , Ohio, December 27, 1825.	Douglas County, March 4, 1874.	Leavenworth Co.
Benedict, M. R., N. Y.	Lawrence May 9, 1867	
Bannister, W.		
Beard, John, N H , March 10, 1810.	Monmouth Tp., Shaw County, December 1, 1868	Monmouth.
Bailey, F. A., Mass , October 21, 1827.	Lawrence, September 15. 1854.	Lawrence.
Bailey, Mrs. F. A., Vermont	Lawrence, September 15, 1857.	Lawrence.
Barnes, A., Barnesville, O., July 15, 1848.	Topeka, April 12. 1870	Topeka.
Barnes. Emma, Madison, Wis., January 7, 1854.	Leavenworth, September 1, 1862.	Topeka.
Bauman, Miss Carrie, N. Y. City, February 17, 1867.	Wilson County, June 15, 1871.	Lawrence.
Bryant, W H. Jr., Nashville, Tenn., May 5, 1856.	Lawrence, May 30, 1879.	Lawrence.
Bruce, H. C , Chester, Vt., April 15, 1821.	Rensselaer, Ind., 1857.	Rensselaer.
Baldridge, Geo W , Lawrenceburg, Ind , May 7. 1853.	Lawrence, October 1. 1870.	Lawrence.
Bache, Anna C., Harrisonville, Mo., August 18, 1842.	Paola, January 14, 1868	Paola
Burton, Martha, Maquon, Ill , November 15, 1843.	Franklin County, October, 1859.	
Bailly, Elizabeth A.		Lawrence.
Burnton, Ella, Brooklyn, N. Y., June 1, 1862.	Lawrence.	Lawrence.
Bond, W. H , Platte County, Mo., July 19, 1840.	Leavenworth, November 21, 1862.	Leavenworth.
Brown, Sarah A., New York, January 12, 1838.	Lawrence, July, 1857	Lawrence.
Brown, Elizabeth B., Mass., November 26, 1845.	Hutchinson, July 6, 1862.	Lawrence.
Bowen, H. W., Ohio, September 4, 1851.	Lawrence, March, 1857.	
Banta, C. J., Illinois, February 28, 1837.	Osawatomie, October 25, 1855.	Douglas Co.
Buttons, F. H., Pittston, Pa., February 28, 1759.	Lawrence, April 1, 1878.	Kansas City.
Byrd, John H., Vermont. December 28, 1816.	Leavenworth, May, 1855.	Lawrence.
Byrd, Elizabeth I., New York, August 30, 1821.	Leavenworth. May, 1855.	Lawrence.
Byrd, Abby E., Michigan.	——, May. 1855.	Lawrence.
Byrd, Alice H., Kansas, December 21, 1862.	Leavenworth	Lawrence.
Bowman, Mary L., New York April 9, 1852.	Topeka, October, 1857.	Wakarusa.
Butler, E. Jr., New York, March 16, 1860.	Wallace, 1868.	Lawrence.
Beggs, J. L., Indiana, November 11, 1819.	Lawrence, November 12, 1873	Lawrence.
Baldwin, Cyrus, Indiana, December 25, 1842.	Leavenworth Co., Oct 1, 1868.	Lawrence
Booth, William, Bradford, Eng., January 18, 1829.	Leavenworth, March 7, 1871.	Leavenworth.
Brown, Ira, Vermont, February 23, 1831.	Lawrence, March 20, 1855.	
Brown, Mrs. Ira, New York, October 27, 1834.	Lawrence, December 20, 1857.	
Banta, J. C., England, July 14, 1856	Linn County, July 1, 1863.	Lawrence.
Banks, Alex. R , Ohio, August 9, 1835	Douglas County, April 3, 1855.	Lawrence.
Brown, Mrs. M. E. A., Frankfort, N. Y., Aug. 15, 1821.	——, September, 1867.	Topeka.
Bowman, C., Pennsylvania, March 1, 1828.	Near Hyatt, Anderson County, April 16, 1857.	Topeka.
Buckminster, J., Jeff. County, N. Y., August 10, 1839.	Douglas County, Nov. 18, 1869.	Topeka.
Byles, Chas J., Princeton, N J., November 18, 1839.	Leavenworth, July 6, 1866.	Leavenworth.
Byington, Mrs. D., Guilford, N. Y., June 15, 1835.	Leavenworth, January, 1864	Leavenworth.
Booth, L. S., Connecticut, June 12, 1873.	Leavenworth, April 19, 1876.	Leavenworth.
Burriss, W. E , Peru, Ind., June17, 1858.	Topeka.	Topeka.
Banks, Jennie S., Pittsburg.	Lawrence, April, 1863.	
Banks, Emma R., Lawrence.	Lawrence.	
Banks, Annie B., Lawrence.	Lawrence.	
Boughton, L. J., England.	——, 1863.	Lawrence.
Boyd, Abner H., Donnelson, Ill., November 7, 1859.	Pomona, October 10, 1874.	Lawrence.
Bell, J P., Pennsylvania, January 15, 1842.	——, September 18, 1865.	
Barrett, J. R., Ohio, October 30, 1825.	Franklin, Douglas County, Sept. 1, 1857.	
Blinn, W. B., France, November 24, 1854.	Leavenworth Co , June 30, 1867.	Smith Co.
Brewster, E. C , Georgia, September 14, 1858.	Lawrence, January 6, 1876.	Junction City
Bristol, J. A., New York, February 11, 1831.	Lawrence, June 25, 1879.	Lawrence.
Baldridge, Geo. W , Lawrenceburg, Ind., May 4, 1853.	Lawrence, October 18, 1870.	Lawrence.
Bowen, Addison, Peru, Mass., July 11, 1825.	Olathe, Johnson Co., February 25, 1858.	Olathe.
Bowen, M. A., Illinois, 1833.	Olathe, Johnson County, 1857.	Olathe.
Bonham, John C.		Kansas City.
Bannister, W. H., Cincinnati, O., February 26, 1851.	Topeka, March 27, 1879.	Topeka.
Butts, George D., Wisconsin.	Lawrence, 1860.	Lawrence.
Bush, Chas. D., Dayton, O., August 13, 1846.	Tecumseh, 1857.	Leavenworth Co.
Bookout, W. N., Kentucky, August 16, 1831.	Wyandotte Co , April 22, 1861.	Johnson Co.

Name, Place and Date of Birth.	Place and Date of Settlement.	Present Residence
Bruce, Wm., Blairsville, Ind., July 20, 1824.	Reno Station, June 20, 1869.	
Bowman, Annie, Lawrence, September 20, 1862	Lawrence, September 20, 1862.	Topeka.
Baker, Catherine E., Pennsylvania, June 31, 1831.	Baldwin City, April 27, 1857	Baldwin City.
Barnes, Ida C., Rock Creek, Kan., January 23, 1861.	Rock Creek, January 23, 1861.	
Brett, C. H., New York, July 15, 1847.	Lawrence, April 9, 1878.	Lawrence.
Boles, Nettie E., Kentucky, April 18, 1867.	Lawrence, September 1, 1877.	Lawrence.
Brown, G. W. Jr., Kansas, September 21, 1861.	Paola, September 21, 1861	Key West.
Barber, O. P., New Paris, O., December 23, 1846.	Bloomington, Douglas Co., March 23, 1857.	Lawrence.
Barber, Mrs. O. P., Pittsburg, Pa., October 1, 1854.	Lawrence, 1863.	Lawrence.
Badger, E. W., Girard, Erie Co., Pa., June 9, 1850.	Lawrence, May 9, 1879.	Lawrence.
Breese, S. A., Mt Gilead, O., October 4, 1836.	Cottonwood Falls, Oct. 27, 1858.	Chase Co.
Breese, L. Ressie, Washington, Ia., April 22, 1851.	Plymouth, Lyon County, August 8, 1871.	Chase Co.
Burdick, J. M., Orleans Co., N. Y., October 14, 1826.	Sherman, Leavenworth Co., Feb. 15, 1876	Linwood.
Bishop, William, Scotland, December 9, 1823.	Lawrence, October 20, 1858.	Salina.
Burt, O. M., Massachusetts, December 8, 1847.	Lawrence, July 17, 1878.	Lawrence.
Bullene, Wm. L., Wisconsin, October 30, 1849.	Lawrence, August, 1867.	Lawrence.
Broughton, F., Pennsylvania, August 5, 1857.	Lawrence, September 25, 1869.	Lawrence.
Bell, Millie J., Broad Ford, Pa., December 8, 1848.	———, September 18, 1869	
Baldwin, Mrs. Lucy J., Ohio, February 24, 1825.	Kanwaka, October 29, 1859	Kanwaka.
Boughton, J. S., New York March 2, 1830.	Lawrence, November 4, 1861.	Lawrence.
Brown, Alice E., Osage Co., Kan., January 4, 1859.	Osage County, January 4, 1859.	
Baker, Wm. S., New York City, November 11, 1809.	Topeka, 1861.	Topeka.
Benson, A. P., Sweden, May, 1832.	Topeka, 1863.	Topeka, Kan.
Bullen, T. W., Canada, March 16, 1829.	Clinton, August, 1868.	Clinton.
Blunt, Nancy C., New Madison, O., December 10, 1842.	Anderson County, March 3, 1858.	Leavenworth.
Blunt, Kate P., Leavenworth, August 2, 1867.	Leavenworth, August 2, 1867.	Leavenworth.
Beal, J. M., Allentown, Pa., June 13, 1811.	Anderson Co., March 19, 1861.	Jefferson Co.
Biggs, Bill H., Johnson Co., Kan., January 20, 1858.	Vinland, January 20, 1858.	Coal Creek.
Blake, John Henry, Caswell Co., N. C., Dec. 17, 1831.	Gum Springs, Johnson County, March 4, 1857.	Olathe.
Burnett, C. H., Lawrence, June 12, 1861.	Lawrence, June 12, 1861	Lawrence.
Bates, A. M., Ohio, October 4, 1846.	Shawnee County, March 15, 1872.	Shawnee Co.
Burgard, A. A., Wyandotte, January 1, 1859	Wyandotte, January 1, 1859.	Wyandotte.
Brown, C. W., Vermillion Co., Ill., March 5, 1847.	Clinton, November 2, 1857.	Clinton.
Barnes, Delos N., New York, January 28, 1831.	Quindaro, April, 1859.	Leavenworth.
Bloss, Harry H., Rochester, N. Y., January 10, 1859.	Leavenworth, January 10, 1865.	Lawrence.
Billingsley, H. M., Ladoga, Ind., October 27, 1837.	Topeka, September 20, 1870.	Topeka
Breeze, T., St. Louis, Mo., March 20, 1843.	Palmyra, Doug Co., June 4, 1854.	Palmyra Tp.
Breeze, Mrs. M., Kentucky, May 28, 1841.	Willow Springs, 1855.	Palmyra Tp.
Brown, P. B., Arrow Rock, Mo., October 23, 1854.	Douglas Co., March 18, 1871	Centropolis
Brown, E. E. Lawrence, January 20, 1863.	Lawrence, January 20, 1863.	Lawrence.
Bruce, Chas., Windsor Co., Vt., June 7, 1828.	Douglas County, April 1, 1858.	Lawrence.
Brooks, Frank, England, June 16, 1849	Topeka, May 6, 1867.	Topeka.
Brown, W. H., Pennsylvania, October 12, 1800.	Big Springs, June 15, 1856.	Big Springs.
Bachelor, Chas. E., Hamilton Co., O., 1840.	Topeka, 1861.	North Topeka.
Babcock, C. W., Vermont, 1839.	Lawrence, 1854.	Topeka.
Brown, Geo. Lee, Providence, R. I., Feb. 28, 1838.	———, November, 1876.	Lawrence.
Beam, C. I., Pennsylvania, 1832.	Lawrence, April, 1872	Lawrence.
Bardell, Chas. F., Sydney, Ill., 1857.	North Lawrence, 1866.	Bismarck Grove.
Bower, Sol., Summit County, O., November 7, 1832.	Lawrence, [April, 1859.	Olivet, Osage Co.
Beeks, Ed., Ohio, February 19, 1850.	Baldwin City, Douglas County,	Baldwin City.
Booth, R. E., Ohio, April 18, 1850.	Lecompton, July 10, 1867.	Lecompton.
Burroughs, Oscar, Bridgeport, Conn., May 31, 1835.	Lawrence, October 7, 1854.	Lawrence.
Bowes, Chas. C., Halifax, N. S., September 23, 1856.	Lawrence, November 4, 1869.	Topeka.
Bowes, George W., Boston, Mass., October 14, 1827.	Lawrence, November 4, 1869.	Lawrence.
Brooks, George G., Philadelphia, Pa., June 9, 1832.	East of Lawrence, Sept. 18, 1857.	East of Lawrence.
Hancroft, A. R., Michigan, November 24, 1835.	Emporia, February 28, 1857.	Emporia.
Barker, Thomas J., Bedford Co., Va., Dec. 11, 1828.	Wyandotte, April 28, 1855.	
Buckingham, C. J., Miamiville, O., July 11, 1839	Lawrence, December 5, 1868.	Reno Tp.
Bedale, Wm. and wife. Sarah, England, Dec. 20, 1825.	Lawrence, November 12, 1870.	Lawrence
Byers, J. L., Montgomery Co., O., July 17, 1833.	Leavenworth, October 20, 1855.	Leavenworth Co.
Bush, Mrs. Alice, Atchison Co., October 7, 1858.	Atchison, 1856.	Leavenworth Co.
Brown, Ethel, Indiana, October 12, 1821	Douglas County, 1850.	Baldwin City.
Bleakly, Ella, Nebraska, October 12, 1872.	Douglas County, 1877.	Bismarck Grove.
Badger, Mrs. S. A., South Port, Eng., Aug. 20 1856	Lawrence, July 10, 1879. [1, 1854.	Lawrence
Barber, Oliver, Franklin Co., Pa., December 11, 1810.	Bloomington, Douglas Co., June	Lawrence.
Burnett, J. C., Lamoille Co., Vt., March 19, 1825.	Mapleton, Bourbon Co., April, 1857.	Russell, Kan.
Baldridge, Minnie, Lawrence.	Lawrence, March, 1855.	Lawrence.
Blood, J., Vermont, March 21, 1819.	Lawrence, July, 1854.	Lawrence.
Barnum, W. B., Vermont, May 21, 1822.	Lecompton, April 20, 1859.	Reno.
Barnum, Mrs. E. A., New York, September 23, 1832.	Lecompton, April 20, 1859.	Reno.
Bishop, Emma B., Kentucky.	Lawrence, November, 1858.	
Blythe, J. H., New York, January 10, 1840.	Tonganoxie, February 16, 1875.	Tonganoxie.
Burnett, S. W., Waynesville, O., July 4, 1837.	Leavenworth Co., March 1, 1865.	Lawrence.
Barber, Mrs. John, Cincinnati, O., February 13, 1852.	Lawrence, July 11, 1872	Lawrence.
Barber, John, New Paris, O., February 28, 1842.	Douglas Co., March 25, 1857.	Lawrence.
Brown, John H., Illinois, January 6, 1826.	Lawrence, March 20, 1865.	Wyandotte.

Name, Place and Date of Birth.	Place and Date of Settlement.	Present Residence
Berkey, Geo. A., Kansas, 1859	Lawrence, 1859.	Winfield, Cowley Co
Brown, Joe, Lawrence.	Lawrence.	Lawrence.
Bangs, John E., Canada, August 1, 1807.	Lawrence, 1869.	
Bliery, Jacob, Germany, 1821.	Lawrence, 1863.	Lawrence.
Bloss, Wm. W., Rochester, N. Y., March 31, 1831.	Lawrence, September 25, 1858.	Kansas City, Mo.
Blayney, Mrs. Fannie J., N. Y. City, Sept. 14, 1854.	Lawrence, October 1, 1855.	Lawrence.
Blayney, G. M., Washington Co., Pa., Feb. 6, 1816.	Lawrence, April 6, 1855	Lawrence.
Beack, Mrs. S. C., Hamilton, Scotland, Apr. 6, 1821.	Mission Creek, Wabaunsee Co , May 3, 1858.	Mission Creek.
Bacon, Ligarius S., Hartford, Ct., October 24, 1816.	Lawrence, November 8, 1851.	In Lawrence.
Billings, Tobias, Newport, Me., December 18, 1829.	Topeka, April 2, 1860	Topeka, Kan.
Billings, Mrs. C. F., Knox, Me., February 15, 1833.	Topeka, April 2, 1860. 　[1, 1854.	Topeka.
Barber, Oliver, Franklin Co., Pa., December 10, 1816.	Bloomington Douglas Co., June	Lawrence.
Banta, J. C., S. A., July 14, 1850	Linn Co., Kan. August 1, 1860.	Lawrence.
Brown, A. D., Livingston Co., N. Y., January 1, 1833.	Leavenworth, May 1, 1856.	Burlington, Kan.
Bassett, Jane A., Bristol, R. I., August 22, 1809.	Lawrence, May 30, 1870.	Lawrence.
Bassett, Owen A., Troy, Pa., July 16, 1834.	Lawrence, April 5, 1856.	Lawrence.
Bassett, Josephine E., Baltimore, Md., Nov. 27, 1836.	Quindaro, Kan., Dec. 12, 1857.	Lawrence.
Bassett, May V., Lawrence, Kan , August 2, 1866.	Lawrence, August 2, 1866.	Lawrence.
Bassett, Thomas B., Lawrence, Kan , October 21, 1870.	Lawrence, October 21, 1870.	Lawrence.
Bassett, Frederick L., Lawrence, Kan , May 19, 1873.	Lawrence, May 19, 1873.	Lawrence.
Bassett, Josephine E , Lawrence, Kan., Sep. 28, 1875.	Lawrence, September 28, 1875.	Lawrence.
Bookout, Emly A , Wyandotte, Kan., April 30, 1861.	Lenexa, Kan.	Shawnee.
Bookout, Charlotte N., Shawnee, January 14, 1863.	Lenexa, Kan.	Shawnee.
Burlingame, M. J., Bennington Co., Vt., 1828.	Kanwaka, 1857.	Lawrence.
Butts, H. D., Valley Falls, Kan., 1862.	Valley Falls, Kan., 1862.	Valley Falls.
Brown, E. E., Lawrence, Kan , January 20, 1863.	Lawrence, January 20, 1863.	Lawrence.
Beach, David C., Indiana, August 2, 1844.	Douglas Co., March 22, 1867.	Winfield, Kan
Bowers, Joe, Illinois	Lawrence	Lawrence.
Baker, Ryrus, Franklin Co., N. Y., March 31, 1822.	Washtenaw Co., Mich., February 1, 1852.	North Lawrence.
Bayles, Robert, England, March 22, 1832.	Pottawatomie Co., March, 1868.	Greene Tp., Potta. Co.
Bangs, Francis S , Warren, Mass., June 12, 1852.	Lawrence, September 30, 1855	Lawrence.
Brockson, Wm. A., Illinois, January 22, 1854.	Lawrence, December 21, 1876.	Lawrence.
Bliss, J. A., Wilbraham, Mass., February 13, 1843.	Lawrence, October 1, 1862.	Lawrence.
Bell, R. H., Malone, N. Y., May 4, 1837.	Lawrence, February 17, 1872.	Lawrence.
Blodgitt, Jessie, Illinois, September 17, 1857.	Mound City, 1869.	Lawrence.
Bayne, Thomas R., Shelby Co , Ky., May 16, 1836.	Jefferson Co., October 13, 1854.	Jefferson Co.
Bayne, Susan, Indiana, January 28, 1839.	Jefferson Co., Kan., May 4, 1857.	Jefferson Co.
Bromell, Mrs. Harriet, York State, August 9, 1809.	Leavenworth, Kan., May 1, 1857.	
Brass, Kate, Kansas, January 5, 1860.	Near Lawrence, 1860.	Near Lawrence.
Brown, Thomas R., Lawrence, December 11, 1860.	Lawrence, December 11, 1860.	
Baker, Isaac L., Pennsylvania, July 10, 1828.	Baldwin City, April 27, 1857.	Baldwin City.
Barker, Lucena A , Rochester, N. Y , August 16, 1844.	Lawrence, Douglas Co., October 5, 1867.	Lawrence.
Banta, J. C., Ridge, Kan., July 14, 1856.	Lawrence, April 15, 1860.	Lawrence.
Bartell, Alice F., Riley Co., Kan., February 24, 1858	Riley Co., Kan., Feb. 24, 1858.	Junction City, Kan.
Baker, Charles S., White Co., Ind., October 25, 1840.	Topeka, February 4, 1864.	Topeka.
Baker, Carrie M., LaSalle Co., Ill., August 3, 1852.	Topeka, September 5, 1855.	Topeka.
Benjamin, Alexina, New Lexington, O., Sept. 26, 1846.	Kanwaka, February 14, 1867.	
Brown, W. R., Buffalo, N. Y., July 16, 1840.'	Lawrence, May, 1864. 　　[1857.	Hutchinson.
Byrne, John O., Ireland, May 16, 1826.	Cottonwood, Chase Co., July 3,	
Barricklow, G. R., Indiana, March 23, 1835.	Baldwin City, April 29, 1856.	Topeka.
Bond, Thomas, Indiana, March 31, 1848.	Lawrence, November 17, 1854.	Clinton.
Banker, F. H., Pittston, Pa., February 28, 1859.	Marion, April 4, 1879.	Lawrence.
Brown, James P., New York, August 21, 1859.	Lawrence, May 10, 1869.	Lawrence.
Barnes, William C., Mansfield, O., August 18, 1831.	Oskaloosa, April 4, 1858.	
Bardell, John C., Rush Co , Ind., January 19, 1832.	Lawrence, September 15, 1861.	North Lawrence.
Baker, Floyd P., Fort Ann, N. Y., Nov. 16, 1820.	Nemaha County, May 15 1860.	Topeka. 　[Co.
Barchell, Elizabeth, Green Co., Pa., October 7, 1811.	Lawrence, October 28, 1861.	Reno Tp., Leav.
Barnes, W. E., Dracut, Mass., September 21, 1833.	Vinland, March 29, 1856.	
Byerley, G. W. Jr., Pennsylvania, April 6, 1821.	Clinton, Doug. Co., Mar. 4, 1855.	Clinton.
Byerley, Wm., Ohio, April 13, 1817.	Clinton, Doug. Co., Mar. 4, 1855.	Palmyra.
Badger, S. A., Girard, Pa., August 29, 1855.	Lawrence, 1879.	Lawrence.
Bliss, J. F., Shoreham, Addison Co., Vt., Apr. 13, 1820.	Lawrence, May 25, 1856.	Oskaloosa.
Bliss, Mrs. Julia, Salsbury, Addison Co., Vt., November 28, 1824.	Lawrence, March 31, 1857.	Oskaloosa.
Bliss, Miss Nellie C., July 28, 1866.	Valley Falls.	
Brewer, D J., Smyrna, A. M., June 30, 1837.	Leavenworth, Sept 13, 1859.	Leavenworth.
Benedict, S. A., New York, November 8, 1831.	Lawrence, May 1, 1867.	Lawrence.
Bowman, Mrs. Mary S., Washington Co., N. Y	Lawrence 1857.	Topeka.
Baldwin, Mrs. Nora, Newton, Pa., February 22, 1841.	Lecompton, May 1, 1859.	Lawrence.
Bauker, F. H., Pittston, Pa., February 28, 1858.	Marion, April 4, 1878.	Lawrence.
Cone, A. F., Delaware, O , November 20, 1832	Douglas Co., April 1, 1861.	Lawrence.
Carr, E. M., Davis Co., Ia., March 5, 1854.	Miami Co., February 15, 1857.	Wichita.
Conway, Thomas W., Ireland, December 13, 1840.	Bismarck Grove, 1879.	Bismarck .
Cradit, N. C., Tompkins, N. Y., March 11, 1827.	Palmyra, Doug. Co., Mar. 16, 1857.	Leavenworth.
Carter, Paschal, Monroe Co., Ky., October 20, 1819.	Douglas County, April 19, 1855.	Douglas Co.
Cummins, J. S., Corydan, Ia , May 17, 1864.	Great Bend, 1877.	Great Bend.
Cox, Mrs. M. L., Berlin, Wis., Nov. 23, 1854.	Lawrence, August 1, 1859.	Jefferson Co.

Name, Place and Date of Birth.	Place and Date of Settlement.	Present Residence
Curtis, H. W., Piqua, O., October 8, 1821.	Shawnee Co., November, 1855.	Shawnee Co.
Curtis, Mrs. Sarah, St. Clair Co., Ill., March 17, 1822.	Shawnee Co , November, 1855.	Shawnee Co.
Cherry C M., Kansas. May 23, 1858.	Lawrence, April 1, 1870.	Lawrence.
Collier, A. A., Pennsylvania, June 21, 1860.	Lawrence, 1865.	Lawrence.
Conwell, J H., Maine, May 17, 1850.	Ft Dodge, Iowa, May 17, 1855.	Ft. Dodge, Iowa.
Cherry, Arthur. Ohio August 24, 1860.	Lawrence, April 7, 1870	Lawrence
Charlton, Kate, Illinois, January 14, 1867.	Lawrence, August 19, 1867.	Lawrence.
Charlton, Ada, New York.	Lawrence, November 15, 1857.	Lawrence.
Carpenter, John C., Indiana, Pa.. February 5, 1838	Allen County, June 6, 1857.	Leavenworth.
Crosby, M. J., Brattleborough, Vt., February 2, 1821.	Baldwin City, March 17, 1869.	Baldwin City.
Cracklin, Joseph, Boston. Mass , May 2, 1816.	Lawrence, September 26, 1854.	Lawrence.
Cretors, Horace. Paris, Ill , October 10, 1857.	Emporia, April 18, 1879.	Emporia.
Cooke, Geo. W., Comstock, Mich., April 23, 1848.		Indianapolis.
Clarke, Alf. L.		Round Rock, Tex.
Cartwright. C J., Batavia, N. Y., June 29, 1813.	Lawrence, March 10, 1869.	Clinton.
Charlton, Miss Mary. Illinois, November 13, 1867.		
Cline, A. E., Missouri, 1844.	Lawrence, January 2, 1865	Lawrence.
Cline, Mary, Kentucky, 1823.	Lawrence, 1861.	Lawrence.
Cline, Ellen, Tennessee. 1856.	Lawrence, 1871.	Lawrence.
Cline, William, Missouri. 1840.	Lawrence, 1870.	Lawrence.
Converse. Miss Stella, Uniontown, O. , Oct. 26, 1855.	Wyandotte, Nov. 20, 1859.	Wyandotte.
Cutler, H. A., Highgate, Vt., May 30, 1830.	Lawrence, October 20, 1857.	Lawrence.
Collins, Hattie Lexington, Ky. September 4, 1859.	Olathe, October, 1860.	Olathe.
Collins, John C., Keene, Ky., February 30, 1830	Olathe, March, 1860.	Olathe.
Collins, Elizie C., Lexington, Ky., August 4. 1835.	Olathe, March, 1860.	Olathe.
Cornell, Annie M., Pennsylvania, May 16, 1849.	Wyandotte, June, 1857.	Wyandotte.
Conger, Mrs. Eliza. Genesee Co., N. Y., August 1821	Douglas Co., June, 1857	Hesper.
Campbell, G. W. Warren Co., Md., May 21, 1837.	Douglas Co , October 10, 1861.	Douglas Co.
Corey. A. S., West Springfield, Mass., Jan. 1, 1824.	Quindaro, April 21, 1857.	Plowboy.
Campbelle, Mary E , Highland Co , O., May 11, 1827.	Leavenworth, April 15, 1870	Baldwin City.
Charlton. Kate R., Pennsylvania, March 26, 1834	Lawrence, May 6, 1857.	Lawrence.
Canaday, J. R , Macoupin Co., Ill., Feb., 22, 1855.	Wichita, February 28, 1874	Wichita.
Cleland, P. S., Washington Co., Ky., Nov. 27, 1811.	Topeka, July 28, 1869.	Topeka.
Cleland. Mary B., Mercer Co., Ky.	Waveland, November 4, 1855	Topeka.
Cook, Mrs S C , Greenwood, Ind.	Waveland.	Topeka.
Clark, Geo. E., Rochester, N. Y., January 10, 1831.	Wyandotte, May 22, 1857.	Great Bend.
Clayton, Thomas, Kansas City, Mo.. August 29, 1859.	Johnson County, 1859.	Great Bend.
Crole, Wm. A., St Louis, Mo., March 25, 1852.	Lawrence, November 25, 1874	Lawrence.
Cosley, Geo. W , Berkley Co., Va., Aug. 4. 1805.	Kanwaka, April 10, 1855	Lawrence.
Cosley, Mrs. G. W., Franklin Co., Pa.. Feb. 8, 1809.	Kanwaka, April 10, 1855.	Lawrence.
Cole, W. H., Rome, Adams Co., O., Sept. 17, 1833.	Nemaha Co., September 14, 1857.	Eudora.
Cordley, Richard, Nottingham, Eng., Sept. 6, 1829.	Lawrence, December 2, 1857	Emporia.
Crutchfield, W., Jamestown, C. E , May 22, 1829	Lawrence, March 8, 1856	
Cosley, H. A., Berkley Co , Va., January 29, 1825.	Lawrence, May 1, 1855.	Belvoir.
Cosley, Rebecca, Xenia. O., June 29, 1835.	Lawrence, May 1, 1855.	Belvoir.
Crocker, Annie L., Lawrence. Kan.. Oct. 10, 1859.	Lawrence, October 10, 1859.	Lawrence.
Cochran, L. C., Cadiz, Harrison Co., O., Aug. 1, 1814.	Leavenworth Co , Oct. 1. 1865	Leavenworth.
Coffman, W. T., Lewisburg, W. Va., Aug. 27, 1849.	Carbondale, September 13, 1869	Carbondale.
Chapman, W., Plymouth, N. H., May 1, 1860.	Lawrence, August 18 1866.	Lawrence.
Clark, M. T., Decatur, Ind , April 21, 1850.	Richland, March 6, 1877	Richland.
Conger, Cynthia, Gibson Co , Ind., March 15, 1850.	Lawrence, October, 1854.	Hesper.
Cheney, D., Vermont. Nov. 8, 1815.	Douglas Co., January 28, 1856.	Greenwood Co.
Crane, Jeanie Howell, Easton, Northampton Co., Pa., June 23, 1839.	Topeka, August, 1855.	San Francisco, Cal.
Climenson. E. L., Crawford Co., Pa., June 16, 1839.	Shawnee Co., March, 1855.	Topeka. [Co.
Cardwell, Wm. A., Henry Co., Ky., August 16, 1816	Big Springs, Douglas Co., June 5, 1855.	Richland, Shawnee
Climenson, Wm. W., Waynesburg, Chester Co., Pa., August 11, 1829.	Topeka, March 25, 1857.	Topeka.
Cotton, John W , Park Co., Ind., Nov. 19, 1851.	Jefferson Co., April 10, 1870.	Oskaloosa.
Cross, Ozitia, Illinois, August 30, 1855.	Ohio City, April, 1860.	De Soto.
Christian, James, Ireland. September 30, 1810.	Lawrence, October 25, 1854.	
Charlton, Joseph Jr., England. July 12, 1833.	Lawrence, September, 1866.	Lawrence.
Carpenter. W. T., Washington, Ill., July 28, 1857.	Lawrence. June, 1869.	Lawrence.
Crowder, James A. Salem, September 12, 1831.	Cottonwood Falls, May 15, 1856	Cottonwood Falls.
Chapman, Amasa, Rochester, November 5, 1842.	Americus, October 15, 1858.	Duck Creek.
Cunningham, J. B., Ohio, October 18, 1836.	Lecompton, June 1, 1865.	Lecompton.
Cook, G. P., West Virginia, August 7, 1826.	Douglas County, Sept. 28, 1870.	Douglas Co
Crothers. Charles, Greenfield, O., June 17, 1860.	Belvoir, April 20, 1876	Panhandle.
Cresse, Philip, Cape May, N. J., February 10, 1843.	Jefferson Co., September 1, 1868.	Oskaloosa.
Cutick, Rachel, Shawnee Co , Kan , Aug. 22, 1858.	Shawnee County, August 22, 1858.	Topeka.
Chadwick, F. G , Hanover, N. H., Sept. 9, 1852.	Lawrence, August 15, 1862.	Lawrence.
Cook. Austin D., Cardington, O., Sept. 26, 1852.	Lawrence, March 16, 1860.	Hesper.
Colville, John H. Kentucky, October 13, 1832.	North Lawrence, April 9, 1879	Lawrence.
Clarke, H S., Rushville, Ill., April 14, 1845.	Lawrence, August 17, 1869.	Lawrence.
Clarke, Lucy J., Findly, O.	Lawrence, July, 1855.	Lawrence.
Corcoran, John, Ireland. February 4 1834.	Ft. Leavenworth, August 4, 1857.	Leavenworth Co.
Coombs, J. M., Bangor, Me., December 8, 1824.	Lawrence, May 15, 1858.	Brookville.
Colman, Mary J., Massachusetts, October 16 1818.	Lawrence, November 1, 1854.	Kanwaka.
Colman, F. A., Ashley, Mass., August 10, 1814.	Lawrence, November 1, 1854.	Kanwaka.
Crocker, Geo. H., Providence, R. I., April 7, 1828.	Lawrence, April 22, 1855.	Lawrence.

14

Name, Place and Date of Birth.	Place and Date of Settlement.	Present Residence
Crocker, E. F., Hartford, Ct., Aug 19, 1850.	Lawrence, October 2?, 1855.	Lawrence.
Crocker. Mrs. E F., Champaign, Ill., Feb. 19, 1854.	Leavenworth, April 21, 1874.	Lawrence.
Campfield, Jos. L., Newark, N. J., October 12, 1856.		Lawrence.
Campbell, Frank M., Pennsylvania, March 13, 1862.	Leavenworth, April 13, 1870.	Lawrence.
Chrisman. John T, Kentucky, April 6, 1859.	Hutchinson, March 15, 1875	Hutchinson.
Crocker, Ernest, Lawrence, Kan., March 23, 1868.	Lawrence, March 23, 1868.	Lawrence.
Crocker, Betsy B., Liberty, Me., February 27, 1329.	Lawrence, October 22, 1855.	Lawrence.
Crew, John W., Owensville, Ky., Sept. 23, 1812.	Lawrence, May 10, 1858.	Monsey.
Curless, John W., Bluff City, Ill.		Brown Co., ().
Carmean, C. K., Kossuth, Ia., April 3, 1857.	Baldwin City, November 1, 1859	Lawrence.
Curtis, Charles, North Topeka, January 20, 1859.	North Topeka, January 20, 1859.	First white child born in N.Topeka.
Cartlidge, Mrs. Nettie, nee Weymouth, Topeka, Nov. 10, 1858.	Topeka, November 10, 1858	Topeka.
Coleman, A. W., Ohio, May 29, 1833.	Douglas Co , October 29, 1858.	Douglas Co.
Campbell, J. F., Newberg, N. Y., November 14, 1844.	Fort Scott, Feb. 27, 1867	Eudora, Doug. Co.
Crawford, James, Cincinnati, O , January 15, 1846.	Kansas City, September 2, 1870	Lawrence.
Cayton, Meddie, Lawrence, October 21, 1866.	Lawrence, October 21, 1866.	Lawrence.
Cayton, Bertie, Lawrence, December 9, 1868.	Lawrence, December 9, 1868.	Lawrence.
Corbin, J. N , New York, February 14, 1847.	Lawrence, July 8, 1868.	
Collier, E. E., Hampshire, Va , June 22, 1836.	Leavenworth.	Leavenworth.
Campbell, A. W., Canada, March 8, 1837.	Leavenworth, October 21, 1865.	Clyde
Cramer, C. B., Grangerville, N. Y., Sept. 24, 1857.	Lawrence, 1858.	Lawrence.
Campbell, Wm. H., Indiana, June 30, 1854.	Lawrence, September, 1869.	Lawrence.
Churchill, S J., Rutland, Vt., November 1, 1842.	Lawrence, March 1, 1879.	Lawrence.
Churchill, Lue, Westville, N. Y., February 24, 1840.		Lawrence.
Chase Henry V., Dover, N. H., April 27, 1852.	Shawnee, Johnson Co., May, 1863.	Lawrence.
Cook, Austin D , Cardington, O , September 26, 1852.	Lawrence. March 16, 1860	Hesper.
Carr, H. H , Wayne Co., O., November 23, 1835.	Eudora, December 10, 1866.	Eudora.
Crothers, J. Y., Greenfield O., July 30, 1830.	Lawrence, April 20, 1876.	Douglas Co.
Croll, J. E., Old Keystone, May 26, 1856	Eudora, June 7, 1878.	Eudora.
Clock, J. W., New York City, October 2, 1811.	Baldwin City, April, 1869.	Clinton, Doug. Co.
Crombie, James, Ireland.	Topeka.	
Chase, Enoch, Newburyport, Mass , Aug. 29, 1824.	Topeka, November, 1854.	Topeka.
Chase, Mary J , Litchfield, Me., June 22, 1822.	Topeka, March, 1855.	Topeka
Cavaness. A. A B , Morgan Co. Ill. Aug. 12, 1838.	Lawrence, May, 1856.	Baldwin City.
Ch ster, E. P., Ohio, September 26, 1847.	Lawrence, September 26, 1847.	
Carothers, Maggie E., Franklin Co., Pa.	Leavenworth Co , Nov. 15, 1854.	Leavenworth Co.
Clarke, H. S., Canada West, April 30, 1833.	Lawrence, April 10, 1857.	Lawrence.
Clarke, H. M., Massachusetts, February 21, 1834.	Lawrence, June 21, 1858.	Lawrence.
Collamore, Hamlet, Boston, Mass , February 11, 1848.	Lawrence, 1857.	Ellis.
Codington, Thomas V., Ohio, January 26, 1833.	Topeka, March 11, 1867	Topeka.
Cavaness, U C., North Carolina, May 10, 1810.	Lawrence, April 15, 1856.	Baldwin.
Cradit, Mrs. N. C., Sharon, N. Y., May 24 1831.	Prairie City, September, 1857.	Prairie City.
Curry, Mrs. Sallie E., Wabash Co., Ind , Nov. 17, 1849.	Lawrence, November 17, 1831.	Grant.
Conger, T. S., Genesee Co., N. Y., October 19, 1817.	Hesper, June 15, 1858	Hesper.
Cretors, Horace, Edgar, Ill., October 10, 1857.	Emporia, April 18, 1878.	Emporia
Crawford, J. W., Harrison Co., Mo., April 12, 1845.	Sedgwick Co , October 28. 1870.	Kinsley.
Casmire, C. A., Revenna, O., February 8, 1860.	Iola, 1845.	Iola.
Coffin, W. G., Guilford Co., N. C., Feb. 22, 1811.	Leavenworth, May 1, 1861.	Leavenworth.
Chrisman, John T., Louisville, Ky , April 6, 1859.	——, March, 1875.	
Crothers, Carrie, Ohio, December 28, 1856.	Belvoir, April 18, 1876.	Lawrence.
Crothers, Florence, Ohio, March 16, 1859.	Belvoir, April 18, 1876.	Kaw Valley.
Cannon, G. C F , Locust Grove, O . June 24, 1847.	Topeka, June 14, 1863.	Topeka.
Cole, Carrie, Lawrence, April 4, 1867.	Lawrence, April 4, 1867.	Lawrence.
Connor, Alfred P , Alexandria, October 15, 1860.	Lawrence, May 11, 1874	Lawrence.
Crowder, John J., Sangamon Co., Ill., April 29, 1859.	Lawrence. 1878.	Lawrence
Cretors. Granville, Lebanon O., September 10, 1855.	Emporia, April 18, 1869.	Detroit, Mich.
Cadwalader, Rees, Cadiz, Ind., March 31, 1854	Tonganoxie, March 12, 1879.	Tonganoxie.
Crowder, Thomas J., Ill , May 28, 1835.	Crawford Co., April 29, 1874.	Douglas Co.
Crowder, J. William, Ill., February 17, 1874	Crawford Co., April 29, 1874	
Clare, J. C., Mifflingtown, Pa., October 28, 1851.	Woodstock, November 8, 1870.	Woodstock.
Campbell, Will M., Ind., June 20, 1838.	Lawrence, March 27, 1866.	Lawrence.
Clarke, Sidney Jr., Lawrence, January 15, 1861.	Lawrence, January 15, 1861.	Lawrence.
Cohunn, William, Lawrence March 15, 1855.	Lawrence, March 15, 1855.	Kanwaka.
Culbertson, W. M , Zanesville, O., August 6, 1837	Lawrence, November 30, 1872.	Lawrence.
Crawford, I. L., Ohio, May 3, 1832.	Council Grove, Nov. 15, 1859.	Chase Co.
Clark, Joseph, Greensburg, Decatur Co., Ind., April 24, 1836.	Vinland, Doug. Co., Mar. 28, 1857.	Vinland.
Cherry, E. Ellen, Leesburg, O., December 20, 1856.	Lawrence, April, 1857	Lawrence.
Crawford, L. M., Ohio, July 24, 1845	Topeka, November 16, 1858	Topeka.
Clark, J. T , Isle-La-Motte, Vt., August 3, 1814.	Topeka, October, 1868	Topeka.
Clough, E. N. O., Virginia, May 28, 1835.	Leavenworth, October 16, 1861.	Leavenworth
Chase, Geo. A., Charleston, Mass., Oct. 27, 1850.	Topeka, April, 1855.	Topeka.
Chase, Alice M., Mt. Pleasant, Pa., April 2, 1852	Bourbon Co., May, 1855.	Topeka.
Corey, F. M., Sparta, N. J., January 23, 1851.	De Soto, February 2, 1878	Johnson Co.
Coxe, William H., Cleveland, O. December 8, 1854.	Topeka, February 26, 1864.	Topeka.
Crutchfield, Mrs A , Canada West, March 2, 1839	Eudora, September 1, 1860.	Wakarusa.
Cox, Mrs M , Canada West. November 9, 1828.	Eudora, September 1, 1860.	
Crane, F. L , Hartford Co., Ct., January 10, 1808	Topeka. M rch 19, 1855.	Topeka.
Crandall, LeRoy, Madison Co., N. Y., Oct. 4, 1826.	Fremont, Lyon Co., May 21, 1858.	Lawrence.

Name, Place and Date of Birth.	Place and Date of Settlement.	Present Residence
Crandall, Sarah A., Allegheny Co., N. Y., Dec. 18, 1830	Fremont, Lyon Co., May 21, 1858.	Lawrence.
Cooke, Annie, Ohio, June 22, 186-.	Lawrence, September 15, 1870.	
Carton, H. G., Paris, Ill., October 10, 1847.	Emporia, April 18, 1879.	Emporia.
Chapman, Mrs. Edward, Vermont, August 28, 1834	Lawrence, October 20, 1856.	Lawrence.
Cameron, J. L., 1840.	Bourbon Co. [1872	Lawrence.
Crouch, T. J., Galway, Saratoga Co., N. Y., Apr. 7, 1828	Americus, Lyon Co., March 14,	Topeka, Kan.
Conant, A. P., Wisconsin, September 7, 1849.	Lawrence. June 8, 1868.	Lawrence.
Case, M. H., Troy, Bradford Co., Pa, Aug. 26, 1826	Topeka, November 19, 1865.	Topeka.
Case, Mrs M H., 1837.	Topeka, November 19. 1865.	Topeka, Kan.
Conklin, T. L., Clarke Co, O., June 17, 1827.	Topeka, March 7, 1867.	Topeka.
Cornutzer, C A., Davis Co., N. C., Feb 7, 1827.	Johnson Co., March 18, 1850.	Lawrence.
Colman, O. A., Chelsea, Mass., January 20, 1850	Douglas Co., October 18, 1854.	Douglas Co., Kan.
Campbell, C. D., Philadelphia, Pa., Aug. 19, 1857	Leavenworth, April 9, 1869.	Leavenworth.
Chadwick, Mary M., New London, N. H., November, 20, 1820.	Douglas Co., December 1, 1867.	Lawrence.
Clark, L M., Petersburg, N. Y., Dec. 19, 1831.	Lawrence, April 9, 1857.	Nortonville.
Crowe, George F., Nova Scotia, February 12, 1812.	Topeka, November, 1854.	Emporia.
Crowe, Jane F., Nova Scotia, April 19, 1817.	Topeka, May 10, 1857.	Emporia.
Cayton, R. M., Fulton Co., Ill., April 23, 1843.	Neosha Falls, May 19, 1858.	Lawrence.
Carter, John. Jiles Co., Tenn., March 31, 1831.	Topeka, May 10, 1862.	Topeka.
Cox, Isaiah, August 14, 1822.	Monmouth Tp., June 11, 1855.	Monmouth Tp.
Cook, Joseph P., Richmond, Ind., October 13, 1828.	De Soto, Johnson Co., February 20, 1879.	De Soto.
Cuppen, J. J., Roxbury, Mass , January 24, 1848.	Lawrence, April 30, 1873.	Salina, Kan.
Cowen, Lucy E., N. Y., March 27, 1855.	Lawrence, August 22, 1874.	Lawrence.
Cole, J. A., Ohio, September 11, 1851.	Blue Mound March 1, 1860.	
Clogston, J. B., Washington Co., August 19, 1840.	Topeka, May, 1861.	Eureka.
Cole, Harvey, Boston, Mass., June 7, 1860.	Lawrence, November 28, 1867.	Lawrence.
Casperoon, A. M., O., May 10, 1851.	Topeka, 1871.	Topeka.
Caldwell, E. F., Park Co., Ind., September 6, 1859.	Carlyle, Allen Co., Mar. 10, 1870.	Lawrence.
Cramer, B. J., Saratoga Co., N. Y., July 31, 1838.	Lawrence, October 10, 1858.	Lawrence.
Clarke, N. S., Rushville, Ill. April 14, 1845.	Lawrence. August 17. 1869. [1868	Lawrence.
Cooley, John T., Manorville, Pa., Sept. 2, 1856.	Perry, Jefferson Co., December 6,	Perry.
Crane, Mrs Ada, Sandusky, O., June 17, 1841.	Wyandotte, July 31. 1843.	Wyandotte.
Cansdell, A., London, Eng., August 28, 1836.	Anderson Co., April 6, 1856.	Willow Springs.
Cameron, N. J., Zanesville, O., December 14, 1834.	Eldorado, April 25, 1870.	Eldorado.
Cormer, Mollie A., Willow Springs, Nov. 10, 1861.	Lawrence.	Eudora.
Cummings, Henry A., Pittsburg, Pa., Aug. 26, 1845	Belvoir, April 1, 1858	Belvoir.
Croll, Henry C , Berks Co., Pa., April 29, 1820.	Douglas Co., April 12, 1878.	Douglas Co.
Croll, Sarah A., Berks Co., Pa., June 29, 1820	Douglas Co.. June 7. 1878.	Douglas Co.
Curless, Jennie, Lawrence, May 25, 1856	Lawrence, May 25, 1856.	Barton.
Clarke, Sidney, Southbridge, Mass., October 13, 1831	Lawrence, March, 1858.	Lawrence.
Carnes, Harriet R., Pennsylvania, March 2, 1857.	Lawrence, March, 1855.	Lawrence.
Chapman, Katie S., Plymouth, N H , March 17, 1837.	Lawrence, January 12, 1867.	[Co.
Coxson, Wm., Canada, November 11, 1829.	Franklin Co., May 20, 1856.	Tonganoxie, Leav.
Coxson, Mrs T., Indiana, November 15, 1838.	Douglas Co., May, 1861.	Tonganoxie.
Coxton, Horace Greeley, New York City, Oct. 10, 1855.	Emporia, April 18. 1879.	St Paul, Minn.
Clark, J S. Pittsburg, Pa., January 13, 1847.	Wyandotte, April 14, 1869.	Wyandotte.
Carmean, Cyrena B , Iowa, 1859.	Baldwin City, 1859.	Lawrence.
Cottrell, H. M., Mendon, Ill., July 20, 1863	Wabaunsee, November 18, 1875.	Wabaunsee.
Collins, Mrs. Vallentine.		
Chadwick, Chas., New York.	Quindaro, February 21, 1857.	Lawrence.
Campbell, J. R , Franklin Co., Pa., October 25, 1825.	Leavenworth City, Mar. 13, 1870.	Douglas Co.
Cornell, Fred D., Wyandotte, July 20, 1869.	Wyandotte.	Wyandotte.
Cone, Wm. W., Monroe Co., N. Y., Dec. 18, 1836.	Topeka, June 1, 1869.	Topeka.
Crane, C. H., New York, February 5, 1823.	Osawatomie, March 18, 1855	Osawatomie.
Coutant, Charles G., Ulster Co. N Y., Oct 16, 1840.	Topeka, March 15, 1878.	Hutchinson.
Conley, Harry, Buffalo, N. Y., May 17, 1855.	Kansas City, Kan., Feb. 14, 1878.	Kansas City, Kan.
Cameron, Noah, Fulton Co., N. Y., April 20, 1831.	Wakarusa, Douglas Co., October 29, 1854.	Wakarusa, Douglas Co.
Cotton, G. W., Jefferson Co., Kan., May 31, 1860.	Jefferson Co , May 31, 1860.	Williamstown.
Cutter, Alfred, Massachusetts, July 12, 1837.	Vinland, October, 1858.	Douglas Co.
Cox, A. B , Knoxville, Tenn., November 30, 1854.	Eudora, Kansas, May 22, 1880.	
Cruise, J. H., New York, February 16, 1844.	Wyandotte, October 22, 1863.	Wyandotte.
Cruise, Belle A., Clinton, Pa., January 22, 1847.	Wyandotte, November 17, 1857.	Wyandotte.
Cruise Edgar D., Wyandotte, February 22, 1867.		
Cruise, Mary Belle, Wyandotte, April 30, 1871.	Wyandotte, April 30, 1871.	Wyandotte.
Canavan, Edward, Ireland. April 20, 1851.	Linn Co , Kan., May 1, 1854.	Jefferson Co., Kan.
Cravatt, Eldridge A., Philadelphia, October 11. 1853.	Lawrence, June 9, 1879.	Baldwin City.
Carter, Mrs Dicy, Barren Co., Ky., July 8, 1824.	Lawrence, April 19, 1855.	Lawrence.
Crew, Dan, Lawrence, December 24, 1865.	Lawrence, December 24, 1865.	Lawrence.
Corel. J. P., Tazewell Co., Va., February 16, 1832.	Wakarusa, Kan , Sept., 1854.	Wakarusa.
Corel, Susan C., Centre Co., Pa , December 25, 1828.	Wakarusa, May 20, 1855.	Wakarusa.
Corel, Jennie E., Douglas Co., Kan., April 20, 1858.	Wakarusa, April 20, 1858	Wakarusa.
Corel, Ollie, Douglas Co., February 15, 1860.	Wakarusa, February 15, 1860.	Wakarusa.
Corel, Ella, Douglas Co., December 17, 1862.	Wakarusa, December 17 1862.	Wakarusa.
Corel, Kate, Douglas Co., March 27, 1863.	Wakarusa, March 27, 1863.	Wakarusa.
Corel, James H., Douglas Co , June 3, 1865.	Wakarusa, June 3, 1865	Wakarusa.
Corel, Charley W , Douglas Co , December 9, 1868.	Wakarusa, December 9 1868.	Wakarusa.
Corel, Anna, Douglas Co., August 12, 1870.	Wakarusa, August 12, 1870.	Wakarusa.

Name, Place and Date of Birth.	Place and Date of Settlement.	Present Residence
Cavanaugh, Thomas H., Vincennes, Ind., Mar. 8, 1844.	Salina, April 22, 1869.	Salina.
Chadbourn, Allen W., Greenville, O., July 18, 1857.	Ft. Scott, June 7, 1860.	Wallace.
Coole, William A., St. Louis, Mo., March 25, 1852.	Lawrence, November 24, 1874.	Lawrence.
Carter, Robert, Ill., July 21, 1849.	Lawrence, February 25, 1855.	Lawrence.
Chadwick, W. W., Hamilton Co., O., March 11. 1835.	Lawrence, November 20, 1875.	
Crane, F. D., Monroe Co., Mich., March 25, 1839.	Wyandotte City, Sept. 8, 1863.	Wyandotte.
Chrisman, J. M., Ky., June 12, 1839.	Tecumseh, Kan., Mar. 12, 1866.	Grantville, Kan.
Cade, Lizzie W., Matoon, Ill., November 12, 1859	Leavenworth, Nov. 18, 1861.	Lawrence.
Connell, Howard M., Wyandotte, October 23, 1870.		
Cosley, Frank D., Chambersburg, Pa., Feb 23, 1842.	Kanwaka, April 6, 1855.	
Cutler, Florence E , St. Albans, Vt., June 19, 1864.	Lawrence, 1869.	Lawrence.
Casmire, B. A., Portage Co., O., September 23, 1858.	Iola, Allen Co., Sept., 10. 1863.	Lawrence.
Coach, John M., Ireland, June 10, 1810.	Bloomington, Douglas Co., April 22 1859.	Clinton.
Corbin, Mrs. A L , New York	Lawrence, May 11, 1859.	[1860
Campbell, M. T , Bloomington, Ind., May 2, 1847.	Monrovia, Atchison Co., May,	Topeka.
Carlson, I , Sweden, July 25, 1810.	Lawrence July 13, 1865.	Lawrence.
Cretor, Horace G., Paris, Ill., October 10, 1857.	Emporia, April 18, 1879.	Emporia.
Cobb, A. H , Beloit, Wis., August 8, 1859.	Wyandotte, October 8, 1859.	Wyandotte.
Cramer, N. Augusta, Medway, Mass., Feb. 7, 1845.	Lawrence, May 20, 1856.	Lawrence.
Canniff, H. J., Stillwater, N. Y., March 1, 1814	Prairie City, June 2, 1857.	Lawrence.
Culbertson, Kate W., McConnelsville, O., May 15, 1843.	Lawrence, March 15, 1873.	Lawrence.
Culbertson, Howard D., McConnelsville, O., December 14, 1870.	Lawrence, March 15, 1873.	Lawrence.
Culbertson, Charles W., Lawrence, Kan., July 10, 1878.	Lawrence, July 10, 1878.	Lawrence.
Carothers, S. N., Franklin Co., Pa., Dec. 10, 1836	Leavenworth Co., Nov. 25, 1854.	Leavenworth.
Cartwright,Mrs. Victoria.Angelica, N. Y.,Nov. 13,1818	Lawrence, Kan., May 6, 1856.	Clinton, Kan.
Drinkwater, Mrs. Ida, Mercer Co., Pa., Sept. 29, 1859.	Cedar Point, Chase Co., June 17, 1871.	Chase Co.
Downs, W. F., Seneca Falls, N. Y., April 18, 1837.	Wyandotte, February 27, 1857.	Atchison.
Dassler, C. F. W., St. Louis, Mo., April 3, 1852.	Salina, Saline Co., June, 1868.	Leavenworth.
Dillard, Jesse, Henry Co., December 15, 1827.	Lawrence, June, 1868.	Lawrence.
Deal, Mattie K., Ill., February 8, 1841.	Lawrence, September, 1869	Lawrence.
Deal, Mabel, Kansas, April 3, 1873.	Lawrence, April 3, 1873.	Lawrence.
Davidson, John R., Jefferson Co., Mo., June 10, 1837.	Lawrence, September 25 1854.	Lecompton.
Davidson, Sarah, O., July 27, 1833.	Lecompton, Kan., Sept. 10, 1859.	
Douglas, Frank, Clayton, Ill., February 27, 1838.	Lawrence November 16, 1869	Lawrence.
Dickerson, Luther, Washington Co., O., April 12, 1823.	Atchison Co., June 25, 1854.	Atchison Co., Kan.
Daugherty, George, Me.	Lawrence, March 20, 1857.	9 mls. e. of Lawr'ce.
Daugherty, Lucy T., Me., January 29, 1837.	——, October 20, 1857.	
Dresser, Ben P , Dayton, O., August 28, 1857.	Lawrence, March, 1864	Lawrence.
Dies, Leslie, Canada, March 8, 1840.	Topeka, April 7, 1879	Kansas City.
Durngham, I. W., Md., March 3, 1855.	Jefferson Co., April 1, 1866.	Perryville.
Davis, Willard, Madison Co., Ky.	Neosho Falls, September 11, 1870.	Topeka.
Dumars, Mollie, Baldwin City, Kan.	Stoney Point, November 10, 1859.	Vinland.
Duncombe, Wm., New York City, March 27, 1831.	De Soto, Kan., June 15. 1860.	Vinland.
Day, John W., Adams Co., Pa., April 12, 1833.	Leavenworth, May 14, 1856.	Topeka. (One of the "Old Guard."
Drinkwater, Orlo H., Le Raysville, Bradford Co., Pa., September 1, 1835.	Topeka, April 13, 1855.	Cedar Point.
Dutton, W. P., Charlestown, N. H., October 1, 1817.	Miami Co., March 1, 1857.	
Doom, J. C., Bloomingburg. O., August 13, 1846.	——, 1878.	Baldwin City.
Dawson, W. J., Pittsburg, Pa , April 7, 1834.	Palmyra, May 23, 1856.	Lawrence.
Dumars, James, Mercer Co., Pa., July 4, 1815.		Palmyra.
Dale, Nellie F., Lawrence, January 10, 1866		Melvin.
Draper, E. C., Plymouth, N. H., May 1, 1856.	Lawrence, May 1, 1879.	Lawrence.
Dean, James D., Ross Co., O., July 15, 1832.	Clinton Tp., 1858.	Clinton.
Duncan, Wesley H., Rockbridge Co., Va., Apr. 18,1815.	Lawrence, May 5, 1855.	Lawrence.
Davis, W. R., Circleville, April 1, 1845.	Baldwin City, 1858.	Baldwin City.
Downs, S. H., Utica, N. Y., November 14, 1839.	Topeka, February, 1870.	Topeka
Dumars, J. S., Pa., May 1, 1851.	Coal Creek, May 21, 1856.	Coal Creek.
Devereux. John P., Washington City, April 29, 1821.	Lawrence, March 1, 1860	Lawrence.
Dawson, Mrs. Barbara E., Lexington, O., 1832.		Lawrence.
Davidson, James A., Ky., October 28, 1829.	Near Lawrence, Nov. 11, 1854.	Lecompton.
Deal, Clara E , Philadelphia.	Lawrence.	
Davy, Milton, Green Co , Ky., December 25, 1833.	Douglas Co., March 15, 1871	Johnson Co.
Donovan, Daniel, Cork Co , Ireland, March 17, 1825.	110 Shawnee Co , March 22, 1857.	Lawrence.
Donnelly, John, Ireland, July 4, 1844.	Illinois, May 4, 1857.	Lawrence.
Doud, M. T. Jr., Pulaski Co., Ind., Feb. 29, 1856.	Miami Co., November 1, 1863.	Topeka.
Dix, Edward E., Lawrence, March 21, 1860.	Douglas Co., March 21, 1860.	Lawrence.
Dudley, B. S., New York, May 10, 1830.	Shawnee Co., March, 1857.	
Dudley, Guilford, New York, March 19, 1835.	Shawnee Co., March 25, 1858.	Topeka.
Dickson, L. A., Me., October 7, 1823.	Douglas Co., November 10, 1854	Osage Co.
Dobbins, Dr. R., Ind., May 13, 1828.	Olathe, August 4, 1870.	Lawrence.
Daniels, J G., Springfield, Mass., September 15	——, May, 1870.	
Davis, Joseph R , Brown Co., O , February 22, 1832.	Emporia, November 2, 1868.	Lyon Co.
Davis, Caroline G., Brown Co., O , May 27, 1837.	Emporia, March 1, 1871.	Lyon Co. [Co.
Duffee, Mrs. M , Westmoreland Co., Pa., May 18, 1835.	Lawrence, April 7, 1855.	Kanwaka, Douglas
Dickinson, Miss Philena F., Mo., April 18, 1860.	Baldwin City, March, 1869.	Baldwin City.
Drisdom, Bedford, Ky., June 4, 1815.	Shawnee Mission, March, 1833.	Lawrence.
Drew, John.	——, 1855.	Burlingame.
Dickinson, S. S., Oswego Co., N. Y., Sept. 22, 1837.	Lawrence, September 10, 1865.	Larned,Pawnee Co

Name, Place and Date of Birth.	Place and Date of Settlement.	Present Residence
Devereux, E. C., April 10, 1847.	Wyandotte, October 18, 1859.	Topeka.
Dillon, Miss Mammie, Pa., April 18, 1859.	Council Grove, Sept. 10, 1867.	Lawrence.
Davis, Mary Ann, Amble Tp., N. Y., August 31, 1805.	Blanton's Bridge, May 22, 1854.	Rock Creek.
Denton, Shelly W., Middlefield, O., June 11, 1859.	Traveler.	Lawrence.
Draper, Wm., New York, August 5, 1831.	Clinton, Doug. Co., April 26, 1855.	Kanwaka.
Draper, B. A., New York, April 15, 1835.	Clinton, April 20, 1855	Kanwaka.
Dutton, J. W , Ill., July 20, 1848.	Douglas Co., March 1. 1857.	Douglas Co.
Dickinson, C. W., Mo , January 20, 1834.	Baldwin City, November 10, 1864.	Baldwin City.
Dillon, Wm , O., September 23, 1835	Lawrence, April 15, 1860.	Lawrence.
Dail, C. C., Girard Co., Ky., January 5, 1851.	Leavenworth, March 1, 1808.	
Dessroy, A. B., France, June 2, 1846	Lawrence. 1866.	Leavenworth.
Douthitt, James V , Topeka, March 24, 1858.	Topeka, March 24, 1858.	Topeka
Dawson, B F., Vigo Co , Ind., Dec. 2, 1829.	Topeka, September 12, 1855.	Topeka.
Dawson, Mrs. B. T., Ill., May 25, 1843.	Topeka, September 12, 1855.	Topeka.
Dick, Will S., Pa , March 1, 1861.	Lawrence, September 12, 1878	Grant Tp.
Dick, Harry, Pa , June 1, 1863.	Lawrence, September 12, 1878.	Grant Tp.
Dick, George, Pa., August 20, 1865.	Lawrence, September 12, 1878.	Grant Tp.
Disney, J. C., Ire and, August 15, 1834	Topeka, March 26, 1855.	Topeka.
Deering, Mrs. Cornelia J., Elgin, Ill., Oct. 27, 1841.	Prairie City, Nov. 30, 1857.	North Lawrence.
Dole, A W., Fitchburg. Mass., March 4, 1835.	Lawrence, March 15, 1856	Osage Co.
Dinsmore, Frank F , Ind., April 3, 1851.	Lawrence, November 10, 1857.	Lawrence.
Dudley, Coleman, Putnam Co., N. Y., Nov. 12, 1818.	Osawatomie, June 10, 1856	Topeka.
Dean, W. A., O , September 23, 1862.	Clinton, 1868.	Clinton.
Dean, Ollie, South Salem, O., June 22, 1860.		Clinton.
Dow, Mary, Bourdown, Me., May 10, 18—	Douglas Co., November 3, 1854.	
Dole, Martha E , Indianapolis, April 1, 1838.	Willow Springs, October 2, 1857.	
Davis, S. C., Ind., November 20, 1855.	Shawnee, January 23, 1877	Lawrence.
Davis, J. L., Ill., July 12, 1836.	Lawrence. May 21, 1865.	Lawrence.
Durubauch, M., Pa., October 21, 1854.	Belle Plaine, Sumner Co.	
Darragh, James W., Ky., October 7, 1837.	Lawrence, February, 1879.	
Doty, Mrs D. H., Cleveland, O , December 11, 1845.		
Dudley, Mary E., Greenwich, Conn., June 10, 1848.	Topeka, April 8, 1867.	Topeka.
Dudley, Amanda, Hastings, Minn., August 17, 1858.	Topeka, April 8, 1867.	Topeka.
Doddridge, John S , Ind., March 16. 1818.	Lawrence, October 10, 1868. [1860.	Lawrence.
Dickinson, David, Green Co., Ky., July 13, 1806.	Oskaloosa, Jefferson Co , Apr. 10,	Topeka. (Died Oct. 5, 1879.)
Doan, A., Mass., November 20, 1826.	Topeka, April 2, 1855.	Topeka.
Deechmann, F., Germany, November 27, 1831.	Lawrence, April 18, 1857.	Lawrence.
Davis, E. W., Kosciusko Co., Ind., September 9, 1841.	Palermo, Doniphan Co , Nov., 1859.	
Dean, C. D., Douglas Co., Kan., September 11, 1858.	Douglas Co., Sept. 11 1858.	Clinton.
Disbrow, E., Conn., March 27, 1827.	Lawrence, October 15, 1854.	Clinton.
Disbrow, B. B., New York, August 28, 1829.	Clinton, May 12, 1855.	Clinton.
Disbrow, C. V., Clinton, Kan., December 31, 1859.	Clinton, December 31, 1859.	Clinton.
Disbrow, Lulu E., Clinton, Kan. January 25, 1861.	Clinton, January 25, 1861.	Clinton.
Disbrow, Frank H., Clinton, Kan , August 23, 1872.	Clinton, August 23, 1872.	Clinton.
Davidson, Mrs. David, Ky., December 1, 1852.	Lenape, August 11, 1868.	Near Tonganoxie.
Davidson, David, Mo., August 25, 1851.	Douglas Co., March 21, 1853	Near Tonganoxie.
Dickson, Nettie A., Kansas, October 17, 1856.	Wakarusa, October 17, 1856.	Lawrence.
Dobbins, Mrs. Amelia H , Harbor Creek, Pa., October 4, 1831.	Lawrence, October 15, 1866	Lawrence.
Darnall, Callie, Bainbridge, Ind., October 12, 1861.	Baldwin City, November 17, 1871.	Baldwin City.
Doane, Levi A , Spencer, Mass., February 13, 1836.	Neosho Co., December 4, 1860.	Lawrence.
Doane, Laura A., Spencer, Mass., March 25, 1840.	Neosho Co , December 4, 1860.	Lawrence.
Deal, I. W., Shippensburg, Pa., January 22, 1828.	Junction City, October 28 1869.	Lawrence.
Downs, A. D., Seneca Falls, N. Y., January, 1824.	Wyandotte, June 1 1858.	Wyandotte.
Dodd, J. W., Quincy, Ill., December 14. 1837.	Lawrence, November 20, 1870	Armstrong.
Duck, Daniel, Center Tp., Pa., August 23, 1826.	Lawrence, July 10, 1857.	Clinton.
Dutton, A. M., Bath, Ill., August 30, 1850	Lawrence, June 21, 1858.	
Dutton, Mary A., Portland, Me., January 20, 1817.	Lawrence, June 7, 1858.	Lawrence.
Dean, F M., Clinton, Kansas, August 17, 1863.	Clinton, August 17, 1863.	Clinton.
Davis, I W., Petersburg, Ill., September 27, 1828.	Franklin, February 27, 1862.	Lawrence.
Dallas, Chester E., Sewellville, O., 1850.	Baldwin, Douglas Co , 1859.	Baldwin.
Dunmire, W. M., Hall, Pa., September 3, 1809.	Leavenworth, February 1, 1865.	Tonganoxie.
Dunmire, J., Mo , March 12, 1841.	Leavenworth Co., Feb 1, 1865.	Tonganoxie.
Demming, W. D., La Grange Co., Ind., Dec. 20, 1855.	Lawrence, October 4, 1865.	Lawrence.
Davis, J. A	Leavenworth, 1856.	Wyandotte.
Daboney, Nelson, Williamson Co., Tenn.	Topeka, April 10, 1876.	Lecompton.
Douglas, W. W., Peru, Ind , July 28, 1863.	Topeka, 1868.	Lawrence.
Douthitt, James V., Topeka, March 24, 1858.	Topeka, March 24, 1858.	Topeka.
Davis, J. F., Topeka, December 25, 1862.	Topeka, May 20, 1875.	Topeka.
Douglas, James, Xenia, O., March 4, 1828.	Shawnee Co., December, 1867.	Topeka.
Dutton, M. R., Litchfield Co., Conn., May 15, 1829.	Jefferson Co., March 20, 1855.	Topeka.
Dutton, Marion H., Wayne Co., N. Y., Sept. 20, 1828.	Jefferson Co., March 20, 1855.	Topeka.
DeHoff, Peter S., Columbiana Co., O., Nov. 11, 1857.	Salina, August 16, 1878.	Douglas Co.
Dole, Artemas W., Fitchburg, Mass., March 4, 1835.	Lawrence, March 15, 1856.	Melvern, Osage Co
Dill, Wm., Hillsboro', O., April 16, 1846.	Leavenworth. Sept. 22 1869.	Leavenworth.
Dershern, John A., Pa.	Black Jack, February 3, 1859.	Lawrence.
Deal, Katie D., Shippensburg, Pa.	Lawrence, January, 1870.	Lawrence.
Davis, G. W., Orleans Co., N Y., October 7, 1838.	Oskaloosa, April 27, 1858.	Perry
Dickinson, L. E., Ky., March 31, 1837.	Baldwin City, November 10, 1864.	Baldwin City.
Deming, B. H., Ind., August 9, 1864.	Lawrence, Spring of 1865.	Lawrence.

Name, Place and Date of Birth.	Place and Date of Settlement.	Present Residence
Deming, N. P., Chautauqua Co., N. Y., Aug. 1, 1826.	Lawrence, October 22, 1865.	
Day, S. A., New Albany, Ind., November 4, 1842.	Fort Scott, March 14. 1869.	Fort Scott.
Donnelly, James, Ireland, December 24, 1840.	Lawrence, April 3, 1857	Lawrence.
Davis, John C., Bloomington, January 14, 1858.	Lawrence, January 14, 1858.	Clinton.
Daniels, C. R., Essex, N. Y., August 12, 1814.	Black Jack, Douglas Co., Sept. 15, 1867.	Black Jack.
Deskins, John, Va., February 25, 1810.	——, 1866.	Lawrence.
Davis, Thomas C., Gorham, Me., September 8, 1809.	Topeka, June 24 1873	Topeka.
Disbrow, W. D., Clinton Co., O., February 15, 1836.	Shawnee Co., October 6, 1858.	Topeka.
Dustin, Mrs. Marietta, Toledo, O., March 6, 1838.	Leavenworth, Sept 27, 1858.	
Diehl, Mrs. Charlotte, Waukesha, Wis., Mar. 30, 1850.	Leavenworth, May 1, 1857.	
Dowdell, J., Ind., January 23, 1823.	Lexington Tp., Nov. 1, 1858.	Olathe.
Doane, Frank A., Mass., January 29, 1862.	Osage Mission, Dec. 15, 1869.	Lawrence.
Dutton, J. B., Walo, O., September 4, 1827.	Fairmount, Leavenworth Co., May 1, 1864.	Fairmount.
Duffet, L., Chester Co., Pa., December 8, 1834.	Lawrence, April 7, 1855.	Kanwaka.
Davenport, Blanche, New York, February 29, 1861.		Lawrence.
Draper, G. W., Texas, January 17, 1863.	Lawrence. 1864.	Abilene.
Dean, Thomas J., O., November 18, 1835.	Atchison Co., May 1, 1857.	Lynn Cr'k, Topeka.
Duncan, Mrs. C. S., Harrodsburg, Ky., 1827.	Lawrence, May 11, 1855.	Lawrence.
Duncan, Lucetta D., Lawrence, January 7, 1863.	Lawrence, January 7, 1863	Clinton.
Duncan, Charles S., Lawrence, February 4, 1860.	Lawrence, February 4, 1860.	Lawrence.
Dickson, C. H., Mass., August 10, 1839.	6 mls s Lawrence, Mar. 21, 1855.	Quenemo, Doug.Co.
Downard, Ed., England, February 27, 1837.	Elwood, 1859.	Topeka.
Dennis, Wm.		
Dean, R. A., Salem, Ross Co., O., November 2, 1821.	Clinton, June 1, 1857.	Clinton.
Dean, M. N., Ross Co , O., July 15, 1827.	Clinton, July 15, 1857.	Clinton.
DeMoss, J. A., Ind., February 5, 1850.	Iola, Kansas, 1868.	
Eastey, F. H., Rockford, Ill., September 27, 1850.	Great Bend, Sept. 7, 1872.	Great Bend.
Eberhart, A., Pa., 1835.	Douglas Co., 1854.	
Eggers, L. F., Center county, Pa., 1848.	Jefferson County, 1869.	Hays City, Kan.
Emery, James S., Industry, Me	Douglas Co , September 14, 1854.	Lawrence.
Evens, Levina, Randolf Vt., December 2, 1805.	Sherman, Leavenworth County, April 1, 1872.	Leavenworth Co.
Ecke, Josephine, Germany, January 11, 1837.	Lawrence, July 3, 1858.	Lawrence.
Ecke, Josie, Kansas, March 30, 1862	Lawrence.	Lawrence
Ecke, Amelia, Kansas, November 4, 1868.	Lawrence.	Lawrence
Elwell, Mary G., England, October 9, 1827.	Missouri May 1, 1844.	Vinland.
Elliot, Mary, California, June 5, 1823.	——, July 17, 1865.	
Elliott, John, Buckfastleigh, England, April 15, 1833.	Topeka, December 15, 1856.	Topeka.
Eaton, Gertrude, New Haven, Vt., January 28, 1862.	Russell, Kan , Dec. 26, 1876.	Russell.
Estabrook, Lucy, Weston, Mass.	——, April 5, 1855.	
Eberhart, Emma J., Crawford county, Pa., Nov 8, '52	Franklin County, June, 1856.	Vinland.
Epley, James, Pennsylvania, August 3, 1816.	——, 1857.	Eudora.
Elwell, Charley, Galena, Ill , December 25, 1863.	Near Lawrence, 1865.	Vinland.
Edwards, William, Wellington, England, July 16, 1836.	Lawrence, October, 1878.	Lawrence.
Edwards, Catharine A., June 20, 1840.	Lawrence.	
Eckman, D M., Lancaster, Pa., February 25, 1858.	Leavenworth Co., Mar. 10, 1870.	Lawrence.
Elias, Gideon, Huntingdon county, Pa., Aug. 26, 1831.	Prairie City, Douglas County, April 1, 1857.	Washington Creek.
Elias, Isabella C., Huntington Co., Pa., Dec. 16, 1832	Prairie City, April 1, 1857.	Washington Creek.
Elias, Juniata A., Prairie City, Kan., January 8, 1858.	Prairie City	Washington Creek.
Emerson, J. R , Maryland, February 6, 1843.	Lecompton, March 31, 1858.	Topeka
Eidemiller, C. M , Miami county, O., October 1, 1844.	Wyandotte, March 1, 1870.	Lawrence.
Edwards, T. H., Charleston, Pa., November 14, 1849.	Larned, June 15, 1875.	Kansas City, Mo.
Edwards, W. C., Charleston, Pa., April 12, 1853	Larned, January 11, 1876.	Larned.
Ela, Charles N., Lebanon, N. H., April 22, 1836.	Lawrence, Sept. 15, 1856.	Topeka.
Elam, E., Tennessee January 26, 1829.	Bourbon Co., January 2, 1861.	Douglas Co.
Elam, Elizabeth, Missouri, August 18, 1843.	Bourbon Co , January 2, 1861.	Douglas Co.
Elam, Edward, Kansas, Apri, 13, 1864.	Douglas County, April 13, 1864.	Douglas Co.
Eberhart, H. S., Mercer county, Pa , May 20, 1831.	Lawrence, June 15, 1854.	Willow Springs.
Eidemiller, A G., Frederick City, Md., Aug. 22, 1833.	Lawrence, June 16, 1867.	Lawrence.
Eidemiller, M. J., Troy, Ohio, February 16, 1835.	Lawrence, August 1, 1867.	Lawrence.
Eidemiller, Nellie E., Troy, O.	Lawrence.	
Eidemiller, Magg e R.	Lawrence.	
Ellison, A G., St. Thomas, Can., March 6, 1880.	North Lawrence, 1869	North Lawrence.
Ellis, E., Lewis county, N. Y., February 14, 1848.	Lawrence, October, 1865.	Leavenworth Co.
Elliott, J. G., Ohio, September 24, 1852.	Clinton, September 2, 1878.	Clinton.
Elston, John, Wayne county, Ind., June 13, 1812.	Johnson County, Oct 17, 1857.	Lawrence.
Elston, Eliza H., Auburn, Me., November 3, 1834.	Douglas County, Nov. 3, 1854.	Lawrence.
Etherington, Thomas, Durham, England, Aug. 4, 1827	Ridgeway, Osage Co., July 20, 1857.	Ridgeway.
Earl, George F , Massachusetts, February 11, 1834.	Lawrence, Sept. 13, 1854.	El Dorado.
Essic, Emanuel, Missouri, 1850.	Lawrence, 1861	Lawrence.
Eberhart, Paul C., Butler county. Pa., April 3, 1838.	Douglas County, June 20, 1854.	Douglas Co.
Eoke, F. J., Germania, July 10, 1831.	Lawrence, April 28, 1857.	Lawrence.
Edwards, Mrs. C L., Hadley, Mass., March 2, 1837.	Lawrence, September 26, 1866	Lawrence.
Edwards, Virginia S., Southampton,Mass., Dec. 13. '64.	Lawrence, September 26, 1866.	Lawrence.
English, David C . District of Columbia, Mar. 20, 1853.	Leavenworth Co , May 20, 1870.	Jefferson Co.
Elliott, R. G., Indiana. July 23, 1828.	Lawrence, Nov. 15, 1854.	Jefferson Co.
Elliott, Hattie A., Ohio.	Lawrence, November, 1857.	Jefferson Co.

Name, Place and Date of Birth.	Place and Date of Settlement.	Present Residence
Evett, William, Lockland, O., June 1, 1825.	Butler Co., October 4, 1866.	Wakarusa Tp.
Evans. William J., Pittsburg, Pa., November 25, 1852	Lawrence, April 10, 1865.	Lawrence.
Elwell, S. R., Ohio, November 23, 1816.		Vinland.
Eberhart, Obadiah, Westmoreland county, Pa.	Willow Springs, Douglas Co., April 16, 1859.	Willow Springs.
Emery, Charles C., Saco, Me., May 30, 1830.	Kanwaka, May 30, 1855.	
Emery, Anna C., Saco, Me., July 19, 1829.	Kanwaka, September 19. 1857.	
Evans, Thomas, East South Wales, June 16, 1824.	Lawrence, April 10, 1857.	Lawrence.
Elston, Mrs. R. C., Kansas, February 14, 1857.	Johnson County, February.	Jefferson Co.
Elston, R. C , Olathe, July 3, 1857.		
Eberhart, Saty, Montgomery, O.	Willow Springs, Sept 19, 1861.	Willow Springs.
English. Thomas A.. Indiana December 14, 1840.	Hutchinson. Nov. 17, 1866.	Clifton.
Edney, F. J., Woodsfield, Ohio, January 21, 1858.	Lawrence, June 10, 1873.	Douglas Co.
Evans, Henry, Massachusetts, January 19, 1828.	Kanwaka, March 15, 1855.	
Eddy, George A , New York, 1834.	Leavenworth, March, 1857.	Leavenworth.
Eddy, Mrs M. L., Ohio.	Leavenworth, November, 1856.	Leavenworth.
Edgar, W. I., Greenbrier county, Va., May 19, 1850.	Leavenworth Co., Sept. 8, 1868	Leavenworth Co.
Eberhart, L. J., Pennsylvania, Sep 8, 1833.	9 mls. s. Lawrence, June 12, 1854.	Douglas Co.
Ellwell, J. K , Galena, Illinois, Obtober 28, 1860.	Lawrence, July 4, 1876.	Vinland.
Essow, G. T., Canada West, February 22, 1856.	Williamstown, Jefferson County, March, 1864	Lawrence.
Fasley, F. H., Chicago, Illinois, September 27, 1859.	Sedalia, Mo., Sept. 7, 1872.	Great Bend.
Emmert, D. B., New Cumberland, Pa., Aug 1, 1836	Topeka, August 15, 1859.	Wichita
Edwards, C. L., Southampton, Mass., Oct. 19, 1828.	Lawrence, Nov. 26, 1855.	Lawrence.
Ely, A. F. Susquehannah Co., Pa , Dec. 22, 1838	Mound City, Sept. 1, 1867.	Mound City.
Embry, Josephine A , Northeast Pa., Jan. 17, 1841.	Lawrence, Nov. 12, 1851.	Ottawa.
Embree, A , Fayetteville, Indiana, January 22, 1850.	Eudora, August 21, 1879.	Eudora.
Eldridge, Wm. T., Berkshire Co., Mass., Dec. 23, 1831.	Clinton, Doug. Co., Mar. 18, 1870.	Clinton
Etherington, Albert, Kansas, March 11, 1862.	Ridgeway.	Topeka.
Foster, W. S., Indiana, March 27, 1833.	Leavenworth City, Feb., 1856.	Media, Kansas.
Fox, James W., Ohio, February 22, 1843.	Topeka, Oct. 14, 1856.	Topeka.
Fisher, Peter, Glasgow, Scotland. August 27, 1829.	Topeka, 1857.	Topeka.
Fairchild, T A., Iowa, July 22, 1854	Holton, 1857.	Topeka.
Francis, John. Norfolk, England, April 24, 1837.	Lykins Co., Sept. 20, 1858.	Iola, Allen Co.
Francis, L., Jonesboro, Indiana, March 2, 1841.	Allen Co , July 5, 1860.	Iola, Allen Co.
Fry, John, England, November 25, 1832.	Lawrence, Nov. 1, 1854.	Linwood.
Falley, George M., Mt. Gilead, Ohio, May 4, 1855.	Lawrence, May 1, 1857	Douglas Co.
Fultz, Henry, Indiana. May 12, 1859.		
Frazier, M., Rockville, Indiana, May 30, 1845.	Lawrence, Mar. 1, 1877.	Douglas Co.
Filley, H. W., Cleveland, Ohio, June 9, 1816.	Lawrence. Mar., 1863.	Burlingame.
Fugate, J. W., South Carolina, May 2, 1832.	Douglas Co., May 6, 1866.	Lawrence.
Finley, Richard, Ashfield, Ontario, June 22, 1856.	Parallel, Kan , April 1, 1870.	Baldwin City.
Foster, Frank S., Bloomfield, Iowa, Nov., 12, 1863.	Ellsworth, Ellsworth Co., Mar 1876.	Lawrence.
Fitzpatrick, J. C., Agency City, Iowa, Jan. 6, 1847.	Osawatomie, Feb 5, 1859.	Lawrence.
Fitz, Mary Ann, Vinland, Kansas, December 25. 1858.	Stony Point.	Vinland, Kansas.
Fitz, Mrs. G. W., Limerick, Ireland.		Vinland.
Fitz, Laura A , Vinland, Kansas, March 27, 1866.		Vinland.
Fitz, Almira W., Vinland, Kansas, December 9, 1863.		Vinland.
Flanery. C. T., Virginia, August 8, 1850.		
Finch, H. O., Monroe Co., Ohio, May 31, 1821.	Jefferson Co., Mar. 13, 1855.	
Foster, James P., Ross Co. Ohio, January 19, 1835	Douglas Co., Mar 1868.	Douglas Co.
Foster, M. F., Ross Co., Ohio, July 30. 1840.	Douglas Co., April, 1868.	
Frey, Henry, Switz Republic, December 28 1837.	Lawrence, Aug. 1864.	Lawrence.
Force, Jennie E., March, England, February 5. 1845.	Lawrence, June 21, 1870.	
Findley, W F., Dayton, Pennsylvania, August 24, 1857	——, April 21. 1873.	McPherson Co.
Fletcher, Mary E., Ripley, Ohio, February 21, 1830.	Prairie City. 1856.	Prairie City.
Field, A. H., Peterborough, N. H., December 22, 1810.	Wakarusa Tp., 1869	
Field, Jane E., Vassaboro, Maine, June 27, 1821.	Wakarusa Tp , 1869.	
Faucett, J. F., Indiana August 12, 1825.	Palmyra, Mar. 18, 1857.	Palmyra.
Fugate, W., Virginia, May 10, 1862	Lawrence, Nov. 11, 1875.	Lawrence.
Farrell, John, Ireland. August 9, 1849.	Reno, Aug. 1, 1861	Leavenworth.
Felin, Flavia, Buffalo, New York, October 16, 1860	Lawrence, July 4, 1869.	Albany, N. Y.
Fincher, A. T., Columbia county, Pa., August 12. 1847.	Lawrence, January 17, 1869.	Lawrence.
Fritshe, Frederick, Lachsen, Altenburg, Germany, February 28 1820.	Topeka, October 26. 1866.	Topeka.
Farrar, Mrs D. K., Springfield, Ill., Nov. 26, 1840.	Burlingame, May 14, 18 0.	Burlingame.
Flagg. Mrs John, Weston, Mass., January 5, 1827.	Manhattan, March 17, 1855.	Manhattan.
Fitz, E. G., Massachusetts, October 19, 1851	Douglas County, 1855.	Vinland.
Foote, A. H., Middlefield, Ohio. Dec. 24, 1838.	Lawrence, March 24, 1866	Lawrence.
Flinn, Ella, Lebon, January 16, 1840.	Lawrence, December 13, 1868.	Lawrence.
Flinn, Jennie, Lawrence, October 19, 1869.		Lawrence.
Forney. J W., Lancaster, Pa., September 30, 1817.	Topeka, May 12, 1856	Philadelphia.
Farnsworth, H. W., Vermont, October 13, 1816.	Leavenworth, August 11, 1868.	Topeka
Fortescue, W. M., Philadelphia, April 1, 1833.	Lawrence, October 19, 1869.	Leavenworth.
Flick, George, Illinois, January 5 1862	Hutchinson, June 7, 1872.	Lawrence.
Fellows, Francis W , Attleboro, Mass., Jan. 27, 1829.	Ontario, Jackson County, Sept. 1, 1869	
Faas, Gustav A., Philadelphia, Pa., March 6, 1848.	Lawrence, June 7, 1878.	Lawrence.
Faas, Helen S., Allentown, Pa., January 17, 1856.	Lawrence, June 7, 1878.	Lawrence.
Flinn, Julia G., Canada, July 19, 1866.	Lawrence.	Lawrence.

Name, Place and Date of Birth.	Place and Date of Settlement.	Present Residence
Fugate, Mrs. J. W., Griggsville, Illinois, May 12, 1839.	Lawrence, March 1, 1876.	Lawrence.
Field, L. A, Davenport, Iowa, October 30, 1858.	Blue Rapids, Sept. 29, 1870.	Lawrence.
Foster, Richard, Tabor, Iowa, July 15, 1858	Osborne County, July, 1871.	Osborne City.
Foster, Suard, Lincoln, Nebraska, August 8, 1863.	Osborne County, July 15, 1870.	Osborne City.
Forbes, Charles F., Brookfield, Mass , Jan. 25, 1845.	Douglas County, January 1, 1879.	Lawrence.
Frazier, Mrs Olive L., Ridge Farm, Ill., Aug 12, 1853.	Lawrence, March 1, 1877.	Douglas Co
Farrell, Thomas, Ft. Bliss, Texas, July 1, 1856.	Leavenworth Co., August, 1861.	Leavenworth Co.
Franklin, Wilson, Tennessee, about 1829.	Lawrence, 1861.	Lawrence.
Fortuer, Riley, North Carolina, 1811.	Eudora, 1861.	Eudora.
Foster, F. R., Pennsylvania, April 1, 1832.	Topeka, November 9, 1854.	Topeka Tp.
Foster M B , Pennsylvania, August 10, 1835.	Topeka, September 20, 1857.	Topeka Tp
Fellows, Cara, Cahaba, Alabama, December 18, 1860.	Ontario, Jackson County, Sept. 1, 1869.	Lawrence.
Fish, W. L., New York, January 4, 1813.	Lawrence, February 12, 1879.	Shelbina, Mo.
Flinn, Sarah T., Niagara, Ontario, June 30, 1857.	Lawrence, July 12, 1868	
Frank, Henry, LaFayette, Indiana, December 21, 1853.	Leavenworth Co., Nov. 6, 1877.	North Lawrence.
Fincher, I. D., Berks, Pennsylvania, January 21, 1845.	North Lawrence, Oct. 20, 1860.	North Lawrence.
Furgason, J. D., Iowa, August 17, 1853.	Lawrence, April, 1870.	Fall Leaf.
Foreman, James B., Xenia, O., September 1, 1851.	Topeka, July 25, 1879.	Topeka.
Fitz, George T., Cambridgeport, Mass., Feb. 18, 1843.	Palmyra, Nov. 12, 1859.	Willow Springs.
Fitz, Mrs. L. E, Mercer county, Pa., Feb. 9, 1847.	Palmyra Tp., Douglas Co., May 21, 1856.	Willow Springs.
Farnsworth, Charles, Groton, Mass., February 5, 1822.	Topeka, Nov., 1854.	Shawnee Co.
Foley, Peter, Missouri, March 23, 1860.	Lawrence, July 5, 1879.	Lawrence.
Freyhofer, Jacob, Switzerland, 1806.	Riley Co., 1861.	Riley Co.,Randolph
Fensky, Herman, Prussia, 1843.	North Topeka, 1864.	North Topeka.
Falkner, Daniel, Ohio, November 15, 1818.	Clinton, 1867.	Ridgew'y,OsageCo.
Falkner, A. C , Ohio, May 17, 1858.	Clinton, 1867.	Ridgeway.
Frazier, C. N., Indiana	Lawrence, 1868.	Tonganoxie.
Feister, J. M , Lancaster Co., Pa., December 17, 1813	Peabody, April 1, 1878.	Peabody.
Foster, Mrs. M A., Bristol, Conn., July 26, 1812.	Atchison, Nov. 22, 1857.	Wyandotte.
Flinn, George, Ontario, Canada, February 19, 1830	Lawrence, May 9, 1868.	Lawrence.
Fillmore. H. S , New Brunswick, November 25, 1833.	Lawrence, April 25, 1859.	Lawrence.
Fields, Michael, Philadelphia, January 1, 1819.	Reno Co., June 15, 1877.	Floating.
Fluke, W. W., Ohio, Oct. 4. 1827,	Lawrence, Mar. 10, 1865.	Lawrence.
Fry, M. Lulu, Shelby, O., September 9, 1864	Lawrence, June 9, 1877.	Lawrence.
Fry, E. E., Ohio.	Lawrence, June 9, 1877.	Lawrence.
Fry, Mrs. M. B , Richland connty, O., April, 1811.	Douglas Co., June 17 1877.	Lawrence.
Fry, T. E., Crawford county, O., October 12, 1833.	Douglas Co , Jan. 17, 1877.	Lawrence.
Flinn, Annie, Florence, Can., 1860.	Lawrence, 1869.	Lawrence.
Flinn, Julia G., Canada, 1865.	Lawrence, 1869.	Lawrence.
Finney, Frank, Mt. Vernon, Ohio.	Lawrence, Sept., 1865	Lawrence.
Freeland, J. S , Owens county, Ind., August 7, 1826.	Shawnee Co., Feb. 27, 1854.	Shawnee Co.
Freeland, Mary J , Vermillion, Ill , November 25, 1852.	Shawnee Co., Aug. 13, 1857.	Monmouth.
Frye, D. F., New Hampshire, Mar. 19, 1834.	Palmyra Mar. 1, 1857.	Wyandotte Co.
Fletcher, Clara A., Kansas, February 13.	———, 1879.	
Faucett, Mary E., Kentucky, January 19, 1836	Douglas Co., Mar. 18, 1857.	Douglas Co., Kan
Fogle, Ella.	Williamsburg, Aug. 20, 1869.	Lawrence.
Farnsworth, Mrs. A. C., Piqua, O., December 20, 1852.	Lawrence.	Lawrence.
Fluke, Fannie, Mt. Pleasant, Ia., July 18, 1870.	Lawrence, May 6, 1875.	Lawrence.
Flinton, William J. , Higate, Vt., March 19, 1849	Lawrence, Oct. 16, 1869.	Lawrence.
Fuel, Henry, Osceola, Mo., April 22, 1840.	Lawrence, Douglas Co., July 4, 1866	Lawrence.
Fisher, Julius. Germany, May 23, 1827.	Lawrence, Kansas, Apr. 17, 1857.	
Fisher, Thockla, Wilden Spring. Ger., Feb 21, 1847.	Lawrence, Kansas, May 16, 1857	
Faxen, James D., Plymouth, Mass., April 29, 1843.	Lawrence, Douglas Co., Dec. 2, 1856.	Lawrence.
Flinn, Julia G., Canada. July 19, 1865.	Lawrence, July 18, 1868.	Lawrence.
Fager, J. Foreston, Ogle county, Ill., April 26, 1819.	Wichita, Nov. 12, 1871	Haysville.
Franks, James, County Cork, Ireland, August 25, 1815	Leavenworth City, Sept. 24, 1855.	Leavenworth City.
Franks, Mary Ann, County Cavan, Ireland, Aug. 22, '42.	Leavenworth City, April 15, 1857.	Leavenworth City.
Fitz, George W., Sundown, N. C., April 22, 1815.	Coal Creek, Douglas Co., April 29, 1855	Coal Creek, Douglas Co.
Fox, Thomas, London, England, April 2, 1829.	Wakarusa, Dec. 13, 1860.	
Flinn, George, Niagara, Ont., May 19, 1800	Lawrence, May 9, 1868.	
Fugate, W. T., Bloomington, Ill., September 24, 1861	Ottawa, 1876	
Flanders, Mrs Mary A., Pittsburg, Pa., Aug. 15, '38,	Lawrence, May 9 1856.	Manhattan.
Foos, Otto, Philadelphia, Pa., January 19.	Lawrence, June 7, 1878.	Lawrence.
Falknor, Andrew,Montgomery county, O., May 24 1844.	Bloomington, Sept. 21, 1860.	Lawrence.
Franks, Lizzie S., Leavenworth, June 28, 1859.	Leavenworth.	Leavenworth.
Gilbert, Eli, Morgan county, O , October 16, 1822.	Lawrence, June, 1856.	Larned.
Gowen, J W., Farmington October 22, 1800	Lawrence, March, 1877.	Lawrence.
Gallaher. William, Pennsylvania, January 22, 1833	Ft. Scott, August 1, 1857	Ft. Scott.
Green, T. C., Naples. N. Y., June 12, 1830.	Lawrence, March 10, 1865.	Perry.
Green, L. C., Ohio, April 10, 1840.	Lawrence, March 10, 1865.	Perry.
Grefkaw, Fred, Germany, October 15, 1831.	Eudora, March 30, 1857	Lawrence.
Gilliland. R. M., Brown county, O., Sept. 20, 1812	Lyon Co., July 12, 1871.	Lyon Co.
Goodin, J K., Somerset, Perry Co., O , Feb. 24, 1824	Wakarusa. May 26, 1854.	Ottawa.
Goodin. Mrs. J. K , Canal Fulton, O., March 31, 1836.	Palmyra, Douglas Co., Jan. 1857.	Ottawa.
Geller, W. G., Germany, September 13, 1856.	Great Bend, April 7, 1856.	Great Bend.
Griffith, Mrs. T. E., St. Johns, N. B., 1857.	Lawrence, 1866.	Lawrence.

Name, Place and Date of Birth.	Place and Date of Settlement.	Present Residence
Grovenor, G., Suffield, Conn., September 13, 1840.	Lawrence, Oct. 1, 1857.	
Green, Charles H., Illinois, November 10, 1860	Anderson Co., Sept., 1878.	
Gentry, Mary, Missouri, 1835.	Leavenworth, 1863.	Lawrence.
Griswold, W. S., Guilford. Conn., May 6, 1827.	Wabaunsee Co., April 15, 1856.	Wabaunsee.
Gellert, W. G., Ft. Wayne Ind , September 13, 1861	Great Bend, April 3, 1878.	Great Bend.
Gordon, G. S., Rushford, N. Y., September 28, 1826.	Topeka, May 22, 1856.	Topeka.
Going, James W., Rolla, Mo , October 19, 1862.	Salina, March, 1866.	Salina.
Geyer, Jonas, September 21, 1794.	Douglas Co , April. 1874.	
Gould, M. A , Pendleton, Ind., December 3, 1841.	Lawrence, August 6, 1856.	Lawrence.
Gardner, John, Ireland, August, 1832.	Lawrence, August, 1856.	Lawrence.
Gardner, Mrs.	Lawrence. 1858.	
Gleason, J. H., Saratoga county, N Y., Nov, 10, 1821.	Willow Springs, 1854.	Willow Springs.
Gleason, Janie L , Windham Co., Conn., May 2, 1832.	Willow Springs, 1859.	
Greene, Albert R., Mt. Hope, Ill., January 16, 1842.	Ridgeway, Osage Co , May 18, 1857	Lecompton.
Gray, G. B., Johnson county, Mo., March 12, 1851	Jefferson Co., Kansas, Oct., 1857.	Jefferson Co.
Godding, Frank, Lunenburg Mass., February 21, 1855.	Douglas Co., September 17, 1878.	Kanwaka, Doug. Co
Grout, A. D., Westfairlee, Vt , September 14, 1844.	Lawrence, March 18, 1877.	Lawrence.
Gregg, E. H., Frederickstown, O., March 20, 1840.	Ottawa, Franklin Co., March 7, 1878.	Ottawa.
Gilbert, R. L., England, February 1, 1835.	Lawrence, Kansas, Nov.. 1, 1855.	Chester, Jeff'n Co.
Gates, H. W., Ohio, August 2, 1849	Ottawa, November 1, 1870	DeSoto.
Gates, Huldah S., Ohio, December 7. 1851.	Ottawa, November 1, 1870.	DeSoto.
Greene, M M., New York, May 14, 1842.	Shawnee Co , May 18, 1857.	Lecompton.
Garvin, J. M., Fulton county, Ill , February 14, 1835.	——, November 1, 1854.	
Gilson, Simeon, Cambridge, Mass., April 14, 1819.	Wakarusa, Douglas Co., March 21, 1855.	Wakarusa.
Gilpatrick, W. C., Blue Hill, Me , August 3, 1836.	Shawnee County, Nov , 1854.	Topeka.
Gunn, Charles H.	——, 1857	Lawrence.
Gillmore, John, Gosport Ind , January 15, 1854.	Lawrence, March 25, 1871.	Lawrence.
Graeber, G. A., Sheffield, Ill., February 27, 1855.	Lawrence, 1856	Lawrence.
Griggs, W. D , Naples, N. Y., February 18, 1845.	Lawrence, May 1, 1870.	Lawrence.
Griggs, Mrs. Sarah J., Sandusky, O., January 26, 1845.	Lawrence, May 1. 1870	Lawrence.
Guernsey, Lutie, Fulton county, Ill., July 19, 1857.	Neosho Falls, October 21, 1858	Lawrence.
Guernsey, Robert C , Newton, Kan., Sept. 16, 1878.	Newton, September 16. 1878.	Lawrence.
Gilman, George, Georgia, July 2, 1860.	Lawrence, August, 1860.	Lawrence.
Gevens, Rev., Wellsborough, April 3, 1808.	Sherman Tp., Leavenworth Co , October, 1869	Leavenworth Co.
Glathart, J. H., Ohio, May 5, 1836.	Lawrence, February 1, 1857.	Lawrence.
Gingerich, M. E., Pennsylvania, August 3, 1850.	Lawrence, May 5, 1855	Lawrence.
Green, M. E., Ohio, September 22, 1847.	Baldwin City, June 7, 1857.	Prairie City.
Grover, Mrs. A. B., Hartford, Conn.		Gardner.
Guild, F. B., New York, March 19, 1841.	Lawrence, 1860.	Topeka.
Gilbert, Mrs. J. E., Buffalo, N. Y., August 22, 1846.	Topeka, August 16, 1878.	Topeka.
Gunn, Vara H., Kansas, October 6, 1857.	Wyandotte. October 6, 1857.	Lawrence.
Green, L. F., West Liberty, O , August 31, 1835.	Palmyra, March 31. 1855.	Prairie City.
Griffin, A. J., Milton, N. C., November 15, 1842.	Lawrence, March 21 1857.	Lawrence.
Gordon. H. A., Allegany county, N. Y., Jan. 2. 1832.	Topeka, May 22, 1856	Topeka.
Green, E. H., Scituate, R. I., June 29, 1800.	Near Ridgeway, Osage County, May 10, 1857.	Lecompton.
Gipfert, P., Germany, February 9, 1852.	Lawrence, August 30, 1878	Lawrence.
Griggs, E. W., Wisconsin, July 28, 1850.	Lawrence, November 20, 1860.	Lawrence.
Green, Flora A., Paris, Ill , December 21, 1860.	Peabody, March 26, 1876.	Baldwin.
Gilmore, A. O., Kansas, November 15, 1858	Lawrence, November 15, 1858	Kaw Valley.
Good, E B., Madison county, Ill , October 19, 1832	Lawrence, May 3, 1863	Lawrence.
Good, A. G., Madison county, Ill., February 6, 1837.	Lawrence, May 3, 1866.	Lawrence.
Good, T. W., Lawrence, January 27, 1868.	Lawrence, January 27, 1868.	Lawrence.
Good, O. L. , Madison county. Ill., December 3, 1863.	Lawrence, May 3, 1866	Lawrence.
Good, F. L , Lawrence, December 4, 1869.	Lawrence, December 4, 1869.	Lawrence.
Grossette, M A., Pennsylvania, January 8, 1859.	Prairie City, 1863.	Lawrence.
Grossette, J M., Kansas, November 30, 1864.		Lawrence.
Guest, A. H., Albany, N. Y., February 10, 1842.	Lawrence, March 1, 1857.	Lawrence
Gardner, R., Donegal county, Ireland, 1820.	Lawrence, May, 1858.	Jefferson County.
Gardner, Charlotte, Juniata county, Pa., Aug. 14, 1833.	——, 1858.	
Gunn, O. B., Montague, Mass., October 20, 1828.	Leavenworth, March 20 1857.	Lawrence.
Gunn, Mrs. O. B.	Lawrence, 1857.	Lawrence.
Gleason, Mrs M. F , New Hampshire, May 1, 1828.	Lawrence, May 7. 1857.	Lawrence.
Gleason, F., New Hampshire, April 20, 1824.	Douglas County, May 7, 1857.	Lawrence
Coolman, A. T., Springtown, Indiana. June 6, 1852.	Osawatomie, August 12, 1868.	
Gill Mrs. Angeline. Mercer county, Pa , Sept. 13, 1828.	Douglas Co , Nov. 10, 1855.	Douglas County.
Greenwood, J E., Grafton, Mass., March 4, 1825.	Topeka, Dec. 10, 1854.	Topeka.
Greenwood, A. W., Maine, August 2, 1832.	Topeka, Nov. 12, 1855	Topeka.
Grow, J. B , New York, December 25, 1831.	Lawrence, February 9, 1860.	Lawrence.
Griffing, J. S , Tioga county. N. Y., October 28, 1822.	Lawrence. October 15, 1854.	Manhattan.
Griffin, E. K., Greenville, N Y., February 14, 1835	Topeka, July, 1856.	Topeka.
Goodwill, H. C , Chicopee, Mass., August 22, 1838.	Lawrence, April 1, 1879.	Lawrence.
Griffith, Mary, Lawrence, Kansas, March 17, 1864.	Lawrence, March 17, 1864.	Lawrence.
Griggs, A. D , Naples, New York, February 18, 1815.	Lawrence, May 21, 1870.	Lawrence.
Greer, John P , Dayton, Ohio, October 21, 1820.	Topeka, 1856	Topeka.
Griffith, R. S., Mass , February 18, 1819.	Lawrence, July, 1856.	Topeka.
Gillpatrick, J. H., Topsham, Maine, October 18, 1830.	Shawnee County, June 1, 1855.	Leavenworth.

15

Name, Place and Date of Birth.	Place and Date of Settlement.	Present Residence
Gillpatrick, Sadie R., New Madison, Ohio, Nov. 18, 1851.	Anderson Co., March 3, 1856.	Leavenworth.
Gillpatrick. Phebe, New Madison, Ohio, May 13, 1848.	Anderson Co., April 17. 1854.	Leavenworth.
Goodrich, E. F., Somerset county, Maine, June 14, 1843.	Lawrence, March 6, 1869.	Lawrence.
Goodrich, L. R., Somerset county, Maine, Dec. 6, 1845.	Lawrence, March 6, 1869.	Lawrence.
Giffen, John M. Belmont county, Ohio, 1830	Shawnee Mission, Johnson Co., Sept. 20, 1855.	Olathe. Was present when the candle box was found.
Goulding, Dora L., England, August 14, 1858.	Topeka, May 6, 1870.	Topeka.
Griffeth, Mrs. N. C., Tecumseh, Mich , Sept. 4, 1836.	Ft. Riley, January 1, 1862	[rence.
Gilmore, John, New York, March 27, 1835	Lawrence, March 7, 1857.	5 miles S. of Law-
Gilmore. Sus'nh C., Crawfordville, Ind., Mch. 28, 1837.	Lawrence, September 27, 1857.	
Gilmore, Frank L., Kansas, September 18, 1878.	Kansas.	Douglas Co.
Grant, O. H., Oneida county, N. Y., November 7, 1841.	Miami Co., May 12, 1855.	
Geelan, P. H., Cavan county, Ireland, March 15, 1833	Big Springs, Douglas Co., April 28, 1855.	Big Springs.
Grant, A J , Ohio, November 23, 1846.	Lawrence, November 2?, 1867.	Vinland.
Grim, Jacob, Maryland, October 20, 1852	Douglas Co., March 28, 1879.	Lawrence.
Gentry, Abram, Lafayette county, Mo., April 10, 1835	Douglas Co., June 11. 1862.	Lawrence.
Giles, F. W., Littleton, New Hampshire, May 30, 1819.	Topeka, December 4, 1854.	Topeka.
Giles, Caroline A. Salisbury, N. H., August 2. 1821.	Topeka, April, 1855.	Topeka.
Gill, Eliza J., Glasgow, Kentucky, September 3, 1813.	Lawrence, May 11, 1864	Lawrence.
Gregg, S. C., Warren county, Ohio, October 12, 1844.	North Topeka, May 15, 1869.	North Topeka.
Gregg, M. H., Green county, Ohio, October 29, 1847.	North Topeka, May 27, 1869.	North Topeka.
Gamble, I. C., West Newton, Pa., Feb. 6, 1844.	Tonganoxie, Leavenworth Co., March 6, 1869.	Tonganoxie.
Gleed, J. W., 1843.	Lawrence.	Lawrence
Green, H. T., Virginia, October 16, 1824.	Leavenworth, September, 1854.	Leavenworth.
Green, Susan M., Kentucky, December 7, 1835	Leavenworth, November, 1855.	Leavenworth.
Gilmore, John S., Rochester, N. Y , December 6, 1848.	Lyon Co., Kansas, Oct 31, 1857	Fredonia, Kansas.
Gould, George E , Kansas City, Mo , Aug. 27, 1864.	Kansas City, Mo., Aug. 27, 1864	Lawrence, Kansas.
Griffis, Joseph, Michigan, May 23, 1842.	Vinland, Douglas Co., April 10, 1857.	Vinland.
Griffith, Prucilla A., Pennsylvania, Sept. 26, 1833.	Prairie City, 1855.	
Griffith, Geo. W. E., Indiana, December, 22, 1833.	Franklin Co., October, 1855.	Lawrence.
Garvin, David, Fulton county, Illinois, May 1, 1810	Wakarusa. Douglas Co., December, 1854.	Wakarusa.
Green, B. F., Sullivan county, Tennessee, Jan. 18, 1842.	White Church, Wyandotte Co., November 20. 1868.	White Church
Gibbons, Wm C., Bermuda Isles, April 7, 1834.	Lawrence, November 3, 1854.	Topeka.
Gibbons, Mrs. Eda, Indianapolis, Ind., March 10, 1850.	Topeka, January 8. 1869.	Lawrence.
Gill, W. W , Wisconsin, September 8, 1858.	Lawrence, April 10, 1868	Topeka.
Gregory, Wes Muncie, Indiana, August 5, 1851.	Lyndon, May 1, 1870.	Topeka.
Greer, Julia E., Yellow Springs, Ohio, Feb. 27, 1817.	Shawnee Co., October 3, 1863.	Topeka, [1873.
Gray, Alfred. Evans, Erie county, N. Y., Dec. 5, 1830.	Quindaro, Kansas, Mar. 27. 1857	Topeka, Kan. since
Gray, Sarah C., Livingston county, N. Y., July 31 1834.	Quindaro, Kansas, August, 1857.	Topeka, Kansas.
Glynn, O. M., New York, Feb. 14, 1838.	Lecompton, May 2, 1856.	Oskaloosa.
Green, M. L., French Valley, Kansas, Jan. 16, 1863.	Lawrence	Lawrence.
Greig, James H., Scotland, December 5, 1857.	Lawrence, September 5 1878.	Lawrence.
Gaylord, G. L., New York, September 16, 1826.	Atchison July 3, 1858.	
Glymm, T W., New York.	Oskaloosa, November 20, 1867.	Oskaloosa.
Gill, Wm. H., Cornwall county, England, July 1, 1830.	Lawrence, August 6, 1856.	Coal Creek.
Graton, Adelaide H., Genesee county, Michigan, December, 15, 1840.	Lawrence, August 1, 1856	Lawrence.
Graton, Allie L., Lawrence, August 24, 1861.	Lawrence, August 24, 1861	Lawrence.
Gordon, J. C., Allegany county, N. Y., May 13, 1831.	Lawrence, November 20, 1854.	Topeka.
Gordon, Mrs. J. C. Tompkins county, New York, February 16, 1831.		
Gilliland, J. B , Brown county, Ohio, April 27. 1828.	Lawrence, October, 1855.	Topeka.
Gilliland, J. A , Brown county, Ohio, Nov. 13, 1828.	Douglas Co., June 26, 1857.	Douglas Co.
Gilliland, Mary, Brown county, Ohio, Feb. 27, 1818.	Douglas Co., June 26, 1857.	Douglas Co.
Griffith, Charles E , Kansas, August 17, 1858	Lyon Co., October 13, 1871.	Lyon Co.
Gingerich, E. J. Pennsylvania, December 25, 1829	Lawrence, May 10, 1855.	Lawrence.
Gingerich, J. M., Pennsylvania, August, 4, 1847.	Lawrence, May 10, 1855.	Lawrence.
Gleed, Charles S., Vermont, March 23 1855.	Lawrence, May, 1866 (?).	Lawrence.
Gordon, J. W , North Fork of Deep river, North Carolina, June 13, 1815.	Johnson Co., May 4, 1869.	Johnson Co.
Grant, H. C., Oneida county, New York, Nov. 12, 1844.	Miami Co., May 12, 1855.	Lawrence.
Gregg A. H., Ohio, October 22, 1832.	Olathe, Kansas, May 15, 1857.	Lexington Tp.
Gardner, G. W., Jefferson county, N. Y. July 4, 1826.	Leavenworth Co., April 15, 1855.	Leavenworth
Hunting, E. H., Penobscot county, Me., Dec. 3, 1832.	Lawrence, March, 1856.	Russell, Russ-ell Co.
Hutchinson, Wm., Randolph, Vt., January 21, 1823.	Lawrence, April 1, 1855.	Washington, D C.
Hubbard, D., New Hampshire, 1855.	Marion Tp., 1857.	Olathe.
Holsinger, Frank, Bedford county, Pennsylvania, 1836	Douglas County, 1856.	Rosedale, Kan.
Hadley, D. B., Genesee county, New York, 1819.	Wyandotte City, 1857.	Wyandotte City.
Hadley, Willard J., Milwaukee, Wis., Sept. 17, 1836.	North Lawrence, Dec 16, 1869.	Lawrence.
Hasbaugh, W., Shelby Ohio, July 17, 1859.	Lawrence, November 28, 1877.	Lawrence.
Hayenes, J. C., Betheny, Missouri June 7, 1854.	Lawrence, October 28, 1861.	Lawrence.
Hadley, Mrs. Sarah E., Ohio, February 6, 1838	Lawrence, June 7, 1855.	Lawrence.
Henshaw, Newton, Chatham, N. C., December 28 1833.	Eudora, 1855.	Hesper.
Hyde, Ella, Chicago, Illinois, January 22, 1857.	Atchison, October 16, 1866.	Lawrence.

Name, Place and Date of Birth.	Place and Date of Settlement.	Present Residence
Horne, Maria L., Cambridgeport, Mass., June 26, 1826.	Topeka, April 3, 1855.	Topeka.
Horne, Daniel H., Dover, N. H., February 26, 1828	Topeka, Dec. 4, 1854.	Topeka.
Horne, Georgia W., Woburn, Mass., April 24, 1852.	Topeka, April 3, 1855.	Topeka.
Holan, James, New York, June 8, 1856.	Lawrence, September 14, 1865.	Lawrence.
Hoffman, Harry, Montgomery county, Pa., Aug. 27, 1858.	Lawrence, April 17, 1876.	Lawrence.
Hamelton, E. E., Barton, N. Y., January 3, 1855.		
Houghton, Effie, Florida, November 3, 1862.	Lawrence, September 6, 1864.	Lawrence.
Hidden, John, Sutton, Vermont, June 17, 1814.	Garnett, Anderson County, July 1, 1864.	Lawrence.
Henderson, Robert, north of Ireland, January 8. 1833.	Junction City, Sept. 10, 1855	Junction City.
Harmon, Angelena, Gentry county, Mo., March 10. 1841.	Douglas Co., Nov. 12, 1854.	Douglas Co.
Hutchinson, G. W., Hartford, Vt., February 22, 1822	Lawrence, August 1, 1854.	Kansas City, Mo.
Hall, A. W., Lamoille county, Vermont, July 30, 1842.	Trading Post, Linn County, Apr. 7, 1857.	Trading Post.
Hutchinson, Josiah, Tennessee, 1830	Wakarusa, July, 1854	Sigel.
Hadley, W., North Carolina, December 12, 1817.	Lawrence, April 8, 1866.	
Hadley, Naomi, Richmond, Indiana, July 31, 1819.	Lawrence, April 8, 1866.	
Houghtelin, Grace, Kalamazoo, Mich., Nov 11, 1861.	Lawrence, July, 1874.	Lawrence.
Harman, B F., Rockingham county, Va., Dec. 20, 1832.	North Lawrence, Dec. 31, 1868.	North Lawrence.
Hiatt, Oliver S., Indiana, February 4, 1839	Leavenworth, September, 1866.	
Hatch, George W, Great Bend, Pa, Feb. 27, 1818.	Lawrence, September 15, 1869	
Hatch, Mrs. Matilda, Danville, N. Y.	Lawrence, October 8, 1870.	
Hook, S. K, Berlin, Somerset county, Pa, Dec 4, 1837.	Lawrence, May 15, 1866.	Douglas County.
Hook, Martha A., Preston county, Va., Sept. 23, 1840.	Lawrence, July 28, 1878.	Douglas Co.
Holloway, Dora L., Douglas Co, Kan., Feb. 4, 1860.	Lawrence, February 4, 1860.	Douglas Co.
Horsley, J. W., Virginia, June 6, 1847.	North Topeka, November 30, 1870.	Lawrence.
Heine, Libbie, Douglas county, Kan., Sept. 22, 1862.		
Hayes, J. L., Industry, Ill., April 7, 1853.	Willow Springs, April, 1877.	Franklin Co.
Harris, W. C., Zanesville, O., March 31, 1825.	Leavenworth, March, 1857.	Lawrence.
Hale, John H., Lawrence, July 25, 1858.	Lawrence, July 25. 1858.	Lawrence.
Hale, E., England, June 21, 1820.	Douglas Co, March 15, 1857.	Lawrence.
Hale, Mrs. L., England, August 18, 1833.	Douglas Co, March 15, 1857	Lawrence.
Hale, Fred, T., Lawrence, December 2, 1865.	Lawrence, December 2, 1865.	Lawrence.
Hughes, William, Wales, April 9, 1833.	Lawrence, March 15, 1855.	Lawrence.
Hunt, William, North Carolina, September 15, 1834	Tonganoxie, August 26, 1876.	Lawrence.
Hawarth, Jonathan, Guilford Co., N. C., Aug. 15, 1800.	Leavenworth Co, July 1, 1868.	Leavenworth.
Haskell, D. C., Springfield, Vt, March 23, 1842.	Lawrence, March 28, 1855.	Lawrence.
Haskell, J G. Milton, Vt., February 5, 1832.	Lawrence, July, 5, 1857.	Lawrence.
Haskell, Mary E. B., Massachusetts, October 22, 1837.	Lawrence, January, 1860.	Lawrence.
Hoag, Benjamin W., Genesee Co., N. Y., Feb, 23, 1813.	Lawrence, May 17, 1855	Lawrence.
Hughes, Joseph R., Baltimore, Md, Sept 23, 1857.	Lawrence, November 9, 1869.	Lawrence.
Hurd, George R., Lowell, Mass., July 10, 1841.	Lawrence, May 2, 1855	Kanwaka.
Hughes, Ellen Jane, Pittsburg, Pa., June 29, 1829.	Lawrence, August 20, 1858.	Lawrence.
Hermar, Frank, Philadelphia, Pa , November 24, 1850.		Vinland.
Hillyer, Justin, Massachusetts, January 5, 1800.	Valley Falls, March 29, 1867.	Topeka.
Himoe, S. O.	Bourbon Co., April, 1857.	
Hellstrom, Rudolph, Sweden, August 26, 1841.	Clinton Tp , 1860.	Clinton.
Hellstrom, Laura, Sweden, December 13, 1840.	Clinton Tp., 1859.	Clinton.
Hanselman, Emanuel, Shelby county, O , July 14, 1855.	Michigan, September 10, 1855.	Lawrence.
Hartbaugh, Dell F., Attica, O., September 4, 1858.	Topeka, November 25, 1877.	Lawrence.
House, B. M., Virgil, Courtland county, N Y., December 27, 1826.	Syracuse, March 20, 1873.	Newton.
Hadley, J M., Randolph county, N. C., Jan. 25, 1835.	Johnson Co., March 18, 1855.	Olathe.
Hay, Matilda, Pennsylvania, September 5, 1836.	Lawrence, April, 1855.	Lawrence.
Harrison. J. H., Alabama, December 22, 1828.	Douglas Co. June 14, 1854.	Douglas Co.
Heister, Jacob, Leavenworth county, May 24, 1822	Leavenworth City, May 14, 1854	
Hollowell, Silas, Salem, Ind , September 10, 1825.	Bloomington, April 8, 1857.	Lawrence.
Holliday, Francis E , Wooster, Ohio, Dec 22, 1852.	Topeka, January 4, 1878.	Topeka.
Hoyt, Charles C. Coventry, New York, May 18, 1852.	Manhattan, November 15, 1850.	Lawrence.
Hunter, Wm. J., Xenia, Ohio, April 7, 1838.	Manhattan, December 25, 1856.	Hays City.
Hunter, Mrs. Susan, Cincinnati, Ohio, April 11, 1840.	Manhattan, June, 1857.	Hays City.
Haywood, J. M., Monmouth county, New Jersey, July 17, 1814.	Monmouth, Shawnee Co., March 1, 1857.	Monmouth.
Hill, Hettie M , Lawrence, Kansas, Dec. 16, 1859.	Lawrence, December 16, 1859.	Lawrence.
Holm, C. W., Denmark, December 16, 1815	Paola, April 5, 1857.	Paola
Hill, Oliver, Pennsylvania. June 13, 1858.	Leav. Co., April 1, 1871.	Leavenworth Co.
Hosmer, Mrs. C. A , Potsdam, New York, Feb 20, 1813.	Lawrence, 1875.	
Hughes, James R., Baltimore, Maryland, Jan 6, 1831.	Lawrence, November 10, 1869.	Lawrence.
Horne, J L., Cloverdale, Indiana, January 18, 1859.	Carbondale, Kan., Oct. 1, 1870.	Lawrence.
Hollingbery, S. M , 1858.	Lawrence, May, 1871.	
Hollingbery, J , England, 1856.	Lawrence, May, 1871.	
Hard, Inez L , Lawrence, November 24, 1860.	Lawrence, Nov. 24, 1860.	Lawrence.
Himoe, Eva A., Ft. Scott, November 28, 1858.	Ft. Scott, November 28, 1858.	Lawrence.
Hubbell, Ella, Paola. March 31, 1861.	Lawrence, April, 1874.	Lawrence.
Holcomb, N K., Meadville Pennsylvania, Feb 22, 1840.	Washington, June 10, 1873.	Washington.
Hoag, P. M., Connecticut, April 27, 1811.	Lawrence, May 5, 1855.	Lawrence.
Harmon, H. E , Kansas, December 11, 1860.	Douglas Co., December 30, 1860.	Lawrence.
Haskell T. H., Maine.	Topeka, April 10. 1856.	
Harbison, A. K., Pennsylvania, August. 19, 1830.	——, April 15, 1860.	Jefferson County.
Hiatt, Maggie M., Ross county, Ohio, Dec. 7, 1849.	Edwardsville, July 30, 1874.	Tiblow.

Name, Place and Date of Birth.	Place and Date of Settlement.	Present Residence
Hutcheson, Mervila, Clinton county, Mo., Oct. 15, 1854.	Douglas Co., October 15, 1854.	Jefferson Co.
Harding, James M., Mass., 1812.	Topeka, June, 1856.	
Howard, John B., New York, August 6, 1815.	Wakarusa, June 15, 1857.	
Hallett, C. H., Marietta, Ohio, May 2, 1865.	Ft. Scott.	
Hubbell, Frank R., Paola, May 19, 1865.	Lawrence, May 18, 1865.	Lawrence.
Holmes, Samuel, Orange county, Ind., March 25, 1830.	Eudora Tp., April 14, 1866.	Eudora.
Huntoon, A. J., Unity, N. H., February 29, 1832.	Shawnee Co., April 23, 1857.	Topeka.
Huntoon, Lizzie P., Walpole, N. H., Nov. 12, 1829.	Shawnee Co., April 23, 1857.	Topeka.
Harbaugh, D. F., Seneca county, Ohio, Sept. 4, 1858.	Lawrence, October 12, 1877.	Lawrence.
Hanscomb, Anna, T., New York, October 9, 1831.	Lawrence, October, 1854.	Lawrence.
Hurlbert, Mrs. W. S., Leoni, Michigan, March 15, 1847.	Blue Tp., March 15, 1864.	
Herrick, Mrs. E. E., Buffalo, N. Y., Feb. 20, 1838.	Highland, Sept. 26, 1858.	Highland.
Hyde, Charles A., Ohio, March 17, 1861.	Lawrence, April 22, 1869.	Lawrence.
Hughes, J. W., Indiana, August 23, 1859.	Topeka, June 3, 1869.	Topeka.
Hathaway, Marion, Indiana, August 5, 1850.		
Hegmann, H., Rhode Island, August 1, 1861.	Lawrence, July 3, 1876.	Lawrence.
Hamleryer, J., Baltimore, Maryland, Oct. 1, 1854.	Lawrence, October 3, 1878.	Lawrence.
Hickok, G. B., Malone, New York, June 8, 1860.	Lawrence, September 1, 1875.	Lawrence.
Hester, J. M., Huron county, Ohio, August 28, 1846.	Lawrence, December 31, 1878.	Lawrence.
Hard, A. B., Arlington, Vermont, January 5, 1816.	Lawrence, September 8, 1862.	Lawrence.
Heine, Mary A., Clinton, Kansas, October 16, 1859.	Clinton, Kan., October 16, 1859.	Clinton.
Herz, T., Germany, July 25, 1822.	Lawrence, January 1, 1863.	Lawrence.
Hartshorn, Edward C., Lynn, Mass., July 26, 1859.	Topeka, March 15, 1879.	Lawrence.
Hudson, J. K., Carrollton, Ohio, May 4, 1840.	Jim Lane's Brigade, July 1, 1861.	Topeka.
Hudson, Mary W., Fayette county, Pa., June 10, 1840.		Topeka.
Hale, Geo. D., Massachusetts, February 19, 1829.	Topeka, May 1, 1867.	Topeka.
Hale, Frank C. Mansfield, Ohio, January 20, 1841.	Topeka, February 25, 1868.	Topeka.
Higgins, Sophia, Vandalia, Illinois, November 5, 1824.	Leavenworth, October, 1859.	
Henarlin, L. A., Trumbull county, Ohio, March 5, 1833.	Leavenworth, November, 1853.	
Harmon, John, Ireland, March 22, 1839.	Leavenworth, March 22, 1857.	Leavenworth.
Hester, Mrs. Irene Brink, Plymouth, O., May 16, 1847.	Lawrence, December 31, 1878.	Lawrence.
Hitchcock, A. E., Illinois, January 1, 1865.	Wakarusa, July, 1855.	Wakarusa.
Hollaway, L. R., Wakarusa, February 22, 1862.	Wakarusa, 1862.	Wakarusa.
Holloway, C., Ohio, January 18, 1832.	Wakarusa, 1855.	Wakarusa.
Hodge, J. W., Ohio, November 27, 1832.	Ellis County, March, 1878.	Ellis Co.
Hubbell, W. O., New York, November 7, 1834.	Lawrence, May 15, 1851.	Lawrence.
Hamlen, E. M., Iowa November 29, 1838.	Douglas County, June 5, 1860.	Reno.
Hart, J. W., Ohio, March 31, 1852.	Emporia, June, 1869.	Abilene.
Haywood, Mrs. J. M., Seneca county, New York, December 17, 1828.	Shawnee County, April 2, 1858.	
Hass, George S., Germany, June 15, 1852.	Willow Springs, 1858.	
Harden, Allie, Indiana, February 2, 1862	Coffey County, 1870.	Dexter.
Hogeboom, Sophie, Ohio, July 7, 1837.	Leavenworth, March, 1858.	
Hogeboom, G., New York, December 8, 1832.	Leavenworth, May 20, 1857.	Topeka.
Harden, Alpha, Iowa, July 22, 1859.	Labette County, Feb. 21, 1868.	Dexter.
Harden, J. J., Indiana, March 26, 1846.	Dexter, February 15, 1879.	Dexter.
Henderson, J. S., Findley, O., March 25, 1839	Ottawa, September 20, 1870.	Lawrence.
Henderson, Emma H., Massilon, O., June 25, 1841.	Lawrence.	
Horne, Dan H., Dover, N. H., February 20, 1828.	Topeka, November 30, 1854.	Topeka.
Higgins, William, Pennsylvania, April 2, 1842.	Leavenworth, May 2, 1855.	Douglas County.
Halm, Frank D., Urbanna, O., April 8, 1859.	Topeka, June 15, 1870.	Topeka.
Harris, William A. H., Ireland, November 3, 1850.	Lawrence, July 29, 1870.	Lawrence.
Hill, Noah, Green county, Pa., June 10, 1834.	Leavenworth, April 1, 1871.	Leavenworth Co.
Hurd, Clarissa, Connecticut, February 10, 1801.	Lawrence, May 2, 1855.	Kanwaka.
Horve, J. B., New Hampshire, August 20, 1835.	Topeka, June 12, 1855.	Topeka.
Hunt, Jacob, Bloomingdale, Ind., January 7, 1860.	Tonganoxie, August 26, 1876.	Lawrence.
Hammat, John, Germany, May 17, 1835.	Lawrence, December 11, 1859.	Eudora.
Hoadley, D. L., Genesee, N. Y., November 27, 1831.	Ellwood, March 10, 1858.	Lawrence.
Howell, James, New York, August 10, 1859.	Lawrence, September 8, 1874.	Lawrence.
Ham, G. D., Kentucky, August 2, 1868.		
Hughson, E. D., New Jersey, October 1, 1855.	Wakarusa, October 1, 1855.	Lawrence.
Hughson, Jane, New Jersey.	Wakarusa, October 1, 1855.	Lawrence.
Hughson, C. A., New Jersey.	Wakarusa, October 1, 1855	Lawrence.
Hickerson, Logan, Washington Co., Ky., Jan. 7, 1847.	Woodstock, August 10, 1866.	Woodstock.
Hood, W. E., Columbus, O., June 6, 1854.	Topeka, April 28, 1868.	Topeka.
Heiter, Jacob, Germany, May 24, 1822.	Leavenworth, May 14, 1854.	Leavenworth.
Hughes, E. J., Pitthburg, Ala., June 19, 1829.	Lawrence, September 10, 1858.	Lawrence.
Howell, Lewis, Slanbrynmair, Wales, March 23, 1812.	Wakarusa, September 15, 1854.	Pleasant Valley.
Howell, Mary J., Wales, June, 22, 1829.	Wakarusa, August 2, 1855.	Pleasant Valley.
Harbaugh, J. W., Bedford county, Pa., July 5, 1835	Topeka, August 28, 1877.	Lawrence.
Hanscom, O. A., Portsmouth, N. H., October 13, 1831.	Lawrence, September, 1854.	Decatur.
Horton, Albert H., Orange Co., N. Y., March 12, 1837.	Atchison, April, 1860.	
Horton, Carrie, April 22, 1865		
Holbert, Ida Kansas, July 19, 1860.	Atchison, July 19, 1860.	Atchison.
Henshaw, Abbie A. Middletown, O., Feb. 28, 1840.	Olathe, March 9, 1857.	Hesper.
Hughes, J W., Indiana, August 23, 1859.	Topeka, June 2, 1869.	Shawnee.
Harttmann, Dr. M., Germany, 1817.	Lawrence, March, 1855.	Lawrence.
Hook, Enos, Waynesburg, Pa., February 4, 1832.	Leavenworth, 1857.	Leavenworth.
Hill, Livingston, Warrenville, Mo., March 27, 1834	Atchison, June 20, 1863.	
Hubbard, Mrs. M. J., New Hampshire, Dec. 22, 1836.	Douglas Co., September 12, 1860.	Olathe.
Hemmingway, J. R., Oshkosh.		

Name, Place and Date of Birth.	Place and Date of Settlement.	Present Residence
Haskell, N. G., Lawrence.	Douglas County, 1861.	
Halloway, Mrs. Kate, Ohio, December 18, 1830.	Lawrence, June 4, 1855.	Lawrence.
Hollingbery, George, London, England, Dec. 26, 1843.	Lawrence, August 28, 1871	Lawrence.
Hopper, Letish, Virginia, July 13, 1839	Shawnee Co , Dec. 28, 1851.	Lawrence.
Hopper, William M., Iowa, April 22, 1861.	Shawnee County, July 4, 1861.	Lawrence.
Hopper, Arminda M., Osage, March 4, 1863.	Shawnee County, March 4, 1863.	Lawrence.
Hopper, Charles A., Shawnee county, March 28, 1865.	Shawnee County, March 28, 1865	Lawrence.
Hopper, B. F., Shawnee county, September 19, 1867	Shawnee County, Sept. 19, 1867.	Lawrence.
Hopper, Lanar J., Shawnee county, February 28, 1870	Shawnee County, Feb. 28, 1870.	Lawrence.
Hopper James J., Shawnee county, January 23, 1872.	Shawnee County, Jan. 23, 1872.	Lawrence.
Higgins, Hiram, Mass , April 3, 1817	Topeka, October 10, 1854.	Topeka.
Hanson, Ohio Otto, Palermo, Kan., October 17, 1856	Palermo, Kan., October 17, 1856.	Louisville, Pott. Co.
Heathman, Solon, Devonshire, England, June 26, 1814.	Sigel, Douglas Co., Nov. 7, 1873	
Hupp, Minor B., Stafford, Monroe Co., O., June 20, '36.	On Wakarusa, 4 miles south of Lawrence, Nov. 12, 1854.	Richland, Shaw. Co.
Haynes, C. H., Rensselaer Co., N. Y , Nov. 27, 1832.	Fort Scott, April 2, 1858.	Fort Scott.
Haynes, Mrs. C. H., Orange Co., N. Y., March 20, '36.	Fort Scott, April 2, 1858.	Fort Scott.
Hallister, Mrs. A. J., Spencer, Ind., Sept. 11 1856.		
Herboldsheimer, August, Germany, Sept. 10, 1859.		
Harbison, H. M , Pennsylvania, October 5. 1856.	Leavenworth Co., April 12, 1869.	Jefferson Co.
Hogeboom, George W., New York, December 8, 1832.	Leavenworth City, May 20, 1857.	Topeka.
Hawk, Simon, Pennsylvania, November 11, 1827.	Shawnee County, April 16, 1857.	Topeka.
Hill, Forester, Massachusetts, January 3, 1822.	Lawrence, December 12, 1854.	Wakarusa.
Hosmer, L. M., New York, April 9, 1819.	Lawrence, November, 1875.	Lawrence.
Hadley, Hattie H., Lawrence, October 17, 1863	Lawrence, October 17, 1863.	Lawrence
Halstead, Sophia, Norway, Europe, Sept. 24, 1837.	Mapleton, Bourbon Co., March 25, 1858.	Reno.
Hamilton, J. F., Illinois, January 21, 1858.	Lawrence, October 9, 1866.	Lawrence.
Havens, Lou, Jackson county, Mo., October. 1851.	Prairie City, Douglas Co.	
Hutchings, John, Caroline, N. Y., December 31, 1836.	Lawrence, June 13, 1863.	Lawrence
Hutchings, Josephine E., Litchfield, Conn., May 3, '44.	Lawrence, June 13, 1863.	Lawrence.
Hunt, Mrs. G. W., Leominster, Mass., March 17, 1813.	Lawrence, May 23, 1856.	Lawrence.
Hanson, Wm. H., Belmont county, Ohio, July 22, 1831.	Pottawatomie Co., June 2, 1855.	Louisville.
Hayes, C. A.	Osawatomie, February 29.	
Huson, R., New York, May 12, 1798.	Tecumseh, April 22, 1856.	Lawrence.
Harris, E. B., Robertson county, Tenn., Mar. 20, 1824.	North Lawrence, Dec. 3, 1869.	North Lawrence.
Honnold, A.G., Muskingum county, O , April 20, 1837	Lawrence, January 1, 1870.	Lawrence.
Hughes, Jos. R., Baltimore, Md., Sept. 23, 1857.	Lawrence, October 9, 1869.	Lawrence.
Haslet, James B., Pittsburg, Pa., December 3, 1827.	Lawrence, March 4, 1871.	Lawrence.
Haskell, A. S., Portland, Me., October 30, 1848	Lawrence, November 2, 1866.	Kanwaka.
Hebbard, J. C., Lisbon, Conn., November 16, 1830.	Sabetha, May 15, 1858.	Topeka.
Hebbard, R. N., Deerfield, N Y., Sept. 19, 1836.	Seneca, September 16, 1864.	Topeka.
Hebbard, Mary F., Seneca, Kan., Jan. 30, 1870		Topeka.
Huggins, Jas. L., Troy, N. Y., October 29, 1814	Lawrence, May 5, 1856.	
Hoar, Albian L., Waltham, Mass., October 28, 1819.	Manhattan, May 5, 1868.	Manhattan.
Hoar, Mrs. A. L., Portland Me., May 30, 1853.	Manhattan, March 17, 1855.	Manhattan.
Higby, John, Lewis county, N. Y., November 4, 1818.	Lawrence, October 28, 1863.	Lawrence.
Hunt, D. E, Delavan, Wis., August 30, 1858.	Ottawa, January 4, 1877.	Ottawa.
Himoe, A. H., Norway, Europe, January 15, 1835.	Fort Scott, July 20, 1857.	Lawrence.
Himoe, S. E., Mapleton, Kansas, September 14, 1861.	Mapleton, September 14, 1861.	Lawrence.
Himoe, H. C., Ft. Scott, Kansas, August 27, 1864.	Fort Scott, August 27, 1864.	Lawrence.
Hutcheson, John, Illinois, February 22, 1832.	Lawrence, August, 1854	Jefferson Co.
Howe, I. E. Worcester, Massachusetts, July 5, 1851.	Lawrence, January, 1877.	Lawrence.
Howell, Justus, Northampton county, Pa., Aug 5, 1832.	Lecompton, March, 1870	Lecompton.
Huey, Marsh. H., Bellefonte, Pa , July 28, 1853.	Leavenworth, Sept. 5, 1873.	Lawrence.
Hoadley, S. M., Brockport, N. Y.	Lawrence.	
Harvey, Florinda Crowe, Economy, N. S., November 8, 1840.	Topeka, May 10, 1837.	Topeka.
Henley, A. A., Indiana, October 4, 1858.	Hesper, Kan., October 29, 1858.	Hesper.
Hoene, Sophie, New York City, December 9, 1852.	Prairie City, Douglas County, April 5, 1857.	Jefferson Co.
Hollingbery, A. G., London, England, October 3, 1854.	Lawrence, March 6, 1871.	Lawrence.
Hurst, Albert, Iowa, 1848.	Osawatomie, 1857.	Lane.
Hicks, Amos, Ohio, 1824	Douglas County, 1855.	Leavenworth Co
Harris, E P., Hudson, N. H., June 11, 1834.	Lawrence, August 7, 1856.	Lecompton Tp.
Hanson, L. C. Norway, August 23, 1838.	Scandia, Republic Co., Nov. 23, 1868.	Scandia, Republic Co
	[1868 .	
Hanson, Mrs C. C., Sweden, February 11, 1837.	Scandia, Republic Co., Nov , 23,	Scandia.
Hughes, S. E., Iowa, July 11, 1852.	Lawrence, Sept. 15. 1854.	Lawrence.
Hood, Lewis W., Hillsboro, O., June 2, 1848.	Topeka, Nov. 1, 1872.	Topeka.
Hoar, John L., Lancaster county, Pa., May 9, 1858.		Lawrence.
Hindman, L. W , Sardinia, O., June 9, 1841	Willow Springs, June 1, 1857.	Willow Springs.
Hamilton, S H., Circleville, O., April 19, 1836.	Lawrence, July 30, 1879.	Lawrence.
Hubbell, Frank G., Paola, May 19, 1865	Paola. May, 19, 1865.	Lawrence.
Hollaway, E A., Lawrence, June 22, 1856	Lawrence, June 22, 1856.	Lawrence.
Hathaway, Mary M , Monroe Co , N. Y., July 22, 1816.	Douglas Co , Sept. 1869.	Douglas.
Hughes, John L., Des Moines Co., Ia., March 20 1848.	Douglas Co., Oct. 1854.	Douglas.
Hughes, Willie, Lawrence, February 11. 1862	Douglas Co., Feb. 11. 1862.	Lawrence.
Honnold, Mrs. A. G., Muskingum Co., O., June 15, '45.	Lawrence, Jan. 1, 1870.	Lawrence.
Honnold, Avri, Lawrence, September 20, 1871.	Lawrence, Sept. 20, 1871.	Lawrence.

Name, Place and Date of Birth.	Place and Date of Settlement.	Present Residence
Hollister, A. J , Marietta, O., May 21, 1846.	Lawrence, Nov. 14, 1877.	Lawrence.
Hanway, James, London, England, September 4, 1809.	Lane, Franklin Co., March, 1856.	Lane, Franklin Co.
Hutchinson. G. W., Hartford, Vt., August 22, 1822.	Lawrence, Aug. 1, 1854.	Kansas City.
Holloway, J. M. D , Richmond, Ind., February 21, 1820.	Douglas Co., Nov. 1876	Douglas Co.
Hume, G. W., Sterling, Cayuga co., N. Y., July 23, 1836	Marshall Co., Sept. 15, 1858.	Lawrence.
Hunt, Charles W., Massachusetts.	Lawrence, May 23, 1856.	Lawrence.
Hutchinson, J. B., Lawrence, January 10, 1861.	Lawrence, Jan. 10, 1861.	Lawrence.
Howe, George W., Plattsburg, N. Y., Sept. 30. 1835.	Lawrence, June 1, 1856.	Lawrence.
Howe, James, New York City, February 8, 1801	Wyandotte, April 1, 1868.	Tiblow, Wyandotte Co.
Hiatt, D. B., Henry county, Indiana, December, 9, 1832.	Wabaunsee, Sept. 1, 1854.	Tiblow, Wyandotte Co.
Hinman, D G., Ohio, June 29, 1838.	Lawrence, April 18, 1856.	Lawrence.
Hollingsworth, Wm., Knox county, Ind., Jan. 13, 1817.	Emporia, March 1, 1861.	Near Emporia, Lyon Co.
Hollingsworth, C. P., Dublin, Ind., January 11, 1859.	Emporia, March 1, 1861.	Emporia, Kan.
Hoyt, Sarah E., Boston, Mass., June 1, 1811.	Lawrence, Oct. 17, 1854.	North Lawrence.
Herd, James, Douglas county Kan., April 20, 1855.	Douglas Co. , April 30, 1860.	Williamston.
Hicox, A J., Union, Conn , August 7, 1847.	Cheyenne, March, 1879.	Barton Co.
Hughes, R. W., Paulsboro, N J., July 12, 1843.	Leavenworth Co., Dec 20, 1868. 1858.	Leavenworth.
Harris, C. B , Pennsylvania, 1838.		Lawrence.
Hillyer, W. J , Valley Falls, Kansas, 1862.	Valley Falls, 1862.	Valley Falls.
Henderson, T. W., N. C , 1845.	Lawrence, 1868.	Lawrence.
Hall, W. N., Newcastle, Maine, March 8, 1842.	Lawrence, Oct 10, 1870.	Lawrence.
Hyde, Emma, Ohio, August 7, 1850	Lawrence, Apr. 22, 1869.	Lawrence.
Herd, R. R., Philadelphia, February 17, 1830.	Lawrence, Apr. 18, 1856.	Atchison.
Heil, F. J., Jefferson, N. Y., November 4, 1838.	Shawnee Co., June 9 1859.	Shawnee Co.
Henderson, O. C., Iowa, September 18, 1855.	Oskaloosa, March, 1858.	
Herrington, J. D., Pittsburg, Pa., February 8, 1831.	Franklin. May 28, 1855.	Lawrence.
Herrington, Sarah H., Pittsburg Pa., January 7, 1835.	Franklin, K., May 28, 1855.	Lawrence.
Herrington, Mollie E., Franklin, Kan., Nov. 27, 1856.		Lawrence.
Herrington, Lina V., Pittsburg, Pa., January 2, 1845.	Lawrence, May 16, 1855.	Lawrence.
Howard, L. D., Saline Michigan, August 22, 1849.	Wakarusa, June 15, 1857.	Wakarusa.
Hoar, Jno. L., Lancaster county, Pa., May 9, 1858.	Lawrence, Apr. 1, 1879.	Lawrence.
Herrick, Frank L , Corinth, Me., September 12, 1848.	Lawrence, Oct 1854.	Jefferson Co.
Hollinger, G. W., Lancaster, Pa., February 1, 1842	Marion Co. , Jan., 1871.	Sterling, Kan.
Heine, Henry, Germany, June 4, 1830.	Clinton, Douglas Co., Apr 15, 1855.	Clinton, Kan.
Hale, John H. Lawrence, July 25, 1858.	Lawrence, July 25, 1858.	Lawrence.
Helwig, John H., Tuscarawas county, O., Mar. 26, 1828	Atchison, Co , Nov 15, 1854.	Topeka, 12th Reg., Price Raid.
Hindman, W. T., Brown county, Ohio, Dec. 20, 1825.	Lawrence, Oct 8, 1858.	Linwood. Leavenworth Co.
Hurlbert, C. O., Middle Haddam. January 14, 1822.	Topeka, Jan. 1, 1878.	Lawrence.
Hamlin, Samuel Somerset county, Pa , Nov. 1, 1832.	Atchison Co., Aug. 20, 1856.	Lawrence.
Hale, Edward E., Boston, Mass., April 3, 1822.		Roxbury, Mass.
Hale, Ellen Day, Worcester, Mass , Feb. 11, 1855.		Roxbury, Mass.
Hersh, S. S., Pittsburg, April 13, 1844.	Kanwaka, March 1, 1855.	Grant Tp. , Douglas Co.
Howard, John Jay, East Evans, N. Y., Mar. 6, 1828.	Council Grove, May 15, 1860.	Kansas City.
Head, Mrs. S. W., Madison county, O., Dec 14, 1853.	Topeka, April 20, 1869. [19, 1858	Topeka.
Harris, Jonathan, Franklin county, O., May 10, 1839.	Middle Creek, Lykins Co., Sept.	Olathe, Johnson Co.
Husas, John, Lawrence, February 7, 1863.	Lawrence, 1863.	Lawrence.
Hart, Mrs. M., Canada, Oct. 21, 1851.	Lawrence, March 1, 1859.	Lawrence.
Haas, Sarah, Douglas county, November 21, 1851.	Lawrence.	Lawrence.
Hopkins, Ettie, Douglas county, March 30, 1863.	Lawrence.	Lawrence.
Hollister, Simpson, Woodsfield, Monroe county, O Sept 6, 1828.	Lawrence, Feb 1, 1867.	Lawrence.
Herman, Frans, Widstrand, Stockholm, Sweden, Oct. 10, 1821.		Buffalo, Minn.
Harris, M. C., Mariah, Essex Co., N. Y., Nov. 3, 1841.	Maria, Leavenworth Co , July 4, 1866.	Leavenworth Co.
Harris, O. J., Columbia, Ohio, January 30, 1844.	Leavenworth, Sept. 1, 1870.	Leavenworth Co.
Holcomb, Mary, Hagerstown, Ind., March 13.	Lawrence, Nov. 1869.	Lawrence.
Hunt, Jacob, Bloomingdale, Ind., January 7, 1860.	Tonganoxie, Aug. 26, 1876.	Lawrence.
Hadley, F. W., Leavenworth, June 12, 1861.	Leavenworth, June 12, 1861	Lawrence.
Hutcheson, Emeline Janet, Belle Mount, Dec. 15, 1826.	Douglas Co., Apr. 1, 1855.	Douglas Co.
Hopper, A. R , Scott county, Ky., January 8 1834.	Lawrence, May 9, 1854. [1861.	Douglas Co.
Houston, E. W., Spring Hill, Ky., August 10, 1846.	110 Creek, Osage Co , July 13,	Lawrence.
Hendricks, Homer J., Indiana, August 9, 1859.	Iola.	Lawrence.
Herron, G. W., Ohio, September 1, 1832.	Topeka, Apr. 1, 1863.	Topeka.
Howell, Walter, Hillsdale county. Mich., Aug. 30, 1842.	Lawrence, Oct 1864	Lawrence.
Harris, Mrs. Minerva B , Zanesville, O , April 13, 1834.	Leavenworth City, March, 1857.	Lawrence.
Harbine, John F., Franklin county, Pa , June 16, 1853.	Topeka, July 17, 1878.	Topeka.
Hubbell, Mrs. M. G., Spring, Crawford county, Pa., February 20, 1848.	Lawrence, May 20, 1855.	Lawrence.
Hupp, Samuel L., Monroe county, Ind., Feb. 18, 1843	——Aug. 23, 1873.	
Howe, Dr. O. R , Chillicothe, Ohio, March 26, 1840.	Lawrence, June 8, 1876.	Lawrence.
Havens, Mrs R. F., Michigan.	Wyandotte, 1858.	Ft. Scott.
Hughes, J L. Baltimore, Md., January 14, 1852.	Lawrence, Nov. 15, 1870.	Lawrence.
Haskell, Mable Bliss, Lawrence, Aug. 12, 1866.	Lawrence, Aug. 12 1866.	Lawrence.
Hunt, G. W., Midway, Mass., February 12, 1842.	Lawrence, May, 1856.	Lawrence.

Name, Place and Date of Birth.	Place and Date of Settlement.	Present Residence
Ingersoll, William M., Cambridgeport, Mass., June 8, 1847.	Lawrence, March 28, 1858. [1863.	Kanwaka.
Ice, A. R., Marion county, W. Va., March 11, 1835.	Cedar Point, Chase Co., Sept. 12,	Cedar Point, Chase Co.
Irvin, W. S., Crawford county, Pa., April 5, 1854.	Lawrence, Apr. 10, 1855.	Blue Mound.
Ingersoll, Caroline A., Cambridge, Mass., May 19, 1819.	Lawrence, Nov. 1, 1858.	Kanwaka.
Irvin, J., Blue Mound, Kan., November 27, 1858.	Douglas Co., Nov. 27, 1858	Blue Mound.
Irvin, Robert, Pennsylvania, October 18, 1820.	Blue Mound, March, 1855.	Blue Mound.
Irvine, Thomas E., Ireland, May 5, 1841.	Topeka, July 13, 1869.	Topeka.
Inman, Henry, New York City, July 3, 1837.	Ellsworth, May 17, 1860.	Larned.
Irwin, J. A., Pennsylvania, December 5, 1829.	Wakarusa, Apr. 10, 1855.	Wakarusa.
Irvin, Robert, Pennsylvania, December 26, 1820.	Wakarusa, Apr. 10. 1855.	Wakarusa.
Irwin, George S., Alton, Ill., April 4, 1851.	Holton, Jackson Co., Sep. 1, 1857.	North Topeka.
Irwin, William, Ohio, October 12. 1847.	De Soto, Aug 20, 1854.	Johnson Co.
Irvine, O. P., Pulaski county, Ky., May 5, 1846.	Perry, Jeff. Co., Dec. 12, 1868.	Rural, Jeff. Co.
Jewett, L. B, Ohio, Oct. 1, 1830.	De Soto, Oct. 8, 1865.	De Soto.
Jewett, Miss Emma J., Ohio, March 9, 1850.	De Soto, March 1, 1877.	De Soto.
Jewett, A. W., Ohio, Oct. 22, 1828.	De Soto, Oct. 9, 1865.	De Soto.
Jones, Joseph W., Park Co., Ind., March 29, 1862.	Lawrence.	Osage Co.
Jones, J. D., Briton, Milfield, Lampeter, Wales, March 23, 1844.	Bala, Riley Co., Feb. 26, 1871.	Osage City.
Jackson, Nellie, Kansas, December 13, 1863.	Lawrence, Dec 13, 1863.	Lawrence.
Jones, J. L, Enfield, Mass., December 4, 1831.	Kanwaka, March, 1857.	Kanwaka.
Johnson, Jno. P., Pocahontas, Ill., Dec. 6, 1821.	Highland, July 25, 1851.	Highland.
Johnson, A. D, New York, August 25, 1846.	Lawrence, July 1, 1877.	Lawrence.
Johnston, J. W, Westmorland Co., Pa., Nov. 22, 1817	Lawrence, Feb. 22, 1872.	Lawrence.
Johnston, Mary L., McMinnville, Tenn, Oct. 4, 1827.	Lawrence, Feb. 22, 1872.	Lawrence.
Jenkins, Wm. Hall, Philadelphia, Pa., Dec. 31, 1828	Lawrence, Feb. 26, 1868.	Topeka
Jenkins, Mrs. Anna W., Kidderminster, England, January 2, 1830.	Lawrence, Feb 26, 1868.	Topeka.
Jennings, Charles, Bourbon Co., Ky., July 9, 1825.	Allen Co, Nov. 18, 1856.	Douglas Co.
Johnson, I. W., Missouri, 1855.	Lawrence, Jan., 1861.	Lawrence.
Jordon, William, Poland, Maine, March 14, 1817.	Lawrence, Nov. 15 1855.	Topeka.
Johnson, H. H., Yates county, N. Y., Aug 24, 1819.	Lecompton, June, 1857.	Lawrence.
Jones, Endsley, Howard county, Ind, June 16, 1844	Leavenworth Co., Oct 24, 1866.	Lawrence.
Jones, H. W., North Carolina, September 30, 1820.	Leavenworth Co., July 4, 1868.	Lawrence.
Johnson, H. W., Bath, New York, January 5, 1840.	Fort Scott, June 1, 1857.	Kinsley.
Johnson, J. J, Elmira. New York, March 29, 1846.	Fort Scott, June 1, 1857.	Salina.
Johnson, W. H., Corning, New York, Feb., 1843.	Fort Scott, June 1, 1857.	Salina.
Johnson, W. F., Amity, Pennsylvania, Nov. 13, 1811.	Auburn, July 15, 1854.	Silver Lake.
Johnson, Jane, Nova Scotia, June, 1827.	Topeka, Sept 15, 1857.	Silver Lake.
Jones, Geo. V., St. Catharenes, Canada, July 7, 1842.	Lawrence, Aug. 27, 1870.	Osage City.
Jackson, J. W., New Leads, Md., October 9, 1824	Topeka, Nov. 1865.	Osage City.
Jacobs, S. P., Shanesville, Tuscarawas county, Ohio, January 14, 1837.		Lawrence.
Jacke, A. D, Decatur county, Indiana, July 10, 1852	Eureka Mar. 12, 1879.	Lawrence.
Jacke, Mrs. M. E., Millersburg, Ohio, Nov. 28, 1829	Eureka, Mar. 12, 1879. [20, 1859.	Lawrence.
Jones, Lucinda, Cocke county, Tenn., Feb. 25, 1827.	Baldwin City, Douglas Co., Mar.	
Johnson, P. F.		Douglas Co.
Jacobs, J. H. Poland, February 18, 1829.	Eudora, Nov. 20, 1857.	Lawrence.
Jacobs, R. A, Clinton county, New York, Aug., 1831.	Lawrence, April 14, 1865.	Clinton.
Jacobs, J., Clinton county, New York, July, 1840.	Lawrence, Nov. 6, 1860.	Twin Mound.
Jones, R. O, Kansas, October 8, 1857.	Lawrence, October 8, 1857.	Willow Springs.
Johnson, A. S., July 11, 1832.	Johnson Co., July 11, 1832.	Topeka.
Jackson, W. H., Illinois, July 8, 1855.	Douglas Co., July 8, 1872.	
Jones, Fred R, London, England, October 10, 1853.	Topeka, Nov. 2, 1875	Topeka.
Jones, S. R., Harlan county, Ky., Dec 29, 1827.	Hickory Point, Jefferson Co., Oct. 1, 1854.	Jefferson Co
Jones, Carrie, Brown county, Ohio, Dec. 21, 1842.	Lawrence, May 14, 1868.	Wakarusa, Douglas Co.
Jones, Mattie S., Brown county, Ohio, June 19, 1852.	Lawrence, Nov. 22, 1868.	Vinland, Douglas Co.
Johns, D. G., Montgomery county, Ky, Aug. 14, 1849.		Topeka.
Jones, Morgan, Wales, G B., September 4, 1819.	Douglas Co., June 16, 1858.	Douglas Co.
Jones, E. L, Fayetteville, Pa, August 17, 1835.	Lawrence, March 21, 1857.	Lawrence.
Jenkins, P. F., New York, October 4, 1834	Lawrence, May 15, 1879.	Lawrence.
Jenkins, W. S., Zanesville, Ohio, April 13, 1834.	Leavenworth, Apr. 10, 1857.	Kansas City, Mo.
Jones, Rebecca, St. Louis, Mo., July 6, 1807.	Clinton, June 15, 1864.	
Jones, Sarah, St. Louis, Mo., July 6, 1807.	Clinton, June 15, 1864.	
Joergen, J., Baltimore. Md., June 24, 1851.	Topeka, Aug. 15, 1867.	Leavenworth.
Jones, Milton, Vermont, Ill., September 2, 1849.	Brown Co Aug. 5, 1869.	Lawrence.
Jones, David G, Brecon, Wales, December 19, 1833.	Topeka, Mar. 3, 1877.	
Johnson, Annie M., Missouri, October 17, 1845	Jefferson Co., Aug. 5, 1855.	Topeka.
Jacobs, Mrs J. H., Prussia, August 7, 1848.	Eudora, March, 1861.	Lawrence.
Jones, L. M., Oxford, New York	Lawrence, 1856.	Lawrence.
Jemison, Alice M., Trenton, N. J., February 3, 1865.	Lawrence, Feb. 5, 1877.	Lawrence.
Johnson, E. G., Sweden, 1822.	Vinland, 1868.	Vinland.
Johnson, C. O., Sweden, June 17, 1802.	Lawrence, Aug. 10, 1865.	Lawrence.
Johnson, H. H., Wayne county, Ohio, June 24, 1835.	Allen Co., March 13, 1879.	Lecompton.
Johnson, Susan G., Macon county, Ill., Aug. 6, 1849.	Allen Co., March 13, 1879.	Lecompton.
Johnson, Jas. H., Cass county, Mich., Nov. 21, 1848.	Lawrence, April 15, 1871.	Lawrence.

Name, Place and Date of Birth.	Place and Date of Settlement	Present Residence
Jewett, E L., Jefferson county, Ohio, May 8, 1821.	Lexington, Johnson Co., March 1, 1878.	De Soto.
Jones, J. W., Rockville, Indiana, April 27, 1845.	Independence, Kas., Mar. 29, 1863	Lawrence.
Judd, Byron, Otis, Mass., August, 13 1821.	Wyandotte, Nov 10, 1857.	Wyandotte.
Johnson, B., Pennsylvania, April 5, 1821.	Lawrence, Nov. 12, 1854.	Ottawa.
James, C. C., Cass county, Mich., Feb. 20, 1846.	Lawrence, Jan. 21, 1869.	Lawrence
Johnstone, C. C., Mount Pleasant, January 22, 1850.	Lawrence, May 14, 1879.	Lawrence.
James, M. M., Plymouth, Conn., April 8, 1829.	Lawrence, April 15, 1857.	
Joyner, J. M., Sumner county, Tenn., July 12, 1849.	Topeka, April 7, 1876	Topeka.
Johnson, Louise M., Naples, N. Y., October 17, 1862.	Lawrence, Nov. 1867.	
Jones, Robert M., Cincinnati, Ohio, July 15, 1850.	Lawrence, Aug. 25, 1858.	Lawrence.
Jones, A. J., Bloomington, October, 25, 1858.	Douglas Co., Oct. 25, 1858.	Echo City.
Jackson, Walter, Leavenworth, April 27, 1865.		
Jaquith, M. H., Vermont	Milford, April, 1865.	Milford.
Johnson, Mrs. L. A., Topeka, March 9, 1857.		Topeka.
Johnston, L. A., Guernsey, Ohio, July 31, 1854.	Topeka, Oct. 13, 1870	Topeka.
Jones, William, England, February 6, 1827.	Douglas Co., April, 1855.	Lawrence.
Julian, Geo. W., Centerville, Indiana, May 5, 1817.		Irvington, Ind.
Jones, Edward, Bala, N. Wales, November 26, 1817.	Lawrence, Oct. 23, 1854.	Willow Springs.
Johnson, Jennie J., Naples, New York, July 25, 1857.	Douglas Co.	
Junkermann, Julius, Prussia, November 14, 1841.	Wichita, Nov. 10, 1878.	Topeka.
Jaques, Will F., Geneseo, Ill., March 24, 1855.	Pleasant Prairie, Graham Co , April 5, 1879.	
Johnson, Benjamin F., North East,Erie Co ,April 5,'21	Lawrence, Nov. 12, 1854.	Ottawa.
Johnson, Mary M , Mayville, N. Y., October 21. 1826.	Lawrence, Nov. 12, 1854.	Ottawa.
Jenkins Mrs. A. M., Andover, N H., May 2, 1823.	Lawrence, Oct 1855.	Lawrence.
Jamison, R. G., Milford Center, Ohio, July 19, 1825.	Lawrence, May 28, 1872.	Lawrence.
Jamison Serena C , Urbana, Ohio, March 11, 1828.	Lawrence, May 18 1872.	Lawrence.
Keen, Cordelia, Mercer county, Pa., April 27, 1850.	Cedar Point, Dec. 1878.	Chase Co.
Kellam, C. C., Irasburgh, Vt., March 17, 1830.	Topeka Nov. 2, 1856.	Topeka
Kellogg, Josiah, Palmyra, New York, January 8, 1831	Leavenworth, Oct. 11, 1854.	Leavenworth
Kennedy, Levina S., Brown county, Ill. , June 16, 1837	Doniphan Co , Oct 10, 1855.	Highland.
King, Larry, Delaware, July 7, 1838.	Leavenworth, March 3, 1865.	Leavenworth.
Katzenstein, L., Leavenworth, March 15, 1863.	——March 15, 1863.	
Kelly, J. A., Washington county, Va., Nov. 19, 1823.	Kanwaka, Nov. 9, 1865.	Douglas Co.
Keys, M. J., Valley Farm, Iowa, June 3, 1862.	Delphos, 1876.	Lawrence.
Kuncli, Alfred C., Wabaunsee, February 20, 1868.	Alma, April 6, 1858.	
Kreiser, John, New York City, May 21, 1854.	Lawrence, March 20, 1876.	Lawrence.
Keleher, Joe A., Baltimore, September 12, 1859	Lawrence, Aug. 19, 1869.	Lawrence.
Knight, Wm. M., Indiana, November 28, 1824.	Lawrence, April 16, 1878.	Lawrence.
Karr, E. A., Bartholomew county, Ind., May 16, 1840.	Miami, Mo., March 1, 1858.	Kingman, Kingman Co.
Karr, H. J., New Berlin, Wis , April 12, 1842.	Miami Co., July 11, 1860.	Kingman, Kingman Co.
Kingman, F. H., New York City, March 31, 1855.	Lawrence, March 13, 1877.	Lawrence.
Kennedy, Belle, Wakarusa, May 21, 1862.	Lawrence, May 21, 1862.	Lawrence.
Kimball, Warren, Mass., Dec. 2, 1830.	De Soto, May 1, 1856.	
Knight, J. Lee, Indiana, July 6, 1837.	Topeka, April 18, 1868.	Topeka, Kan.
Knight, M. A., Indiana, January 28, 1839.	Topeka, Aug. 1, 1868.	Topeka.
Knight, S. L., Indiana, August 25, 1861.		Topeka.
Knight, F. I., Iowa, December 4, 1865.		Topeka.
Knight, M. L., Kansas, May 15, 1872.		Topeka.
Knight, M. G., Kansas, July 23, 1874.		Topeka.
Kulin, E. N., Annapolis, Indiana, April 20, 1842.	Lawrence, Oct 27, 1876.	Franklin, Kansas.
Kennedy, T. H., Brown Co., Ohio, Oct 25, 1831.	Wakarusa, May 10, 1855.	Wakarusa.
Kennedy,W. B., Brown county, Ohio, Feb. 16, 1822.	Wakarusa, May 10, 1855.	Lawrence.
Knight, Elizabeth, Rockford, Ind , Feb. 19, 1831.	Tonganoxie, Oct. 10, 1834.	
Kunckl, Joseph A., Chicago, Ill., Feb. 9, 1859.	Lawrence, Sept. 1, 1870.	Lawrence.
Kunkel, Jerome, Pennsylvania, March 11, 1827.	Jefferson Co , July, 1856.	Rising Sun Farm.
Knight, I. A., Vandurburg Co., Ind., June 19, 1852.	Lawrence, April 12, 1879.	Lawrence.
Kennedy, Ella A., Kansas, February 22, 1860.	Douglas Co.	
Kennedy, Oscar, Illinois, August, 27, 1855.	Douglas Co., Oct. 3, 1855.	Wakarusa.
Kennedy, Laura, Kansas, April 6, 1857.	Douglas Co.	
Kleinhaus, Mrs. A. J., Virgin ia, April 28, 1834.	Jefferson Co , Oct. 29, 1855.	Grantville.
Kennedy, O. P , Brown county, Ohio, April 15, 1834.	Wakarusa, May 20, 1855.	Wakarusa.
Koons, W. H., Findley, Ohio, January 1, 1866.	Lawrence, April 7, 1871	Lawrence.
Knight, J. C., Topeka Band.		
Knapp, Dora M., Coxsackie, N. Y., Dec. 5, 1856.	Ottawa, April, 1870.	Osawatomie.
Kimball, Geo., Masonville, N. H., May 30, 1817.	Lawrence, April 15, 1865.	Lawrence.
Kimball, Mary A., County Caven, Ireland. Oct. 13, '32	Lawrence, April 15, 1865.	Lawrence.
Kimball, Cora L, Lawrence, Kas , Jan. 28, 1867.	Lawrence, Jan. 28, 1867.	Lawrence.
Kreyhill, J E., Penn., January 9, 1820.	Leavenworth, May 1, 1870.	Leavenworth Co.
Keen, A. B., Platte county, Mo., February 7, 1845.	Leavenworth, 1854.	Leavenworth.
Kimball, Mrs. Adeline A., New Ipswich, N. H , October 20, 1831.	Lawrence, March 24, 1855.	Lawrence.
Kennedy, Mrs. Eugene, Michigan, Dec. 29, 1852.	Douglas Co., Dec. 18, 1869.	Douglas Co.
Kennedy, L. J , Brown county, Ohio, Sept. 21, 1835.	Wakarusa, May 1, 1855.	
Kennedy, Amanda E., Indianapolis, Ind., Nov. 22, '41.	Wakarusa, April 15, 1855.	
Kennedy, Wm. I., May 21, 1832.	Near Lawrence, Oct. 12, 1855.	Near Lawrence.
Kennedy, J., March 19, 1829.	Near Lawrence, Oct 12, 1855.	Near Lawrence.
Kennedy, May, Kansas, August 28, 1863	Wakarusa, Aug. 28, 1863.	Wakarusa.

Name, Place and Date of Birth.	Place and Date of Settlement.	Present Residence
Kennedy, Effie, Kansas, July 14, 1871	Wakarusa, July 14, 1871.	Wakarusa.
Kennedy, Mrs. E., Ohio May 19, 1829.	Wakarusa, May 5, 1855.	Wakarusa.
Keezel, J. C., Limestone, Tenn., Feb. 14, 1857.	Ottawa, May 3, 1875.	Ottawa.
Katzenstein, A., Germany, October 28, 1831.	New York, 1859.	Lawrence.
Kelcher, David, New York, August 29, 1850.	Franklin, March 11, 1857.	Lawrence.
Kelso, C. Z., Indiana, June 29, 1852.	Lawrence, Nov. 17, 1866.	Lawrence.
Kessler, Michael, York county, Pa., Sept. 25, 1834.	Russell Co., Aug. 24, 1872.	Russell Co.
Keys, M. J., Linn county, Iowa, June 3, 1862.	Junction City, 1876.	Lawrence.
Kenderdine, Fannie, Iowa, June 1, 1862	Topeka, 1874.	Topeka.
Kimball, Sam'l, Mason Village, N. H., Aug. 27, 1827.	Lawrence, Oct 9, 1854.	Lawrence.
Kessler, Michel, York county, Pa, Sept. 25, 1834.	Russell Co., Aug. 24, 1872.	Bunker Hill.
Kelly, Peter, Altoona, Pa., June 18, 1849.	Reno Station, June 25, 1869).	
Kerr, James M., Dayton, Ohio, July 13, 1844.	Montgomery Co., 18—	Douglas Co.
Koons, Mada, Findley, Ohio, January 23, 1864.		Douglas.
Kretzinger, Lue E., Pennsylvania, February 7, 1847.	Kanwaka, July 2, 1858.	Winfield, Cowley Co
Kingen, Lydia M., Pennsylvania, February 16 1847.	Lawrence, Sept. 5, 1877.	Lawrence.
Kennedy, Eugene, Illinois, March 21, 1850.	Lawrence, June 25, 1855.	
Kimball, Frank, Mason Village, N. H., Jan. 6, 1824.	Lawrence, Sept. 1857	Lawrence.
Keeper, Abraham, Luzerne county, Pa., Feb. 9, 1809.		
Knight, Mrs. Mary, Ky, September 1, 1828.	Lawrence, April 16, 1879.	Lawrence.
Knight, Lutie, Evansville, Ind.. Nov. 23, 1864.	Lawrence, April 16, 1879.	Lawrence.
Knight, Eunice, Evansville, Ind., Dec. 22, 1860.	Lawrence, April 16, 1879.	Lawrence.
Knight, Mary E., Evansville, Ind., Sept. 5, 1854.	Lawrence, April 12, 1879.	Lawrence.
Kennedy, Eva, Lawrence, Aug. 17. 1861	Lawrence, Aug. 17, 1861.	Lawrence.
Kingman, Samuel A., Washington, Mass., June 26, 1818.	Brown Co., April 27, 1857.	Shawnee Co.
Kingman, Mrs. M. W, Catawissa, Pa., May 14, 1822.	Brown Co., April 27, 1857.	Shawnee Co.
Kingman, Lucy D., Smithland Ky., January 8.	Brown Co., April 27, 1857.	Shawnee Co.
Klodt, John N, Brooklyn, Long Island, 1823.	Atchison, 1869.	
Kastenbader, A., Union county, Pa, Aug 17, 1818.	Wakarusa, March 27, 1857.	Wakarusa, Douglas Co.
Kastenbader, Elizabeth, Center county, Pa., May 12, 1818.	Wakarusa, March 27, 1857.	Wakarusa, Douglas Co.
Kastenbader, D. N., Stephenson county, Ill., April 14, 1818.	Wakarusa, March 27, 1857.	Wakarusa, Douglas Co.
Kastenbader, Rose, Stephenson county, Ill., June 6, 1852.	Wakarusa, March 27, 1857.	Wakarusa, Douglas Co.
Kastenbader, Anna, Douglas county, Jan. 26, 1865.	Wakarusa.	Wakarusa, Douglas Co.
Kennedy, D. G., Butler, Pa., May 14, 1821.	Black Jack, Douglas Co., June 24, [1861.	Black Jack, Douglas Co.
Kennedy, Margaret, Adams, county O., Oct. 27, 1800.	Wakarusa, Oct. 19, 1855.	Wakarusa.
Kistler, G. W., Cass county, Ind., May 10. 1833.	Shawnee Co., March 10, 1856.	Shawnee Co.
Knitle, Albert, Pennsylvania, January 19, 1849.	Lawrence, April 1872.	Lawrence.
Kellam, E. P., Vermont, February 28, 1832.	Topeka, March 29, 1857.	Topeka.
Kennedy, Frank, Lawrence, May 16, 1862.		Lawrence.
Lindsey, H. C., Iowa City, 1844.	Shawnee Co, 1856.	Topeka.
Lockwood, Mrs. J. T., Danville, Ky, March 15, 1843.	Leavenworth City, Dec. 11, 1857. Lawrence, 1870.	Lawrence.
Lake, B. F., Jackson, Ohio, Februry 14, 1824.	Lecompton, 1856.	Lecompton.
Leamer, Wm., Pennsylvania, September 8, 1826.	Kanwaka, Aug. 1, 1850.	Leavenworth Co., Kan.
Leonard, Mrs. A. H., Erie county, N. Y., May 16, 1825.		
Lovejoy, Julia L., Lebanon, N. H., March 9, 1812.	Manhattan, May 6, 1855.	Baldwin City.
Little E. V., Newark, Ohio, December 11, 1858.	Olathe, May 5, 1866.	Abilene.
Lemon. W. T., Michigan, February 16, 1853.	Humboldt, Oct. 6, 1857.	
Longfellow, Charles, Machias, Maine, May 28, 1812.	Wakarusa, Dec. 23. 1855. [1871.	Lawrence.
Lester, E., Dark county, Ohio, March 29, 1842.	Ridgeway, Osage Co., Aug. 16,	Ridgeway.
Lewis, Miss M., Harvard, N. Y.	Lawrence, Aug. 1, 1879.	
Leamer, E. B., Lecompton, Kansas, May 18, 1862.	Lecompton, May 18, 1862.	Lecompton.
Loper, T. L., Troy, Kansas, July 31, 1860.	Troy, July 31, 1860.	Troy.
Lindner, T. G., Germany, Feb. 23, 1833.	Lyon Co, Jan. 1862.	Lawrence.
Loesch, M., Baden, Germany, May 2, 1831.	Lawrence, Jan. 4, 1857.	
Lindley, Alfred, Orange county, Ind., Jan. 29, 1822.	Douglas Co., Oct. 17, 1866.	Lawrence, Kan.
Lindley, Joe, Orange county, Ind., Nov. 11, 1849.	Douglas Co., Oct. 28 1866.	
Lane, V. J., Washington county, Pa., Jan. 7, 1828.	Quindaro, March 6, 1857.	Wyandotte.
Leonard, C. C., France.	Topeka, 1855.	
Lambers, L. I., St. Louis, Mo., Oct. 18, 1850.	Lawrence, March 4, 1866. [5, 1857.	Lawrence.
Leonard, Henry B., London, England, Jan 20, 1842.	Prairie City, Douglas Co., April	Emporia.
Long, H. C. Zanesfield, Ohio, July 41, 1824.	Wyandotte, Aug. 7, 1748.	Wyandotte.
Long, Martha M., Circleville, Ohio, May 18, 1833.	Wyandotte, Sept. 7, 1852.	Kansas City, Mo.
Lovejoy, I. R Manhattan, Kansas, Sept. 17, 1855.	Manhattan, Sept. 17, 1855.	Coal Creek, Douglas Co. 1st white child born in Manhattan.
Longfellow, M. E., Loudon county, Va., Jan. 17, 1849.	Lawrence, Jan. 12, 1861.	Lawrence.
Littell, D. W., Beaver county, Penn., June 29, 1838.	Coffey Co, March 28, 1859.	Lawrence.
Lamb, C. W., Ohio, March 27, 1850.	Detroit, Nov. 1. 1858.	Detroit.
Lamb, John E, Orange county, N. Y., Nov. 16, 1843.	Junction City. Oct. 22, 1866.	Lawrence
Lowe, Elizabeth, Granger county, Tenn., Mar. 20, 1820.	Lecompton, Oct. 10, 1861.	Lecompton.
Long, T. E., Miami, county, Ohio, August 18, 1858.	Douglas Co., March 19 1869.	Lawrence.
Leamer, Kate K., Steamer "Keystone," March 10, 1856.	Lecompton, July, 1856.	Lecompton.
Leamer, C. W., Lecompton, July 2, 1866.	Lecompton, July 2, 1866.	Lecompton.

16

Name, Place and Date of Birth.	Place and Date of Settlement.	Present Residence
Limbocker, J. N., Monroe county, N. Y., Dec 22, 1830.	Pottawatomie Co., April 9, 1859.	Manhattan.
Linton, Eli H., Penn., June 15, 1844.	Tonganoxie, Dec. 9, 1846.	Tonganoxie.
Leigh, Mrs. M. R., Juniata, Penn., Oct. 7, 1839.	Highland, Feb. 10, 1859.	Highland.
Lyman, Wm., Kentucky, January 15, 1831.	Lawrence, 1865.	Lawrence.
Lynde, Edward, Saybrook, Conn., Oct. 16, 1820.	Jefferson Co., Nov 1, 1855	Kansas City.
Lagerquest, L. A., Armstrong, Pa., Oct 22, 1842.	Near Lawrence, July 4, 1854.	Lawrence.
Ludington, George W., Syracuse, N. Y., May 10, 1832.	Topeka, May, 1857.	Topeka.
Ludington, Sate E., Burlington, Vt., Feb 9, 1836.	Topeka.	Topeka.
Lyon, A. C.	Lawrence, March 11, 1857	Lawrence.
Lecompte, Samuel D , Md., Dec. 13, 1814.	Leavenworth Co., Dec 11, 1855	Leavenworth Co.
Livingston, C. C., Sharon, Pa., Oct. 28, 1855.	Topeka, May 8, 1873.	Topeka.
Louland, L. J., Rutland, Vt., Feb. 3, 1814.		Clyde, Kan.
Lynch, John C., 1814.	Leavenworth Co., 1861.	Leavenworth.
Leiby, Nancy, Holly, Pennsylvania.	Lawrence.	
Leiby, Lily G., Kansas.	Lawrence.	
Lowe, Allen, Kentucky, April 21, 1816.	Auburn, June, 1859.	Topeka.
Lowe, Mary E., Pennsylvania, March 29, 1817.	Topeka, June, 1859.	Topeka.
Lyon, J. H., Buffalo, N. Y., June 7, 1841.	Leavenworth. Aug. 1857.	Leavenworth.
Lewis, Rees Jones, Breckenshire, England, Aug. 24, 1831.	Bourbon Co., May 30, 1861.	Westport, Mo.
Lightcap, S. B., Greensburg, Pa., Oct. 7, 1842.	Wamego, May 1, 1870.	Wamego.
Ludington, R. W., Holyoke, Mass., Sept. 1, 1827.	Lawrence, March 20, 1857.	Lawrence.
Lincoln, Eben, P., Louisville, Ky., Dec 5, 1852		Lawrence.
Lincoln, Merwin C., Hancock county, Ill., Jan. 1, 1855.		Lawrence.
Lincoln, Geo. E., Hancock county, Ill., July 7, 1857.		Lawrence.
Lyon, L. D., Illinois, March 16, 1843.	Lawrence, Jan. 24, 1868.	Lawrence.
Leonard, A. R., Vermont, Nov. 28, 1828.	Kanwaka, Aug. 10, 1859.	Tonganoxie.
Lescher, George M. Kansas, September 28, 1862.	Shawnee and Osage.	Topeka.
Lew, Samuel, Kentucky, 1857.	Lawrence, June, 1864.	Lawrence.
Lewis, P. B., Parke county, Indiana, Nov. 7, 1848.	Lawrence, Nov. 6, 1865.	Lawrence.
Lindner, Wm., Chicago, June 20, 1861.	Council Grove, March 8, 1863.	Lawrence.
Love, Alexander, N. Y., November 25, 1835.	Lawrence, April 28, 1858.	Lawrence.
Lowe, Imogen P., Virginia, August 23, 1854.	Lecompton, Oct. 15, 1859.	Lecompton.
Long, Edward, Columbus, O., February 27, 1851.	Marion Co.	
Lowe, P. G., Coos county, N H., Sept. 29, 1828.	Ft. Leavenworth, Dec. 25, 1849.	Leavenworth.
Lincoln, Andrew J., Putney, Vt , March 10, 1815.	Lawrence, May 10, 1877.	Lawrence.
Leis, Wm. J., New York, January 11, 1847.	Lawrence, March 4, 1855.	Lawrence.
Lane, S. J., Galena, Ill., June 20, 1833.	Quindaro, March 6, 1857.	Wyandotte.
Lunkins, J. W., Chester, S. C., May 23, 1827.	Lawrence, April 13, 1854.	Lawrence.
Lunkins, Mrs. J. W., Chester, S. C., Oct. 15, 1836.	Lawrence, April, 1856.	Lawrence.
Long, Anna E., Marietta, Lancaster county, Pa., November 14, 1829.	Iowa Point, April 12, 1848.	½ mile south of Highland.
Lamb, Ella, Illinois, April 12, 1855.	Douglas Co., 1857.	
Lafgren, F. Theodore, Malmo, Sweden, Dec. 11, 1838.	Franklin Co., July, 1859.	Lawrence.
Litchfield, Alice L., Lawrence, March 5, 1859.	Lawrence, March 5, 1859.	Lawrence.
Lawson, James, Illinois, September 8, 1857.	Lawrence, March 19, 1862.	Lawrence.
Lovejoy, H. F., New York, February 25, 1851.	Topeka, Sept. 17, 1877.	Topeka.
Leonard, F. H.		
Loveless, M., Illinois, December 13, 1859.	Seneca, Kan., May 1, 1865.	Centralia.
Lischer, Augusta W., Kentucky, Sept. 12, 1838.	Shawnee Co., April 27, 1855.	Topeka.
Lischer, T. H., Pennsylvania, March 18, 1829.	Shawnee Co., March 14, 1857.	Topeka.
Laurence, Annie M , Henderson, Ill., June 18, 1862.	Lawrence, Sept. ——	Lawrence.
Longfellow, Mary C., Augusta, Maine, April 26, 1815.	Wakarusa, Oct. 20, 1857.	Lawrence.
Lamb, C. A., Elbridge Tp., N. Y., Feb. 16, 1846.	Clinton, Nov. 25, 1867	Clinton.
Lapham, W. W., Illinois, March 7, 1838.	Lawrence, Aug 15, 1878.	Lawrence.
Lake, Maggie W., Ohio, November 20, 1832.	Lawrence, April, 1870.	Lawrence.
Lewis, M. D., Indiana, May 4, 1853.	Lawrence, Nov., 1865.	Douglas Co.
Lovejoy, I. R., Manhattan, Kas., Sept. 17, 1855.	Manhattan, Sept. 17, 1855.	Baldwin City.
Lundy, I. S., New Jersey, August 18, 1810.	Wyandotte, Nov. 1863.	Lawrence.
Leonard, Sophia, London, Eng., April 1, 1818.	Prairie City, April 5, 1857	Lawrence.
Leonard, Anna, Cedar Rapids, Iowa, March 12, 1852.	Leavenworth, April 14, 1865.	Emporia.
Leonard, Bernard, Enniskillen, Ireland, Dec. 25, 1813.	Prairie City, April 5, 1857.	Lawrence.
Langdon, J. W., Crystal Lake, Ill., July 12, 1851.	Washington, March 15, 1872.	Washington.
Lowe, A. K., Monroe county, Tenn., Feb. 11, 1830.	Lecompton, Oct 10, 1861.	Lecompton
Lines, Chas. B., New Haven, Conn., March 12, 1807.	Wabaunsee May 1, 1856.	Wabaunsee.
Lansdown, L B., Fleming county, Ky., March 24, '53.	Lawrence, Aug. 18, 1856	Lawrence.
Ladd, Miss Annie H , Franklin Co., O., Aug. 14, 1815.	Wyandotte, July 31, 1843.	Wyandotte.
Leonard, George, Prairie City, June 9, 1859.	Lawrence, June 9, 1859.	Lawrence.
Lynch, Mary.		Lawrence.
Lowe, P. G., Coos county, N. H., Sept. 28, 1828.		Lawrence.
Long, Henry C., Banesfield, Montgomery county, O., July 31, 1824.	Ft. Leavenworth, Dec. 25, 1849.	Leavenworth City.
Long, Martha M., Circleville, Ohio, May 18, 1833.	Wyandotte City, Aug. 7, 1843.	Wyandotte.
Lyman, Cordie, Osceola, Mo., June 28, 1854.	Wyandotte City, Sept. 7, 1852.	Wyandotte.
Lyman, Zuez, Lawrence Kansas, January 15, 1879.	Lawrence, May 11, 1864.	Lawrence.
Lyman, D. O., Ashtabula, Ohio, May 2, 1851.		
Lugenbeel, Charles W., Ross county, O., March 29, 1849.	Geneva, Allen Co., Sept. 12, 1866.	Lawrence.
	Four miles East of Lawrence, Oct. 11, 1879.	East of Lawrence.
Lewis, P. M., Delaware, Indiana, February 20, 1841.	Linn Co., Nov. 7, 1857.	Lecompton.
Lewis, W. S., Malone, N. Y., January 19.	Lawrence, Nov. 1872.	Lawrence.

Name, Place and Date of Birth.	Place and Date of Settlement.	Present Residence
Lewis, George A., Malone, N. Y., October 2.	Lawrence, Nov., 1872.	Lawrence.
Lewis, Emma A., Malone, N. Y, September 18, 1864.	Lawrence, Nov., 1872.	Lawrence.
Lecompt, Eugene D., Cambridge, Md., 1845.	Leavenworth, Dec. 1, 1854	
Lecompt, Mrs Eugene D., New Bedford, Mass., 1850.	Manhattan, March, 1857.	
Leis, George, New York, February, 18, 1842.	Lawrence, Feb. 19, 1855.	Lawrence.
Lovejoy, C. H , Hebron, N. H., October 11, 1811.	Manhattan, March 14, 1855.	Baldwin.
Lee, Mrs. G. W., Maine, March 20, 1827.	Manhattan, April, 1855.	Manhattan.
Levy, Abe L., New York City, March 23, 1862.	Lawrence, May 1, 1868	Lawrence.
Lovejoy, C. H., Manhattan, September 17, 1855.	Coal Creek, Sept. 17, 1855.	Coal Creek.
Laloge, C. F., France, May 31, 1830.	Chase Co., Feb. 15, 1859.	Cedar Point, Chase Co.
Lawson, Mrs. E. J., Massachusetts, July 3. 1845.	Lawrence, Feb., 1869.	
Lawson, John, Lowell, Mass., August 26, 1840.	Lawrence, Oct. 2, 1869.	Lawrence.
Love, Alexander, Seymour, Ind., April 10, 1845	Leavenworth Co., Mar. 13, 1868.	
Loar, John W., Muskingum c unty, O., July 15, 1816.	Leavenworth Co., Oct. 28, 1854.	Wamego, Kan.
Loar, Lucinda, Gillia county, Ohio, March 3, 1828.	Leavenworth Co., Oct 28, 1854.	Lawrence
Lynch, John C.	Leavenworth, ——, 1861.	Leavenworth.
Livingston, C. C., Mercer county, Pa., Oct. 28, 1855.	Topeka, May 3, 1873.	
Liggett, J. M., Brown county, Ohio, Dec. 27, 1825.	Fort Scott, July 24, 1858.	Johnson Co.
Lamasney, James, Ogdensburg. N. Y., July 9, 1842.	Olathe, April 10, 1860.	Olathe.
Legate, Ivory H., Edinburg, Ind., Aug. 21, 1855.	Olathe, Feb. 7, 1870.	Olathe.
Lamorean, Geo. W., Wisconsin, 1860.	Mound City, ——, 1869.	Kansas City.
Lamorean, D. R., Scoharie, November 10, 1829.	Linn Co., Nov. 12, 1868.	Mound City.
Larue, Mrs. Sarah J., Connecticut, Nov. 20, 1850.	Franklin, June 15, 1861.	Baldwin City.
Lee, John, Lawrence, November 12, 1858.	Lawrence, Nov. 12, 1858.	Lawrence.
Lemmon, Allen B , Freeport, Ohio, August 21, 1847.	Winfield, March 11, 1871.	Winfield.
Lawson, Emmet R., Illinois, February 8 1863	Lawrence, Mar. 19, 1862.	Lawrence.
Lapham, S., Cumberland county, Me., Feb. 28, 1832.	Coal Creek, Douglas Co., Nov. 16, 1851.	Coal Creek, Douglas Co.
Little, E. C., Newark, Ohio, December 14, 1858.	Olathe, May 5, 1866.	Abilene.
Laws, Emma, Malone, N Y., February 13, 1862.	Lawrence, Dec. 13, 1872.	Lawrence.
Leonard, G. F., Prairie City, June 9, 1859.	Lawrence, Mar. 23, 1860.	Lawrence.
Legate, James F., Leominster, Mass., Nov. 23, 1829.	Lawrence, July 5, 1854	Leavenworth.
Lawson, Sarah E., November 16, 1844.	Lawrence, ——	
Levy, Chas., Germany, August 8, 1828.	Lawrence, May 1, 1865.	North Lawrence.
Leeper, Allen, Ohio, August 24, 1830.	Paola, Jan. 23, 1857.	Lawrence.
Leeper, Vinna, Indiana, January 21, 1833.	Paola, Jan. 23, 1857.	Lawrence.
Leeper, Vidalia S., Kentucky, August 6, 1858.	Lawrence, Aug. 10, 1878.	Topeka.
Leeper, C. G., France, December 10, 1853.	Paola, Jan. 23, 1857.	Topeka.
Montgomery, P. D., Genesee county, N. Y , Nov. 29, 1831.	Cedar Point, Oct. —, 1873.	Cedar Point.
Morgan, A. P., Framingham, Mass., Feb. 17, 1813.	Lawrence, Nov. 1, 1854.	Lawrence.
Martin, William, Bedford county, Pa , May 1, 1801.	Lawrence, April 5, 1855.	Lawrence.
Miller, W C , McLean county, Ill., Oct. 3, 1839.	Lawrence, Feb. 26, 1869.	Lawrence.
Michael, Wm. H., Hardy, W Va., Jan. 5, 1843.	Douglas Co., Nov. 28, 1871.	Marion Tp.
Marckle, Wm. D., Preble county, O., Aug. 26, 1848.	Douglas Co., Mar. 24, 1859.	Willow Springs.
Meserbey, E. C., Halowell, Me., March 4, 1861.	Lawrence, Feb. 15, 1877.	Lawrence.
Murray, Lucetta, Ohio, July 15, 1860.	Big Springs, ——, 1862	Wamego.
Mann, Nannie E., Delaware, O., August 15, 1860.	Leavenworth, May 26, 1877.	Leavenworth.
Morgan, Ellen, Johnson county, December 7, 1859.		
Marble, Orin C., Sturgis, Mich , March 5, 1848.	Lawrence, Mar. 6, 1867.	
Mitchell, Mrs S. D., Ottawa, Ill., April 29, 1838.	Osage City, June 18, 1879.	Osage Co.
Murphy J. H , Paris, Edgar county, Ill , July 12, 1843.	Tecumseh, May 20, 1856.	Tecumseh.
Moore, Alonzo W., Penn., June 29, 1825.	Topeka, Oct. 30, 1854.	Topeka.
Mann, J. A., Montgomery county, Pa., Nov. 7, 1836.	Grasshopper Falls, May 9, 1858.	Jefferson Co.
Morris, W. F., Ill., May 22, 1858.	Lawrence, June 4, 1874.	Lawrence.
Moody, H. C., Peoria, Ill., March 23, 1856.		
Moore, Dr. John S., Woo'wich, Eng., May 19, 1855.	Lawrence, Sept. 22, 1871.	Lawrence.
Maxson, P. B , Hopkinton, R. I., July, 20. 1828.	Fremont Tp., Lyon Co., May 8, 1858.	Fremont Tp., Lyon Co.
Maxson, Mrs. Mary S , Courtland county, N. Y., Dec 11, 1829.	Fremont Tp., Lyon Co., Dec. —, 1858.	Fremont Tp., Lyon Co.
Mitchell, D. T., Kentucky, April 8, 1832.	Douglas Co., April 2, 1855.	Lawrence.
Mails, Mrs. Martha, Center county, Pa., Jan. 9, 1821.	Manhattan, May 1, 1855.	Manhattan.
Macy, E. G., Preble county, O , October 13, 1817.	Near Bloomington, Oct. 22, 1854.	Near Bloomington.
Meeker, Mrs. P., N. Y , July 20, 1811.	Lawrence, ——	Lawrence.
Melendry, Henry L., Vermont, Feb. 7, 1860.	Linn Co., June 19, 1867.	Lawrence.
Matney, Julia, October 23 1832.	Richland, April 15, 1857.	Richland.
Maxwell, Joseph, Greenville, March 11, 1795.	Lawrence, May 30, 1858.	Lawrence.
Martin, George W., Holidaysburg, Pa , June 30, 1841.		
Martin, Mrs. George W., Columbiana county, Ohio, March, 1845.	Lecompton, Mar. —, 1857.	Topeka.
Moore, G. W. H., Russell county, Va , July 17, 1824	Pottawatomie Co., Mar. —, 1857.	Topeka.
Miller, A., North Carolina, Sept. 17, 1827.	Jefferson Co., April 20, 1859.	Leavenworth Co.
Mexel, A., Germany, February 14, 1833.	Lawrence, Sept. 25, 1859.	North Lawrence.
Maitland, A. W., Reading, Pa., Dec. 26, 1854.	Leavenworth, ——, 1858.	Wichita.
Mead, Mrs. Etta, Boston, Mass., Dec. 14, 1837.	Lawrence, Sept. 16, 1869.	
Moore, Harry J., Camden, N. J., Sept. 25, 1859.	Manhattan, June 11, 1856.	Manhattan.
Martin, Pierre, France, July, 4, 1822.	Lawrence, May 10, 1861.	Lawrence.
Mann, Cynthia, Frankfort, Ky., Aug. 9, 1853.	Cedar Point, Chase Co., Kansas, Aug. 15, 1854.	Cedar Point.
	Near Lawrence, ——, 1868.	Lawrence.

Name, Place and Date of Birth.	Place and Date of Settlement.	Present Residence
Martin, Leon R., Topeka, May 9, 1864.	Topeka, ——	Topeka.
Moore, Maggie, Lecompton, Sept. 11, 1862.	Lawrence, ——, 1866.	Lawrence.
Moore, M. A., Evansville, Ind., Dec. 1, 1852.	Western Mo., ——, 1856.	Lawrence.
Moore, Susie, Lawrence, Dec. 15, 1866.	Lawrence, Dec. 15, 1866.	Lawrence.
Moore, Nellie, August 17. 1871.	Lawrence, Aug 17, 1871.	Lawrence.
Menger, Christian A., Saxony, March, 1828.	Leavenworth, ——, 1854.	Lawrence.
Morgan, Ellis, Johnson county, Dec. 7, 1858.		
Miller, Alzina M., Michigan, Dec. 3, 1839.	Douglas Co., May 25, 1860.	Lawrence.
Morgan, Mrs. W. A., Elkhart, Ind., March 16, 1835.	Paola, Sept 1, 1855	
Murphy, Mary, Indiana, September 16, 1855.	Johnson, Sept. —, 1857.	Lawrence.
Murphy, Eliza, Kansas, August 28, 1861.	Kansas, Aug. 28, 1861.	Lawrence.
Morrill, E. N., Maine, February 12, 1831.	Hamlin, Mar —, 1857.	Hiawatha.
Moore, Hugh, County Down, Ireland, Oct. 14, 1804.	Lawrence, July 9, 1870.	Lawrence.
Miller, Lloyd W., Miller, Hancock county, O., March 31, 1863.	Lawrence, Aug. 6, 1870	Lawrence.
Marshall, I. R., Pittsburg, Pa., Nov. 13, 1839.	Leavenworth, May 9, 1856.	Leavenworth.
Marshall, T. L., Indiana county, Pa., July 17, 1840.	Douglas Co., July, 1867.	Scranton.
Marshall, Margaret, Belfast, Ireland, Nov. 15, 1842.	Douglas Co., May, 1869	Scranton.
Moore, Ely, New York City, Dec. 7, 1834.	Miami Mission, July 11, 1854.	Lawrence.
Massey, C. C., LaSalle county, Ill., August 2, 1842.	Lawrence, Feb. 6, 1878.	
Massey, E. J., Marion county, Ind., April 28, 1847.	Lawrence, Feb. 6, 1878.	
Manwaring, Henry, Kent, Eng. Feb. 28, 1839	Wakarusa Tp , Mar. 14, 1871.	
Manwaring, Esther, Brighton, Eng., Feb. 1, 1845.	Wakarusa Tp., Mar. 14, 1871.	
Markley, O. M., Wabash county, Ind.. Aug. 4, 1854.	Lawrence. Mar. 8, 1879.	Lawrence.
Miles, Dessie C., Ridgely, Mo., Sept. 17, 1859.	Russell, Russell Co., Mar. 25, 1875.	Russell, Kan.
Moore, Wm., North Carolina, July 25, 1805.	Ottawa Creek, Franklin Co., Aug. 1, 1854.	Ottawa, Franklin Co.
Moore, J. C., Park county, Ind., July 12, 1842.	Ottawa Creek, Franklin Co., Aug. 1, 1854.	Norwood, Franklin Co.
Mackey, Thos. I., Lewis county, Ky., Oct. 23, 1831.	Franklin, Douglas Co., Oct. 10, 1856	Douglas Co.
Montfort, F. P., Warren county, Ohio, May 2, 1816.	Highland, Doniphan Co., June 28, 1856.	North Topeka.
Mull, G. W., Penn., September 19, 1819.	Lawrence, April —, 1867.	Lawrence.
Miller, W. K., Hamilton county, Ohio, May 10, 1827.	Illinois, ——, 1870.	Lawrence.
Miller, A. R., Glasgow, Scotland, August 29, 1827.	Johnson Co., July 1, 1859	Johnson Co.
Morse, Charley, Topeka, August 19, 1869.	Shawnee Co., Aug, 19, 1868.	Topeka.
Marshall, W. N., Pa., June 30, 1850	Douglas Co., April 19, 1857.	Prairie City.
Mason, L. P., Pennfield, N. Y., April 12, 1833.	Lawrence, July 15, 1866.	Lawrence.
Morrice, Chris , Henry county, Ind., 1862.	Franklin Co., 1876.	Douglas Co.
Milner, Frank E., Erie, Pa., January 14, 1853.	Iola, Oct. 22, 1857.	North Lawrence.
Mador, J. D., Jackson county, Mo., December 25, 1848.	Douglas Co., Feb 24, 1862.	Lawrence.
Montgomery, Jess. S , Ireland, April 28, 1844.	Lawrence, March 25, 1877.	Lawrence.
Mendenhall, C. F., Lewisville, Ind., December 9, 1851.	Shawnee, Johnson Co , April 1, 1855.	Lawrence.
Moah, J. E , Lawrence, Kan., February 26, 1856.	—— — 1863.	Lawrence.
Marckle, Mrs. M T., St. Geneva Co., Mo., Dec. 16, 1824	Near Siegle, April 7, 1854.	Near Siegle.
Meairs, Wm., Butler Co., Ohio, March 3, 1829.	Blanton Bridge, Doug. Co., Apr. 7, 1855.	Blanton Bridge, Douglas Co.
Miller, William, Chester county, S. C., Aug. 7, 1841.	Lawrence, May 6, 1858.	Lawrence.
Marshall, J. B., Topeka bend.		
Mitchell, W. P., Leavenworth, May 21, 1857.	Leavenworth, May 21, 1857.	Williamston.
Miller, John S., Rush county, Ind., March 1, 1850.	Leavenworth Co., Jan. — 1870.	Leavenworth.
Miller, A. P., Hamilton county, Ind., July 17, 1846.	Douglas Co. Dec —, 1856.	Douglas Co.
Mull, Geo., Iowa, July 14, 1860.	Douglas Co., ——, 1868.	Lawrence.
Modin, John E., Korsta, Hopta, Sweden, Nov. 4, 1856.	Lawrence, Jan 14, 1869.	Lawrence.
Mason, Myron, Robinson, Lawrence, May 9, 1871.	Lawrence, May 9, 1871.	Lawrence.
Marple, E., Ohio, October 3, 1826.	Shawnee Co., April 19, 1856.	Shawnee Co.
Monelle, Newton II., Burlingame, Nov. 24, 1860.	Burlingame, Nov. 24, 1860.	Burlingame.
Maynard, F. A., Wellsboro, Pa.	Osawatomie, May —, 1861.	
Maynard, H. S., Wellsboro, Pa , March 3. 1854.	Randolph, Oct. —, 1865.	Randolph.
Moyes, Nay, Lawrence, December 18, 1861.	Lawrence, Dec. 18, 1861.	Lawrence.
Marvin, Mina E., Warren, Ohio, September 23, 1860	Lawrence, Dec. 24, 1874.	Lawrence.
Miller, A. G., Kentucky, October 17, 1833.	Topeka, May 4, 1857.	Topeka.
Miller, Mrs. A. E , Indiana, Oct. 2, 1833.	Topeka, May 4, 1857.	Topeka.
Mart, A. P., Indiana, January 14 1836.	Miami Co , March 15, 1857.	Lawrence.
Millard, Mrs. F. O , St. Charles, Ill., October 26, 1852.	Mound City, —— —, 1859.	Lawrence.
Mathias, Mrs. William G., Columbus, O., Apr.26, 1836.	Leavenworth, May 1, 1857.	Leavenworth.
Moore, G. W., Boston, Mass., October 1. 1846.	Crawford County, March 3, 1870.	Lawrence.
Mills, Virginia. St. Joseph, Mo., Aug. 6, 1852.	Leavenworth, ——	Leavenworth.
Mills, Catherine, Schuyler county, N. Y., Oct. 17, 1828.	Fort Leavenworth, —— 1852.	Leavenworth.
Mitchell, M. P., Leavenworth, May 21,1857.	Leavenworth, May 21, 1857.	
Myers, M. F., March, 1829.	Marion, Douglas Co. — —, 1857.	
Murray, M. V., Ohio, October 22, 1859.	Lawrence, —— —, 1861.	Lawrence.
Moore, Helen L.		Decatur, Ill.
Miller, Mrs. E., Ohio, March 15, 1844.	Miami Co., Sept 3, 1860.	Lawrence.
Mauzer, S. J., Harvard, Ill., October 11, 1860.	McHenry Co., Ill., — —	Lawrence.

Name, Place and Date of Birth.	Place and Date of Settlement.	Present Residence
Moore, Milton R., Madison Co., Ind., Sept. 27, 1846.	Bloomington, Douglas Co., Nov. 8, 1858.	Topeka.
Milner, Mrs. Margaret, Ft. Covington, N. Y., March 13, 1825.	Cofachique, Allen Co., Nov. 23, 1857.	North Lawrence.
Mueller, Rev. John Adam, Germany, May 24, 1830.	Baldwin City, Nov 18, 1860.	Baldwin City.
Miles, Joseph, Pennsylvania, Jan 19. 1839.	Lawrence, Jan 22, 1876.	Leavenworth.
Morris, Isaac, Dearborn county, Ind., Feb. 22, 1824.	Bourbon Co , March 20, 1857.	Tecumseh.
Markson, Herman, Germany, July 13, 1834.	Leavenworth, Oc., —, 1857.	Leavenworth.
Markson, Mrs H., Germany, July 33, 1836.	Leavenworth, Oct. —, 1865.	Leavenworth.
Mahaffie, J. B., Fayette county, Ohio, April 25, 1820.	Olathe, Johnson Co., Oct. 15, 1857.	Olathe.
March, George, Ohio, Feb. 2, 1828.	Lawrence, Oct. 25, 1873.	Lawrence.
Matney, Charles, Taswell county, Va , Feb. 1, 1829.	Richland, Aug. 17, 1854.	Richland.
Mitchell, D. H., Indiana, May 29, 1830.	Leavenworth Co , May 29, 1854.	Williamstown.
Mobely, R. D., Graves county, Ky., June 24, 1833	Reeder, Solomon Valley, May 20, 1855	Minneapolis.
Murch, A. B., Essex county, N. Y , March 4, 1824.	Franklin Tp., Ottawa Co , Sept. 15, 1871.	Fount Tp., Ottawa Co.
Miller, Mary G., Ohio, September 16, 1832.	Shawnee Co., April 17, 1856.	Tecumseh.
Marshall, Jennie, Topeka, Jan. 13, 1861	Topeka, Jan. 13, 1861.	Topeka.
Morris, Geo W., Port Republic, Va., Feb. 28, 1823.	Douglas Co., May 20, 1857.	Douglas Co.
Mason, J. H., Ireland, April 20, 1857.		
Mann, C., Indiana, Jan. 3.	Lawrence. —— ——	
Maine, M. P , New York, May 10, 1843.	Richland, Shawnee Co. Aug. 1, 1874.	Shawnee Co.
Martin, J. S., Blair county, Pa., August 2, 1852.	Lecompton, March, 1857.	Lecompton.
Mason, J. N., Whiteside, Ill., September 30, 1857.	Douglas County.	Clinton, Kansas.
Mendenhall, D. W., Indiana, June 21, 1847.	Shawnee, Johnson Co., April 1, 1855.	Lawrence.
Mendenhall, S. E , Virginia, July 6, 1832.	Shawnee, Johnson Co., April 1, 1855.	Lawrence.
Mauzer, S. J., Illinois, October 11, 1860.		Lawrence, Kansas.
Meek, C. M., Indiana, September 24, 1824.	Leavenworth, Feb. —, 1858.	Kansas City, Mo.
Merriman, Wm.		Lynchburg, Va.
Miller, Lizzie J., New Paris, Ohio, January 21, 1861.	Lawrence, Oct. 4, 1872.	
Mendenhall, S A., Nausemone Co., Va., Nov. 9, 1811	Shawnee Mission, Apr. 1, 1854.	Lawrence.
Montgomery, Minnie M., Westfield, N. Y., Jan .31, 1861.	Lawrence, Oct 1867.	Lawrence.
Mason, Ernest Gordon, Lawrence, September 18, 1873.	Lawrence, Sept. 18, 1873.	Lawrence.
Monroe, Frank H , Fairfield Co., Conn., Apr. 22, 1832	Lawrence, May 5, 1855.	Lawrence.
Miller, J. B., Pennsylvania, May 28. 1828.	Tecumseh, April 27, 1856.	Tecumseh.
Moore, J. C., Belvoir, Kan., December 20, 1843.	Bloomington, Kan., Nov. 5, 1858.	Belvoir, Kan.
Miller, Robert H., Chester county, S. C., Dec. 6, 1796.	Lawrence, May 6, 1858.	Lawrence.
Mason, A. L., Dubuque, Iowa, February 22, 1857	Paola, Kan., April 1860	Lawrence.
Mason, Dorcas, Westford, Mass., December 8, 1826.	Clinton, Douglas Co., Oct. 1869.	Clinton.
Meeker, C. W., Harrison, Ill., Aug 31, 1848.	White Cloud, May 10, 1875.	Lawrence.
Myer, I. J., Ringgold county, Iowa, October 22, 1858.	Woodstock, Jeff. Co. Sep. 15, 1861	
Morgan, James, Putnam Co., Ind., October 17, 1824.	Jefferson County, April 15, 1856.	Sarcoxie.
Mendenhall, C., Shawnee Mission, Johnson Co., Kan., Feb. 14, 1850.	Osawatomie, Sept 1, 1854.	Lawrence.
Meade, F. A., Centervill·, Ind., January 15, 1859.	Lawrence, December 22, 1869.	Lawrence.
Morgan, O. A., N. Y , July 14, 1833.	Lawrence.	Lawrence.
Miller, Mrs. Charles H., Platte Co., Mo., July 29, 1845.	Leavenworth, Co., May 1854.	Leavenworth.
Mosher, Arch., Rutland Co., Vt , Nov. 3, 1811.	Franklin Co., April 14, 1857.	Prairie City.
Myers, F. A., Licking Co., Ohio., June 9, 1846.	Auburn, April 3, 1869.	Douglas Co.
Martin, W. H., Mercer Co., Ky., September 18, 1836.	Douglas Co., March 13, 1868.	Lawrence.
Morgan, H. H., Bethel, Ohio, April 14, 1854.	March 24, 1876.	Lawrence.
Mason, Ernest G., Laurence, September 18, 1873.	Lawrence, September 18, 1873.	Lawrence.
Maine, Laura E., Green county, Wis., Nov. 13, 1850.	Shawnee Co., Nov 10, 1854	Shawnee Co.
Maine, Laura E., Shawnee county, March 18, 1878.	Shawnee Co.. March 18, 1878.	Shawnee Co.
Monroe, Ed., Reeding, Conn., Nov. 11, 1834.	Lawrence, May 5, 1855.	Lawrence.
Meade, Frank A., Indianapolis, January 15, 1859.	Lawrence, December 23, 1870.	Lawrence.
Markley, S., Pa., October 10, 1828.	Douglas, Co , March 9, 1879.	Lawrence.
Mitchell, S. A., Tyler county, Va., January 5, 1838.	Leavenworth, Dec. 15, 1854.	Lawrence.
Moys, Emily J., Holland, Vt., February 2, 1837.	Lawrence, April 7, 1857.	Lawrence.
Miller, Chas. H., Germany, April 15, 1838	Leavenworth, June 1857.	Leavenworth
Moore, H. Miles, New York, Sept 2, 1826.	Leavenworth, June 13, 1854.	Leavenworth.
Moore, Linna F., Virginia, Jan. 23, 1841.	Atchison, April 2, 1856.	Leavenworth.
Martin, R. G., Mercer Co., Pa., June 25, 1837.	Topeka, Kansas, May 1855.	Topeka.
Meinke, P. D., Hannover, 1833.	Eudora, 1867.	1873, Tex.
Morgan Jonathan F., New London, N. H., April 3, 1818.	Lawrecne Kansas, Aug. 1, 1854.	Deceased, Oct. 19,
Morgan, Edward W , Holliston, Mass., May 30, 1842.	Lawrence, Kansas, Nov. 1, 1854.	Osawatomie.
Morgan, G. H., South Framingham, Mass., Feb. 27, 1852.	Lawrence, Nov. 1, 1854.	Lawrence, Kan.
Morgan, Jonathan F., jr , Lawrence, Kas., Jan. 20, 1856.		Lawrence.
Morgan, Anna M., Lawrence, Kas , Nov. 25, 1857.		Lawrence, Kan.
Marshall, D. A., Virginia, Feb. 10, 1842.	Jefferson Co., May 20, 1871.	North Lawrence.
Martin, Louis, Kentucky, 1827.	Lawrence, 1867.	Lawrence.
Morse, D. L., Bradford, Pa., Oct. 11, 1827.	Topeka, April 12, 1857.	Topeka.
Myers, F. J., Pennsylvania, April 15, 1857.	Black Jack, Douglas Co., April 12, 1877.	Black Jack

Name, Place and Date of Birth.	Place and Date of Settlement.	Present Residence
Matney, Solomon. Richland, Dec. 28, 1859.	September, 1878.	Big Springs.
Morille, Z. M., Switzerland, March 24, 1827.	Burlingame, June 1, 1855.	Osage City.
Murphy, Emma Nilson, Upper Sandusky, June 25,1853.	Wyandotte, Nov. 16, 1857.	Wyandotte.
Mugler, Mrs. Anna, Germany, Jan. 19, 1833	Burlingame, April, 1858.	Lawrence.
Morris, Charles, Niles, Mich., Jan. 25, 1850.		Lawrence.
Mason, Frank, New York, 1825	Lawrence. 1875.	Manhattan.
Mendenhall, A. S , Indiana, March 26, 1856.	Osawatomie, Jan. 1, 1855.	Lawrence.
Millikan, I., Monroe Co., Ind., Jan. 7, 1827.	Johnson County, May 29, 1857.	Johnson Co.
Millikan, E. L., Manchester, N. H., Dec. 5, 1830.	Olathe, May 28, 1857.	Olathe.
Merrit, Francis, Canada, May 3, 1838	Lawrence, Oct. 1867.	Lawrence.
Maberly, Augustin Wm., jr., London, England, Dec. 26, 1834.	Blue Mound, May 25, 1855.	Lawrence.
Maberly, Mrs. Ruth S , Romsey, Hampshire, England, Oct. 3, 1835.	Eudora, Tp , Jan 11, 1878.	Lawrence.
Morris, Sarah, Franklin Co , Ohio, March 15, 1828.	Lecompton, May 20, 1857.	Lecompton Tp.
Morris, Alice, Franklin Co., Ohio, Jan 3, 1854.	Lecompton, May 20, 1857.	Lecompton Tp.
Mitchell, C. B., Miami Co., Ohio, April 18, 1849.	Lawrence, March 25, 1879.	
Mitchell, Mrs. Emma C., Miami Co., Ohio, Jan. 20, 1844.	Lawrence, March 25, 1879.	
Miller David, North Carolina, 1805.	Lawrence, 1860.	
Miller, Susie I., Keokuk, Iowa, Jan. 14, 1857.	Lawrence, Jan. 2, 1870.	Lawrence.
Mustard, M. E. Pittsburg, Pa., Nov. 6, 1838.	Lawrence, April 10, 1859.	
Marks, A., Bainburg, Jan. 6, 1814.	Lawrence. Nov. 30, 1858.	Lawrence.
Montgomery, J M., Jasper Co., Mo., Oct. 20. 1860.	Douglas County, 1862.	Kanwaka Tp.
Moore, R. R., Farmington, Ohio, Feb. 13, 1841.	De Soto, Nov. 1, 1808.	DeSoto.
Moore, John D., Farmington, Ohio, June 8, 1858.	De Soto, Nov. 1, 1868.	DeSoto.
Marshall, S. A., Boston, March 25, 1818.	Leavenworth, May 9, 1856.	Leavenworth.
Miller, Richard, Indiana, Jan. 2, 1839.	Two miles west of Lawrence, June 12, 1854.	Leavenworth Co.
Morris, R., M. D., Ohio, April 15, 1824.	Lawrence, Nov. 1, 1865	Lawrence.
Muzzy, H. C., Oxford, Mass., March 9, 1834.	Lawrence, Nov. 4, 1854.	Lawrence.
Manning, E. C., Redford, N Y., Nov. 7, 1838.	Marysville, Marshall Co., Oct. 23, 1859	Winfield.
Martin, Nelson, Hudson, N Y., Jan. 31, 1815.	Baldwin City, Oct 1867.	Topeka.
Martin, S. E., Greenville, Pa., Jan. 18, 1826.	Lawrence, Nov. 26, 1854.	Topeka.
Martin, Maria M., Cincinnati, Ohio, July 5. 1834.	Topeka. May 7, 1868.	Topeka.
Mason, R. D., Portsmouth, N. H. March 1, 1847.	Lawrence, Aug. 10, 1868.	
McAllaster, C. A., Jefferson Co., N. Y., Dec. 8, 1848.	Marquette, McPherson Co., Aug. 25, 1876.	Lawrence.
McAllaster, Mrs. C. A , Des Moines Co., Ia., June 8, 1860.	Lawrence, Oct. 30, 1872.	
McAllaster, J. E., St. Lawrence Co., N. Y., Aug. 19, 1829.	Lawrence, Oct 30, 1872.	Douglas Co.
McAllaster, Laura, Little Valley, N. Y., Dec 13, 1836.	Lawrence, Oct. 30, 1872.	Douglas Co.
McFarline, B. W., Bellville, Canada, May 3, 1860.	Lawrence, June 12, 1864.	Lawrence.
McCurdy, F. A., Maine, Jan. 22, 1852.	Lawrence, Dec. 15, 1876.	Lawrence.
McFarland, Hattie, Oskaloosa, Aug 17, 1861.	Lawrence, ——, 1869.	Lawrence.
McFarland, C. W., Iowa, June 1, 1856.	Oskaloosa, —— -. 1857.	Lawrence.
McPherson, W. D., Henry Co., Ia , July 25, 1848.	Woodstock, Jefferson Co., Nov. 23, 1870.	Woodstock.
McCarty, Wm R., Kentucky, Jan. 7, 1841.	Linn, June 21, 1857.	
McQuiston, Will, Ohio, Dec. 15, 1857.	Lawrence Sept. 14, 1869.	Lawrence.
McKinney, David R., Kentucky, March 27, 1850.	Palmyra, Sept. —, 1855.	Palmyra Tp., Douglas Co.
McPhail, Vinnie, Toronto, Canada, July 24, 1855.	Osage Co., June 20, 1879.	Osage City.
McIntire, L. O., Wooster, O., March 10, 1856.		
McCormick, J. F. Nova Scotia.		
McFarland, John, Indiana Co., Penn., July 12, 1832.	Douglas Co., Sept. 10, 1854.	Lawrence.
McIntire, Susie, Pennsylvania, March 11, 1862.	Lawrence, March —, 1869.	Lawrence.
McCall, Moses, Green Co., O., April 8, 1827.	Lecompton, Sept. —, 1854.	Lecompton.
McFarland, Mrs. S. J., Ohio, Feb. 12, 1833.	Oskaloosa, Sept. 15, 1857.	Lawrence.
McKenney, E. J., Ohio, Sep. 15, 1849.	Clinton. Douglas Co , March 4, 1855.	Clinton.
McFarland, Thomas, Indiana Co., Pa., Sept. 20, 1835.	Franklin, Douglas Co , Sept. 24, 1854	Eudora.
McLaughlin J., Topeka band.		
McWhorten, A. H. Hebron, N. Y., Dec. 15, 1838.	Lawrence, Jan. 14, 1869.	Lawrence.
McDonald. C. B., Fort Scott, Dec 25, 1860.	Fort Scott, Dec. 25, 1860.	Fort Scott.
McFarland, J. N., Ohio. Dec. 8, 1832.	Oskaloosa, April 20, 1857.	Lawrence.
McGill, Alice, Olathe, Kas., Aug. 30, 1859.		Lawrence.
McCan, S. S , Dubuque, Iowa, Oct. 31, 1839.	Fort Scott, Nov. 15, 1856.	Woodstock.
McCan, E. F., Maysville, Ky., Jan. 18, 1851.	Franklin, Aug. 15, 1857.	Woodstock.
McFarland, W. G , Kaw Valley. April 8, 1865.		Kaw Valley.
McFarland, N. J , Fulton Co., Ill., April 11, 1838.	Wakarusa, Dec. —, 1854.	Parsons.
McMillen, M., N. Y , March 9, 1834.	Douglas Co., March 18, 1870.	Marion Tp.
McClees, Nelson Oliver, Nov. 8, 1861.	Wichita, Jan. 14, 1870.	Lawrence.
McCoy, Chas., May 14, 1858.	Lawrence, ——	Vinland.
McKinney, Page, Otoe and Omaha Missions, old territory of Nebraska, Sept. 29, 1846.	Bellevue, Old, Ter. of Neb., 1814.	Lawrence.
McIntire, Jennie B., Pennsylvania, Dec. 30, 1857.	Lawrence, March 11, 1869.	Lawrence.

Name, Place and Date of Birth.	Place and Date of Settlement.	Present Residence
McLaughlin, James, Indiana, June 22, 1851.	Topeka, March 23, 1868.	Topeka.
McClurg, J. K., Ohio, Oct. 23, 1857.	Larned, ——	
McKee, Elijah, Pennsylvania, June 26, 1838.	Lawrence, April 11, 1858.	
McNees, J. A , Butler Co., Pa., April 19, 1840.	Edgerton, Johnson Co , Nov 3, 1876.	Lawrence.
McMeekin, H. D., Nelson Co. , Ky., Jan. 3, 1822.	Fort Leavenworth, Oct. 5, 1850.	Topeka.
McAllaster, O W., Morristown, N. Y., Jan. 11, 1834.	Osawatomie, March 1857.	Lawrence.
McAllaster, E. P., Indian Ter., June 23, 1846.	Lawrence, Nov 2, 1862.	Lawrence.
McCabria, Melissa, Pennsylvania, July 22, 1853.	Lawrence, Nov 18, 1870.	Leavenworth.
McMeekin, Ben, Shelbyville, Ky., 1850	Fort Leavenworth, —— - , 1850.	Topeka,
McClure, N. B., Indiana, Feb. 12, 1830.	Miami Co., May , 1857.	Perry.
McDaniel, G., Valley Falls.	Valley Falls, ——	Valley Falls.
McConnell, J. F., Niagara, Canada, Feb. 22, 1860.	Lawrence, May 7, 1869.	
McDonald, Chas., Pennsylvania, May 3, 1815.	Topeka, Sept. - , 1859.	Topeka.
McDonald, Mary J., Pennsylvania, March, 1820.	Topeka, Sept. —, 1859.	Topeka.
McKinn, Robert B., County Tyrone, Ireland, April 6, 1818.	Lawrence, April 7, 1865.	Lawrence.
McCoy, J. C., Indiana, Sept 28, 1811.	Various Places, Aug. 15, 1830.	Johnson Co.
McNees, D. E., Butler Co., Pa., March 19, 1847.	Lawrence, ——	Lawrence.
McCoach, John, Philadelphia, Pa., June 9, 1841.	Bloomington, Douglas Co., Apr. 22, 1859.	Lawrence.
McQuiston, John, Venango Co., Pa., May 5, 1827.	Shawnee Co., June 14, 1859.	Shawnee Co.
McQuiston, Barbara, Crawford Co., Pa., Dec. 22, 1828	Shawnee Co , June 14, 1859.	Shawnee Co.
McQuiston, H. R., Coffey Co., Kas. , Aug. 27, 1868.		Shawnee Co.
McCombs, Marion, Henry Co. , Ind, Nov. 15, 1852.	Lawrence, Kan., Apr. 12, 1879.	
McNees, Henry, Ohio, '22.	Lawrence, ——	
McGee, J. J., Center Co., Pa., April 9, 1836.	Wakarusa, May 20, 1855.	Wakarusa, Douglas Co.
McGee, Olivia G., Tazewell Co., Va., Jan. 14, 1838.	Wakarusa, Sept. --, 1854.	Wakarusa, Douglas Co.
McGee, Jas. C., Douglas Co., Dec. 25, 1858.	Wakarusa, ——	Wakarusa, Douglas Co
McGee, Chas. M., Douglas Co., Nov. 7, 1860.	Wakarusa. ——	Wakarusa, Douglas Co.
McGee, Birdilla, Douglas Co., Kas., Feb 12, 1861.	Wakarusa, ——	Wakarusa, Douglas Co.
McGee, Carla, Douglas Co , Kas., Sept. 15, 1862.		Wakarusa, Douglas Co
McGee, John J., jr., Douglas Co., Kas.,March 24, 1864.		Wakarusa, Douglas Co.
McGee. Gertrude, Douglas Co., Kas., March 12, 1866.		Wakarusa, Douglas Co.
McGee, Richard, Douglas Co. , Kas, June 5, 1871.		Wakarusa, Douglas Co.
McGee, Albert E., Douglas Co , Kas., Aug. 27, 1873.		Wakarusa, Douglas Co.
McGee, Solon, Douglas Co., Kas., Oct. 11, 1875.		Wakarusa, Douglas Co.
McGee, Oliver P., Douglas Co., Kas., April 20, 1878.		Wakarusa, Douglas Co.
McGuire, M., Dark Co , O., March 8, 1833.	Leavenworth Co., May 5, 1860.	Lawrence.
McIlvain, Margaret, Washington Co., O., Aug. 11, 1843.	Lawrence, May 24, 1855.	Lawrence.
McNees, H. S., Armstrong, Pa., Nov. 6, 1870.		Lawrence.
McCoy, Justus, Indiana, June 7, 1835.	Grantville, Kan., May 13, 1871.	Grantville, Ks.
McMillian, Mrs. I., Arkansas, Feb. 5, 1838.	North Lawrence. Feb. —, 1865.	Lawrence.
McCoy, J. E. Circleville, Ohio, July 30, 1830.	Wakarusa Tp., Douglas Co., Apr. 8, 1860.	Lawrence.
McKee, B. W., Muscatine Co. Iowa, March 11, 1854	Iola, Kan., —— -, 1861.	
Norton, S. B., Massachusetts, Aug 1, 1823.	Lawrence. May 21, 1858.	Douglas Co.
Niles, A. B., Williamsburg, Mass., November 6, 1858.	Lawrenceburg, Cloud Co., 1869	Clyde, Cloud Co.
Niles, F. A , Vermont, May 5, 1839.	Fontana, Kansas, 1869.	Fontana.
Newby, C. H., Arcadia, Ind., July 24, 1861.	Leavenworth, Sept. , 20, 1869.	Lawrence.
Newby, T. F., Hamilton county, Ind., August 26,1848.	Tonganoxie, Kansas.	Tonganoxie, Leavenworth Co.
Neill, B. J., Ohio, Nov. 5 1859.	Leavenworth, 1872.	Lawrence.
Nye, Sam W., Illinois, Dec 25, 1856.		Vinland.
Newhall, S. M , Lincoln, Mass., July 20, 1827.	Lawrence, Nov. 1, 1856.	Lawrence.
Nolnn, N F., Ireland, September 3, 1847.	Lawrence, March 21, 1857.	Lawrence.
Newlin, J. H., Howard Co , Ind., April 7, 1852.	Douglas County, Nov. 20, 1867.	Lawrence.
Naidley, Anslem, Ironton, Ohio, January 26, 1880.	Fort Scott, April 10, 1860.	Lawrence.
Nills, E. T., Cattaraugus, June 16, 1833.	Centropolis, March 25, 1857.	
Neese, David Ohio, March 18, 1833.	Richland, June 6, 1872.	Shawnee Co.
Noland, S. W., Jackson county, Mo., Sept. 20, 1850.	Lawrence, Sept. 15, 1877.	Lawrence.
Neisley, J. K,, Lancaster county, Pa., May 24, 1824.	Lawrence, April 1, 1878.	Lawrence.
Neisley, L. B., Cumberland Co., Pa., February 11,1827.	Lawrence, April 1, 1878	Lawrence.
Noyes, John N., Abington, Mass., March 20, 1820.	Lawrence, Oct. , 1868.	Lawrence.
Nichols, Cora, Branch Co., Mich., February 23, 1862.	Lawrence, March 4, 1873.	Eudora.
Nelson, Topeka Band.		
Nelson, F , Topeka Band.		
Nichols, R., Rushford, N. Y., August 28, 1837.	Topeka, July 3, 1865.	Topeka.
Neals, P. D. K., Quincy, Ill , Oct. 14, 1846.	Humboldt, May 1, 1860.	Larned.

Name, Place and Date of Birth.	Place and Date of Settlement.	Present Residence
Neill, Victor, Springfield, Ohio, May 6, 1859.	Lawrence, Sept. 12, 1870.	Lawrence.
Nary, O. B. M., Washington, Pa., February 1, 1823	Leavenworth, Oct. 14, 1866.	Leavenworth.
Norton, Mrs. H. J., Cooperstown, N. Y., Oct. 10, 1834.	Atchison. Oct. 1, 1873.	Topeka.
Nace, William M., Virginia, December 19, 1826.	Lecompton, July 10, 1851.	Lecompton.
Nesbitt, Houstin, Ohio, June 23, 1846.	Leavenworth, March 1, 1864.	Topeka.
Norton. Willis, Ohio, July 22, 1846.	Topeka, August, 1871.	Topeka.
Newlin, M. U., Indiana, Oct. 27, 1823.	Lawrence, November, 1866.	Lawrence.
Neal, Albert, Pennsylvania, April 24 1854.	Garnett, April 15, 1856.	Lawrence.
Newby, Henry, Jackson Co., Ind., December 28, 1826.	Leavenworth Co., Sept. 23, 1869	Lawrence.
Newby, Naomi, Wayne Co., Ind., January 20, 1827.	Leavenworth Co., Sept. 23, 1869.	Lawrence.
Newby, Elma, Indiana, December 28, 1863.		Lawrence.
Northway, F. A., Onondaga, N. Y., August 23, 1832.	Lawrence, April 15, 1870.	
Neal, Henry, Clarion Co., Pa., November 20, 1826.	Garnett, Anderson Co., April 15, 1856.	
Neal, Henry, Jefferson Co., Pa., September 21, 1826.	Lawrence, Sept. 20, 1856	Lawrence.
Nichols, F. P., New Hampshire, July 2, 1832.	Highland, Doniphan Co., March 1, 1859.	Council Grove.
Nichols, Mrs. A., N. Y., June 13, 1840.	Highland, Doniphan Co., March 1, 1859.	Council Grove.
Neisley, Bertie K., Harrisburg, Pa., June 30.	Lawrence, 1878.	Lawrence.
Noecker, Mrs. J. C., Maryland, September 4, 1820.	Lawrence. Kan.. Nov. 6, 1860.	
Northruk, D. L., Valley Falls.	Valley Falls, 1855.	Valley Falls.
Nyc, J. W., Woodstock, Ct., August 31, 1828.	Leavenworth, April, 1856.	Leavenworth.
Neville, R. H., Rivervale, Ind., August 8. 1853.		Oxford.
Norton, John, Q. A., Ohio, April 30, 1844.	Lawrence, May 5, 1866.	Lawrence.
Oliver, M. M., Illinois, Dec. 15, 1857.	Lawrence, Oct. 3, 1868	Lawrence.
Osmond, S. M., Oxford, Pa.	Lawrence, April —, 1879.	
Osmond, H. S. Cornwall. Vt.	Lawrence, April —, 1879.	
Osmond, R. M., Perry, Ill.	Douglas Co., April 2, 1879.	Leavenworth Co.
Ogden, John H., Lawrence, Kas., Aug. 21, 1856.	Lawrence, Aug. 21, 1856.	Topeka.
Owen, A. E., Plainfield, Ind., Aug. 11, 1843.	Leavenworth Co., Sept. 25, 1859.	North Lawrence.
Oles, Maurice, Toledo, Ohio, June 17, 1855.	Emporia, — —, 1870.	Cottonwood Falls.
Oliver, J. J., Philadelphia, Sept. 10, 1845.	Osawkee, Aug. 25, 1857.	Silver Lake.
Oswald, M., Switzerland, Jan. 8, 1834.	Lawrence, March 28, 1857.	Topeka.
Oliver, J. B., Philadelphia, Pa., Aug 28, 1832.	Ogawkie, Jefferson Co., March 13, 1856.	Silver Lake.
O'Brien, Mrs. J. E., Illinois, Oct. 6, 1838.	Topeka, — 1879.	
Olney, F. Z., Berkshire, Jan. 16, 1816.	Burlingame, March 23, 1857.	Eureka.
Ortman, Fred, Prussia, Nov. 28, 1882.	Shawnee Co., May 1857.	Topeka.
Ophir, Sophereth, Warren, Pa., Jan. 24, 1834.		Lawrence.
Oliver, Thomas S, Pittsburg, Pa., Oct. 4, 1841.	Lecompton, March 21, 1857.	Rural Tp.
Osburn, Samuel E., Illinois, Dec. 25, 1857.	Lawrence, Feb. 11, 1879.	Lawrence.
Oure, Chas., Prussia, Germany, July 10, 1821.	Eudora, Douglas Co., May 8, 1878.	Eudora.
Oliver, Adam, England, Oct. 15, 1823.	Lawrence, May 21, 1860.	Lawrence.
Owen, N. W. Luzerne Co. Pa., Jan, 8, 1824.	Kansas Bottom, Nov. 3, 1860.	Lawrence.
Ogee, L. H., Peoria, Ill., 1827	Silver Lake, — 1847.	Silver Lake.
Otis, J. D., Perry, N. Y., May 26, 1820.	Topeka, Nov. 2, 1871.	Topeka.
Ossmann, Justus, Germany, July 16, 1825.	Douglas Co., March 28, 1858.	Lawrence.
Oagel, John C. Ohio, June 2, 1856.	Leavenworth, Kan., — 1858.	Leavenworth.
O'Neil, M A., Summerfield, Ohio, June 18, 1832.	Black Jack, May 24, 1860.	Black Jack.
O'Neil, Eleanor, Middle Lancaster, Pa., Oct. 25, 1832.	Black Jack, May 18, 1861.	Lawrence.
Oberholtz, Lou, Ohio, April 8, 1857.	Lawrence, —	Lawrence.
Oliver, Charles, England, June 28, 1828.	Lawrence, Feb. 9, 1863.	
Osmand, R. M., Illinois, May 2, 1850	Osawatomie, —	Lawrence.
Owens, Wm., jr., England, April 17, 1842.	Marion, Douglas Co., July 21, 1867.	Richland.
Owens, Wm., sr., Wales, England, Nov. 19, 1820.	Marion, Douglas Co., July 21, 1867.	Richland, died Nov. 20, 1868.
Pierson, F. M., Bedford, Pa., October 21, 1820.	Kanwaka, April 7, 1855.	Wakarusa.
Pamhan, Rachel A., Fulton Co., Ill., April 1, 1843.	Lawrence, —, 1855	Lawrence.
Pamhau, J. B., England, January, 1842.	Leavenworth, — 1858.	Lawrence.
Phillips, C. B., Ohio, June, 1852	Waterville, — 1870.	Waterville.
Petrie, A L., Edinburg, Scotland, May 11, 1841.	Butler Co., July 4, 1860.	ElDorado.
Platts, Susie Kanwaka, Kansas, February 21, 1858.	Kanwaka, Feb. 21, 1858.	Kanwaka.
Pardee, John, Illinois, July 25, 1841.	Lawrence, May 8, 1865.	Lawrence.
Pierson, James H., New Castle, Ind., April 4, 1854.	Lawrence, April 11, 1855.	Lawrence.
Phenicie, W. C., Ohio, December 19, 1841.	Leavenworth, March 10, 1866.	Leavenworth Co.
Pearce, George W., Providence, R 1, 1816.	Lawrence, April 1, 1865.	Lawrence.
Penchard, J. S., England, May 20, 1839.	Lawrence, Jan. 20, 1869.	Lawrence.
Phillips, Oliver, Luzerne Co., Pa, June 21, 1816.	Lyon Co., April 2, 1855.	Lyon Co.
Pike, J. A., Westboro, Mass., February, 19, 1843.	Lawrence, October 8, 1854.	Florence.
Pike, Mary E., East Douglas, Mass., June 1, 1833.	Lawrence, October 8, 1854.	Florence.
Pike, Jessie A., Lawrence, March 4, 1863.	Lawrence, March 4, 1863.	Florence.
Pettengill, E. D., Terre Haute, Ind., June 9, 1831.	Lawrence, —.	Lawrence.
Propper, C. F., Yankton, Dak., February 9, 1858.	Lawrence, May 30, 1868.	Atchison.
Phinney, Chas. H., Henry Co., Iowa, Aug. 20, 1845.	Woodstock, Jeff. Co., Nov. 20, 1860.	Woodstock, Jeff. Co.
Peairs, O. A., Janesville, Ohio, May 31, 1855.	Coal Creek, Nov. 23, 1860.	Vinland.
Pearce, W. J., Kanwaka, Kansas, December 3, 1860.	Lawrence, Dec 3, 1860.	Lawrence.

Name, Place and Date of Birth.	Place and Date of Settlement.	Present Residence.
Phillips, Mrs. A. J., Leominster, Mass., April 15, 1839.	Lawrence, March 9, 1859.	Lawrence.
Patterson, Frank, Jefferson Co., Ohio, July 11, 1829.	Junction City, June 24, 1866.	Junction City.
Perkins, Eli, Florida, May 1, 1850.		
Parker, A. E., Indiana, Sept. 17, 1856.	Plymouth, 1860.	Wellington.
Patterson, J. L., Steubenville, Ohio, April 9, 1830.	Lawrence, Jan. 1, 1856.	Lawrence.
Palmer, Barnabas Dorr, Boston, Mass, Jan. 13, 1842.	Lawrence, April 14, 1856.	"Rosebrook Farm," Wakarusa Tp.
Palmer, Mrs B. D., Illinois, May 13, 1847.	Lawrence, April 10, 1858.	Wakarusa Tp.
Priestly, J., Ohio., October 6, 1862.	Lawrence, Jan. 10, 1869.	Lawrence.
Patrick, A. G., Salem, Ind., May 21, 1824.	Leavenworth, February 14, 1856.	Valley Falls. An old Hickory Point prisoner.
Pattison, Wm. B., Bracken Co., Ky., January 17, 1825.		Indiana.
Picard, Mary L., Hudson, Ohio, January 26, 1821.	Topeka, Dec. 1869.	Topeka.
Pennypacker, Gen. G., U. S Army.		Ft. Riley, Kan.
Parah, J. W., Indiana, May 13, 1843.	Lawrence, March 9, 1870.	North Lawrence.
Penny, J. C.	Lawrence, ——	
Patterson, H. C., Lewis Co., Ky., May 27, 1844.	Leavenworth Co., Nov. 1, 1875.	Lawrence.
Perce, Wm., Circleville, Ohio, Nov 9, 1817.	Russell Co., Oct. 31, 1871.	Russell Co.
Perce, Mrs. R. V., Ohio, August 12, 1821.	Russell Co., Oct. 31, 1874.	Russell Co.
Powers, H. W., Lyons, Iowa, September 24, 1858.	Irving, Kansas, Jan. 1, 1859.	Manhattan.
Pettibone, Milton, Genesee Co., N. Y., Jan. 15, 1823.	Franklin Co, Aug. 20, 1858.	Lawrence.
Parks, W. H., Erie, Pa., August 28, 1836.	Blue Mound, April 10, 1855.	Cottonwood, Chase Co.
Petefish, G. B., Rockingham Co., Va., August 7, 1833.	Douglas Co., April 5, 1867.	Douglas Co.
Petefish, Mrs. G. B., Springfield, Ill., Jan. 22, 1838.	Douglas Co., Sept. 1,——	Douglas Co.
Pigott, George M., Dublin, Ireland, Sept 11, 1834.	Fort Leavenworth. July 20, 1858.	Lawrence.
Plaskett, Wm., Clark county, Ind., April 10, 1824.	Baldwin City, Douglas Co., Feb., 1869.	Baldwin City.
Palmer, Luther, Washington Co., Ohio, April 29, 1829.	Topeka, April 4, 1857.	Topeka.
Pearson, Ella., Plainfield, Ind.	Lawrence, ——, 1872.	Lawrence.
Platts, Susan W., Rindge, N. H., November 30, 1832.	Douglas Co., April 8, 1855.	
Priestly, Wm., Ohio, April 8, 1827.	Baldwin City, April 10, 1869.	Lawrence.
Peteet, W S., Mass., August 18, 1831.	—— 1856.	
Pearson, C. E.	Lawrence Sept. 30, ——	Lawrence.
Powell, E., Ohio, October 11, 1847.	Bellville, April 12, 1870.	Bellville.
Pease, C. A., Vermont, March 7, 1831	Lawrence, May, 1855.	Lawrence.
Patee, Clair M., Ashland, Riley Co., Kan., March 6, 1857.		Manhattan.
Poter, C. H., Dalton, Mass., January 1, 1845.	Lawrence, June 2, 1857.	Lawrence.
Pennel, W. M., Indiana, June, 1848.	Russell, June, 1873.	Russell.
Pell, C. B., Jr., Brookfield, Mass., Oct. 5, 1827.	Lexington, Johnson Co., Sep. 10, 1857.	Lexington.
Pickett, J. C., Bethlehem, Ind., May 18, 1850.	Lawrence, June 5, 1876.	
Pickett, Mrs. Ida, Bartlet, Ohio, February 8, 1852.	Lawrence, Sept. 19, 1876.	
Penchard, W, E, N. Y. City, September 13, 1859.	Lawrence, June 29, 1869.	Lawrence.
Parney, Grace, Chicago, Ill., June 28, 1842.	Tonganoxie, Nov. 22, 1866.	
Parney, E. J., Canada, August, 17, 1835.	Tonganoxie, Nov. 22, 1866.	
Petzold, Mrs. Kate, Grandview, Ill., July 22, 1860.	Lawrence, June 1, 1875.	Lawrence.
Prentiss, S. R., Massachusetts. 1817.	Lawrence, ——, 1855.	Lawrence.
Prentiss, I. L., Coventry, N. Y., 1812.	Lawrence, ——, 1855.	Colorado.
Pearson, John, Indiana, April 17, 1838.	Wakarusa, Nov., 1854.	Jefferson Co.
Pooley, Chas. F., Stanford, Conn., February 4, 1829.	Lawrence, ——	
Payne, Mrs. Acie, Susquehanna, Pa., Oct. 24, 1858.	Atchison, Oct. 1, 1873.	Topeka.
Persey, Emma., Ogdensburg, N. Y., June, 1862.	Burlingame, June, 1865.	Osage City.
Potter, A. S., Crawford Co., Pa., August 4, 1832.	Lawrence, Oct., 1854.	Lincoln Center.
Pinkston, Mrs. W. M., Cincinnati, O., Nov. 4, 1847.	Leavenworth, ——, 1854.	Leavenworth.
Parrott, Mrs. Marc J, Alexandria, La, Oct. 15, 1836.	Leavenworth, Sept., 1854.	Leavenworth.
Phillips, A. J., St. Lawrence Co., N. Y., July 11, 1833.	Burlingame, April 20, 1859.	Lawrence.
Page, William N., Chelsea, Vt., April 4, 1837.	Leavenworth, June 1, 1873.	Leavenworth.
Potter, Otis, Providence, R. I., February 27, 1807.	Lawrence, April 5, 1855	Lawrence.
Plummer, Taylor, Kentucky, February 12, 1819.	Rising Sun, April 11, 1854,	
Platts, Aaron E., New Hampshire, May 4, 1828.	Kanwaka, April 9, 1855.	Kanwaka.
Phelps, A. H., Illinois.	Blue Rapids, Aug. 21, 1872.	Lawrence.
Pryor, M. B., Pa., June 24, 1854.	Black Jack, April 20, 1879.	Black Jack.
Purd, Jacob, Chester Co., Pa., August 19, 1824.	Lawrence, Nov. 22, 1878.	Douglas Co.
Price, W. C., Pennsylvania, September 3, 1823.	Douglas Co., July 13, 1858.	Willow Springs.
Pettingill, Mrs. Eliza, Canada East, Sept. 5, 1852.	Douglas Co., June 8, 1856.	Leavenworth Co
Powell, Mary C., Cedar Rapids, February 14, 1857.	Baldwin City, ——, 1869	Clinton
Pinkston, Sarah A. Lyon, Lexington. Ohio, May 2, 1837.	Near Lawrence, July, 1854.	Cedar Point.
Pinkston, Hattie May, Cedar Point, May 31, 1869.	Cedar Point, May 31, 1860.	Cedar Point.
Pinkston, Florence L, Cedar Point, May 6, 1871.	Cedar Point, May 6, 1871.	Cedar Point.
Potter, Ezra A., North Scituate, R. I., June 2, 1830.	Lawrence, April 5, 1855.	
Potter, George A., North Scituate, R. I., March 25, 1842.	Lawrence, April 5, 1855.	
Pinneo, Harry W., Philadelphia.		Lawrence.
Patterson, J. D. Ohio, February 9, 1848.	Lawrence, April 22, 1867.	Lawrence.
Pease, Wm. H., Hartford, Vt., June 16, 1821.	Lawrence, March 18, 1868.	Wakarusa.
Preisach, Alice, Lawrence.	Douglas Co., ——, 1861.	
Preisach, L., Lawrence.		
Patee, E. L., M. D., Delaware Co., Ohio, Feb. 13, 1832.	Ashland, near Manhattan, April 7, 1855.	Manhattan.

17

Name, Place and Date of Birth.	Place and Date of Settlement.	Present Residence
Palmer, Alpheus, Marietta, O.. February 8, 1831.	Topeka, Aug. 20, 1856.	Topeka.
Palmer, Bell J., Plymouth, Me , June 10, 1855.	Topeka, May 10, 1875.	Topeka.
Pike, Mrs. H. S., Groton, N. Y., Nov 15, 1835	Lawrence, April, 1870.	Florence, Marion Co.
Perkins, J. B., Ohio, April 8, 1860.	Douglas Co , July 11, 1866.	Lawrence.
Potter, A. S., Crawford Co., Pa.. August 4, 1832.	Lawrence, Oct., 1854.	Lincoln Center.
Peirce, Samuel, Ohio, September 12, 1822.	Leavenworth Co., April 3, 1878.	Tonganoxie.
Pearson, R. H., England, April 1, 1828.	Palmyra, May, 1851.	Baldwin City.
Pressach, P., France, Dec. 24, 1829.	Lawrence, Aug. 28, 1860.	Lawrence.
Pettibone, John, N. Y., Dec. 20, 1827.	Blue Mound, May 1856.	Miami Co.
Peters, D. T.		Lynchburg, Va.
Place, John T., Chester Co., Pa., April 5, 1827.	Lawrence, Aug. 4, 1865.	
Place, P. M., Lockport, N. Y., July 16, 1833.	Lawrence, Aug. 4, 1865.	
Patterson, Angie, Findley, Ohio, July 18, 1843.	Lawrence, July 24. 1855.	
Pierson, E. B., Batavia, N. Y., April 16, 1856.	Lawrence, May 1874.	Lawrence.
Pound, Belle, Ripley, Ohio, August 1, 1826.	Lawrence, April 1, 1858.	
Pinkston, E. W., Indiana, March 1, 1828.	Leavenworth, April 25. 1857.	Cedar Point.
Payne, B. T., Maysville, Ky., June 7, 1826.	Indianola, Oct. 15, 1857.	Shawnee Co.
Pierce, A. C. Cooperstown, N. Y., Sept. 13, 1835.		Junction City.
Pierce, H. L., Otsego Co., N. Y., March 29, 1837.	Junction City, May 13, 1865.	Junction City.
Phenis, I. R., Franklin Co., Ind., April 20, 1825.	Eureka, Greenwood Co., Dec. 14, 1867.	Eureka.
Phenis, Emily, Union Co., Ind., Jan. 16, 1825.	Eureka, Greenwood Co., Dec. 14, 1867.	Eureka.
Perry, S. A., Nantucket, Mass.. Feb. 6, 1844.	Lawrence, Sept., 1879.	
Powell, L. M., Cedar Rapids, Iowa, Aug. 30, 1858.	Baldwin City, March, about 10, 1871.	Clinton.
Presley, Wilbur F., Nashua, N. H., 1860.	Cottonwood Falls, 1870.	Hutchinson Grove.
Porter, J. W., Ohio, Sept. 23, 1841.	Miami Co , May 20, 1868.	De Soto, Johnson Co.
Porter, M. J., Columbiana Co., Ohio, June 27, 1845.	Eudora, Douglas Co., April 1, 1864.	De Soto, Johnson Co.
Pennel, W. M., Ohio, June, 1832.	Russell, June, 1873	Russell.
Parsons, James, Somerset, England, June 20, 1816.	Atchison Co., March, 1855.	Shawnee Co.
Parsons, Jane, Devonshire. England, March 13, 1819.	Atchison Co., Nov., 1855.	Shawnee Co.
Pettingill, Z. H., Auburn, Me., April 30, 1839.	Douglas Co., Nov., 1854.	
Pettingill, Frederick B., Cole Creek, Oct. 14. 1858.	Douglas Co., Oct. 14, 1860	Jefferson Co.
Pettengill, Nathan, Cole Creek, Oct 2, 1860.	Douglas Co., Oct. 2, 1858.	Jefferson Co.
Pettengill, Kitty L., Cole Creek. June 7, 1863.	Douglas Co., Oct. 7, 1863.	Jefferson Co.
Pettengill, F. H., Maine, May 30, 1845.	Douglas Co., 1855.	Leavenworth Co.
Pratt, John G., Hingham, Mass., Sept. 9, 1814.	Wyandotte, April 2, 1837.	Near Wyandotte.
Powers, B. F , Kentucky, April 25, 1846	Lawrence,——.	Wyandotte.
Prentis, C. T. K., Connecticut, March 2, 1847.	Lawrence, May 16, 1857.	Lawrence.
Phillips, Walter W.., Guernsey Co., Ohio, July 11, 1831.	Shawnee Co., April 23, 1855.	Topeka.
Place, Harry, Philadelphia, March 29, 1860.	Lawrence, Kan., Aug 5, 1864.	Lawrence.
Prentis, Noble L., Mount Sterling, Ill., April 8, 1839.	Topeka, Nov. 10, 1869.	Atchison.
Parr, J. W., Harmony, Ind., Jan. 26, 1856.	Topeka, Kan., Oct. 13, 1865.	Shawnee Co
Pursel, E B., Chester Co., Pa.	Lawrence, Dec 25, 1878.	
Peer, Rebecca, Michigan, 1839.	Coal Creek, ——, 1866.	Coal Creek.
Peer, Carrie, Michigan, 1860.	Coal Creek, ——, 1866.	
Perry, H. L., Troy, 1862.	Troy, ———, 1862.	Troy.
Patton, J. E., Lancaster Co., Pa., April 11, 1834.	Lawrence City, Kan., April 12, 1878.	Lawrence.
Patterson, Mary Buckingham, Howland, Ohio.	Lawrence, ——. 1865.	Lawrence.
Powell, W. L., Ohio, July 4.	Olathe, Jan. 16, 1878.	Lawrence.
Peepels, R. A., Jefferson, Ohio, April 11, 1831	Lawrence, Oct 15, 1876	De Soto.
Penchard, Emma F., New York, March 4. 1857.	Lawrence, April 30, 1870.	Lawrence.
Palmer, Minnie, St. Louis, 1861.	Kansas City, ——, 1875.	Black Jack.
Payne, J. W., Indiana, Oct. 30, 1858.	Leavenworth. Aug. 9, 1876.	
Phillips, E. D. F., Morgan Co., Ind., Aug. 7, 1841.	Tonganoxie, Feb. 11. 1870.	Lawrence.
Pike, Perley, Plymouth, N. H., Jan. 16, 1862.	Quindaro, Jan. 16, 1857.	Wyandotte.
Phillips, Bertie, Waterville, Kas., Feb. 14, 1873	Waterville, Feb. 14, 1873.	Waterville.
Phillips, Clara B.. Bucyrus, Ohio, June 5, 1853.	Waterville, April 20, 1871.	Waterville.
Perine, A. B., New York, May 4, 1836.	Topeka, Oct. 1, 1854.	Topeka.
Perine, Mary E., Conn., July 31, 1842.	Topeka, Sept., 1858.	Topeka.
Prentice, Mrs. Thaddeus, Connecticut.	Lawrence, May 11, 1859.	Lawrence.
Pellt, Kate L., Hollidaysburg, Pa., January, 1837.	Lecompton, Aug., 1860.	Lexington, Johnson Co.
Pellt, H. L., Lexington, Feb. 1, 1862.	Lexington, ——, 1862.	
Paramore, H, B., Arcanum, Ohio, March 28, 1860.	Ottawa, March 28, 1805.	Ottawa.
Prouty, S. S., Onondaga Co., N. Y., July 31, 1835.	Prairie City June, 1856.	Topeka.
Pierson, Cora, Batavia, N. Y., Feb. 3, 1862.	Lawrence, April 7, 1875.	Lawrence.
Pease, Mrs. C. A., Boston, Mass., Jan. 20.	Lawrence, Kan., Spring of 1855.	Lawrence.
Palm, Mrs. Charlotta, Sweden, Oct. 10, 1835.	Lawrence, Kan., April 1, 1864.	Lawrence.
Palm, A., Sweden, April 30, 1835.	Bloomington, Kan., Aug. 7, 1858.	Lawrence.
Quinton, A. B., Iowa, January, 1855.	Topeka, ——, 1876.	Topeka.
Quick, A., Moorestown, N. J., July 16, 1828.	Topeka, Kan., Oct. 1, 1873.	
Quick, Mrs. A M., Tiffin, Ohio, July 10, 1835.	Topeka, Oct. 1, 1873.	
Quinon, W. M., Brown Co., Ohio, Dec. 24, 1852.	Leavenworth, Oct , 1876.	Topeka.

Name, Place and Date of Birth.	Place and Date of Settlement.	Present Residence
Ricker, Anthen S., Cherryfield, Me., April 23, 1817.	Kanwaka, Douglas Co., Nov. 5, 1866	Kanwaka.
Ricker, Jane M., Hingham, Mass , April 10, 1816	Kanwaka, Nov. 5, 1866.	Kanwaka.
Ricker, Leonora S., La Prairie, Ill , October 12, 1856.	Kanwaka, Nov. 5, 1866.	Kanwaka.
Ricker, A. S. M., Portland, Me., October 10, 1817.	Kanwaka, Nov. 3, 1866.	Douglas Co.
Robinson, M. L., Fitchburg, Mass., May 29, 1846.	Lawrence, Nov. 11, 1867.	Lawrence.
Robinson, J. M., Barre, Mass., May 28, 1821.	Lawrence, Nov. 11, 1867.	Lawrence.
Richardson, Asa, N. H., April 9, 1812.		Lawrence.
Rothrock, J. B., Pa., January 26, 1836.	Lawrence, March 10, 1858.	
Read, Fred W., Bedford, Westchester county, N. Y., December 25, 1831.	Lawrence, ——, 1857.	Lawrence.
Rowley, J. P., South Byron, N. Y., July 4, 1849.	Topeka, ——, 1860.	Topeka.
Read, A. M , New Haven, Conn , March 18, 1842.	Wabaunsee, ——, 1856.	Wabaunsee.
Reading, James A., Frankfort, Ky., May 16, 1819.	Lyndon, Osage Co., ——, 1867.	Lawrence.
Ross, Mrs. Abigail L., N. J., April 17, 1843.	Atchison, Aug. 10, 1873.	Baldwin City.
Reed, Hona, Warsaw, Ill., September 3, 1859.	Topeka, May, 1869.	Topeka.
Rahskopf, Jos., Canada West, May 10, 1835.	Wisconsin, October 18, 1847.	Lawrence.
Rahskopf, M. J , Illinois, December 6,1844.	Lawrence, ——	
Reid, G. N., Kansas, September 8, 1863.	Wyandotte, September 8, 1863.	Lawrence.
Rowley, Emmet, Ohio, October 1. 1850	Topeka, January 3, 1871.	Tecumseh.
Ritchie, John, Uniontown, Ohio, July 17. 1817.	Topeka, April 3, 1855.	Topeka.
Roberts, Samuel S., Massachusetts, May 21, 1833.	Council Grove, May 4, 1803.	Cedar Point.
Roberts, Lillian, Cedar Point, August 8, 1870.	Cedar Point, August 8, 1870.	Cedar Point.
Roberts, Ellen M., England, June 8, 1859.		
Root, Frank A., Binghampton, N. Y., July 3, 1837.	Lawrence, April 21, 1857.	Topeka.
Root, George Allen, Atchison, March 13, 1867.	Atchison, March 13, 1867.	Topeka.
Richardson, Mrs. E. W., Medfield, Mass., 1819.	Lawrence, June 2, 1870.	Lawrence.
Reisner, Henry, Lebanon Co., Pa., October 29 1831.	Leavenworth, April 5, 1853.	Topeka.
Roberts, W. I., Lyon Co., Kas., September 6, 1823.	Near Emporia, April 17, 1855.	Near Emporia.
Roberts, S. A., Manchester, Vt , June 3, 1839.	Lawrence August, 1869.	Topeka.
Rote, L. J., Oneco, Ill , September 3, 1854	Franklin, March 1, 1856.	
Ricksecker, G. V., St. Joseph, Ind. August 4, 1837.	Ottawa, Kansas, Oct. 5. 1866.	Hutchinson, Kan.
Reynolds, Samuel, England, April 12, 1823.	Lawrence, March 30, 1855.	Lawrence.
Reynolds, A. T., Canada East, May 21, 1818.	Lawrence, March 10, 1857.	Lawrence.
Richey, W. S., St. Charles, Mo., July 18, 1817.	Lawrence, Kansas, ——	
Richardson, M. E., Wisconsin, May 14, 1854.	Lawrence, Oct 6, 1870.	Lawrence.
Richardson, Mabel E., Wis., February 2, 1865.	Lawrence, October 6, 1870.	Lawrence.
Rushmer, G. E., Columbus, O , December 19, 1860.	Lawrence, ——	Douglas Co.
Rossington, Wm. H., Galena, Ill., July 31, 1848.	Topeka, November 23, 1870.	Topeka.
Ray, John W., Madison Co., O., August 21, 1833.	Douglas county, March 30, 1857.	Douglas Co.
Reeder, Ida B., Hollidaysburg, Pa., December 14, 1854.	Lecompton, June 15, 1872.	Lecompton.
Randolph, W. W., Illinois, April 1, 1831.	Douglas county, June 11, 1854.	Douglas Co.
Richmond, M., Washington City.		Denver, Col.
Richey, J. T., Adams Co., Ill. January 20, 1847.	North Lawrence, Jan. 20, 1870,	Lawrence.
Reedy, Lewis, Ross county, Ohio, July 14, 1860.	Lawrence, October, 1870.	Lawrence.
Richardson, A. M., Franklin, Mass. July 28, 1822.	Lawrence, Kan., June 2, 1870.	Lawrence.
Ridgway, J C., Ohio county, Ky. January 25, 1814	Shawnee county, April 10, 1855.	Tecumsuh Tp.
Reed, Wm., Mercer county, Pa., January 20, 1824.	Shawnee county, May 21, 1857.	Monmouth Tp.
Richardson, James C., Madison Co., Tenn., Jan. 12, 1825.	Leavenworth Co., Apr 10, 1855	Douglas Co.
Root, Charles, Bucks Co , Pa., November 1, 1830.	Lecompton, May 1, 1859.	Lawrence.
Rastall, John E , Cheltenham, Eng., July 23, 1840.	Topeka, August, 1856.	Burlingame.
Roe, Wm., Yorkshire, Eng., January 6, 1831.	Coal Creek, Douglas county, May 15, 1855.	Vinland.
Roe, Margaret, Toronto, Canada, November 27, 1832.	Coal Creek, Douglas county, May 15, 1855.	Vinland.
Roboler, Mrs. E. A., Kentucky, March 5,1825.	Jefferson county, April 16, 1857.	
Radges, Samuel, Birmingham, Eng., May 24, 1840.	Fort Dodge, September. 1867.	Topeka.
Rush, Irena, Indiana, November 18, 1857.	Lawrence, September 30, 1868.	Lawrence.
Rush, Anna, Indiana, May 12, 1862.	Lawrence, September 30, 1867.	Lawrence.
Rose, W. A., N. Y., November 15, 1836.	Leavenworth, April 14, 1858.	Leavenworth.
Robinson, C., Hardwick, Mass , July 21, 1818.	Lawrence, July, 1854.	Lawrence.
Ridlon, Peter W., Saco, Me., August 20, 1810.	Gardner, March 5, 1869	Gardner.
Robertson, S. E., Peru, Ind., May 28, 1857.	Topeka, November 28, 1869.	Melvern.
Robenson, J , 1st Tenor.		
Ripley, J , Bb. Clarionet.		
Rankin, W. A., Ripley, Ohio, Sept. 15, 1831.	Black Jack, Douglas Co., April 23, 1857.	Lawrence.
Rankin, L. Lou, Paris, Ill , Sept. 20, 1857.	Black Jack, Douglas Co , Sept. 1, 1857.	Lawrence.
Rankin, Dora J., Black Jack, Kan., Oct. 26, 1858.	Douglas county, Oct. 26, 1858.	Lawrence.
Rankin, P. D., Columbus, Ohio, Dec. 29, 1831.	Douglas county, Sept. 1, 1857.	Lawrence.
Raynolds, Arthur Palmyra, Nov 19, 1859.	Palmyra, November 19, 1859.	Baldwin City.
Rote, Paul W., Clinton Co., Pa. Sept., 30, 1838.	Douglas county, July 4, 1854.	Lawrence.
Rote, Sarah, Fulton Co., Ill., January 6, 1842.	Leavenworth, April, 1855.	Lawrence.
Rote, Mary L., Douglas Co., Kansas, Jan. 12, 1860	Douglas county, Jan 12 1869.	Lawrence.
Rote, Ida B., Douglas County, Kan., April 12, 1870.	Douglas county, April 12, 1870.	Lawrence.
Rote, Clara J , Douglas Co., Jan. 27, 1872.	Douglas county, Jan 27, 1872.	Lawrence.
Rote, Elmer P., Douglas Co., Nov. 12, 1874.	Douglas county, Nov. 12, 1874.	Douglas Co.
Rigby, Geo. W., Kennebeck Co , Me., July 30, 1834.	Topeka, October, 1877.	Topeka.
Russ, Wm. W., Vermont, May 12, 1862.	Junction City, Sept. 12, 1876.	Lawrence.
Ross, Kate J., Topeka Kansas, June 8, 1861.	Topeka, June 8, 1861.	Topeka.

Name, Place and Date of Birth.	Place and Date of Settlement.	Present Residence
Rushmer, H. J., Quebec, Canada, April 25, 1833.	Lawrence, April 19, 1867.	
Rushmer, Gorten E., Columbus, O., Dec. 19, 1860.	Lawrence, April 19, 1867.	
Rushmer, H. F., Columbus, Ohio, June 14, 1863.	Lawrence, ——, 1867.	Lawrence.
Richardson, M. E.. Wisconsin, May 14, 1854.	Lawrence, October 15, 1870.	Lawrence.
Rayson, Thomas, England, Jan. 9, 1832.	Eudora, December 10, 1864	Eudora.
Rankin, Amanda J., Columbus, O., Dec. 29, 1853.	Lawrence, September, 1857.	Wakarusa.
Ryan, A. J., Virginia, May 4, 1813.	Topeka, April 15. 1860.	Topeka
Rankin, John K., Indiana, Nov. 3, 1837.	Douglas county, May 1, 1859.	Lawrence.
Ross, J. B., Ohio, Dec. 18, 1822.	Jefferson county Aug. 20, 1854.	Baldwin City.
Raymond, Lizzie D., Michigan, Feb. 18, 1838.	Douglas county, April, 1861.	
Rowley, Mrs. Lyman, Adams Co., Pa., June 1, 1837.	Douglas county, May, 1855.	Leavenworth.
Raymond, Harry L , Battle Creek, Mich., Sept. 4, 1858.	Lawrence, ——, 1861.	Lawrence.
Raymond, W. G., Iowa, March 2, 1859	Leavenworth, ——, 1870.	Kansas City, Mo
Richards, Sophia D., Germany, July 5, 1849.	Ohio, May, 1856.	Douglas.
Ross, J. E., Warren, Mass., March 2, 1855.	Lawrence, September 30, 1855	Lawrence.
Roseburg, Emma B., Pittsburgh, ——	—— October, 1866.	
Reed, W. S., Lawrence County, Pa., June 26, 1854.	Lawrence, Sept. 11, 1878.	Lawrence.
Richey, Mrs. R. C., St. Louis, January 24, 1849.	North Lawrence, Jan. 20, 1870.	Lawrence.
Rice, Harvey D., Massachusets, November 8, 1821.	Topeka, April 1, 1856.	Topeka.
Rice, Mary A., New York, December 4, 1827.	Tecunseh, October 1, 1859.	Topeka.
Reynolds, J , Ohio, October, 20, 1848.	Cottonwood Falls, March 4, 1869.	Elmdale.
Reynolds, Wm., Rhode Island, June 11, 1819.	Lawrence, March 30, 1863	Lawrence.
Reynolds, P. G., Elmira, New York, Nov. 3, 1827.	Lawrence, May 9, 1857.	Dodge City.
Reicheniker, George B., Ohio, November 10, 1843.	Wyandotte, August 1, 1857.	Wyandotte.
Reynolds, S. M., North Carolina, Sept. 21, 1828.	Douglas county, Nov 15, 1855.	Douglas County.
Richards, C. H., Michigan, Oct. 20, 1833.	Douglas county, March 30, 1857	Lawrence.
Reading, I. W., Alton Ill., Jan. 28, 1851.	Osage county, October 15, 1867.	Topeka.
Ridenour, P. D , Union Co., Ind , May 5, 1831.	Lawrence, March 15, 1857.	Lawrence.
Ridenour, Sarah L., Green Co., May 38, 1836	Lawrence, March 15, 1858.	Lawrence.
Ridenour, Katie L., Douglas Co., Aug. 14, 1861.	Lawrence, August 14, 1864.	Lawrence.
Ridenour, Eddie M., Douglas Co., April 9, 1867.	Lawrence, April 9, 1867	Lawrence.
Ridenour, Alice B., Douglas Co., April 7, 1872.	Lawrence, April 7, 1872	Lawrence.
Ridenour, Ethel B., Douglas Co., Oct. 15, 1877.	Lawrence, October 15, 1877.	Lawrence.
Rutherford, O. R , Lancaster, Ohio, Nov. 4, 1855.	Lawrence, February 20, 1879.	
Rushmore. G. H., Albany, N. Y., Nov. 7, 1827.	Leavenworth, May 12 1858.	Grantville.
Ripley, J. W., Coventry, Vt , March 23, 1804	Topeka, March 10, 1869.	Topeka.
Riggs, Jos. E , Portsmouth, Ohio. August 31, 1837.	Lawrence, September 27, 1863.	Lawrence.
Rule, J. W., Virginia, Aug. 23, 1834.	Leavenworth Co., April 26, 1877.	Leavenworth Co.
Rule, Peninah. Wayne Co., Ind., June 30, 1832.	Leavenworth Co., April 26, 1877.	Leavenworth Co.
Roberts, W. H	Paola, Kansas, ——	
Reed, Fitch, Richmond, Ontario Co., N. Y., July 28, 1814.	Wakarusa, July 20, 1869	Wakarusa.
Rue, C. B., New York, Dec. 1, 1824.	Near Black Jack, April 11, 1856.	Near Black Jack.
Roberts, A. S , Ohio, Jan. 7, 1841.	Shawnee county, April 15, 1856.	Tonganoxie, Leavenworth Co.
Russell, J., New London, N. H., Oct. 13, 1833.	Lyon county, March 1, 1857.	Wakarusa.
Rippey, W. D., Indiana, 1833.	Doniphan county, ——, 1856.	Severance, Doniphan Co.
Rushmore. H. C.. Leavenworth, Sept. 6 1858.	—— —— 1858.	Grantville, Jeff. Co.
Richards, Frank W., Ogdensburg, N. Y., June 22, 1844.	Topeka, May 5, 1879.	Topeka.
Rankin, Alexander, Ohio, 1834.	Douglas county, May 1857.	Lawrence.
Rogers, H. B , Susquehanna Co., Pa., Sept. 5, 1830.	Lawrence, March 1, 1871.	Lawrence.
Roach, H. T., Estell, Co.. Ky., April 28, 1836.	Leavenworth, June 7, 1854.	
Rogers, Clarkson, Eudora, June 29, 1839.		
Read, Fred W., Bedford, N. Y., Dec. 21, 1831	Lawrence, March 17, 1857.	Lawrence.
Rice, Samuel, Colored, Missouri December. 1838.	Douglas county, March 11, 1868.	Douglas Co.
Russell, Sheldon C., New York City, April 1. 1836.	Lawrence, April 19, 1856.	
Rushmore, Helen A., New York, June 4, 1837.	Leavenworth, ——, 1858,	Grantville.
Richards, O. G., Michigan, Jan. 12, 1836.	Douglas county, Aug. 15, 1856.	Douglas Co.
Rogers, George C., Piermont, N. H., Nov. 22, 1839.	Eureka, Greenwood county, Jan. 18. 1871	Eureka
Reynolds, Clarkson, Randolph Co., N. C., July 7, 1828.	Baldwin City, June 10, 1857.	Baldwin City.
Reynolds, Olinda B., Wayne Co , Ind., Jan. 16, 1832.	Baldwin City, June 10, 1857.	Baldwin City.
Rogers, James, Oxford, N. H.,(Oct. 18, 1826.	Burlingame, April 20. 1856.	Burlingame.
Rawlings, Thomas E., Pennsylvania, Sept. 26, 1840.	Barton county, March 4, 1877.	Great Bend.
Rawlings, Sarah C., Virginia, Sept. 7, 1847.	Barton county, March 4, 1877.	Great Bend.
Rottman, Mrs. Anna E., Versailles, Ky., 1835.	Lawrence, ——. 1865.	
Rudolph, Edward W., Philadelphia, Pa , Jan. 1, 1821.	Shawnee county, near Topeka, March 15, 1855	Wakarusa, Shawnee Co.
Richards, John F , Virginia, Oct. 23, 1834.	Leavenworth, March 4, 1857.	Leavenworth.
Reese, Samuel, Dayton, Ohio, Dec. 17, 1825.	Lynn Creek, Shawnee Co., May 10, 1856.	North Topeka.
Roberts, H. M., Lyon Co , Kas., Oct. 21, 1858.	Lyon county, Kansas, ——	Lyon Co., Kansas.
Rankin, M. A., Ironton, Ohio.	Lawrence, July 4, 1869.	Lawrence.
Bankin, A. V.		Lawrence.
Ridgway, R. M., Warren Co., N. J., Sept. 13, 1833.	Lawrence, October 15, 1865.	Lawrence.
Ryus, W. H., Monterey, N. Y , July 12, 1841	Wyandotte, Kansas, ——	Wyandotte.
Rogers, Solon, Hendricks Co , Ind., June 2, 1843.	Hesper, Douglas connty, March, 1867.	Prairie City.
Ross, Henry T., Warren, Mass., Dec. 12, 1845.	Lawrence, Sept. 30, 1855.	Lawrence.

Name, Place and Date of Birth.	Place and Date of Settlement.	Present Residence
Riddle, J. R., Clintonville, Pa., April 1, 1844.	Lawrence, May 30, 1868.	Topeka, Kansas.
Russell, Josephine, Coles Co., Ill., March 6, 1846.	Clinton, October 1, 1854.	
Russell, Carl, Lawrence, Oct. 4, 1867.	Lawrence, October 4, 1867	
Reed, Chas. H., Williamstown, Mass., March 25, 1859.	Lawrence, November 4, 1878.	Lawrence.
Randall, Reuben, Bolton, Mass., Oct. 4, 1832.	Lawrence, ——, 1855.	
Randall L., Missouri.	Lawrence, ——, 1854	
Randall, Susan, Kansas, November, 1868.	Lawrence, ——	
Randall, Nellie, Kansas, February, 1870.	Lawrence, ——	
Randall, Jennie, Kansas, May, 1873.	Lawrence, ——	
Randall, Carrie, Kansas, January, 1875.	Lawrence, ——	
Randall, C. R., Kansas, December. 1879.	Lawrence, ——	
Ross, J. P., Warren, Worcester Co., Mass., April 6, 1839.	Lawrence, September 30, 1854.	Lawrence.
Ross, Mrs J. P., Dundee, Yates Co., N. Y., May 21, 1845	Lawrence, November 2, 1855	Lawrence.
Ryan, Mrs. A. J., Ohio, Miami Co., March 27, 1827.	Topeka, Shawnee County, April 20, 1869.	Topeka.
Reinheimer, Samuel, Ohio, April 19, 1846.	Lawrence, September 10, 1869.	Lawrence.
Redmon, Mrs. J T., St. Louis.		
Rogers, E. F., Kentucky, Nov. 29, 1830.		Kansas City.
Reeine, W. K., Tiffin, Ohio, March 9, 1856.	Lawrence, July, 1872.	Lawrence.
Ross, Pitt, Milwaukee, Wis , Dec 8, 1855.	Topeka, August, 1856.	Lawrence.
Rutherford, W. F , Baltimore, May 5, 1858	Ottawa, Franklin, County, Feb. 20, 1879.	
Rayson, E. A., Philadelphia, Pa , Feb. 19, 1860.	Eudora, June 3, 1865.	Eudora.
Rayson, M. A., Warrickshire, Eng. Feb 27, 1833.	Eudora, June 3, 1865.	Eudora.
Rice, John H , Greenville, Tenn , Nov. 14, 1824.	Miami County, Sept., 21, 1865.	Paola
Russell Ed., Plymouth, N. H., Feb., 9, 1833.	Doniphan County, August, 1856.	Lawrence
Russell, Iohia, Blackiston, Guernsey Co., Ohio, July 20, 1842.	Doniphan County, May, 1854.	Lawrence.
Read, A. M., New Haven, Ct., March, 28. 1842.	Wabaunsee Co., April 22, 1856.	Wabaunsee Co
St. John, John P., Franklin Co., Ind., Feb. 25, 1833.	Olathe, April 7, 1869.	Topeka.
Smith, C. C. Patrick Co., Virginia, Oct. 11, 1831.	Cottonwood, October, 1857.	Chase Co.
Sturgis, Dr P. M , Uniontown, Pa , ——, 1816	Iowa Point.	Topeka.
Sherman, Pat., Ind., ——, 1840	Leavenworth, 1866.	Topeka.
Sheafor, Frank P., Fairfield, Ia., Aug. 11, 1855.	Coffey county, Nov , 1865.	Kansas City.
Shimmons, J. H., Manchester, Eng , Feb. 6, 1827.	Lawrence, March 12, 1855.	Lawrence.
Sawyer, James, Thetford, Vt., Dec 25, 1825.	Lawrence, Sept., 1854.	Vinland, N. J.
Smith, F. M., Ala., ——, 1823.	Ft. Leavenworth, Dec., 1842.	Leavenworth.
Smith, E. F., Missouri, ——, 1837.	Leavenworth, August, 1856.	Leavenworth.
Sheats, R., Pennsylvania, Feb. 8, 1830.	Douglas Co., April 5, 1879.	Leavenworth Co
Savage, I. O., Moravia, N. Y., Sept. 30, 1833.	Bellville, 1871.	Bellville.
Sykes, J. B., Philadelphia, Jan. 25, 1834.	——, 1866.	
Streeter, Ellen E., Erie Co., Pa., Oct. 27, 1833.	Douglas county, May, 21, 1856	Abilene.
Simmons, S. A., Ohio, Dec. 25, 1833.	Lawrence, March, 1878.	Lawrence.
Spurlock, J. H., Platte Co., Mo., July 15, 1857.	Lecompton, March, 1850	Perry.
Stanton, A. L., Newport, Ind., Sept. 8, 1845.	Hesper, September 10, 1868.	Lawrence
Scrogge, Maggie E., Ohio, Feb 1, 1843.	Wyandotte, April 27, 1858.	Wyandotte.
Stubbs, S M., Wayne Co , Ind., Dec. 23, 1849.	Lawrence, May 16, 1879.	Lawrence.
Sedgwick, M., Oneida Co , N. Y., March 4, 1818.	Kanwaka, April 1, 1864.	Douglas Co.
Speer, John, Kittanning, Pa., Dec. 27, 1817.	Lawrence, September 27, 1854.	Lawrence.
Searl, A. D., Southampton, Mass., July 6, 1831.	Lawrence, September 15, 1854.	Lawrence and Col.
Searl, R. S , Southampton, Mass., Aug. 18, 1844.	Lawrence, September 15, 1865.	Solomon.
Spaulding, Stella E . Illinois, Oct. 5, 1859	——, August 9, 1877.	
Still, S. S. Mrs., Holten. Me., Feb. 8, 1856.	Lawrence, October 20, 1857.	Near Eudora.
Smith, G. C., Phillips, Me., Oct. 3, 1860	Lawrence, September 1, 1877.	
Stocker, W. F., Scranton, Pa., Oct. 4, 1850.	Topeka, Nov. 11, 1876	Anthony.
Shortridge, Mrs., West Virginia, April 13, 1833.	Manhattan, Sept. 1, 1859.	Manhattan.
Seymour, A. B., Haverhill, N. H., July 26, 1850.	Irving, August 6, 1867.	Clyde, Kan.
Strong, N. Z., Spafford, Onandaga Co., N. Y., Aug. 31, 1827.	Leavenworth, May 7, 1856.	Lawrence.
Shoner, A., Germany, March 25, 1837.	Leavenworth, July 15, 1857	Newman.
Starkey, G. A., Waynesville, Ill., May 9, 1858.	Humboldt, Kan., Sept. 12, 1862.	Lawrence.
Sloan, C. M., Indianapolis, Ind., May 26, 1833.		Newark.
Simpson, Mary L., Lawrence, Aug. 11, 1861.	Lawrence, August 11, 1861.	Lawrence.
Strahan, A. P., Scott Co., Ill., Jan. 2, 1835.	Kanwaka, July 1, 1860.	Kanwaka.
Strahan, Mary J . Callaway Co . Ky , May 15. 1846.	Kanwaka, Feb 1, 1856.	Kanwaka.
Shank, William, Hancock Co., Ill., May 12, 1856.	Southern Kansas, Fall of 1850	Douglas Co.
Sayer, J. P.. Attica, N. Y., Dec. 26, 1845.	Paola, Kansas, August 14, 1874.	Lawrence.
Sutliff, Charlie B., Kansas. Sept. 6, 1869		Lawrence.
Sutliff, Frankie D., Kansas, June 22, 1867.		Lawrence.
Stevens, W. J. T., Ill., Nov. 13, 1867.		Cass Co , Kan.
Stauffer, J. S., Fayette Co., Pa., July 24, 1842.	Atchison Co , June 1, 1857.	Leavenworth City.
Short, Celia C., Oneida Co, N. Y., June 20, 1836	Lawrence, October 16, 1865.	Lawrence
Shaw, W. F , Maryland, June 11, 1847.	Wyandotte, Kan., Aug 12, 1857.	Wyandotte.
Speck, W. W., Duncannon, Pa., Dec. 2, 1849.	Douglas Co., Jan. 20, 1861.	Douglas Co
Sands, J. Irving, Lawrence, Jan. 20. 1861.		
Shaft, D. P., Howell, Livingston Co., Mich , Dec. 2, 1840	Silver Creek, Chase Co., Dec. 23, 1857.	Silver Creek.
Simmons, J. D., Jackson Co., Mo., Dec. 22, 1848.	Palmyra, May 14, 1857.	

Name, Place and Date of Birth.	Place and Date of Settlement.	Present Residence
Stark, Howell D., Franklin Co., Pa., July 20, 1841.	Independence, July 19, 1870.	Topeka.
Stark, Mary J., Ohio, Sept. 14, 1847.	Independence, July 19, 1870.	Topeka.
Stark, Caray D., Independence, March 9, 1873.	Independence, March 9, 1873.	Topeka.
Sherman, W. P., New Haven. Conn., Feb 15, 1837.	Douglas Co., May 1, 1876.	Lawrence.
Skeet, Wm, Ufferton, Eng., May 8, 1842.	Jefferson Co., April 16, 1869.	
Spencer, Rooka, Wis, Feb. 17. 1860.	Lawrence.	Lawrence.
Sternberg, Leo. Nuremburg, Bavaria, April 8, 1840.	Lawrence, 1865.	Lawrence.
Smith, Peter, Abington, Ind., Aug 24, 1851.		North Topeka.
Swift, Frank B., Brunswick, Me., Jan. 17. 1835	Lawrence, March 28, 1855.	
Stuart, E. A., North Carolina, Sept. 10, 1856.		Lawrence.
Simmons, R E., Hancock Co., Ind., Jan. 20, 1854.	Holton, Jackson Co., Feb 22, 1879.	Hays City.
Shurp, George W., England, ——	Lawrence, April 25, 1857.	Washington, Kan.
Simpson, S. N., Deerfield, N. H., Oct. 3, 1816.	Lawrence, Sept. 28, 1854.	Lawrence.
Savage, Forrest, Hartford, Vt., Sept. 27, 1827.	Wakarusa, Sept. 1, 1854.	Lawrence.
Seiler, Martin, Reading, Pa, March 31, 1822.	Ridgeway, Osage Co., May 14, 1857	Ridgeway.
Scott, C. C., Union Co., Me., Oct. 5, 1841.	—— ——, June 15, 1857.	
Simons, Harry, Troy, Ohio, Jan. 15, 1840.	Lawrence, Dec. 7, 1867.	Lawrence.
Seman, W. H., Mansfield, Ohio, April, 28, 1840.	Fort Scott, Sept. 9, 1853.	Lawrence.
Simmons, C. J., Union City, Ind., Feb. 25, 1858.	Lawrence, June 19, 1868.	Lawrence.
Shirley, W., Illinois, February 26, 1828.	Douglas Co., August, 1854.	
Smith, E. A., Andover, Vt., May 4, 1833	Lawrence, December, 1859.	Lawrence.
Starnel, G. W, Tennessee, August 24, 1827	Leavenworth, March 14, 1855.	Leavenworth.
Sheets, James W., Pennsylvania, January 21, 1861.	Lawrence, March 19, 1879.	Lawrence.
Stevenson, Wm. G., Ripley county, Ind., Dec. 25, 1822.	Clinton, Doug. Co., Feb. 20. 1857.	Clinton, Doug. Co.
Scott, Chas. F., Kansas, September 7, 1860.	Allen Co., September 7, 1860.	Lawrence.
Stirling, S. J., Philadelphia, Pa, Feb 22, 1835.	Leavenworth Co, April 5, 1855.	Lawrence.
Smith, J. C., Ridgely, Mo., February 28, 1834.	Medina, May 8, 1856	
Smith, W. K., New Jersey, August 14, 1816	Osawkie, Jeff. Co., Oct. 13, '55.	Lawrence.
Starr, J. T., Fairfield county, Ct, Oct. 31, 1806.	Baldwin City, Oct. 15, 1856	Baldwin City.
Simmons, H., Ohio, March 1, 1828.	Lawrence, August 1, 1868.	Lawrence.
Simmons, Mrs. E. A, Ohio, June 10, 1838.	Lawrence, August 1, 1868.	Lawrence.
Shannon, Osbun, Belmont Co., Ohio, Feb. 7, 1842.	Lecompton, May 7, 1857.	
Smith, Ed. G., Brown Co., Kansas, Aug. 22, 1859.	Brown county, August 22, 1859.	Topeka.
Sawyer, S. W., Maine, February 20, 1832.	Leavenworth, 1875	Lawrence.
Skofstad, M. J., Wisconsin, January 27, 1842.	Howard county, July, 1869.	Lawrence.
Skofstad, Julia N., Wisconsin, October 14, 1848	Lawrence. April 1, 1871.	Lawrence.
Spivey, R. M., Alabama, April 27, 1845.	Shawnee Co., January 20, 1869.	Topeka.
Staggers, B. S, Ohio, August 21, 1840.	Lawrence, June 2, 1855.	Lawrence.
Staggars, N. L., Iowa, April 30, 1861.	Lawrence.	Lawrence.
Smith, E. T., Ohio, September 15, 1822.	Douglas county, Oct 1, 1857.	Lawrence.
Sanderson, Thomas, Orkney, Scotland, Dec. 24, 1858	Lawrence, October 2, 1868.	Lawrence.
Schinn, Dr. Charles, Germany, October 13, 1839	Lawrence, August 6, 1869.	Lawrence.
Schell, Frank M, Iowa City, Iowa. July 18, 1856.	Douglas Co., November 20, 1878.	Lawrence.
Steel, John McLeon, Clinton, Kansas, April 12. 1860.	Clinton, April 12, 1869.	Lawrence.
Steel, Charles A, Clinton, Kansas, April 26, 1867.	Clinton, April 26, 1867.	Lawrence.
Steel, James L., Clinton, Kansas, Sept. 13, 1871.	Clinton, Sept. 13, 1871.	Lawrence.
Stout, Cora, Boston, January 17, 1861.	Emporia, April 18, 1879.	Lawrence.
Smith, C. W., Portage Co. Ohio, Dec. 7, 1832.	Lawrence, Sept. 12, 1854.	Lawrence.
Seymore, D. K. C, Erie, Penn., July 21, 1838.	Irving, June 1, 1861.	Clyde.
Sears, Chas., Herkimer Co., N. Y., Jan. 20, 1811.	Franklin Co., June 1870.	Williamsburg.
Shield, Joseph, Harrison, Ind., April 18, 1811.	Eudora, Doug. Co, Nov. 15, 1855.	Eudora.
Still, J. M., Lee county, Va., February 5, 1826.	Blue Mound, Douglas Co., Oct 22, 1854.	Eudora.
Sears, C. M., Lewis Co., N. Y., Nov. 26, 1829.	Eudora, July 6. 1859	Eudora.
Scudder, T. W., Huntington, N. Y., Sept. 15, 1833.	Lawrence, April 29, 1855.	Topeka.
Scudder, Helen B., Albany, N. Y., April 25, 1839.	Topeka, Dec. 17, 1878.	Topeka.
Scott, Lewis, B., Bucks Co, Pa., Jan. 14, 1821.		
Savage, Miss G W., Reading, Penn., June 11, 1855.	Lawrence, March, 1867.	Lawrence.
Smith, J. D., Corning, N. Y., Feb. 4, 1804.	Topeka, August 30, 1841.	Topeka
Soule, J. S, Wilksville, May 27:	De Soto, April 10, 1861.	El Dorado.
Stearner, Harry, 2 Topeka Band.		Topeka.
Stevenson, Topeka Band.		
Slagle, Topeka Band.		
Smith, Ed., Lancaster Co., Pa., Feb. 28, 1818.	Twin Mound, Oct. 25, 1857.	Osage Co.
Snyder, G. H., New York, Jan. 12, 1828.	Lawrence, Oct. 15, 1854.	Jefferson Co.
Sherman, D. S., Bridgeport, Conn., Oct. 27, 1828.	Topeka, Dec. 3, 1869.	Lawrence.
Speer, Georgiana, Hodge Ohio, March, 1849.	Ellis Co, March 20, 1878.	Ellis Co.
Siler, A. C., Ohio, April 21, 1840.	Douglas Co., Jan. 15, 1871.	Jefferson Co.
Snedden, Mrs. Mary C., Selinsgrove, Pa., Mch. 25, '51.	Wyandotte City, June 21, 1857.	Wyandotte.
Smith, Anna G., Blue Mound, Kansas, June 30, 1860.	Douglas Co., June 30. 1860.	Blue Mound.
Stimpson, Fred. E, Boston, Mass., May 13, 1837.	Lawrence, Jan. 10, 1872.	Lawrence.
Stimpson, Mrs. Fred. E, Boston, Mass., Nov 19, 1834.	Lawrence, Sept 22, 1872.	Lawrence.
Stimpson, Mary G., Boston, Mass., Sept. 14, 1865.	Lawrence, Sept. 22, 1872.	Lawrence.
Stimpson, Edwin Fiske, Jamaica Plains, Mass., Aug. 11, 1867.	Lawrence, Sept. 22, 1872.	Lawrence.
Stimpson, Wm. C., Jamaica Plains, Mass., June 8, '70.	Lawrence, Sept. 22, 1872.	Lawrence.
Stone, A P., Rowe, Mass., Sept. 25, 1836	Reno, Leav. Co., March, 12, 1874.	Reno, Leav. Co.
Strong, E. T., Leavenworth, Kansas, Jan. 2, 1860.	Leavenworth, Jan. 2, 1860.	Ottawa.
Sharp, Lydia S., Salem, Ohio.		Visiting at Topeka.
Stuart, Fannie, Monroe, Mich., Jan. 21, 1856.	Lawrence, August 29, 1877.	Lawrence.

Name, Place and Date of Birth.	Place and Date of Settlement.	Present Residence
Sanders, H. B., Germany, Nov. 2, 1835.	Kanwaka, February, 1860.	
Sanders, C. B., Willow Springs, Kas., Aug. 18, 1871.	Willow Springs, Aug. 18, 1871.	
Sawyer, L. M., Cleveland, Ohio.	Topeka, Sept. 16, 1855.	
Storms, Geo. T., Girard county, Ky., Jan. 19, 1830.	Douglas Co., November, 1862.	Douglas Co.
Sutliff, Addie M., Lawrence, Kas, Feb. 23, 1861.	Lawrence, Feb. 23, 1861.	Lawrence.
Sutliff, Jennie S., Lawrence, July 27, 1863.	Lawrence, July 27. 1863.	Lawrence.
Sutliff, J. B., New York, April 1, 1838	Lawrence, March, 1860	Wakarusa.
Skinner, Mrs. E., Yates Co., N. Y., Dec. 2, 1834.	Lawrence, November, 1855.	Lawrence.
Saunders, H. F., Mass., November 14, 1822.	Lawrence, Oct. 6 1851	Lawrence.
Smith, Miss Nannie, Wellington, Ohio, March 4, 1854.	Holton, September, 1869.	Topeka.
Spencer, W., New Haven, Conn., Oct. 18, 1866.	Lawrence, 1866.	Lawrence.
Stanley, Mr and Mrs. H. A., Mass, July 13, 1853.	Lawrence, December, 1863.	Lawrence.
Stevens, Geo. W., Ohio, June 12, 1822.	Lawrence, May 12, 1867.	Lawrence.
Simon, D., Germany, August 7, 1832.	Leavenworth. March, 1858.	Leavenworth.
Smith, H. B., Wellsboro, Pa., Feb. 22, 1832.	Osawatomie, May, 1858	Osawatomie.
Sands, James G., Gilbertstown, Pa., Aug. 21, 1833.	Lawrence, May 29, 1855.	Lawrence.
Sands, Mrs. Susie E., Winchester, N. H., Jan. 3, 1843.	Kanwaka, 1858.	Lawrence.
Sternberg, T. J., New York, Oct. 25, 1837.	Lawrence, Oct 15, 1857	Lawrence.
Stephens, Richard, England, June 30, 1820.	Palmyra, Feb. 16, 1856	Lawrence.
Schmidt, John M., Bayern, Ger.. July 25, 1835.	Peace, Reno Co., March 10, 1879.	Peace
Slonecker, J. G., Savannah, Ohio, March, 1851.	Topeka, April 27, 1872.	Topeka.
Sutliff, Helen B., Lawrence, Oct. 3, 1861.		
Swan, D. M., Jefferson Co., N. Y, Aug. 13, 1843.	Leavenworth, October 22, 1866.	Leavenworth.
Swan, Mrs. D. M., Maysville, Ky., Feb. 22, 1847.	Leavenworth, September, 1865.	Leavenworth.
Stuart, Sarah R., Monroe, Mich., April 3, 1846.	Douglas Co.. Aug. 25, 1877.	Lawrence.
Seervir, Dr. John G, Berne, Switz., March, 1827.	Lawrence, 1858.	Lawrence.
Seervir, Sarah C., Camden, N. J., 1831.	Lawrence, 1858.	Lawrence.
Shields, Prudence, Indiana, Jan. 3, 1855.	Neosho Co., 1869.	Douglas Co.
Shields, A. H., Illinois, September 9, 1850.	Douglas Co., 1855.	Douglas Co.
Spivey, Lina, Iowa, October 11, 1854	Jefferson Co., Aug., 1855.	Topeka.
Summerfield, M., Prussia, August 15, 1842.	Eudora, Aug. 1, 1857	Little Rock, Ark.
Summerfield, Mrs. M., Fulton, Ill., May 30, 1857.	Eudora, September, 1859	Little Rock, Ark.
Stevenson, E. H., New York, Nov. 10, 1846.	Leavenworth Co., Jan. 1, 1869.	Leavenworth.
Smith, Sarah A, Sheffield, Eng., Feb. 4, 1839.	Blue Mound, Douglas Co., March, 1855	Blue Mound,
Smith, Charlie F., Wakarusa, Dec. 11, 1868.	Blue Mound, Dec. 11, 1868.	Blue Mound.
Sutliff, Mrs. W. E., Bristol, Va, Dec. 14, 1831	Lawrence, October 19, 1857.	Lawrence.
Steele, L. S., Ross county, Ohio, Sept. 15, 1833	Clinton, Dong Co.. Jan. 1, 1857.	Lawrence.
Smith, Wm. H., Chatham, New York, Sept. 20, 1813.	De Soto, May 20, 1860.	DeSoto.
Stiner, Lizzie G, Garrettsville, Ohio, July, 1836.	Lawrence.	
Stevens. Esther R., Ohio, Feb. 13, 1828.	Lawrence. May 9, 1867.	Lawrence.
Sherman, Hattie A. Mrs, Ohio, Aug 14, 1842	Topeka, January 1 1870.	Lawrence.
Sherman, Ettie Miss, Iowa, Dec. 16, 1860.	Topeka, June 15, 1870.	Lawrence.
Snow, J. B., Westminster, Vt., June 28, 1850.	Salina, October 30, 1878.	Salina.
Seewin, Charles C., Oneida Co., N. Y., Nov. 29, 1855	Lawrence, November, 1859.	Lawrence.
Sille, George W.. Portage Co., Ohio, Feb. 12, 1823.	Neosho Rapids, Sept. 13, 1858	Eureka.
Sparaw, J S., Lancaster, Pa., April 26, 1843.	Holling. Sept. 27, 1860.	Holling
Shearer, George, Pennsylvania, March 20, 1856.	Lawrence, September, 1865.	Lawrence.
Stanton, S., Ohio, Aug. 20, 1832.	Marshall Co , June 19, 1858.	Tonganoxie.
Snider, G. N., Pennsylvania. Feb. 1, 1825.	Douglas Co , March 1, 1856	Topeka.
Shaw, Thos., Hawkins Co., Tenn., Aug. 28, 1847.	Kanwaka, October, 1854.	Kanwaka.
Shaw, Wm., Hawkins Co , Tenn., Feb. 11, 1849.	Kanwaka, October, 1854	Kanwaka.
Seaman, J. W.. Mt. Vernon, Ohio, ——, 1832.	Fort Scott, 1852.	Lawrence.
Steele, Alexander, Kentucky, May 15, 1826.	Douglas Co , Nov. 15, 1877	Wakarusa.
Smith, Mary B., Mound City, Kas., Dec. 21, 1860.	Linn Co., December 24, 1860.	Lawrence.
Stufel, A. J., Germany, Sept. 2, 1849.	Lawrence, February 29, 1877.	Lawrence.
Stufel, Ida, Germany, May 24, 1850.	Lawrence, February 29. 1878	Lawrence.
Stufel, Sophia, Germany, May 24. 1854.	Lawrence, February 28, 1875.	Lawrence.
Smith, Martin, Germany, Jan 1, 1832.	Leavenworth, June 15, 1857.	Leavenworth.
Smith, M. Mrs., Barreu Co., Ky.. Dec. 10, 1837.	Leavenworth, Nov. 20, 1861.	Leavenworth Co.
Strong, Charles F., Leavenworth, Aug. 2, 1856.	Leavenworth, August 2, 1856.	Lawrence.
Smith, H. T., Bucks Co., Pa , Oct. 24, 1850.	Mound City, April, 1860	Lawrence.
Smith, H. T. Mrs., Cincinnati, Ohio, Jan. 30, 1827.	Lawrence, October, 1866.	North Lawrence.
Savage, Joseph, Hartford, Vt , July 28, 1824	Lawrence, Sept. 15, 1854.	Lawrence.
Savage, Joseph Mrs., Deanstown, Scotland, March 5, 1834.	Lawrence, April, 1858.	Lawrence.
Storm, Anson. Ann Arbor, Mich , June 6, 1838.	Lawrence, March 18, 1857.	Lawrence
Scouten, D. W., New York, Feb. 12 1833	Douglas Co , August, 1856.	Douglas Co.
Stanley, E , Hendricks Co., Ind., April 7, 1847.	Douglas Co , Sept. 30, 1868.	Lawrence.
Sutherland, S. H., Lawrence, Jan. 2, 1858	Douglas Co , January 2, 1858.	Lawrence.
Saunders, Frank M , Wakarusa Tp., Dec. 9, 1856.	Near Lawrence, Dec. 9, 1856.	Lawrence.
Spencer, Selden P., New York, Dec. 19, 1835.	Lawrence, July 15, 1860.	Lawrence.
Stewart, Charles, Clark Co., Ky., Feb. 24, 1805.	Clinton, Doug. Co., Nov. 27, '59.	Leavenworth Co
Stirling, R., Scotland, Nov. 15, 1829.	Ft. Leavenworth, April 16, 1852.	Lawrence.
Sampson, T., Londonderry, N. H , Dec. 1, 1814.	Lawrence, Nov. 20, 1851.	Lawrence.
Sutliff, A. A., Marietta, Ohio, Nov. 27, 1836.	Lawrence, Nov. 24, 1859	Lawrence.
Stripp, R. C., New Haven, Conn., Jan. 11, 1858.	Topeka, June 8, 1878.	Topeka.
Safford, J., Royalton. Windsor Co , Vt., Aug. 27, 1827.	Lawrence,	Topeka.
Sterling, Wilson, Independence, W. Va. Dec. 25, 1835.	Abilene, October 9, 1871	Lawrence.
Simmons, J. D., Jackson, Mo., Dec. 22, 1848.	Baldwin City, May 14, 1854	
Simmons, Mrs. E. B., Montgomery, Ky., July 25, '25.	Baldwin City, May 14, 1857.	

Name, Place and Date of Birth.	Place and Date of Settlement.	Present Residence
Simmons, Adda B , Douglas Co., Dec. 30, 1859.	Baldwin City, December 30, 1859.	
Saunders, F. A , Haverhill, N. H., Feb. 23, 1829.	Irving, May 29, 1867.	Clyde.
Smith, W. H., Ohio, November 21, 1841.	Leavenworth Co., June 15, 1865	Leavenworth Co.
Swift, S. P., Ohio, April 15, 1822.		
Stevenson, Susan, Illinois, Jan. 10, 1843.	Clinton, May 12, 1856.	Clinton.
Swallow, John R., New Jersey, April 30, 1821.	Breckenridge county (now Lyon), July 15, 1857.	Topeka.
Stephens, C. B , New York, March 4, 1844.	Wyandotte, November, 1863.	Wyandotte.
Stout, Perlie, Ohio.		Lawrence.
Scripps, Herman C , Rushville, Ill , March 10, 1860.		
Sholes, D. C., Easton, Pa., May 8, 1859.	Lawrence, July 19, 1854.	Lawrence.
Schleifer, John, Chicago, Ill., Sept. 15, 1855.	Eudora, Douglas Co , Mar. 20, '57.	Lawrence.
Stevens, Phebe Gillpatrick, New Madison, Ohio, May 13, 1848.	Anderson Co., April 17, 1854	Leavenworth.
Stevens, Charles N., Livingston Co.,N. Y., Jan. 22, '44.	Leavenworth, September 1, 1868.	Leavenworth.
Searing, Clinton, Park county, Ind , July 1, 1827.	Twin Mound, Douglas county, October 14, 1864.	
Searing, Purlina, Park county, Ind.,'Oct. 31, 1829.	Twin Mound, Oct. 14, 1864.	
Stumbaugh, F. S., Franklin Co., Pa., April 14, 1817.	Rush county, Nov. 17, 1877.	Walnut City, Rush Co.
Stevenson, Frank, Green Castle, Ind., April 1, 1859.	Ottawa, July 11, 1879.	Ottawa.
Smith, C. W., West Granville, Wis , June 12, 1850.	Stockton, Rooks Co., Feb. 1, '79.	Stockton.
Stansfield. I. G., England, July 3, 1828.	Columbus, O., December 25, 1831.	Topeka.
Simmons, E. F., Ireland, Aug. 25, 1825.	Lawrence, April 1, 1857.	
Smith, H. C., Clinton county, Ohio, May 30, 1831.	North Lawrence, April 7, 1868.	North Lawrence.
Seckler, Oscar, Atchison, August 16, 1860.	Leavenworth, August 16, 1860.	Leavenworth
Stillmen, M. P., Berlin, N. Y., Nov. 27, 1833.	Lawrence, April 1, 1857.	Nortonville, Kan.
Stocks, Fred. A., Lena, Ill., March 25, 1863	Blue Rapids, April 17, 1872.	Lawrence.
Shannon, Geo., Knoxville, Tenn., Jan. 20, 1844.	Kansas, May 12, 1868.	DeSoto, Kan.
Schuls, C., Bavaria, Germany, August 29, 1852.	Douglas Co., March 1, 1876.	Blue Mound.
Surber, M. D., Indiana, March 30, 1829	Lawrence, December, 1858.	Perry, Kansas.
Surber, F. J., Indiana, February 28, 1842.	Clinton, June, 1858.	Perry, Kansas.
Stone, E. E., Akron. Ohio, Nov. 12, 1831.	Douglas county, May, 1858.	Lawrence.
Stone, James A , Hartford, Conn., May 28, 1833.	Pawnee, September, 1860.	Douglas Co.
Seetin, C. M., East Finley, Washington Co., Pa., Feb. 23, 1814.	Lawrence, October, 1850.	Lawrence.
Seetin, Thomas, Donegal Co., Ireland, March 15, 1813.	Lawrence, May 21, 1855.	Lawrence.
Stoul, Andrew, Circleville, Ohio, Jan. 30, 1837.	Baldwin City, May, 1857.	Baldwin.
Spraw, A. M., Ill., Feb. 28, 1858	Palmyra, March 3, 1860.	Holling, Kansas.
Starkweather, Charles, Missouri, Oct. 31, 1861.	Lawrence, March, 1862.	Lawrence.
Smith, Sidney W., Vermont, ——, 1812.	Topeka 1847.	Topeka.
Smith, Reuben F., New York, ——, 1840	Doniphan county, 1859.	Atchison.
Smiley, T. W., Buchanan Co., Mo., April 29, 1843.	Franklin county, 1856.	Leavenworth.
Speck, Fred., M. D., Carlisle, Pa , Nov. 24, 1818.	Wyandotte, May, 1857.	
Speck, Adelaide M., ——		
Smith, Mrs. M. O., Tennessee, Jan. 1, 1826.	De Soto, Kansas, 1860.	DeSoto.
Simpson, Wm. H., Lawrence. Jan. 19, 1858.	Lawrence, January 19, 1858.	Lawrence.
Shaft, John, Howell, Mich., Dec. 28, 1849.	Chase county, Dec. 22, 1857.	Chase Co.
Sutton, P. A., Blairsville, Pa., Feb. 2, 1850.	Burlingame, April 10, 1872.	Topeka.
Smith, H. H., Huron Co., Ohio, Sept. 14, 1817.	Kansas River, Jefferson county, April 20, 1857	Jefferson Co.
Sharp, Isaac, Lancaster Co , Pa., May 5, 1832.	Morris county, March 25, 1857.	Council Grove.
Smith, R. H., York Co., Pa., Oct. 10, 1834.	Topeka, April 25, 1876.	Lecompton.
Skinner, D. S., Albany Co., N Y, March 18, 1823.	Topeka, November 27, 1868.	Topeka.
Spencer, Selden G , Madison, Wis , June 17, 1860.	Lawrence, September 12, 1861.	Lawrence.
Stevens, A L., Bridport, Eng., July 5, 1842.	Jackson county, 1867.	Leavenworth.
Scouten, R., New York, May 4, 1808.	Deer Creek, Douglas county, October 14, 1855.	Belvoir.
Scouten, D. G., New York, June 24, 1757.	Deer Creek, Nov. 9, 1857.	Belvoir.
Shearer, V. I., Ellisville, Ill., April 15, 1850.	Lawrence, May 27, 1859	Lawrence.
Stevens, George F., East Brooksfield, Mass., May 17, 1850.	Topeka, May 17, 1855.	Douglas Co.
Springer, J. H., Monroe Co., Ky., Jan 25, 1819.	Coffey county, 1859	Jefferson Co.
Skiles, John K., Pennsylvania, Sept. 7, 1841.	Rice county, July 15, 1876	Rice Co.
Spencer, C. T., Kansas, Oct. 21, 1859	Douglas county, Oct. 21, 1859.	Big Springs.
Serene, Charles H., Ill., Nov. 16, 1860.	Lawrence, September 2, 1878.	Lawrence.
Stuart, Helen R , Kansas, Jan 1, 1876.	Lawrence, January 1, 1876.	Lawrence.
Stuart, Annis I., Mo., Sept. 13, 1843.		Lawrence.
Stimpson, Willie C., Boston, Mass , June 8, 1810.	Lawrence, September 22, 1872.	Lawrence
Stark, Andrew, North Lyme, Ct , March 8, 1831.	Lawrence, September 25. 1856.	Topeka.
Stark, Susan M., Chesterville. Ohio, August 14, 1836.	Linn county, Nov. 20, 1859.	Topeka.
Squires, H. C., Kentucky, Nov. 6, 1838.	Atchison county, March I, 1858.	Leavenworth.
Smith, N. R., Green county, Tenn., March 6, 1820.	Perry, October 22, 1858.	Perry.
Simmons, Fred., Lawrence, May 9, 1842.	Vinland, January 24, 1856.	Douglas Co.
Scott, George. Hopkins New York, 1860.	Atchison, 1869	
Schott, John F., Baltimore, Md.	Marion, Douglas county, 1857.	
Scroggs, J. B , Ohio, November, 24, 1837.	Wyandotte, August, 1866.	Wyandotte.
Simpson, Louisa, Prentiss, N. Y., March 15, 1846.	Lawrence, 1855	Lawrence.
Springer, C. H., Morgan county, Ill., Dec. 27, 1856.	Coffey county, May 8, 1861.	Jefferson Co., P. O. Lawrence.
Smyth, L. R., Illinois, Nov. 2, 1842.	Lawrence, October 31, 1876.	Lawrence.

Name, Place and Date of Birth.	Place and Date of Settlement.	Present Residence
Spencer, J. M., Depauville, N. Y., May 18, 1832.	Lawrence, September 30, 1877.	Lawrence.
Stanley, E. H., Attleboro, Mass., Feb. 26, 1854.	Miami county, Dec. 28, 1879.	
Simpson, B. F., Belmont county, Ohio Dec. 24, 1837.	Paola, March, 1857.	Paola.
Stanley, T. A., Attleboro, Mass., Oct. 6, 1826.	Osawatomie, April 8, 1869.	Lawrence.
Sears, L. A , Lawrence, August 15, 1860.	Lawrence, August 15, 1860.'	Lawrence.
Stiefel, B., Bavaria, Ger., November 19, 1851.	Lawrence, 1877.	Lawrence.
Smith, James, Eldersridge, Pa , Jan. 29, 1837.	Marshall county, March 25, 1860.	Marysville.
Smith, Jane, Galesburg, Ill., Jan. 17, 1844.	Marshall county. May 1. 1860.	Marysville.
Stonebraker, Sam A., Huntington Co., Pa., July 16, '32	Black Jack, April 23, 1856.	Black Jack.
Sprague, Sarah J., Lexington, Ky., March 27, 1828.		Lawrence.
Smith, J. G., Missouri.	Jefferson county, 1862.	Valley Falls.
Shirar, David, Indiana, A gust 14, 1848.	Lawrence, November 5, 1868.	Lawrence.
Smith, Jacob, Pennsylvania, June 24, 1831.	Topeka, March 17, 1857.	Topeka.
Smith, Chas. C., Nuremberg, Germany, Dec. 20, 1830.	10 miles south of Lawrence, Apr. 28, 1855	Same place.
Smith, Elizabeth, Leicester, England, Jan. 11, 1829.	10 miles south of Lawrence, Sept 20, 1855	Same place.
Shepley, F. B , Massachusetts, January 6, 1832.	Topeka, September 15, 1879.	Topeka.
Smith, William, Kansas, November 3, 1858.	Topeka.	Topeka.
Suttan, I. P., Osage county, Mo., Dec. 9, 1843.	Anderson county, June 1, 1855.	Garnett.
Still, S. S., Macon county, Mo., Dec. 7, 1851.	Douglas county, October 20, 1854.	Douglas Co.
Searl, Susie J., Southampton, Mass., Nov. 18, 1832.	Lawrence, November 18. 1857.	Lawrence.
Searl, A. D , jr., Lawrence, February 1, 1864.	Lawrence, February 1, 1864.	Lawrence.
Searl, Ella A., Lawrence, January 11, 1859.	Lawrence, January 11, 1859.	Lawrence.
Stone, David, England, June 19, 1836.	Lawrence, December 20, 1878.	Lawrence.
Savage, W. W , Vermont, May 17, 1850.	Wakarusa, October, 1855.	Wakarusa.
Smith, Henry, Madison Co., Ky., March —, 1819.	Mill Creek, Johnson county, Apr. 20, 1842.	Lawrence.
Stevenson, Mrs. J. A. Illinois, Nov. —, 1859.	Douglas county, November, 1859.	Hutchinson.
Sherman. Lillie V., Rockford, Ill., Feb. 26, 1865.	Lawrence, May 6, 1876.	
Smith, Kate S., Osawatomie, March 12, 1863.		
Searle, R. H. C., Montgomery Co., N. Y., April 14, 1831.	Topeka, December 25, 1865.	Topeka.
Searle, Amelia B , Ohio, July 28, 1835.	Topeka, December 25, 1865.	Topeka.
Sutorius, Charles, Cologne, Prussia, June 18, 1858.	Ottawa, June 18, 1868.	Lawrence.
Straffon, C. W., Sparta, Ontario, Dec. 9, 1858.	Ottawa, November 4, 1869.	Lawrence.
Smith, W. R., Terre Haute, Ind., Aug. 19, 1833.	Ottawa, April 25, 1857.	Reno, Leav. Co.
Steinberg, Simon, Batavia, October 3, 1833.	Lawrence, December 11, 1864	Lawrence.
Scagell, Mrs. M J., Lisbon, Maine, July 27, 1827.		Topeka.
Selig, A. L., Hamburg, Germany, August 6, 1846.	Lawrence, 1858.	Lawrence.
Scholes, Thomas, Illinois, September 10, 1846.	Holton, April, 1872.	Lawrence.
Sterner, H. C., Penn., November 10, 1857.	Topeka, May 30, 1877.	Topeka.
Sperry, L. J., New York, January 5, 1829.	3 miles east of Lawrence, June 5, 1856	Lawrence.
Searl, Hattie E., Fitchburg, Mass., January 9, 1847.	Lawrence, May 20, 1856.	Solomon, Kansas.
Spray, L. M., New London, Indiana, July 23, 1856.	Springdale, Kansas. 1870.	Lawrence.
Strong, Mrs. C. A., Tioga, New York, Feb. 27, 1832.	Highland, Kansas, May 6, 1872.	
Smith T. B., Connecticut, March 5, 1836.	Blue Mound, near Lawrence, December 6, 1854	Blue Mound.
Stanley, Sino, Buchanan Co., Mo., August 12, 1841.	Doniphan Co , May 27, 1857.	
Snoddy, James D., Lycoming Co., Penn., September 11, 1838.	Mound City, February 25, 1861.	La Cygne.
Speer, John, Kittanning, Penn., Dec., 27, 1817.	Lawrence, September 27, 1854.	Lawrence.
Stouffer, Mary R., Pennsylvania, Aug., 29, 1837	Lawrence, March, 1855.	Onaga.
Smith, Mrs. Elizabeth, Pennsylvania, June 4, ——	Lawrence, March, 1855.	Lawrence.
Sherman, Christiana, Edinburgh, Scotland, May 20, 1831.	Quindaro, June 5, 1857.	Quindaro.
Sherman, Morris, Maine, January 29, 1829.	Quindaro, June 5, 1857.	Quindaro.
Sterling, J. A., Brandonville, W. V., Nov. 18, 1853.	Abilene, October 9, 1871.	Lawrence.
Smelser, Lydia A., Indiana, December, 26, 1855.	Miami county, 1860.	Leavenworth Co.
Sawyer, Mary W. G., Union Co., Ind., Jan. 27, 1842.	Bloomington, February, 1857.	Lawrence.
Sherman, Ike Lycurgus, Cleveland, O., July 11, 1860.	——, January 6, 1864.	Topeka.
Stuart, J. H., Guilford, N. C., June 20, 1836.	Lawrence, February 1, 1872.	Lawrence.
Taylor, A. B., Ohio, 1831	Franklin, 1865.	Rosedale.
Turrell, N. S., Lexington, Ind., May 17, 1817	Wakarusa, April 10, 1867.	Lawrence.
Taylor, George A., South Windsor, Ct , Sept. 24, 1836.	Leavenworth, September 30, 1855.	Junction City.
Thomas, J , Bucks county, Penn., March 20 1841.	Topeka, October 18, 1871.	Topeka.
Taylor, D. B., Pittsburg, Pa , January 8, 1857.		Emporia.
Taylor, Moses W., Illinois, November 22, 1831.	Douglas county, August 20, 1854.	
Taylor, Janie, Kansas, September 27, 1866.	Douglas county, Sept. 27, 1866.	
Taylor, Emma, Kansas, September 18 1868.	Douglas county, Sept 18, 1868.	
Trent, T. S., Barry county, Mo., March 20, 1862.	Shawnee county, Feb. 24, 1875.	
Tefft, Mrs. Emma A., Ohio,	Topeka, December 11, 1866.	Topeka.
Thomas, Erven, Calloway county, Mo., March 25, 1841.	Lawrence, September 5, 1861.	Lawrence.
Thralls, Will H., Lawrence, June 24, 1878.	Lawrence, June 24, 1878.	Lawrence.
Tabor, Mrs. R. K , Rochester, New York.	Lawrence.	
Tolles, Ada C., Lawrence, November 2, 1860.	Lawrence, Nov. 2, 1860	Lawrence.
Tolles, Abbie F., Lawrence, August'2, 1864.	Lawrence, August 2, 1864.	Lawrence.
Thompson, E. D., Saratoga county, N. Y. July 6, 1837.	Lawrence, 1857.	Lawrence.
Tucker, Charles H., Cornwall, Eng., May 6, 1857.	Lawrence, September 24, 1870.	Lawrence.
Taylor, D. B., Alleghany City, Pa., Jan 8, 1857.	Council Grove, January 1, 1879.	Clay Center.

18

Name, Place and Date of Birth.	Place and Date of Settlement.	Present Residence
Tosh, Andrew, Preble county, Ohio, July 12, 1821.	Lawrence, November 9, 1870.	Lawrence.
Thurber, W., New York, December 25, 1831.	Lawrence, April 8, 1856.	Twin Mound.
Tennis, Anne E., Kentucky, May 18, 1863.	Lawrence, Nov. 11, 1871.	Lawrence.
Tennis, Mattie M., Kentucky, March 1, 1855.	Lawrence, Nov. 30, 1870.	Lawrence.
Thacher, T. Dwight, Hornellsville, N. Y , Oct. 22, '31.	Lawrence, April, 1857.	Lawrence.
Taylor, C. H., Ohio, August 14, 1822	De Soto, August 30, 1865.	DeSoto.
Taylor, C. P. W., Kansas, November 30, 1860.	Douglas county, Nov. 30, 1860.	Oskaloosa.
Tisdale, H., Norfolk, New York, February 17, 1833.	Lawrence, Feb. 17, 1857.	Lawrence.
Thompson, Mrs. Laura Bell, Cin., O., May 22, 1847.	Ft. Riley, May 12, 1855.	Lawrence.
Thacher, W. M., Lawrence, Kansas, March 24, 1862.	Lawrence, March 24, 1862.	Lawrence.
Thurber, Orville, La Grange Co., Ind., Jan. 8, 1854.	Douglas county, May, 1855.	Twin Mound.
Trimper, A. A., Columbia county, N. Y., Feb. 17, 1816.	Lawrence, April 1, 1873.	Lawrence.
Thompson, C. L., Clinton, Mass., June 27, 1832.	Lawrence, April 27, 1857.	Thompsonville, Jefferson Co.
Thompson, Mrs. C. L., Lubec, Maine, Sept. 10, 1836.	Lawrence, June, 1858.	Thompsonville, Jefferson Co.
Tefft, F., Hamilton county, N. Y., Dec. 27, 1818.	Topeka, spring of 1859.	Topeka.
Tilly, T. J., St. Louis, Mo., October 23, 1852.	White Cloud, Sept. 1, 1862.	Topeka.
Thralls, O. E., Fairmount, W. Va., May 18, 1862.	Paola, October, 1867.	Lawrence.
Topping, Kate L., Carbondale, Ill., Sept 3, 1856.	Topeka, July 6, 1877.	Topeka.
Tolles, Mary B., Gardner, Mass., August 19, 1832.	Lawrence, March 30, 1855.	Lawrence.
Tisdale, Mrs. H., Compton, Canada, Oct 26, 1832.	Lawrence, May 17, 1862.	Douglas Co.
Thompson, J. F., Shelbyville, Ind., Jan. 13, 1852.	Lawrence, Nov. 21, 1878.	Lawrence.
Thacher, S M., Hornellsville, N. Y., Dec. 21, 1834.	Lawrence, September, 1857.	Hornellsville, N. Y
Telford, Wm. B., Ohio, December 6, 1854.	De Soto, Johnson county, April 28, 1870.	DeSoto.
Telford, Mattie, Ohio, May 28, 1855.	Spring Hill, April 1, 1865.	DeSoto.
Telford, Eliza, Ohio, July 12, 1858.	De Soto, April 28, 1870.	Gardner.
Taber, Ira l., Delaware county, N. Y., Aug. 22, 1836.	Holton, Jackson Co., May, 18, '58.	Holton.
Taber, Homer Galen, Holton, Jackson county, Kansas, March 12 1873.	Holton, March 12, 1873.	Holton.
Todd, Frank A., Leavenworth, September 26, 1859.		Atchison.
Taylor, Elizabeth, Ohio, October 4, 1836.	Jefferson county, October, 1859.	Topeka.
Taylor, Lucy H., N. Y., March 14, 1833.	Lawrence, Nov. 27, 1867.	Lawrence.
Tunnell, Robert M, Illinois, October 17, 1830.	———, September, 1867.	Wyandotte.
Telford, J C., Steuben county, N. Y., March 13, 1829.	De Soto, April, 1870.	Gardner.
Telford, Susetta, Seneca county, Ohio, Feb. 15, 1820.	De Soto, April, 1870.	Gardner.
Tefft, H. K., Illinois, September 8, 1848.	Topeka, July, 1859.	Topeka.
Thralls, F W., Fairmont, W. Va., October 6, 1852.	Lawrence.	Lawrence.
Ten Broeck, Frank, Annapolis, Ind., March 8, 1858.	Lawrence, August 26, 1879.	Lawrence.
Taylor, Mrs. R. B., New York.	Wyandotte, July, 1858	Wyandotte.
Tomson, T. K., Youngstown, Ohio, Sept. 20, 1866.	Topeka, May 5, 1861.	Topeka
Thornton, Annie, East Tennessee, April 28, 1831.	Lawrence, September 9, 1861.	Franklin Co.
Tefft, C., Rhode Island, September 28, 1827.	Douglas county, Nov. 19, 1851.	Lawrence.
Thompson, Mrs. Carrie, Ohio, August 25, 1856.	Lawrence, Nov. 23, 1879.	Lawrence.
Trask, Mrs. J. C., Cortland, N. Y., Jan. 1, 1840.	Lawrence, Nov. 23, 1862	Williamsport Tp., Shawnee Co.
Tice, Perry, Myerstown, Pa., May 26, 1821.	Shawnee county, May 4, 1859.	Williamsport Tp., Shawnee Co.
Tice, Sarah C., Lycoming county, Pa , Oct. 31, 1820.	Shawnee county, May 4, 1859.	Topeka.
Temple, J. S., Galena, Illinois, November 6, 1857.	Topeka, November, 1876.	Leavenworth Co.
Taber, Tillford J., Jackson county, Ind., Aug. 17, 1833.	Douglas Co., Nov. 20, 1854.	Jefferson Co.
Turley, E. B , Miami county, December 4, 1861.	Douglas Co., Nov. 5, 1862.	Lawrence.
Tennis, Mattie M., Kentucky, March 1, 1865.	Lawrence, Nov. 30, 1870.	DeSoto.
Taylor, Sallie, Wales, September 27, 1840.	Lawrence, April 10, 1865.	Lawrence.
Treadway, Mrs. D. C., Wisconsin, January 29, 1851	Lawrence, June 26, 1879.	Edwardsville.
Thompson, Mr. L., Goshen, Conn., August 9, 1820.	Baldwin City, Nov., 1858.	Lawrence.
Thornton, W. F., Hannibal, Mo., January 5, 1850.	Leavenworth, Sept. 10, 1870.	Valley Falls.
Thacher, Charles C., Hornellsville, N. Y., March 27, 1847.	Lawrence, April 10, 1868.	Topeka.
Taylor, Eva, De Soto, Kansas, July 5, 1842.	Lawrence, May 3, 1871.	Lawrence.
Tefft, E., Madison county, New York, Dec. 27, 1818.	Topeka, May 25, 1859.	Leavenworth.
Thew, W. A., Ohio, December —, 1860.	Oxford, March 4, 1876.	Lawrence.
Taylor, James S., Philadelphia, December 28, 1847.	Leavenworth, April 7, 1858.	Hesper.
Thralls, Ed., West Virginia, May 29, 1850.	Paola, Nov. 28, 1860.	Hesper.
Thomas, Phebe R., Bolton, Mass., October 18, 1841.	Lawrence, Feb. 28, 1865.	Lawrence.
Thomas, Barclay, Newport, Indiana, July 1, 1841.	Hesper, Nov. 20, 1864.	N. Topeka.
Thurber, Ada, Lawrence, October 14, 1858.	Lawrence, October 14, 1858.	N. Topeka.
Thompkins, Charles T., New Bedford, Mass., Feb. 4, 1833.	N. Topeka, May 15, 1869.	Denver.
Thompkins, Mrs. M. L., Cameron, Vt., Feb. 24, 1830.	N. Topeka, May 15, 1869	Atchison.
Taber, Hannah S., Holland, Vt., July 21, 1834.	Lawrence, April 7, 1857.	Lawrence.
Todd, Frank A., Leavenworth, September 26, 1859.	Atchison.	Douglas Co.
Turner, James, Kentucky, ———, 1810.	Lawrence, 1864	Charleston, S. C.
Thomas, L. W., Fairmont, West Va., Oct 9, 1856.	Paola, Nov. 12, 1868.	Shawnee Co.
Tucker, John, M. D. San Francisco, Jan. 1, 1855.	Chicago, April 18, 1871.	Topeka.
Tweedale, E. W., Castine, Maine, August 31, ——.	Lawrence, July 20, 1867.	Grantville
Thompson, Wm. P., Mercer Co., Pa., Dec. , 18, 1832.	Shawnee Co., July 20, 1867.	DeSoto.
Tebbs, John, Missouri, December 18, 1846.	Topeka, May 26, 1855.	Lawrence.
Terrey, H. O., Oswego, New York, April 13, 1829.	Grantville, Kan., Mar. 17, 1868.	
Tyner, E. B., June 3, 1801.	De Soto, Johnson Co , Feb. 4, '70.	

Name, Place and Date of Birth.	Place and Date of Settl ment.	Present Residence
Tosh, I.. D. L., Upshur, Ohio, August 2, 1851.	Lawrence, October 31, 1870.	Lawrence.
Thomas, Chester, Troy, Penn., July 18, 1810.	Topeka, April 28, 1858.	Topeka.
Thomas, Frank S., Canton, Pa , Oct., 22, 1857.	Topeka, April 28, 1858.	Topeka.
Taylor, J H., Allegheny City, Pa., Nov. 18, 1855.		Lawrence.
Tanner, Wm., Chautauqua Co., N. Y., Oct. 7, 1819.	Leavenworth City, Oct. 23, 1854.	
Tanner, Ellen F., Mount Vernon, O., April 29, 1847.	Leroy, October 12, 1869.	Leavenworth.
Tabor, L. R., Barton, Vt., February 6, 1826.		
Tabor, C. D., Topsham, Vt., July 23, 1799.	Lawrence, May 9, 1857.	Lawrence.
Underwood, Nelson, Carter county, Ky., Apr. 20, 18..8.	Jefferson Co., Kan., Oct. 7, 1868.	Near Williamstown, Jeff. Co.
Underwood, Delila, Fleming Co., Ky., March 20,1828.		Near Williamstown, Jeff. Co.
Umberger, David, Ohio, May 15, 1841.	Clinton, Douglas Co., March 4, 1855.	Clinton, Doug. Co.
Umberger, John, Ohio, September 26, 1845.	Clinton, Douglas Co., March 4, 1855	
Underwood, Prescott, Wayne Co., Pa., Feb. 22, 1835	North Lawrence, Feb., 1868	N. Lawrence.
Umberger, R. O., Indiana, April 29, 1834.	Kanwaka, August 6, 1856.	Clinton.
Vern n, John E., Ohio, October 12, 1849.	Lecompton, Oct 15, 1808.	Lawrence.
Vincent, J. C., Dutchess Co., N Y., March 7, 1824.	Kanwaka, March 28, 1857.	Kanwaka.
Vanderpool, T. B., Decatur Co., Iowa, June 22, 1846.	Jefferson Co , Sept. 12, 1867.	Douglas Co.
Vrooman, H. P., Johnstown, New York, July 24, 1828.	Council Grove, May 26, 1876.	Eureka.
Vermilyea, E. W. G., New York, Nov. 28, 1825.	Lawrence, Sept. 17, 1855.	Douglas Co,
Vanderveer, W. R., Avon, O., July 28, 1842.	Lawrence April 8, 1879.	Lawrence.
Van Winkle, R. A., Wayne Co., Ky., Nov. 25, 1818.	Kapioma Tp. Atchison Co., Feb. 11, 1855.	Arington, Atchison Co.
Vernon, Walter A., Ohio, May 14, 1861.	Lawrence, 1877.	Lawrence.
Van Hoeson, Kinder Hook, N. Y., Dec., 25, 1841.	Manhattan, Feb. 1, 1866.	Lawrence.
Vincent, Wm. E., Deer Park, Illinois, Nov. 7, 1857.	Lawrence, June 4, 1878	Ridgeway.
Vestal, J. M., Mooresville, Ind. January 15, 1840.	Shawnee, Oct. 24, 1865.	Prairie Center.
Van Houten A., Ithaca, N. Y, August 15, 1834.	Eureka, June, 1871.	Eureka.
Vandersburgh, S. G , Ohio, May 16, 1854.	Aurora, Oct. 12, 1863.	Aurora.
Voorhees, Peter, New Jersey, March 7, 1845,	Lawrence, March 4, 1877.	Lawrence.
Van Nordstrand, A. S., Illinois, February 14, —	LeRoy	
Vincent Anna E. Preble county Ohio, June 1, 1844.	Douglas Co., March 28, 1857.	Douglas.
Van Wormer, P. A., Oneida, New York, Nov. 29, 1831.	Lawrence, May 5, 1868.	Lawrence.
Van Wormer, J A., Albany, Co. N. Y., July 13, 1830.	Lawrence, May 5, 1808.	Lawrence.
Valentine, D. M., Shelby Co., Ohio, June 18, 1830	Leavenworth City, July 5, 1859.	Topeka.
Valentine, D. A , Fontanelle, Iowa, April 16, 1856.	Franklin Co., July, 1859.	Topeka.
Vestal, John H.. Morgan Co., Ind., Jan. 15, 1840.	Shawnee, Oct. 24, 1865.	Tonganoxie.
Van Fossen, C. H , — —.	Wyandotte, Feb 1, 1856.	Kansas City, Kan.
Varnum, F. B , Bluehill, Maine, July 33, 1837.	Vinland. Douglas Co., May 10, 1856.	Vinland, Douglas Co.
Vaneil, Amelia, Kentucky, May 29, 1808.	Lawrence, Dec. 15, 1854.	Clinton.
Van Laer, H. E., Auburn, N. Y., May 9, 1853.	Leavenworth. Kan , July 20, 1878.	Topeka.
Van Fossen, Mrs. C. M., Ohio, —	Wyandotte, Kan., 1848.	Kansas City, Kan.
Van Hoeson, Mrs. J. N., Glasgow, Ky.	Leavenworth, Spring of 1879.	Lawrence.
Van Hoesen, Rilla B., Lawrence Kan., Jan. 1, 1872.	Lawrence, Jan. 1, 1872.	Lawrence.
Wear, Martin S , Butler county, Ohio, Jan. 11, 1815.	Edward's Co., August 1, 1876.	Edwards Co.
Wood, Mary A., Columbiana Co., Ohio, Sept 9, 1832.	Chase Co., April 10, 1865.	Elmdale.
Wood, D. M., October 25, 1825.	Wakarusa Tp., Nov. 10, 1878.	Wakarusa.
Wilkin, R. S , Indiana, August 17, 1837.	Douglas Co., December, 1876.	Topeka
Wilson, Mrs. J. N., Madison, N. Y.	Lawrence.	Lawrence.
Wilson, John S., Rome, Richland Co., O., July 2, 1831.	Garnett, March 1, 1869.	Lawrence.
Warrington, A. P., Iowa, 1853.	Cherokee Co., Dec., 1867.	Leavenworth Co.
Watt, J K., Indiana, March 10, 1861.	Twin Mounds, 1861	Lawrence.
Williams, Henry, Louisville, Ky., March 24, 1863.	Lawrence, Sept 15, 1879	
Walker, J. E., Franklin county, N. Y., July 24, 1847.	Douglas Co., April 10, 1860.	Baldwin City.
Wood, Frances, Illinois, July, 8 1849.	Vinland, April 4, 1863.	Vinland.
Wood, Caroline A., Vermont. May 6, 1813.	Vinland, April 4, 1863.	Vinland.
Wood, J. Z. D., New York, March 29, 1817.	Vinland. April 4, 1863	Vinland.
Wallace, P. W., Kentucky, February 7, 1829.	Lawrence, March 1, 1869.	Wellesley, Mass.
Walton, Ray A., Indiana, May 10, 1858.	Hesper, April 1, 1870	Lawrence.
Wosbache, Chas , Overton, Pa., Dec. 1, 1855	Lawrence, June 5, 1874.	Lawrence.
Winchell, G H., Lawrence, August 6, 1862.	Lawrence, May 8, 1865.	Lawrence.
Williamson, Chas.. London, Eng., Feb. 8, 1824.	Atchison Co., April 10, 1856.	Washington Co.
Wilkinson, Wm., Jo Daviess Co., Ill., Sept. 14, 1854.	Wakarusa, Sept. 15, 1864.	South of Lawrence.
Way, Arthur P.. Mansfield, Kas , Nov. 21, 1862.	Linn Co., Nov. 21, 1862.	Lawrence
Webster, Frank L , Sandusky, Ohio, April 22, 1861.	Wyandotte, Nov 15, 1865.	Lawrence.
Wenrick, S. E. S., Hopkinton, Iowa, March 8, 1857.	Elgin, September, 1879.	
Walton, J. B., Pennsylvania, January 4, 1852.		
Wakefield, Wm. H. T. Vandalia, Ill., Dec. 13, 1834.	Douglas Co , June 8, 1854.	Lawrence.
Wilkinson, Rachel, Indiana, July 25, 1831.	Douglas Co., Sept. 14, 1851.	Wakarusa, Douglas Co.
Whiteside, George P., Muncie, Ind., Sept. 18, 1845.	Topeka, Sept. 10, 1880.	Topeka.
Willard, J. B., Salem, Illinois, May 3, 1859.	Leavenworth, July 1, 1878.	Leavenworth.
Wherry, E. J., Washington Co., Pa , March 1, 1844.	Eudora, April 5, 1865.	Edgerton.
Wherry, F. A., Columbiana Co., Ohio, June 28, 1845.	Eudora, April 5, 1865.	Edgerton
Way, Amanda M., Winchester, Ind., July 10, 1828.	Lawrence, October, 1870.	Lawrence.

Name, Place and Date of Birth.	Place and Date of Settlement.	Present Residence
Woffindin, Thomas, England, March 25, 1815.	Lawrence, August, 1859	Lawrence.
White, Nettie E., Carlinville, February 12, 1861.	Lawrence, April 19, 1870.	Lawrence.
White, E. A., Holliston, Mass., March 19, 1829.	Lawrence, April 19, 1870.	Lawrence.
Watts, P. N., New Orleans, June 18. 1854.	Douglas Co.	
Westheffer, Eli, Pennsylvania, December 12, 1842.	Douglas Co , April 12, 1866	Douglas.
Wheeler, J. B., Chenango county, N. V., Feb. 28, 1844	Lawrence, 1866.	Lawrence.
Wilhelmi, Emma, Washington, Mo., Oct. 13, 1858.	Lawrence, Jan. 27, 1879.	
Wamsley, W. P., West Virginia. January 8, 1854.		
Weseman, Theo., Prussia, April 23, 1832.	Camped out three days in Douglas Co., June 17, 1849.	Lawrence.
Weaver, I. T., Montgomery Co., Ky., Nov. 4, 1824.	Olathe, Kan., June 1, 1860.	Olathe
Walker, O. D., Emporia, December 3, 1860.	Lawrence, June 1, 1866.	Lawrence.
Watt, J. M. G., Ohio, July 28, 1854.	Anderson Co., March, 1856.	Lawrence.
Wells, E. S		Leavenworth.
Willet, H W , Pennsylvania, August 29, 1835.	Lawrence, May 23, 1856	Media.
Willet, Susie E., Akron, Ohio, May 10, 1843.	Lawrence, July 29, 1857.	Media.
Winter, M S , Virginia, September 21, 1833.	Lecompton, Jan. 10, 1855.	Lecompton.
Wood, K. M., Darlington, Ohio, February 24, 1841.	Kansas City.	
Whitlock, John F., Missouri, November 11, 1848.	Wakarusa, Oct. 1, 1854.	
Ward, Chas. J., Butler, Mo., December 18, 1856.	Stanton, April 16, 1857.	Lawrence.
Wilson, E. B., Lawrence, April 27, 1861	Lawrence, April 27. 1861.	Lawrence.
Whitlock, Della, Missouri, November 11.	Wakarusa, Oct. 1, 1854.	Wakarusa.
Winchell, Henry H., Springfield, June 23, 1865.	Lawrence, May 8, 1866.	Lawrence.
Williams, Charles, Kansas, July 30, 1859.	Vinland	Vinland.
Wentworth, H., Otsego county, N. Y., Sept 6, 1830.	Russell, Russell Co., May 19, '71.	Russell.
Wentworth, Charlotte B., Jamaica, L. I., Oct. 8, 1835.	Russell, May 19, 1871.	Russell.
Wentworth, Frances E., Ripon, Wis., April 29, 1862.	Russell, May 19, 1871.	Russell.
Wood, S N., Mt. Gilead, Ohio, Dec. 30, 1825.	California Road, June 25, 1854.	Chase Co.
Way, J. P., Winchester, Indiana, Sept. 8, 1826.	Mound City, Linn Co., June 12, 1861.	LaCygne.
Watt, D. G., Eaton, Ohio, July 15, 1828	Franklin Co., April 17, 1856.	Near Lawrence.
West G. C., Scott county, Va., January 30, 1842.	Parsons, Jan. 1, 1870.	Topeka.
Wilder, John H , Bolton, Mass., June 19, 1829	Lawrence, October 8, 1854.	Lawrence.
Woodard, J. S., Jamestown, Ind., Nov. 9, 1836	Bloomington, March, 1854.	Riley Co.
Washburn, A., Connecticut, October 23, 1818.	Topeka, March 27. 1857.	Topeka
Washburn Mrs. A., New York, March 10, 1820.	Topeka, March 27, 1857.	Topeka.
Warner, Mattie, E., Schoharie, N Y., April 28, 1839.	Wyandotte, Feb. 10, 1856.	
White, E. J., Blairsville, Penn., June, 1859.	Wamego, May, 1870.	
Willard, W. S., Wellsboro, Pa., June 4, 1841.	Lawrence, July 18, 1878.	Lawrence.
Wilber, Luella, Sharon, Ohio, October 1, 1880.	Lawrence, Dec. 23, 1877.	
Wilson, Homer, Paris, December 16, 1855.	Emporia, April 18, 1879.	Emporia.
White, E M., Cloverdale, Indiana, October 1, 1831.	Willow Springs, Sept. 1, 1854.	DeSoto.
Walton, John, Washington Co., Pa., Dec. 16, 1831.	Coal Creek, Douglas Co., Oct. 15, 1856	Vinland.
Walton, Amos, Green county, Pa., July 29, 1838.	Coal Creek, June 1, 1857.	Arkansas City.
Walker, Samuel, London, Pa., October 22, 1822.	Kanwaka, Douglas Co , April 8, 1855.	Lawrence.
Williamson, S. S , Somerset Co , N. Y., July 4, 1831.		Kansas City.
Winslow, Edward, Barnard, Vermont, July 20, 1831.	Wakarusa, August, 1854.	
Welles, Wm. D., St. Louis, Mo., May 23, 1858.	Gardner, June 17, 1879.	Gardner.
Wilcox, S., Topeka, Band		
Winchell, George H., Lawrence, Kas., Aug. 6, 1862.	Lawrence, September 21, 1865.	Lawrence.
Walker, S. N , Burlington, Vt., Aug. 18, 1816.	Baldwin City, February 1, 1859.	Baldwin City.
Weymouth, Will. H., Topeka, Kas., Nov. 21, 1855.	Topeka, November 21, 1855	Topeka.
Williams, A. C., Ohio, July 7, 1819.	Leavenworth Co., May, 1869.	Cowley Co.
Winter, Jacob, Washington Co.. Pa. Oct. 8, 1811.	Leavenworth Co., March 1, 1870.	Leavenworth City.
Ware, W. W., Iowa, June 14, 1857.		Fairview.
Webber, Horace, Terre Haute, Ind., March, 1858.	Topeka, June 1, 1869.	Topeka.
Wild, Elizabeth B., Boston, Mass., May 28, 1806.	Lawrence September 22, 1872.	Lawrence.
Woods, Mrs. N. J., Louisville, Ky., Jan. 16, 1826.	Topeka, June 5, 1855.	Topeka
Woodard, F. T., Rockville, Ind., Sept. 22, 1853.	Hesper, Kansas, Dec. 1, 1865.	Wichita.
Wood, L J., New York, May 9, 1834.	Douglas Co., Nov. 25, 1862.	Lawrence.
Ward, M. E., New York, March 22, 1862.	Eudora. November 19, 1869.	Lawrence.
Williams, Mary M., Vinland, Kansas, July 4, 1861.	Vinland, July 4. 1861.	Lawrence.
Winey, Thomas G. Pennsylvania.	Lawrence.	Lawrence.
Whitcomb, A. Vermont, August 14, 1827.	Lawrence, April 3, 1855.	Lawrence.
Whitcomb, Mrs. A., Vermont, January, 9, 1832.	Lawrence, April 3, 1855.	Lawrence.
Winchell, H. H., Springfield, Mass., June 23, 1865.	Lawrence, 1866.	Lawrence.
Wilcox, Robert, Cambridge, N. Y., August 16, 1843.	Lawrence, March 10, 1868.	Lawrence.
Webber, James B., Ohio, January 30, 1821.	Topeka, December 12, 1868.	Topeka.
Worrell, Mrs. I. P., Illinois, August 25, 1835.	Larned, August 27, 1873.	Larned.
Worrell, I. P., Alexandria, Virginia, April 8, 1833.	Larned, May 14, 1873.	Larned.
Woodard, O. J., Wayne county, Ind., Aug. 10, 1854.	Douglas Co. 1856.	Lawrence.
Waugh, E. H., N. C , December, 25, 1815.	Linn Co., June 24, 1856.	Clinton, Doug. Co
Walton, J. C., Indiana. March 8, 1842.	Lawrence, April 16, 1866.	Lawrence.
Watson, A. B., Ripley county, Ind , Feb. 28, 1835.	Cottonwood Falls, July 10, 1859.	
Washburn. C. F, Columbia, Ind., Feb 5, 1862.	Ridgeway, Sept. 15, 1868.	
Webber, Mrs. A. B , Watertown, N. Y., Nov. 22, 1842.	Lawrence, Oct. 1, 1871.	Lawrence.
Wells, Mrs. Elijah, Westfield, Mass.		St. Louis, Mo.
Wyman, George, Potsdam, N. Y., Sept. 14, 1816.	Topeka, May 27, 1868.	Topeka
Wheat, M. A., Harrison county, Ky., July 29, 1836.	Leavenworth, Nov. 6, 1859.	Leavenworth.

Name, Place and Date of Birth.	Place and Date of Settlement.	Present Residence
Warren, J. R., Kentucky, March 29, 1829.	Shawnee Co. Sept 4, 1854.	Shawnee.
Williams, Allen, Rush county, Ind., January 23, 1811.	Lawrence. October 7. 1866.	Abilene.
Willis, Mrs. S. J., Fulton Co., New York, July 9, 1820.	Lawrence Sept., 1854.	Skiddy, Morris Co
Walker, Mrs. P. A., Washington Co., O., March 1, 1838.	Garnett, Sept. 10, 1873.	Lawrence.
Watson, James E., Connecticut, May 3, 1830.	Lawrence, March 10, 18:7	Lawrence.
Wanemaker, N., Madison. Wis., March 29, 1857	Washington Co., July 4, 1869.	Lecompton.
Wood, Andrew J., New York, March 14, 1833.	Sac and Fox Reservation, April 29, 1869.	Topeka.
Waters, G. E.. Northfield, Minn., June 20, 1860.		Douglas Co.
Wardlow, S. W, Kentucky, 1851.	Leavenworth Co., 1868.	Lawrence.
Woodward, S E., Iowa, August 20, 1859	Lawrence.	Lawrence.
White, W. B., North Carolina, January 1, 1833.	Lawrence, Nov. 4, 1868.	Lawrence.
Wood, John, Versailles, Morgan county, Mo., April 15, 1835.	Clinton, Oct. 13, 1854.	Twin Mounds.
Wright, Robert H, St. Louis, Mo., September 15, 1861.	Dodge City, June 12, 1861.	Dodge City.
Weber, Gus., Canada, August 16, 1860.	Lawrence, Sept 29 1870.	Lawrence.
Wild, H C, Baltimore, May 24, 1845		
Wonneberg, Adolph, Hanover, Germany, February 15, 1856	Leavenworth Co., July, 16, 1878.	Tonganoxie.
Woodward, J. W, Chester county, Pa, Feb. 14, 1834.	Lawrence, May 18, 1855.	Lawrence
Wells, Thomas, Bedfordshire. England, August 15, 1809	Lawrence, October 20, 1850.	
Wumps, Mrs A., Goshen, Indiana, August 19, 1849.	Ottawa. Nov, 1866	Leavenworth.
Waters, Aaron P, Ohio, April 15, 1832.	Leavenworth, Sept 18, 1879.	Wyandotte Co.
Willey, S P., Chautauqua county, N. Y., June 22, 1809	Baldwin City. April. 1860.	
Wood, Louis M, Pennsylvania, November 22, 1846.	Lawrence, Dec. 2, 1872.	Lawrence.
Walter, M. I., Lawrence	Douglas Co., 1861.	
Waltermire. E. B., Ohio. April 9, 1858	Douglas Co., April 2, 1878.	Reno, Leav. Co.
Webber, Ellwood P., Indianapolis, Indiana, Nov., 1854.	Topeka, 1868.	Topeka.
Watkins, J. B.. Indiana. Penn., June 25, 1845.	Lawrence, August 16, 1873.	Lawrence.
Wood, E W., Lebanon, Maine, April 26, 1833.	Lawrence, April 5, 1800.	Lawrence.
White, G. W., Kentucky. July 30, 1844		
Wiggins, Miss Ida, Kansas, September 15, 1864.	Lawrence. Sept. 15, 1864.	Lawrence.
Wilson, V. P., Pennsylvania April 1, 1828.	Abilene, Feb., 1870.	Abilene.
Wallace, Josie B., Rochester, New York, March 23, 1850.	Lawrence, Jan. 10, 1856	Lawrence.
Warren, A. B., Berkshire, Mass, March 25, 1848.	Lawrence. Dec. 15, 1868.	Lawrence.
Winan, H. K., Pennsylvania, April 13, 1831.	Auburn, Shawnee Co., October 10, 1856.	Topeka.
Welsh, C. W, December 13, 1816.	Shawnee Co., April 7 1859.	Williamsport Tp., Shawnee Co.
Williams. Henry, Wales, England, November 27. 1822.	Willow Springs. Sept., 1855.	Douglas Co.
Weatherby, S. S., Knox county, Ohio, February 1, 1841.	Pleasanton, Linn Co., Sept. 30, 1871.	Baldwin City.
Waysman, James R., Port Republic, Va., Sept., 5, 1816.	Tecumseh. May 5, 1854.	Tecumseh.
Willey, I. W., Pennsylvania, September 25, 1807.	Blue Mound, Douglas county, March 26. 1857	
Walgamot, L., Millersburg, Ohio. June 17, 1832.	Wyandotte Co., April 17, 1865.	
Woodard, Sarah A, Highland county, Ohio, March 31, 1831.	Douglas Co., April 12, 1857.	Camden.
Willis, C. H., near Lawrence, Kansas. October 14, 1856.	Lawrence, October 14, 1856.	Lawrence.
Winnis, M. A, New York, December 25, 1842.	Lawrence, May 25, 1871.	Reno, Kansas.
White, Samuel, Indiana, July 17, 1854.	Leavenworth Co., April 11, 1871.	Lawrence
Wyler. C. R., Thun, Switzerland, December 4, 1826.	Lawrence, Sept. 23, 1861.	Twin Mound.
Woodward, Mary, Pennsylvania, July 16, 1815.	Clinton, March 30, 1855.	Lecompton.
Woodard, J. M, Illinois, May 19, 1851	Clinton, March 10, 1855.	
Wood, Lucie A., Cherry Valley, New York, August 26, 1845.	Lawrence.	Lawrence.
Watkins, Emma, New York, October 13, 1862.	Osawatomie, May 26, 1856	Lawrence.
Watkins, John, England, November 23, 1842.	Lawrence, April 10, 1865.	Lawrence.
Waugh, W. C. Harrison county, Ohio, June 15, 1855.	Lawrence, April 10 1865.	Lawrence.
Way, A. P., Linn county, November 21, 1862.	Lawrence, August 3, 1873.	Lawrence.
Whitney, H. C, Vermont, June 28, 1862.	Lawrence, April 16, 1863.	Lawrence.
Wheeler, Joshua, England, February 12, 1827.	Pardee, Atchison Co., October 1, 1857.	Nortonville.
Williams, N. L., Springfield, Ohio, October 30, 1807.	Shawnee Co., May 14, 1855.	
Williams, Susan, Coshocton, Ohio, October 2, 1809.	Shawnee Co., May 14, 1855.	
Wallace, James E., Marshall county, Kentucky, Aug 7, 1833.	Leavenworth, August 24, 1851	Shawnee Co.
Walker, H A, Chester county, S. Carolina, May 15, 1855.	Lawrence. Nov., 1865.	Lawrence. Burrton.
Wright, L. C, Simpson county, Ky., February 17, 1851.	Burrton, Feb. 1, 1877.	Leavenworth.
Wellhouse, F., Ohio, November 16, 1828	Leavenworth, Oct., 1859.	Douglas Co.
Wiggs, R., Indiana, March 9, 1879.	Lawrence, March. 1879.	Lawrence.
Walker, S. Jennie, Indiana. May 22, 1857.	Lawrence, Nov., 1869.	Douglas Co.
Weaver, J. F., Ohio, December 31, 1848.	Douglas Co., April 1, 1865.	Lawrence.
Wartner, A. B., New York, September 15, 1879.	Lawrence, April 29, 1859.	
Woodruff, Frank L., Independence, Mo., Jan 1, 1859.	Lawrence, Dec. 23, 1861	Lawrence.
Williams Lizzie A., Cold Springs, Ill, Jan 9, 1853.	Franklin, Kan., March 17, 1857.	Eudora.
Wilder, John, Skaneatelas, N. Y, Nov. 10, 1822.	Lawrence, 1857.	
Wilson, A. D., Dundee, Scottland, Aug. 2, 1840.	Scandia, Republic Co., Nov. 5 1870.	Scandia.
Watson, J. S., Ohio, December 2, 1843.	Emporia, Sept., 1858.	Emporia.

Name, Place and Date of Birth.	Place and Date of Settlement.	Present Residence
Woodard, Levi Indiana, August 29, 1830.	Hesper, April 6, 1857.	Lawrence.
Watson, G. B., Virginia, November, 1, 1806.	Lecompton, March, 1856.	Lecompton.
Watt, Sally B., Mt. Gilead, Kas., Nov. 26. 1859.		Lawrence.
Watt, Mary E., Franklin Co., Kas., June 6, 1857.		Lawrence.
Watt. Phebe J., Lawrence, November 24, 1870.		Lawrence.
Whitford, A. I.. Jefferson Co , N Y., April 12, 1836	Manhattan, June 1, 1856.	North Lawrence.
Woods, George H., Erie, Pa., August 21, 1825.	Topeka, June 25, 1855.	Topeka.
Walker, Mrs. Lydia B., Kent Co., R. I , May 18, 1817.	Wyandotte, July 31, 1843.	Wyandotte.
Walker, Miss Louise, Sandusky, Ohio, April 11, 1843.	Wyandotte, July 31, 1843.	Wyandotte.
Wick, Carson. Erie county, Pa , March.	Clinton, April 12, 1857.	Clinton.
Walnhouser, E. J., Portland, Maine, Feb. 8, 1841.	New Chicago, June 18, 1869.	Kansas City.
Willits, Jacob, Jericho, L. I., February 24, 1824.	Topeka, May, 1855.	Topeka.
Willits, Elizabeth, Babylon, L, I.. August 26, 1834.	Topeka. June, 1856.	Topeka.
Weeks, Robert E., Oneida Co , N. Y., Dec. 24, 1812.	Lawrence, October-10, 1870.	Lawrence.
Watson, Julia M., Lawrence, January 23. 1817.	Douglas Co., January 23, 1861.	Lawrence.
Wood, S. N., Morrow county, Ohio, Dec. 25, 1825.	Near Lawrence, June 24, 1854.	Elmdale, Chase Co.
Wood, Margaret L., Richland Co., Ohio, Oct 15, '30.	Near Lawrence, June 24, 1854.	Elmdale, Chase Co.
White, C. E., Whiting, Vt., April 25, 1822	Lawrence. Jan 29, 1876.	Lawrence.
Walker, Fannie, Pennsylvania, Nov. 27, 1854.	Lawrence, March, 1855.	Lawrence.
Wade, A B., Franklin Co , Mo., Aug 26, 1829.	N. W. of Lawrence, June 5, 1854.	N. W. of Lawrence.
Wade, N. E., Fayette county, Ky., March 13, 1828.	N. W. of Lawrence, June 5, 1854.	N. W. of Lawrence.
Wilson, F. H., Ross county, Ohio, Jan 5, 1829.	Lawrence, October 20. 1871.	
Webber, A. B., Cincinnati, Ohio, June 14, 1852.	Topeka, May 1, 1809.	Topeka.
White, James, Westmoreland Co., Pa., Aug. 25, 1833.	Wamego, Kansas, April 7, 1870.	Lawrence.
Wilson, James C., Warren Co., O , March 9, 1830.	Leavenworth Co., Oct. 23, 1855.	Douglas Co.
Watkins, Mrs. Charlotte. Fredonia, Mich , Nov. 20, '36.		Ann Arbor, Mich.
Witbeck, Mrs. Sarah. O., Feb. 22, 1838.	Lawrence, April 7, 1871.	
Willits, T. E., Ind., Nov. 5, 1824.	Newman, Jeff Co., March 1, 1865.	Newman.
Weybright. J. B , Elkhart Co., Ind., June 11, 1835.	Willow Springs June 1, 1860.	Lawrence.
Woodruff, Thomas P , Meadville, Pa., March 27, 1835.	Council City, November 10, 1854.	Lawrence.
Woodward, H. P., Homer, Courtland Co , N. Y., Apr. 17, 1824.	Lawrence, Kansas, April 15, 1865.	Wamego, Kan.
Woodward, E. A , Lenawee Co,, Mich., Oct. 11, 1841.	Lawrence Kansas, April 15, 1865.	Wamego, Kan.
Weeks, Mrs. Matilda L., Philada., Pa., Nov 7, 1817.	Lawrence, April 29, 1871.	Lawrence.
Weeks, Mary L.. Sandusky, Ohio, May 24, 1856.	Lawrence. April 29, 1871.	Lawrence.
Weeks, Joseph H., Newark, O., Aug 17, 1851.	Lawrence, April 29, 1871.	Lawrence.
Wabintz, Wm., Kan., Sept. 14, 1860.	Lawrence, September 14, 1860.	North Lawrence.
Wilder, A. V., Bethel, Vt , Apr 29, 1832.	Lawrence, January 15, 1877.	Lawrence.
Wight, Ruth L., Leicester, Mass , June 4, 1832.	Near Lawrence, April, 1858.	Lawrence.
Wight, Annie, vicinity of Lawrence, July 25, 1860.	Near Lawrence, ——.	Lawrence. `
Wight, Lucy, Lawrence, March 27, 1864.		Lawrence.
Whaley, Geo. W., Athens Co , O , June 7, 1842.	Dimon, Jefferson Co., November 15, 1874.	Dimon.
Wood, W. R., Morrow Co., O , June 2, 1857.	Cottonwood Falls, April 14. 1865.	Elmdale, Chase Co
Wood, J. M., Norridgewock, Me., Jan. 20, 1824.	Lawrence, January 15, 1872.	Lawrence.
Woodard, J. N., Park Co., Ind., June 7, 1843.	Lawrence, October 20. 1868.	Lawrence.
Whipple, F. B., Brockfort. Oct 23, 1843.	Lawrence, November 20, 1865.	
White, Joel S., Lancaster Co , Pa., Dec. 25, 1831.	Lawrence, August 16, 1864	Lawrence.
White, Almeth, Burlington, N J., Oct. 29, 1847.	Atchison, November 1, 1878.	
Walruff, John, Prussia, June 11, 1830.	Ohio City, Franklin Co., April 25, 1857.	Lawrence.
Warren, Mrs. Ann, Garry, Ireland, Nov. 5, 1805.	Eudora, September, 1859.	Lawrence.
Watson, E. P., Darien, N. Y., June 13, 1833.		North Lawrence.
Watts, Elsie Kan , Apr. 20, 1875.		
Watts, Lottisa, Mo., Feb. 15, 1850.		
Willey, J. W., Clark Co., Ind., Jan. 22, 1836.	Lawrence, May 20, 1864.	Lawrence.
Willey Mrs. M. W., Va , Oct. 5, 1839.	Lawrence, March 20, 1877.	Lawrence.
Way, T. A., Richmond, Ind., Sept. 18, 1826.	Franklin, April, 1855.	Lawrence.
Wight, H., Mass. , Feb. 27, 1827.	Mound City, June 12, 1861.	Leavenworth.
Wharton, S. R., Newton, Hamilton Co , Pa., March 24, 1861.	Lawrence, April 8, 1858.	Lawrence.
Wilhite, Charles, Morgan Co., Ind., June 9, 1854.	Hamlin Tp., Brown Co , February 23, 1872	Lawrence.
Winchell, G. H., Lawrence, August 6, 1862.	Emporia, March, 1858.	Emporia Tp
Willard, Mrs. N. F., Canada. November 4, 1851.	Lawrence, June 8. 1865.	Lawrence.
Wilson, George, Linwood, January 29, 1859.	Lawrence, July 17, 1878.	Lawrence.
Watts. J. C., England, Sept. 3, 1836.	——, September 11, 1869.	
Wilder, Daniel W., Blackstone, Mass., July 15, 1832.	Lawrence, December 15, 1856.	Lawrence.
Woodard, J. W., De Witt Co., Ill , July 7, 1848.	Leavenworth, June 15, 1857.	St. Joseph, Mo.
Woodard, Lemuel, Lee Co , Va , May 23, 1799	Bloomington, March 15, 1855.	Osage Co.
Weymouth, Wm. H., New Market, N. H., Feb. 23, 1824.	Bloomington, March 15, 1855.	Died May 27, 1877.
Weymouth, Mrs. Susie M., Boston, Mass., Nov. 27, 1836.	Topeka, February 10, 1855.	Topeka.
Wiggs, Al. D., Tampico, Darke Co , O , March 17, 1855.	Topeka, February 20, 1855.	Topeka.
Worcester, Leonard, Union Mission, C. W., March 8, 1836.	Hutchinson, Reno Co., April 5, 1873.	Clinton
Willson, J. E., Peru, Ind., Feb. 11, 1856.	Lawrence, March 2, 1856.	Greensburg, Ind
Whicomb, Ansel H., Lawrence, July 7, 1864.	Topeka, October 18, 1869.	Osage City.
	Lawrence.	Lawrence.

Name, Place and Date of Birth.	Place and Date of Settlement.	Present Residence
Wade, Ida May, Lawrence, Kas , June 18, 1867.	Lawrence.	Lawrence.
Whittick. H. A., Germany, July 18, 1839.	Big Springs, Kansas, March, 1857.	
Wilber, Miss Florence E., Dundee, New York.	Lawrence, Kansas, October, 1856.	Lawrence.
Walruff, Adelade, Ottawa, Feb. 13, 1864.	Ottawa, Kansas.	Lawrence, Kan.
Whitbeck J. Elmore, Newark, N. J., Feb. 6, 1850.	Louisville, July, 1878	Lawrence, Kan.
Weybright, Sarah, Lewistown, Pa., Oct. , 15, 1840.	Lawrence, October 4. 1858.	Valley Falls.
Wilhelmi, Max, Washington, Mo., Nov. 5, 1856.	Lawrence, September, 1878.	Lawrence.
Wilson, E. A., North Carolina, July, 24, 1824.	Lawrence	Lawrence.
Whittemore, Gordon, Huntley Grove, Ill , July 9, 1851	Atchison, April, 1860	Beatrice, Neb.
Whittemore, Ida M., Beatrice, Neb., April 26, 1863	Beatrice, Nebraska, April 26, 1863.	Topeka, Kan
Yelington, A. E , India, February 2, 1844.	Douglas county, October 14, 1860.	Leavenworth Co.
Yemdall, Joseph Bradford, Yorkshire, England, Sept. 26, 1823.	Douglas county, April 11, 1866.	Lawrence
Yates, G. W. W., Pittsfield, Ill., September 2, 1844.	Lawrence, August 12, 1854.	Lawrence.
Yoakum, S. T., Georgia, September 6, 1860.	Leavenworth, March 1, 1857.	Fairmont, Kan.
Yeats, Mrs. S. G., Jonesborough, Tenn., August 21, 1828.	Franklin county, September, 1870.	Iola.
Young, J B., Indiana, October 30, 1833.	Humboldt, May 9, 1857.	Iola.
Yates, Wm., Barren county, Kentucky, Jan. 30, 1820.	Lawrence, August 12, 1854.	Lawrence.
Yarrington, M. S., New York, March 21, 1826.	Wakarusa, Shawnee Co , May 20, 1860.	Wakarusa.
Young, W. G., Braddocksfields, Pennsylvania, July 7, 1837.	Franklin, September 15, 1858.	Ottawa
Yetger, Lizzie, Germany, August 17, 1861.	Lawrence, August 8, 1859.	Lawrence.
Yeager, Miss Isaac, June 10, 1867.	Lawrence, August 8, 1859.	Lawrence.
Young, Mrs. Isaac, Columbus, Ohio, September 14, 1828.	Leavenworth, May, 1857.	Leavenworth.
Young, Jas. W., Rolla, Missouri, October 19, 1862	Salina, May, 1866.	Salina.
Young, Geo. L., Shelby county, Ky., Sept. 16, 1832.	Indianola, Shawnee Co., November 17, 1831.	Shawnee Co.
Yeats, Robert A., Kentucky, November 10, 1810.	Pomona, September 15, 1871.	Lawrence.
Yosthup, Fred M., Williamstown, Mass., June 23, 1857.	Lawrence, February 16, 1879.	Sigel.
Zeigler, Logan, Stone county, Mo., April 3, 1825.	Wyandotte county, October 15, 1829.	Leav. Co. Oldest inhabitant.
Zerby, John V., Lancaster, Penn., March 23, 1855	Lawrence, August 14, 1868.	Lawrence.
Zimmerman, E., Montgomery county, Penn., Sept. 9, 1824.	Douglas county, Dec. 31, 1864.	Grant Tp., Douglas Co.
Zinn, Laura N., Virginia, December 18, 1831.	Lecompton, October 15, 1869.	Lecompton.
Zinn, Geo. W., Ohio, December 21, 1809.	Lecompton, September 15, 1854.	Lecompton.
Zimmerman, J. P., Center county, Penn., August 29, 1837.	Perry, Jefferson county, April 5, 1878.	Perry.
Zimmerman, Ella, Center county, Pennsylvania.	Perry, Jefferson county, April 5, 1878.	Perry.

Kansas State Historical Society.

This is an institution recognized by the laws of the State of Kansas. The character of the work of the Society is thus stated in its constitution: "'The object of the Society shall be to collect, embody, arrange, and preserve books, phamphlets, maps, charts, manuscripts, papers, paintings, statuary, and other materials, illustrative of the history of Kansas in particular, and of the country generally; to procure from the early pioneers, narratives of the events relative to the early settlement of Kansas; and of the early explorations, the Indian occupancy, overland travel, and immigration to the Territory and the West; to gather all information calculated to exhibit faithfully the antiquities, and the past and present resources and progress of the State, and to take steps to promote the study of history by lectures and other available means."

The collections of the Society are the property of the State; and provision is made by law by which apartments are furnished in the State House for their deposit and care, and where they are open at all times to the public.

INDEX.

www.ingramcontent.com/pod-product-compliance
Lightning Source LLC
Chambersburg PA
CBHW020354030726
47496CB00007B/2141